"Farris is a real master ... a giant of contemporary psychological horror."

— Peter Straub

"Few writers have Mr. Farris' talent for masterfully devious plotting, the shatteringly effective use of violence, in-depth characterizations, and scenes of gibbering horror guaranteed to turn one's blood to gelatin."

— *The New York Times*

"Farris has a genius for creating compelling suspense."

— Peter Benchley

"His paragraphs are smashingly crafted and his images glitter like solitaires."

— *The Philadelphia Inquirer*

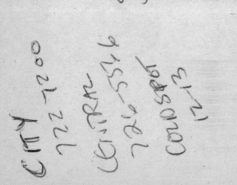

Tor books by John Farris

JOHN FARRIS

KING WINDOM

TOR

A TOM DOHERTY ASSOCIATES BOOK
NEW YORK

KING WINDOM

Copyright © 1967 by John Farris

A TOR Book
Published by Tom Doherty Associates, Inc.
49 West 24 Street
New York, NY 10010

Cover art by Gary Smith

ISBN: 0-812-51793-8

First Tor edition: April 1990

Printed in the United States of America

0 9 8 7 6 5 4 3 2 1

FOR MY DAUGHTER
Julie Marie

PART ONE

THE TENT

1

Prophet Charger

In the fall of the year and just before the first cold snap, when the leaves were turning an indifferent yellow or a coarse red-brown if they turned at all, two men left the Great Southern Livestock Exposition in Tennessee and walked through the scrub woods behind the amusement area, ducking the wasps, which were mean and sluggish from prolonged heat, raising the dust of the clay ground with each step. The late-afternoon sky was half darkened and it was raining, but the rain was not quick enough or wet enough to disturb either the men or the wasps, or the parched leaves; it was a jewel-like rain in the low-lying sun and it was nearly over by the time they reached the open field on the other side of the woods.

The field was irregularly divided by a deep ditch. Below the ditch and next to the woods were the lean-to stables and corrals where the rodeo cowboys kept their horses. Across the ditch, to the south, the land rose to form a ridge shaded by several oaks whose ancient trunks were a silvery gray. Between the trees and downwind from the stables, within range of the flies and animal odors, stood a four-pole revival tent, and it was to this tent that the two men leisurely made their way through the high, heat-curled grass of the field.

The tent of the man who called himself the Prophet Eli Charger was old canvas, a rough ocher in color, sewn in many places with an awl, or patched with strips of cloth; it sagged

3

somewhat dispiritedly against its stays in the still air. Yet to King Windom this tent, steeped in a sunlit squalor, was uniquely valuable. He was a born evangelist, and in one sense, after many years he was home at last. His heartbeat quickened as he passed beneath the banner with the unreal Kewpie-doll portrait of Prophet Charger on it and entered the tent.

The Negro, whose name was Age, went with King only as far as the edge of the sawdust, where he waited. He was wearing an old yellow slicker ornamented with a hundred faceted red reflectors of the type commonly found on bicycles. He was tall and as thin as a coach whip, blue-black in the theatrical light. Despite his getup and the prominence of his scarred bald head, there was a calmness about him, a combination of silence, severity, and self-possession that few Southern Negroes dare to achieve. His eyes were on his friend, and as he watched King prowling the length of the tent, from the makeshift pulpit to the back row of metal folding chairs, a smile curled catlike across his dark face. But the smile quickly faded, and his jaw set worriedly.

King was trying, on his fourth visit to the tent, to look around with an unsparingly critical eye, but he wasn't having much success. His amber eyes shone with enthusiasm as he measured distances with a long stride. He was a big man, six feet four or five, not symmetrical like an athlete, but with thick, squared-off shoulders and the long ungainly hands of a mountaineer. Except for the uncharacteristic light eyes, he had an Indian's coloring and taut features. At first glance his was a cruel face, handsome as a well-turned arrowhead.

He paused in his pacing to lean against the hip-high pulpit, made from a double thickness of boards across sawhorses, and deliberately caught Age's eye. He smiled fitfully, squeezing the edge of the pulpit with both hands.

"I know," he said. "I know, Age. We'll need new lashing right away, and any kind of decent wind'll tear this canvas to ribbons. But it's got to be mine, that's all there is to it." A note of pleading came into his voice. "I have to have this tent. I have to start *now*, Age. Or else it never will happen."

Age nodded, as if he was unwilling to dispute King's feeling of urgency. But he said, "The Prophet will cheat you some way. Question is, does he cheat you a little, or a lot?"

"I can handle him," King replied. "Pocket-picking evangelists or carnival grifters, they wear the same stripes." His

4

eyes darkened with thought, and he looked around once more. "Or it never will happen," he repeated, half aloud, then kicked at the sawdust and smiled, contentiously. "Well, Age? Reckon we ought to go sound him out?"

On the other side of the ridge they came upon a gray board house, part of a small farm. An emerald screen of kudzu grew between two posts of the front porch. The sun burned hotly against the windows, and except for the variety of cats on and under the porch, the house looked deserted. But there were signs that people not only lived there, but lived cleanly. The hard clay before the steps was swept, the vines were trimmed, the screen door was freshly whitewashed, and there was a clear-glass light bulb in the porcelain fixture beside the door.

As they entered the yard Age left King's side and walked across the clay to a stunted and unproductive peach tree off to one side of the house. There he settled down between sprawling exposed roots, the reflectors on his prized raincoat winking dolorously in the sun.

King glanced at him, then at the modest fairgrounds with its rickety colossus of roller coaster, and the familiar carnival encamped beyond. When he turned back to the house he saw that a girl with an apron full of pecans had appeared; with her free hand she was filling a quart can at a spigot near the kitchen door. She gave King her attention and waited for him to explain himself.

"I'm here to see the Reverend Mr. Charger."

The girl didn't reply; instead she carried water to the stoop, gently pushed one of the half-grown cats away, and began dropping pecans into another large can. She was slender, eighteen or so, with straight, honey-colored hair, and a healthy heart-shaped face pleasantly reddened by a summer of sun. Despite the condition of her cotton dress, which was faded and sewn here and there, there was no visible canker of poverty about her.

"Are you his girl?" King persisted. "Is he here?"

"Inside," she said, raining fistfuls of nuts into the can. "But he's been sick."

"I need to see him, though."

"What's your name?"

"King Windom."

She brushed her apron clean and came closer, carrying the water. He noticed the imperfection then, the numbing ugliness

5

of a distraught, outward-looking eye, duller brown than its mate, and he felt a sharp, transient pity for her, for that unfortunate eye in the mint-fresh and lovely face.

"I'm Jeremy," she said, and pronounced it Jere-*my*. "Are you the sheriff?" At a glance she had taken in Age, sitting obliviously under the blighted peach tree, and was studying King again, a little worriedly, but not as if she thought he would really amount to much in a long succession of worries and crises.

"I'm a preacher," he replied, and smiled consolingly. "I know about his ailing. I won't be but a little while."

"What did you want to see Eli for? So I can tell him."

"I've got some money for him."

"Well, he'll like *that*," she said, with a faint pull at the corner of her mouth that might have been from amusement, or from pain, and went up the steps to the porch. There she hesitated, then turned and beckoned and said, just before she disappeared inside, "I'm not his girl."

King swallowed his tension and followed. He waited on the porch, where he could hear the girl talking in monosyllables; the voice of Eli Charger was sleepy and peevish. Presently she appeared again, ghostlike behind the whitened screen, and beckoned once more.

The furnishings in the long front room of the house were primitive, but here too—despite the juxtaposition of kitchen, dining room, and sleeping area—King was impressed by a sense of order and neatness; there was oilcloth and clean china on the table, and a bright Mexican-style spread covered the couch. The girl had drawn away somewhat self-consciously after opening the door and was rearranging the crockery on the table as if she was aware of his thoughts and pleased by his reaction to her housekeeping.

Sunlight had gathered like golden wool in one corner of the kitchen, where a folding screen partly concealed a claw-footed bathtub. Jeremy nodded toward the tub. King heard a floundering, followed by a grumpy oath.

"Over here, Preacher, if you want to talk to me."

Sitting in the bathtub, which was partly covered over by a sheet, was a stubby man, ugly as Socrates, with blue-white skin gone rosy in spots from the heat, and prying, intelligent eyes. His head lolled above the margin of the sheet; the air around the tub smelled hotly of sulphur.

"Sit down," said Eli Charger, lifting a dripping hand in invitation. "Not too close if you can't abide the stink. Jeremy? Bring me here some more mineral salts for my bath, if you please."

King removed several towels from a straight-back chair and hung them on a length of line above the rusty sink. As he sat down he eyed the girl again. She skimmed by him with a lithe turning of her hips, and a preoccupied grace, hurrying, efficient, like a swan with a duckling's moody eye.

"King Windom," Eli mused, his eyes half closed. "She said you come to talk about money. Sorry, but there's no money here." He offered a beleaguered grin. "All the same, you're invited to take part in our revival. What church you from?"

"No church," King said. "I work at the carnival across the way."

Eli frowned, and lifted his gnarled hand again as the girl approached with a packet of mineral salts. "Jeremy, didn't you tell me he was a preacher?"

"I *am* a preacher, but I don't have a church. I wouldn't want one, anyway. I'm an evangelist, like you. That's why I'm here. I want to buy your tent and furnishings. The truck too, if I can make it run."

Eli spilled the mineral salts into the tub and closed his eyes all the way, emitting a short sigh. He sank deeper, so that his chin was below the edge of the sheet. "Jeremy, I think I could do with another kettle of hot water."

"You've been in there two hours already," she said.

"No matter. I'm just before feeling the soak in my bones."

She threw back her head in a gesture of indifference, sneaked a glance at King, and turned away. Eli's febrile eyes opened wide for a second, taking in the preacher, the length of him, the hard width of shoulder, the Tartar's features.

"Tent's not for sale," he said.

King shifted his weight in the uncomfortable chair and smiled, a little skeptically. He had expected bluntness from the Prophet Charger, but he could be blunt himself. "I heard you *would* be selling—now that you're laid up and forced to give over preaching to another man."

As if an electric charge had passed through his bath water, Eli sat up, his expression wrathful. "That's a lie!" he said. "I've been laid up before. Worse than this! Why, I can get around some during the heat of the day if I make up my mind to it—"

"But you can't preach nights," King said, more softly. "And it's a shame. You're as good a preacher as I've heard."

He leaned forward slightly, hands on his knees, eyes intent on Eli's pug face, a sympathetic turn to his mouth. "Oh, I know. There's nothing harder on a man than preaching cold nights in a tent. I've lost my voice many a meeting. And young as I am, I've had joints stiffen so I couldn't get out of bed in the mornings—"

"Jere-my!" Eli cried.

"Water's not hot yet," she answered.

King sniffed the sulphur-laden air. "I've heard sulphur will soothe a swollen joint," he said politely. "Never tried it myself. Now, about your tent—"

"Damn," snapped Eli. "Tent's not for sale. Are you after putting me out of business?"

King ignored the Prophet's scowl. "As I see it, you're just about there already. I begged some time off my job last night and attended your meeting."

It had been the sorriest spectacle of revivalism he'd ever seen. The congregation had numbered less than a hundred. There hadn't been a choir, nor any deeply felt singing, and only three preachers, from obscure churches, were huddled together on the barren pulpit, their faces avid for whatever share of the collection would fall to them. The young preacher who was standing in for Eli had spent most of the evening trying to fatten the collection, clumsily applying those techniques for wringing dollars out of poor people that Eli probably had spent a lifetime perfecting. The faithful, who were eager to please but still not fools, had finally stopped listening to the preacher altogether, so the Spirit of Christ never had had the chance to stir their hearts. King had been further offended by the "healings" which the wretched preacher attempted as a climax to his service. He had slept poorly, troubled by what he had seen, and at the moment he was thinking that it might not be a bad idea if the Prophet Charger *did* go out of business.

His face must have revealed part of his feelings; Eli's eyes became sullenly lidded, and he muttered, "Last night was Tuesday. If you know anything about revivals you know week nights are slow. Friday and Saturday that tent will be full. I'll be preaching myself by then."

"But if you can't?" King shook his head sadly in the face of

8

Eli's suppressed wrath. "Who is that young preacher I heard last night?" He asked this politely, but there was no mistaking what he thought.

"His name's Philemon," Eli replied. "Philemon Love. Nephew of mine. He's all right. Yes, give Philemon a little time, and he'll do. I've been working with him every day. . . ."

Jeremy came with a kettle and Eli lay back, wincing as she poured the hot water into the tub. His face was much redder than it had been; it began to set in lines of effort as if, beneath the sheet, he was pitting all of his will against the needle-like pain in his joints. For several moments he strained, his chin trembling. Then his mouth loosened and he gasped; his eyes looked old and tired with the sense of his predicament.

"Any better?" Jeremy asked, somewhat concerned by his expression.

"I'm all right," Eli said, without conviction. "Few more minutes and I'll be ready to get out. Fetch my robe for me."

As the girl passed him, King rose, with a half-smile of regret. Eli quickly raised his eyes. "Where you going?" he asked ungraciously. "Sit down."

"Well, it'll be suppertime before you know it, and I—"

"You just got here. Sit."

"If we can't bargain, then—"

"How long have you traveled with that carnival show?" Eli interrupted.

"About five years," King replied. He studied the Prophet for a few moments, then pulled up his chair again.

"What do you do over there?"

"I'm a grinder."

"What the devil is that?"

"I talk, mostly. For the ten-in-one. That's a freak show. Used to be a bingo caller, but the freaks needed me more." He smiled. "There's good money in talking games, but the hardest job in the world is to turn the tip for a collection of freaks. In a way it's a lot like preaching."

Eli shook his head impatiently at the stream of unfamiliar carnival lingo. "What gives you the right to call yourself a preacher?" he demanded.

"I was ordained in the Old Saints' Original Church when I was twenty years old—right before I went into the Army."

"That's a good Fundamentalist church," Eli admitted. "Are you seminary trained?"

9

"No. I don't have a speck of college. But from the time I was fourteen on I studied just about every night with my uncle, the pastor of my home-town church. Down there in Curtlow, South Carolina. He was a seminary man himself and he owned a library I wasn't about to get through if I read to be a hundred, so I feel like I'm educated almost as good as if I'd put in some college. I didn't just study the Bible. I studied the great thinkers, whether they were Christian or not. I reckon I've read—"

"No need to say. I don't have any use for seminary preachers myself. Have you read your Bible? Do you *know* your Bible? Are you a born-again, blood-washed believer?"

"I am."

"That's all I cared to know. If I thought you'd polluted yourself with a lot of modernist books and neglected the Bible, I wouldn't waste time talking to you. Now then. Where've you preached at?"

"Well, when I came home—I was just shy of twenty-four then—I caught on with an evangelist named Bonner"—he hesitated to see if Eli would recognize the name—"who is in his grave now, I expect, and I traveled with him and learned the ropes."

"How long?"

King tilted in his chair and looked around, restlessly. Jeremy had returned with Eli's robe and was standing by, her eyes on a kitten swiping at a moth in the kitchen window. The flared line of her jaw seemed to curve directly to his heart, cutting as a memory. He stirred; he was aware of Eli's stare, and his mouth felt dry.

"Six months is all. But I learned a lot from the Reverend Mr. Bonner."

Eli was puzzled. "I peg you at about thirty now. Is that all the preaching you've done in six years' time?"

"No." And as if his following silence held some meaning for her, Jeremy turned her head, quizzically, her face glowing from the coal of the sun held up to the west window. "I had a church for a while," he said to her. "In a place called the Sugar Tree Valley."

Jeremy shrugged, as if she was disconcerted by the intense look in his eyes. "Where is that? I never heard of it?"

"Oh . . . it's a place in—" He hadn't intended to mention the Sugar Tree Valley, or even the church, but since it was done he

10

continued. "It's deep down in some dark blue hills just over the Virginia border, a pretty but a poor place too. And in winter as stark as if a soul never had taken breath there." He lowered his head, caught up by his vision, and said in a low voice, "That's where I was, and after that, not too long after, I joined the carnival, and now what I'm looking for"—he raised his eyes and found the girl gently lifting the half-grown cat from his window perch, and looked from her to Eli, earnestly—"what I want now is a tent of my own, and a chance to make my peace. And that's why I've come to you."

"What else is on your mind?" Eli asked. "You're craving more than a chance to preach."

King shook his head.

"Do you want to be a great man?" Eli persisted. "Is that why you're looking for a tent? Plenty others have done it, like Harlan Gray. Do you think you can follow him?"

"How do I know what I can be?" I only know I have to preach God's Holy Word, and—"

"Maybe you think you'll make a lot of money and preach in auditoriums, wearing two-hundred-dollar white suits; but look at me. You said I was as good as any preacher you've heard, and . . . look at me." Eli seemed about to lift himself from the tub and Jeremy turned, unfolding his robe, but he sat back, grimacing. "Dirt poor and ailing," he mused, his expression indignant and then resigned.

"I don't have ambition for myself," King protested. "I want to do for God, serve God, and that's the whole truth! I want to reach souls, Prophet. If it takes a great man to reach a hundred thousand souls in torment, then maybe God will make me a great man."

"Who'll listen to you? Who cares what you have to say?"

"Why do you have to talk to him like that?" Jeremy said, but the two men were intent upon each other.

"I need a tent to preach Jesus the way He should be preached, but I've looked everywhere. Rents run steep. All I can afford to own is a secondhand tent and furnishings and a truck for haul—"

"How much money have you got?" Eli asked, cutting him off.

His sudden shift to the attack was unsettling. "Are you meaning to make me an offer?"

Eli nodded contentedly, as if the prospect of money talk was more soothing than all the mineral salts in his bath.

Now that they were actually coming to grips, King had misgivings, but he said unfalteringly, "I figure twenty-five hundred for the canvas and furnishings. The truck—well, if it runs, if it doesn't need *too* much work, another two thousand."

"Hunh," said Eli, as the sweat rolled down his cheeks. "You're ready to spend forty-five hundred dollars for nearly all of a man's life." He thought over this implied indignity, looking baffled and worried and perhaps a shade away from tears, but soon he recovered and muttered to himself, enigmatically, "Forty-five hundred dollars," and his eyes became opaque. "I'll tell you what," he said, "I ain't even a little bit interested in that kind of money. I'm not dickering with you, understand. I'm just plain not interested. Jeremy, I could do with a cold soda, and open up one for the preacher too." He smiled, almost gaily. "No sense in your going off without a little refreshment."

"What would you be interested in?" King asked, not stirring.

"You wait," said Eli. "I want my soda."

King settled back, feeling perplexed but calm. He knew one thing for sure: the day hadn't dawned when Eli Charger wouldn't be interested in the lump sum of forty-five hundred dollars, so the bargaining wasn't over, and there was hope after all that the Prophet might sell, once he was certain he had a firm grip on every nickel which King was capable of paying.

He accepted his soda from Jeremy, and the two men swigged away in silence. Jeremy went about preparing supper, slicing a loaf of bread with a long black knife, putting a mixture of okra and corn to heat on the relic of a gas stove. King shifted his gaze and recoiled slightly at the look of the wise old dog in Eli's face, and wondered what had been in his eyes as he stared absently at Jeremy.

"You say you're a preacher," Eli began abruptly, "and I'd like to hear you. If you're good I'll hire you away from the carnival. You'll board with us"—he flicked a glance at Jeremy—"and take your wages from the collection. So you might do all right for yourself. You'll likely make more than that flat-wheel carnival can pay you. Yes or no?"

"That's mighty quick."

"Has to be. I figure a rest wouldn't do me harm. The last thirty-two years I've worked a sixteen-hour day for the Lord's sake, and I'm tired."

"What about Philemon?" Jeremy asked.

"I'll worry about Philemon," Eli growled, not taking his eyes

12

from King. "What do you say? You'll have a better chance at reaching all those souls that are troubling you if you're with an old established revivalist, who is widely known in the South, than if you were on your own hook."

King was silent until Eli said impatiently, "Well, what are you thinking?"

"What happens to me when you're wanting to preach again?"

"You'll still have your turn."

King gravely shook his head. "It's a fine offer, but I just don't think I can accept. You see"—he leaned forward, his eyes sharply golden in the twilight—"I believe God hasn't been happy with me. I failed Him once, I transgressed in an awful way. The past few months I've prayed to the Lord to show me His will, and I think—I *know* that He means for me to go into cities, unstop deaf ears and pour in the Love of Jesus, unblind dim eyes and reveal to them the Light and the Way. I'll preach if I have to in a bare field, or any old country church along the road, but as you say, who'd hear me? Who'd listen to a man in my hurry, a man with no time to spare?" He relaxed somewhat, spreading his hands. "If Gods means for me to be redeemed, then He means for me to stand alone, to preach alone, not to use a man with your . . . reputation for a crutch. So there you can see what's been on my mind since I set eyes on your canvas. There's my dream. Reckon now what I need to do is pray a little more, look a little further, and wait for the Lord to trust in me."

Eli nodded slightly, looking drowsy in the diminished light of day, and skeptical. "You strike me as an upright man," he murmured, "even with that bloodthirsty face of yours. And I expect what you know about sin doesn't amount to a blight on a daisy. The Lord probably trusts you more than you think—Now there you go again jumping up. What did I do?"

"I've overstayed," King replied stiffly. "There's no more I can say and I've got a man waiting on me outside."

Eli ignored him. "Jeremy," he said, "I'm sleepy as the devil in here. Help me up. And, Preacher, you might lend her a hand; soaked as I am, I ain't easy to pull out of the water."

King extended a hand, which Eli grasped tenaciously; he emerged dripping, with the sheet clinging to his boiled skin. Behind him Jeremy opened a heavy soft cotton bathrobe. Eli backed into it, then discarded the sheet, which Jeremy took outside to wring.

13

"I've been studying what to do about you," Eli said, lowering himself into a chair. "I have to admit I'm curious. Most preachers now days are bland as marshmallow, or else they're raving madmen. Now, you've got brass and sense and a way of making a girl like Jeremy, who I'm sorry to say is not all there, turn on her heel. Maybe you can preach too. I'll find out tonight."

"Tonight?" King said, startled.

"And if you've got the right kind of fire in your throat to go with the love of Jesus in your heart, then we'll come to terms."

"You're selling?"

"Don't get ahead of me. If you're the preacher you think you are, and *if* you can come up with six thousand dollars, then I'll sell you a *half* interest in everything, including—and this ain't no small item—the goodwill of the Eli Charger Evangelical Crusade."

"Six thousand dollars?" King repeated, frowning, wondering by what divination Eli had hit on a figure within fifty dollars of all he'd managed to save in his years with the carnival. "Why, I couldn't afford anything like—"

"I don't know what kind of money you've put away," Eli interrupted, "but I consider six thousand a reasonable price for a half share. If you won't preach for hire, then that's the only offer I can make, and one I wouldn't consider making in ordinary times. I think you'll do right well by your . . . investment. There's no need to haggle over dollars. I won't come down. Yes or no?"

Since he hadn't anticipated Eli's move, King didn't know what to say, but he didn't relish the idea of joining up with Eli Charger even on the basis of proprietorship. The Prophet was, as he had bragged, well known in the South, at least by other evangelists and by the large number of the faithful in every Delta junction and mountain hamlet who turn out for traveling preachers, for whom a tent revival is an event of magnitude on the horizons of slow-moving summers. He was a preacher of thunder and sham; he was far from a good man. Still, he had scruples behind his greed, he preached a solid, sensible, come-to-Jesus sermon when he was in the mood. And he had never stooped to the sordidness of "healing" services. He had never pretended to be a miracle worker. Possibly he didn't know what was going on in his tent these nights with cousin Philemon in charge, but more likely he was too broke and desperate to care.

14

Eli's expression, as King hesitated, was untroubled, but there was a nervous bobbing in his throat, and King knew what the thought of six thousand dollars in cash had done: Eli Charger was burning with the need for that money. King had no doubt that the man had made his final offer, and that the sacrifice involved selling half his name was considerable, as if he were selling half his small store of pride. In a way he admired Eli, but he wasn't sure at the moment if he had Eli, or Eli had him.

"Fifty-fifty," King said, thinking aloud; he had pinned a lot of hope on that canvas.

Eli focused on him, and waited, his eyes dimmed by pain. Jeremy came in by the back door and stood, half turned, looking at something in the distance.

"Yonder comes Philemon for his supper," she said. "And he's got that brute dog with him."

"Who calls the shots?" King asked Eli.

"I do," Eli said instantly.

"No," said King.

Anger burned briefly in the Prophet's eye.

"Has to be," King said gently.

The screen door banged and King glanced up. "He's let that dog off the chain," Jeremy advised. "Maybe you'd better look to your nigger."

Without responding, King returned his attention to Eli, who sat perfectly still, seemingly without a breath, for over a minute, before nodding and speaking in a parched voice. "Deal," he said, and again anger—and hostility—glinted like a spark in his eyes.

"Deal," King repeated, and smiled.

"What about your nigger?" Eli asked indifferently.

"Age has been with me a long time. He'll come in handy, and he's no bother to any man."

"Preacher . . ." Jeremy said, warningly.

This time King heard her, and he looked up, frowning. He heard the dog then too, coming on, past the house, a terrible sound in its throat. Outside a man laughed shrilly and excitedly as Age cried out. King bolted for the front door, a step ahead of Jeremy. Behind him Eli shouted wrathfully, "Philemon, you damn fool, lay hold of that dog before he kills the nigger!"

There was a small storm of dust in the softly lighted yard, where Age lay kicking and struggling to protect his face and throat. King was frozen for a few moments on the porch; he had

15

never seen anything quite like this lion-colored dog, but from its size and shape and the deadly way it used its forepaws he knew that it must be one of the breed of Louisiana pit fighters. The head was like a maul, blunt, almost earless, the jaws unusually wide and powerful. The body was similar to a mastiff's, thick-chested, muscular, and scarred.

"King!" Age pleaded, fear in his voice.

King glanced at Philemon, who was circling the Negro and the dog, his face alive with pleasure, and at the length of chain and the studded collar which Philemon held in his hands. He leaped from the porch, caught Philemon by the collar with one hand, and with the other snatched the chain away. For a moment he was dimly aware of Philemon's eyes, round and startled behind dark glasses, then he yanked the man right off his feet and sent him wheeling to the ground.

Face red with anger, King whirled, the chain doubled in his hands, and bent over the fighting dog, dropping his makeshift noose below the black, dust-caked muzzle. Before the brute could turn on him, King braced and lifted the dog straight up off the ground. Philemon scrambled up, a broken brick in his hand. The dog was threshing and strangling horribly and blood came in a jet from its bitten tongue.

"You'll break his neck!"

Wordlessly King turned and as Philemon lunged he hurled the hundred-pound animal squarely at him. One of the dog's flailing paws tore the sunglasses from Philemon's face as they went sprawling together. On the porch Jeremy shouted with laughter. King's eyes lingered on the inert dog; then he kneeled beside Age, who was holding a knife in one bloody hand.

Age's eyes flashed. "Watch the man!" he warned.

King turned almost disinterestedly as Philemon charged. He hunched his shoulders, lowered his head, took two quick steps, and hit Philemon head on and low, driving him hard across the clay and onto the porch as the left-side railing cracked like a shot and the metal roof trembled overhead.

Dazed, Philemon lay beneath the windows and lifted one hand in a weak gesture of self-defense, but King, instead of following his advantage and stomping the daylights out of the fallen man, stood back and slowly shook a bruised hand. For several moments there were no sounds except for a groan from Philemon and the hacking breath of the semiconscious pit dog.

16

Then the screen door creaked and Eli came out. He looked first at King and then, disgustedly, at Philemon.

"What's the matter with you?" he demanded. "You've got a strong back. Get up!"

"Can't," said Philemon. "I'm hurt."

"Age!" Eli said.

Age came forward, limping.

"You got a good sharp knife there?"

"It's sharp," Age murmured, looking down at the narrow blade in his hand.

"Cut that dog's head off with it."

Philemon sobbed. "Don't let him hurt Cosh! He wasn't doing that nigger no harm! He ain't never killed nothing but other dogs in his life!"

"How about that nigger's ear he chewed off over there in Chilowee last spring?" Jeremy asked.

"An ear!" Philemon cried indignantly, as if she were making too much of an insignificant matter.

Age looked mutely at King.

"You hurt much?" King asked quietly.

"No. But my heart's pounding like it won't ever quit."

"It's your dog," Eli said to Age. "You do with him any way you like."

"How do you expect Cosh to act with a strange nigger in the yard!"

"And you shut up," Eli said ominously.

Age looked at the injured dog over with inbred loathing. "He's had enough. I don't want to do more to him." He folded his knife and put it away.

Philemon took advantage of Age's decision by rising and dusting off his suit and going to his dog, which greeted him with a slow lifting of its monster head from the clay. Tenderly Philemon wiped blood from the dog's muzzle with his pocket handkerchief and looked long and meaningfully at King, who returned the stare patiently, without malice. Philemon was large and unmannerly, with a silo-like chest and a round pug face reminiscent of Eli's, but not so ugly. There was a permanent dark glower in and around his eyes. He was, all at the same time, delicate as a prodigy, youthfully soulful, and baby-menacing, like an eaglet. Emotion swirled in his face, big as a tide, leaving behind a salty bitterness and discontent and small unnamed fears.

17

"I don't know who you are," he said, "but I don't like the way you did my dog and so you remember that."

The blood and the fight had depressed King. He had no use for this boy, and little use for Eli, and as a confirmed loner he felt unhappy about the family he had suddenly acquired by his commitment. But he knew making amends with Philemon would be difficult, so he held his tongue for another time.

"His name's King Windom," Eli said, "and he's going to be with us for a while, so get acquainted."

Philemon came straight up from the ground with an expression of shock.

"Doing what?"

"Preaching," Eli said, with a tone of savage satisfaction.

"Preaching!" Philemon echoed, even more shocked.

Eli turned away. "Bring Age in the house," he said to King, "so Jeremy can have a look at that hand. And I reckon you've missed your supper call at the carnival by now, so you might as well sit down to the table with us; there's enough."

"That's mighty fine," King said, doubtfully.

"And Philemon . . ." Eli hesitated, then swung around with a frosty eye in a grim face and said, as if in afterthought, "King Windom here is calling the shots from now on. You'd better bear that in mind."

The screen door scraped again and Eli went inside, leaving three silent, isolated figures in the darkening yard and a smiling Jeremy on the porch.

2

The Strong and the Rapt

King preached that night with less than three hours to prepare himself, and for a while it seemed as if his first meeting under the Eli Charger canvas was going to be as dismal and fruitless as the meeting he had witnessed the night before.

The congregation numbered around two hundred, and most of them were white. There were children, including one babe sitting obliviously in the sawdust with a bottle of orange pop between her knees. There were many old women, some as cool as gladiolas, some red-necked and work-horse heavy, others wrinkling down into their bodices. There were taffy-tailed girls, boys shaven clean as milk around the ears and men with old gray bludgeon heads, gangling men, rope and knots from a gourd. They had one thing in common: they were worshipers, and they would have been an excellent congregation, if they had been better prepared.

Strategy for successful revivals, whether they were held in sultry tents or in pineboard tabernacles, varied little. First there was a warm-up period of about an hour. A handsome, good-natured preacher (if one could be found) welcomed the congregation with announcements, brief prayers, and a promise that Jesus would indeed be with them tonight. The faithful were then led in a hymn to wake up their voices, a slow-paced sing-along followed by livelier music featuring tambourine, guitar, organ, and sometimes drums and accordion. Skillful musicians could whip a congregation to the flash point of frenzy in practically no time. There were periods of dancing, writhing, and shouting, with quieter moments of singing and praying interspersed; the worshipers were never allowed to become tired by or bored with their own excitement. Visiting preachers spoke out if they were so moved; testimonials were given, cheers were raised, and finally another hymn, sung sweetly and with restraint, closed the hour.

King had no choice but to let Philemon handle the first hour of the service, since he needed time to return to the fairgrounds for a change of clothes and a chance to meditate in his trailer, surrounded by the holler and hokum of a carnival in full cry. Unfortunately Philemon wasn't good at jollying or inspiring a congregation, and he was in a sulking mood anyway, indisposed toward helping King. By the time the tall preacher rose to deliver his sermon, the boredom of his flock was visible; they were silent and attentive, but their faces were glazed. Children lay with their heads in their mothers' laps. He came forward unannounced, neatly turned out in a blue blazer with brass buttons and a striped tie, his Schofield Bible open in one hand, mulling over the sermon he had pieced together between the supper table and the pulpit, and their eyes, accustomed to

19

the sulking Philemon, shut him out too, and tried to turn him away.

Eli, along with Jeremy, arrived after King had begun. Eli took a seat at the back and thereafter sat immobile, buttoned up in a thick cardigan sweater, a rakish golfing cap pulled down to his ears. His appraising eyes never left King, and his expression remained unchanged, even when the preacher's first words struck falteringly against the barrier separating him from his congregation.

Yet despite King's uncertain beginning, the preliminary artlessness of his text (" '. . . Payday is every day—when you failed to pay to Me then you lavished on the devil. He's bought you with every unspoken prayer, with every careless lie, with every mean-spirited wish that's crossed your mind . . .' "), the power of his presence was enough to draw the attention of every man and woman in the tent, and hold it. Every line of him was cut cleanly against the lights; there were no flaws of flesh or bone that Eli could see. Even the preacher's mass of untrimmed black hair was not unsavory to the eye, nor dissatisfying in the total portrait of physical integrity. The preacher handled his body well, like a man who could swing a double-bitted ax better than any other man, and do a day and a half of work between morning and evening without growing very tired. This sort of endurance and vitality was written into every movement, yet he was in control, neither stiff with the suppression of the available space, nor antic and excitable.

He had a hangman's face, and perhaps that disturbed some of the congregation, but his voice reassured them. He was quiet, speaking without the hoarse rhythm of a Pentecostal shouter. He spoke as effortlessly as another man might sing. His sound was that of a Southerner inspired by more than clay hills, sloughs, and poverty. They listened, and warmed to him, and there was yea-saying. In turn compassion and dedication lighted King Windom's face; he sensed willing hearts perishing to obey him. As he preached on and became more urgently involved with his flock, his sense of timing and his showmanship returned. An undisciplined current of excitement, or raw force, began to flash from him. It was not a warming current; at times it seemed to set the preacher's teeth on edge, and Eli frowned, forgetting for a stretch the nagging pain in his joints.

King had left the pulpit early to make his way back and forth along the front row of chairs, beneath the lights, so that he might be in more intimate touch with the congregation. Now he was saying, sternly:

"Maybe you think when the time has come for the White Throne Judgment that is your lot and the lot of every soul on this earth that the Lord will be in a fine mood of charity and forgiveness, and will hold out His hand to you and say, 'So you don't have the spiritual price of admission? Well, that's all right, I love you just the same.'"

He stopped and singled out a teen-age Negro girl with a look and drew a reluctant "No, suh" from her.

"Hunh," the preacher said approvingly, then bound them all with the arc of his gaze.

"Sinner friend, listen. It's *not* all right, because He *doesn't* love you just the same! That's harsh truth, but it is the truth! If you don't like my telling it to you, then just wait till you hear it from the *Lord*—and see how you like it!

"He'll have only *one thing* to say to you."

King turned and cracked his Bible down flat on the pulpit.

"'Today's payday! And as far as I'm concerned, Brother, you're a pauper.'"

Silence. The preacher's eyes burned with authority.

"Well, then it will be *your turn*. What do you say? What do you say? What words can you find to explain yourself to a God who is sickened and angered by the sight of your wretched self? What *can you say* with that white throne blazing in your eyes? How can you justify your presence for *another second* in the presence of absolute purity and goodness? If that prospect doesn't fill the throats of each and every one of you with dry and bitter sand, well then . . . all I can say is the devil has been working harder here tonight than I have. And let me say this: the smartest lawyer in the world, the fastest talker who ever lived, is going to be at a loss same as you when it comes his turn, because there is *no answer*, no possible reply when the Lord says, 'Your turn, Brother.'"

He leaned back against the pulpit.

"'Your turn, Brother,'" he said, reflectively.

"'Your turn, Brother,'" he said, apprehensively.

"'Your turn, Brother—to go to hell!'"

He sprang at them, and crouched.

"'You spent your life lavishing on the devil, and now you belong to him, not to me! Get you to the devil, sinner friend, get you to the fiery lakes of hell!'"

21

"Amen!" Eli spoke, harshly.

King turned his back, and stood tensely with his hands on the pulpit contemplating the cross on the alter, and the faces of the two preachers who had shown up for the night's meeting, and Philemon, who was combing his hair with his fingers and who looked unsettled. When he began again, he spoke rapidly.

"How many of you would invite a thief into your house, uncover the silver for him, show him that place in the cupboard where you keep the Town Day money and help him load his pickup with your television and your heirloom keepsakes? No, not *one* of you would; that doesn't make sense, and you are all *hard-working, sensible* people!

"Well . . ." His voice was down to a whisper, and as he faced them he cast down his eyes and thinned his lips as if in despair of knowing how to continue. "Why . . ." And then he raised his eyes and trembled, and knotted his fists at them. "Why in the name of sense, friends, do you keep company with the devil? Why have so many of you brought the devil with you tonight? *Why* have you paid to the devil instead of to God and placed your immortal souls in the most terrible jeopardy?

"Because, oh, you have paid to the devil.

"With every drunken spree you've ever been on!

"With every speck of lust that's lodged in your thoughts.

"With every . . . filthy oath that's passed your lips.

"Paid!

"And he's here, hunh. He's gloating! He knows his power, and make no mistake: *he is powerful!*

"There is no greater power on this earth, except:

"The love of man for his Lord and Master Jesus Christ.

"Who, I think, is still here tonight, despite the devil.

"Despite him.

"Do we have what it takes, to let ourselves love Jesus?"

He paused, and studied them, flushed and intent, hands on hips.

"Do we have what it takes to say, 'Go, devil—come, Jesus'?

"Try it. 'Go, devil.' "

They murmured.

"I don't think," the preacher said, softly and cruelly, "that you *want* the devil to go. You want him to keep on robbing from your soul, so that when payday comes—*as it must come*—you'll have nothing left for the Lord's due."

"Go, devil," they said.

22

King Windom smiled grimly. "It's work. Pull harder."

"Go, devil, come, Jesus!"

"Go on, devil," he sang, to show them how. "Go on, devil!" He began to jig in the sawdust in front of the pulpit, his head bobbing from shadow to light. He repeated himself, many times. He was not playacting, nor was he abandoned. He was merely joyful, and they quickly caught the spirit, and began to shout with him.

"Go on devil, gone devil, gone, gone, gone gone gone . . ." The preacher set himself and then whirled, like a discus thrower, and uncoiled, and flung himself across the tent, where he recovered and with a flourish pointed to a space in the canvas and the dark sky beyond and announced, "Devil's *gone!* Oh, ho, ho, *shout!*"

They shouted.

"Whyyyyyyy, ohhhhhhhh, whyyyyyyy ohhhhhhh wheeeeee!" he chanted.

"Lord, Lord!"

They cried with relief and pleasure.

"Let me hold you, Jesus! Oh, isn't this wonderful? Spirit is moving! Come on, preachers, come on down here where the Spirit moves. Join in! Yea! Lord, Lord, Lord, O Lord, feel like singing? Sing! Want to dance? Who's stopping you? What have we got that piano up there for! This is a *happy* night! Ohhhhhhh, Jeeeeeeesssussss . . ."

Fifteen minutes later, when the late-blooming excitement had subsided, when the last praying was over, and as the congregation was breaking up and the cold night air was coming in under the raised sides of the tent and the proselytes he had invited were meeting with the preacher down near the pulpit, Eli stirred himself and straightened out his arms and said, "Now, *that's* a preacher. . . . Jeremy, you get Philemon and tell him I need help home."

There was no response and he turned his head. She was still praying, and her face was pale. He started to speak curtly and then changed his mind and waited until she looked up, her expression mild and astonished.

"Something come over you?"

"No," she said, intent on the preacher and the circle of proselytes.

"Well, watch yourself. We don't have use for another one of your spells any time soon."

Color came into her cheeks. "I'm all right," she insisted, looking angry as she rose—angry not because of his rude warning but because something comforting and important had slipped away from her at the sound of his voice. She went in search of Philemon and found him outside, just beyond the light, looking in on the new preacher and his converts; the strong and the rapt. Philemon's face was anguished. Jeremy stood by him silently for a few moments, unnoticed. She knew that she could have her turn at Philemon now, if she chose to take it. She struggled with her temptation, and lost.

"Isn't he good, though?" she said deliberately.

He started. "What do you want?"

"Eli says to come on."

Obediently Philemon turned and followed her, the lockbox which contained the night's collection clenched under one arm. Eli surveyed his face, then pointedly ignored him. The three set off for home across the rough field lighted by a gap yellow moon, Eli in the center supported by dutiful hands. Under a religious sky the carnival played boldly. Thinking of what he had observed in his tent, Eli smiled to himself, for the while not concerned with the pain in his calcified joints. Then he became regretful, aware of Philemon's thinly held passion.

"Eli, he can't stand in my stead!"

"He will."

"He's just some stranger walked in off the road. I'm your own family!"

"Why do you want to preach so bad?" Jeremy asked. "You're no good at it." Then, as if to soften this judgment. "Words get stuck on your tongue."

"Ohhh," Philemon groaned, his head down as he walked.

"Let him alone," Eli said, and then to Philemon, "We need a new preacher. *I* need him, so I can get important work done. Let King Windom carry us for a while. Just wait and get along, that's all I ask from you. Hear?"

"Oh, Eli!"

They went on, and Philemon's passion continued, and soon he said, "I never been allowed to have what I wanted in my *life*, Eli!"

"Phew," Jeremy said, softly and scornfully.

"Eli, the Lord means for me to heal sick bodies! How can I do that if *he's* going to preach all the time?"

"When did the Lord say—" began Jeremy.

"You *know* I can do it. I can heal! But you won't let—"

"I don't know anything of the kind," Eli said disgustedly. "No more about it."

"Eli," Philemon said pleadingly, "I have healed and you won't believe, you just won't accept that one of your own has the Power—"

"You stop!" Eli demanded, and set his teeth as pain clawed at him. He went on in a level voice: "There's no such thing as a healer."

"The Bible—"

"You don't need to remind me about the Bible. Jesus healed. Jesus had the Power. Who are you holding yourself up to? Jesus? A healer! Healers are back there in the Bible, they're not here and now. Listen. My own daddy was a preacher and a fool for every fanatic that came down the pike. He gave bed and board to pilgrims who shouldn't have been allowed to stand in the barn, yes, and I've seen him wash their filthy feet. From the time I was five on I saw healers, and every one was a scheming fake. Oh, they made eyes see and unstopped deaf ears but it was not the bodies of those wretches suffered, it was their souls, all they wanted was touching and praying over, and strong sympathy. But I'm telling you, I heard of a boy no older than me jumped in the Obed River and cracked his neck on a log. He was so paralyzed he couldn't lift a finger nor do for himself, and his folks carried him from healer to healer, not a one of which would look at the boy, because they were fake, and afraid. Everybody's heard stories of the dead raised and severed arms and legs joined back to the body, but I never have seen it done. All I ever saw in my life was sick people made sicker by the uproar, and I saw a woman die because some fool made her get up and walk; she died right in front of me." His voice was ragged from the cold, and emotion. "Don't you know if there was such a thing as a genuine healer I would have bumped into him long since?"

"I'm no fake," said Philemon, humiliated and saddened.

They walked on. Eli felt his nephew's weakness, and soon relented. "If that dog of yours is right by Saturday next, I might let you hie him to the pits over in Beersheba County."

"You never have liked me," Philemon moaned, ignoring the peacemaking gesture. "I don't know why I stay."

"Be careful now with my tender elbow," Eli warned. They had reached the steps of the dark house and Jeremy went ahead to spring the lights. "Like you?" he said. In the glare from the porch he turned for a look at the chastened Philemon. "Sometimes I'm liking you and sometimes not, which is the best I can do for any man. But I know I've always meant well for you, Philemon, and that's why I took on about the healing."

"You let me hold healing services before," Philemon said dejectedly, opening the door for Eli. "It was all right until *he* came along."

"I only said you could pray for the sick, and you're smart enough to know the difference. Praying for the sick can't never to harm. But I've seen a hundred boys like you, who can't be satisfied just praying, they have to bear real fruit for the Lord, so they go from prayer to laying on hands, then they get caught up themselves in the ecstasy and lose their senses, and after that nothing's left but damnation. . . . Jeremy, is my bed all ready for me?"

"I just now turned down the covers," she said from the kitchen.

"What are you up to?"

"The preacher only picked at his supper; I thought I'd fix him something to eat."

"If he wants eats, there's a pronto pup wagon right outside the tent there."

"That kind of grease would kill his stomach."

"Never hurt *my* stomach," Philemon muttered.

"He needs some decent coffee, anyway. Eli?"

"What the devil. He's done a full night's work."

"And maybe a couple of fried egg sandwiches?"

"Them too," he agreed. "And mind you don't stay out late; I've never seen the bums like they have around this part of town."

"I'll watch out," Jeremy said, pleased, and she dropped a scoop of lard into the skillet.

Eli and Philemon sat down on the daybed with the lockbox between them. Philemon opened it and dumped the contents on the Mexican spread. They began to count the silver and the dollar bills, that were nearly worn out from too many death grips. Except where Jeremy worked in her own little square of lamplight and warmth from the stove, the house was chilly and Eli's fingers were blue and awkward as he worked at his counting. He counted with only a part of his mind. He was still thinking of Philemon's yearning, and his disappointment. Seeing the soreness that remained in Philemon's eyes, the defensive hump of his shoulder as he lay sprawled across the bed, he was sorry that Philemon was not a good preacher, and never would be. Philemon knew this too, in his heart, which partly accounted for his infatuation with the art of laying-on-of-hands, his hunger to be separate, singled out, gifted by the Lord. Eli gritted his teeth to hold back a spasm of shuddering, and longed for his bed. He sighed. He had more to say to Philemon, and didn't know quite how to begin.

"I hope I've made plain to you why I've always been against so-called healing, and why," he ventured. "I do believe that there is a miracle-working Power in the world today—"

"I *know* there is," Philemon said, perking up, "an—"

"*God's* own invisible and miraculous Power to accomplish all things. The Power that all the fakes and fanatics that ever lived claimed was theirs too. Now," he was quick to add, as Philemon jarred the heels of his boots against the floor and began to rise, "I never have named you for a fake, just *mis*guided is what I said. You want to set the world on fire like any other young evangelist, like King Windom over there, and maybe you thought if you prayed long enough and wept over the sick and afflicted that the Lord would take pity, and heal them, with you as His instrument."

"Sick folks . . . has always moved me to tears, Eli," Philemon said, with a clenching of his fists.

"Exactly. Exactly," Eli said. "And you have always wanted to be of use to them."

"I suffer too. I suffer for every one of their cancers, and their poor twisted bodies. I just can't stand away from folks in torment." Tears had formed in Philemon's eyes, and he was rigid with a distress that bordered on excitement.

"Exactly," Eli said again, soothingly. "But you know by now that all the wretches you've prayed over and pressed on and pried at ain't been made one bit better for the experience. You *know*. Maybe God heals in His own way, in His own time, if it be His inscrutable Will. But *you* can't, Philemon."

"Oh, Eli," Philemon said, hopelessly, "pain and suffering's on my mind!"

27

"You can't be a healer. All you can do is pray long and hard for God to move and be merciful. That's all any of us can do."

"There are men," Philemon said, pacing, "there are men who can heal! I've heard, I know!"

"Then feel sorry for them!"

The harshness of Eli's voice stopped Philemon. "Sorry . . . Why?"

"Why? God's Power in a man's hands? Don't you know what a man must suffer to be such an instrument? Unthinkable, to me!"

Philemon leaned forward, hands braced on either side of the left-hand window, gazing out, his chest rising and falling, and then he lowered himself to the floor, forehead against the sill, and stayed there, not praying, just sitting with his nose lonesomely at the landscape, eyes white as frost and unblinking.

"I would suffer it, Eli. I would gladly."

"Philemon, that dog of yours is moaning and threshing in his box like he has a fever." Jeremy stopped beside Eli and glanced sidelong at him. "I'm off now." She carried a gallon lard pail in which there was a pitcher of hot coffee and sandwiches wrapped in napkins, placed next to the pitcher to keep them warm. "Are you hungry? I can fix up another egg sandwich easy as not."

"No. Run on," Eli said, and turned his eyes on the collection before him. "Tell King Windom I want to see him in the morning. He's going to have to learn how to ask for money."

Philemon lifted his head. "I'll come walk you home if you want me to."

Jeremy hestiated at the screen, patterned with the last of summer's moths. "I guess I won't need you to," she said, after truly thinking it over, and let herself out.

Philemon raised and watched her go, then cocked an ear to the whimpering of his dog. After a while he stretched out, but was uncomfortable. He turned, became rigid; breathed; turned again; sat up distractedly, hands clasping his knees. He rocked. He breathed. His face became fiery with his efforts to speak. Eli gazed down at his silver, entranced, his back to Philemon.

"I had six . . . older brothers and sisters, Eli," Philemon said, chewing out the words.

Eli raised his eyes calmly and questioningly to heaven.

"And all my life it's been take, take, take. I never have had what I wanted! Bless me, Lord." He rocked more violently.

"Glory, God," Eli said approvingly, nodding.

"He's got his eye on her, Eli," Philemon said, warningly. "But you said she was to marry me! I *sin*, Jesus!"

"She's not right in the head, Philemon. Preacher'll see that, and he won't want her. Let him weep, Lord."

"Sho lo me set tai lo sholem o so con dai!"

"Go on, Philemon," Eli urged, his pale tongue flickering across his lips. "Cry out unto the Lord, Philemon!"

Unmindful of this encouragement, Philemon continued in the unknown tongue, in which he could be eloquent, and speak of his deepest self without the threat of immediate madness. His heart burst open in praise, and confession; he had his say of abuse and abomination and black sin, of gall, lost pride, dispossession, and murder. And of hell, which he feared, which delighted him. Gradually he was transported by the hidden words, while his neglected body thumped and flailed.

"Colum we etai shem set abeth!"

At last he grew cold in his rapture, and was silent to the Listener. Half an hour had passed.

"Dear Lord, Amen," Eli the Prophet pronounced, breaking the silence when he felt that it was time. Rising, he went his hobbled way and fetched a blanket for the gray and prostrate boy, whose cheek he kissed, humbly, before going to his own bed.

3

White Sleep

When Jeremy reached the tent with his late supper, King Windom was drinking from a spigot down by the rutted road that crossed the ridge; he was bare to the waist and there was a towel across one shoulder as if he had just finished washing.

29

When he raised up, his back had a tired curve to it, and he cupped his neck with his free hand, pressing gently with the ball of his thumb, gradually lifting his head toward the sky. Jeremy stood stock still, watching. Obviously the energy which had sustained the preacher for the past few hours had fallen low. With his barbarous features in profile, there seemed to be nothing about him now that was out of the ordinary; he would have passed for just another impoverished country boy lifted momentarily in contemplation far above the slight land and the workaday scheme that bound him and would always bind him. She felt disappointed, as if at the lessening of a mystery.

Turning, he saw her, and snatched at a towel to cover his naked chest, not an unusual gesture for a white Southern boy to make in the presence of a strange female, even in this day. Jeremy smiled, held up the pail for him to see. King turned his back, lifted a sweater from the dead jut of a nearby branch, slipped it on, and came up the ridge with a boy's stoop-shouldered, hulking, hill-climbing strides.

Lifting a hand in greeting, he said, "I didn't know you right off, Jeremy. What's this?" He smiled delightedly at the dinner pail. "Oh, you didn't have to do all that! My, my!"

She made a face. "Just a couple fried egg sandwiches; nothing to get worked up over."

"And there's hot coffee?"

"Fresh made."

"Oh, that's wonderful! But, Jeremy, you ought not be out by yourself this time of night."

"It's no matter," she said, shrugging. "Better get inside before all this is stone cold."

He looked around, his head moving like a hunting bird's, the sharp, slightly tilted eyes picking at every shadow on the tent ground. "Well, I really ought to get straight for the night. Just look at the trash around here. Kids do like this at home, they get a broom handle laid across their ribs."

"Eli gives quarters to a couple nigger boys for cleaning up; don't you worry about it." She took him firmly by the elbow and led him toward the ocher puff of canvas with lights swung deep and bright in its belly. The skirts of the tent were lifted, and the rows of folding chairs askew. King righted a couple of chairs and fashioned a trestle with a plank from the pulpit. With his first mug of coffee clenced in his fist, he went behind the altar

30

and the hangings of black cheesecloth there and returned carrying a bulky old portable radio.

"Sometimes I get those Mexican stations that play country and sacred music all night long," he explained, dialing in the Chuckwagon Gang from south of the border. "Good company in the small hours."

"When do you go to bed?"

"I don't. That is, not often." He made himself as comfortable as possible in one of the small chairs, knees high and feet gripping the square rung. In addition to his sweater, nearly out at the elbows, he wore a pair of faded Levis, indelibly grease-stained, and Indian-style moccasins. "I'm one of those insomniacs," he went on. "Doctor I went to says I sleep more than I think I do. Probably get three hours' sleep a night when I'm not gnawing on something, but it's white sleep, whatever you want to call it, no sawing logs till half the morning's gone. . . . Jeremy, this is *coffee*."

She unwrapped a sandwich for him. "Must get tiresome for you, awake all the time."

"Well, I read a lot." He sat munching and staring, and Jeremy was aware, as she had been before, of his fatigue.

"Eli liked your preaching," she murmured, pulling her sweater more tightly around her shoulders and settling down.

King's eyes lighted briefly. "I expect it wasn't half bad," he said modestly, but then he turned sad. "Only a handful of proselytes, though. So looks like I was a failure when you get right down to it." He bolted up with his half-eaten sandwich and began to prowl around the cold tent, sunk in thought. Jeremy turned in her chair to keep him in sight.

"The Spirit of Jesus stirred in my heart," she said simply. "I know it was the same with others. If they didn't come forward when you said to, well, then I reckon it was because they were . . . afraid of you." She paused, and he caught her eye. "It was a powerful job of preaching," she explained, lamely. "It took my breath away. Ask Eli."

King laughed suddenly, delighted with her oblique praise, and came to sit beside her. "Thank you, Jeremy. Give me a little time and this old tent will be a truly fine tabernacle—What's the matter?" He had seen a spark of irritation in her eyes.

She shook her head, curtly, and poured coffee for herself. "It was nothing."

31

"I wasn't bragging," he said, shamefaced. "I've got plans. . . . Just as soon as I talk to Eli again I'll get started."

"What do you want with this old tent?" Jeremy said indignantly. Instantly she bit her lip, but she couldn't keep silent. "The way you can preach! The way people listen to you! You ought to have a church of your own in town, and a thousand people to come on Sundays and hear you, instead of beating the bushes with old Eli. Turn your money over to him? For what? You'll never see a red cent again. You'll never see a sizable town neither if I know Eli, and I think I do. There are Christian folks lenient about the use of their land, but if we go to pitch the tent inside the town limits where it's handy for everybody, the sheriff or the tax assessor or the man from the Board of Licenses comes around sounding out Eli on just how much he's worth, and then they slap on penalties for the privilege of setting up in their town. Eli says he'd rather preach in the middle of a slough five miles from the nearest road than pay tribute to Mattan, and sometimes that is exactly the way it works out."

"Why, I know all those things," King replied, surprised by her outburst.

"You ought to know, then, Eli won't give a fig for any plans of *yours*. He's used to small-town ways. Eli says if the Lord had meant for him to wear a fine suit of clothes and carry the Gospel to Arabs and foreign niggers, He would have gifted Eli with a dozen tongues instead of the one that never stops wagging in his head."

"Whew," said King admiringly. "You can talk when you want to."

"Just watch out before you give him any money," Jeremy said with finality, and she gulped some of her coffee, wincing as it burned her tongue.

"I've learned how to take care of myself, Jeremy. I know how to do business, all kinds of business."

"Then your mind's made up, and you're going to stay with us?"

"Sure."

She thought about that, and a smile came tentatively to her lips. "Reckon it'll be nice to have you," she said graciously. "The three of us been together so long . . ." She brushed her cheek with the back of one hand, her expression thoughtful. "I didn't mean to paint Eli entirely black. He's a worthwhile man, and has his saintly days. He's managed to provide for Philemon and me, if nothing fancy."

"Are you and Philemon related?"

"Just about. He's on Eli's side of the family, and I'm on the other side. But Philemon's been with Eli longer than I have. Since he was ten years old. He was a sickly coot and the others in his family would have pecked him to death if Eli hadn't come along and kindly taken him in. Didn't he grow up to be a big brute, though," she finished, with a hint of grimness.

Her voice was soft and pleasing, and even in a simple tan dress and sweater that had been overwashed she seemed far removed from the dreary circuit of small time revivalism; nowadays any country girl who can read and who has the spending money may get herself up in a fair imitation of New York fashion, and many do, and look like bums. Jeremy was clean and mannerly and dignified, most of the time, and despite the stricken eye, so pretty that he found it hard to think of much else. He wondered what had possessed the Reverend Charger for him to say that this girl was "not all there." King was warmed by Jeremy's attentions, and charmed by her ways, and felt as if they were quickly going to be friends, without fuss.

"How *did* you come to be with Eli?" he asked tentatively.

She took a while to answer. "Well, I didn't have any place to light. My folks were real young when they died; neither one of them was twenty years old, if you can imagine that."

Kind made a clucking sound of sympathy. "I reckon then you made the rounds."

Jeremy nodded. "Till Eli sent for me. That was five years ago. He was already having trouble with his bones then. He wanted somebody to keep house." She grimaced. "You should have seen the way they were living! I threw a fit. Philemon was down on his hands and knees scrubbing for two days straight." She giggled, uncharacteristically, at this thought. "That place we're living in now—I guess you don't think too much of it, but it was all we could afford at the time." She turned, restlessly, toward him. "The reason I said that about the money—you'd better hold back some for your own sake, no matter what kind of arrangement you figure to make with him. Because every piece of bread you eat at his table, Eli'll make you feel like you're stealing it out of his own fingers."

King was struck, and chagrined, by the hopelessness in her voice, by the deeper lament of poverty which she had never been able to express fully, but which showed now in the thinning of her lips, and the look of puzzled endurance in her eyes. He resolved, then and there, that before too many days went by he would hustle Jeremy away from that dispirited house, take her to see sights and indulge in frivolous things, allow her the treat of being no more than a young girl. He would take her to the fair, because he was quite sure she hadn't been, hadn't let herself think of going. The prospect filled him with pleasure and, unexpectedly, a dim foreboding, and so he put it temporarily away.

"You didn't eat," she said, reprovingly. "There's another sandwich to go."

"Jeremy, I never have enjoyed food so much, but I couldn't take another bite. I'm still swelled up inside from all that's happened tonight."

"Maybe if you'd eat right once in a while you wouldn't have trouble sleeping," she said reasonably. "But no sense to force yourself." She stood, straightening her dress. "Time for me to go; I just meant to drop that dinner pail off anyhow. You keep it, you might get hungry. Staying here all night?"

"No, Age is going to watch the tent. I've got some things to attend to back at the carnival."

She glanced sympathetically at his sleepless face. "What sort of reading do you like?"

"Mostly religious books, history, and the writings of great Christian theologians. Started with Justin's *Apology* a few years back, and I'm up to Menno Simons now. I'm still an ignoramus on the subject of Oriental religions, but I'll get around to all of them one of these days."

"You will if you stay up enough nights," Jeremy said, wide-eyed. They walked together toward the back of the tent. "Maybe if you think about it," she continued, uncertainly, "you could let me have one of your books to read sometime."

"Why, sure, Jeremy."

"I probably *won't* understand it," she said defiantly. "I had to quit school after the eighth grade. But I read, and I copy a good hand for Eli. I like to read. And . . . if there was a part I didn't understand . . ." She gave him a level look, waiting for him to deride her, but he nodded gravely.

"I own a real fine *Life of Christ* I think you'd enjoy. I'll see about it when I get back to my trailer."

Jeremy seemed able to cope with anything but small

kindnesses, so a strained silence unexpectedly came between them, until they were outside, under a cool rib of stars. There she swung around to him again, and the look they exchanged was a bond, of a sort. Jeremy nodded her favor, and her thanks. King was about to say good night, but he saw that something else was on her mind.

"I meant to tell you," she said, "but I couldn't there, inside. When you asked me about coming down to be with Eli? What he really had in mind then was for me to marry Philemon. He was twenty-one, and crying for a wife, but in nowise able to get one by himself." Her lip curled. "So Eli, remembering me somehow, thought I'd do."

"You're not married now," King said, when she paused.

"No. I was just fourteen, and sure not thinking about marriage myself. He scared me."

"How?" King asked sharply.

Jeremy deflected that question with a side glance. "Expect you know. But he only tried one time. I don't hold that against him now; he was in love or so he said, but just didn't know how to act." Her face became bitter. "There's no excuse for me, though; I deserved what I got."

"I don't understand, Jeremy."

"To begin with, he tore my dress," she said, her explanation coming hard, as if she was afraid of offending the preacher. "Two days after I laid eyes on him. Tore my dress in a patch of woods near where we pitched the tent that summer. I could have just run away from him, but instead I cried. That was no way for me to keep my head."

"Wasn't your fault. A fool like that, why—"

The clenching of her fist was enough to quiet him. "The more I carried on, the more upset Philemon got, and the more . . . determined. My knees were jelly. I couldn't do but crawl, and him with his hand on my ankle. That's when I picked up a chunk of limestone about as big as an old-time bath sponge and raised it high up. He scrambled off then, but I couldn't hit him. I just sat there, shaking and sore all over, knowing I couldn't hold that stone over my head for long; it was too heavy. Knowing I couldn't let him come close again, ever."

Her voice had fallen low, and, studying her in the pale light that filtered through the body of the tent, his sorrow and outrage were leavened by the calmness in her face.

"Jeremy, if he hurt you, I think I might—"

"Wait," she pleaded. "I hurt myself. Grieved as I was, I couldn't think of another thing to do. So I knocked my head against the stone, four or five times, until there was blood on it, until I couldn't feel any more and blacked out. The last I recall was Philemon with tears running down his cheeks begging me to stop, but not trying to take that stone away from me, either." She took a step toward King, a hand raised to her head. "You'll hear I'm addled because of what I did, and, I don't know, maybe I am, though a whole lot better than I used to be. In a good light you can see one of the scars about here, and"—she lowered her fingers deliberately to the orbit of her wandering eye—"you can see *this* anytime, which I did to myself too. I wasn't born with this mean eye, and no accident caused it."

Involuntarily he reached out and framed Jeremy's face with both his hands, and for a second she was startled, almost seizing his wrists; then she relaxed, accepting his touch.

"Your hands are scarred," she said, wonderingly. "Burned once. I noticed that tonight at dinner, and inside just now. How did you scar the palms of your hands like that?"

"With live coals, Jeremy."

"Then you've hurt yourself too. Why?"

"It was atonement, Jeremy. It happened years ago."

"Because . . . I think I know."

"Because it was the Will of God."

"Yes. Why?"

"I have done plenty to be ashamed of in my life, Jeremy, but I never have questioned the Will of God." He heard something then, and turned his head to see the figure of Age standing close by, reflecting the fire against the background of the long yellow coat. Almost reluctantly King took his hands from Jeremy's face. "Sometimes, Jeremy, His Will is powerful enough to bring down whole nations, and sometimes it's like a wraith, invisible as air. And sometimes men mistake the Will of God, so they suffer. Jeremy: once He condemned me, and then He let me live. I'll never rest until I know the reason why."

"Because He knows you love Him. Because you honor Him with your preaching."

He smiled unexpectedly, a cold, unpleasant smile that startled her. "Don't hold me too highly for that, Jeremy. You heard old Eli: Is it for God's greater glory, or my own?"

"You're a fool to talk like that," she said severely. The

closeness they had experienced a few moments before was completely gone with those words, and she turned, with a sigh, toward home.

"I wish I knew," was all he had to say. Together they walked partway down the ridge, now white as the sea with frost, until Jeremy stopped him.

"You don't have to go on with me," she told him. "Eli'll talk your ear off about all the mistakes you made if you set foot in the house tonight."

"I don't have the stomach for much of his talk tonight," King admitted. "Then——" But she was running, her dress gathered in one hand.

"Good-bye," she called. "Good-bye, come in the morning!"

4

The Woman on the Roller Coaster

It was after midnight by the time King entered the fairgrounds by the stockmen's gate, and there was little activity under the misty sodium-vapor lights which illuminated open-sided barns packed with prize black Angus, brown Swiss, and burly sheep carrying all their brains in their eyebrows. But in the midst of the amusement park he found some excitement: a city fire truck with a long extension ladder was parked beneath the ancient scaffolding of the roller coaster, or Pippen, as it was known in those parts, and three police cars were on the scene, turret lights revolving, casting a red spell on the ranks of soundlessly rearing enameled horses across the way. A sizable crowd had gathered; at a glance he saw that most of them were carnival people. He thought first, Accident, and began to stride out.

Two policemen were standing on the loading dock of the Pippin; one of them had pointed his electric torch upward and was poking through the lofty rafters with its strong beam. King looked toward the top of the structure but could see nothing. It wasn't a case of cars being stuck somewhere along the route. The train was parked below and locked in for the night.

A middle-aged Negro wearing a robe and boxer's shoes made room for him in front of the grill of one of the police cars. "What do you know, King?" he said in a voice blurred by many punches to the side of the neck.

"Kirby, how was the tip tonight?" He was an old fighter whose life with the carnival depended on his ability to bulge his eyes, frighteningly, from his head, and roll them in opposite directions, a sight which had been known to make the more susceptible faint dead away before his stage. Kirby was also still fast with his fists and gave exhibitions on the light and heavy bags as an assist to the grinders trying to work up a crowd.

"Only fair," the ex-fighter replied. "Missed you, I expect."

"What brought out the fuzz, Kirby?" the preacher asked, slipping easily into carnival vernacular.

"Woman up there," Kirby explained, pointing to the highest bend of the Pippin.

"Good Lord. She climb?"

"That's right. Not up through all that trestle, but along the track while the train was below. There she sits, half hour gone, high but not dry."

"Drinking, you mean?"

Kirby nodded. "According to him in the little bitty tight suit over there." He singled out a hulking gent, whose sideburns ended a discreet inch above his shirt collar, being intently questioned by a ring of patrolmen. The man was angry and loud, and—King thought—scared beneath it all. He didn't know anything about the woman on the Pippin; they had met on a blind date less than two hours ago; he, Jerry, wanted to go home; it was the business of the police to deal with nuts like that. The policemen were noncommittal but they didn't let Jerry budge, and, as King watched, the man suddenly ran out of words and look all around him, mouth gaping open, misery in his eyes.

"What are you doing down there, you hillbilly white trash?"

King looked up, along with everybody else, but the woman on the Pippin was still invisible.

"Jerry? Where'd all your company come from, lover? Move

over into the light where we can get a good look at you! La-dies and gentle-men, may I introduce my good friend of the past two hours and my escort for the evening, Mr. Jerry Dee Binsford!"

King shot a look at Mr. Jerry Dee Binsford, who was staring upward with the rest but not believing that any of this could possibly be happening to him. The following few seconds of silence were broken by a slow, solitary, sarcastic clapping of hands, after which the woman resumed:

"Now, la-dies and gentle-men, I admit that looking at this prime example of unwashed hill ape is not enough to move a single one of you to tears of joy, but wait—I'm going to tell you plenty about Mr. Binsford, while I have your attention. You'll gasp! You'll weep! You'll drop your stitches! Don't go away, friends, the beeeeg show is about to begin."

Kirby was slumped against the front of the police cruiser, laughing helplessly, and King grinned. Her voice was thin and there was a definite rasp to it, but although she was shouting to be heard she did not sound hysterical. She sounded as if she was relishing every moment.

"Anybody try to bring her down?" he asked Kirby.

Kirby wiped his eyes. "One of the fuzz climbed partway up just before you came. She threw a plaster Jesus at him, and he nearly took a fall."

"Anything to say for yourself, Jerry, old bugger? Swell, I'll do the talking. Now, folks, we have conceded that Mr. Binsford has a little too much crud behind the ears and he's won a few acne tournaments in his time, but give ear, give ear! He has a talent! Hidden talent! Rare old talent! I can't describe exactly what it is that Mr. Binsford, by his own admission, excels at, but I can paint a picture for you. Ready? Think of a barnyard! Think of a whole chicken house full of contented . . . tender . . . young . . . hens! Do you all begin to comprehend me down there? Now, what is absolutely necessary to keep those chickens contented? Hah? Hah! You said it! Why, nothing but the biggest, fattest, hardest-working young . . . cock in the barnyard! Yippeeee! I give you my good friend and escort of the evening, Mr. Jerry Dee Binsford, who has . . . fine feathers!"

"You old whore!" Jerry Dee roared back. "What are you trying to do, get your name in all the papers? Well, just leave me out, hear? I don't have a thing to do with you, lady!" And at

39

that he pushed his way past the policemen, and half ran, with a scarlet face, to the nearest gate.

"Jerry! I like those fighting words! Yes, baby, there may be some hope for the two of us yet! Climb on up here and we'll . . . jump over the moon together."

Her voice, at the end, was almost too hoarse to be heard, and she sounded forlorn to King. He made his way to the Pippin entrance, where a patrolman stopped him.

"Do your sightseeing back there with everybody else, pardner."

"My name's King Windom. I'm a preacher with the Eli Charger revival. We're camped there on the ridge back of the rodeo." He glanced up at the Pippin. "I think that woman's about ready to come down. I'd like to help her."

"Why? Do you know her?"

King shook his head. "But now that she's had her fun, I think she'll be reasonable. She might be a little scared up there all by herself. And she ought to be a lot more sober than when she climbed; it's colder than the dickens out."

The patrolman looked dubiously at King's sweater and Levis. "Preacher, you say?" He danced his nightstick past his knee several times, then lifted it decisively. "No need to bother yourself. When she wants down, we'll get her down."

A man with a patrol captain's bars had detached himself from the group on the platform and come through the gate in front of the Pippin, an electric torch clamped in his fist. King glanced at him, then said, clearly, "She might decide to come down the hard way."

The captain heard him and changed course, looking him over. "Who are you? Relative?"

"Claiming to be a preacher," the officer said.

"Claiming is right," the captain said, with heavy emphasis. "How do you know she's a leaper?"

"I don't know it at all; I just know she's a lost soul or she wouldn't be there in the first place."

The captain was an old horse, with challenging, thorough eyes behind rimless glasses. "Planning to save her soul while you're up there?"

King decided not to be baited. "I'll just talk to her, same as you would do. Chances are she won't bolt at the sight of me"—he passed a hand over the front of his sweater—"where a

40

blue coat could set her off, depending on her temper right now."

"Every time," the captain said, speaking to the broad air, "we get one like this, we get one like you too. I don't understand it. . . . What makes you think you're a preacher?"

"I'm ordained in the Old Saints' Original Church."

"That's rolling on the ground, isn't it? Snakes and all the rest?"

"Nothing but pure Gospel in our church, Captain. I guess you're not going to let me help that woman?"

"When she gets out of jail you're free to latch on to her and there's not a thing I can do about it; till then I'd say you'd better make yourself highly inconspicuous."

Without hesitation King sprinted, cleared the fence, and bounded up the ramp to the roofed platform in two strides. He saw, in passing, the face of one of the patrolmen as he turned, the lift and blaze of his light, and then he was beyond the shed where the mechanism for the Pippin was housed, over the wooden guardrail and down on the depressed railroad-gauge track. There he stopped and looked up, through the long black tunnel to the sky. Light picked at him, dashing off the walls and inclined track.

"I want him!" he heard the captain shout. "I want that man. *Now, don't you come back without him!*"

King needed no more spurring, and there was no sense in looking back; he knew that the two officers he had glimpsed outside would be on top of him in a matter of seconds. Stooping, hands on the catwalk outside the track, he began a swift, monkey-like ascent, finding the going easy despite the dark and the somewhat slippery walk. He reckoned that the two officers, burdened with their electric torches and handicapped by slick-soled shoes, would be having their troubles as the slant became more pronounced. Sure enough, before he reached the mouth of the frame tunnel he heard one of the men slip and clatter backward into the other, and the shafts of light that had been probing and buzzing around him suddenly vanished. He hoped no one was hurt, but he was glad for extra time; he would have had a hard time trying to cope with the woman above while the law was breathing down his neck.

For a few moments he regretted his rashness, though he did not question the impulse that had sent him on his way toward the woman. What had she thought about the uproar? By now she must have realized he was coming, if she couldn't see him, and that might be enough to send her scrambling farther along the curved track to the point where it plunged steeply downward again. And if she lost her balance . . .

One hundred feet, and the end of the tunnel; he stood, hands on hips, under the open sky, finding the track empty away and above. He glanced down at the crowd below, at the whirligig of red lights, and was heartened by the sight of many familiar faces; most of the carnys had turned out for the action, and he heard a concerted cheer as they spotted him. With a hand on the outside railing he began to climb again, twice slipping despite himself. He frowned; going up was nothing compared to what it would be like going down, and if the woman decided to throw some sort of fit she could make it rough on them both. But at the moment he wasn't thinking too hard about that, because he still hadn't had a glimpse of her.

When he was only a few feet from the top and the long inward curve of the Pippin, lights suddenly flashed on all over the structure.

"Who-whee, it's party time, y'all!"

King smiled, wryly, at this bravado, and followed the voice around the level bend.

She was sitting to the outside of the track, on the strip of catwalk, one arm propped against the insubstantial railing; there was a lot of space just inches from her right hip. Her reckless perch made him feel a little weak in the stomach, and he whistled, softly. She was looking right at him, expectantly, her face washed out by the bare lights strung above. She was wearing a red coat with a fur collar into which her chin was rakishly set. One of her stockings had come down in a puddle below her knee, and she was shoeless. She had either red or auburn hair—the light was washing that out too—and it was done in a style that could best be described as tizzy. Hers was a thin face with an occasional sprawling freckle, like a tiny pawprint, a wide catlike barrel of a nose, a small rounded chin and a pantherish mouth, which opened long and deep but not wide and showed little flat seedling teeth, neat and white, and two pointed eye-teeth. She also wore glasses, with black frames, and her eyes, perhaps because of the frames, or the light, or the sky around her, were also jet black. Something of a wild face,

42

but for the moment he detected no wildness in her manner; her seat was forlorn, her attitude plaintive.

"I expected some sort of company," she said, "but I wasn't prepared for *you!* Another redneck! It must be cosmic month. Otherwise how to account for all my good fortune?"

"I'm no redneck," King said severely; it was a word he hated. "You ought to be able to tell the difference."

"What are you then?" she asked mildly, laying her head to one side, and making a show of inquisitiveness. "Are you a cop?"

"Not that either."

"But they're not far behind, I expect," she said, regretfully. "And they'll be hunkering down beside you presently, not too close, and all of you will be soft-spoken, sympathetic, and kind-hearted, and secretly sweating blood wondering how to get close enough to grab me before I decide to do a roll-out off this thing."

"You're not thinking about that, are you?" he asked.

She considered her state of mind. "No. But I'll tell you the truth: I hope we're not going to have any more company, you and me. In fact, I'm asking that, polite as you please, because I just don't think I could stand it right this minute."

King nodded and returned to the front side of the Pippin, where he could look out over the fairgrounds. "Captain!" he called.

"Here!"

He saw the policeman with a knot of men which included Frank Henderson, the owner of the carnival King worked for.

"I'm up here with the woman and everything's going to be all right!"

"King?" Frank Henderson shouted. "Do you want some help?"

"No! Just keep everybody down off here for now!" He lingered to make certain that they had heard and understood him, then returned to the woman.

"Now," she said, when he was within twenty feet, "don't come all the way because I don't think I'm used to you yet. I won't make you go down, though. I like the way you sounded just then. Plenty of authority in that voice! I take back the crack about your being a redneck. You might not even be a—a *rustic,* even if it does look as if you wrestle hogs in those clothes."

43

"This rig? I get into it every time I feel like spending the late hours tinkering with my cycle."

"One of those nuts?" she remarked, with a measure of approval. "What kind of cycle do you own?"

"Harley-Davidson fifty-five, modified for scrambling."

"I went through the cycle phase myself, probably when I was younger than you," she said. Her voice was hoarser still from the cold, but companionable. He was further convinced that this sweet-and-sour woman wasn't a crackpot, or bent on suicide, but he wasn't lulled, because despite her offhand manner he sensed rigidity and despair.

She turned her head. "See that?" He could barely make out the pink scar on the side of her neck. "Cycle accident. Throttle jammed open. Damned thing went roaring round and round in a circle with me pinned underneath it. Believe me, one time was all it took." She fought against a yawn. "Since I may decide to elect you Samaritan," she said, her eyes a little bleary, "maybe we ought to exchange names, unless of course you'd prefer to be anonymous. I'll understand. I'm Molly Amos."

"King Windom," he said.

"That's a marvelous name! How did you think of it?"

"One of my great-grandfathers thought of it; name's been in the family ever since."

"Well, my God, apologies are *due,*" Molly Amos said, unaccountably cross, and looked aside, at the tarnished treetops and the dark fields and the lights of Clearwater half hidden by hills. She seemed to have forgotten he was there. "I came up here expecting anything but stars. They're sort of hard to bear when you don't expect them, aren't they?" she sighed, and ended her search. "I think I'm going to have a splitting headache," she said, through her teeth. "What a time to be stranded without a drink." She took off her glasses and seemed to get a little wobbly without them. King poised on the balls of his feet, ready to lunge if she should wobble too far. Molly Amos was aware of his tension, and smiled meanly.

"What happened to my loving cup, Jerry Dee?"

"Turned tail and ran; what else?"

"What else indeed?" she said with the hint of a sneer, and then became contrite. "I don't know why I wasted my time cutting him down. He wasn't a fit victim. Aren't they quiet down there! Maybe I ought to yell out something vulgar and witty to keep them all amused, but just now I can't think of a thing." Molly made a face and spat. "I hate the taste of ashes," she complained, dully. She replaced her glasses and began searching in a coat pocket for something and nearly upset herself.

"Whoops," she exclaimed, with a ghastly smile, clutching the railing. She appealed to King with a glance. He responded quickly and helped her to her feet. Molly clung to him, trying to breathe more slowly. There was gin on her breath. They swayed together, and King felt a contrary tenderness for Molly Amos as he inched around hoping for some place to plant his feet; she was slender and not too tall but solid as concrete and he was afraid they both might topple through the unsafe railing.

"I'm not as fearless as I thought I was," she admitted, pressing her face against his sweater. "In fact, I think I'm scared right now. The joke is over, and it wasn't a very good joke to begin with, and now I'm stuck with it."

"What chased you up here in the first place?"

"Chased?" She puzzled over his choice of words. "I hadn't thought about it that way but you're right." The fingers of her left hand dug into his ribs below the sweater. "Hard muscle there," she murmured, unabashed by her casual exploration. "You don't smell sour and defeated like most young men. And it does, it smells, defeat smells like the smoke of worms. There's no treachery in you either. Just warmth. You don't mind if I soak for a little while, do you? I've been so miserably cold the past few days." Molly looked up at him sharply. "You flinched just then. You don't want to touch me, do you?"

In answer he cupped one hand against the back of her neck and, with a vague smile, she rested her head against him.

"Just a little more," she promised, "and I'll be steady as a rock. Where were we? Oh, *chased*. To begin with, there was Jerry Dee, and as soon as I got close to him, as soon as we were sharing the same atmospheric bath, I knew he was not, *not* for me. Because, you see, without my glasses my eyes are bad; without my glasses I can survive anything for one night. But I have very sensitive fingers and a sensitive nose, and one whiff of Jerry Dee convinced me I'd did a blunder again. It wasn't so much the lotions and tonics, though they were bad enough, it was the sweats. All the sweats that had dried like insect poison on his skin. And the hot sweats of his insignificant soul. Unsmellable to him, to almost anybody else, but one whiff and I almost gagged. Right there I made my first mistake. I should have run out then, but I didn't, I stayed because Jerry Dee had come highly recommended to me, and I was . . . I had the shakes, I was in need." Again Molly felt or thought she felt him flinch but this time held him more tightly, possessively. "I should have realized before ten minutes had gone by that Jerry Dee's reputation was mostly based on the uncritical reactions of a bunch of underfed pokebottoms with starched hair and eyes like targets—that place where we met was full of them—but by then I was busy wrecking my better judgment with gin. Well, I almost wrecked it. But the fair was nearby, and I got to longing for fresh air. On the way I did something I *never* do, have done; I drank straight from the bottle in a man's car. And I tried, really tried to find some genuine body warmth, but all I drew was poison to shrink my lip, so when we reached the fairgrounds, I was in a disastrous low mood; I wasn't so sure I would make it through the night, with nothing to breathe but the dead air of my self-disgust."

Someone was yelling up from below again but a long freight had begun to rumble past the fairgrounds a hundred yards from where they were standing and the voice was obscured. King looked down through the dark maze of trestle beneath his feet and thought he saw the weaving of lights, but he was silent as Molly Amos continued.

"The lights and those awful roasting odors you smell around a carnival hit me worse than any hangover, and I was over my head in faceless faces. Through all of *them* I managed to shove my way to the fence around the merry-go-round, and I hung on there with Jerry Dee tugging at my elbow and bawling me out. I suppose that's what he was doing because I wouldn't budge, and I wasn't paying attention to him either. The merry-go-round was stirring up the sweetest songs in my bygone ear, reminding me of my little-girlhood; I almost felt sublime. My old daddy brought me here to the amusement park on Sundays when he came to town, each time with a new lady on his other arm. He liked to set me high on my horse to whirl around and around, sometimes for an hour, while he made himself comfortable outside on a bench with his friend, and I could see him in my mind's eye, Horatio, there in the sun, his head back with laughter, oh, elegant, his white teeth flashing, as if he could take a bite from the sky. Ugh, hold on to me! And I would ride, ride on my way, leaning forward for that first glimpse of him, leaning way back until we had rounded out of sight and then all those chilly seconds when I was utterly alone, hoping on the next round that he would be smiling at me when I appeared, not chuckling over his lady or patting her hand. I thought of this, I thought of all the Sundays and the different ladies and then I thought of the Sunday when I leaned too far on the indifferent wooden horse and fell off on my head, and *that* memory was too much for me, all those tears, all the hatred I hadn't known I felt for my daddy, and I woke up with a snap and Jerry Dee was chinning in my ear. He had just said something—oh, it wasn't bad, considering the source, God knows—but it just struck me as humiliating and . . . *unforgivable;* I was still a child, a child, with a child's feelings and sense of horror. So I ran away from him, straight across to the roller coaster, where they were shutting down for the night. I ran up to the platform, and then, and then, nowhere else I could ride, nothing I could do but . . . go back to *him.*"

Abruptly, and with a cry, she straightened, pushing King hard away. He caught her wrist to keep her from falling. Head jutted forward, glasses askew down her nose, Molly glared at him. "But I didn't come up here to kill myself! Go ahead and think that, I suppose everybody will! But I came up here to be free. I came up here because I . . . dared myself, and I never have turned down a dare! I've done good things and bad things, but I've done them knowing what I was doing, because I wanted to!"

"What do you want to do now?" he asked calmly, still holding her fast.

Almost instantly the flushed, wild look was replaced by softness, by a moping dependent smile. He had seen, though, in the moments of her wildness, how old Molly Amos was, or at least he thought he could tell. She was in her late thirties. The college-style coat, the feline-demure face in the flattering light along the periphery of the roller coaster had fooled him for a time into thinking she was a youngster.

"Well, as I said, the joke is over, and it never was much of a joke. And now the high sheriff and police are waiting and I'm going to have to swallow my medicine neat and bitter. You can let go now, please. I know one thing, I'm not going downstairs looking hagridden, so . . ." Molly reached into her coat for a flat purse and took out lipstick and compact. She held the mirror far enough away from her face so that her breath wouldn't cloud it, perhaps so that she wouldn't have to face too much of the truth right off, and there, balancing herself besides the rails, over seventy feet above the ground, she carefully began to make up her face, talking to him between swipes with the lipstick. "Now that I think about it, how do we get down? I'm in your hands completely. Oh, straighten me out on one thing before I forget. Did *they* send you up here? I mean as a calming influence until they could bring a hook and ladder?"

"I asked for permission to come up, but they wouldn't give it, so I came anyway."

"Good for you!" she said approvingly, dusting her nose and chin with powder. "Maybe they'll arrest you too. It's going to be a long night yet, and I wouldn't mind company down at the station house. There." She tucked her makeup kit away. "OK; why?"

"Why what?"

"Why did you risk your neck? And it *is* a risk. I could have fallen several times on the way up. Nothing kept me going but sheer terror."

"I reckon I knew that," he said. "I could hear you down there. I don't mean those things you said to Jerry Dee. All the things you were saying to yourself."

"Not all of them, I hope," Molly murmured, not looking too pleased with his answer. She bent to straighten her fallen stocking. King turned and walked to the front of the Pippin, where the people waited below. He signaled and shouted, "We're coming down!" and waited for Molly Amos to join him.

"King!" Frank Henderson shouted back, *"They say do you want the ladder?"*

He studied the glittering arrow of rails into the tunnel below. He did not relish taking her down that way, but it would be dangerous, despite the help of firemen, climbing down a nearly vertical ladder. As he studied his problem he remembered that the back-side grade had not seemed as precipitous as the track just below.

"Molly?" She had come within a few feet of him, but would not take another step.

"I'm afraid to look," she said, eyes shut. "He's down there now—"

"Who? Jerry Dee?"

Molly shook her head. "No. My father. Sitting on a bench in front of the merry-go-round, cast in white marble, durable as the moon, and just as dead and unloving. A museum of long-ago ladies arranged behind him." She shuddered. "You'll tell them, won't you? That I never intended to kill myself. I'll pay the cost for this, I'll pay it all right, but I won't abide some fat judge sentencing me to a psychiatrist for six months because I . . . did a blunder."

"Don't worry, Molly," he said, with such conviction that she was moved to smile, weakly, half-believing that somehow within his sphere all things must turn out right. She groped for his hand. King signaled to the watchers the direction he and Molly Amos were taking, and they started down, she in front, he anchoring on the grade, talking to her soothingly, trying to distract her from the danger. Twice her foot slipped and she almost yanked both of them off balance. Each time they stopped until the fright subsided.

"Oh, you'd better be right," she muttered, "you'd better be right. I don't think I want to go down after all; I can't even see the stars now!" But they were more than halfway down, and they resumed. "Who are all those?" she asked, peering anxiously at the ground.

"Friends of mine, standing by in case we need help."

"Spooks and freaks . . . You mean you work for the carnival?"

"Have for the past five years. I'll be quitting soon, though."

"To do what?" She gasped, and paused again to catch her breath.

Her wrist had become too slippery for him to hold tightly and he wiped his palm on his Levis. "To preach, Molly."

As she looked up, her lenses were turned to ice by the lights overhead. "Oh," she said, softly and grievously, "you're *not.* *Too* much, just too much. I've written this corny story a dozen times, and here it is *hap*pening to me. I wish you hadn't told me you were a preacher. I was getting to like you so much." She smiled, a strained, jaunty smile. "Now I know what you were doing up there. Let me see; the church needs a new recreation hall, and a little publicity never hurt at fund-raising time. Did it? Did it!"

"Molly—"

"How come you're not talking to me about *goad*, and the *lard*, and all of them? While you had me cornered up there why didn't you give me a real going over for the sake of my immortal soul?"

He winced at her raging mockery. "Wasn't the time or place

49

for a sermon, Molly. And I don't need one from *you*. I'm tired and my knees are fixing to buckle from hauling back on you; let's just get off this thing."

"You bet I'm going to get off!" she snapped, turning her back on him and plunging the rest of the way down the grade. He thought she would fall and there was nothing he could do except hold his breath. But Molly managed to stay upright until she had reached the bottom, where she kneeled, breathless, on the section of catwalk there, hair billowed in her face. There she stared in dread at the lights, the police, the carnival faces, and drew back from the hands raised to assist her. She sobbed and looked for King.

"I'm sorry," she cried. "I'm sorry!"

"Are you hurt?" he asked, holding her by the shoulders.

"No . . . only stay with me. Don't let go. Don't."

Her appeal was so genuine and urgent that King quickly forgot he was angry, angry because of her attack on him and his motives, angry because she had run from him, and again he felt only sympathy for her predicament. "I'll stay with you, Molly," he said. But in making this promise he had the insecure feeling that he might have committed himself more fully than he intended to Molly Amos.

5

Fire in the Water

By three in the morning the thunderous sounds of an empty freight train being put together in the nearby marshaling yards of the Southern Railroad began to penetrate the shield of concentration which had hardened around Frank Henderson as he worked on his ledgers; he looked up in annoyance at a particularly loud coupling of cars and put down his pen. The coffee in the shaving mug at his left hand was cold, as he discovered by dipping his ink-stained finger into it, and when he lifted the elderly enameled coffeepot from the hot plate on his workbench and gave it an experimental shake, he heard nothing but the swish of dregs in the bottom.

There was a sharp pain in his back below the right shoulder blade, which he couldn't quite reach with his hand; one of the rewards of the accountant's life, he thought, and rose from his chair to stretch. His eyes, accustomed to the ledger, were not easily distracted, and he continued to gaze down at the lines and columns of figures, the occasional scoldings of red ink, feeling neither pleasure nor pain, but a modest satisfaction. He had learned bookkeeping because the budget of the Henderson Brothers' Exposition America Shows did not allow for the services of either a professional auditor or a regular paymaster. Despite the name, which seemed to indicate an extravaganza on the order of a world's fair, the unit which he ran was a small one, pared down to the essentials of such outdoor entertainment: games, freaks, rides. His brother Averill had the other half of the family carnival, which spent most of its season on the rodeo circuit. Years ago, because of increased operating costs and mounting disinterest on the part of the public, they had found it necessary to split Exposition America and play only the smaller cities and fairs. Despite all economies, they counted their net profits in hundreds of dollars, but, thought Frank, dimly assessing the pages of his ledger, they still managed to come out ahead somehow, the interest on the mortgage was paid, the payroll would be met, as usual, and there would be at least one more season for the Henderson Brothers.

Three more days in Clearwater, Tennessee; after that, the winter layoff. The weariness which he felt at this hour told him that he was more than ready for a long rest, for a few weeks of small-game fishing, for sessions of lies and reminiscences with the other owners who wintered their shows on the Florida Gulf Coast. For mapping out the season which would be the Best Ever. Perhaps during the months to come he would be able to find that Spectacular Ride, the unique Thrill Attraction, that incomparably Fascinating Geek to endow *his* show with a glamour all the others lacked. Perhaps . . . but the dry air of the trailer was making him edgy and depressed, and he found it almost impossible to think beyond the next three days, and the end of the current season. This time pulling up stakes meant losing a friend, he was certain of that, and he didn't know what to do about it.

Taking his old twill jacket from a wardrobe, he left the small office in the back of his trailer home and went outside, bracing himself in the cold air. The bellowing of metal had ceased in the railroad yards and his people, his troublesome, endearing, irreplaceable family, slept; he felt both warmed and saddened by a sense of their common breath as he crossed the sawdust-filled yard of the trailer compound, which lay just outside the silent promenade of the carnival itself.

The night watchman was nodding himself to sleep in his shack at the gate and Frank caused hardly a ripple in the old man's dreams as he let himself into the fairgrounds. His carnival had been brought in to supplement the meager attractions of the permanent amusement park there and they had done well in the first week of a ten-day stand; they would be invited back. He strolled past the outlandish machines, with names like Wild Mouse and Roman Circus, rides that were expensive to maintain and haul around. But even the newest and most complicated rides didn't interest the kids much anymore. The kids had their drag races and motorbike rallies and some of them even jumped out of airplanes for fun. He had a notion of what might interest them: he would buy a freight train loaded with old autos, junk but still intact, windows and all, and lay in an arsenal of various-sized hammers, and then he would charge all comers a buck apiece for a quarter hour of unrestrained destruction.

This sort of pessimism for the future of showmanship annoyed him; he roused himself from his lethargic pace and walked more briskly along the paved streets of the deserted fair, in the direction of the stock pens and rodeo arena.

From far back on the ridge the lights of the Eli Charger revival tent became visible to him, and he studied the tent as he walked across the soft earth chewed by the hoofs of horses and steers. He leaned against the slat side of an empty pen, chin against his arms, thoughtless, half-alert. Before long he became aware of the figure of a man, sitting bow-backed on the fence not too far away, also facing the ridge.

Frank stayed where he was, not wanting to let King know he was there. He wondered how the preaching had gone tonight, who had liked him and who hadn't. Of course, all kinds of women liked King, and so did teen-agers. The kids like him because he was near their age and incapable of talking down, and the frustrated mothers . . . He looked as if he needed a mother, most of the time, with his hair slumped down around his ears and growing down the back of his neck. A woman would see that he might possibly need taking care of. A man would see only King's size, and face, and be glad that he had a good disposition. Frank shook his head. It was a mystery to him why he should have such thoughts. Why should he be disturbed by King's choice of a way of life? He resisted an impulse to shudder, remembering too well the look in a haunted boy's face, some five years gone. . . .

"Frank, you turned to stone down there?" King said, with a trace of amusement in his voice. A steer, disturbed by the talking, bumped against one of the fences, grunted irritably, and settled back down to sleep. Frank buried his hands in the pockets of his jacket and joined King.

"I thought you'd still be in town, trying to talk your way out of a night in jail."

"Oh, there wasn't any trouble. That captain's a bullheaded man and he gave me a good-sized piece of his mind on the way, but I think he was glad none of his men had to go up there." He glanced briefly over one shoulder at the Pippin.

"What's going to become of the woman?"

"She was sweet and quiet and worried, and they let her call a lawyer she knew, and he had her home in an hour. She'll get a hearing and she'll have to pay for the city's time and trouble."

"At that she's lucky," Frank said, thinking of the whiteness in her face as King brought her down, wondering what might have been. He turned his attention to lighting a cigarette, not sure yet if this would be their time to talk. King had invited his company, but his eyes had turned away to the distant tent, bright as a bird against the steel-gray sky. He was steadfast and watchful, but with an air of resignation.

"I had a letter from down home, today," Frank said, when their silence began to burden him. "One of the kids drove over to Sanibel after the hurricane to see what was left standing. Dardy's old shack was scattered along the beach, but all we lost was one shutter; she hardly leaked a drop. We built even better than we thought." He smiled slightly, thinking of the fishing retreat which he and King had put up, doing all the carpentry themselves. Two winters of hard work, and he could just see the place now, weather-tight, solid, the cypress silver-gray by

53

morning light. He longed for home, for the first big family weekend at Sanibel, but without King there to help him brag . . .

"What do you want to do it for?" he asked abruptly, knowing that King was not going to be swayed by his talk of Florida. "When you aren't even sure if it's *right*. I don't mean right in the eyes of the Lord, I mean right for you."

King nodded, as if the same thoughts had been in his mind. "That's a fair question, Frank, and I intend to give you an answer." He climbed down from the fence and gently slapped his friend's elbow with his hand, indicating that he wanted to walk on; together they left the stock pens and started back. "Because," King continued, "I've loved you, and you deserve the best I can give to any man. You kept me alive when I didn't particularly want to live, and saved my soul from hell."

For a few moments Frank Henderson's thoughts were filled with the smoldering brilliance of an afternoon sun. It had been more than five years. A wet spring had plagued them, they were deep in the red and far behind schedule. He'd had enough to keep him occupied during the headachy drive from Johnson City to Asheville, through the tip end of the Appalachians; it was only by the wildest chance that he saw the Negro and the boy in the gorge by the side of the road. No reason at all for him to pull off on the shoulder and wave the rest of them on. But he'd had a glimpse of the efforts the Negro was making to bandage the gaunt boy's hands, using river mud as a poultice. He'd seen a vacant white face, and curiosity had distracted him.

So he clambered down, into the gorge, and the smell of char was as strong as the odor of spring pine across the stony chute of the river. The soles of the boy's boots were nearly burned through and his clothing was saturated with smoke. The boy was going to die, that was clear. He asked no names, no questions, and the Negro volunteered nothing. They might have been fugitives, but Frank didn't care. He'd never seen a human face so close to the bone before, or suffering like that reflected in the dry, pale, unseeing eyes. Between the two of them they lifted the boy up the side of the gorge and carried him to the trailer, there laid him across Frank's bed. To die, Frank thought again. He'd seen men hurt, some mangled badly, and never doubted they would recover. But the look of

54

this boy, who showed no wounds except for his poor hands, gave Frank a forlorn chill.

"There was nothing I could do but drive on for Asheville," he said, thinking aloud, "and let the nearest hospital dispose of you. But you were still alive. The doctor told me your lungs hadn't been cooked in that fire, and you might pull through once you were over the shock that had hold. There was no bed for you in the hospital so I thought, Well, a couple of days. Anyone with a name like King Windom deserved a chance to show what sort of grit he had."

"It wasn't a lot," King said with a morose smile. "But you made me fight. Gave me something to fight. Frank Henderson was rough medicine for me to take. First thing I remember hearing you say was, 'Nobody is going to die in my bed but me!' And then you put me out. I had to swallow everything at once. The rawness of people. Lights that scraped my eyes. Music that made me want to vomit. I kept going, looking for a place to drop. And every time I made as if to lie down and quit, you snatched me up again and said, 'Look!'"

King stopped; in a fit of nervousness he had been about to leave his friend behind. "I want to go home with you, Frank," he said. "I want to go home where I'm welcome and wanted, where I've learned to be loved; I want to teach Tip how to sail the moth when he gets a little older, and I want to go gigging with Marsh and Patty. I want to get by, and not take any more chances in my life. I don't want to gamble on anything but the fact that the wind might keep the fish away from the pass tomorrow. Only I have to. You asked me why I'm throwing money at a man I don't even trust, for a piece of goods like that tent back there, and I promised an answer. It's because God has said to me, Show me who you are."

"He spoke to you?" Frank asked, quietly.

"Oh, not in so many words, Frank," the preacher said impatiently. "I know good and well God hasn't spoken directly to a man in over nineteen hundred years, and I've not been hearing any strange voices lately. But he provided me with a sign I couldn't miss."

"What sort of sign?"

"I'll have to tell it to you this way. Last winter I took the pirogue down the coast and poled my way through the islands. I told you I was off for a little still-water fishing, but I had a different purpose: I was planning a retreat, two weeks of meditation and prayer. I had to know, once and for all, if I should let go of my dream of ever preaching again.

"I set up camp on a strip of beach between blue water and a mangrove swamp, just a good-size fire to keep the varmints away, a raised pallet to sleep on, and a square of canvas over that. I kept a two-gallon can of fresh water with me and nothing else. Oh, and clothes were a torment in that air, so except when I was back in the mangrove I went naked as a savage."

"It's a wonder the mosquitoes didn't kill you right away."

"It was so sultry the first three days they followed me like a fog; I couldn't even go into the bay for a swim. I had to stay close to swamp water, and bathe twenty times a day to flush the salt from my skin. I was so miserable I couldn't keep my mind on praying. Then the wind changed and it rained three days, a steady cold torrent. I stayed dripping wet, and my toes swelled up with fungus."

"Good Lord. Were you fasting all this time?"

"No. Each day I ate a single small fish from the black water. Each day the meat of the fish was cold and bitter, bitter as salt, or clay, but I ate it, to remind myself of the meanness of my own flesh. By the seventh day I was talking out loud to myself, so weary I could hardly raise up from my pallet and go to wash in the stream. But on the seventh morning the weather was fair, and I thought, Today I'll pray. Not long after, I had my first sign that the Lord was attending me."

King stopped and lifted his head, expelling a cold mass of breath. "Shooting stars," he murmured, his eyes on the horizon. "It's that time of year, isn't it?" They joined a Negro watchman who was warming his hands over a flaming barrel. Frank was absorbed by what he had heard, by the touch of leopard in the preacher's eyes as he bent to the fire, and although the heat gave him an instant headache and he felt a yearning for sleep, he was content not to force the end of the story from King. Presently the Negro, with a nod and a smile for his fellow nighthawks, left them alone. King brushed a hot swirl of ash from his forehead and looked up, apologetically.

"I lost myself for a little while there. What was I telling? Oh, the day—"

"Something about a first sign," Frank reminded him.

"On the seventh morning I went to bathe in the stream again, but as I was so done in, so blind tired I could hardly

56

find my way. I was trembling, retching, nearly as cold as a corpse. I slipped down to rest when I thought my heart was about to burst, but I chose a poor place: a water moccasin, thick as my wrist, was hanging on a root not five feet away." He sucked in his breath, appalled by the memory. "Even if I'd had all my wits about me I couldn't have escaped. I was never so close to death, not even in that church fire. But instead of striking me, the snake just edged back, flicked his tongue, and went away. Can you imagine? A water moccasin, the meanest kind of snake that lives! I knew then God would be listening to me that day. I rushed down to the beach, into the open, and without a thought for the sand flies or anything else I kneeled down. After an hour—two hours?—in the hot sun I made my way back to my pallet and fell sound asleep.

"When I woke up I couldn't tell if it was dawn or dusk. A mist had gathered over all, and through the mist the sun was shining, a perfect radiance. Frank, I just never have seen anything so beautiful. The bay was dark blue and motionless; I didn't hear the slightest sound, or see a flying thing. I propped myself on an elbow and drank in all that beauty; it was meat for my hungry belly and drink to quench my thirst. I was dumb with the reverence I felt for my Lord and my God, but I felt too the same old terror, for the earth was empty, and I was alone. The Lord's own silence in that cloister of water and cloud caused me to tremble from doubt, from fear of His final Judgment." King's expression was scornful as he recreated the scene. "My naked knees about knocked together from terror when I left my pallet and went down to the water's edge, to the mist that was swirling inches above the surface. And there I saw—" His voice weakened and he was mute, staring off into space, his lips moving slightly, as if he could not find words to share the most disturbing, or most precious, experience of his life. "I saw the salt water of that little bay *consumed* beneath its surface by fire. I'm not lying! I saw it. I was overcome, for it is written in Genesis that the Spirit of God was moving over the face of the waters. No man should witness such a sight. But I witnessed it. I saw Him in the water, Frank. I saw His name written in the glowing pool: YHWH—God. Written in a fire more beautiful and mysterious to behold than the lights in the depths of the most precious jewel on earth."

"You saw . . . " Frank murmured, his love and respect for King weighted with doubt that what he had experienced could be more than a dream provoked by desperation. "You saw God. Was that all?"

"Not all. When those letters of fire had perished of themselves, there was more writing in the salt. 'Go . . . ye. Go, ye,'" King repeated, triumphantly, but Frank saw a worried, almost feverish light in his eyes.

With a slight nod of his head Frank suggested that they walk on toward the trailer compound. King was excited; he went headlong. His passion—a steady inward turbulence—was evident in every motion; it whipped away the chip of a smile he showed to his friend. He said:

"Isn't it plain, Frank? Judging from your expression you— But the words were written, *there*. They were the Lord's sign, and His will. *Go ye and preach the Gospel!* Show me who you are. Because it's time, it's late—"

Frank looked back, uneasily, at King's abrupt silence. The preacher had stopped as if struck and his face was pale and queer in the cold light. Frank had no way of knowing what thought had so completely changed King's expression of joy, and urgency; he said only, "I'm here."

"The sign, Frank," King said, with such effort that Frank shared his pain. "If I've misread the sign and His Divine will, this time I'm damned to hell for good and all, and no way to be redeemed!"

"What makes you think—"

"GO YE! That was the message of the Lord. But did He mean to preach the Gospel, or did He say: *You are a guilty man; go ye to the Sugar Tree Valley and humble yourself before those you have wronged?*"

Frank listened, and felt a shock of despair. Then, as he studied King's taut face, flinched at the exhaustion and will to ruin he saw there, he recalled his original judgment upon a burned and hollowed youth: He will die. Frank became, for one of the few times in his life, shatteringly angry. And, for the first time, he was able to suppress his anger, use it to forge the words that would help him retrieve this boy, his unexpected, cherished son, from the edge of a new disaster. In the corner of his eye the faraway tent of Eli Charger burned like a sore. But the tent at least meant life for King, which was all that mattered now.

"You're as saintly a man as I've ever known," he said, sharply enough to call King from his anguish, "and I believe in you and trust you. When you say that you saw the Will of God burning in salt water at your feet I don't doubt you for a second, because I'm not a proper judge of miracles. And I never have denied the Will of God; didn't He give you over into my hands? Don't we know that He is our God, and He is just? Don't we? I've told you, and Age has told you, time and again, there's no reason for you to go back to the Sugar Tree Valley. You've listened, you can tell common sense when you hear it. If He *is* a just God, who sent you away from the Valley and healed your spirit so that you could live again and rejoice in your stewardship, why would He send you back? Son, don't turn away from me, I'm talking to you! Would He do that? Send you back there just so some fool could shoot you in the head? What kind of saint or martyr do you think you have to be? You're a preacher, that's all, with God's help and His blessing—"

"Frank!"

Frank stopped, but there was a warning in his eyes. "No," he said.

"I killed!"

His cry of guilt and self-hatred stunned them both, like a pistol shot, and Frank stared helplessly.

"Demon . . . demon . . ." King muttered, and folded. Frank caught him.

"There's no *demon*. And you never *killed*. That little girl died of pneumonia, and nothing on this green earth could have saved her life! It's to your credit that you tried to save her. God knows, God forgives."

"Then why can't I be easy in my mind?" He was sitting on the ground, sick with remorse, his head loose as a drunk's against his hand.

"You didn't commit any crime; there's no reason for you to go on feeling sorry for yourself, and grieving over trouble most sensible people have put out of their minds entirely. Don't you see that you're a different man now? That's God's true will, He wants you to have a good life, He wants you to preach and be happy, and not drive yourself half insane with thoughts of demons living in your body."

Frank continued to lean over King, protectively, not knowing what to do next. But King steadied himself, and gained color slowly, and looked up with rimmed, haggard eyes.

"I may be a better man, or a worse man, than I was," he said tentatively, "but still I belong to God."

"Yes, and He suffers you gladly. Remember His sign. There have been sinners in the Bible, great men, and they were able to overcome their sins. Don't just sit now; you're too much of a man to grovel there in the dirt."

"I'm a sorry sight—a sorry sinner," King said with an awkward smile, and he rose with Frank's assistance. But he was nearly out on his feet.

"A few hours' sleep—"

"I'm so afraid I never will sleep again," King said, his tongue dull and slow.

"You will. With a warm blanket over you, and warm milk in your stomach." And, Frank thought grimly, with the help of a potent sedative in that milk. The insomnia had always been a problem, but of course King brought that on himself. For an educated man he had an almost superstitious fear of medicines, and doctors too, and refused to take anything to relieve his sleeplessness. Frank had seen King worked up like this before, when mental strain and long hours outrode his fantastic stamina. He would be stronger in just a few hours; he would be himself again. But when the next crisis came, who would be there to help him? For a few seconds Frank was weak with fear, and he cursed himself.

"Oh, I ache! Which way, Lord Jesus, which way? There's so much for me to do!"

"This way," Frank Henderson said, sadly leading him along.

6

The Agreement

When eleven o'clock came and went and King still hadn't stopped by, Jeremy grew restless and snappish in her kitchen and went outside to sweep the front porch a second time. She'd already had a busy day. Barely past daybreak, Eli had got up and dressed in his meeting suit and, with Philemon to accompany him, had gone into town to pay a call on a lawyer he knew of. Once they were out of the house Jeremy had taken advantage of the opportunity to give the place a thorough cleaning, annoyed by the fact that old houses seemed to have a special attraction for dirt.

It was a gorgeous morning, she thought; last night's hard freeze had brought out the wine tones of a parcel of sweetgum and hornbeak close by. As she swept, her mind wandered to thoughts of a certain elegance: to freshly painted or papered walls, pink, or peach (her favorite color); to red curtains and pleasant ovals of carpet and no sounds of mice in the walls at night. Jeremy had lived in small comfortable houses as well as places like this, she had good memories on which to base her practical longings, but unaccountably, this morning her daydreams of the decencies of life were bound up with her desire to see King again; it was the first time she had thought that boldly of loving him, and instantly she felt glum, as if she were playing an unforgivable trick on herself.

Jeremy set her broom aside and sat down on the steps, reaching for a kitten to hold. The paws and breath of the kitten gradually made her feel better, and the cramp that had been threatening her midsection went away. She felt sufficiently good to be scornful of herself. Someday she would be married, all right. To someone willing to overlook her black spells and mean eye, someone a little more decent and presentable than Philemon, but no more manly or interesting. That was her woman's luck, born into her. Why then, she wondered, dreary again—her moods were too changeable to keep track of today—if God was generous and had given her a man like King Windom to love before the fact of that endless, inescapable marriage, did she have to feel such pain? What kind of generosity was that? She could make herself miserable enough with everyday things, if she wanted.

This blasphemy brought a flush to her cheeks. She looked up to see King coming at last, over the ridge, in a rattling hurry.

"Jeremy? Morning," he said by way of greeting as he crossed the clay yard, and thrust a paper sack at her with a smile. "Are you liking pears? Take a look at those beauties."

"Pears!" Jeremy repeated, glowing; she dipped into the sack and chose one for herself. She was half-hoping that after their closeness of the night before King would spend a few minutes with her, but before she could turn her head he had bounded up to the porch, a preoccupied look in his eye. Well, the treat was unexpected and wonderful, and her glow continued. She trailed him into the house with an unnecessary, "Eli, King's here."

Eli was sitting at a nearly worn-out card table in a spate of sun from the windows, surrounded by water-stained cardboard boxes jammed with papers and thick, bound envelopes. He looked up from his writing, unkinked his rusty fingers and scowled at the railroader's watch open in front of him.

"Thought you'd changed your mind," he grumbled.

"No, I had some things to do in town, and I made a late start." King shook his head, perplexed. "I slept until almost nine, and I *never* do that."

"Well, pull up a chair and we'll get this over with." There was an inexplicable trace of animosity in Eli's voice and he looked unwell, his face seamed and grained and poorly shaven, his eyes burning with a fiery light; King found it uncomfortable to look into them.

Because of his unaccustomed deep sleep, the past twelve or fourteen hours were crowded dimly in King's mind. He had awakened alert, shaky, troubled, and ravenous, and had gone immediately downtown to a bank to make arrangements which he had been considering for a week. He was still laboring with a headache, with a ghost of the terror that had almost overcome him on the deserted fairgrounds, but generally he felt vigorous and sure of himself. He wanted to question Eli closely about the meeting the night before, but decided to shut out all but the business at hand.

Eli produced a folder which contained several typed sheets of paper.

"This here is an agreement between us which I had a lawyer draw up this morning. It's simple and to the point. You sign, I'll sign, Jeremy'll witness, and it's done."

King nodded politely and scanned the six paragraphs. They were to the point, as Eli had said, and in sum made him and Eli equal partners.

"Six thousand dollars," Eli said, to make sure King hadn't missed that. "Payable to me within three days."

King nodded again, reached for a pen, signed all copies. He passed them to Eli, who inscribed his name with care and effort, then called for Jeremy. She came bearing a bottle of table wine and two glasses, glanced at King as if she were still concerned about his involvement with Eli, then put down her name in an admirable hand and left them alone.

With the signed agreements in hand, Eli's manner altered: he smiled, showing his teeth fretfully, and tilted his head in a courtly manner.

"Help yourself to the wine," he said. "I don't have much else to offer by way of celebration. . . . And a glass for me if you please." When King hesitated, he added, cheerfully, "Some of our own frown on spirits and drinking, but wine is the water of the desert after all, and made from honest grape; it can't ever do harm to a temperate man."

"No, it can't," King said, still taken aback. He poured a generous portion of the honest grape into Eli's glass, an ounce into his own, and settled back in his chair. Eli sniffed his glass like a connoisseur and drank deeply.

"Now, about the money . . ." King began.

Eli's smile hung, motionlessly, from the jut of his upper teeth. King went into a pocket of his hopsacking jacket, withdrew a green card, and reached across the table to place it squarely in front of Eli.

"What's this?" Eli said, scowling down at the card.

"Oh, just something the savings and loan needs to establish our joint account. I went into town this morning and arranged it all." He contentedly patted his stomach at the beltline. "Sure was a relief to get all that money off my own person and safe in a bank. I've been carrying it with me most of the summer." He held up two identical passbooks and opened one so that Eli could read the entry. "You'll have to jot your name in the savings books too. Then when we want to take out some of that money, all we do is sign the withdrawal slip together. Easy as can be. In the meantime the money's there in the savings and loan earning better than four percent a year for us."

Eli, staring, wet his lips meticulously, and his right hand fell vengefully upon the agreements which they had just been celebrating. King decided he needed that ounce of Concord wine he'd been hoarding in his glass, and swallowed it down in a lump, feeling vaguely sinful as he did so. Eli's hand trembled, and the tremor spread; the reddish, marbled eyes lifted briefly, to meet King's own. Tension had clotted the air in the sunny room.

Eli smiled, as before, but his face seemed to blow up with derisive, hidden laughter for an instant.

"I'm delighted with you," he said, "delighted! And I know we're going to be happy in the Lord and each other."

"I know we are," King echoed, surprised at the ease with which Eli had accepted all the strings King had attached to the six thousand. Eli beckoned for the passbooks in order to sign his name to them; he did this good-humoredly, saying, "The Lord had replenished our barrel of meal and pitcher of oil, but how shall we render unto the Lord?"

"God is blessing us here today," King asserted, throbbing with relief and happiness, now that the way to God's appreciation and greater love seemed unmistakable. He looked for Jeremy, wanting her reaction, but she had gone outside by the back door.

"Amen!" Eli said rejoicing. "We'll all surely profit from your inspiration and your zeal. You're young, and the spectacle of revivalism inflames your soul! You want to give to God, give God His due, give God His tithe!"

"Amen, that's what I want to do."

"You want to see that old devil whimpering on his knees, and know it was you who put him there. Glory, God! But, Preacher . . ."

King's fervor burned a little lower as Eli, who was suddenly all business again, reached into his shirt pocket for a nickel notebook and began to fumble through the pages. At each page his tongue darted rapaciously over his lower lip.

"A thousand dollars," Eli continued, "is only a speck of dust in Satan's eye. A hundred thousand dollars is a bone in his throat. But it takes a *million* dollars to stagger that old devil, to put him down on his knees crying for mercy." He drove this point home with a meaningful look. "Now, there's no need for us to chew over the fact that you're an ambitious man, so I'll get on. I wrote down some figures you'll find of interest and I urge you to study them. There are plenty of preachers with fancy tents and big followings who travel all over the world. These are the expenses of one such preacher I know.

"His tent cost him over twenty-five thousand dollars, new, when he bought it three years ago. It was made to order, out of vinyl plastic instead of canvas, and it holds three thousand people. He requires a staff of twenty, and his payroll is six thousand dollars a month. Five days a week he's heard on radio stations across the country, and that's another forty thousand dollars a month, every month, for air time. His printing bill runs one or two thousand most months, even though he doesn't put out a magazine like others do. Mind you, this man's not famous like Harlan Gray. He's what I'd call an ordinary preacher with a sense of mission that's too big for him to handle. He works so hard he's already suffered two heart attacks, but he's in it, and can't quit. Most months he only meets expenses."

King ignored this calculated dim view and the figures, since he was being permitted to see only one side of the ledger. He knew perfectly well what Eli was getting at, and he tried to feel tolerant of the old evangelist's short-sightedness. But he only half listened.

Jeremy had returned to the kitchen in time to hear part of Eli's lecture. "You're talking about an ordinary preacher," she said. "King can raise a riot on a street corner without half trying."

Eli put Jeremy in her place with a look, his smile having worn down to a humorless gleam. To King he said, "Harlan Gray, who is the greatest evangelist in the world today, can stun the devil with his power and divert men from debauchery and evil by the strength of his will. But he has the faith of a Joshua, who stops the sun in the sky. What about your own faith? Is it all-powerful, or is it small and perfect like a pearl, the kind of faith that inspires God to tears of happiness for such a man at His bosom? Will you grow weary and cold from the sins of the world, and be driven into yourself?"

King knew when he was being caressed with a hickory switch, but Eli's suggestion of his limits hit home. Somehow Eli saw this, and was content with his advantage.

"Remember that a small tent such as ours can be a mighty fortress against the devil. Many nights we've had nothing but the tent itself over our heads. That was enough. We are where we belong. You're a man of considerable experience in the world—I may judge you on short acquaintance—and practical too; I know you see the wisdom of singing God's praises day by day and being content."

"That is nothing but good advice," King said, feeling a little sullen for allowing himself to be put on the defensive by Eli. But just now he didn't feel like a showdown over matters of policy.

"Jeremy," Eli said, "serve up our lunch." And he smiled like a canny horse once more.

Philemon came in after they were all at the table, dropped a look on King that was enough to break his back, and sat down at his place with no words other than those necessary to get him through a private grace.

King had run out of compliments for Jeremy's excellent vegetable soup, which she had accepted with regal aplomb to hide her pleasure, and, looking for a way to give the conversation a lift, he asked politely of Eli:

"Are you fixing up a book of your sermons? I noticed your writing table piled high."

The evangelist put down his spoon—he had eaten little—and blinked his reddish eyes. For several moments he stared thoughtfully at King as if trying to decide whether to entrust him with something uncommonly precious, such as the hard-won wisdom of Eli Charger.

"Not just one book that occupies me, King," he allowed, "but twenty-one. The Books of Fundamentalist religion."

"Oh, I see. You're writing a history."

Eli smiled serenely at that statement. "Yes, a history of our Southern religion, but also of our Southern people, from the middle eighteenth century up to now." His face lighted with a rare enthusiasm. "I correspond with upward of four hundred preachers of the Fundamentalist faiths from here to Borneo. You say, how can one man find the time? But those preachers do most of the work on the Books. It's no secret. My mission is to set down the whole magnificent story in my own words, in prose poetry. I have a gift for language. My models are the great poets and historians of the Old Testament. I don't imitate them, mind. The story of our time ought to be written in the speech of our time, the speech of home folks. I've also included in the Books sermons and epistles by those of my friends I judge to be among God's holiest men. The survivors of our earth will turn to the words of these men for guidance in the clouds of darkness that surround them after civilization as we know it shall perish."

Part of this was familiar to King, but he felt a little surprised to hear that Eli was at heart a Doomsday preacher. At the same time Eli seemed to have a few special ideas that disturbed him. Apparently he had set himself to compiling a sort of Third Testament, which would be instrumental in the rebirth of religion after some calamity, self-inflicted or otherwise, had reduced men to sticks and stones once more.

"The look on your face tells me you think I'm engaged in

66

child's play," Eli said. From the tone of his voice he wasn't offended; any preacher thrives on resistance. "As a religious man I don't have to tell you about God's Day of Terror. The Day of Terror is prophesied in many books of the Bible, and with good reason, for it has come before. During the centuries the Old Testament was being written, the original Day of Terror still lived in the memory of men. I call it the *original* Day of Terror because it happened not more than one thousand years before civilization, as we reckon it today, began in the plains of northern Iraq. That was almost fifteen thousand years ago, and the new Day of Terror is imminent; God in His wisdom foresaw that the numerous races of men would again rush to the brink of self-destruction within fifteen thousand years. We are hell-bent to destroy one another; we have made an overcrowded dung heap of our Lord's green earth. That's why I say the time has come for cataclysm. Do you know that not only our own civilization, in which we set such store, but all the civilizations of the world are doomed to perish in a few seconds' time?"

"I'd heard some talk," King said soberly.

"Likely I know what you're thinking. The bomb!" His lips shriveled disdainfully. "That thing is a toy. It's *highly* overrated. I'm talking about an earth-shattering cataclysm that only God could imagine. It is upon us. But—"

As he buttered a third piece of crumbling cornbread, King found that he was losing his appetite; Eli cast a lugubrious spell. His Southern voice was basically as sweet as a melon, somewhat dim like a long-lived wind that sighs against the ear, and at times unexpectedly rusty, undoubtedly from years of shouting in drafty tents.

"There will be survivors," Eli went on. "For the Lord has said, Never again shall all flesh be cut off by the waters of a flood. The men who live on next time—only a handful—will again be entrusted with the earth, and it'll be up to them to fashion a civilization pleasing to the senses of the Lord. These are the men who will need the truth everlasting of the Fundamentalist Books."

"I see," King said, glancing first at Jeremy and then at Philemon. He had the notion that he was involved in an intricate practical joke, but he could tell nothing from their expressions; Philemon's eyes were fixed deliberately on his plate and Jeremy was gazing out the window as if she had heard all this many times before. The cartons of papers around the writing table seemed to lend impressive weight to what Eli was telling him, however. King decided he was not being gulled.

"Do you wonder what I mean by cataclysm?" Eli said.

"I always thought it would take a war to—"

"War has sufficed, war has sufficed," Eli said, nodding. "Where are Susa and Shahabad, Ur and Ugarit and Babylon today? Them places, and a thousand others, are bits of pottery and ruined walls, once mighty cities pillaged by war. But the world was small then; billions of people living now. Famine can't destroy those billions. Wars can't destroy them. Man multiplies in his sins faster than he dies; hence God's wisdom in preparing for the cleansing of His earth is revealed. Who knows how many perished on the last Day of Terror? Who knows what cities lie on the floors of the oceans and beneath the icecaps of Greenland and Antarctica?"

"How could that be?"

"It not only can be true, it is. The cataclysm which God has provided for our Day of Terror is a fact of nature which has been demonstrated by the greatest prophet of modern time, a twentieth-century Isaiah named Nicholas Crenshaw."

King's disappointment in having been deprived of knowledge about Nicholas Crenshaw was evident in his face.

"No, you never have heard the name. Dr. Crenshaw was a professor of physics at the University of Western Canada. He also happens to be one of my proselytes. Unfortunately, few have listened to his warnings, or read his theories. All that men remember of catastrophe is written in the Bible, yet in their concern for the here-and-now they have ignored all historical signs and prophecies. This is God's *own* prophecy:

" 'I am God and there is none like me, declaring the end from the beginning. . . . ' "

He paused to let that sink in. King listened attentively, frowning.

" 'The end from the beginning.' The earth is stone and fire and mud, but it also suffers the infirmities of man." Eli's eyes blazed a little brighter. "For nearly fifteen thousand years, on the frozen continent of Antarctica, a great tumor has been growing. As the earth spins each day, it carries along this bulging tumor of ice, a tumor now over six million square miles in size, more than two miles thick at its heart—think of it! And each year this

68

tumor increases in size by nearly five trillion tons. Do you believe the earth will go on rotating faithfully forever, with its burden of ice? I can tell you it won't."

With laborious intensity Eli took the notebook from the pocket of his shirt again and sketched the earth for King.

"Not round, is it? Some say it looks like a pear. Scientific fact, as we know." He went on to describe the land bulge at the equator, and the slight wobble of the earth as it turns. The reason for that wobble—he was now quoting Dr. Crenshaw— was the mass of ice off-center at the South Pole.

"That's physics, and I don't understand physics. But it's simple enough, to hear him tell of it. Right now the bulge at the equator compensates for the ice so the wobble won't get out of hand. But the ice is building up, and one day it will become too much of a burden for the earth. On that day the earth will wobble like a top about to fall. But the earth's not a top; it has to keep moving. When it can't rotate on its present axis, it'll flop over and rotate on a different axis altogether. The poles will be changed, hemispheres reversed. Do you begin to see the possibilities of such a change?"

"Dimly."

Eli spelled it all out. The whole atmosphere would be churned into violent winds. The seas would be snatched from their beds, and torrents of water would fall on the great cities, obliterating them at a stroke. There would be earthquakes and volcanic eruptions and chaos. The lower Mississippi Valley, not far from where they were sitting right that minute, would be so deep undersea that no light might penetrate the depths.

"All you have to do is look at the history of our earth to understand I'm not talking myth. Where did civilization begin? In valleys once covered by the sea. Near arid land, blighted by salt. But fresh-water rivers, running from the mountains, across continents, flushed away all that salt, so the land could become fruitful in the valleys of the Nile and Euphrates. Men who survived that great flood of long ago descended from their mountain homes, cast aside their weapons, and fashioned the tools of the fields. A lovely picture, isn't it? Genesis! Eden! The tribes of Abraham! The whole Biblical story come to life, just as it will again after the Day of Terror. But next time, because a few of us foresaw to provide our descendants with the Word of God as it is spoken and sung today, they will not long suffer without awareness of their God. The grass withereth, the flower fadeth, but the word of our God shall stand forever. He has promised a *new* earth—wherein dwelleth righteousness. . . . Jeremy? Coffee!"

King felt a measure of sympathy as he glimpsed the yearning in the aging man's eyes. He allowed his imagination free rein and saw Eli as Eli might see himself, as a man born out of his time, truly Biblical in his passions for the Lord and the raw beginnings of civilization. Yes, he could picture Eli on a goat-skin pallet before a campfire, in a sheltered valley, instructing numerous families in the wisdom of elders. At the same time Eli's vision—he hesitated to call it an obsession—made him distinctly uneasy.

"Dr. Crenshaw sounds like an imaginative man," King said. "But can he prove any of his theories?"

"He has proof, all right, if you can understand it. A hundred pages solid with mathematic equations, then another hundred pages about magnetic lines of force, arctic fossilization, and, Chaldean mythology."

"When does he say the cataclysm will begin?"

"He's not knowing . But the icecap is already thick enough to cause plenty of trouble. It might happen in my lifetime. Surely in your own."

Jeremy had returned to the table with the coffeepot. "Or maybe God will move to stop the cataclysm forever," she said, in a low worried voice.

"The Lord has despaired," Eli answered. "For who has seen His bow among the clouds?"

King glanced up as Jeremy poured a cup of coffee for him. Clearly she was having a struggle to contain herself. "Then Lord Jesus will come," she said with conviction. But her hand trembled, and drops of hot coffee splashed on the oilcloth.

"At the Advent," Eli said. "But the Day of Terror is not the Day of Judgment. The time for the dead to be judged is not yet. First He must fulfill the prophecies of Isaiah, and Revelation."

There was a look of desperate earnestness on Jeremy's face, but she lacked assurance. Even Philemon was watching her now with a half-smile of enjoyment and King felt that this was a scene which had been repeated many times, with Jeremy always at a disadvantage.

"What about God's other prophecies?" she said reluctantly. "What about the Kingdom? God's prophecy of the Birth, the Life, the Death, the Resurrection—they're all in the Bible." A definite but short-lived anger appeared in her downcast eyes. "Jesus *was* in the beginning. He is God the Son. His birth was told seven centuries before it happened. God told the Virgin Birth to Adam. To Micah the city, to David the seed, to Abraham the tribe, to Daniel the time, to Zachariah the betrayal, to the Psalmists the Cross and the Resurrection, to the Disciples the Kingdom. It's all there. And all the Apostles tell of His coming. John says, The hour is near."

"Saul of Tarsus saw His face," King murmured, in support of Jeremy, "and became Paul, the great teacher."

Eli's red eyes flicked about, growing sharper. "The hour is near," he conceded, respecting the Scripture, "but what is an hour of God's time? One day is with the Lord as a thousand years, and a thousand years as one day."

"When we need Him He'll come! We'll see Him. I know, I believe!"

Eli shook his head. "The earth is thistle and thorn, and we are all Esau, and those of us who seek to repent with tears may not do so. That's in your Bible the same as mine, Jeremy. No, the Day of Judgment is a millennium away, but the Day of Terror is coming swift. And when it does, only the Saints among us will go directly to Heaven. The rest will await the seventh trumpet in their graves, and the chosen will be few, for even the righteous man is scarcely saved."

There was outright fear in Jeremy's face. King knew that Eli had chosen to wound her for some reason, and the look of womanish meanness he saw in Philemon's eyes confirmed this. But how was she at fault? He felt uncomfortable; it was up to him to stop this by a turn in the conversation, but Philemon, with a desire to humble Jeremy in front of her admirer, spoke first.

"Some sins the Majesty won't ever forgive," he said insultingly. "You named me for a fornicator, and the mark of the beast is in your head. Even Lord Jesus can't change that."

With a howl of misery Jeremy hurled the half-empty coffee-pot at him, missing, but splattering coffee on his sleeve. She ran instantly from the house, in tears. King rose from his chair to follow her but Eli said sharply:

"Let her be. When you're in my house you'll *let her alone.*"

"She's due for one of her spells," Philemon observed, angrily drubbing at his stained shirt with a spit-moistened napkin.

"Then why pick?" King said challengingly, his face hot.

They were going to have to work together, and so he had hoped for some sort of reconciliation with Philemon today, but this latest clash ended that possibility. Philemon, however, was not so ready to tangle as he had been the night before; he only shrugged and left it up to Eli to do the talking.

"Jeremy'll be all right," Eli said in a mollifying tone. "After she's had her cry."

King felt a low shame because he was still standing there, eating Eli's crow, and not trying to comfort the stricken girl. But the moment had passed when he might have gone without causing a real stricture, so he took his seat, to Philemon's open amusement, and said, indignantly, "Why did you tell her she couldn't be saved? No matter what she's done. She's just a girl!"

"Did I?" Eli said indifferently. "I tell only the truth from the Bible as I know it, the plain truth, the Fundamental truth. She put her own soul in jeopardy, it's not my doing." He sucked at his teeth and glanced at Philemon somewhat disapprovingly, a look King couldn't fathom. He kept a clamp on his tongue while he drank his coffee, not liking Eli at all, feeling afraid of his hostility and the possible consequences. In a sense he was a prisoner of Eli's as well as the Lord's and this realization filled him with regret, doubt, and sadness.

A fresh breeze came through the windows. King looked out, hoping he might see Jeremy. He wanted to soothe the wounds with which she had fled before they deepened and poisoned her spirit. But there was no telling where she had gone. He ached to say to her, You're not alone. I believe too that the Saints will rise in their bodies incorruptible. I believe Jesus will return and we will be called to meet Him in the clouds. I believe in the White Throne Judgment, but not—not in the Day of Terror. No, not in punishment of souls that could be saved if only preachers would look to their duty and trust in the Lord, and not spend their days occupied with false bibles and false prophets.

King didn't like to think about the Fundamentalist Books or their purpose. The warnings of Revelation were explicit, and Eli was courting disaster with some of his—this time King named them—*obsessions*. But maybe Eli, who was harassed by illness, had only temporarily lost sight of his duty. Maybe, he thought, I should be praying for him, and not finding fault. Praying that soon he'll be able to get out among the people and preach. He's spent far too much time cooped up with himself.

While this was going through King's mind he had turned to look again at Eli's heaped writing table, and Eli, seeing the direction of his curiosity, nodded approvingly.

"Maybe you've wondered what's going to happen to the twenty-one Books when the cataclysm begins," he said. "Cinch they won't do anybody good buried under a few thousand feet of water."

"Well, I—"

"Dr. Crenshaw and I studied the problem for some little time," Eli admitted. "When he retired last year he left his home in Manitoba and along with a small colony of loved ones and believers trekked to the east slope of Osprey Mountain up there in Montana. They settled down, six thousand feet above sea level, to ranching and farming and preparing for the future. Next spring Dr. Crenshaw plans to go even higher up the mountain with two of the followers and build a tabernacle complete with workrooms. In those rooms they'll settle down to copying onto scrolls the Books I've finished so far. These scrolls are treated to last for centuries. Soon as one is finished it'll be packed in a drum of chrome steel. All the drums will be stored in caves on Osprey Mountain and on other mountains around the world where we believe life will go on after the cataclysm. Some of Dr. Crenshaw's faithful are already at work carving symbols in the rock of Osprey Mountain and elsewhere. These symbols explain in simple terms about the Books and tell where they can be found. The work is hard. We know most of the scrolls will be lost. But surely the Word of God will live on, through our efforts."

King could think of nothing appropriate to say; the scheme of Eli Charger and Dr. Crenshaw sounded mad to his ears. He was both dazzled and repelled by the wealth of ego, the manic self-righteousness which seemed to rule the evangelist.

"You can probably tell from my description how expensive all this has been, and will be, before the work is done," Eli said in a sober voice. "My poor tithe has gone forth every week to further the work of the colony, and I've taken up special offerings in meetings, or leastwise I did before I was confined. Of course, it's not for me to say what you do with your tithe but I know you'll want to think over the great work that Dr. Crenshaw has undertaken."

"Making an offering to the Lord is a serious matter," King said.

73

"Exactly! That's a matter between you and your God; I have no say, no say. But if you want my help or prayers, stop by any time; you'll be welcome."

King took these words as an indication that he might go whenever he wanted without seeming rude, so he rose with as much of a smile as he could muster. Eli was watching him with an expression of missionary intensity and Philemon's eyes were speculative.

He stooped to retrieve the coffeepot, which had rolled under the table. It was clear to him now why a preacher with Eli's ability to take in dollars had not profited by and greatly expanded his ministry, why he lived in a poor house and preached under a left-over canvas and wore shoes that were coming out at the toes: all of his greed had been dedicated to the fulfillment of Dr. Crenshaw's earnest cause. Now he better understood the terrible anger that had flashed in Eli's eyes as he learned that King's six thousand dollars was not readily available. Oh, he understood a great deal now, enough to give him a griping bellyache. He thought of how boldly he had stood up to Eli yesterday and told the evangelist that he would be calling the shots. And Eli, thinking of his worth, thinking of the flow of dollars to that mountain colony in Montana, had humored him. Suffered him like a fool.

Well, King reassured himself, Dr. Crenshaw—a man whom he was now picturing as some sort of Antichrist—would never see a penny of the six thousand dollars. And the nightly offering, so long as he preached, would be dedicated to God and not to some wild scheme. He was going to have to keep a sharp eye on Eli, and he accepted that condition grimly.

"Reckon I'd better run," he said. "I'm making calls on pastors this afternoon."

"Commendable," Eli said, nodding. "But watch what kind of promises you make to them. We don't have money to pay preachers for sitting on our stage."

"I'm aware. If it's all the same to you, I believe I'll put off preaching again until Saturday night. Philemon here can take my turn."

"No," Eli said deliberately, "I think I'll handle that chore myself."

"You know best, Eli. Are you certain you can stand for that long a time?"

"I'll lean on a chair if I have to; don't worry about me.

Philemon, choose a couple of passages to read tonight. Maybe Jehoash's admonition to the priests will do. Second Kings." Eli fastened on King again. "The message tonight will be short and to the point. Dig! Dig! Dig! You stop by. Could be you'll learn something about how to ask for money. That ain't beneath your dignity, you know."

"I know," King said shortly, and took his leave.

7
─────

Molly's Humble Pie

The fair had opened at midday and, blessed by flawless Indian summer weather, it was doing a thriving business. Apparently the schools had been let out for the day; everywhere King looked he saw gangs of children in school and community-club sweaters. But there were signs that the fair had passed its peak: half of the corrals by the rodeo arena were empty, and at the stock barns exhibitors were gingerly loading tons of prize beef into long and dusty trailers. King had foreseen that the closing of the fair would bring about a plunge in the already scant attendance at the revival tent. Many of the congregation during the past week had been farm people, in town for the day to take in the sights of the fair; more than likely they had climbed the ridge to the tent seeking no more than a place to sit down and rest their aching feet. Eli couldn't have chosen a worse location to set up his tent, which was a good three blocks from any street. One thing was sure: he was there because he didn't have to pay a penny for tent space, or for the use of the house, however he'd been able to work it out.

For now the ridge would have to serve, King decided. Over the weekend he could puzzle out a new location, one where they wouldn't be gouged for rent, where the people could find them without having to hunt all over that end of town.

"Hey! King!"

He turned to see a group of the girls who danced in the show that traveled with Frank's carnival. One of them, who was named Emily and who called herself, for professional reasons, Sandi Dare, waved him to a stop and came at a jog to join him. Like the others, Sandi wore a tight-fitting sleeveless jersey and slacks that were almost as snug as leotards, and all she had to do was break into a run to turn every male head within fifty feet. Unlike some of the others, she was a naïve and frequently lonely little country girl who had been alternately thrilled and horrified by her season as a carny. Since the first week on the road King had been her unofficial chaperon and confessor and he had gone out of his way to keep her dependence on him inside the bounds of friendship, with limited success.

They walked together for a little way, Sandi chattering about something that had just popped into her head, and then she struck herself lightly on the forehead with the heel of one hand and exclaimed, "Holy cow, I just about forgot. That woman is looking for you!"

"What woman?"

"You know, the one you climbed up the roller coaster after." There was a veiled look of envy in her blue eyes.

"When did you see her, Sandi?" King asked, surprised by this piece of news.

"No more'n fifteen minutes ago, at the trailer compound. What do you think she wants? Isn't she supposed to be in jail?"

"She didn't really do anything wrong, Sandi, outside of causing an uproar." Sandi skipped a couple of steps to keep up with him. "The others'll be going on without you," he reminded her.

She shrugged indifferently. "They're just planning to kill time with some cowboys until the two-o'clock show. I can see all the cowboys I want in Sallisaw. Oh, listen, King, do you know what? Seriously, now." She stopped him with a hand on his elbow, eyes agog. "Penni"—she mentioned another of the dancers, most of whom had adopted first names ending in *i* for their careers in show business—"knows this Hollywood *impresario,* who is putting together a troupe of dancers for a show in Las Vegas this winter, and Penni says I might have a chance to get on with them." She was all innocence now. "What do you think of that idea?"

"You know what I think, Sandi," King said severely.

She toed in and held her hands in such a way as to look

76

banished and defenseless. "Well, I don't see where living in Las Vagas for a few weeks is going to hurt——"

"You stop by after dinner and I'll tell you what I know about Las Vegas," he said, more kindly, and put a hand on her shoulder. He shook her playfully. "Then you can come to your own conclusions."

The question was evident in her face before she spoke. "What are *you* going to do this winter?"

He smiled. "A spell of preaching, Sandi."

"Well . . . " She came up with her own grudging smile. "Anyway, I'll drop by tonight. My mind's not made up yet. . . . Oh, there's George, I have to ask him——" She whirled suddenly and dived through the crowd, but he heard her say, in a gayer voice, "I talked to that woman and I think she's after you, so *watch* yourself!"

King caught a wink of sun off one golden hip as Sandi disappeared and he scowled amiably after her, wondering if she was trying to show off with her maverick talk of tackling Las Vegas. No, she was a little more than half serious, motivated by the simple conviction that nothing really bad could happen to you if you didn't want it to. King, during a brief stint with Averill Henderson's half of the circus, had spent some time in Las Vegas and had disliked the city, not with a self-righteous scorn for its apparent immorality and Godlessness, but because it had seemed, for all the blandishments and garish wonders, to be a kind of prison, and the stark, hungry, or merely deadened faces he'd seen by the scores during his sleepless inventory had reinforced this impression. He was anything but a child when it came to the ways of the world. As a boy he had labored in North Carolina turpentine camps, one of the meanest ways to earn a living on the face of the earth. He'd soldiered in Europe and stayed on nearly a year after being mustered out of the Army. In his travels he'd poked his nose into places like the Reeperbahn of Hamburg and the Marseilles waterfront. He knew human sharks when he saw them, and he knew Sandi's average Baptist conscience would be no defense against the variety of sharks he had seen cruising the streets of Las Vegas.

So far, he thought, the day was not turning out well. He'd had his run-in with Eli and Philemon, and now Sandi was acting up. What did Molly Amos want with him?

Apparently she hadn't waited around to see if he would show

up, for there was no one in the trailer compound but carnival people: two young mothers sunning their babies and hanging up wash, an old concessionaire asleep on a tumbling mat with a copy of *Billboard* shielding his eyes. But there was a note for him on the door of his small trailer, a single sheet of wrinkled blue stationery that looked as if it had been stuffed in the writer's purse for several days. He pried the note out from under a snippet of Scotch tape and unfolded it.

> *Dear King Windom:*
>   Right about now you're reading this slightly seedy-looking message with a feeling of dismay, which if you cared to put into words would go something like this:
>   Don't I have enough problems today, without Mrs. Amos intruding again?

King smiled at her accuracy and read on.

>   Believe me, I gave the matter a lot of thought before I decided to try contacting you. Let me here and now skip over a lot of things that are just too painful to go into and say simply, Look, I'd like a chance to thank you properly by the light of a new and I hope better day.
>   If you'll remember, I said something last night about hating the taste of ashes (didn't I say that?) and, because the taste of humble pie is even worse, I promise our meeting won't embarrass you in any way. Just a firm thank you, and a firm good-bye—and maybe a bite of lunch in between.
>   OK, King Windom? I'll be at the Melrose Restaurant, on Clifton Street, which is about six blocks west of here, so if this note catches up to you before two, please do come.
>
> *Molly Amos*

He didn't deliberate for long. He liked the cheerful tone of the letter, and was sympathetic with the struggle she must have had in writing it. He was also pleased with some wry drawings she had made in the margins: after "intruding again?" there was a lugubrious face, in cartoon style, that might have been him, and after the third paragraph she had sketched the two of them on the Pippin; he had a mock-heroic chest and a self-sufficient smile, and she was shedding great drops of tears while pointing at the distant ground.

King glanced at his wristwatch: five minutes past one. He was already late for the suggested meeting, and he had planned to make a lot of calls that afternoon. But the restaurant was close by, according to her note. Besides . . . He shrugged. The plain truth was he did want to see her again, without fully understanding why. Perhaps just to satisfy himself that she was all right, and had done some growing up during the bleak night hours.

West Clifton was a mixed residential and business street. The Melrose Restaurant occupied a former private home set on a terrace away from the traffic and looked expensive enough so that he felt self-conscious about his black hopsacking jacket and faded corduroys. Nevertheless, he found a place to park in the back of the gray frame building and went in.

Molly Amos spotted him as soon as he poked his nose tentatively into the main dining room, and signaled with her hand. She was at a table for two by one of the large bay windows with a slouching gentleman in Western-style clothes, but he got up almost immediately and left without a glance at King.

"Didn't mean to run that man off," King said, sitting opposite Molly.

"We weren't having a tryst. Ordell's about to tape his afternoon show."

"Ordell?" King repeated, and turned for a second look at the departing luminary. "You mean that's Ordell Hawkins?"

"None other. I take it you follow country music." Molly snapped open a gold case, offered cigarettes, took one for herself when he shook his head.

"Oh, I listen a lot. Mostly nights when I'm not sleeping. I've heard a few of Hawkins' tunes, and liked them. Does he work near here?"

"Right next door. KTIP radio. *Kay*-tip, as they say. Biggest dawn-to-dusk country-music station in the South. I work there too." She arched her head back gracefully and let a cloud of blue smoke drift from her lips. "That is, as far as I know now. Have you seen the afternoon paper?" She retrieved her copy from between a couple of window boxes overflowing with artificial plants and handed it across the table. "Read down there in the right-hand corner. That's us."

79

King found the story she meant and scanned it. The few lines contained an account of Molly's escapade the night before and mentioned one "Kin Wendell, a carnival employee" as being responsible for her rescue.

"No reason for that to go on the front page," Molly said as he was reading, "but I used to work down at the *Press* and I still have my enemies there. They must have been jumping up and down for joy over the chance to put the knife in me." She exhaled more smoke, her eyes narrow, petulantly amused. "Just dumb luck they didn't have a picture to run."

A waitress came with a sandwich plate for Molly. She gave the sandwich a disapproving glance, lifted a corner of the bread with two fingers, said, in an infuriating voice, "Didn't you hear me tell you no mayonnaise, dear?" and allowed the plate to be removed without batting an eye. She then smiled at King and, while the waitress was still within earshot, said, "It may take an Act of God to get a menu from the help here, they're all a little dull from hookworm or something, but by cracky we'll try. Oh, you've eaten? Well, coffee then." Her hand trembled slightly as she took back the offensive newspaper and ditched it. "But as I was saying, when Fish—he's the station manager—comes back to town and gets wind of last night, I probably won't have a job. Ordell's promised to go to bat for me and he swings a mighty big bat around the station, but . . . what the hang, I'm tired of the whole situation there; I just may quit."

Molly angled a look at him and her mood changed magically, acrimony and swift brute despair giving way to playfulness. "You have a way of pulling your ears when you're uncomfortable," she observed. "I've gone back on my bargain already, haven't I? Sit awhile; I promise not to drown you in any more of my heart's blood, old blood brother Windom."

King smiled a little stiffly. "I'm not going anywhere." He was still put off by Molly's tireless neat gestures, by the quick leaps and lunges of her mind and tongue, by her taste and skill for surgery on the hapless. By physical paradox. For in the grip of her furies her appearance seemed to change radically, she became old, worn, and leathery, her hair a sight, her eyes waxen; then again, when she came under the spell of a lighter heart, a nonviolent moment, the look of the crone vanished and was replaced by color, passion, a vixenish gaiety. Now she was seeking to please him, and it made her pretty. In some unexpected way he found her exciting; by contrast the other women within his range looked slapped and pinched together, pounded lopsided and stuffed into their shoes. They seemed overwrought, flagrant, foolish, even despicable.

"Your ears are back to normal," Molly said, knowing the work she had done, and she reached out to give his hand an impulsive affectionate pat. "Sorry, I shouldn't have gone after that waitress like I did, but I've eaten lunch here every day for the past year, and . . ." She made a fist and then let her hand fly open in a gesture of defeat. "Care for a cigarette? Oh, I asked before and you don't smoke. Well, I'll have another one." She puffed gladly away. "Three and a half packs a day. That's a fact. Most mornings I wake up feeling as if my lungs are full of bats. Will we ever get off the subject of me, me, me? he asked, with a wistful look in his eye. So you're a preacher. I lay awake last night—what was left of the night—thinking about that."

"Why?"

"I dunno," she brooded. "You don't look the part. If you'll pardon the expression, you're ugly as hell. I mean that as a compliment." She brushed the ashes off a lapel of her beige suit jacket, leaving King to figure out just how she was complimenting him. "Where do you preach? Church here in town?"

"No. I started out as an evangelist, then gave it up for a while." He really intended to say no more about his life, but Molly was interested, she asked good questions to draw him out, and so, in the time it took him to drain two cups of hot black coffee, while smoke from her endless cigarettes thickened in layers over the table, he told Molly quite a lot about himself. He was pleased to make her laugh with a few of his stories about the eight months he had spent in England after his tour of duty with the Army.

"Harlan Gray was in the middle of a big crusade at White City Stadium at about the same time I was preaching down by Guy's Hospital in South London, and a little of his glamour rubbed off on me, I guess. That was before I taught myself not to drawl all day long; those limeys thought I was quaint or anyhow different. One night I looked up to see about twenty extra people crowding into the back of that sooty old hall we'd rented for our meeting, most of them youngsters, not very well dressed even for that part of the city, and they looked so pinched and plain I felt sorry for them. They were dead earnest for Jesus, or so I thought; they hung on my every word and from time to time I'd see a head bob down and lips moving in prayer—even seemed as if some of them were repeating my exact words. Don't think I didn't puff up like a pouter pigeon! Because of the attention they were giving me I preached fifteen minutes longer than usual. But do you know? When I asked souls to come forward to receive the Christ, not a one of those twenty people made a move. I was so puzzled and downcast that I hunted up a few of them afterward in a pub across the street. Turned out they were all Royal Academy actors doing some play about a decadent Southern family, and they'd come just to hear a sample of how South'ners actually talked!"

"So you've made up your mind to give revivalism another try," Molly said, when the anecdotes lagged. "Why the long layoff with the carnival?"

King looked vaguely out the window at the street. "Just to give myself time to think. I had to be sure . . . and I was determined to put a little money away. Harlan Gray started out preaching on street corners, to anybody who'd listen to him—and it was nine long years before anybody did. Twice he quit out of plain discouragement. But by the time he was my age, he had a big tent in Hollywood and movie stars down front every night."

"You're really sold on Gray."

"I just about worship him. I know the Book warns against idols, but that's my feeling toward Mr. Gray: worshipful. I listen to him on the radio Sunday nights no matter where I am. He knows how to talk to people. He knows everything that's going on in the world, he's sat down to the table with kings and scholars, and he also knows there's hellfire waiting for those he can't get at. It makes him fighting mad. You can hear that in his voice. He's fighting mad, but confident too." King looked bleakly at her, having lost most of the good feeling which companionship had given him during the past few minutes. "Sermons! I sit up many a night with paper and pencil, just sit for hours and try to think of ways to write the simple words that'll fire people with the need for Salvation before they are forever lost, and it's *hard*. Hopeless. I know the Bible, I love the beautiful verse in Psalms and Solomon, but it isn't in me to write great words."

"Or in Harlan Gray either; I've heard him. But like you say, he knows how to talk to people. I think you do too. I'm wondering how you'd sound on the radio, or on television."

"I've never heard the sound of my own voice," King said.

"You haven't?" Molly's fingers waggled uncertainly over her cigarette case, but the last one had baked her mouth dry and sore and she decided against another smoke. Besides, she'd enjoyed the taste of her sandwich, which was a wonder, since she wasn't on one of her eating streaks. The food, which she might have expected to sit uneasily on her stomach, had instead helped promote a feeling of warmth and contentment. Part of that feeling, she knew, was due to her increasing interest in King Windom.

Molly was still a little surprised that she was sitting there in the restaurant just as if it were an average day, because the unpleasant scene she had made at the fairgrounds had seemed to be the kickoff for another in a lifetime of nervous upsets. Molly was thirty-eight; she had always been a fragmentary person, unstable as ectoplasm. During the formalities with the law the night before, she had behaved herself, partly because it was her first time to be in serious trouble, but also because, as an old campaigner when it came to her nerves, she was holding some of herself in reserve, anticipating a particularly dreadful climax to her fit of bad temper.

The first hour she spent alone in her apartment after being released by the police served to convince her that she was in for it; the sedatives she had on hand made her woggy as a pup but failed to knock her out. She began tenterhooking, which was her name for a kind of athletic pacing and breathing by which she hoped to put to rest the screeches rising in her breast, but at that point her defenses were inadequate. From there the usual procedure was a quick cab ride to her long-suffering doctor's, a really heavy blast of tranquilizer, and then a week at a good small private hospital nearby.

Before she could commit herself to this course of action, however, she began to think of the clod who had taken it upon himself to climb the roller coaster after her. This was unusual, since in a neurasthenic extremity she seldom thought of anything but her own suffering. Molly considered herself a fine judge of people, and she usually judged them ruthlessly. (By her own lights she was unsparingly honest with herself, which automatically put truth on her side.) She had the habit of arbitrarily separating people into haves and have-nots, with

83

further refinement that included a class she thought of as the Underworld. In the Underworld were all the Jerry Dee Binsfords, teen-age poke-bottoms and other examples of the culturally deprived South—all the trash she had learned to scorn in childhood. She had without even thinking about it assigned King Windom to the Underworld, but for some reason—now that she was at a critical point in her suffering, with sweat on her brow—he had come forth from the Underworld and was there with her, silent and concerned.

This angered Molly. Who was he? Who did he think he was? She ranted, and cursed the *trash* who had the nerve to judge *her*.

She continued to try to dispose of his image in this way, all the while remembering in melancholy detail how desperate she'd been to see *anybody*, and how he had looked up there, with his back to the stars. No, he hadn't judged her, not really; he'd simply cared about her.

With those thoughts the crisis ended, the fist poised threateningly at her temple dissolved into harmless air. Molly, immediately overcome with the delayed effects of the sedative in her slowing blood, had fallen asleep on her bedroom floor, a Persian rug lapped over her.

The note which Molly had expectantly written to King in the light of a better day was mostly a lie. She was only a little contrite over her stupid behavior, for by nature she was generous as well as impulsive, and she always forgave herself quickly. Having escaped confinement in that good little hospital, which was her usual reward for acting up and flinging her emotions around, she had been in a decent enough mood when King dropped into the chair opposite her in the restaurant.

Now that she had spent some time with him, and had studied him in the clear light of the afternoon, her mood was even better. The unexpected deadening plunges into gloom, the hints of black floating death which were side effects of sedation, had ceased altogether. Her hands still trembled, off and on, but that was from excitement, from the pleasure of discovery; for Molly had come across that rarity in her life, an authentic man.

Right away she had seen that, in a sense, he did belong to the Underworld. The way he hunched his shoulders in the too-small coat, the way his hands fell across the table, the sun-

84

chapped neck and the big ears and the paintbrush shock of black hair that needed pruning rather than trimming—all those things contributed to the look of the run-of-the-mine small-town or rural Southerner. Because of his honest envy and hero-worship of the great evangelist Harlan Gray, his apparent fear that he would be neglected in his ministry as Gray had been neglected, it was easy enough for Molly to lump him with the hungry, down-at-heels country musicians who besieged the radio station in droves, looking for a chance to get on the air, looking for someone who would listen to the driveling tunes they had composed.

Yet there was nothing slack, slow, or predictable in King Windom's face, which she had described as "ugly as hell." His eyes—weathered to a lemon yellow by the streaming sun—dictated nearly all change of expression, from intellectual preoccupation to a raw bullish glare at moments of intensity. Only once while he talked did she see his whole face relax, as if the skin sewed tight to the bones of his wide head had softened and blurred like warm wax and become comfortably lined, and that was when an unpremeditated dovelike smile touched upon his lips and warm wings of shadow darkened and gentled his eyes. Molly was transfixed by that smile, by the compassion and humanness which it revealed; she half understood the impulses which had followed her the night before, which had taken shape like a homeless ghost to haunt her out of her crisis. She felt a great, possessive joy.

With his admission that he had never been on radio nor otherwise heard himself speak, Molly had an inspiration which she carefully conserved.

"Now that you've bought yourself half of a tent to preach in," she said, toying with the cigarette case and rapidly giving in to her desire to light up again, "how did you go about attracting a crowd? I was raised high church Episcopalian, so I'm a little vague about revivals. They're wild, aren't they? Lots of shouting and carrying on. You know, *Elmer Gantry*."

King winced slightly at the reference and stacked his long legs beside the table. "Well, there are all kinds of humbugs passing themselves off as evangelists—I mean men who can't even qualify as preachers, except they know how to read a little bit. And there are wild revival meetings; all depends on the folks that are sponsoring them." He reached unself-consciously into a glass for a piece of ice and munched away. "My feeling

is, a good, old-time revival meeting should do three things: give
the believers, those who may have grown a little cold in the
confines of their own churches, a chance to feel real joy in their
stewardship again, to raise a great glorious shout or two in His
name; make the poor sinning backslider so miserable in the
presence of the living church and the Spirit of Jesus that he
can't help but want to be redeemed; and give the unchurched,
the troubled, the sore at heart, and the unbelieving a chance to
cast aside their cynicism, throw down their earthly burdens,
and lay their hands in the nail-scarred hand, accepting the shed
blood, accepting Christ as Savior. I believe in a meeting where
folks can rejoice openly, where they can weep and pray and
shout if they're so moved, but I don't believe in letting a
congregation get carried away; does more harm to the spirit
than good—that's the devil working." He gestured impatiently,
as if slapping a fly-size devil away from his ear. "As for getting a
congregation together—well, even Harlan Gray has to have
help, from the preachers of whatever city he's in. If I'm going to
do any good in Clearwater, I've got to convince a lot of
pastors—Holiness, Adventist, God of Prophecy—that we're
here as friends, that we're not aiming to steal half their congregations and snap up offerings that rightfully belong to
the churches." He looked discreetly at his watch. "Eli hasn't
done much work with the preachers in these parts, unless I miss
my guess. I want to visit around, dicker for a choir or two, do
some inviting, make friends."

"You said you saved some money. How do you plan to spend
it? Advertising?"

"Well, that's right," King said guardedly. "I need to talk to a
printer about handbills, song sheets, and the like, and maybe
I'll take a space in one of the papers for a few days. Of course,
when we move the tent from where it is now there'll be rent to
pay—"

"You're wasting your time with newspaper advertising,"
Molly said, her lip curling. "I know what I'm talking about, I've
worked both shops. The papers are all right to sell beef brisket
and used cars, but no matter what lies you tell in your ads, you
won't whip up much curiosity. People have to know you in
some personal way before they'll come to your tent to see what
you have to offer. Besides, how many people read a newspaper
in this part of the South? What I'm telling you makes sense,
whether you're in politics or religion. I don't think you want to

go around knocking on doors, or making speeches in a parking lot. That leaves radio and television. The TV stations, at least in this town, will put you on the air when most people are either at work or asleep. Radio is you best means of communication, and your best bargain."

"I've known too many preachers who've gone broke trying to be on the radio."

"So have I," she said, undaunted by his scowl. "On any given day we have a dozen mail-order preachers on the air at Kay-tip, quite a few of them deadbeats—whiners and complainers who can't pay their bills, or won't pay. They're frauds a baby could see through. They don't have anything to offer. But you do. How would you like to talk to a quarter of a million people at four-forty-five this afternoon, and invite them all to the evening service at your tent?"

King's scowl deepened. It had never occurred to him just how obvious his longing for a radio program of his own really was, although in conversation with Molly he had made more than one admiring reference to the far flung radio ministry of Harlan Gray. Molly had cracked through the hard bone of caution and exposed a dream.

The immediate effect was to make King distrustful of her, because her words had called back too much for him to handle all at once. He thought of the long spells of after-midnight driving over wretched roads to reach another town, his friend Age asleep in the car beside him, the sleeping countryside seen through a mystical haze of fatigue, the radio alive and crackling, his only real company that time of night the hillbilly howlers and the contemptible, uninspiring prophets who groaned and sobbed and sang hosannas in his ear. He thought of the fits of anxiety he had experienced, the sense of dispossession which he had felt on those lonely roads, the fear of the Angel of Death. Someday, he had promised himself, his ear ringing from the late hours and cries of money-grabbers and self-deluded savants, I'll take my turn. Someday I'll tell all the truth that's in me by the Grace of God, and they'll listen.

But he wasn't ready, he knew he wasn't! A pall of despondency settled upon King despite the brightness of the day which he had enjoyed so much only an hour ago, despite the clatter of diners in the cheerful restaurant. Why had he forced himself upon Eli Charger, what devil had prompted him to make bold plans, to make a fool of himself?

Molly, mistaking his silent agonizing for skepticism, pressed her point. "Those are certified figures I'm giving you, my friend, there actually are that many people in a three-state area who have, if you'll pardon the expression, the Kay-tip habit. Give Ordell most of the credit; he's one of the three top country disc jockeys, according to the latest *Music Reporter* poll. He calls a few of his famous buddies long distance and they chat over the air, and he plays an occasional record and sells dog chow or rebuilt motors and several thousand score hill apes in this part of the world hang breathlessly on every syllable. They'll still be tuned in at a quarter of five, when you come on. That's prime evening time. It wouldn't be available at all, but one of the preachers finally fell too far behind in his payments and our program director dropped him from his spot this morning."

Molly's enthusiasm cut through King's unpleasant self-criticism and caused him to shift uneasily in his chair; he stacked and restacked his legs, creating a traffic hazard for the waitresses plying their way between tables. At least he saw that Molly wasn't just trying to fill a vacant quarter hour in the log-book of her radio station, and his suspicions of her evaporated. With this block out of the way he was able to think more clearly.

Since the day of the Heaven-sent sign, he'd had little on his mind but the pure joy of preaching again, and his lonely nights had been ablaze with extravagant dreams of a great ministry for Christ. Why then was he shying away from the opportunity Molly had suggested? Why had there been a cloud on his mind and fear in his heart after his decision to throw in with Eli? King felt a jolt of apprehension. Because his dealing with the old evangelist meant an *ending*, and not a beginning, as he so earnestly wanted himself to believe. All along what he'd really craved, despite his complacent longings and schemes, was a haven, a scrap of canvas above his head, the surroundings he was used to, and loved. He'd simply grown tired too quickly in his search when the Lord had said unmistakably Go Ye. He'd been willing to settle for too little, because—King's mouth turned down at the corners and his eyes were filled with such a wild light that Molly immediately decided to have the cigarette she had been putting off—because he really hadn't the necessary courage to test the extent of the Lord's will. When Eli had offered the doubtful protection of a partnership he'd been almighty relieved to accept it! He'd lied to himself, over and over; he'd been a fool, not for planning too boldly, but for lagging in his zeal. Molly had pointed out immediately the inadequacy of the steps which he'd proposed to take for the increase of his ministry, and still he resisted the truth!

Well, now he knew the truth of himself, he had rediscovered the coward which still dwelled perfidiously in his heart. It would take vigilance and great strength to slay that coward for all time!

The silence between him and Molly had stretched rather thin and she was beginning to look annoyed by his rudeness when King suddenly threw back his head like a swimmer breaking water, or a long-trapped miner sucking air, and beamed at her.

"Well, Molly, like I said, I'm an ignoramus when it comes to radio. But I've got six thousand dollars that needs spending in a hurry for the Lord's cause, and right now is as good a time as I know to get at it."

8

Cowboy

Entering the studios of Kay-tip radio was almost like entering a fashionable and opulent home.

Molly led the way through two doors of grainy gleaming dark wood with brass saucers in place of doorknobs and King found himself in a sitting room decorated in shades of royal blue, sand brown and russet. Sun filtered through striped drapes drawn over two banks of high windows. There was a grouping of sofa and three chairs around a coffee table like a great stone altar. The walls were a dark, tasteful walnut veneer, with odd handsome inlays. Against one wall there was a cabinet television, and above that a long painting, almost mural-size, of the "Grand Old Opry," depicting fabled "Opry" stars. In an alcove a fountain puttered peacefully away. The only thing that disturbed the tranquility of this sun-filled chamber was the appalling nasal voice of a female country-singing idol which came from a small loudspeaker built into the wall above the painting.

King had worked around woods, both in sawmills and in a cousin's lumberyard, and he knew good quality when he saw it. He paused long enough to draw his finger down one of the wall panels. Just the sort of thing he would choose for his own house someday, he thought, realizing with a pain just how sick he had become of the gypsy's life.

"What did you expect—a potbellied stove and a checkers game in the corner?" Molly said. "I tried to tell you this is a money operation. Eight months from now we'll be on the air with the first all-hillbilly television station in the country." The singing stopped and a folksy disc jockey's voice took over.

"Come on now, I want to show you around."

King followed her obediently to the reception center, which was on a level above the sitting room.

"Budgie, this is the evangelist King Windom," Molly said to the pallid blonde behind a low sweeping wing of desk. "Is Duckworth back yet?"

"He's in one of the studios," the girl replied, staring overhead at King and seeming a little awed.

"I'll find him." Molly took King through a broad door behind which was a long corridor painted a chilly ice-cream yellow. She began opening doors.

"Who's Duckworth?"

"Program director. We need his OK to put you on the air."

"Oh. What do you do here, Molly?"

"A little of everything. I'm down as Director of News and Publicity." She backed out of a small office after a futile, inquiring "Duck?" and glanced back at King. "I worked for NBC once upon a time," she said with good cheer. "I mean the National Broadcasting Company. Quite a comedown, hunh?"

A rotund man wearing a cardigan sweater came around a jog in the corridor with a sheaf of papers in one hand. He inobtrusively took King's measure through a pair of oversized black-rimmed glasses and gave Molly a clenched absent smile.

"Duckie!" she cried. "What are you doing with that time slot after Ordell this afternoon?"

"Nothing much. A few hymns until sign-off."

"Sustaining?"

"What else?" he asked morosely. He stuffed the pipe he'd

been carrying in his right hand into a pocket of the sweater and extended his hand to King. "Dan Duckworth," he said. "Friend of Molly's?"

Molly apologized for her bad manners and, after introducing King, she explained what they were after. The program director nodded, a little bleakly, as she went on, his eyes continuing to peg away at King. At the first opportunity Duckworth cleared his throat and said, "Uh yeh? Well, I don't know if I can just put him on, Molly, without a contract and a guarantee of some sort; that's Fish's procedure." He riffled through his papers, frowning. "In the morning it wouldn't matter so much, but we've got our big audience with us right now." He looked once more at King, a darting, doubtful look.

King knew that the man had thrust him into the company of other preachers who undoubtedly had shown up in just this way, down from the hills and looking more like moonshiners than men of God. Preachers willing to gamble every dollar they'd ever made in hopes of staying on the air long enough to reap handsome returns. He felt both embarrassed and annoyed and wished now he hadn't come in cold, ill-dressed, blinded by impatience, and unprepared to conduct his business intelligently. Color seeped into his face and he said bravely, trying to make some sort of decent impression, "I've got plenty of money if that's what—"

Molly hushed him with an aggressive smile. She said to Duckworth, "When Fish gets back and has a look at the log, he's not going to worry about who King Windom is, as long as the station is paid for the time. But you'll hear from him about sustaining, and you know it."

Duckworth was not cowed, but he looked weary, as if he had barely held his own in other encounters with Molly. "We'll have the time sold quick enough. The fact is, Molly, I had a call from the 'United Mission Appeal Hour' this morning, and they're interested. I told their representative to get in touch with Fish, so I don't see how I can arbitrarily put Reverend Windom on until we hear from the United Mission people again."

"That may be two weeks from now, and Fish will turn them down cold. Why not give King his chance in the meantime? All we can get is a bawling out." Molly was still aggressive and determined but at the same time, King noticed, she had never been more winning. In the heat of contention her face glowed with a pantherish intensity. "I'll tell you what: I'll take all the responsibility for putting him on the air. You can pass the buck to me and I'll handle Fish."

Duckworth smiled as if this was absurd, but he couldn't quite say no in the face of her enthusiasm. At this sign of possible weakness King might have expected Molly to pounce and push her argument, but instead a smile brushed her lips and she held back and said nothing until she had the program director's eye again.

"He's a good friend, Duck; the best I have right now." She spoke sweetly and sadly, and as if King were not standing right beside her. "Won't you give him this chance, for me?"

King had never seen a man so obviously melted; Duckworth lowered his head and fiddled with the bowl of the pipe protruding from his pocket. With the other hand he waved his sheaf of papers vaguely at the hall. "Well, we wouldn't sell the time anyway; I suppose there's no reason . . ." He looked keenly at the preacher. "You're ordained, and all that? I mean there can't be any question about—"

"My ordination papers are back at the carnival," King said, trying not to glower like an ape. "I could fetch them for you in a hurry." He added, unnecessarily, "I've never been in jail either."

"Carnival?" said Duckworth, a line coming deeply between his eyes.

Molly linked arms with King and gave his elbow a steadying squeeze. "You don't have to bother with *that*," she said in a tone of severe goodwill. "Duck, we're ready to go to work this minute. Is there a studio free?"

"Charley-Bob's on the air in number one, Ordell's taping in three, and there are some musicians from the 'Town and Country Show' fooling around in the big studio. We could run them out, though."

"Good. As long as you're not doing anything urgent right now you can lend us a hand. King's never been on the radio before."

"He hasn't?" Duckworth said, becoming dubious all over again.

Molly reached out and fastened a playful but tenacious hand on the back of his neck. "That's why we need you to direct. We have to have technical help; I can't run one of those big tape machines." She turned to King. "This is all coming pretty fast

92

for you. Is half an hour enough time to work up a program? What all do you need? A Bible?"

King produced from his pocket a worn New Testament bound in soft leather. "Scripture will serve. I always like to talk about Paul. Most people don't really know what sort of man he was. Some throw off on him as a cranky woman-hater, but—"

"That's fine," Molly said. She disengaged her arm and grasped King's hand. Her own hand was unfeminine, and hard; he was reminded of the crone that had emerged so vividly from her doldrums in the restaurant. He could see little now in her face that was old, except for the inevitable lines around the eyes and the droop of her chin. He noticed too, for the first time, just how voluptuous Molly was, which surprised him; he had throught her rather thin up there on the Pippin, in the unvarying stark light beneath a black sky.

They went down the hall, through a heavy door, up a rubber-treaded ramp, and into a small control room. A span of glass overlooked the studio below, which was a deep chamber about twenty feet square, with acoustical material on the walls, carpet on the floor, and some oddly hung baffles in the far corners. The studio contained two boom mikes, neither of which was being used by the musicians in view. They were singing lustily but King couldn't hear a sound.

Abruptly the musicians—they were all youngsters with various kinds of banjos and guitars—broke off with foul looks of displeasure over their playing. Molly flipped a switch on the console under the slanted window and said, "Jimbo, how about taking a break? We need the studio for a taping."

The oldest of the boys looked up as her voice filled the studio. He turned his head all around the room in an airy pantomime of surprise, then settled on her behind the double glass. He made a face like a performing chimpanzee, got up, sauntered across the carpet to the window, lifted his face, and with an expression of mellow content put his lips against the glass. Molly leaned over the console and consummated the act of recognition, smearing the glass with her lipstick.

"Hiyeh, Mol-lee," the boy said, his eyes squinched in an elaborate effect of bliss, his lips curled in a dog-happy leer. He was a big bruiser, King thought; he would probably run two hundred and thirty pounds. He was also toting more of a pot than a boy of his age—twenty-two? twenty-four?—should have had, and it looked to King like purely a beer-drinker's belly. His clothes fitted him indifferently, yet he didn't seem sloppy, only good-naturedly unkempt. He had an overlarge, blunt-featured, haughty head, and tufted steer-red hair.

Apparently just because he felt like it, the boy suddenly blazed away at his banjo, capering a little for Molly, who smiled indulgently, and hit another switch so they could hear him in the control room. He played well for an amateur, King thought, claw-hammer style and mile-a-minute.

"Come on up here, you goof, and meet a people," Molly said when she was tired of his shenanigans. She turned off the studio intercom. "The old Cowboy is in a rare mood today," she announced. "King, don't let him put you on; he just might try. Jim Cobb and I go way back and he can be real sweet if he's in the mood. On the other hand, he'll do anything, or say anything. That's an exact definition of honesty—or insanity; take your pick."

With this sobering thought still hanging in the air, the control room door thudded open, nearly catching the hapless Duckworth flush in the face, and Cowboy Jim Cobb came in, nimble as a dancing bear, a foaming can of beer in one hand. A girl with a frozen kind of prettiness, whom King hadn't noticed in the studio, followed him.

As soon as he was inside, the Cowboy stopped and looked around with a pleased idiotic grin on his face. "You want me to me-yut some paypul?" he drawled, and stuck out a beer-wet hand to King.

Once he had the preacher's hand, he pumped it like an automaton and continued in his corn-pone accent, "Is this the paypul ri-yut he-yah, Mol-lee?" He gazed up into King's eyes, as if totally absorbed, but there was a faint, mocking simper about his brutish mouth. One whiff of the Cowboy and one look into his reddened eyes told King that he'd been doing a lot of drinking. He also realized that Cobb was older than he had first guessed: Cobb was a grown man and looked boyish only because of the clothes he chose to wear and the company he kept. King decided with uncharitable speed that he had no great use for the old Cowboy.

"Are you maken it all right, chief?" Cowboy asked, still hanging on to the hand. "Mol-lee, ah swayah ah din know you had In-yun fray-ends."

"Jimbo, you nut, calm down. This is the Reverend King

94

Windom. He's an evangelist, and he's starting a new program on Kay-tip."

"Ohhh," the Cowboy said, with a great grave nodding. "Ah be-le-yuhv ah've heard a yew, chief. They call yew the Apache Apostle." He swayed and grinned happily.

King turned his head casually toward Molly as if to say, I don't think I'll be responsible if this goes on any longer, and the Cowboy, who was perhaps not as drunk as he appeared, suddenly released King's hand, reached past him, lifted Molly's hand by the fingers, and tenderly planted a kiss. Under the circumstances, this gesture should have seemed like additional buffoonery, but his movements were so restrained, his manner so circumspect and courtly, that the kiss seemed proper and unremarkable, despite his ill-fitting ranch clothes and ungentlemanly reek of beer.

"Honey, when are you going to grow up?" Molly said, smiling indulgently.

Duckworth's eyes were on the can of beer and it was obvious that being slammed by the door and then ignored had hurt his feelings. "Cowboy, you've been told about bringing beer into the studio!" he snapped. "Do you want us to lose our license?"

Cowboy swung around to him uncertainly, tossed his head in a heavy way, and squinched his eyes.

The girl said, tensely, "Jimbo, why don't we go on?"

She attracted all eyes, and the attention made her suffer visibly. She seemed to King to be very young and strikingly shy, and not unlike Sandi Dare, the carnival dancer he'd befriended. The girl's hair was a frosted, thickety blond, her features small and true, her figure, in white jeans and a light sweater, over-emphasized.

The Cowboy smiled. He made a kissing face that was as crude and vulgarly explicit as his hand-kissing had been correct, and said, "Hey, I din mean to be *rude!* Chief, Molly—you too, Duckbutt, or whatever your name is—this is my girl, Suzie Tucker."

Suzie unfroze enough to nod in their direction, and then her large eyes swung to Cowboy and she stared at him desperately.

He pointed an amiable thumb at Duckworth. "Am ah stoned?" he asked. "Is that what you object to, Duck?"

The program director, who was growing a deep red in color, opened his mouth to speak, but Molly, lounging against the console and rolling a cigarette across her lower lip, beat him to it. "Yes, you are, Jimbo," she said in a steady voice with a note of passing regret. Her eyes were hard on the girl. "You certainly are stoned."

"What?" said Cowboy, utterly astounded. *"Ah am!"*

"Jim," Suzie said in a scared, halting voice, "I haven't been home since seven o'clock this morning."

"Hmmm," Cowboy said, deep in thought, an elbow in the palm of one hand, his massive head propped on the other fist.

"Come on, Jimbo," Molly urged, "clear the studio. We've got work to do."

"Ah guess ah have had two or three quarts of beer already today," the Cowboy allowed. He shrugged convulsively and beamed at his girlfriend. "Well, let's get in the car and go down to the Hi-Hat Café so ah can sober up and get started all over again."

The girl's mouth was open, soundlessly, and she trembled. Molly's mouth had hardened into a line of steely distaste, and she seemed once again to wither, just a little, to King's eyes. Something was going on in the small room that he didn't understand. The young girl's inexplicable fear had created a nasty tension.

Cowboy lunged forward suddenly and awkwardly patted Suzie's shoulder. He wasn't being funny, he really meant to comfort her. He turned his head to take them all in and his eyes were shining happily. "She's eighteen years old today, and do you know what—"

"Please," the girl whimpered, tugging at his shirt.

"That's all right, that's all right," Cowboy said soothingly. "Come on now, let's jest get out of here, and ah promise ah won't drink another beer until we—" He stopped because her hand was across his mouth. He freed himself gently and muttered to them all, "We've got plans . . . big plans." With this pronouncement he stared inscrutably into the girl's eyes and she gradually offered up a smile, gazing back at him blindly and adoringly.

Satisfied with her devotion, Cowboy opened the door and daintily ushered her out. He turned in the doorway and peered back at King.

"You're a preacher? That's not a bunch of bull?"

King nodded.

"Where do you"—Cowboy made vague circles in the air with one hand—"you know, preach? Where's your church?"

King unbent a little. "Tent tabernacle, back of the rodeo at the fairgrounds."

"Oh," said Cowboy, his expression wide-eyed and blank. "Thanks." He turned and stumbled out and the door clicked shut behind him.

Molly had her cigarette going. She was still leaning on the console, looking down at the now empty studio. King made a fist and stared bleakly at it. Molly said, meanly, "Jimbo's taste for underage pelt hasn't deserted him, obviously."

"How well do you know him?" King asked.

She looked up, startled and suspicious. "Hah?"

"He won't do anything to hurt that girl, will he?"

"Depends on what you mean by hurt," Molly said indifferently.

Duckworth was still red in the face. "I'm going to have a talk to Fish about the way Cobb acted. There's no telling what trouble—"

"Duck," Molly said, with fierce patience, "just lay off. Jimbo may have some stripped gears, he may act like the most ignorant overbearing hick who ever came down the pike, but it *is* an act, and he's not stupid. He knows where he can make trouble and where he can't. Revenge knows its bounds. There's Cobb money in this place, and that's enough said." Her eyes were hooded as she smoked. "Also, he wasn't half drunk, he was delirious with victory. He's fooled around with kids younger than Suzie, and always gotten burned. Half of the fun, as he sees it. Nobody's been able to impress upon him that Grandmother Cobb hardly blinks an eye anymore when she hears Jimbo has bagged another one." Molly looked straight at King. "Part of Jimbo is not an act, though. I'm convinced part of him is pure evil. He's driven hardened psychiatrists to rage."

King nodded, thoughtfully. "From what I've seen of him, and from what you've told me, I'd say he's possessed by the devil."

Molly said, "Well, there's an explanation the Menningers would be thrilled with. They had Jimbo for a while. A *very* short while."

King said, "I've read that book by Dr. Karl Menninger— about self-destructive people. I know there are sicknesses of the mind, breakdowns, that a medical man can treat and be successful. But I also believe that there are devils, real devils, who cause what we call mental illness, and only the Holy Ghost can cope with them."

"If you've got an idea in your head of carrying the Gospel to Cowboy Cobb, spare yourself."

King smiled. "I'm not a fool for hard times, Molly. A great man filled with great inspiration might be of some use to Cowboy, but I don't think I would."

Duckworth opened a drawer of a work desk and pulled out a new box of recording tape. "Can we get started now, Molly? I *do* have a few other things to take care of this afternoon."

Molly sprang up from her contemplation of King and patted Duckworth on the rump. "Bless you, Duck, we'll do just that! Come on, King; I'll get you squared away in the studio while he sets up in here."

Except for metal folding chairs and a small desk, there was no furniture in the studio. Molly had him sit at the desk while she manipulated the boom mike, responding to hand signals from Duckworth, who was at the same time threading tape on the refrigerator-size recorder inside. King leaned on the desk, eyes on the New Testament open between his elbows. He sucked on a clove Life Saver Molly had given him and pondered his text while Molly and the program director consulted in the control room. Then the intercom was turned on, he heard a couple of screeches and the high-pitched whir of tape on the machine, and they were ready.

"I'll signal you when to start talking," Molly said over the intercom. "Keep an eye on the clock and try to hold it down to about fifteen minutes. But if you spill over, no difference, we'll edit the tape. Anything you want to know? Good. All right—fire away!"

King lifted his head, glanced at the small steel basket of the microphone a few inches from his nose, picked up his New Testament and began to read.

". . . as he journeyed, he came near Damascus: and suddenly there shined round about him a light from heaven: And he fell to the earth, and heard a voice saying unto him, Saul, Saul, why persecutest thou me?"

When he had finished he closed the book, laced his fingers on the desk top and stared off at the wall for a few seconds, as if in contemplation. But the seconds stretched on, and he fidgeted, and scowled, and glared both at the microphone and at Molly in the control room.

Her voice came over the intercom. "Duck stopped the tape. What's the matter, mike fright?"

"I don't think so," he said dryly. "I usually spend eight hours a day with a mike in my hand. I feel hemmed in, Molly, my knees are bumping the underside of this table. I never have preached like this; it's cold potatoes. I need to move around, warm up a little."

Within a couple of minutes Duckworth had outfitted him with a button mike, plugged in several yards of cord, and pushed the desk back out of the way.

King began again, after a spell of pacing. He spoke haltingly at first, with several long pauses. He tried to work himself up into the spirit, but, confronted with blank and slightly soiled walls and the remote faces of Molly and Duckworth behind a glare of glass, with the sound of his own voice bouncing back at him everywhere he turned, he did neither well nor badly, and was in a cold sweat by the time he glanced up at the clock and discovered that he'd rattled on for over twenty minutes. He concluded his talk with a terse prayer and stripped off the offensive microphone.

"Come on up, King," Molly said. "We'll play it back for you."

The playback was gruesome, and he squirmed all the way through it. As he had told Molly, King had never heard his recorded voice; once he adjusted to this uncomfortable experience and was able to concentrate on what he was saying, he was angered at how little content the message contained, how little feeling! It was not due to the fact that he'd had no preparation; he'd preached hundreds of times at impromptu meetings, just opened his mouth and let his love for the Lord carry him through. But this was hopeless, he thought, gritting his teeth as the spools ran on, and he made up his mind to ask Duckworth to erase the tape and forget the whole thing. The endless glances he sneaked at his audience of two confirmed what he believed to be a total failure. Duckworth looked sound asleep in his swivel chair in front of the console—although from time to time he reached out to make an adjustment of the dials on the board—and Molly was doodling industriously on a pad and avoiding his eyes altogether. Foolishness, he thought, and felt a newborn sympathy for all the radio preachers he'd ever heard, particularly those who worked from a studio like this one.

When the playback was over, and before King could have the face-saving pleasure of getting in the first critical jabs, Molly straightened up, threw down her pencil, and said, *"Very* good. Comes through fine, doesn't he, Duck?"

The program director nodded and smiled wanly. "Good radio voice."

"I was awful!" King said vehemently.

They both looked at him. Molly smiled understandingly. "Of course it sounds that way to you."

"Why," King said, "why, I fumbled words and tripped all over my tongue—"

"Some small mistakes," Duckworth conceded. "It's what you manage to convey with your voice that matters. You speak well. You've got that touch of drawl, the boyishness, and the load of grit in your throat. Mind if I call it a whiskey baritone? A few popular actors have grown rich because people recognize them before they've spoken half a dozen words. That cowboy actor—you know, Wayne. People will recognize you." He set to work stuffing his pipe.

"We're going to do some more work on the tape," Molly said, and Duckworth favored her with an inquiring glance. "All we have now is a sermon, but not a program. We'll edit out some of the stumbling in the beginning, and Duck can pull a hymn from the record library. What's your favorite?"

" 'Under His Wings I Am Safely Abiding,' " King said mechanically, staring at the floor.

She wrote it down. Duckworth dropped his empty tin of pipe tobacco in the wastebasket and rose with a yawn. "I've got a couple of telephone calls to make. Back with you in a minute, Molly."

"I have to be going myself," King said quickly. He motioned toward the tape recorder. "I don't suppose I can talk you into burning that?"

"You'd be doing the wrong thing," Molly replied. "When you hear yourself on the radio this evening you'll get a whole new perspective."

The two men shook hands perfunctorily, and Duckworth left. Molly said, "How can I convince you this will be a terrific program? That theme you brought out in your sermon was a beautiful appeal. 'How far would you walk to meet Jesus?' That struck me, and it'll strike others too. I wouldn't be surprised if you found your tent overflowing this weekend."

King scarcely heard her; he was only anxious to get away, and make the rounds he had promised himself he would make that afternoon. "Maybe we ought to get down to business, Molly. About the cost of the time——"

"Don't worry about it now. Don't even think about it. If you decide that you want to broadcast on a regular basis, then we'll negotiate some sort of contract with Fish when he gets back."

King shrugged. "I doubt if I'll want to do that. But thanks anyway, Molly, for your trouble. I can find my way out all right."

Molly passed off his depression and his rudeness with a somewhat rueful smile and bade him good-bye. When she was alone she rewound the tape and began playing it back in the silence of the control room. Occasionally she made a swift note on the pad in front of her. After five minutes Duckworth came back and sat down with her.

"I'll tell you what I want to do, Duck," she said. "It's a good tape but there's no excitement—he's just a preacher talking in a studio. You're an old hand at this sort of thing, you've taped live revivals. Can we give King Windom some of the live quality? Crowds behind him? Choirs of angels?"

"We've got a binful of old tapes; I could snip sound effects out of those. Funny up the hymn so it sounds like a live performance. And I'll tell you another thing—an announcer would be helpful."

"Would you do it, Duck?"

"Takes time," he complained. He sucked on his pipe for a while, gazing at the vacant studio. Then he said, "King Windom. Is this the new one?"

"I don't know what you mean by that, Duck," Molly said, but she couldn't keep the edge out of her voice.

"Where'd you meet him?"

"Where'd you get the idea it was any of your business?" But she told him anyway. "I met him on a roller coaster last night. Late last night."

He puzzled out the message. "Uh yeh. I see. He's the one in the newspaper."

"That's right. Duck, we've had some battles, but by and large you've been a good friend. Don't ask me any more." She started to get up, but sat down again and faced him, hands on knees, a girlish pose requesting confidence. Her face was puzzled. "You know, he saved me last night. I don't mean from taking a plunge off the Pippin, but afterward. When I was alone. He was *there,* somehow. A few hours' sleep and I've been fine today, no danger of a bash like poor Jimbo seems to be on." When he said nothing Molly's face flamed. "Well, look, Duck, just what reasons do I have to have for liking a man? I'm attracted to him, that's all."

Duckworth shrugged, but he was discomfited. "Molly, like you said, it's your business."

"Sure." Again she bounced up. "Going after coffee."

"I'll start editing that tape."

In passing Molly touched the nape of his neck with her fingertips, a gesture of endearment and gratitude. "Duck, all I've ever asked out of life is a man I can mean something to."

"This one's strange, Molly," he said, not turning his head.

"Let him be." And then she whispered, fervently, "Just don't let him disappoint me."

At twenty minutes of five that Thursday afternoon King found himself bogged in a southbound traffic snarl not too far from the fairgrounds.

The sun was setting peacefully and the sky above the autumn trees had dark-blue streaks of weather in it. On another day he might have settled back and enjoyed the onset of dusk until cars were moving again, but he'd had a rocky afternoon and so leaned over the wheel and glared impatiently down the static lines of traffic. He had gone down his list of preachers and made his calls, he had been met with jolly indifference and outright rebuff—and also, just possibly, he'd made a friend or two—but what loomed large in his mind at the moment was the prospect of listening all over again to the abominable sermon he had preached in the Kay-tip studios.

With a grimace of displeasure he recalled the halfhearted—or so it had seemed at the time—praise which Duckworth and Molly Amos had offered, so that he wouldn't feel like a complete dolt. For a while he had petulantly debated not listening, but the program was costing him hard cash; the lesson he'd already learned would be indelible if he suffered through the tape a second time.

The radio was already on, tuned to a small-town station near

102

Clearwater, and as King waited he found himself attending, through the horn blasts and the racketing of his own unreliable motor, the appeals of a mail-order missionary.

This preacher, after his wife had wailed out a hymn of her own composition while accompanying herself wretchedly on the guitar, began to speak frantically about money. He nearly got sick in the pit of his stomach, the man said, when he went down to the mailbox every morning and found it almost empty. Lord God, how he needed money to carry on his work in the prisons and jails across the Great Southwest! He had made appeals before, brother, but this time things were really grim. The transmission on his car was all fixed—King regretted having missed the last installment—but the man at the garage out there in Roswell wouldn't give up the car on his, the preacher's, pledge alone, and this eminently reasonable condition provoked the preacher to a new tantrum of sorrow. Being poor didn't bother him—he'd scraped along all his life and was none the worse for the experience—it was the thought of not being able to convey the Word to all the prisoners in the lockups that grieved him so. By this time his wife was hawking miserably into an open microphone somewhere, and strumming along on the guitar, despite some really formidable clinkers that almost brought sweat to King's brow.

Gradually King grinned, the muscle bunched in his jaw yielding reluctantly; then he laughed aloud. The absurd predicament of the jailhouse missionary had lent perspective to his own fears. Maybe his hail and farewell as a radio evangelist wouldn't be so hard on his nerves now.

The first thing he heard was a magnificent mixed chorus apparently singing from the depths of a great tent or hall. He thought immediately that he had tuned to the wrong station, but a glance at the dial told him he hadn't. And the hymn which was being sung was the one he had named for Molly, "Under His Wings I Am Safely Abiding." He'd expected the usual chocolaty-rich male baritone, but the multitude of voices sent a chill of excitement through him.

He was totally unprepared for the sounds he heard next: a congregation sighing, scuffling, settling into place while the last organ notes were dying away. And he gaped in astonishment at the radio when a man began speaking over this faint, familiar hubbub. It wasn't his voice.

"On behalf of King Windom I want to welcome all of you as

103

we begin the second week of our revival here at the Great Southern Stock Show and Exposition in Clearwater, Tennessee. Already hundreds have come forth in Jesus' name, hundreds have found new hope of life in the Lord. . . . "

Incredible, King thought, still feeling astonished, and also somewhat eerie. He looked vaguely out the window at the long furled shadows across the sun-splashed parkway, at the cars beginning to roll by him in the left-hand lane. And who was the man speaking for him in a measured, buoyant voice? And when had this revival—*his* revival—that was now being so realistically presented over the air taken place?

"Now it is my pleasure to turn the pulpit over to one of God's outstanding young men of faith and works, a man who already stands tall in the company of the great apostles, the Reverend King Windom!"

Again all the traffic came to a standstill, and horns blew dismally. King slumped lower in the seat, one hand hooked over the wheel. He heard himself reading the words of Acts 9 just as he had recorded them, and then, following the Scriptural passage, he began speaking incisively, commandingly, without all the muddled pauses and stumblings which had pained him so. With only the slyest turn of the imagination, through the sleight of hand of dreams, he saw tier upon tier of listeners where there had been only blank walls a few hours ago. Molly had done quite a job of editing! If he could somehow have torn his truck free of the tieup that instant, he would have chased her down and told her what he thought of this embarrassing fakery. But even as he was damning Molly in his thoughts, King was listening to his quick challenging voice, and little by little his anger, and his humiliation, subsided.

The cars ahead started up; absently he set his pickup in motion and drove on toward the fairgrounds.

The eerie feeling had grown stronger; he was dazed by it. This is the way I sound, he said to himself. This is the way I sound. I am King Windom.

He realized now that what he was hearing was good, and powerfully stated. The false setting which Molly had provided only added authority to his message. It was wrong for her to have done it, but he understood her reasons, or thought that he did.

King's first radio sermon had ended by the time he drove into the carnival compound. He went straight to his trailer, shutting the door against the dulcimers and drums of the midway. In his darkened, tiny bedroom he went down on his knees to lift the Schofield Bible from atop a mountain of paperback books. He was jittery, cold, badly frayed; yet he felt exalted. He kissed the Book many times, until his exaltation was made bearable. Then he threw himself across his untidy bed and stared upward, fists clenched.

Quite unexpectedly he became choked with tears, and he could not fight them.

9

The Southern Cross Crusade

For the second time that day King had slept, an almost unheard-of occurrence for him, and he might have gone on sleeping another hour if Sandi hadn't barged in at six-thirty, lugging a hot ham casserole which she'd spent most of the afternoon preparing in somebody else's kitchen. Her busy presence in his trailer jarred him awake and he found himself the wrong way in the bed, head jammed up against the trailer wall, hands beneath him, closed and aching. He had dozed off with his fists clenched and now pain ran up his forearms, such scalding pain that he almost groaned.

"Age?"

"King, it's me," Sandi replied. "The crack-the-whip broke down about half an hour ago and Age is working on it with Larry."

He heard her coming light-footedly through the trailer and struggled up in time to straighten his shirt before she appeared in the gloom, looking, in her thick stage makeup and grotesque eyelashes, not unlike some of the more enigmatic demons he'd now and then encountered in dreams.

"Hi," she said. "Dinner's almost ready." She had been in his trailer many times, but she had never ventured as far as his quarters, and her manner was overly bright to cover a certain trepidation. "I saw you drive in about five but you looked so tired I thought you'd want to lie down and nap for a little while before you ate."

"Sandi, why do you want to go and put yourself out fixing me a meal?"

"That sounds cranky," she said in a stricken voice. "I wanted to cook you *something*. You said I could stop by after dinner, so I thought we'd just eat together."

King had a whiff of the casserole bubbling in the kitchen, and discovered that he was ravenous. With a strained smile he apologized for his churlishness, praised Sandi for her consideration, and sent her happily off to the kitchen to brown biscuits. He then lunged up from the low, narrow bed that was hardly big enough for a growing boy, let alone a man his size, and went into the bathroom. There, hunched over the washbasin, he pounded open the hot-water tap and thrust both of his painfully knotted hands into the basin. The water became smokily hot right away, and he winced, but held his fists down as long as he could stand it. The heat served to unlock his frozen muscles, and he was then able to open his hands. He stared at them in soft amazement. As a boy he had experienced muscle spasms associated with severe growing pains, but nothing like this.

The experience was oddly terrifying and he had never been more glad for company. With a brush he went over his thick coarse hair until it was as wet as a seal's back, chose a fresh shirt from the wardrobe in his room, and went pensively to the kitchen. Fortunately Sandi was in her element, and as full of small talk and carnival gossip as ever, and it was pleasant for him to sit at the drop-leaf table in the kitchen with his back nearly against the stove, soaking up warmth and filling his stomach with her good rich casserole and blanketing his mind with trivialities.

King had no conceit when it came to women, and little psychology. Sandi was only one of many carnival girls, and women, who had taken to him since the day Frank Henderson had adopted him and bullied him back to life. Men were seldom jealous of King's appeal because he generally accepted the attentions of all women with a thick-skulled absent-mindedness which seemed to them to resemble a self-sufficient indifference, and they admired him for it. Actually he needed female attention, and companionship, as much as any other lonely and susceptible thirty-year-old man.

106

As they ate—or rather as he ate and she kept a hawk's eye on his plate, rushing in with another large helping of casserole when it seemed as if he was making a serious dent in the preceding helping—Sandi gradually worked herself up into a more serious frame of mind. She was not devious or particularly clever, so the hints which she chose to rain on him about her immature plans for the future, and the totally different future she had coveted since laying eyes on him, fell as solidly as hailstones.

King knew what was up and he was not indifferent; he felt like any man faced with the thinly restrained love of an appealing and good-looking young girl. He was stirred and flattered and inclined to soul-searching, because as late as three weeks ago, in his deeper brooding moments, he had considered marrying Sandi. During the summer, when they found themselves alone and she had made known her willingness, he had nearly given in to a combination of low morale, sexual desire, and a yearning for some sort of permanence in his life. But he had never made love to Sandi. By his ethics sex outside of marriage was unthinkable and even a kiss was sacred, an acknowledgment of deep love and purpose.

He should have answered her own seriousness by being frank, but at times he could be the world's worst at just speaking his mind. So to avoid her he began to argue vigorously against the dancing troupe she proposed to join. Sandi was hurt by his apparent insensitivity and obtuseness, she became defensive and then adamant, committing herself to a threat she'd never meant seriously. The convivial little dinner which she had created as a milestone in their wrong-way courtship ended in a bog of tension and strained nerves.

King could resist almost anything but a woman with wounded feelings—and the resultant reflection on his boorishness and lack of maturity—so, despite the harsh lecture which had left Sandi silent and struggling with her pride, he might have weakened then and there and taken her tenderly in his arms, thereby turning his life neatly upside down. But Frank Henderson picked that moment to stop by, open the trailer door, and ask King, in a sarcastic voice, if he minded putting in a little time on the midway that evening, since he hadn't worked for the better part of two days.

This was all the excuse King needed to take flight from his own home, leaving Sandi behind. His parting smile withered quickly on his face as he slogged through the sawdust toward the fairgrounds, a crumpled khaki jacket in one hand. He had behaved badly where Sandi was concerned, acting like a witless boy, and he was suffering for it. His only hope was that she would somehow see just how unfit and unrewarding a husband he would have made, that she would get over her crush quickly now that he had been cruel to her, and do the sensible thing—whatever that might be. If only he could have been truthful about himself! He might then have eased his mind, and given Sandi some consolation, or a reasonable way to settle her dilemma. The truth was simple, as he saw it. Six years ago he had loved, and he had no hope of loving again. There was no more to be said. There would never be another Mary Kate.

He spent the next two and a half hours hard at his old job, assembling the curious before the long outside platform of the freak show, and keeping a steady flow of customers moving up to the ticket booth and into the tent. He had Kirby, the ex-boxer with the remarkable eyes, to help his spiel, and, at various times during his stint, the Great Rodrigues, a sword-swallower and fire-eater, and Madam Sphinx, the Woman of Stone, also appeared on the platform.

By the time King got around to actually letting something happen outside, several hundred people had grown tired of waiting, bought their tickets, and filed past the various cubicles behind the canvas. As the Madam was borne grandly away in a sedan chair by four self-conscious Negro boys in pantaloons and turbans, King decided to give his voice a rest until the show's Incomparable Prestidigitator and Master of the Somnambulistic Art made his appearance. Since seven o'clock King had been immersed in the world of the carny, concerned with nothing but the crowd, alert for those who showed even a flicker of interest in the fright pictures of geeks in bold color above his head. His pause brought back to him the commitments he had made to another, more demanding way of life. It gave him an uneasy, sad feeling to realize that in another forty-eight hours the carnival which had been his home, and a good home, for so long would vanish almost magically from under his feet.

"I thought you were a pretty good preacher, but you're a better con man."

The voice of Molly Amos cut through the confusion of sound

all around him, the gravel and caw of other pitchmen, the confectionery music, and the heart-stopping rumble of machinery. He discovered her lively, angular face near the ticket stall, and moved along the platform with a rather fierce expression which brought a grin to her face.

"You didn't like it," she said.

"Molly what gave you—" He stared down at her, perplexed, troubled all over again by her audacity. "You could get me in a mess with all the lies you told on one radio program."

Molly, realizing that he wasn't really angry, brightened. She looked fetching in flats, a culotte, and a denim jacket. Apparently she had spent part of the afternoon having her hair done: it was whipped and lacquered in a handsome way. "What lies?" she asked blithely. "We gave you a solid introduction. I was tempted to throw in an appeal for money at the end, but before I did that I had the sense to call a man named Handwerker—he's one of the local Baptists who buys time on Kay-tip—and he said that wouldn't be the thing to do at all. It would leave you open to a charge of using the mails in an attempt to defraud, since you don't represent anybody but yourself."

"Why, I know all that, Molly. Preachers get hauled into court right and left on that charge."

"Well, the point is, *I* didn't know any better, but I've since had a nice talk with the Reverend Mr. Handwerker about the business—he's interested in you, by the way—and with my lawyer, the boy you met last night. I'm full of ideas, but"—she glanced around at the carnival—"I don't want to spend any more time than I have to in this infernal place; it gave me a stomachache as soon as I walked in the gate. Could you knock off long enough to have a cup of coffee? I promise, I'll just steal you for five minutes."

King nodded and signaled his assistant, an eager boy whom he'd been training as a grinder that summer, just as Frank Henderson had once trained him. He led Molly to a refreshment booth run by the Order of the Eastern Star, which was away from the mainstream of the carnival. Molly gave him a couple of appraising glances as they waited for their coffee, then squeezed his elbow tightly. "I wish you'd do away with the grim face. You were just out to let me know I wasn't getting away with anything. All right, I'm properly chastened. Now let me tell you the news, and you might look interested."

"What news?"

She took several seconds to get another of her interminable cigarettes going. "First off, Fish, our station manager is due back tomorrow afternoon. I'm going to collar him right away and sing your praises, hoping he'll give you a contract for the time slot you were in today. I could hear Mr. Handwerker crackling with envy over the phone when I told him what I'd done for you; he'd love to have that time for himself. Any preacher would. The problem is money, of course. For class-A time Fish can gross over a hundred dollars in a quarter hour selling spot announcements. At the most you're worth fifty. That's two hundred fifty dollars a week you'd bring in. So the station will lose money at a time when advertisers are competing for spots, hoping to catch a big part of Ordell's audience. But I think I can convince Fish that he'll be doing more than throwing money away for your sake. I don't have any doubt once you get going you'll hold Ordell's audience, and you might increase it—which would be quite a feat, since Ordell is one of the holies in a very clannish business. When the station gains an extra hour and a half of air during the summer, spot advertisers will be begging for time. In the long run you'll profit the station just as Ordell has."

"*If* anybody's listening to me," King grunted. "Summer's a long time coming. And two hundred fifty dollars a week!"

"Don't get rattled," Molly said. From a floppy leather purse she took three folded sheets of onionskin paper. King looked curiously at them, but in the foggy light of the refreshment stand he could make out only the typed heading THE KING WINDOM EVANGELICAL ASSOCIATION.

"As I told you," she resumed, after a glance at her handiwork, "I did some phoning around this afternoon, and while I was sitting under the dryer tonight I ran this through my portable. You sort of blanched at the idea of laying out two hundred fifty dollars a week for radio, but Mr. Handwerker assured me you could make that kind of money easily from donations, without any kind of hard sell. But first you'd better be incorporated." Molly handed him the copy of the prospectus she'd written. "Everything is down here in a more or less orderly manner; you can ponder these pages later tonight when you have time. Cy, my lawyer, thinks it will cost you about a hundred dollars to incorporate on a nonprofit basis here in Tennessee—which is as good a state as any for your purposes."

110

" 'The Southern Cross Crusade'?" King said, reading his way down the first page.

"That was just a brainstorm on my part. You don't have to like it. Mr. Handwerker told me that several of the successful evangelists use 'Crusade' to describe their revivals, and people respond favorably. It suggests bigness and a sense of high purpose. I'm going to go more deeply into all this, of course; that prospectus is nothing but surfaces. Still, it's exciting, at least to me." She drank hot coffee, her bold black eyes centered on his face. "You have adequate working capital, and other assets—that tent you described, and the old truck. If we start right away, the incorporation procedure will only take three or four weeks. It's a must, as I said. Cy, by the way, is a whiz at that kind of paperwork; bailing me out of jail was an oddity for him. I recommend Cy highly to you. In the meantime . . ." She paused while King calmly flipped over to page two and went on reading, his taut face without expression. "In the morning you ought to come in and cut three more tapes; they'll be useful when I make my presentation to Fish."

"Ummm."

"That is, if you agree with everything I've written there."

King lifted his head, and his eyes were a stark yellow in the bug-repellent light beneath the canopy of the refreshment stand.

"This is well done, Molly; you're way ahead of my own figuring."

"You've thought mostly about preaching," she said, taking out a handkerchief to cover her sensitive nose as a stench of frying grease enveloped them.

"That's true," King admitted, refolding the prospectus. "Of course, we're both forgetting one thing. Old Eli. I haven't told him a word yet about going on the radio."

"I meant to bring him up," Molly said. "I haven't met the man, but I know you would have been better off if you'd put some of your savings into a rented tent, and, if you thought you had to have one, a rented truck."

"Well, I had reasons for going halves with Eli," King said uncomfortably. In fact his reasons seemed less realistic than ever to him. But he continued to hold stubbornly to the notion that it was better to own half a canvas than rent a whole one. Then no matter what turn his fortunes might take, he would

111

always have a place to preach. That was all he really cared about, as Molly had discovered.

"Whatever your reasons were, you ought to think them over," Molly said, talking through the scented handkerchief. She had begun to drift away from the refreshment booth as if it were filled with plague. "What sort of agreement did you sign? By all means show it to Cy before he goes to work drawing up the incorporation papers. He shouldn't have too much trouble voiding the agreement, or sweet-talking Eli into a small settlement." Molly's voice had become slightly sharp and her manner officious; she was beginning to suffer deeply from her surroundings. Again King felt unsure of himself with her, as he had on two or three occasions that afternoon; his reaction was to—as Molly had put it—pull in his ears.

"Well, I'm not so sure I'd want to break my agreement with Eli," he said.

"For Pete's sake, why not?" Molly cast a sick hopeless glance at the refreshment stand. "Can we get away from here?" she begged. "All those odors of stale fried chicken and mummified frankfurters are making me reel."

"Reckon I'm used to them," King murmured, draining his coffee and tossing the paper cup away. They strolled back toward the midway. "I can't break with Eli because the fact remains I need a place to preach."

"You've *got* a place. Kay-tip radio."

"No, I mean a tent."

"A tent. All right, you won't rent one; native caution forbids, or something. After you've incorporated there's a possibility you can bag a good loan from one of the banks and buy. And you'll certainly be making money from your radio programs."

"That's a maybe, not a certainty, Molly." He shook his head broodingly. "No, the prospectus is fine and I'm mightily impressed with the work you've done on my behalf. Grateful. With your help I'd like to go through with the incorporation and continue my radio ministry too. But I don't think you can catch the Holy Ghost fever over the radio, like a lot of preachers say you can. Remember what I told you about the importance of people coming together to make a living church of their flesh, wherein the spirit of Jesus could dwell? Jesus visited Eli's tent last night, Molly. He blessed me by His presence. That tent is a

112

Holy place to my way of thinking, no matter how badly it's been used by others. And it's a lucky place for me."

Molly had been aware of the streak of religious mystic in King since their meeting in the Melrose Restaurant that afternoon. Of course, it had to be there—religious conviction made him the man he was—but at the same time Molly felt an odd anger and impotence when he spoke like that. She said, "I'm just thinking ahead. Once you lock yourself into a corporation with old Eli, as you call him, you may regret it. . . . But we can talk later about it, if you want to." Out of the corner of her eye she had caught the beginning of a curt smile on his face.

Possessiveness had begun to grind away in Molly like the mad energy of the carnival, and she had to set her teeth to keep from ranting at King about his lack of business judgment—about everything in him which she found unsatisfactory. After all, she had done well with the prospectus, he was impressed by it, and surely by her. But Molly knew that their relationship was still tenuous; he was ready to draw away from her on any pretext, because—she told herself with a nervous amusement—he was afraid of her. The racketing of the Pippin nearby, the thin shrieks of its delighted and frightened passengers, broke in on her thoughts, and depressed her. Some of the things she had babbled to him last night! But even if she hadn't said a word, it still would have been clear to King what she had wanted with Jerry Dee Binsford.

It was not possible for Molly to bear the thought of Jerry Dee for long; she was even now passing within a hundred feet of the scene of her disgrace. Molly fell back on a tried-and-true defense of herself, as if the accusations which she had raised had been on King's lips instead. She was a creature of superior sensuality, seething with creative energy. In search of life, and fulfillment of herself as a person, she sometimes made mistakes. It was up to King to understand that, to realize that her unpredictable behavior was not the same thing as immorality. She still attended the Episcopal church in which she had been baptized, and had formed lasting notions of a somewhat philosophical and uncommitted God. Morally speaking she had no reason to hang her head. Unfortunately—she'd better make up her mind to it—King had seen her worst side, seen her deeply sensual nature commanded and cheapened by lust. Despite her best efforts since then, he didn't really know her, and so,

113

notwithstanding his forgiving Christian heart, he still equated her with Jerry Dee Binsford. She would need time to overcome this block, Molly conceded, and she felt in better spirits as they walked on and the body of the carnival lay behind them. He probably had never known a woman of her experience and outlook. That was part of his fear—or call it wariness—of her; his "women" had most certainly been nothing but rattle-brained girls, love-struck and unsophisticated, the pack of them with a common thought: to land him, and tie him down. Molly smiled softly and contemptuously. It was a wonder he hadn't been landed by now. But she was too full of pride in herself, too certain that she was the only woman of consequence who had ever taken an interest in King Windom, to feel inquisitive about his past loves.

Three or four minutes had gone by while Molly was making these corrections in her attitude toward King; they reached the main gate without having spoken a word to each other in that time.

"Well," Molly said lightly, turning to him, "I've used up more than the five minutes you promised me. I didn't want to bother you while you were working, but I didn't know how else to get in touch. You were in a tearing hurry to leave the station this afternoon." She pointed to the prospectus which he still held in his hand.

"I was excited over that; I had to show it to you or bust."

King smiled absentmindedly; he looked as if he too had done some wrestling of thoughts during their silence. Suddenly he glanced her way and blurted, "I don't know how I can thank you for all this, Molly. 'The Southern Cross Crusade.' That strikes me fine. I'm truly in your debt. But why in the world should you go to this kind of trouble on my account?"

Molly decided that he was not trying to remind her, in an oblique way, of the risk he had taken the night before. He had not flexed his muscles once over the incident, as other men would have done. He was sincere, and she was warmed by his appreciation. She offered a gay smile.

"Oh, I had fun. The work I've done the past year and a half has been a glorified drudgery. Editing wire-service news, writing spots, and handling a few publicity chores for Ordell on the side. This was something I could get my teeth into." She peeked at her watch. "I'd better run on. My night to visit Mother. Once a month, like clockwork. If I'm not on time the

114

fight starts as soon as I sit down; otherwise we wait until we've had a good stiff drink apiece."

"From around here, Molly? I wouldn't have known that; you don't sound like a South'ner."

Molly put her hands in the pockets of her denim jacket and stared down at the ground for a few moments. "The people of quality in this city are the Stranahans, the Cobbs, the Mendenhalls, the Houstons, and the Wheelwrights. I'm a Houston; Amos is a remnant of a marriage I've almost forgotten." She looked up with an uninspired smile. "My mother has some time-honored ideas of what a Southern lady should be. 'Let the niggers do it, dear.' I'm afraid I was a sickening example of a precious Dixie belle until I was almost old enough to vote. Can you imagine me in organdy and tulle? I was more of a horse than I am now, with these wide shoulders, and skinny to boot. What a bad joke to play on a sensitive and self-conscious girl. Then I heard the rest of the joke: I was a Houston by decree. Adopted. Do you know what it means when there's *no trace* of your birth at all?" The heaviness of an old anxiety lay across her forehead; King looked on in mute sympathy. "My foster father had been dead a little over a year, but I think I told you that even when he was living he never paid any attention to me. Small wonder! For years every time I passed a country shack or looked down a slum street I asked myself if that's where I belonged—I mean where I'd been *born*." She lifted her chin, giving King a level and almost unfriendly look; her face was terribly pinched. "Any guess what blood I am? I've been mistaken for Mexican, and Armenian Gypsy, and, for all I know, Negro." She sounded the last with particular gusto, as if she were eager to shock him. Then she let her hand fly out in a vigorous gesture of unconcern. "Mother knows who I am, and where I came from, and she'll go to her grave without telling me. I don't know why I go sit in her house, even for a couple of hours, and let her browbeat me. She has the notion that it's my *duty* to come home as an unpaid companion to her. Imagine that!"

She began tearing through her pockets in search of a smoke, looking redly cheerful. King felt as if Molly had been peeling herself down layer by layer—absorbing work for her—and the closer she had come to the labyrinth of her soul, the more skittish he had felt.

He was baldly relieved when she looked up, damned her lack

115

of cigarettes, and said again that she had to run. They made arrangements to meet the next day. Then Molly reached up and gave his shoulder a quick pat.

"Mother's a better person than I made her sound. She's a cultured woman, remarkable in many ways. It's a sad life, being that last leaf on a dying tree." A moment's aimless curiosity prompted her to ask, "Do you get along with your mother? I'd imagine she dotes on you."

"Actually she died when I was about twelve."

"I'm sorry to hear it. What sort of woman was she?"

He could have passed off the question with a meaningless answer, but he said, "She was a spiritualist, a medium. I had an unusual childhood."

"I should *say*. You mean she could talk to—"

"I never knew; I never asked her." King yawned, his eyes bleak. "But I never believed in her, either. Well, Molly, I'll be meeting you in the morning. Thanks again. Reckon I'd better head back now and drum up some more business before we close."

10

Jeremy's Dream

King did not return to work; a few seconds' study of the midway convinced him that the boy whom he had left in charge of the show was doing a good job with the mike. His own voice was tired, it was close to ten o'clock, and the crowds were beginning to thin out. He decided to look in on the revival meeting and avail himself of the lesson in how to fill the collection buckets which Eli had promised.

Because of his radio sermon that afternoon he had half hoped to find the tent crowded, but if anything the congregation was smaller than it had been the night before, and the people were as silent as if attending a funeral. Philemon and the same three vulturous-looking preachers who had been in attendance most of the week were sitting at the rear of the small stage, and Eli was leaning heavily on a straight-back chair as he addressed the flock. Diligent work with a brush had taken some of the wildness out of his hair, and he was presentable in his rumpled meeting suit. Apparently he had been talking about money for some time. Such was his ability that King remained longer than he had intended. Eli was by turn ingratiating, amusing, waspish, threatening, and tearful before his flock. He scratched their bellies and flayed their backs and walked them barefoot at the edge of brimstone. He was obvious when he had to be: he spelled out GIVE ME in foot-high letters a dozen times. He had his faults and long-windedness was one of them. But as King looked at the assembly he saw that many of the people had accepted Eli's simple equation—give to the Lord, and the Lord will repay you many times over. King felt a measure of disgust for Eli's mendacity, knowing what harm such a suggestion could do in the mind of a decent Christian plagued by financial troubles.

As he listened he searched the tent for Jeremy, but she wasn't there. He scowled, thinking of how she had been baited into a violent fit of temper at lunch. He'd done nothing—nothing. Eli's judgment of Jeremy was like a chill in his mind. But perhaps by now she had forgotten the whole thing.

The dust of the tent ground had given him a thirst. Although there was a spigot nearby, he decided to walk down the ridge to the house.

He left the tent and circled the parked truck. Philemon's dun-colored fighting dog appeared like a ghost from beneath the cab and King stood stock-still. The dog was secured by a rope and a halter to the front bumper, and made no sound—undoubtedly it had a badly bruised throat from the choking he had given it. King let his breath go cautiously. The dog continued to study him with a slow turn of its hellish head as he went on by.

From the top of the ridge he looked down on small ponds of mist and the blunt shapes of cattle, then outward to a sky of great oaks and a Negro settlement by the railroad. It would be a good place for a cross-country ramble on his motorcycle, he decided; the pasture was clean, the ravines shallow, and the trees widely spaced. He vowed to finish cleaning the big sprocket which he had recently bought so he could use the motor again. He'd had time for few amusements while on the road with the carnival, but there was nothing like a long, bone-jolting ride on his motor to set him right with the world again.

He ran the rest of the way to the house, blood pounding in his head, and capered in the front yard for a while, swinging like a boy from a thick leafless arm of the peach tree. "Jeremy!" he called, but there was no answer; the house which she had made habitable was silent.

Growing tired of his solitary play, he dropped from the tree and waded with a heavy breath up to the front door. "Jeremy?" he said again, rapping his knuckles against the screen door. A single lamp burned inside. He entered. The folding screen which had shielded Eli in his bath had been removed, and now squared off the other end of the kitchen, by the back door. There was a narrow mattress on the floor, half-hidden by the screen. By the light coming through the glass in the door he saw Jeremy lying in a mass of bedding on the mattress. He approached quietly, thinking that she was asleep. But he heard her sniff.

"I came for a drink of water," he said.

"Help yourself. Bottle there on the sink."

King went. Jeremy said wanly, not stirring, "I'd get it for you, but I'm too fat to fly and too lazy to walk."

"That's all right." She sounded in the worst possible spirits, and he was worried. He drank two glasses of water, and stared somberly at the mattress. He said, unforgivably, "Is that where you sleep?"

"Do you see another bed?" Jeremy asked.

"Well, no, but Philemon's a strapping boy, the floor wouldn't hurt him. I missed you at the meeting."

"I'm getting an eyestrain from time to time," she said, her voice muffled, "so I stay out of the light."

"Is there anything I can do for you, Jeremy?"

"I reckon there's not."

She had made it perfectly plain that she wanted to be left alone, but King pulled up a straight chair. Almost immediately he was aware of a strong draft under the door, so he got up, prowled through the house, and found a bath towel that smelled of sweat and the shaving lotion which Philemon used excessively, and stuffed that in the space to keep the cold air off Jeremy. She had not stirred. He kneeled beside her, eyes alight.

"Jeremy, I went on the radio today!"

118

For several seconds he thought she had gone to sleep after all, and he was disappointed. Then the bedding quaked, Jeremy sat up, and kittens fell darkly out of the patchwork folds. She swept her hair out of her face with one hand and picked up the kitten, which was crying most piteously.

"You didn't!" she said, genuinely excited.

"And another thing—it's possible a quarter million people were hearing me. That's the number tuned in to the station late in the afternoon." King thought of the miserably silent few he had seen in the tent a few minutes ago and his own excitement climbed. He answered her eager questions and recited the high points of his sermon, but he said nothing about the additions which Molly and the portly program director had made to his tape. Jeremy then wanted to know more about "Mrs. Amos" and gradually drew out of him the whole story of his encounter with Molly on the Pippin the night before. Jeremy listened thoughtfully and at times incredulously.

"Is she a drunkard? If she could act the fool that way, there's no telling what else she might do it she took a notion."

"Well, Molly'd had a few snorts," King said a shade impatiently. "But today she was straightened out and just as pleasant as could be."

"Hmmm," Jeremy went on, wide-eyed. "What do you know about that?" She patted the mattress behind her to make sure there were no kittens in the way and fell back. King was sitting on the floor now with his arms around his knees. "And you're going on the radio every day!" she said, emphatically changing the subject.

King frowned. "Now that's not definite. I won't know for sure until tomorrow, or maybe next week."

Jeremy said, responding to the caution in his tone, "You don't want Eli hearing about it yet."

"I'll tell him," King said resolutely, "just as soon as I have contracts for him to look at. But everything has to be cut and dried." He had, so far, resisted thinking about Eli's probable reaction to the spending of two hundred and fifty dollars a week for air time. He was reminded of Molly's qualms about his partnership with Eli, but he beat down these thoughts without difficulty. After all, in terms of attendance for their nightly meetings, they could do nothing but profit from a radio ministry. Eli, despite his fixations, would realize that.

"I'm glad to know you were right busy this afternoon,"

119

Jeremy said, contentedly crossing her arms outside the quilt. "When you didn't come even at supper I thought you were real sorry I'd made a spectacle of myself and didn't care if you never came again or not."

"Jeremy, I understand. A person can just swallow so much meanness from others, and then that person has to hit back. Why, I've got a terrible temper myself; there's a split porch railing outside will testify to that."

Her mouth thinned out to a rueful line, an expression which touched him deeply. "If you understand, it's no difference. But I'm apologizing here and now." She turned over on her side, one hand dropping to the edge of the mattress. King dwelled on her hands, which were long, with only a hard hint of bone or down on the smooth surfaces. His eyes lifted to the unspoiled line of her throat and a long wisp of hair over one cheekbone. Her ears were small and, as he remembered, a healthy red. He felt a heady sensual pleasure, no more than he had felt when Jeremy had first confronted him with a load of pecans in her apron.

"I don't know what reason Eli had for saying you couldn't be saved, but it isn't true and you shouldn't believe it for a second. Jesus paid the sin debt for us, and all we have to do is love Him and accept Him for God's grace to shine upon us."

Jeremy could not see the question in his eyes, which was impossible for him to ask; but she realized what he wanted to know. "Philemon was right in saying I named him a fornicator, because I did. And it was a lie."

"Why did you do it, Jeremy?"

She looked thoughtfully at him. "Knocking myself in the head with that rock caused all sorts of trouble. I had to stay in a little country hospital for a week, and Eli dug deep on my account. The doctor had to be paid, and there were medicines to buy." She made a face, recalling some of those medicines. "I had the worst dreams you could think of, and I'd wake up in fits. Well, they cured the fits there in the hospital but I still had dreams, which was an unusual thing, because I never dreamed before in my life. Some of the dreams were good, just as splendid as Bible stories. I didn't mind them. But there was this one dream . . ." She rolled her eyes in a dreary embarrassed way. "I was married to Philemon, if that isn't something, and I was going to have a baby."

"You mean you dreamed you were pregnant?"

Jeremy gripped the quilt tightly in one hand. "That's right. But when I woke up, I still believed I was going to have that baby. I realized the part about being married wasn't true, but I couldn't help believing the other. I should have known better, but at that age, well, you have to understand I didn't know much about life."

King nodded. Jeremy was terribly embarrassed, and he suffered with her. But she seemed determined to finish her story, even if she made a mess of it.

"After three or four weeks I didn't any the less believe in the baby, because at that time I was starting to swell up." She smiled wanly. "Did you ever hear of such a thing? I almost died of humiliation. I had to talk to somebody about what was happening to me, and who could I turn to but Eli? At first he thought I was just telling a tall tale to get back at Philemon. He was so mad he got red in the face. But I cried like a lunatic and scared him, and he began believing me. He went looking for Philemon with a big belt in his hand."

"Good," King said grimly.

Jeremy, misunderstanding, raised up. "But you see, Philemon hadn't done anything to me. Not even at night when I was sleeping off my medicine, which was what Eli suspected. Philemon was as upset as I was, terrified actually, because he could see that he was in for a whipping. There we were, both white as spooks, carrying on, yelling at each other; I'll bet Eli was wishing he could crawl in a hole to get away from us. He just knew somebody was telling lies. So the upshot was he took me to a doctor, a specialist. I'm forgetting what he was called. This doctor examined me"—despite the poor light King thought that she had blushed a deep red—"and said that there was no chance I was going to have a baby, even if I did look like it and have all the symptoms."

"It's called false pregnancy," King said.

"Yes, that's what it was," Jeremy affirmed, and sat up straighter. "The doctor explained everything. But still I believed I was going to have a baby. Nobody could talk me out of it."

"Something changed your mind, though."

She nodded. "Along about a week later I dreamed I was having my baby, and it hurt me. I suffered! And afterward an angel came down from above and told me that he was going to take my baby with him. My heart broke, because I thought my

121

baby was dead. But he said no, the child was going to Heaven to live with Jesus. In the morning, when I woke up, I wasn't... swollen anymore." She sat with her hands on her knees, pensive, not looking at King. "I know I never was ... pregnant. But still, now and then, I catch myself thinking about my baby in Heaven, who is with the Lord Jesus, who may grow up to be as good and strong as Jesus. .... Do you think I'm crazy?"

She blurted out the last with such an expression of shame and unhappiness that King instantly grasped one of her hands and held it tightly. "I don't think that, Jeremy. And neither should you."

"But why did it happen?"

"You know, Jeremy, a baby is the most precious gift a woman can give. And I do believe that because you love our Lord, who died for your sake, you've always wanted to give Him something precious."

Jeremy drew a sharp breath, then shook her head in bewilderment. "You must be right," she said, after a long pause. "You must know. . . ." She leaned toward him as if to see his face better; instinctively he lifted his hand and cradled one shoulder. Jeremy came willingly into his arms, tangled bed-clothes and all.

King felt only a mild shock, and the sensation of deep grief thickened by passion. Even as he unthinkingly kissed Jeremy, part of his mind was icy clear. What was he doing, what was the matter with him? Barely three hours ago he had almost taken Sandi in his arms, and had just escaped being overwhelmed by his emotions then. Hadn't he learned? However, his sensible mind had no great voice and he continued to hold Jeremy and to kiss her. Jeremy, though not exactly wooden, was unresponsive, but her breath came in gusts against his cheek.

Within seconds King's sense of sin and disgrace unlocked his hands and brought a taste of bitterness to his tongue; he released Jeremy and her head slipped below his shoulder. He felt the pressure of her cheek against an inner arm. He was too stunned by his behavior to speak. Then Jeremy began to quake, as if she was throttling tears. At that moment he could gratefully have given himself over to a horsewhipping.

"Oh, my," Jeremy said in a joyful voice, "and a dozen times today I wished I could die, because I didn't know what you were thinking of me!"

He had expected tears from Jeremy, or disgust—almost anything but delight. The grief which he had felt in the beginning, as he clumsily bound her with his arms, suddenly tore loose inside and smashed heavily against his heart. He lunged to his feet, caught the surprised glint of her upraised eyes, and was swept by panic.

"King!" she said, in an astonished voice, but he was running, stumbling over a loose floorboard, banging his elbow painfully against the doorframe as he pushed open the screen.

It was not Jeremy he was running from, but the image of another.

Realization brought King to a breathless halt some twenty yards up the ridge. The night was deep and quiet; the sounds of the carnival, blunted by distance, failed to fill it. In the toy tent voices were shakily out of tune: "I'll Be Singing up There." He sank down on a windfall that had been lying in the pasture for most of his lifetime and stared back wretchedly at the broken-looking house, its tin roof glazed like stale water under the stars.

Jeremy reminded him of his dead Mary Kate, that was all there was to it. Mary Kate had been smaller, more delicate, with black hair worked into a single braid the thickness of her wrist. But the contours of their youthful faces were disturbingly similar. True, the bad eye at times made Jeremy seem homely, but he had not been aware of this imperfection while they had talked in the dark. He had seen only the pensiveness, the absorbing glances.

Because he'd been so close to her, exposed to her most intimate feelings, he'd comforted Jeremy, and kissed her. But it really had been Mary Kate he was seeking when he impulsively reached out.

As quickly as he had come, King left his seat on the windfall and ran back to the house, bent on apologizing to Jeremy for what he considered to be his humiliating misuse of her. His thoughtless and unrestrained approach—a pounding run that shook the whole porch when he hit it—was probably not very reassuring to Jeremy, who had been appalled by his unpremeditated flight just after a wholehearted bout of kissing.

King fumbled with the sticking screen door, calling "Jeremy! Jeremy!" and finally entered the house.

She came rushing out of the dark in her nightclothes, arms outstretched. But her head was lowered and, instead of

123

embracing the preacher, she hit him with all her strength, using both hands like a ram. He was slightly off balance to begin with, and her accurate charge bowled him backward through the still-open doorway with a grunt of surprise. He landed butt first on the porch and went sprawling down the steps in a tangle of legs, coming to rest in the clay yard. His teeth had clicked together so hard upon being hit that he tasted sparks, and his head lolled in a dazed way. Distantly he heard the front door slammed and the wild shape of a cat leaped across his distorted field of vision.

"Jeremy?" he said, unbelievingly.

His head cleared slowly. He rose, favoring a strained muscle under his right arm, and tottered up the steps to the porch. The front door was locked. He rattled it experimentally. There was no response from inside. He thought of a thing or two to say in defense of himself, but at the same time he was aware that if Jeremy'd had a gun it would have been nothing but fair play to shoot him, so none of his silent eloquence rose to his tongue.

Long after he knew that she wasn't going to come, and unlock the door, and give him a chance to explain, he continued to stand there in a fine forlorn fit of shivering, like a lean old dog after his master's funeral, wincing at the pain in his side. Likely, he thought with tight-lipped satisfaction, he'd pulled every shred of rib gristle. He considered the possibility of climbing through a window to get to Jeremy, but how would that strike her? Besides, he'd have troubles enough just walking the way his side hurt. In the morning . . . well, in the morning something would occur to him; he'd make his peace with Jeremy.

Then he limped down the porch steps and went away, finding a path that would take him around the fairgrounds to the trailer compound, a distance of about a mile.

Was Jeremy loving him, then? King thought as he went stiffly along, bent slightly forward at the waist, a hand against his sore side. This possibility made his treatment of her seem even more grotesque, but with a strange vibrancy he remembered the gentle yielding of her parted lips. Someone like Sandi, why, she was miserably disappointed in him and would settle on another man in a hurry. The other carnival girls—and there had been several before Sandi who had responded to his solitariness, his look of taut brooding, and had more or less lost their heads—had gone their ways without suffering too much from his meanness, but Jeremy was entirely different. She was not apt to treat a kiss any more lightly than he himself would.

A half mile passed slowly, and King's thoughts shaded away from the freshness of Jeremy to the scarce memories of his beloved Mary Kate, and the short life they'd had together in the Sugar Tree Valley. The terror with which that life had ended was as fixed and immovable in the reaches of his mind as a troll of stars in the sky, but for a little while Mary Kate filled the larger emptiness of his thoughts, and he was absorbed.

Age was in the living room of the trailer, putting a razor crease in his slick gray twill trousers with an iron, when King came in.

"Whoever you had over here for supper left a mess in the sink," Age complained, not looking up from his chores.

King did not reply but went straight back to his room and slid the door shut.

Utter silence from King was nothing new, but Age's instincts told him that King was not doing his usual brown study, so he frowned, and pulled lint from the path of his iron, and scratched the top of his scarred head where a wildcat had clawed him, years ago. How many years he did not recall; he was unconcerned with the passing of time. He called himself Age because he had no age. This was only partially a conceit, an expression of a dark sense of humor, just as the ornamented yellow rain slicker was both a conceit and a fierce expression of individuality. Age had no knowledge of name or parents. He had faint memories of being cared for in a marginal way, but otherwise life had begun for him as soon as he was old enough to fend for himself in the wild but game-filled hills of eastern Virginia. The First World War was over, or had begun. He didn't know which. He hunted and trapped and maintained an acre or two and grew up. Later he buried a woman and buried a wife, and moved around some, always sticki..g close to the wilderness. He had no formal education but some instinct always drove him to the nearest church o..ce a week. He was properly baptized, and he spoke well, like a backwoods Negro preacher might speak.

When he finished with the trousers Age began to iron his three shirts. He stood in the middle of the living room in his underwear, stooping slightly, his limbs long and thin, the cords and muscles in them like twisted iron rods. He and King had found the trailer a fire-blackened wreck, bought it for a few dollars, and spent a whole winter restoring it. Age slept on the sofa in the living room, kept nearly all of his belongings in an Army-surplus footlocker under the sofa, and maintained their quarters spotlessly, despite King's tendency to strew. His devotion to King was absolute and unthinking. In five years of living with the carnival he'd had only fragmentary longings for the wilderness. Most of his old skills had gathered rust, and despite his undetermined years he sensed that long winters in a mountain cabin would be harsh indeed for him now.

Twenty minutes had gone by, and he'd heard nothing behind King's door. Age buttoned the last of his shirts and hung them all in the closet, dressed in his gray trousers, and put a pot of coffee on the two-burner stove in the kitchen. When the coffee was hot he carried some back to King.

King did not answer his rap on the door, so Age slid the door open with one sharp elbow and looked in. The tiny bedroom was in a familiar mess. King was lying lengthwise on the floor with his head on a mound of soft-cover books, his back to the door. There were some objects on the carpet in front of him: an old-fashioned bone comb, an antique brooch, an informal color portrait of newlyweds taken by an itinerant photographer. Age stared at these things with a feeling of despair.

King lifted his head and looked back at his friend with a preoccupied smile. His eyes were deeply reddened and hollow.

"I brought coffee," Age said. "Why do you want to lie there on the floor?"

"Oh, I pulled gristle in my side and this is comfortable." He held the photograph, which was printed on heavy dull-finished paper, at an angle and studied it intently. "Can't believe I was as young as all that, Age. And Mary Kate—just look at the sweet light in her eyes; wasn't she a beauty?" His voice had a dreary edge of tears. "You know, I've never put a single flower on her grave, nor kneeled on the earth where she's buried to say a prayer for her soul in Heaven. It's all so far away from my mind. Did it really happen? It hurts me, Age."

Age set the coffee tray on the only chair in the room and poured a cupful, villainously black. He handed the cup to King, who set it unmindfully aside, and went on staring, morbidly, at the photograph, a tense smile pulling at one corner of his mouth.

"I put flowers on her grave for you," Age said in a calm voice.

126

"I roamed half a day in the woods finding the ones she favored. And they were as wet as my eyes could make them."

"And what was her tombstone like? Did you ever tell me?"

"Told you lots of times. It was a white stone, fine-cut marble, the best in that tiny graveyard."

"And the two of them were lying together?"

"Not far apart," Age said, his eyes unwavering despite the disturbance he felt. "If you've got a stitch in your side, let me tape your ribs, before you make it worse."

To Age's surprise King rose obediently, his treasures in his hands. The photograph he replaced in a worn gray folder, which he put away in the bottom of a dresser drawer. The comb and the brooch he left out, and studied them in absorption while he clumsily unbuttoned his shirt.

"I don't understand how you managed to save these things for me, Age, but I'll always be grateful."

"It wasn't no trouble at all," Age said with an almost inaudible sigh. "The picture was in the mailbox, gathering dust from the road. It belonged to you, so I took it. The house was stripped clean and standing empty, but I found the comb lying on the floor. Nothing the least valuable about a comb; that's why it was left." With delicate appraising fingers he probed King's ender side. Once the preacher drew his breath sharply, but if he found Age's examination very painful he didn't otherwise show it.

"There's swelling," Age muttered. "Now move your arm, easy over. That's it."

"And the brooch? Tell me again about the brooch, won't you?"

"I recalled how Mary Kate had sent me to Jerrold's Camp with the brooch to have it fixed, just a few days before . . . and I expected it was still there at the jewelry store, waiting to be claimed." He straightened. "No need to wrap those ribs. You'll mend. I'll rub you down good with my atomic balm." This was Age's prime cure-all, for everything but toothache.

By the time he had finished his doctoring, King seemed to have broken clear of his lethargy, and his eyes had lost much of their former ghostly, reddened look. "Age, you've been as true a friend to me as a man could want," he said with great earnestness as he rebuttoned his shirt.

"I only give as good as I get," Age replied in a surly,

127

discouraging voice; he customarily took that tone whenever King impulsively brought up the matter of personal loyalty.

"That isn't so, since I owe my life to you. More often than not we bicker to hide our feelings—but the fact is I love you, and want what's best for you."

Age grunted something skeptical as he wiped his hands clean of atomic balm; the room was filled with the hot smell of the salve.

"I've got hard traveling ahead before I can hope to make a success of preaching. I'm so lonely now a few thousand more miles won't matter; there's years, yet, for me to have a home. But you're getting on, Age; if you don't mind my saying so, you've slowed down considerable from last season. I just can't ask you to stay with me this time. My conscience won't let me! I know Frank would want you to hire on with the carnival, and more than once I've heard you say how much you'd enjoy to spend the rest of your days by blue water down there in Florida. You'll build yourself a small place and maybe find another wife—"

This well-meant but thoughtless recital caused Age to stiffen, and when King mentioned "wife" his indignation overcame him. Where did King get off saying that he, Age, was slowing down? What was he angling after, with all this talk talk talk about his poor conscience? He didn't have to try to be subtle if he was tired of having Age around, all he had to do was say so! And another thing: what gave King the right to assume he had the slightest interest in acquiring another wife? . . . And so went Age, frequently shading into nigger dialect in his anger and anxiety; King blinked in astonishment. Age, taking full advantage of the opportunity to unburden himself of the load of small grievances that normally accumulate when two men share a common living space, became so impassioned that he trembled, and stamped his foot on the floor; the trailer shuddered from the force of his outrage. Dimly he realized that he was carrying on like this because of the fear he had felt upon seeing King with the mementos of his brief marriage.

King had never heard such a tirade from his friend, although he'd stood through an occasional well-deserved upbraiding when Age was in the mood. He set his jaw, and tried to lodge a word or two against the flood and at last gave up and simply took the blast full in the face, hands dangling awkwardly at his sides. Only then did Age run out of emotion, and when his voice also dried up on him he simply turned around and walked out of the room with his shoulders back. His eyes were dry, but they stung him. He went to the kitchen and stood resolutely looking out the tiny window over the sink, at the dark ground paved with glints of silver light. Five minutes went by. He heard King rummaging and coughing, and then he heard him striding through the trailer to the door. He felt King's eyes like twin drills at his back; his shoulders twitched but he held firm.

King cleared his throat. "Age, I—" He faltered immediately, and began over. "I never meant that you should go if you didn't strictly want to. I reckon that I . . . speak badly sometimes. And this night I've done a real job of speaking badly—or not at all when I should have said something." Pure bitterness underlined this added thought. He resumed, with a sigh. "If you can forgive me, I want you to stay. I need you to stay and that's the Lord's truth, because I'm scared I won't have another friend for a long time to come." He opened the door. "I'm going up to the tent to sit the night. No use trying to sleep; I've never been less in the mood."

After King was gone Age relaxed and mopped his perspiring head with a handkerchief. He was cluttered with the slag from a rather pointless quarrel, and he felt slightly ashamed of himself. But the fear was still there.

He finished dressing, put on the yellow, many-eyed slicker, and went straight to Frank Henderson's trailer.

The carnival owner was working on the payroll when Age arrived, but he set aside his vouchers promptly when he saw that the tall Negro had something urgent on his mind.

He listened thoughtfully while Age explained King's renewed interest in the pitiful keepsakes from his marriage.

"King's gone through this stage before. When he's overtired, upset, with nothing on his stomach but loneliness, it's natural for him to look back, to remember happier times. I don't see why you're making so much of the situation He needs a good woman, and he'll eventually find one."

"He's talking again about putting flowers on Mary Kate's grave," Age reiterated patiently. "That's why I'm worried. Three years ago we nearly had to tie him down to keep him away from the Sugar Tree Valley. What if he takes a notion to slip off some night? Where will he wind up?"

Frank lighted a small cigar and settled down in an armchair. "He won't slip off. Three years ago he might have, I agree with that, but now he has too much to keep him busy." He closed his eyes for a few moments, and some of the lines eased from his face. "King showed me Mary Kate's picture a time or two. Just a young thing. It was hard for me to believe that she was a widow with a three-year-old child when he married her." He savored his cigar, and studied Age in a leisurely way. "What was Mary Kate like?"

"She was a boss. Pretty, but all that temper. She'd fly at him four or five times a day, sometimes with a broom, then forgive him just as quick. He was a strong man taking a child's whipping. Why he put up with that, I don't know."

Frank grinned, sadly. "He loved her. And she loved him, you can bet on it, even if she was something of a shrew."

"Yes, she did," Age said, with the faintest hint of irony.

Frank's tone changed. "I wonder what killed Mary Kate. There are times I've been sorry you didn't stay there long enough to find out."

"Her baby was dead and she thought her husband had burned to death. I imagine it was nothing but grief that took her." He paused. There was a dubious look in Frank Henderson's eyes. "I stayed in the Valley as long as I thought it would be safe," Age said. "If certain ones had seen me, questions would have been asked. I went to the churchyard burying ground where Mary Kate's people had been laid to rest for a hundred years. I saw a child's grave, no more than six months old. The grave next to it hadn't been dug long. That was all I needed to know." He clenched his hands, powerfully. "No need for King to ever go back there."

"Of course not," Frank said. He got up and prowled around his workroom. "I suppose everyone in the Sugar Tree Valley is satisfied that King died in the fire. Likely they don't even talk about him anymore. There'll be a new church, and a new preacher, and no one to mourn Mary Kate."

"No one," said Age. "She was the last of the Ransoms."

"But was she? I don't suppose there's any chance you mistook that second grave? Could it have been, say, another member of the family, brought back for burial in the family plot?" He had a blind look, as if he was trying to visualize the church graveyard. He cleared his throat several times. "Or was a stranger buried in the Ransoms' corner? That could happen, if there was no room left—"

"I didn't make a mistake. It was Mary Kate's grave." Age's

130

nostrils twitched as some of the rank smoke from Henderson's green cigar irritated his nose. "The stone had her name on it."

Frank nodded absently and went on staring into space. Age watched him for a while, expecting more questions; then he hunched his shoulders grumpily and yawned. The sound brought the carnival owner from his reverie.

"Well, keep a close eye on King the next couple of days. I'm sure he'll come around." He glanced at Age uncertainly, as if a thought to contradict Age's assurance had occurred to him. But the hour was late, and serious thinking required all the effort of catching goldfish with a greased hand. He stretched until he felt light-headed, and said, "One other thing. I'm damned glad, Age, you're going to stick with King after we're gone. If ever there should be any reason why you need me, *any* reason, all you have to do is let me know, and I'll come."

Age regarded him stolidly, then smiled a close-mouthed smile that was a shade grim. "When he's lost all his money he'll quit. He'll get tired of it all when winter comes along. He's forgot what winters are like up here." Age trembled with conviction. "He'll soon enough be down. You watch for him."

"I'll watch for him, Age," Frank Henderson said hopefully, and smoked his green cigar.

11

The Grandmother

> "... On my farm in Louisianner
> Where the old Red River flows ..."

King heard the car radio, tuned impossibly loud, long before he heard the car itself grinding up the ridge. He had been alone in the tent for some time, sitting in one of the folding chairs with his feet on another, reading in the fuzzy light.

He looked up, startled by the hillbilly lament booming

through the cold early-morning air, and shuddered. Two paperback books slipped off his lap and fell to the ground. The pockets of his stadium coat bulged with other books, two of them by the modernist theologians whom the Prophet Charger scorned. But King had been raised on what might be called New Testament Fundamentalism. While he had some routine Fundamental prejudices—he never read from the Revised Standard Version of the Bible—he preached the broad redemptive love of Jesus and believed strongly in Augustinian *caritas*. As he usually did when he was feeling heartsick from conviction of personal failure and unworthiness, he had gone back to St. Augustine, and in the past few hours he'd done a lot of reading, making a familiar reconnaissance through the labyrinth of human desire and Christian *agape*. He had just begun to feel reaffirmed in his dedication to the highest good and to ponder anew Luther's *"amor crucis ex cruce natus"*—the love of the Cross born of the Cross—when the wild surge of music battered him into awareness of the world.

He laid aside his book and went out, yawning and stretching. The music suddenly stopped as if the radio had been turned off, then roared again for a split second. The automobile, a brand-new Buick, came at a precarious clip up the terrible road, headlights a shattering blue-white to King's eyes. Dust from the tent ground swirled over him. The red Buick slid softly to a stop and Cowboy Jim Cobb stepped out, pounding the horn with one hand. He smiled like a prince.

"Quit leaning on that horn," King said sharply.

"Howdy-dew, chief!" the Cowboy bawled. "Thought we'd nevah track yew down. God damnedest place ah evah saw to git tew!"

King had glanced at his watch in the glare and seen that it was two-thirty in the morning. He looked reluctantly at the Cowboy, who had, mercifully, quit blowing the horn. The hefty red-haired man was draped over the Buick door, grinning hammily, his feet at odds with the ground. He wore a stockman's boot on his left foot but the other boot was missing. Was he drunk or just moderately oiled and playful? King shivered a little, partly from a premonition. He was going to have trouble convincing Cowboy Cobb that he should turn around and drive himself home.

"What do you want?" he asked, and looked hopefully under the cab of the truck to see if Philemon's dog, Cosh, was still

132

there. One look at that monster would probably sober the Cowboy up in a hurry. But the dog was gone; apparently Philemon had taken him away.

Cowboy left the car and walked toward the tent, his gait awkward because of drink and the missing boot. Near King he stopped and with open mouth inspected the sorry canvas.

"This is yore place uh worship, good buddy?"

King nodded.

Cowboy swung around so abruptly he almost pitched into the dirt. King tensed. He had an aversion to drunks and drinkers, and, at the moment not too much self-control.

"Well, it's the thought thet counts," Cowboy said, with a wise squint and a loll of his head. His remark was not particularly offensive, but behind his shaggy-dog leer, his outbursts of maniacal good humor, King sensed something unresolved, sad, and perhaps dangerous.

"Listen," Cowboy said earnestly, and reached out for a hold on King's arm. "Listen. Are yew listening."

"What is it, Cowboy?"

"Ah din come all the way up here just to admire your tent, yew know." He licked his lips and glanced back at the Buick, almost unsetting himself again. King hated standing there in the man's grip, with the smell of liquor staling the raw air, but behind the blaze of headlights he had caught a glimpse of the girl named Suzie sitting in the front of the car. "Ah come to—to—" the Cowboy muttered, and fell silent.

"Isn't that your girlfriend?"

"By gawd it is! By gawd you're observant!"

"You're standing on God's holy ground; let's just take it a little easy, Cowboy."

"Oh, ah—ah've got a big mouth," Cowboy said with a contrite smile.

"And you've had too much booze. Why don't you let her drive you home? I mean Suzie there. It's way late for her to be out as it is."

Cowboy responded to King's forced reasonableness by trying to drag the preacher right up against his chest, the better to speak to him. When this maneuver failed, he squared his shoulders as they stood toe to toe, two powerful flushed men in the throes of getting along with each other. "Ah'm liquored up, all right," the Cowboy said with a manly snort. "Sheet, ah have drunk it today, man!" His voice broke in a titter. "An' now—ah, uh, we've had damn' fine time tonight, an' we're ready get married." In a religious hush he repeated, "Get married."

"Married," King said, grimly.

Cowboy's eyes popped and he bellowed, *"Yew din think ah broke mah goddam transmission and mah ass long with it just to come up here and admire your goddam tent, did yew?"*

The other door of the Buick opened and the girl slipped out. She was wearing the kind of coat with a bushy fur collar that King had seen on Molly Amos the night before. Her ankles were thin and bare and her hair looked like a snowbank in the harsh light. Her sudden appearance enabled King to hold on to the slipping reins of his patience. He reached up and seemingly without effort pried the Cowboy's hand from his biceps.

"I'm going to talk to Suzie," he said, "and you stay here."

"Yew fixin' to marry us? She won't let me have mah way if we don't git married first. Know what ah mean?"

"Shut up," King said, and brushed past him. The girl stared at him blankly as he approached. She was trying to control her shudders by gritting her teeth. She still seemed pretty enough, but her lips were livid and the light ruthlessly hollowed her cheeks.

"Suzie, what is this? Did you really come up here tonight expecting to get married?"

"Y-yes," she stuttered. "We want to get m-married."

"Like this? In a tent tabernacle in the middle of the night? No family or friends?"

"P-please," she said, a cloud of vapor rushing from her lips.

"Does your family know about this?"

Suzie clenched and unclenched her hands. "I'm eighteen."

"When did you take out the license?"

"Yesterday." She motioned toward the car. "We brought everything we need. Can't we j-just—"

King shook his head. "You can't *just* get married, because there's a three-day waiting period in this state, eighteen or not." Suzie looked astounded at this piece of news. "And let me make something else clear. I wouldn't marry the two of you if I could. He's drunk, but I'm more disappointed by the way you're acting. I don't think I need to tell you that it's a sin to marry outside of your church." He indicated the gold ring which she wore on the third finger of her right hand. "That's the Blessed Mother, isn't it? I've seen a couple of rings like that one, and I know you wouldn't wear it if you weren't true to your faith. It's

134

beyond me why you'd let Cowboy bluff you into this thing, but I've got a hunch getting married is mostly his idea"—she shook her head weakly, but King ignored her—"and I'm willing to bet if you make Cowboy leave you alone for a week or so and give yourself time to think all this through, maybe visit your priest, you'll see where you're going wrong."

With a roar of protest that included several of the obscenities King liked the least, Cowboy bore down on them. "Get in the car!" he said to Suzie. "Ah know a preacher in Mississippi that'll marry us if this goddam Indian won't!" He gave King a blunt shove into the front of the Buick. King recovered quickly and, with a finesse learned the hard way in a dozen turp-camp brawls in his youth, he knocked the Cowboy down.

Suzie had backed away from the anticipated battle; when she saw Cowboy fall a peculiar expression of torment and relief appeared on her face. She shook her snow-covered head and said in a tone of mild annoyance, "Oh, what are you doing anyway, Jimbo?" And then she took to her heels.

King chased her, but she had long legs and a stride that was far from girlish; he called several times to Suzie as she disappeared down the dark ridge in the direction of the fairgrounds, then gave up, half hopeful that she would find her way home without difficulty and maybe take to heart some of the advice he had given. At least there wasn't going to be a quick drive to Mississippi and a fugitive marriage. He turned back to the tent ground. Cowboy was sitting up in the dust holding the wrist of his left hand.

"What's the matter, hoss?" King asked him.

"I fell on my wrist."

"Hurting you?"

"I've got weak wrists," the Cowboy said in a low voice. He had lost much of his heavy drawl. "They break easy."

Even in the unreliable light King could tell that the man's color was bad, although his wrist didn't look broken. He reached down to help Cowboy to his feet but Cowboy moaned slightly, his eyelids twitched, and he lay back on the ground in a faint.

King stared at him in dismay. He now regretted having hit the Cowboy, but probably it had been a case of hitting him or taking a licking himself. He hunkered down beside Cowboy and pinched his earlobe sharply, but there was no response.

He touched the injured wrist—slight bones for such a sizable man—but could tell nothing from a gentle pressure. There might have been some swelling. But if the wrist was broken the break wasn't a bad one; he could probably move Cowboy without doing more damage.

King grasped the thick tooled leather belt with one hand and, with a weight lifter's grunt, hoisted Cowboy off his wallet. According to the driver's license inside, Cowboy lived at an address on Kennesaw Parkway. There would be an all-night filling station somewhere, King thought, and someone to give directions. He didn't like the idea of leaving the tent unwatched, but he would be back in an hour at the latest, and Cowboy needed more attention than he was willing or able to provide.

With cold water from the spigot, he splashed Cowboy Cobb into a state of walking unconsciousness and loaded him into the nearby Buick.

It was one of the ugliest houses King had ever seen, massive, square, and stony, with a cavelike marquee extending over the drive from the front porch. He would have thought it was an old mansion fallen to the status of a rooming house—how else could the Cowboy live there?—but the neighborhood was rich and well-preserved. By gaslight the long shape of a black Cadillac limousine was visible in the carriage-house-garage. King turned on the inside light and confirmed the address, which left him with a difficult choice. Leave Cowboy sitting in the car all night, and walk several miles back to the fairgrounds, or wake up the household? Well, cinch he wasn't going to walk it; that would be foolish. Besides, his ribs, which had been hurt again in his short brawl with the Cowboy, were as sore as a boil.

He glanced dispassionately at the still-sleeping man. Cowboy was somebody else's problem now. With a sigh he went up to the porch. There was a beautiful array of stained glass in the oaken front door, and behind the glass a night light glowed. He pulled decently at the bell until a shadow blew into the light like a sudden storm cloud and an elderly Negro man in a robe opened the door.

"What is it you want?"

"I brought the Cowboy home."

"You're at the wrong house."

"No, he lives here. Cobb? Cowboy Cobb? Jim, I think it is."

136

The old man had been holding his ear to the door crack, but now he turned his head and looked out.

"He's sick," King explained. "He's had far too much to drink, and on top of that he might have a sprained or broken wrist."

Without a word the Negro slipped the chain latch from the door and came outside, his feet bare on the cold porch. He whistled with pain under his breath and nipped down the steps to peer through the window at the dark shape of Cowboy on the front seat. Then he ran back to the house.

"I'm after shoes," he explained to King. "Step inside."

While the servant was gone, King warmed his hands over a floor furnace outlet and looked around curiously in the half-dark. The foyer had the proportions of a museum and was studded with examples of heirloom furniture. His eye measured a serpentine staircase. On the landing there was a churchlike window with a yellow radiance; before the window stood a robed and hooded figure resembling a madonna.

King smiled as if he'd been spooked. The madonna had come to life and was descending. She was a small woman in a floor-length beige peignoir, and she wore a turban instead of a hood. She came silently across the foyer and paused to light a lamp, the better for them to see each other. Her skin was so delicate it looked as if it would tear at a touch, like cellophane. There were dark cats' paws of age on her face. But her hazelnut eyes were steady, ageless, and businesslike.

"I'm Jim's grandmother, Mrs. Cobb," she said. "Are you a friend of his?" Her tone expressed no interest, and her mouth was set in a line of cold despair. "It was a kindness. You may go now and leave us alone."

"I think you'll need some help packing him out of the car."

Mrs. Cobb walked deliberately past King and with a hand that was mostly knuckles she drew open the massive door and regarded the dark. "Where has he been?" she asked in a strained voice. "I saw him last on Monday. Has he stayed with you?"

"No, ma'am. I hardly know Cow—Jim, there, I met him today through Mrs. Amos. Molly Amos." He paused; Mrs. Cobb closed the door and stood with her back to it.

"Yes, I know who she is," the old lady said expressionlessly. "Her mother . . . But tell me what's happened, so I will know what to do for Jim."

"Could we bring him in? Right now he needs a warm bed more than anything."

The Negro man reappeared, bundled up in an overcoat. Mrs. Cobb addressed him as Judd. Together the two men worked out tactics for getting Cowboy free of the automobile and into the house. Mrs. Cobb looked on from the doorway, a steadfast lift to her emaciated chin.

The Cowboy was uncooperative in his slumbers, and when they moved him he spit up like an infant, which disgusted King. Somewhat roughly the preacher folded Cowboy's arms on the mound of his stomach and they lugged him up the steps, King taking the heavy end. As they went in Mrs. Cobb reached down with a knot of tissue to wipe the dribble from her grandson's fleshy chin, a gesture that was both fussy and pathetic.

A bedroom on the first floor had been made ready by a woman who might have been Judd's wife. Here Mrs. Cobb took over, and she gave orders almost soundlessly, relying on hand signals which the two servants were able to interpret perfectly. King realized just how long the Negroes had been a part of the household. The Cobb house no longer seemed as dismal as it had from the street. But Jim Cobb, the self-styled Cowboy, looked out of place in an old-fashioned bed in a room of dark walnut.

"Ring Dr. Matthews?" the Negress asked gloomily.

"I don't know." In the cove of light by the bed the old lady's hand was as artful as a soaring bird, and King came to attention, knowing he was meant. "How much has he drunk?" she asked. "Has he poisoned himself?"

"No, I don't think so. He was in shape to drive his car up until an hour ago. I'd say he's out from nerves as much as anything. Also I hit him. A good lick. You can see the lump raising there on the side of his chin."

"Yes, I see it." Mrs. Cobb thumbed back one of Cowboy's eyelids and leaned over him. The hulk was snoring. She straightened, disdainfully. "No need to bother Dr. Matthews. But Jim is going to be sick when he wakes. Geneva, lay down newspaper and fetch a basin. Judd, I would like some coffee." She spoke again with her hands, the two servants exchanged the whisper of a glance, and King obediently followed her from the room.

"Now then. You look wide awake to me; you won't mind if we

sit in the library for a few moments. I'll see that you get home, wherever it is you live."

She led him across yards of carpet on carpet, bright Persian and zodiac Chinese. The living room apparently was for great occasions; the library had clutter—cut flowers, portraits, a bowlegged sofa like a fat favorite uncle that seemed to call out to King, and he slumped on it gratefully. Mrs. Cobb sat on the edge of a shovel-back bench with her gleaned face angled his way.

"I've been rude not asking your name. . . ."

"It's King Windom, Mrs. Cobb."

She nodded formally. "If you're not a friend of my grandson's, then I don't suppose there's much you can tell me about his activities the past few days. But I would appreciate hearing anything you have to say about Jim. Anything at all." There was a note of anguish in her voice, but her lovely, soft, brindled face gave away no emotion. He had been wondering about her Southern origins until hearing her say, in the Virginian manner, "a-boot."

King felt at a disadvantage. He had wanted to be on his way upon handing Cowboy over, and he now had that edgy feeling, again, of being cooped up in other people's lives. It was clear to him that the old lady had suffered because of her grandson. She loved him, and still had hope. King knew very little about old people, and he was put off by her outward fragility. Did she want him to be polite and say that he thought Cowboy was a decent enough fellow who was bound to straighten himself out one of these days? But Mrs. Cobb smiled tautly, as if she was well aware of his indecision, and encouraged him with a beggarly clasping of her hands.

"Anything," she said again. "I know you don't like Jim. Why did you hit him? Did he provoke you? And why did you bother to look after him?"

"In the first place he hasn't been a whole lot of trouble to me, Mrs. Cobb. I'm a preacher, and myself and another man have a tent over back of the fairgrounds. Cowboy—I mean Jim—came driving up about two-thirty this morning with his girlfriend, and the long and short of it is they wanted to get married." He went on explaining, and she listened, the light dying out of her eyes, and then her hands died too in her lap.

"My feeling is," King said, "that the girl ran off because she knew she was doing the wrong thing. I imagine when Cowboy

139

wakes up tomorrow he'll realize he was rushing her a little too hard. If they're really in love—" But there was no conviction in his voice, and he stopped altogether.

Mrs. Cobb sat without a word, the thin violet line of her mouth as grim as a stitch, her eyes dim in mauve hollows, until Judd came with a silver coffee service that was as handsome as anything King had ever seen, and poured coffee for them. Then she stirred herself, and her eyes became brilliant again.

"He's not in love with this girl," she said quite positively. "I know, although I've never seen her." She sipped at her coffee and thought for a few moments. "Would you mind listening to me while I talk about Jim? Even though you aren't interested in him? I feel afraid tonight, and he hasn't been able to frighten me in quite a while."

King nodded agreement and she went on. "Six years ago he found an unscrupulous preacher in a small town and married a girl he'd known for two weeks. He was twenty-one years old, and she was fourteen—a lovely, utterly senseless girl. After she became pregnant he left her, and to this day he hasn't seen her, or mentioned her name. I still pay for the support of the child. The girl has remarried. Young as she actually is, she could pass for thirty. She's mostly scar tissue. If one human being could treat another more cruelly than Jim treated that girl, I don't want to hear about it. Since then he's gotten two other girls into trouble, but at least they were old enough to know what they were doing, and they seemed to have no more feelings about their predicament than Jim did. Now there's this new girl. What could he want with her? Why marry her? Oh, yes, I begin to see. She's a Catholic girl. If he left her after a brief marriage, the least she would suffer would be an intense religious anxiety. But this time he's stopped, thanks to you, Dr. Windom."

King, who was Brother Windom to some, and Preacher to others, appreciated her courtesy in calling him Doctor, although the title wasn't deserved. He said, "I only tried to talk some sense into Suzie. But if I did any good it's liable to be temporary. From what I know of Cowboy, he's not the kind to be stopped if he has his mind made up."

"He'll be stopped," she promised, anger in her eyes. "Perhaps I could have him committed to an institution. Yes, I could, you know." And then her bravery failed. "And perhaps I could open

140

a vein in my arm with the point of a needle. Both prospects seem fantastic to me, but one would surely follow the other."

King swallowed a small nugget of shock that had lodged in his throat; he was extremely sensitive to any mention of self-destruction. "He's had mental treatment before."

"Molly told you? It's true; I looked for help in the most obvious way. There have been two psychiatrists and a famous clinic. Jim went without resistance—and talked about everything except himself. He seemed to have no self to talk about." Again she looked angry, but composed herself. "Now, you've seen him at his very worst, Dr. Windom. Drunk and, I suppose, belligerent. Bent on some purposeless cruelty. But he's lived in this house for twenty years and I know all the good that's in him. He's not an ugly boy. He has little malice. He treats my friends beautifully, just beautifully, and he can talk to the old by the hour without a hint of condescension or boredom. He's a willing boy—oh, so willing! At my suggestion he attended college. He would go and sit patiently for hours in classrooms, and never hear a word. Never open a book. He has been given a number of good jobs, and he lost each one through idleness and complete indifference to responsibility. He has his life, and friends. He drinks a lot, but not compulsively. He enjoys music. He does not resist, and yet he is unapproachable. Do you know why I'm anxious? If he were a criminal, if he were deficient in some obvious and uncorrectable way, then I could accept it. I could give up. But I don't believe his goodness is a trick, a deceit like his show of obedience. In childhood he was idealistic, as clear-eyed as a saint. There are traces still. I believe that in his heart Jim is incorruptible, that he is more appalled than anyone else could be by his idleness, resignation, and acts of cruelty in the name of love. But then I'm old, and I want to believe it; I'm afraid of dying and leaving him unfound."

Mrs. Cobb wet her dry lips with coffee and leveled her eyes on King, who sat forward on the sofa with his hands clasped between his knees. "What do you think about all this, Dr. Windom?" she asked, with a disconsolate smile and an unconcealed nervousness.

He was sympathetic, but despite her efforts he still saw Cowboy Cobb as a lazy barroom squatter, with a shade more personality than most of them had. He recalled an old phrase: ne'er-do-well. His eyes gave away his honesty. With a Sunday frown he said, "Mrs. Cobb, Jim is twenty-seven years old. And you say he still lives here. Why?"

"Because I let him," she replied, her smile sharpening over coarse yellow teeth.

"That just encourages him in a lot of childishness, as I see it. For instance, this cowboy stuff."

"He was a gawky boy, nervous, on the effeminate side, with a few friends among other chirrun. He was raised in a houseful of women—his sister, his mother, and myself. Other than Judd, the only man to whom he could turn was my husband, who took seven long years to die in his room upstairs. Charles did his best to befriend Jim from a sickbed, but he needed a walking-around father. A wholehearted guide. Many days I saw the little boy dashing around this gloomy house from pillar to post, all worked up, desperate with a sense of death—he was like a hard-pressed sparrow under glass. His mother was a hothouse plant herself. When she died and it was up to me to look after Jim and Natalie—that was his sister—I took the advice of a relative and sent him away for a summer on a Mississippi cattle ranch. When he came back he was Cowboy. Of course I let him be. I was amused and a little proud. But the pose became all too real. Now his friends are his own careless kind, those most amused by his antics. Ignoramuses. He toys with them."

"How does Jim get along with his sister?"

Her eyes were barren. "Natalie died in childbirth several years ago. She was rough, energetic. Jim responded to her, and when she died—Jim was nineteen—he was crushed. I think that's when the game of Cowboy became so vital. Just too many people had died, and in his guarded way Jim adored them all. You might see, now, why he is staying here. Why he will stay until I'm gone. In a sense he has his arms spread over me."

King rose and stretched his spine inobtrusively, and went to a black window, cold to the touch. "I don't understand *that*. He's giving you nothing but grief. If he's so troubled by suffering, why should he hurt people himself? Still . . ." He thought for a few moments, his heart beating apprehensively. "I remember the day when it came to me that everyone had to die. I remember that too well."

The silence which followed his words was long and bleak. He could see her in the surface of the black window, studying him.

"I think it's a shame that the two of you are not friends."

"Why?" he asked, with a smile to temper this piece of rudeness.

"When I first laid eyes on you I thought you were arrogant and obstreperous, another of the drifters who have been in and out of my grandson's life. Then I saw that you had energy to complement your quickness, a directing intelligence and not mere cunning, and—this is important to me—a sense of balance. In my life I've had to work to get along with women; for the most part other women puzzle and exasperate me. But I think my perceptions about men have always been sound. I've been right about them more often than not. Jim has made me very unhappy and unwittingly shortened my life a year or two—at my age what difference?—but I still believe in him. I see the two of you as something alike. Have you had an easy time of it? No. Those terrible scars on your hands . . ." She closed her eyes for a few moments and seemed at a loss for breath; King was alarmed and almost asked if she wanted him to call Judd. But then she breathed deeply and reassured him with a show of calmness. "Whatever your tragedies have been, you've accepted them. Of course, you have your faith."

"Without my Lord Jesus Christ I would be nothing. Maybe less than Cowboy is right this minute. But—"

"I believe that if innocence, or faith, is locked inside him, you could release it. You could find a way."

"No, ma'am."

"No?"

"Because even though I love the Lord and long to imitate His virtues, I fall short. I'm just a country preacher"—this with no twinge of false modesty—"the same clay as every other man. I don't have any great store of patience. No, and my temper's not the sweetest! We'd be at each other's throats. An older and more saintly man might—" He had been pacing, but he stopped because the muted violence of his motions seemed to upset her. He looked down, ashamed, feeling a piercing pain in his heart. He had told as much of the truth as he could. He did not doubt that there was good in Cowboy; Mrs. Cobb believed it and he trusted her judgment. Yet at the same time evil existed. Not insanity; evil. The dilemma which had been slipping in and out of his thoughts while he listened to talk of Jim Cobb's childhood was now resolved. He had casually suggested to Molly the presence of a devil in Cowboy, but now e was convinced that it was true. A devil of dark wind and black blood, powerful as

143

bane, had gained access to Cowboy's soul. Fine psychiatrists had been defeated by this devil, but that was no wonder.

Having faced the reality of the devil's presence, he remembered a moment while Cowboy was being put to bed, when his nerves had sung with alarm and a laughing dread had swept over him. He had prayed automatically, almost unconsciously: Devil, let him go. But the devil wouldn't; oh, no, he wouldn't! Satan had singled out King Windom for a confrontation, a test of strength.

He could not explain to Mrs. Cobb. Yes, he had fought devils, and gladly, fought them in a well-lighted tent, with the Word of God blazing in his fist; he had fought with the help of the prayerful and devout. But he would not answer the challenge of the devil which had a grip on Cowboy. He was simply aware that he could not win in his present state of grace, that his faith was not equal to the task of a cold, solitary grapple with evil.

The old lady took his expression of failure and despair for fatigue, and even though she was disappointed by his refusal to become involved, she smiled.

"I know I've tired you with all my talk. Because I like you, and find a strength to admire in you, and because I have no other resources, I hoped that I could force Jim on you. But of course, you're boys." There was a hint of scolding which he didn't miss. "Rivals, in a sense. And you would force him into a bitter fight, for lack of understanding your strength and your ways."

"I'm just as sorry as I can be, Mrs. Cobb," he said, for he was truly helpless.

"No, no," the old lady protested quickly, shaking her head. Motioning delicately, she suggested that King help her rise. With a hand on his forearm she conveyed him through the house to the foyer. There for a short time she clung to him with a sweetness he found hard to resist, and he thought that she'd probably had half the men in Clearwater—or Virginia—on the ropes when she was younger.

"At least I'm not frightened now. I can resist sitting up the rest of the night with Jim and go to my own room." Reluctantly Mrs. Cobb parted with King, giving the back of his hand a firm pat. "Will you come to dinner one night next week?"

King was startled. "Now *I'm* sorry," she said, with a hard but engaging smile. "You see, I'm determined, and you won't get away from me easily. One or two nights every week I have small dinner parties; entertaining is my one remaining delight. But I've grown a little bored with the same unchanging faces. We are all of the same blood, the same years; even our memories are similar. You'll be doing us a great favor by coming, and you'll make me proud." Despite the faint light in the foyer, she sized up his expression and said gently, "No, I'm certain Jim won't be around. I'm not a devious person. I'm only selfishly in need of your company."

"Then I'll be sure to come, Mrs. Cobb."

"Tuesday at seven, Dr. Windom. And thank you. Judd will be waiting with the car outside."

12

A Highly Technical Document

With a hope of the Lord's stout blessing and the devils of indecision and failure whispering at him, King began his second ministry.

At first his frightening energies threatened to do him in. Despite his size and strength he would have made a poor prize-fighter, because he had no sense of pace. In two rounds he might have whipped any man in the world, and in ten he surely would have whipped only himself. He crackled with the same charge, whether he was improvising an hour-long sermon from a sketch or supervising the laying of a new pulpit. He found it almost impossible to settle down after an evening's work—on Sunday night he went whirling off like a small cyclone on his motorcycle and wandered alone on dangerous country roads until dawn. Fortunately there were two who understood him, and who could quiet him down.

Age and Molly had met, and disliked each other on sight. Molly's prejudice against Negroes was thoughtless and permanent, and she found Age's aloofness and demeanor offensive. Age saw immediately that Molly considered herself King's discoverer and his inspiration; she worried him greatly.

Age was the one who had the ability to distract King with a problem of hand labor. With the carnival gone he was spending most of his time probing the infirmities of the old Mack. He knew from experience that King would not sleep much until he had established some sort of routine in his preaching, and he knew that King was better off sweating with machinery in the small hours than feeding his tension with one scholarly book after another. Molly, on the other hand, took over many of the details of running a revival which King was not able to cope with in his absorption. For several days she devoted only her spare time to her regular job and gave most of her attention to the old tent on the ridge.

Molly learned a great deal about King during this time, while his dependency on her grew. She remained awed by his great energy, which seemed to run on and on past the point where another man, under similar pressure, would have given in and taken to his bed with a case of nerves. She saw that in his slacker moments he was inattentive and permissive, easily influenced. He was not out of touch with reality, but indifferent to it. She realized, as Age did, that he would eventually settle down, compress his power, and commit it more accurately.

In the meantime, however, he had put off an important confrontation with Eli, and seemed willing to go on indefinitely without facing up to the fact that Eli was robbing him. He was willing, but Molly wasn't, and once she had the contracts from the radio station in hand, she spoke up.

"You'll have to have Eli's signature on these. I argued against it, but since you're in partnership and the agreement is binding, Fish insisted. He also insisted that you return a check for five hundred with the contracts tomorrow. That's piggish of him, but it's his station. Do you think you can make it?"

She had interrupted him at his meditation before meeting, and he was giving grudging attention to the contracts. It was Wednesday, and another clear and stellar night was in prospect. Outside the tent it was pitch-dark to the tops of the trees. The sky had become a brilliant turquoise, and to the west a line of hills was not yet burned out.

King shook his head. "Molly, my last pay check from the carnival is about used up. I'll be flat broke by tomorrow night."

She sat down beside him. "Oh, will you? In the last four

146

meetings you've received nearly a thousand dollars in offerings without half asking. I'm only giving an estimate because I haven't seen any more of the money than you have. Philemon's taken every penny straight to Eli."

King handed her the contracts and restlessly prowled around the new pulpit, made of sweet yellow pine with a sealing coat of shellac. "Well, that's all right," he said, but he still looked amazed at the amount named. They eyed each other for a few moments, and then he said what he had to say. "I'll take the contracts to Eli tonight after meeting and let him know what I'm up to. I'll see about the money too. Five hundred?"

"That'll take care of Fish, temporarily. But there are some other expenses. The choir Monday night. And you're going to pay Mr. Handwerker for all the trouble he's—Oh, look," she exploded, and he jerked his head around from contemplation of the altarpiece. "You know as well as I do the problem here isn't money. The problem is Eli, and the agreement you have with him."

"I don't see where that's a problem, Molly," King replied ungraciously, for they had argued about Eli more than once.

Molly knew what she was up against, but she persisted. "I know you feel sorry for him. He's old and he's sick and he hasn't any money. If you hadn't come along he would have gone out of business with the cold weather. And did he see you coming!"

"Molly!"

She had not liked her tone either, and she gestured in apology. "You had the good judgment to tie up your six thousand so he couldn't shovel it away into his doomsday project, but otherwise your judgment is letting you down. It remains that Eli is a greedy man, and because of the agreement he has his teeth in you. Once he's made up his mind that you're going to be a success, he'll set his bite and hang on until he dies. He's home right now with nearly a thousand dollars in hand from your preaching, and he's thinking hard. If you don't get away from him soon he'll be claiming fifty dollars out of every hundred from the offering. Not for himself, but for that colony in Montana. And I don't think you're interested in supporting a loony outfit like that with your ministry."

King settled back against the pulpit, bleakly silent. Molly dug into her Spanish-leather pocketbook and came up with a fistful of letters. "These were in the morning mail at Kay-tip. Some postmarked from as far away as Kentucky. They're from well-wishers who've heard you on the radio, and almost all of the envelopes contain offerings." King looked alarmed. "Fortunately there wasn't any cash. When I saw what was happening I got in touch with the firm of public accountants that has Kay-tip's business. From now until you're legally incorporated as the Southern Cross Crusade all the offerings you receive through your radio program will be handled by accountants. They'll open your mail, acknowledge receipt of the cash gifts, and turn over every cent of money to a religious charity. That'll protect your reputation. Would you like to read some of the letters? They *are* for you." King, still silent, shook his head. Molly replaced the letters in her pocketbook.

"You've been fooling yourself if you think Eli doesn't know about the radio," she said. "We don't see much of him, but he's the kind to keep his nose in the wind. And, as I say, he's weighing your chances. Tonight he may be thinking in terms of a few thousand dollars a year for his project, but it won't be long before he realizes that you may well bring in hundreds of thousands of dollars." She ignored his incredulous look. "That's my opinion, but I think it's well-founded. So if you want to be free of Eli, you'll have to hurry."

Outside a car door popped. King looked up, then went briskly down the aisle to meet the Reverend Martin Handwerker, a Free-Will Baptist pastor whom Molly had introduced to him. Mr. Handwerker was carrying a big potted poinsettia and spilling dirt down the front of his immaculate suit. King took over and carried the flower to the pulpit.

"I think you'll have a fine congregation tonight," Handwerker said, smiling at King and then at Molly. "I noticed a few people already parking along the highway." The pastor looked a great deal like Benjamin Franklin in his prime— domed and stout, twinkling and alert. His enthusiasm for King and his work had been as unexpected as it was welcome. He had energetically shouldered all the responsibility which Philemon, whose hatred of King was steady and wearisome, was eager to duck. He had secured good musicians for the meetings, brought his own church choir to sing. And, whenever he found the time, he was on the telephone to other preachers, extolling King.

King admired the poinsettia from several angles. "It's a handsome gift," he said, and then, sternly, "I hope you didn't pay for it out of your pocket. You've done so much already. . . ."

148

"No, no. One of the ladies of the church raises tropical plants as a hobby and I happened to mention to her . . ." Mr. Handwerker winked at Molly and began brushing the dirt from his dark-grey suit. "Isn't it bright in here?" he said happily. "The new lights make the tent stand out as far as the highway."

Molly nodded. "Nothing's going to change the fact that old and unheated canvas is a poor place for worship on a cold fall night, but a few touches of colors do wonders."

"No one expects to be comfortable at a revival meeting. Chirrun, I'm having to run on. I promised a friend that I'd drive him to the meeting. He's an old preacher, retired, but still beloved in this city. And I know of two other preachers who plan to be here tonight."

"Isn't that something?" King said, giving Molly a strange look, as if his thoughts were really on what she had said about hundreds of thousands of dollars. He saw Mr. Handwerker to his car and then returned slowly, depressed.

"Molly, what's right for me to do? I just don't know. Eli's obsessions—that false bible!—upset me." He waved a hand in a declamatory way. "But I should be helping him, instead of scheming to throw him out. What's right?"

"I don't say you should throw him out, but he's no help to you, doesn't want to be, and his—his connection with the Crenshaw sect is going to mean a lot of trouble, don't you see?" Again she went to her armorial purse and withdrew several letter-size papers. "There's a solution I think will appeal to everybody. Cy worked on this all morning. In effect it cancels your agreement with Eli. In return, you unfreeze the six thousand and make a slight extra payment to Eli in the interests of goodwill. Altogether he'll end up with seventy-five hundred cash for equipment that wouldn't bring a thousand at auction." she made a slight move as if to offer King the papers for him to look over, but he remained braced against the edge of the pulpit with arms folded, eyes stolidly on the ground.

"Now, Eli will go for this if you talk to him tonight," Molly said positively. "But first you ought to browbeat him about the collection money he's squirreled away. And then you should tell him that beginning tomorrow night a CPA will take all the offerings in hand and that the money will be held until after the incorporation proceedings, when a proper corporate bank account can be established. This won't shake him, because Eli

149

is a competitor and he knows where he stands legally, but it'll make him think."

"Where does he stand legally?" King asked; the tone of her voice made him uneasy.

Molly winced. "Oh, now! Didn't you read the agreement? Well, of course you did, but it takes a mind like Cy's, in light of all that's happening, to see just what Eli has done to you. A limited-partnership agreement is a highly technical document; according to Cy, it's not what you put in, it's what you leave out that hurts. Cy knows the old boy who drew up the agreement, and there's not a smarter lawyer around."

"Well, just what has Eli done to me, Molly?" King said impatiently.

"In the first place, Eli is a properly ordained minister in a recognized church and he has every right to conduct revival meetings and collect offerings as he sees fit, provided the bulk of the money is used for furthering some religious work. *That* includes the work which the Crenshaw group is doing, as far as we know now. The time I talked to Eli I asked him a question or two about the Crenshaws, but he was mum. It's sensible to assume that they're a proper religious organization according to the code of the tax department. Therefore Eli can pass on every nickel he begs or borrows to the Crenshaws with the blessing of Internal Revenue. Because Eli exists in a state of poverty I would call dire, I'm sure there's never been the slightest question about his integrity. Of course, your own standing as a preacher is unquestionable. The two of you have entered into a partnership for the purpose of holding revival meetings. Let me be obvious for a second? Each of you has an equal share in various properties, like this tent. But the partnership is inequitable, because Eli has the right to fifty percent of the love offerings for his own purposes: namely, the doomsday project. Oh, yes, it's there, in one neatly typed paragraph."

This was news to King; his reaction was a scowl of consternation which Molly read as skepticism. "Cy has your copy of the agreement, but you can see for yourself in the morning." She fidgeted in her seat and absently reached into her purse for her cigarette case, which she replaced when King looked balefully at her.

"The worst thing about the agreement is that it can't be nullified in a reasonable way. Eli must give his written consent. So in effect you're under contract to him, without limitation. It's

150

quite possible that he can block you from setting up your nonprofit corporation. He would certainly like to do that since he stands to gain very little from such a corporation. Even if he were one of several trustees, he wouldn't be able to appropriate corporate funds for the Crenshaws. As Cy sees it, Eli will use every means to stop formation of the Southern Cross Crusade. So your best move is to buy him out. He'll listen, especially if you start off by being tough about the offerings. He's half-figuring you'll fall on your face, and cold cash will make up his mind in a hurry."

Molly was alight with enthusiasm for her machinations; King only looked troubled. At her urging he took the papers her lawyer had drawn up and stared at them. He could not fully believe that he had made so many mistakes in his dealings with the old Prophet, whose face on the banner outside welcomed all worshipers to the tent. Molly's flat statement that what had been left out of the agreement was every bit as important as what had been put in struck him as incredible; yet there was no mistaking her concern or her authority, another lawyer.

A few people had wandered into the tent and were standing in a knot at the back, undecided about coming down and claiming front-row seats while the preacher was in conference. Molly frowned at their interruption.

King cleared his throat and said in a low voice, "Wonder what will happen to Eli, though? If I buy him out?"

Molly looked at him as if he were simple-minded. "I imagine he'll take his seventy-five hundred dollars and head for Montana with his family. He's in too poor shape to preach, and all he wants to do is work on that bible of his."

"But where am I going to find fifteen hundred dollars more for Eli? Borrow it? What can I borrow money on? My trailer and truck are already pledged to a bank down in Florida. How much can I get for an old scrambler motorcycle?" This he said with a quaver of anger.

"I've got some money in the bank," Molly said after some hesitation. "I'll loan you fifteen hundred. So don't worry about it."

King glanced down at the papers and his hand was trembling. There were red marks on his cheeks. He looked at Molly, and his eyes seemed to be far back in his head. He put the papers inside his coat and said in a voice that wasn't his own, "I'll surely talk to Eli tonight. Your notion about the

151

accountants was a good one. I should have thought of it myself."

"Well, you've had preaching to do." She smiled, willing him not to be angry with her. But he stared through her smile.

"That's so. And those people back there, they've come to hear me preach now, and I don't have a thing to say to them!" With that he scooped up his Bible from the chair next to Molly, turned rudely away from her, and left the tent.

Molly remained seated until the early arrivals trooped down the aisle and began staking out a row of seats. Then, with a sigh, she picked up her pocketbook. He was awake again, and seeing. But Molly felt uncertain; perhaps she had done badly. Despite King's childlike shock at what Eli had done, was doing to him, she had had glimpses of a perverse, incomprehensible loyalty to the old prophet. Why else should he turn his anger on her?

Cy had wanted to handle the situation differently, lawyer to lawyer. But that might have meant a bitter break between the two men. No, only King could help himself now, and only King knew if he really wanted to.

As Molly was leaving—she'd heard King preach three nights out of four, and she had a dozen things to attend to—a pretty dark-haired young girl caught her eye. Molly looked the girl over, adding up points for both sides in an undeclared competition. Then, unexpectedly, envy poured like salt into her blood. She hurried away, stung, feeling unsettled. She realized that she had missed something important about King during the past few days; somehow she would be made to suffer for her lack of perception. All this was clear to her in the shape of envy for an unknown girl, and then, quite quickly, her dread vanished. Under the stars Molly buttoned her coat and felt competent, secure, and blessed once more.

King had no backlog of sermons, and it was not his style to preach from a prepared text. Like many other preachers, he tackled a sermon by reading a great deal of material, Biblical or otherwise, relevant to his theme, trusting in his natural ability to provide the right words and continuity of thought when the time came.

That night he spoke on the temptations of Jesus, a favorite theme, and the reality of the devil, and he had never spoken better. For his congregation, six hundred strong, the eighty-minute sermon was a fascinating ordeal. Attractively gaunt, mesmerically afire, King stalked them one by one and inspired real fear in a great many hearts. With the art of a storyteller he recreated the steadfastness of Christ in the face of the devil's wiles. Then, scornfully, he pitched into the congregation. The devil had offered Jesus all the kingdoms of the earth and their glory if Jesus would only fall down and worship him. But Jesus had refused, because he was secure in the love of God. King said that the devil was now two thousand years older, and that much wiser and more confounding. And what is the price on your soul? he asked, over and over; who among you has the faith and judgment of Jesus? It was essential that they see through all the blandishments of evil, and then commit themselves without delay to the shed blood; otherwise there could be no hope of escape from the devil and eternal pain. He described what the devil was like, and he spared no one's sensibilities. Many of them imagined the figure of the devil in that small tent, sitting in deadly abeyance with souls on his mind; and they were moved.

When his appeal was finished, after the people had come to him in numbers, King was pale and the bones seemed to show through the transluscent skin of his face. He asked in a voice of fog to be excused and turned over the proselytes to Reverend Handwerker for further counseling. Worshipful eyes watched him go.

There was no place he could sit, unobserved, for a period of cooling off and prayerful contemplation after a difficult sermon, except in the cab of the old Mack parked near the tent.

A few members of the night's congregation had dared to drive their cars to the tent ground. Now the cars were moving, circling, wallowing, throwing up dust, lighting the dust and the trunks of trees. From his elevation, through a windshield that was cloudy with accumulated dirt, King saw people passing in and out of the walls of light and dust, fractional and mysterious, their faces dark or white but clean of expression, their steps measured and serious on the pitched, rutted ground.

King rested his head against the steering wheel, and closed his sweltering eyes. It was confining in the cab of the truck, and the worn seat gave off a smell of rot and grime. The dust fell down and down; it drifted over the cracked windshield and became a part of the air he breathed.

153

When he felt alone and restored to himself, he climbed down from the cab. Most of the people had gone. From inside the tent he heard the strong voice of Mr. Handwerker, and he smiled, thanking God for the goodness and the assistance of the Baptist pastor.

Then, with a sense of earth at his fingertips, King Windom walked down the ridge to talk to Eli.

13

The Falling Out

He had visited the house only once since Saturday, and that time he had first made certain that Jeremy was not there.

This was schoolboy behavior, and he had defended it with long silent monologues on the subjects of love, chastity, and desire. He put himself in the worst possible light, and there he was comfortable. By stressing his wrongness in making love to Jeremy, he felt relieved of the necessity of making a decent effort to speak to her. She would, he knew, appreciate his circumspect silence. Characteristically he was unable to see that he was transmuting an awkward but perfectly natural moment of regard into something far more significant. Jeremy, in her young and uncomplicated way, was perfectly free to say to herself, I love him, and stick with her conclusions through the thinnest of times. His way was a hundred times more difficult, and ultimately painful.

Philemon's dog was on the porch, and the dog wasn't about to let him pass. King raised his voice and shouted, "Eli!" Once more his energy was on the rise, lifting him.

The door opened and Philemon peered out, holding the long barrel of an old but expensive shotgun in one hand. Without a word, he untied the fighting dog from the porch, then led him across the clay yard to the blighted peach tree. There the dog lay in his halter, muscled and tense, facing the house, slivers of light in his eyes.

Inside, Eli was sitting at the loaded-down card table, the work of his years heaped in cartons on the floor around him. Despite the fuming gas heater near the door, it was quite cold in the house. Eli wore his bulky sweater and his robe over that, and a blanket drooped from his lap. Apparently he had been deep in concentration when interrupted. A very old, chewed leather Bible lay open in the cleared space before him. His eyes had looked far into the past; raised to King, they were hollow, watery, inquiring. He glanced down at his open railroader's watch, and the folds of his face were altered in a frown.

"Ain't seen much of you since Saturday," Eli said, and in his words was the sense of knowing all that had brought King to the house. With a gesture of decision he reached out a swollen and clubbed hand and closed the Bible.

Jeremy was opposite him, a pile of papers under an old-fashioned pen. When Eli closed the Bible she put down her pen and clenched her writing hand several times. A yawn escaped her. She looked steadily at King for two or three seconds, sealed off her yawn, rose, tugged at skirt and sweater, and went to the kitchen with Eli's "Coffee, Jeremy" trailing after her. King looked steadfastly where Jeremy had been sitting—probably for hours—doing Eli's copying. There were pages covered with her bold but feminine strokes. Without Jeremy, Eli would be more helpless than he already was.

The fact of Eli's helplessness absorbed King. His head was clear; he saw all the unpleasant things that Molly had seen in the old evangelist, and forgave them. He was not aware of himself physically, a rare thing, a blessing brought about by hard preaching; at the moment he had no sense of his future, or of time. Thus the agreement that bound him to Eli did not worry King, and he could even smile at his country-boy gullibility. Despite Molly's efforts to persuade him, he had no thoughts of trying to save himself from a bad bargain. He was not going to pay Eli the money in the savings account, and then pay him again with borrowed money!

His eyes were drawn to the pages which Jeremy had written—pages of what King now thought of as the Book of Charger, the false bible to which Eli was dedicating the end years of his life. Because of these labors Eli was in serious danger of bringing the wrath of God down around his head. As

155

Molly had noted, King's loyalties were curious and sometimes incomprehensible. But he felt responsible for Eli (and for Jeremy, who would go wherever Eli went). He felt a sublime need to protect them both, and to somehow convince Eli that the work he was doing was the devil's own work.

Eli said, "Philemon tells me you preached to more than six hundred tonight."

King glanced at the couch bed, where Philemon sat cleaning and oiling his dismantled shotgun. He wiped slowly, and the sheen of the steel was visible through the thin black of the long barrel. It was a handsome shotgun, undoubtedly handed down. Beside him, on the Mexican spread, was the money box containing the night's collection.

"Was there that many?" King replied, turning back. "I never counted."

"Philemon counted." Eli showed a smile, and a hint of furrowed pink tongue. "You're doing fine."

"Eli, I hope I am."

"Collection sits over there, but I haven't totaled it up yet." He paused but King's expression was neutral and polite, so he went on, in a gruff undertone, "I expect I've been neglecting you. But I count my own work important, and I know you won't mind if I don't come to every meeting."

"I don't mind at all, Eli. As long as we can get together from time to time where there's business to discuss."

"Pull up a chair," Eli said amiably, peering at King, and King was struck again by how much Eli looked like some Jewish patriarchs he had seen during his travels; this observation he had scrupulously kept from the evangelist. He sat down, shied a glance at Jeremy, who was not looking at him, and said, "We're going to have to spend some money, Eli."

Eli nodded, as if spending money was one of his great pleasures. "Spend how much?"

"Well, we've done some fixing up on the tent, which you know about." He picked at his pockets. "I've got receipts on me somewhere, penny for penny, but call it twenty-five dollars."

Eli nodded again, looking as sleepy as a hedgehog.

"Then there's the Reverend Mr. Handwerker I brought down the other afternoon."

"Fine Christian man."

"He's worked four nights out of five now, not to mention all the calls he's made on our behalf during the day. Ten dollars a night isn't much for a man who's blessed us like Mr. Handwerker has, but at least it's something."

"It was his choir I heard singing Monday night?"

"Yes, it was, Eli."

"Years since there was choir music in that tent," Eli said reminiscently. He deliberated. "No, ten dollars a night ain't too much. Now, what else?"

There were items which Molly had paid out of her own pocket, but King decided to skip those and get down to the radio contracts. He knew that Eli knew what was coming, so he said simply, "I've been on the radio every afternoon for a week now. Payment's due, and I'd like for you to look over and sign some contracts the station provided."

On the couch Philemon was fitting the parts of his shotgun together, *click-clack*, his stubby fatback hands skillful at their work. He was blindly intent on the two men.

"That's business we didn't discuss," Eli said.

"I took it on myself, Eli." And he handed over the contracts.

While the evangelist was studying them word for word, King attempted a catalogue of the advantages of the daily radio program, to which Eli was unresponsive. Presently King stopped talking and sat back with his hands on his knees. On the couch Philemon was aiming and reaiming the assembled shotgun.

"I heard you Sunday on the radio," Philemon said, indifferently.

"Did you? Well, I won't be preaching Sundays from now on. Just Monday through Friday."

"I might go on the radio myself," Philemon allowed, with a quick glance at the back of Eli's head.

"Who'd support you?" Jeremy asked argumentatively, coming to the table with the old enameled coffeepot.

"Don't *you* mind." Philemon got up, with the shotgun sagging from the crook of his arm, and walked into the light. He had no casual airs, and when he glanced again at Eli his head jerked; the expression in his eyes was calculating but half-fearful. "There's some who would support me. There's places where I'm wanted to preach."

"Well, well," Jeremy said, pouring coffee. She was standing sideways to King, by the table, and he looked at the length of her hair and the way the light came over her shoulder and created shadows in her face, and he was aware of life stirring

157

again in the brawny lengths of his hands. Behind her Philemon stood with a fist against his mouth, tension plumping his cheeks; he was infested with secrets. In the silence Eli breathed as an old man, each breath an age, or a voyage; and he went word by word.

Philemon said, fatefully, "There's places where healing miracles are appreciated, and healers are loved."

King looked mildly at him.

"Drink your coffee," Jeremy said, roughly, and thrust a cupful at Philemon. She then turned to King and handed down his cup, which he inattentively took from her. He was concentrating on Eli, and the battle to come—not over the radio program, but over the vital matter of Eli's cause and his obsession. Jeremy was a direct person, and indecision was killing her spirit. Her lower lip trembled, and her eyes were momentarily sick. He could say *something*, she thought. Even censure would do. He had been shocked by her kissing him; she wasn't a proper Christian; he had no thought of loving her. All this Jeremy accepted bravely, as her due. But she thought, What sort of Christian is he? At least he could have given her the chance to apologize for shoving him out the door. She went to the couch, hurled an oily rag from the spread, and sat down. Try as she would, she could not feel ashamed because she loved him. Jeremy held her head high, in case King should look her way. Who's asking you to care for me? she thought. Just be fair. Just talk to me.

At the card table Eli raised questioning eyes.

"Two hundred fifty dollars a week sounds like a lot of money," King said. "But, Eli, people have come to me after meetings and said they heard me on the radio, and that was why they were there. Two hundred thousand people hear me every day, and who knows how many of them are still unsaved? Sometimes I get so excited when I think about it, I can't keep still."

Philemon scowled at the mug of coffee in his hand. Eli stared at King in polite absorption.

"How much money has come in by the mail?"

"Why . . . I haven't asked for money, Eli."

The evangelist showed his horselike smile, full of false wonder and sly mockery. "You do that, though. And it may be the faithful will provide tithes enough to keep you on the radio." His eyes sank beneath heavy lids. "In the meantime . . ."

he muttered, and pushed one half-crippled hand beneath his robe. After an interval of searching which brought white spots of pain to his cheeks, he withdrew a large canvas wallet with a heavy zipper, a lock, and a brass chain attached to one corner. His eyes remained closed. He produced a key and unlocked the wallet. Inside was a great sheaf of bills. Eli pulled out a handful, then without delay closed up the wallet and stowed it away beneath layers of clothing.

With a wheeze the evangelist leaned over the table and dropped the rank-smelling money in front of King. "Count that," he said, "See if it ain't about six hundred dollars. Use it any way you see fit."

"Thank you, Eli," an amazed King said, and he counted the money. While he was doing this, Eli signed both copies of the contract and pushed them back at him.

Philemon returned to the sofa with the shotgun and there he began loading it.

"What do you think you're going to shoot this time of night?" Jeremy demanded.

"Anything I see."

"Six hundred ten dollars," King announced; he'd had an easy time counting because the bills were all fives, tens, and twenties.

"You can buy me a radio with the difference," Eli said pleasantly. "I'd enjoy listening in while you're on the air."

Philemon rose and walked to the door with his shotgun on his arm.

"Where you off?" asked Eli.

"Cosh needs a taste of blood."

"You'll get that dog worked up where he's a danger to everything that moves."

"That's so," Philemon said. "But Cosh is sure to win me a lot of money over in Beersheba County Saturday. Enough to—to buy me a good white suit to preach in, and new white boots." He stood rigidly with his back to Eli, waiting.

"You're going to preach in a suit you bought with dogfight winnings?"

"The Lord told me it was all right."

"Oh He did," Eli said, puzzled by Philemon's show of independence. "Where do you think you're going to preach?"

"I don't know for sure," Philemon said in an uncertain voice. "But I had a vision, Eli, and the Lord—the Lord pointed me away from your tent. Pointed me to town. Yes, He did, and Sunday I went to town. Yes, I came upon the Church of the Apostle's Creed down there in town. And the Lord pointed me in. And the preacher there said that if I was moved in a powerful way to speak, they would hear me. And I told them about my vision, and how the Lord had sent me to their tabernacle and bidden me that if they had sick folks present to heal them. And all the congregation said, Welcome, Philemon. Preach to us, Philemon! Stop awhile with us, Philemon!" He hunched his shoulders and winced in ecstasy, then fastened accusing eyes on them.

"So you had a vision," Eli said expressionlessly. "I'm always glad to know these things."

"But, Eli, doesn't mean I want to leave *you*. Even if I preach in town I can't ever be *leaving*. Unless it is you throw me out!"

"I guess you had a vision, all right," Eli said, with a note of sorrow in his voice. He weighted this small rebellion of Philemon's, and was forgiving. "If you can be of some use to the Lord at the Church of the Apostle's Creed, then I ain't willing to hold you back. But you want to see that you're paid for your work on behalf of the Lord, and don't be depending on charity or the goodwill of that preacher."

"Yes, Eli, yes, Eli!"

"And you want to always be mindful of your obligations. It's a robber and a thief who steals the Lord's tithe!" His voice had risen harshly.

"Oh, I know that, Eli!"

Eli's tone changed and there was boredom in his eyes when he shifted them away from the anxious Philemon. "Don't wake me up when you come in tonight," he said shortly, and left Philemon choking on his gratitude.

The burly boy had not been prepared for Eli's swift and unemotional acceptance of his stand. While Eli delved into some papers, he stood awkwardly around, seeming hollow and a little resentful. Then, manfully, he cradled his wicked-looking shotgun and left, whistling and making a show to his dog.

Apparently, for all the attention he was giving King, Eli meant for him to also be on his way, but King remained fast in his chair, until Eli peeked at him questioningly. Then he asked, "How is your work coming along, Eli?"

"Fair," the evangelist grumbled.

"Much to do yet?"

"Right much."

"I've been . . . curious about it, Eli."

"Unh?"

"Your books, I mean. I'd like to know more about what you're doing."

"Tonight?" Eli suspended activity. "What do you want to know?"

"Everything. How much of the Bible is in it?"

"That much of the Bible I deem important to the man of the future," Eli replied, and burrowed into another stack of correspondence.

King could not have been more shocked. He stared at Jeremy, who let him flounder. "What—books—do you think —are important?"

"Some of Genesis," Eli said, after a long and unfriendly silence. "The story of the Creation. Then some of the ancient story: of Moses, Joshua, David. Of course, a big part of the Fundamentalist Books will be the prophecies of Isaiah, retold according to the theories of Dr. Crenshaw."

"Retold? But those are sacred words, Eli, from the lips of God Himself! What have you done with the other books of the Bible? Where is the Book of Numbers? Deuteronomy?"

"Gone," said Eli, with no sign of regret.

"Where are Ezekiel and Zechariah? What about the vision of Nahum?"

"The fall of Nineveh is chronicled in the Fundamentalist Books, just as the expected destruction of our great civilization is chronicled."

"And what—what have you written about Jesus in your books?"

"Everything about Jesus," Eli said in a crashing voice. "He is God the Son. Do you think I'm some kind of blasphemer?"

"Yes . . . yes, that's exactly what I think."

The quarrel was defined, and there was no escaping it. There was a hot light in Eli's eyes, and contempt. King was not angry, only aghast. In the presence of heathen or skeptics he would have known just what to say, but Eli had him stopped.

"What you think doesn't trouble me! When the survivors of the Day of Terror arise in darkness, naked and wretched and deafened, they'll find their God quickly in my Books. Instead of groping for a thousand years, making war on each other, they'll build tabernacles and spend their days in worship and righteous living. The Books will tell them! The Books will tell them all about the Day of Terror, and the fate of sinful peoples! The Books will tell them to trust in Heaven! They'll know their God, and they will prosper! In those so-called time capsules men have sunk Bibles into the earth. A great church has spent millions building vaults in a mountain, with all the wisdom of that church and the lists of its people locked inside. But when the cataclysm comes, the earth will shudder and swallow all the Bibles ever printed. Those great vaults under the mountain in Utah will lie beneath a thousand feet of ocean water. Future generations will know the Lord only through the Fundamentalist Books, which will be safe from any kind of upheaval. And you sit there and name me a blasphemer!"

"Eli, if God means for most of us to perish and for a new nation to rise, won't He make His presence known to that nation by a sign, or a miracle? Won't He speak to the Moses among them? Will your books make men so wise and righteous? What can you say that wasn't written three thousand years ago by the moving finger of fire? If men haven't harkened to the Commandents, will they harken to your words?" He had pressed forward and the card table was in danger of buckling under his hands. "Don't you know that what you're doing is *against* God? The Bible's not to tamper with; the Bible's to love, and cherish, and never, never question, no matter what some physics professor might have to say! And what master does *he* serve?" He stared beseechingly at Eli, but the old man's eyes were cavernous and frightening. "Eli, how many souls have you brought to Jesus in your lifetime? I expect you can't *count* the souls you've won away from the devil! I know you've done some great preaching in your time; oh, and I wish I could have heard you. But I *will* hear you preach again, I'm positive, as soon as you're well and on your feet again."

Eli's lips were set in a pout of loathing, and his hands jumped impotently in his lap.

King should have been warned but he went on, in a fit of anxiety himself. "You know people have been coming out in good numbers to hear me, and if that keeps on, Eli, and we've got every reason to hope that it will, then there's no reason why we shouldn't set aside enough from the love offering to rent a fine little house nearby. With winter coming on, this is no place for you. You'd feel a hundred times better with a warm room to sleep in and the right medicine. Why do you deny yourself medicine, when you need it so much? I think you'd start preaching again right away. Eli, I know how it is when you're down and out and in pain: it's hard to pray and to understand what the Lord really intends. Once you start preaching again, you'll see that all this writing you've done is an abomination, an affront to our Lord. All the words you've written here, all the months you've spent on these books, don't equal *one* human soul brought to the bosom of the Lamb. Eli, there are *lost souls* out there in the wilderness! Sometimes at night when I'm awake and the air is still I think I can hear all their agonized voices in one terrible choir, and feel their unbearable suffering. Help save them, Eli!" His hands hovered over the stack of papers and letters on the table. "Burn this. Burn it all, and be forgiven for your blasphemy. Look to souls. Please, Eli, please!"

He had not seen Jeremy leave the couch, but he felt her hand tugging at his shoulder. "Don't," she said firmly. "Look out. Just leave him alone. Don't you have any sense?"

King glanced up at her, stifled, his face reddened.

"Go on!" Jeremy urged. "You could hurt him with your little finger. But he won't change. He won't quit. Just get out of here!"

King turned in astonishment to Eli, whose lips were looser, and who was a very bad shade of gray, and he felt afraid. Still he said, "I'm having to keep the money from now on, Eli. All the love offerings. I can't let you have another dollar, not for the Crenshaws. Please understand it's for your own good and safety!"

Eli did not raise his eyes from the table, but he trembled. "You can't keep my money," he quavered. "What's mine is mine."

Jeremy cried, "If you say another word to him, I'll call Philemon back with his shotgun. Now you get out of here!"

"Jeremy!" Eli said, a measure of vigor and authority restored to his voice, and she calmed down, with a last muttering to herself. She had stepped in between the two men to spare King, and not Eli; but nothing could be done.

Eli was trembling still, and this weakness seemed to make him angrier than anything King had said. Only his old eyes were motionless, and they studied King with a hint of wonder in them. The preacher faced Eli squarely and endured his silence, but his courage was nearly gone, and his tongue was dry. At last Eli said, speaking to no one, "There stands God's love of me. There stands my deliverer." He spoke slowly and an ironic smile appeared. Then his head jerked and his eyes became heavy and opaque, filled with sleep.

"In the morning," he said, more slowly than before, "if you're ready to bend your knee, come and we'll pray for your forgiveness together. Otherwise never come, and be damned."

King blanched slightly at this curse. "Eli, I'm truly sorry about your infirmity. But that's all I'm sorry for."

For a little longer Eli stared at him, then his head jerked a second time and sagged. He settled in the chair, and closed his eyes.

King glanced helplessly at Jeremy. "What's the matter now?" he asked. "Asleep?"

"Sure," she said, and placed a hand on Eli's forehead. Philemon pounded on him, then you pounded on him. He couldn't fight back. So he went to sleep."

"I had to tell him, Jeremy."

"All you *had* to do was keep the money and not tell him a thing! And not condemn him. Eli's got his faults; he can be small and picky. He was jealous of you, and I expect that's a sin. But you didn't have to make him hate you."

"I hope I haven't done that," King said fervently, but he knew better.

14

Singeing the Devil

Because it was nearing midnight when he returned, King expected to find the tent empty and the grounds deserted: instead there were three cars parked at the top of the ridge, under the single floodlight. One of the cars was a doughty Cadillac with the dust of roads upon it like a veil. The Cadillac was the center of a commotion: eight or ten Negroes were talking, weeping, perhaps praying. In their midst was Pastor Handwerker, trying his best to be a calming influence. Under the tree in which the floodlight burned stood another white man, tall, spare, and detached, watching the proceedings with his hands in his pockets.

Mr. Handwerker, with a sidewise glint, saw King first and broke from the knot of Negroes. "Here comes the preacher!" he said excitedly. "Here's King Windom now!"

"Here come now," one of the Negroes repeated, and others cried, "Praise Jesus—preacher's come in time!" And together they trooped down the ridge to meet King.

"What is it, Sister?" King asked one of the women. Tears flowed down her cheeks and she seemed to be in the worst state of any of them.

"It's my mother—home from California after all these years—home to pass away in my arms."

"Heart set on dying," one of the others murmured.

"But Shelbina put the fear in her."

"Precious God!"

Not more than an hour ago," Shelbina said, addressing King, "Mama sat up in bed and called for a preacher!"

"It's a miracle, Lord," the dark voices enthused.

"She said, 'I want that preacher I heard driving in on the radio. Take me to King Windom!'"

"Yonder she sits," a pretty girl offered, pointing at the old Cadillac. "Still calling for you, Preacher."

"Oh, help her, Lord!"

"Redeem her, Jesus!"

"Show her the way, Brother Windom."

"Fifteen years since I last seen my mother," Shelbina wept. "And now she's at death's door!"

King glanced at Mr. Handwerker, who said, "The old lady's name is Mab Shaw. She used to be called Queen Mab, and when I was a boy there wasn't a finer singer of blues in the country."

"Oh, yes," King said, nodding thoughtfully, "I've heard of Mab Shaw."

"Now she's sixty-three years old, and a slave to the bottle."

King looked toward the Cadillac, but he couldn't see the woman inside. "How did she get here?"

"Three days ago she and her husband—his name is Daniel

and he was a little overcome with the strain of it all; I had him sit in the tent—left California in their car and drove straight through."

"Mama said she wouldn't be laid to rest nowhere but in the land where she was born. And the end is near!"

"Devil of drink won't let her go!"

"Won't you pray for that sick old lady, Brother Windom?"

"Hmm," King said, "sure I'll pray for her. And I may do more than that." Without another word he strode off up the ridge; the Negroes followed, talking among themselves.

"Now, stand back," King said to them when he had reached the Cadillac. "I'm going to need plenty of help from you good people. I'm going to need all your prayers in a little while. Be ready!" He smacked his hands together smartly and opened the back door of the Cadillac.

The taint of corruption greeted him. Inside were whiskey bottles, paper plates stained with food, and one of the most eye-catching women he'd ever seen. She took up fully two-thirds of the seat. The dress she wore was an eel-like black, only a couple of shades darker but no glossier than her skin. Her exposed arms were weighty, great sausages, tied off into small hands and blunt fingers. Her bosom was an earth in itself, above which rose a white-capped head, softly rounded like an elderly mountain peak. Her hair was pure white, coarse and strong, bound up in a corona of braids. She had the eyes of a barfly, but she didn't flinch when King thrust his head inside.

"How do you do, Mab?"

"How do you do, Preacher."

"Woman, one question. Are you dying?"

"I don't know," she said, and seemed calm despite her misery. "I do know the devil of drink has hold on me, and I'd sooner be dead than go through another day of his torment."

King studied her severely, and came to a decision. "It's a downright shame the fix you've got yourself in. Hmm, hmmm! And that old devil is near, I can smell him. But, woman, will you believe me when I tell you that tonight with the Lord's help I'm equal to the devil? Are you ready for a tussle?"

Hope lighted her opaline eyes. "Kin you really lick him?" she asked timidly. "He's a stubborn devil, and I done his work now for many a year."

"I think if you start to pray right now—just as hard as you can—you'll feel that devil begin to stir around inside like he's set on something hot. Have you been a Christian woman in your time?"

"Bless His precious name, I have. When I was a girl I was baptized in the Braw Haw River, not too far south from here." She tensed herself against some internal spasm. "Oh, that devil, that devil! My liver is hot as fire right now." Her overflowing eyes returned to King. "But I like you, and I hold trust in you, else I wouldn't be here. When I heard you on the radio at sundown—we were crossing over Arkansas then—drunk as I was I said to myself, 'There's a preacher who don't strut and rob poor people, he just prays and saves, prays and saves.'"

"I'm going to save you tonight for Jesus Christ. Now, you sit there a minute or two and prepare yourself for the fight. I want to talk to your husband Daniel. Is there heat enough in this limousine for you?"

"Yes, thank you kindly," Mab Shaw said, and she settled back, lips pursed in a prayerful attitude, to await her destiny.

Mab's husband was light-skinned, with a soft persimmon lip, a balding head, and severe rimless glasses that gave him a professorial look. He was much younger than Mab; King estimated he was not yet fifty. Despite his anxiety and fatigue, he bore himself in a gentlemanly way that reminded of Age, and he dressed well, in a fitted white shirt, black vest, and hickory-striped pants. He was immaculately barbered.

"What do you think, Brother Windom?" he asked as soon as King had taken the chair beside him.

"Hard to say. But I'm convinced she wants to love Jesus again. Is it just drink that affects her, or has she had other complaints?"

Daniel took off his glasses and wiped them on a handkerchief. "I don't believe she's suffering from a cancer or nothing like that. Mab's is an old story. She's had four husbands. I'm the fourth. Not one of her other husbands ever did right by her. They stole her money, and her pride. She drank. She played the lewd woman. She fell into disgrace. Couldn't hold a job. An old story." He smiled, touchingly. "I married her two years ago, and managed to build back her self-respect. But by inches. She wouldn't let go false friends, nor give up the bottle." He shuddered. "It was false friends that brought her low, but she was already well on the way to perdition with her smoking, drinking, and loose ways of the flesh."

167

"What false friends, Daniel?"

"Like some of those picture people. She played the fool for those dopers, and sodomites, and adulterers, and sang bawdy songs at their parties. It was a crying shame. They envied her genius, so they had to bring her down. A famous actor recognized Mab on the street one day. He taken her in, offered her friendship, gave her clean rooms of her own, even hired a nurse when she came down with the flu. Yes, he was generous. He's done many generous things in his life. He's also done some cruel things. There's no rhyme or reason to his actions. One day he's kind, the next a maniac. You'd know this man, and his friends, if I described him even a little. But I'm not filled with malice and hate, toward him like some would be. It's all bygones with me. I don't mention names.

"This actor is rich and can have whatever it is he wants. But what he wants most is not to be lonely and bored. He has people with him always. This one plays cards with him, that one tells him funny stories and thinks up practical jokes. The actor gives parties, but still they are all bored people. So it's always a treat when one of them comes up with a new game to play, a new funny man to act the fool." Daniel grimaced distastefully. "He could have helped Mab. He could have done so much for her. You'll see that I'm not sounding ungrateful for his bringing Mab off the street; because he also gave her whiskey. Just enough whiskey to keep her in a bad state. It was his plan to teach Mab bawdy songs to sing like she was some kind of wornout parrot, and spring her on his friends at one of his parties. She learned his filth because she wasn't hardly living those days, just reaching for the bottle and pouring it down. But when the time came she gave a *performance*, never mind the rotten words that had been put in her mouth. Some of them had the grace not to laugh. I happened to be where I could hear, because I've been a chauffeur for picture people a good many years. I couldn't help the tears in my eyes from what I'd seen. I told myself, Daniel, do something for that woman."

"I know you took good care of her, Daniel."

"Yes, but she'd closed her heart to Jesus, so when the devil said drink! she drank; and when she woke up in bed a few mornings ago with shooting pains in her liver, the devil said, with scorn in his voice, Woman, I'm done with you. I'm ready to cast your soul in the fiery pit, and you'll burn forever! Mab said, Daniel, take me home! I could smell perdition rising from her skin. We'll never make it to Tennessee, I thought, but I prayed anyhow." His hand trembled on his knee, and he looked down at the sawdust. "And now I expect the only hope we've got left in this world is you, Brother Windom."

"Daniel, I'll do what I can for Mab. Won't you come with me? Are you able?"

"I'll come," Daniel said, steeling himself, and he joined King outside.

"Now," King said to Mr. Handwerker, "I want you to make a torch for me. A good stout branch of that oak, some rags, and naphtha gas from the truck will do."

The Negroes pressed around King once more and he said, "I'd like for you all to stand around the Cadillac there in a big circle, hands joined together. You can pray or shout or whatever you like, but don't let go hands until I'm telling you."

The tall man, who had been observing King, approached as the Negroes dispersed and said, "Is there anything I can do?"

King, his mind on his mission, asked brusquely, "Are you a preacher?"

"No, I'm a physician. John Matthews is my name."

King recognized the man: he had a broad lonesome face and a thin sizzle of sandy hair on his freckled head. That balding head had been conspicuous for three nights running above the rows of heads in the tent. "You've come to our meetings often, Dr. Matthews."

The man only smiled in an offhand, shy manner, and nodded pleasantly. "I'm interested," he said. And then he added, "I heard you on the radio."

King looked at the figure of Mab Shaw in the back of the Cadillac. "Doctor, that's an old woman there, but her sickness is mostly of the soul and not the body. I think she's ready to be saved, to return to the Fold. She only needs encouragement, and that's what I aim to give her."

Dr. Matthews smiled at that and backed off to a vantage point near the tent.

King went briskly to the car and opened the door again. This time Mab Shaw was trembling, and she seemed to shrink back from his presence. "I don't think I kin make it," she said in a low voice. "I been apart from Jesus too long."

"Look out there!" King commanded, and her besotted eyes struggled with the light and the figures gathered in a ring around the car. "They're praying for you, Mab. They're a bulwark against the devil. Hear them pray!" King glanced over his shoulder. The Reverend Mr. Handwerker had appeared with the torch, and awaited orders to light it. He was as excited as any of the Negroes, Mab's family and friends, who were exhorting Jesus and shuffling their feet.

King's eyes glittered as he leaned closer to Mab and extended his hand. "I'm talking now to you, devil!" he said, eyes on Mab's throat. "I'm commanding you, devil, in the name of the Lord Jesus, to *come out* and leave that poor woman's body be! Hear me!"

Mab groaned in a sickly way.

King felt confident and happy. He shucked out of his coat and thrust a hand at her. "Woman, take hold of my hand! I'm going to *pull* you to Jesus!"

He pulled, but he would have had better luck with a stone statue. He braced one foot against the doorsill, gripped the roof tight with his other hand, and set himself for a hard fight. Mab felt his strength and opened her eyes wide, but she was two hunded eighty pounds of sin-weighted woman, and the devil wasn't letting go such a prize if he could help it. Shelbina cried fearfully. But King was so sure of himself that he laughed out loud.

"*I'm* going to win, devil!" he crowed. "I'm winning. I'm winning!" And he hauled away at Queen Mab, ferociously.

Five minutes passed, and ten. King changed his stance a dozen times. He could not reach in with his other hand because he needed it for an anchor. But little by little Mab began to come up out of the back seat, and every time she gave an inch King sang out, "What's the matter, devil, losing your grip?" And all the Negroes chanted, "Show him, show him, Preacher! Save that woman!" King's arm bulged and ached with strain, but he would not allow himself to become tired or discouraged.

Suddenly he had a premonition that the devil was through, and he gritted his teeth, reaching for extra effort.

"Woman, open your mouth and shout for Jesus!"

Mab's mouth flew open, it yawned as wide as the Pit, but not a word came out. Her face was shiny with perspiration.

"I'm going to squeeze the devil of drink from your body," King promised. "He'll pop out of your throat and never return! Reverend Handwerker, light up that torch, if you please, and stand by." With that he took a new purchase on Mab's wet hand and bore down. She began to heave and writhe, but still not a word.

"Touch her, Jesus!" King implored. "Touch her, Lord!"

And the Lord apparently heard him. Out of Mab's throat came a wailing cry, and the assembled Negroes, still hand in hand, sank back, prayers silent upon their lips.

"Hallelujah!" Mab shouted. *"The devil of drink is gone!"* And up she came, and out she came, and fell down right on top of King Windom.

The preacher was stunned but not winded. The suddenness and completeness of his victory whipped him to his feet. The Negroes had been about to rush forward to embrace Mab, who was sitting in the dirt and joyously reaching up for Heaven, but King stopped them. "Hold tight!" he gasped. "The devil is here and we've got him trapped! If you feel him pushing at your arms, say, 'Turn back, devil!' He can't break through. We've *got* him. We can't see him, but we knowwwww-w he's here. Wahoo!" He turned and seized the burning torch from Mr. Handwerker, and brandished it. "Satan's had his way too long!"

"Amen!"

"Let's make that sinner-devil dance!"

Celebration!

They spread as far apart as they could, giving King plenty of arena for his joust with the routed enemy. King looked high and low, suspiciously. Suddenly he thrust the torch into the Cadillac, with a cry of glee. "Aha!"

"Singe his hide, Preacher!"

Having poked the devil from his hiding place, King began to chase him around and around the car. "Now, there he goes! Lock hands! Feel him brush against your skin? He's looking for another body to pop into, but he won't find one here!" *Swish!* went the torch. "He doesn't like this fire on his tail; he's used to putting souls to the fire, but not"—*swish!*—"getting a taste of it himself. It's not just the fire that makes him run, though. Do you know why the devil's in real agony right now? Because another soul has come home to the Flock. Oh, devil's suffering! Mab Shaw, what do you say?"

"My God, I'm saved! My God, I ain't gwin to die! I'm beginning a *new* life tonight. Thank you, Jesus!"

King held the torch down low where she could see it, and feel a little of its heat, and his voice was low and deliberate.

"Keep your eyes on the flame, Mab. What's left of the devil who lead you to misery and disgrace is burning right now at the end of this torch. Do you believe it?"

"Yes! I believe!"

"From now on you're going to fill yourself with a new kind of spirits. Not that stuff that comes from California, but that stuff comes down from Heaven. Holy Ghost wine! Mab, say goodbye devil, because here he goes!"

King straightened, sighted, drew back the torch, and then flung it. All eyes traced the burning arc up over the top of the nearby oak, followed the torch as it plummeted down upon a mud flat halfway between the tent and the fairgrounds, and burst into a spray of sparks. King wiped his hands on a pocket handkerchief and reached down to help Mab to her feet. But this took a lot of doing, and his right arm had little strength left in it. Daniel sprang to help him, and slowly Mab rose, weeping.

"Bless you, Daniel! Bless *you*, Preacher. I'm born again."

"Get you in that tent and thank God. And don't ever stop thanking Him."

Silently King peeled down his shirt sleeves and watched Mab into the tent. She walked with her head high, purring with happiness. Daniel was at her side. It seemed an unlikely marriage, but there was no mistaking Daniel's devotion to her.

One by one the Negroes came up to King for a few words of appreciation, and they were as hushed as they would have been at a burial; then they too slipped into the tent to pray with Mr. Handwerker. King nodded in satisfaction and looked around for his jacket. It was in the hands of the tall physician, Dr. Matthews, and he came forward, with his durable smile of encouragement, and a look of somewhat wistful caution in his eyes.

"Congratulations," he said, and unself-consciously helped King into his jacket. "For a time I thought she wasn't going to come out of the car."

"Oh, I had to get her out. She was stuck fast in her old life, and there was no room for Jesus in that life." He held up his hands and smiled. "I used to cry in my bed of an evening because I was so much bigger than the other kids, but God knew I'd need extra strength when I grew up and started in preaching. Praise God I had strength tonight."

Dr. Matthews glanced into the tent. "All this is outside my experience," he confessed, "although I've attended a good

172

many revival meetings during the past year. Will that woman be all right now? Do you think she'll go back to the bottle?"

King considered the possibility. "No, I don't. I've seen alcoholics backslide many times, and Mab, from all I'm told, was an alcoholic. But the devil of drink is gone from her body, and she's with Jesus now. She may have miseries for a while, but He'll see her safely through."

"I've known a few alcoholics myself," Dr. Matthews said. He was still not at ease with King; whether this was from his considerable shyness or from a troubled mind, the preacher didn't know. "Treated a few. Alcoholism is a wretched disease, I think more discouraging than some forms of mental illness. If you've been able to cure Mab Shaw here tonight—"

"Hold on, Dr. Matthews," King said quietly. "What you saw tonight was *redemption*, plain and simple. Jesus was claiming His own. He used me to cast out the devil. Mab wanted saving in the worst way, and she helped too. She was a sick woman, sick with sin. Now she's a well woman. If she never feels the craving for drink in her body again, I'd say that's a miracle, but it's God's miracle and not one of my doing. Jesus laid His hand on my heart and said, Pull her to Me. I pulled, and the devil was cast out."

"Do you think Mab was dying when you looked at her tonight?"

"I saw a sick old woman. Sick of her sinfulness. I think any person possessed by a devil of sin is mortally sick whether they recognize that or not."

"But what if it hadn't been alcoholism? What if she'd been suffering from cancer?"

King saw the light and smiled stiffly. "There are preachers who believe all misery is caused by the devil. There's devils of sin, they say, and devils of disease, and one can be cast out in the name of Jesus the same as the other. To my way of thinking there is a great difference in devils, even devils of sin. Tonight with the Lord's blessing we licked a fat old devil of sin. Tomorrow night I might come up against another devil of sin, and lose, for any number of reasons. If a man comes to me crying, 'I have a devil of cancer in my body, cast him out, Preacher!' I would have to say, 'No, I can't do it. Because that which you call a devil may be only the Will of God.' There was suffering in this world long before the advent of men. Cancer kills the devout as well as the sinful, and what's a poor preacher to do?" He looked Dr. Matthews squarely in the eye. "Does that answer questions you might have had about me?"

"Well, I'd say it gives me a good deal to think over." Dr. Matthews had a habit of stuffing and unstuffing his hands in his pockets, part of his air of timidity and indecisiveness; yet his smile was always appealing, and King was attracted to him. He felt a renewed puzzlement. The doctor seemed to have nothing but leisure time and, though he looked to be in his fifties, he was too young to be retired. What had attracted him to the revival?

"I've been trying to get up the gumption to talk to you all this week," the doctor said with a glint of humor. "Now that I've got you cornered, so to speak, I wonder if I might take up a little more of your time? I know it's late, but—"

"Is it spiritual counsel you're wanting, Dr. Matthews?"

"No, I'm Catholic, and I think secure in my faith." He had come up with a pipe during his pocket-crawling and held it, a shade awkwardly, in both hands. King waited, but Matthews seemed satisfied that he had explained enough.

"I reckon I haven't had a bite to eat since midday," King admitted. "We might have a sandwich together if you're willing."

"Perfectly fine. I left my car down at the fairgrounds; it seemed safer than driving up here."

"Isn't that so? Wait on me for a second if you don't mind, Dr. Matthews; I need something from inside the tent."

King returned shortly with a tall brass candlestick in his hands, and the two men walked down a path toward the rear gates of the fairgrounds.

"I've admired your altarpiece," Dr. Matthews said, indicating the candlestick. "It must be very old."

"I came by it in Italy a few years ago. One of those little shops off the cobbles, filled with dusty mirrors and treasures. The proprietor told me the candlestick was a Holy object, as rare as some of those stored away in the Vatican museums. At least that's what I gathered from his make-do English. I wasn't taken in, but still the candlestick pleased me. Old as it was, it seemed to have a special shine when I polished it on the sleeve of my jacket and held it to the light outside the shop. Do you know antiques, Doctor?" He passed the candlestick.

"Not very well, although my house was filled with them. Mrs. Matthews was a collector." The doctor was every inch the strider that King was, and they had covered ground quickly. In the blue-white glow from the fairground lights he studied the configurations of the hand-cast candlestick. "I'm sure she could have told you a great deal more about its history."

"Just something for the altar," King murmured. Perhaps it was true that the candlestick had been in the hands of saints. Whatever its history or worth, it had survived a devastating fire, just as he had survived. The miracle of the bone comb, the wedding picture, and the jeweled brooch of his dead wife was small compared to the miracle of the candlestick, which Age had resurrected, unmelted, almost unmarred, from earth and ashes. When he had begun to preach a few nights ago, he had restored the candlestick to its place on the altar, because its significance in his ministry was equal to that of his Bible. This he accepted unquestioningly.

"By the way, how's Molly?" Dr. Matthews asked, giving back the candlestick.

"Oh, do you know Mrs. Amos?"

"The Houstons were patients of my father's for many years. Not patients of mine, however. Molly and I surprised each other at the meeting Monday night. I didn't know she was in town. Hadn't seen her for years." They passed through the untended gates into the fairgrounds and Dr. Matthews pointed the way to his car, a Continental. "Molly's a talented girl and a hard worker. She's always made her own way in the world, and I respect her for that. She has courage. When she was twenty-one and in college here, she took a fearful beating from a gang of thugs and almost died. But Molly turned even that experience to her advantage."

"What was it all about, Dr. Matthews?"

"Molly uncovered information about a Ku Klux Klan group operating on campus when she was editor of the school paper. She investigated, wrote her story, and was horsewhipped for it. A newspaper chain followed up on the incident and gave it national coverage. Everyone in Clearwater was talking about Molly, and of course some praised her and some thought she deserved what she got for giving the college bad publicity. When she graduated she was immediately hired by one of the New York papers. You're fortunate to have her working for you. I assume she's doing your publicity."

"Molly's been helpful in a lot of ways, Dr. Matthews."

At the car, the doctor held out the ignition keys to King.

"Would you mind? I don't see well at night and I'm a wretched driver as it is."

"Looks like your car would be a pleasure to drive," King said, and got in.

Once they were speeding quietly through the deserted fairgrounds, Matthews slumped down and rubbed his high forehead with his hand. Without a smile he was a melancholy man, a much older-looking man. He said, "Are you opposed to drinking?"

"I don't favor liquor for myself."

"I'm fighting off a cold and I'd like to have a drink," Matthews explained. "Something like a hot buttered rum, although I haven't made one of those in years. Because of the law in this city, the only places you can have a mixed drink are clubs, or in your own home. My apartment is about ten minutes from here. There's half a rare roast in the refrigerator which my cook prepared last night, and a loaf of fresh rye on hand—not the pap available in supermarkets these days, but the real old-country bread which a German woman bakes for me. I could make a sandwich for you and a drink for myself. We'd be much more comfortable in my living room than we would be at a pit barbecue."

"That's agreeable to me, Dr. Matthews. I can't be away from the tent too long, is all. Someone has to keep watch at night, and it's my turn."

"Good Lord. When do you sleep?"

"When I can," King said, dismissing the subject.

"A right here," Matthews said. "Then left on the expressway." He tilted up the headrest and lay back, hands in the pockets of his rumpled trench coat. They drove a couple of miles in silence. King had never been at the wheel of such a car and he was completely absorbed. On the expressway he opened up to eighty miles an hour. He drove with a sure touch that was close to elegance, and Matthews gave him an easy glance.

"Have you ever been a chauffeur?"

"Yes, matter of fact, I have. When I was stationed near Munich I drove for an old brigadier. He liked to take long trips, so I got a good workout on some pretty terrible roads. Mountain driving, especially in a big car, will test your mettle."

"That's a good word to describe a quality you have. Mettle." King did not respond. "It means valor, you know—another disused word—which in turn is more than courage. It's courage with a noble, a spiritual purpose. Courage can simply exist, but valor comes from the intelligent tempering of courage. The Negro family back there embraced you because, before you spoke a word, they sensed a figure of valor among them. This was all perfectly clear to me as I watched; it was electric."

King was prepared to belittle this judgment, but he didn't. Despite the fact that he lived a long way inside himself, Dr. Matthews was a straightforward man, and King knew his words had not been carelessly chosen, or designed to swell the preacher's head. It was possible that by idealizing the courage of an unknown, a stranger, Dr. Matthews was trying to say something difficult about himself. The car sped on, under midnight, past towers and trees.

"If those people had needed a medical man tonight, they would have turned to you with the same trust they showed in me."

Matthews moved restlessly on the seat. "I don't think so. I'm a doctor, but a reluctant, a hesitant one. I think I told you my father was a physician. He had skill, and a rich practice, and he grew rich and prominent himself. Thanks to him I've been able to live graciously and at ease for most of my fifty-seven years. Because of my father—I admired him immensely—and partly because I wanted the prestige of a profession, I studied medicine myself. It isn't conceit when I tell you I had a fairly easy time in medical school. I'm an intelligent man, and my lack of accomplishments and standing are due entirely to self-indulgence. Of all my traits that one borders on a curse." He smiled evenly, without pity. "I like to think I could have become a good doctor, but that would have meant long hours, other sacrifices. I elected to be competent, and so I've had a successful practice in my father's name, referring all cases that might have been troublesome. I've lived my gracious life, and enjoyed it." With this he passed a hand over his eyes and shook his head in a befuddled way.

"I'm speaking of my life as it was until my wife died," he continued, more quietly. "Today I live differently. Sometimes it's hard to believe that I've survived two and a half years without Edith. Her death was the first real shock I'd experienced in a lifetime of pleasant monotony. That's why I admire you, or any man who has been severely tried, no matter what the outcome. That's why I'm filled with envy of you, a man half my age."

"You don't know anything about me," King said.

"But I know you've been tried," Matthews said, with a trace of impatience in his voice. "I've seen. I was there."

"You mean tonight? Mab Shaw?" King shook his head. "That wasn't much of a trial."

"To me it was critical. The other man might have fallen on his knees and prayed conscientiously until dawn, because that was all he could do. But you made a stand and a fight, you risked losing that woman's soul. You risked who knows what of yourself. By valor you won, and put the devil—symbolic as he was—to the sword, or rather to the torch. To me you took your life in your hands. That was what I felt, and I was awed by your fight.

"Every preacher is tried in that way. In fact, you could better name it a long tribulation. The devil is here, to be fought, day by day. We talked about that."

"What you accept with ease I accept with wonder, and dread: the prospect of a trial. For I *am* being tried, and I have the resources of a child, a thin-skinned, naïve child." They were in the city now, with the Gothic geometry of a college campus on a plain nearby. Dr. Matthews took pink-tinted glasses from his shirt pocket and peered through them. "A left turn below the next exit will bring you within two blocks of my home. I've a story to tell, but it can wait until we've had some refreshment." The glasses, or perhaps the sharpness of vision they afforded, made him nervous. He took the glasses off and folded them, then sank back once more, making a hollow of himself. His blade-thin knees were thrust high, and his forehead was heavy with apprehension. "It's a strange story, but—this is the hope I've had in me since I first heard you preach—it may be that you'll find my story familiar and not strange at all."

15

Hébert

Dr. Matthews maintained four spacious rooms in a high-rise building overlooking the moats and guarded canyons of the city's zoo.

"I took this apartment not long after Edith died," he explained, switching on lights. "Sold the house we lived in, and stored our furniture. I've thought day to day of moving into another house, nothing pretentious, but with a garden. I enjoy having a place to dig." He looked around with an expression of disaffection, blinking his poor eyes. Despite the elaborateness of the apartment, the walls were as cold and white as those in a salt cave. Matthews waved his hand past his nose as if lonesomeness were curling there like a fog and said, "Please make yourself at home. I like that corner myself, by the terrace doors. At night, in the spring, you can hear the lions in their pits, and the peacocks' screech. It all nearly drives Hébert crazy; spring is a dog's time to howl too, and even though he's old he remembers well."

The dog he meant came unhurriedly out of the kitchen; he was thin-legged and had too much skin and too much fur, as if all he was wearing he had borrowed. He was a poolroom dog, a dog-pound dog. Although he greeted Matthews in a friendly way, he had no air of proprietorship about the apartment. He wandered on past King into the living room, genteel but careful, one bright eye cocked above a tongue and a grin.

"What would you like to drink with your sandwich? I have just about anything."

"I could do with a taste of sweet milk. Or coffee is fine."

Dr. Matthews went into the kitchen, unknotting his tie, and King followed the dog to an old tub of a chair by the terrace. On a worktable within reach of the chair were books and newspapers, a jar of pencils, and a small typewriter. On the near wall a portrait of a woman whom King took to be the doctor's late wife caught his eye; she looked pleasant and unshakable.

It was Dr. Matthews' chair, so he didn't sit down. He let the dog out on the terrace, which smelled like a neglected kennel run, and bent over the books.

There was a copy of *Science and Health*, which King had never looked into. Two of the books the doctor owned were more familiar to him: William James's *The Varieties of Religious Experience* and Monseigneur Knox's *Conversion*. He had seen *The Devils of Loudun* in bookstores but had never bought it. Other of the books were standard works by famous psychiatrists and religious figures. But most of them were totally unknown to King; some looked old, rare, and friable, and had ponderous titles: *Demonic Possession in the New Testament—Its Relations Historical, Medical and Theological.*

King already had had a sample of Dr. Matthews' interest in Heaven-sent healing, so he was more impressed by the extent of the doctor's investigation than surprised by it. He was tempted to look into one of the loose-leaf notebooks on the worktable, but they were private too. The spiritualist newspapers strewn about were both familiar and offensive. King had seen too many of them in his own house as a boy and the sight of them made him uneasy even now.

He felt no need to be on his guard and so he made himself at home on a low, cushioned bench, adjusted one of the cones on a pole lamp so that the light fell strongly across his shoulder, and began to read *The Devils of Loudun.* He read with the book on the floor between his feet and his head almost between his knees, a favorite study pose, and as always when he was reading, his forehead became severely lined. Dr. Matthews found him like that when he came in carrying a tray with a sandwich, a glass of milk, and a mug of hot buttered rum.

"Did you find one that interests you?"

King glanced up. "All books interest me," he said, "although I've read a good many I didn't like or understand." He closed the Huxley book and set it aside. "From the first couple of pages I'd say this one is worth finishing."

"Take it with you," Dr. Matthews said promptly.

"No, I couldn't do that. To me borrowing books is like borrowing children. If they belong to you—well, you can always have a look-in, study a sleeping face, or a sweet phrase. Let me tell you, if I had ambitions to be a writer, I'd be grateful that man came along first."

"As a gift then," the doctor amended, clearing a space on the bench for the tray.

"May be that I can accept such a gift," King said, "provided I can be of help to you." He added a thick layer of mustard to the ample slices of cold roast and began to eat.

Dr. Matthews smiled absently, sipped his rum, and took up a position by the terrace doors. "You have a love of books. I'm ashamed to say that I don't. And I don't have the fine plodding temperament of a scholar. I found myself turned into a serious man at an awkward age—I was tempted to say in my declining years, but I'm not ready to admit senescence. I've gone through those books on the bench, and a hundred others, at a clip, without proper enthusiasm, looking for answers, for satisfaction."

King had discovered with the first bite that he was wolfishly hungry, and he had been eating his sandwich at an undignified speed. He put down the remains, took a long drink of the ice-cold milk, and sat back, wiping a spot of mustard from his chin with a paper napkin. "I can honestly say I didn't know there were that many books on religious healing, or so many scholars writing on the subject."

"Are you interested in faith healing?"

"The Bible makes it plain that Jesus intended for His church to carry on healing work. A preacher *should* be interested in faith healing. By that I mean intercession and nothing more. But too many preachers are led astray by the miracle stories in the Bible, by the cures of Jesus." King reached and picked up a Bible from the worktable. "You're an educated man, secure in your faith as you say, and I'm sure you've spent many an evening with Scripture. You know, the same as I do, that there's a tremendous difference between the healing miracles of Jesus and the healing wonders of those He sent two-and-two into the cities. 'Stephen, full of grace and power, wrought great wonders and signs.' Wonders, not miracles." King opened the Bible but did not refer to it; the weight of it in his hand was inspiration enough. "The word of Ananias healed Saul of

181

blindness. Paul challenged the faith of the cripple at Lystra, who then stood upright on his feet. Peter and John healed at the Gate Beautiful through the power of their faith. All of the Twelve, and the seventy that Christ appointed later, had unusual powers because of their communion with the *living* Savior. They had great spiritual strength, strength to awaken faith in the sick. Even today if faith is strong enough it can do mighty and mysterious things. Preachers should remember that. It's faith and prayer that heals, and not prying and poking and laying on hands. There's Paul, who was converted by our Lord Himself, whose faith and zeal have never been equaled. Paul failed more often than not when he tried to heal with his hands. We have known only one great miracle worker. We're meant to pray, and have faith. Nothing more."

"Still, healing through touch is almost as old as human suffering. Galen recommended it. So did Pliny. Primitive people believe in the curative powers of touch, especially the touch of hands slicked with spittle. For centuries common people believed that the touch of royalty was therapeutic. The Emperor Vespasian is reported to have restored the sight of a blind man. Crowds gathering in England to receive the touch and blessings of kings from Edward the Confessor to Charles the Second. Several doctors I've known have had uncommon success easing pain and anxiety by the application of their hands. At least one of those doctors was a long way from having some religious conviction."

Dr. Matthews paused to open one of the terrace doors, and the dog-pound dog came in, his head low, his grin as worldly as ever. He found a place for himself on the carpet beneath the painting of the doctor's wife, and eased down, stiffly.

"Of course, Jesus was unique," Dr. Matthews resumed. "But in addition to His miracle-working powers He had the skill of a physician and the insight of a psychologist. He touched many men—the blind, the scabrous, the paralyzed—in performing His miracles. This may be an unasked-for comparison, but in your redemption of Mab Shaw tonight you used many of the techniques Jesus used in His healings: touch, crowd psychology, the power of suggestion. I'm thinking of a particular healing, that of the man with the withered hand."

"I wasn't imitating Jesus. I can't say for sure why I did all that I did. My only concern was saving Mab's soul, to cast out a devil. The Holy Spirit was guiding me."

Dr. Matthews smiled morosely and nipped steadily at his rum. "Do you believe that all genuine miracles ended with Jesus? Or do you think it's possible for the Holy Spirit to take possession of a man so strongly that miracles occur through the instrument of His flesh?"

King put down the Bible and picked up his half-eaten sandwich to find that his appetite had waned. There was a hint of redness in his eyes and a single hard line across his forehead gave him a tired look, a cutthroat look.

"There's one preacher," he said, "and you must be as familiar with his name as I am, who people say has found special favor with the Lord. I've never met him, and what I know of his miracles is hearsay. The story goes that when he was a poor boy working in fields some years ago he joined a man's leg to his body after it had been cut off in an accident. Today this preacher has a successful healing ministry and I've seen his program on television. There are other preachers—who don't strike me as being quite as honest or devout as the man from Oklahoma—who claim to have powers, even a power to raise the dead, which Jesus Himself didn't do. I notice there under the spiritualist newspapers you have magazines put out by such preachers, and I suppose those magazines are full of articles and pictures about healings they claim. They may be frauds, and they may not be. I can't judge. I believe, though, in the man from Oklahoma, and if it is that God has granted him special powers, then he's doubly blessed for using those powers wisely and with compassion."

"I've talked with the man from Oklahoma," Dr. Matthews said, "and he does have compassion—humility as well. He made no claims for himself. He told me what I already know to be generally true—that successful healing depends on the personal conviction and power of suggestion of the healer, and the susceptibility and faith of the patient. He relies heavily on formula, or ritual, in his healing efforts, and never fails to stress that the hoped-for healing must be in the name of Jesus. Like Paul, he has successes and failures, and he is probably too quick to dismiss failures as failures of faith. The man from Oklahoma is not, to my mind, a symbol of Christian healing at its best. I think assembly-line healing is barbarous, grossly unfair to the suffering, because the onus is forever on the patient if there is no recovery."

Matthews sighed, and drained the last of his rum. "Well," he said ruefully, "this is gone and I don't think I've managed to discourage my cold at all. One more, though, might do the trick. Could I make you another sandwich?"

"This one will do me, Doctor, and thanks very much."

While his rum was heating, Dr. Matthews wandered back into the living room. "It must be obvious to you by now that my interest in healing is intensely personal. I've spent the greater part of my time the past two years not only in reading but in travel. I think I've investigated every aspect of Christian—or religious—healing. The man from Oklahoma is only one of many I've interviewed. Before you began preaching there was a boy—"

"Philemon Love," King interrupted, with a wry look.

"That's the one. I questioned him two weeks ago. He was eager to tell me about his gifts, and his accomplishments, but before he'd gone very far I could tell it was all wishful thinking. Well, I've talked to Christian Scientists, Four Square Gospel preachers, proprietors of spiritualist churches, Raphaelites and Emmanuelists, and Baptist, Methodist, and Quaker healing groups. I've discussed healing with cranks and converts, holy men and humbugs. I visited Milton Abbey in Dorset, and was impressed by the work, medical and spiritual, being done there; I visited Lourdes and was repelled. I came to the conclusion that nearly all cases of so-called faith healing can be explained by modern pyschology. This doesn't make them less important or impressive, but there is a great difference in restoring to health someone whose body has been at the mercy of his emotions, and in affecting a cure of someone legitimately sick or injured. Miracles of healing have been performed unthinkingly by ordinary men, miracles which were in no way God-connected or religiously inspired. These are the healings which concern me most, for I've had a healing experience myself, and it is, to my knowledge, absolutely unique."

King gave him a look of polite interest and polished off the quarter of sandwich in his hand. Dr. Matthews smiled dimly, disappointedly. There was a faint odor of steaming spirits in the air; he hurried into the kitchen and returned with his mug. "I hope I haven't boiled the alcohol out of this," he said, and sipped cautiously. King sat back on the bench and clasped his hands behind his head. His expression was the same, but the drowsy, cloudy redness in his eye seemed to have deepened.

"I suppose," Matthews began, after making sure the rum was

184

to his liking, "that I sound like Philemon to you. Imaginative, if not mystical, and possible overwrought." His forehead wrinkled as if that were a joke, and he sniffed thoughtfully at the rum vapors. "I've given you a definite impression of myself tonight, so that you probably see me as restless and impulsive. The truth is I'm reflective; by nature I move slowly, study at length. I'm careful to the point of drudgery. And, while I'm absorbed by the study of healing phenomena which I've made, I'm not enthralled by it. If my approach hasn't been scholarly, it's at least been considered. Do you understand?"

King nodded.

"I was objective about my experience, as soon as I realized what had happened. There were witnesses, and the next day, after I had decided it was extremely important for me to record the details, all my impressions and feelings just before the healing took place, I interviewed those witnesses."

The doctor sat down then, in his leather tub of a chair, which sighed with his weight. A grin flickered on his face. "Not the best witnesses I would have chosen: an eleven-year-old Negro boy, and a rubbery type of old man who lives in the SP Café like a mouse lives in a cupboard. Still, I'm grateful for them; otherwise I might not be assured of my sanity today."

The dog-pound dog named Hébert, who had been sleeping on the carpet, suddenly kicked out a hind leg and awakened fretfully. He cast a look at King, who made a chucking sound of reassurance. "Hébert, Hébert," King said softly, and the dog grinned himself to sleep again. Matthews gazed at his dog until he noticed the silence, and King's waiting, and then he said, working himself slowly into his story, "Like many men suddenly faced with the loss of their wives, I found myself in the deepest depression, in a lock of inertia, for months after Edith died. I continued to practice medicine, in my desultory way, but resuming any sort of normal social life was next to impossible for me. In desperation I left my patients in the care of another doctor and drove down to Louisiana, to a small farm which I own near the town of Scott. I hadn't been on my farm in a dozen years, but I had fond memories from boyhood, of hard labor in the cane, of strong coffee and rich hot Louisiana food, and always lots of laughter and good talk and bittersweet, caterwauling Cajun music. I remembered all of it, pirogue fishing, fighting cocks, Catahoula dogs with eyes like fresh water, and shooting rabbits and rattlesnakes in the swamp cedar. And I needed it all, I needed a completely different approach to life. I needed the Babineuxes, the old couple who have lived on the place for as long as I can remember. They welcomed me with that splendid hospitality which the Cajun people offer those they know, and tried to put me in their own bedroom, but I wanted the small room I had slept in when I was a boy, which was always cool in the summer from the big cistern standing up against the house." He paused, frowning, as if he had lost his way. King nodded and smiled, because he knew the life which the doctor was describing, and loved it just as much.

"I stayed on at the farm, making myself useful in small ways, hunting and fishing most weekends, and gradually I was able to throw off my depression, only to become trapped in another way—by anger and unhappiness over the life I had wasted. I don't mean I was self-pitying. I was alone, and perfectly able to accept that condition." He glanced somberly at the painting of his wife. "I was just not able to accommodate the realization that Edith had had the kindness, and the patience, to take me exactly as I desired to be. I felt that I had shamefully cheated her; the devotion which I had returned for her love and for-bearance seemed pitiful to me. As I've said, I found myself in another trap, awake to my lack of pride, filled with rare energy, anger, the need to justify myself, past complacency but also past middle age, with precious few active years left. This was my frame of mind after a few weeks in Louisiana, and I've gone into it excessively because I think it's important for you to know that I was in a state of struggle and conflict, alive but without definition, at the time of my healing experience."

King slumped a little lower on the bench, bracing with his heels against the carpet, and his eyes were narrowed as if at a glare. Dr. Matthews drank deeply from the mug of rum with a look of tension.

"Scott is nothing but a crossroads, a farming community on the main line of the Southern Pacific Railroad, a few miles west of Lafayette, Louisiana. I think the population must be something like one hundred percent Cajun, and when I was a boy Cajun French, the Lafayette Parish dialect, was spoken exclusively at home and in the meeting places. A good many of the children who came into town from the outlying farms to attend the grade school didn't know a word of English. Now all that's changing, I think because of television, and probably

186

within the thirty years the old language, along with the old customs, will be a rarity.

"Three or four times a week during my most recent stay old Babineux and I found excuses to make the short trip into town during the middle of the day and to spend an hour in one café or another, drinking those little cups of viperish black coffee, enjoying the familiar gossip, the talk of cocks and gambling, the short, volatile arguments that spring up between Cajun men over everything and nothing, and the occasional thunder of a train. One afternoon in mid-October—almost two years ago today—we drove in according to habit in Babineux's pickup truck and parked outside the drugstore on the highway. October in southern Louisiana is rarely different from summer unless an early norther strikes, but we'd had just such a break in the weather. A few sycamores had turned halfway red; the sky was a clear ice blue and there was a brisk wind blowing. To my eyes the children playing in the schoolyard across the way seemed to be so many scraps of paper scattered about by the tail of the norther.

"Babineux had business in the drugstore and I had a telegram to send, so we parted in front of the store and I walked on toward the depot, which was less than a block away down a short, unpaved stretch of road. I can remember every trivial detail of my surroundings, remember every step I took, with amazing clarity. There was loose cotton on the road and in the air, from the gin, and the pin oak beside the ramshackle gin had literally been thatched by flying cotton. The sun was high overhead, the dust of that little street slanting off to the hump of the railroad tracks sparkled with it. The wind, of course, had been coming steadily from the north, but as I walked along, the high frame oblong of the depot shielded me from it for a few moments, and I felt pleasantly warm. Usually during the afternoon you see a good many faces on that little street, but just then I was aware of only two. Across from the gin and standing side by side are two long frame buildings, one white-painted and trimmed with creeper, a rooming house, the other unpainted and abandoned-looking, with a deep front porch. This building is the SP Café, and one of the more popular spots in the community despite its looks. There's always a *bourais* game in progress at a back table, always someone winning or losing and letting the world know about it. On the steps of the SP Café Henry Lynn was sitting asleep in the sun, and although I hadn't been in Scott very long, I was so used to Henry I hardly saw him at all. The other face was that of the Negro boy, who was sweeping the porch of the rooming house. . . . Oh, and I almost forgot to mention Hébert." He offered a slight smile of affection to the sleeping dog.

"Hébert was lying on the porch which the Negro boy was sweeping, drowsing like Henry Lynn. To this day I don't know if he belonged to someone in the house, but my guess is he was a derelict—like Henry—only much more agreeable and able to fend for himself. Remember, now, I'm telling you the impressions of a few seconds of time, and while I noticed, recorded all the sights of the street as I walked toward the depot, I was occupied with thoughts of the telegram I was not to send that day, with the slight stirrings of loneliness and restlessness which I feel whenever I'm near a railroad. A truck was toiling over the track embankment and I saw it too and, I suppose, made a note to move a little closer to the left-hand edge of the street, because from the way the driver was shifting gears and riding the accelerator, it was obvious he was in a hurry. Four strides, or five, and the truck was bearing down on me; I looked up apprehensively, saw that the truck would pass me with room to spare, and lowered my head to shield my eyes from dust. Three more strides, and some powerful instinct drew my eyes to the truck again. It was now past the rooming house on its way to the highway, making a fierce racket. And behind the truck, in the road, lay Hébert, twisted grotesquely on his back, with dabs of blood bright on the white fur of his belly. I hadn't heard him howl; perhaps if he made a sound at all the accelerating truck drowned it out.

"The Negro boy was standing aghast on the top step of the rooming-house porch with his broom half raised and I gathered what had happened: he had taken a swipe at the sleeping dog and in fright Hébert had jumped, or fallen, into the path of the truck."

King looked down at the oblivious dog and rubbed his tense face gently with his fingertips. "Bad hurt?" he murmured.

"Hébert was broken, but not crushed, so apparently none of the wheels had passed over him. When I reached him he was feebly alive, his eyes back in his head and already collecting the blue glaze of death. He could not have had a minute more to live. His left hind leg was cruelly broken, the bone was splintered and exposed. But this was the only outward sign of mutilation. He was probably beyond feeling pain. I felt a detached pity for him, and because there was only a little blood I decided, impulsively, to move him out of the road to a patch of cool grass beside the rooming house.

"Lifting him was grisly—I've always been a little too faint-hearted for a physician—but as I said, he was so near death I don't believe he experienced much pain. Apparently Henry Lynn had been awakened by the truck; I smelled him behind me as I was lifting Hébert. He said something like, 'Dog's a goner,' but I didn't turn around. I walked gingerly toward the grass with their eyes on me, and I was looking for a likely spot to lay Hébert down when a strange trembling came over me, like nothing I'd ever known before: I felt as if breath and blood were draining from my body in a vast whirlpool, and my knees buckled from the force of this whirlpool. I think that my right hand, which was under Hébert's head, tightened involuntarily, but I couldn't swear to it. I do know my vision blurred and I felt like a fool; I was convinced I was going to faint. But the seizure passed swiftly, it couldn't have lasted for more than five seconds, and I regained my balance, only to lose it again when Hébert suddenly came flailing to life in my arms."

Almost before he was finished speaking, King rose and went to the dog, who awoke, feeling his presence, and, at the invitation of the preacher's hand, rolled on his side to have his stomach scratched. "The left hind leg?" King said, not turning.

"Yes, it was a compound fracture. There's not a trace of it, although Hébert does have stiffness in the leg from time to time. But then, he's getting to be elderly, I'd say thirteen or fourteen years old."

"What happened after you felt him kicking in your arms?"

"I dropped him instantly, in complete astonishment. And as soon as he was down he ran across the street, as fast as possible. When he was about thirty yards away he stopped, looked back, then sat down in the shade of the pin oak and rather unconcernedly began scratching himself—with the same leg which I had seen so badly broken only a few minutes before."

"What were you thinking?" King asked.

"I don't know. I was too shocked to think. I remember seeing Henry Lynn studying me with an expression of drunken amazement and suspicion. 'What did you do to him?' And I said, 'I didn't do anything,' or something about as profound, and then poor old befuddled Henry looked at Hébert rolling himself in the dust like a pup and said churlishly, as if he had been made a fool of, 'Dog appeared like he was a goner to me,' and trudged right back to the SP Café."

"What did the Negro boy say?"

"The same as Henry: 'What did you do?' I was just aware that I *had* done something, or that something had taken place, and I was astonished to feel a prayer in my mind, muscular and demanding, because I'm a reluctant offerer of prayer. Physically I felt blunted; I had a sensation of surcease. The sunlight was punishment, so I put on tinted glasses, turned around, and almost fled back to the drugstore and the no-nonsense company of Babineux. I couldn't be persuaded to walk down that street again. In fact, I overbearingly insisted that Babineux drive me back to the farm, and the rest of the day I dozed, with an aching head which no amount of aspirin could soothe and a wet cloth over my eyes. It took me hours, days, to face the fact that a miracle had come to pass through my flesh. I felt awed and resentful, pious and dismayed. Great power had come and gone in my body, and for weeks afterward I was sensitive to the eyes of every man I met. I imagine that you know, have known, all these feelings. For instance, tonight, when you were working so hard for the soul of Mab Shaw. Even where I was standing I was aware of the current that passed between you the instant before she opened her mouth and shouted for Christ—for life."

"Hmmm," King said, standing. He thrust his hands into his pockets and leaned shoulders against the wall. "You were aware of more than I was. All I felt was tired, and grateful that the devil finally decided he was up against more than he could fight and made a run for it. I'm no miracle man, Dr. Matthews. Mab Shaw summed me up tonight. I pray and I save—when I can, when Jesus is with me. The healing experience which you had is fascinating to me. I never have heard of anything like it. To me it's a fine instruction in the many wonders of God. Hébert! Imagine! Just an ordinary street dog run over by a truck, and spared. Why? Who needs to know why? The Almighty made for it to happen. That's all any man needs to know." And he stared, deliberately, at Dr. Matthews.

The doctor reached down and set his empty mug on the carpet. Though he smiled, his fingers trembled, and he clenched his hands together in his lap. "I'm afraid that isn't enough for me," he said in a low reasonable voice. "For one

190

thing, as I told you, I don't believe my healing of Hébert was God-connected. It certainly wasn't a religious occasion. Religion—God Himself—was as far from my mind as the galaxies. The power was in me, not directed through me. Whether or not God put the power there at some time or other is a question I'm not prepared to argue, because I'm not a theologian."

"I don't see how you can doubt it."

Dr. Matthews did not bother to smile. "I don't doubt that God's ultimate plan for us is in many ways invisible and unknowable, at least from our present level of vision. My beliefs about healing, based on all the research which I've told you about, exclude the possibility that they are simply infrequent manifestations of His inscrutable will. I'm not ruling out the miraculous power of God altogether in healing, you see. Just limiting it."

King scowled slightly, but Dr. Matthews' eyes were lowered and he did not see. "What *do* you believe?"

"I believe," Dr. Matthews said, his voice cheerful again, "that even the most insignificant man among us, even a Henry Lynn, has vast amounts of life-giving or psychic energy within him. This isn't a theory, it's demonstrable, a truth commonplace and obvious. Most men struggle with this energy, or convert it into fear. A few unwittingly make strange use of it: consider the small number of genuine clairvoyants and mediums like the late Edgar Cayce, and the poltergeist phenomena, which are probably evidences of erratic, out-of-control life energies.

"I discovered early that if I was going to attempt to understand healing I would have to learn something of current psychic research. I'm not measureably psychic myself, but long before my experience with Hébert I knew that I possessed some sort of quixotic gift. All my life I've had fiendishly good runs of luck at bridge, because I seemed to sense the cards that were being held around the table, and I've also had, in the course of my medical practice, rare, inexplicable hunches about the illnessess of patients that turned out to be right. Of course, I can't compare these hunches with the ability of the famous Mrs. Bendit, who had no medical training but who expertly diagnosed the physical, psychological, or spiritual ills of a person, sometimes without even laying eyes on that person."

"Now, that's something I never have heard of."

Dr. Matthews got up to pace. "Because of Mrs. Bendit, who could control her power at will, I believe it may someday be possible for many men to experience and control the power of healing. The psychic power of a single man is fantastic: multiply that by the population of the world and you have potential energy perhaps greater than the source of all life itself—the sun. I told you that I felt as if a whirlpool were draining through my body. The few men I've talked to who have had a trustworthy healing experience, or several such experiences, report much the same sensation. Of draining, a pouring out of the life force, sometimes accompanied by trembling, or a clonus. One said he felt as if he were a pitcher being emptied. Inside of me, as I carried Hébert from the road to the grass beside the rooming house, a tap was opened through some psychic accident which I could never trace and the world of life energy rushed through it. Of healing light, and air, and love. All this occured in a few moments' time, and the experience, the accident, has never been repeated. How many men have felt this power, and how did they react? I became a serious man. The man from Oklahoma judged his healing gift to be a sign from God, and he took up preaching. How many others have been thoroughly frightened, and hidden their experience away, telling no one of it? How many have lost contact with reality?" He paused before his wife's portrait and looked at it fondly, but with a touch of sadness. "Do you understand," he said, and King didn't know if he was being addressed or not, "what I'm searching for?"

King patted the dozing dog one last time and stood. "You said you hadn't healed but once."

"It isn't that," Dr. Matthews said, shaking his head at the suggestion. "I don't need to heal again. Of course, I've tried. In my practice, meager as it has been the past two years, I've had a good many opportunities to heal by the inconspicuous laying on of hands. With no results at all."

"It may be that you're a lucky man."

"I don't know. But since I haven't been able to heal, I've been compelled to look for one who can. I'm hoping to find that man in a hundred million who not only has the power to heal, but is able to exert some sort of control over his power. A man who has objectivity about his—his gift, who is in neither a state of fear nor religious mysticism because of it."

"I guess that rules out the man from Oklahoma," King said.

Matthews went on, with a twitch of a smile, "When I saw you tonight—a figure of valor, strong, unafraid—when I sensed you drawing on all of us for energy in your fight to save Mab's soul, I thought I'd found my man. Although you've taken pains to distinguish between the redemption of Mab Shaw and a possible healing of her, you were able to accept, as far as I could tell, my story about the healing of Hébert without a flicker of doubt."

"Well, no, I think I can tell a sincere man when I talk to one. You've had a lot to say that was a revelation to me, and you've said a lot about miracles which as a preacher of the pure gospel I can't agree with—but, Dr. Matthews, I'm sorry. There isn't anything I can do to help you, no light I can shed. I'm just not the man you mean for me to be." He spread his hands, helplessly.

Matthews looked sharply at the preacher for several long seconds, then he nodded as if he had been prepared for that answer. "I suppose I've been so impressed with the work I've seen you do, with the power which you bring to your preaching, that I wanted it to be extraordinary power, healing power. . . ."

For the second time since entering the apartment King felt uneasy, and this time for no good reason. He glanced at Hébert, leering in his sleep, and wondered if it wasn't often nerve-racking for Dr. Matthews to look up from his study and remember the dog lying nearly dead behind a truck. Although Matthews had been discreet about drinking in his presence, there were signs in the man's face that he drank a lot. The weight of the doctor's disappointment and isolation and the cell-like mood of the apartment, unenlivened by a woman's touch, was oppressive. King smile sympathetically but his restiveness was obvious. Dr. Matthews quickly apologized for keeping him so long after midnight.

"It was a pleasure for me," King said politely, "and I hope it won't be long before you find what you're looking for."

"Let me get the Huxley book for you," the doctor said, and he pressed it on King despite his protests.

"Any of the other books that I have—if you're at all interested . . ."

King was not interested, but he liked Dr. Matthews and understood his need for an ally; he felt badly about the sometimes haunted look he'd seen in the man's eyes. "I appreciate the offer. And I hope to see you again at meeting if you can spare us the time. Or drop by the tent, whenever you feel like it; usually that's where I'll be."

Hébert, awakened by the stir of their leaving and the opening of the door, grinned like an elderly con man and lay his head on the carpet again.

16

The Wrecked Tent

King drove the Continental back to the trailer park—called Wheel Estates—where he and Age were putting up, and turned the car over to Dr. Matthews.

The doctor agonized behind the wheel, peering at gauges and prying at levers as if he were about to take off for the moon, then punched down the window on his side for a last word.

"I had in mind talking to Mab Shaw if you could arrange it for me—find out where she's staying."

King paused on the trailer steps. He had thought Dr. Matthews' curiosity about Mab's dramatic redemption was exhausted, but he couldn't see any harm in the two getting together. "Mr. Handwerker will likely know where to reach her. I'll ask him this afternoon."

He watched as Matthews negotiated the drive of the trailer park at a cautious ten miles an hour, smiled slightly, and glanced at the moving sky. There was a wind, a fresh southerly wind, he judged, and the air felt warmer than it had for several nights. He decided against taking the truck the short distance to the fairgrounds; he was not overly tense, despite the excitement of Mab Shaw and the dilemma of Eli Charger, but he thought that a fast ride on his motor would likely clear his head enough so that later, in the early-light hours, the peaceful hours, he might doze stretched out flat on the pulpit with an oversize blanket wrapped around him.

They had not been happy about the motorcycle at the trailer park, which was well-managed and like an exclusive little suburb. Age had been somewhat more acceptable because of King's profession and because a precedent had already been set: an old gentleman already lived with his "man" in one of the park's most elaborate mobile homes.

He wheeled his motor to the highway before starting it. There was almost no traffic that time of night and he covered the distance to the fairgrounds in less than three minutes.

The best means of access to the ridge and the tent was through the fairgrounds, but there was another way, by an old dirt farm road drawn like a half-seen scar across the low yellow pasture and a couple of dry creek beds. King like to take this road whenever he was on his motorcycle; the grade was no real challenge for a scrambler, but he was still experimenting with sprockets. He was afraid the one which he had most recently installed had a little too much tooth for his gear ratio, and was killing his clutch.

The moon nudged through the clouds as he turned off the highway and the pasture lay open before him. He felt a bite of joy in his heart as he clutched and changed gears rapidly with his left hand, and his stomach was snatched at as the engine accelerated from twenty miles an hour to fifty within a few seconds. He had two hundred yards of bumpy but rockless straightaway ahead, and then a long plank bridge over a deep brush-choked gully. On the bridge he usually cut his speed by half before the upturn in the road.

The engine snarled flawlessly and the cross wind buffeted him. The pasture growth on either side whipped after him and tears squeezed from his eyes. He angled himself lower over the handlebars, anticipating jolts which the heavy shocks only partially absorbed. As the flat bridge appeared, its image distorted by the water hanging in his eyes, he glanced at the top of the ridge. What he saw, or couldn't see, caused him to clamp on his brakes, and the motorcycle came to a fishtailing stop in the middle of the bridge.

King blinked his eyes and looked again. Under the open sky the wind-billowed tent was dark, and the spotlight nestled in the wide-spreading oak tree also was out. Some sort of power failure, he thought, studying the shape of the tent in the yellow light. But they had just installed all new wiring with supervision from the Light, Gas, and Water Division. Then, it might be that—

The sky was on the move again, duskily lighted, dark-bodied like a swift spotted leopard, and the outline of the tent became indistinct. At the same time King heard the roar of a car motor.

He mounted his motorcycle again and went squealing across the plank bridge to the road.

The ride up was steeper and much rougher, and the engine labored. He was still over a hundred yards from the tent, slanting in toward it on what was left of the road, when he saw a red car backed up against the canvas. On that side, overlooking the backbone of the ridge and the small farmhouse, there were no trees. The car seemed familiar, but he had no time to puzzle over it. For the moon had burst clear of the clouds and in its lights he saw the car racing off, with a drumming of the dual exhausts that was audible above the thinner wasping sound his motorcycle was making. Behind the car the tent shook as if it had been hit by a fist of wind, and then came pancaking down.

King slowed only a notch as he flew across the last of the road and a hard curb of mud and came down with a painful wallop on the level crown of the ridge. The car was headed away, down the ridge, with the tent rising and falling behind it like a comber, snagging on every piece of rock, and on its own broken poles, leaving a scattering of chairs in its wake. He was still too shocked at having seen the tent go down to be angry; he hadn't realized that the driver of the car—a Buick or Oldsmobile—was purposely destroying the canvas. He bore down on the throttle, insanely intent on overtaking the car and stopping it somehow before the tent was dragged to tatters.

Suddenly the headlights of the car blazed; pinned in the glare was a running figure. King recognized Jeremy in her night-clothes and tromped the brake. The car barreled on. Jeremy faltered against the wall of headlights and froze, hands raised defensively. The car swerved and light fell away from her. For an instant she was dimly visible to King against the sky and beneath the moon; then the snaking black canvas rose up from the ground, seemed to swallow her whole, and went whipping on in a squall of dust.

King fought his motorcycle under control and veered off to follow the car. Dust had half-blinded him, and he saw nothing but the car, the dancing lance of his own headlight, and the flying canvas, now partly ballooned by the wind, as the car carried it down the ridge to the bottom land. He had looked hastily for Jeremy while wrestling with the motorcycle, but the dark and the dust had hidden her—or so he thought. Then the horrible conviction that she was caught up in the dragged canvas chilled him. Fearfully he increased his speed, intent on somehow cutting off the car before it was too late, before Jeremy was battered to death against the slope of the ridge.

King cut away at an angle to avoid the canvas, the occasional folding chair which it was disgorging, and the worst of the dust, and plunged downhill at forty miles an hour, an impossibly reckless speed by night. He could see nothing of the land except a huddled group of storm-wrenched trees to his left. By day he had explored this part of the ridge on his motor and he knew it was clean and relatively free of hazards. But in the dark even a stone could cause a fatal accident.

He also knew there was a dry creek bed, not deep enough to be called a gully, where the ridge bottomed out. The bed was loose dirt and sand, troublesome for even the nobbed scrambler tire on his motorcycle. It would probably stop the car altogether. But the driver seemed to sense an obstacle ahead; he slowed and bore left.

King had outdistanced the car by over fifty yards. He was ahead of and slightly below it on a diagonal, and when he saw, over his shoulder, the change of course, he looped and grimly aimed his motorcycle at the oncoming car, to force it into the creek bed below. He acted instinctively, his judgment blinded by anxiety.

The driver of the red car had only a few seconds in which to turn off, either uphill or down, and possibly he wasn't aware of the small bobbing headlight through the haze of dust on his windshield. The car was not going fast but it was wallowing, handicapped by the canvas anchor, and difficult to control. When the motorcycle leaped into view, blinding as a sunrise, the driver leaned in a paralyzed way on his horn and jammed on the brake.

The motorcycle flashed by the left fender, missing it by an inch, and plunged into a chair glutted furl of canvas. The car spurted forward and the motorcycle spun in a half circle. The back end flew high and King was thrown. By a split second he missed being thrown headfirst into the back of the car; instead he landed on his shoulders up the ridge, clear of the canvas and the motorcycle. His chin was tucked in as he landed and so he avoided a badly twisted or broken neck. But one of his knees doubled into the pit of his stomach, knocking him cold.

King lay for four or five minutes on his back on the open ridge until the dog named Cosh sniffed him out and Philemon arrived with his electric lantern. He came to half on his feet with Philemon hauling at his arm.

"Quit," the preacher said irritably, and sat down with a hand on his sore stomach. Each breath he took made him feel sick.

"You'd better hurry on up to the house."

King looked up. "Where—where'd he go?"

"Took off down toward the highway. Stopped there to undo the tent from his car. I let off a shot at him but it was too far. Who was it?"

King thought about the red car, and he could hear the sound of the horn again, blaring in the back of his mind. He remembered Cowboy Cobb, the smart-aleck drunkenness, his insolent use of the girl named Suzie.

So Cowboy had finally come back, on the one night King had been careless enough to leave the tent unwatched. Now the tent was lying, probably ruined, down by the highway. But the worst was—

"Jeremy!" he cried, and jumped up despite his dizziness.

"Up at the house," Philemon advised. "And you better prepare yourself." He shook his head in gloomy excitement. "Because it looks bad, it looks bad. She's lying there white as a stone and Eli said—"

King scrambled up the ridge toward the lighted house, sobbing for breath. Philemon followed with the lantern in one hand and his shotgun in the other, saying, "If you know who it was, tell me and we'll take after him right now! Cosh and me'll handle him. You want to see that poor girl lying there in her pain! It's awful!"

Jeremy was down on the porch with the Mexican spread over her, and in the unshielded glare of the clear bulb inside the door she looked frighteningly white and drawn. But when she saw King a smile edged on her face.

The smile turned to a look of worry as he kneeled beside her. "Oh, what happened to you?"

"Don't touch her," Philemon said. "For God's sake, don't touch her!"

Eli was standing inside the door. He said hoarsely, "Philemon, crank up your car and go for a doctor."

198

"I don't want to make a lot of trouble, now," Jeremy said weakly, but there was pain in her eyes. She studied King, and then her sound eye wandered a little more. "Are you ever skinned up!"

"Flung off my motor. Never mind. I'm doing just fine."

"Don't you try to move her!" Philemon wailed. "It may be her back's broke."

King glared at him.

Jeremy said, with as much scorn as she could muster, "If you didn't break my back hauling me up on the porch, then it can't *be* broke. Now, Philemon, do I have to do everything for myself?" She raised her head and looked at him sternly, but the effort brought tears to her eyes. "Go start up the car and bring it round. Eli? King? I've got a wrenched back and I've felt better in my life, but it's not too bad. See, the tent just caught me by surprise and knocked me flat." She winced, and King lay a comforting hand against her cold cheek. He glanced up, mutely, at Eli.

"Tent's a loss?"

"I'm afraid it is."

"I've preached ten thousand hours in that tent. Where were you at while it was getting wrecked?"

"Off feeding my face," King said through gritted teeth.

"I hope you got plans for getting a new tent somewhere," Eli said, "because you owe me a lot and I'm bound you're going to pay." He stared down at Jeremy for a few seconds, puzzled and fearful, then slowly closed the door and shuffled back to his bed.

17

Lawyers Talking Law

Eli Charger's lawyer was one of the breed that is becoming more rare in the South, but still well worth looking for. His name was Sam Manson and he was, first of all, an Oxford lawyer, which for some old-timers is a designation of great respect. In that part of the country, where the river winds and toils from the snow line to the sea, an Oxford lawyer was a graduate of the University of Mississippi law school, known for the excellence of its curriculum.

Cy Hillgrin had a few words to say about Manson before he and King went up to the lawyer's offices. They had parked on Adelaide Street, which ran unevenly along a bluff above the river and contained some of the oldest buildings in town, three- and four-story brick lofts and warehouses. In this collection of has-been buildings many of the world's most important cotton brokers conducted their businesses. October continued to run dry and warm but the cotton crop was a good one and the street was aswarm with businessmen. Bales of cotton and assorted "snakes" were stacked along the sidewalk and on loading docks; traffic moved fitfully because of the transport trucks.

"It's trite but true that nobody is ever what they seem to be," said Hillgrin, pausing to unwrap a long cigar, "and that goes triple for old Sam. He's past sixty but in the face at least he shows up about forty. His taste in dress runs to red shirts, suspenders, and string ties—you know. Every town has at least one like him. Quite a bit of his business just walks in off the street and he gets some of the damnedest cases you ever heard of that way. Anybody would feel at home in his office. What you don't see on your first visit to Sam are the sharp-eyed kids working down the hall, or the fantastic library he's collected. Some of the best legal talent in Clearwater started out with Sam. Lud Porterfield. Stewart Ambrose. Both the McHale brothers. All are outstanding trial lawyers. Sam molded them. He is also, as you know, a bear on contracts."

King was watching the muddy river glide by, and he only nodded. Cy Hillgrin got his cigar going and rolled down the window on his side a little more to wave the smoke out. The two men had met several times since Cowboy Cobb's arrest the previous week and they were well acquainted. Hillgrin was just past thirty, a tall, confident, almost jaunty man with a square-jawed handsomeness unmarred by goggle-like glasses.

He frowned at the lack of response which his oblique reference to King's agreement with Eli had got, and said, "Sam is going to do some probing about this situation with Eli when we get up there, and I'm going to need something more to say than I've already said."

King stirred and looked questioningly at the lawyer. "I thought he wanted to talk over the trial this afternoon."

Hillgrin smiled patiently. "Sam's not concerned about the outcome of the trial: it's cut and dried. If Jeremy'd had more than a bruised back we could have brought a separate suit for damages against Jim Cobb that would have been the talk of the town. But everybody is going to be satisfied, I hope. Jeremy's medical expenses will be paid, you and Eli will get a new tent, or rather a two-year-old tent that's almost like new and larger than the old one to boot, and undoubtedly Jim Cobb will get off with a fine."

King hunched his shoulders. He knew better. In fact, what he already knew about the fate of Cowboy Cobb would have astonished Hillgrin, if he'd cared to speak up. But King said only, "I hate to see it happen."

Hillgrin looked slightly startled. "You mean you'd rather see Cowboy go to jail? I thought you'd cooled down."

King shook his head. "That's not what I had in mind. Mrs. Cobb is a friend—or at least I count her as a friend. She's asked me over to her house and I've taken dinner with *her* friends. I was out of my class, but you couldn't tell it from the way those people accepted me. I've always dreamed about having a fine new tent to preach in. But I won't enjoy it at Mrs. Cobb's expense. I know the arrangements which the Cobb lawyers have worked out are required by law; still—"

"Believe me, the family is thrilled to be let off so easily. I think the State stood a chance to get Cowboy for attempted vehicular homicide, in addition to the indicated Malicious Mischief charge. And wouldn't that have made great headlines! The Cobbs have been generously dealt with, no matter what you think."

"What I'm thinking," King said in a troubled voice, "is that I'm obligated to Mrs. Cobb, and I'm still not sure what I can do—how I can help her. It worries me."

Hillgrin shrugged and sought to change the subject. "Maybe we'd better hash over what Sam is likely to spring on us when we see him."

"Cy? Have you asked yourself what in the name of peace Cowboy thought he was doing that night?"

"No, sir," Hillgrin said, puffing. "I haven't worried myself too much with Cowboy's predicament. Anyway, I don't know if I follow you. He went up to the ridge bent on destroying the tent, even if he had to walk all over you first. He admitted it freely enough. First he tried kerosene, but it was fire-resistant canvas and wouldn't do anything but smolder. Then he hit on the idea of knocking down the pulpit, cutting half the stays, attaching the tent to the bumper of his car with a couple of tire chains—",

"All I see is that he went to a pack of trouble to get caught. Why, that canvas was so old he could have ripped it with his hands. Instead he drove around the ridge in his red car, making enough noise to wake up everybody in the house."

"He came asking for trouble. Cowboy's not the brightest soul I ever met."

"He'll fool you that way. He *is* bright. Too bright to put himself in such a bad spot without a real good reason." King fell silent again, working at his jaw with his hand.

"You rubbed his nose in the dirt in front of his former girlfriend. To somebody like Cowboy, that's grounds for murder."

King grunted. "Assuming he cared a pot for the girl in the first place."

"I thought you'd be in a celebrating mood when I picked you up today. Maybe a look at the new tent later on will help." Hillgrin pointedly studied his watch. "The problems with Cowboy are about over, but there are other problems which aren't going to work themselves out."

The preacher nodded, glumly. "I reckon I'm going to have to give Eli some money whether I want to or not."

"Very true. Sam's accepted our plan for an accounting of offerings, but once you start to preach again and stall on paying Eli's share, he'll say, 'See you in court,' and that'll be it. The agreement is good; I can't challenge it. I'd say forget about a bad bargain and look to the future. The money that's been coming in as a result of you radio broadcasts is one very good reason for optimism. I think Sam has been a little slow to look into that source of income, which is a small advantage at the moment. Now, if you're set against making up with Eli—"

"I'm not mad at Eli—just can't stomach the work he's doing."

"That leaves two solutions to the whole embroglio. I'm going to stress the first one again. Pay Eli, and pay him generously. All the money that's in the savings account, plus another fifteen hundred. That's what I'll offer. If Sam is in a mellow mood he'll accept on the spot and the yoke will be off your neck."

Again King gazed at the river, and was a long time in replying. "What if he's not accepting?"

"Then we'll just have to see what it is he wants. Will you give me permission to offer fifteen hundred? Of course, you'll have a certain amount of time to come up with that money, if you're dead set against borrowing." King hesitated, and Hillgrin said persuasively, "I think it boils down to a choice of giving Eli what he wants now instead of making him a rich man later on. I'm assuming you'll continue to expand you ministry. Of course, you could drop the radio program and settle down in the new tent for the rest of your life. Make a little money for Eli, a little for yourself—enough to get by on. You might find peace of mind that way, but does it really suit you?"

"No more peace of mind in poverty than there is in ambition," King murmured. He stretched restlessly, but the muscles on the left side of his jaw knotted tightly. The cigar smoke, the heat of the sun on the roof of the car gave him a queasy feeling. "Eleven days without preaching and I feel like I'm in a straitjacket," he complained. "I know one thing, I'm tired of sitting, of being sat on. Let's go up there and see the lawyer. If he's in a compromising mood, then we'll compromise with him."

Sam Manson's office was as unimpressive as Hillgrin had promised, but King noticed immediately that it was immaculate. There was not a trace of grime on the worn, unvarnished floors, and the white plaster walls looked freshly washed down. Washing the walls was probably a good day's work, King reflected, because it was a big room, the size of an indoor tennis court. One of the walls was framed in piping of different sizes and three wood-bladed fans hung from the ceiling. These looked as if they hadn't turned in years, for Manson had allowed himself the luxury of a one-ton air conditioner.

Most of the furniture was crowded into one corner near the windows, which afforded a long view of the street, and a broad view of the river and the Arkansas shore glimmering with hot light and October color. Manson arose from an ancient swivel chair to greet them. He had a swollen body, tough, horny hands, a sweet smile, and liquid, amused eyes. His black hair was oddly cut, like a satyr's. As Hillgrin had said, the face was extraordinarily youthful.

"Well, Cy, I'm glad to see you brought him," Manson said,

giving King's hand a hard, solitary pump. He settled back in his chair. "Nice to meet you, Mr. Windom. I was intending to drop by and hear you preach before that Cobb boy ran off with the tent." He turned to Hillgrin. "What time are they getting under way at the courthouse? Two-thirty?"

"Yeh. And should be all over by two-forty."

Manson looked again at King, in a friendly, appraising way. "I'm sorry we're not going to have as much time to talk as I would have liked; some little emergency I've got to shoot out east to see about. But we do have time for a cup of coffee if you boys are agreeable."

"Sure thing, Sam," Hillgrin said easily. He was enjoying himself, stimulated by the prospect of locking horns with a lawyer whom he admired and respected. King had expected to feel both reticent and foolish in the presence of Eli's lawyer, who had played a large part in forging the agreement which now had him shackled. He had even come with a preconceived dislike which Sam Manson had dispelled with his openness, the sense of pleasure communicated by his handshake. King realized that Manson had only done for Eli what he would do for any other client—drawn the best agreement possible according to Eli's aims and desires.

After ringing his secretary and ordering coffee for the three of them, Manson settled back with a reflective smile and said to King, "Have you seen the new tent?"

"No, it was due in by truck around noon; church group in Missouri had the rental of it this past month. The tent-and-awning company said their men would get to work setting up late this afternoon, so we're going to try to hold a revival tonight. I retaped this afternoon's radio program so people will know what we've been up to and where they can find us now."

"Planning to add more seats?"

"I'm told we'll have the space—for almost a thousand worshipers instead of the five or six hundred that've been coming. But I don't know right now."

"Have you talked it over with the Reverend Mr. Charger?"

"Eli and I have gone our separate ways lately," King said.

"That's one reason I'm glad to have you here today. I'm not sure I understand the nature of the dispute between you and the Reverend." He smiled again, sympathetically. "I'm sorry to admit I'm a church-once-a-year man myself. I've read and loved my Bible, but I don't understand all the interpretations which can cause a falling-out among scholars and preachers."

"Eli and I didn't fall out over fine points, Mr. Manson. Not unless you call rewriting the entire Bible to suit the schemes of a false prophet like that Crenshaw man a fine point. You know about Professor Crenshaw?"

"Mr. Charger's told me about him, and his colony."

"Well, he's got Eli thoroughly mixed up with his prophecies. While I believe Eli is still loyal to the fundamental teachings of the Bible, what he's doing to some of the Old Testament books amounts to nothing short of desecration. That's one way to put it; I could use stronger language. Eventually Eli *has* to get straightened out in his thinking, and then he'll renounce that false bible he's scribbling, but it won't happen so long as he's getting flattery and philosophy in every mail from the antichrist Crenshaw." King squeezed the arms of his chair until the leaders in the backs of his hands stood out like polished marble. "I believe, I pray, that once Eli stops sending him money, Professor Crenshaw will let up and leave Eli alone long enough for him to get his bearings. . . ." He glanced helplessly at Cy Hillgrin.

"I'm not going to judge whether your argument is justified, because it's a personal thing, it's one set of beliefs opposed to another," said Manson. "How much do you actually know about the Crenshaws?"

"What I've gathered from Eli," King said shortly.

Sam Manson reached out, picked up a pair of glasses from the nearest desk with one hand and a stapled report with the other. He propped the glasses on his nose and scanned the brief paragraphs with an up-and-down jerking of his head. "For Mr. Charger's protection and for my information, I did some asking about the Crenshaws. You might be interested. They're a handful—only a hundred twenty members up there on the mountainside at last count—but they seem to be sober, dedicated people, better educated than the average. No fugitives from justice, ex-Communists, or tax-dodgers. They work hard and live simple. Their religion is peculiar, but they make up a legitimate sect of a reputable church—Christ's Tomorrow Pioneers—and they're properly registered with Internal Revenue."

He tossed the report down and dropped his glasses in his lap. "Whatever Mr. Charger's reasons for contributing to the support of this group, he has every right to do so. And, to get down to hard facts, he has every right to expect you to pay him moneys due by agreement and by contract, whether or not you approve of the uses to which that money is put."

Cy Hillgrin spoke up. "Mr. Windom understands that, Sam."

"And he also understands, of course—because I know you've explained it carefully to him—that he owes the Reverend Mr. Charger six thousand dollars according to the terms of the agreement which he signed, and putting that money in a joint savings account amounts to nothing more than default."

Hillgrin smiled. "We could get very technical over that interpretation, Sam."

"We could," Manson said casually, "but in court, not here in my office."

King looked blankly at the floor but his heart had jumped, because Manson's charge that he had already violated the agreement with Eli was news to him.

The swivel chair squeaked. Manson was smiling at him again, and he raised his eyes to meet the man's gaze. "Don't get worried because lawyers are talking law," Manson said, and chuckled. "And don't be worried because I may have made it sound like you've done something wrong—you haven't, you haven't. At least, you haven't done anything you can't straighten out in a hurry, to fulfill honest obligations."

"You're breathing a little heavy there, Sam," Hillgrin said, but the old lawyer ignored him. Manson wheeled over to his other desk, a big rolltop set against the wall, and picked up one of the green-covered passbooks from the savings bank in which King had deposited his six thousand dollars. This he dropped after a moment's reflection, felt around on the cluttered desk, and came up with a withdrawal slip already filled out and signed—by Eli.

"Do you happen to have your passbook with you?" Manson asked King.

"No."

The lawyer rolled backward in his chair and with a slight wheeze handed King the passbook. "You can sign this for me now, and then when you get home tonight, if you'll drop your own book in the mail I'll see to it that the account is closed out tomorrow. That will take care of your preliminary obligations to Mr. Charger. It won't, of course, do much in the way of resolving your differences, and I sincerely wish I could do something about that."

King sat holding the deposit slip with a taut look of rebellion. He said, "Not likely anything can be done. At least not right away."

Hillgrin said, from behind a high curtain of cigar smoke, "King and I have done a lot of talking about the situation, Sam, and—as you say—it's a little hard for laymen to understand. But there's one thing we all understand: that partnership agreement is a farce. Agreement! It's an indenture. Sam, you must have had in mind some of the old shares contracts the plantation owners down in the Delta used to draw up for their niggers sixty, seventy years ago. Oh, in sum it's valid, it's as solid as a pair of handcuffs; I wouldn't waste my breath attacking it. But"—he leaned forward to reach a green glass ashtray on the near desk—"I wouldn't waste King's time by advising him to persist in this partnership, either."

Manson shifted his eyes to King for a moment, then settled back in the chair with a hand on his high stomach. "All those statements you've been making stand a foot or two away from the truth, and I hope they aren't typical of the counsel you've been giving Mr. Windom. This man"—he nodded in King's direction—"was an evangelist who needed a place to preach, a truck to move around in when the time came, and certain intangibles, like the help and advice of an older man, an established preacher with unquestioned prestige. I assume those were the needs that brought him to the Reverend Mr. Charger in the first place. He had a limited amount of money to spend, and Mr. Charger badly needed money. They struck a bargain—on their own, without interference or counsel from lawyers—and as far as I can see, Mr. Charger has lived up faithfully to the spirit of that agreement." Manson's crusty brows moved ominously down toward his eyes as he looked at King, but he refrained from saying the obvious. "Now, if Mr. Windom is unhappy with the agreement, he has every right to take steps toward dissolving it. Is there a word in the agreement that says he can't? If so, I'd welcome your showing me; I'm not too old to learn."

Hillgrin smiled rather bleakly. "Sam, let's don't get bogged down. The agreement specifically states that the dissolution of the partnership depends solely on the graciousness and good will of Eli Charger. Mr. Charger badly needs money, all right.

At his age, and in his condition, it isn't likely he's going to do much more preaching. King wants out, for all the reasons we've discussed. He's willing to sign that deposit slip there and make arrangements for a further, generous settlement in order to get out."

Before Manson could speak, they were interrupted by his secretary, who came in with a pot of coffee and some cups. Instead of being annoyed by the interruption at such a point, Manson smiled and changed the subject. While they had their coffee the talk meandered briefly from duck-hunting to Ole Miss football to local politics. King, being interested in none of these subjects, burned the tip of his tongue and the roof of his mouth with the hot coffee and shifted restlessly about in his chair, wondering what the outcome of this meeting would be. He was wary once more of Sam Manson, who could be so friendly with one breath and so chilling the next. He skipped back over the conversation they'd had, trying to decide how Manson really felt about Eli. Was he just another client, or was Manson actually fond of him? And, if he was fond of Eli and sympathetic to his plight, would he be inclined to let King out of the agreement for seventy-five hundred dollars? It sounded like a lot of money, but to a nearly invalided man burning with the fevers of a Cause, was it so much after all? He wondered if Manson had any means of knowing the amount of money that had been pouring into the post-office box which Molly had rented. Thinking about the accumulation of unsolicited gifts gave him a lumpy throat and he put his coffee cup down just as Manson glanced at the clock on the wall and shifted back to business.

"What sort of settlement were you considering, Mr. Windom?"

"More than he can afford, and I tried to talk him out of it," Hillgrin put in. "He'll have to borrow heavily on his personal possessions to make it."

Manson's lips pressed flat against his teeth as if he had resisted snapping at the younger lawyer, and he waited for King to reply.

"Fifteen hundred," King said, and felt unexpectedly guilty for saying it.

"Well." Manson sighed, but he seemed neither surprised nor pleased. "I'll certainly pass that on to Mr. Charger."

"Come on, Sam," Hillgrin said in exasperation.

Manson gave him a fatherly scowl. "But I sure won't recommend that he accept. I suppose it all depends on how badly he needs money. With that much cash and the tent, which he could lease to other preachers—"

Hillgrin came to his feet. "What's going on here?" he said, and his face reddened slightly as he forced a smile. "That's seventy-five hundred *for the property*. Cash for the whole works. King retains possession, not Eli."

"Then I won't even bother to tell him about the offer, because it doesn't make sense. You know as well as I do how much the new tent is worth. If you're serious about a settlement, why don't you talk seriously?"

"What sort of settlement are you thinking about?" King asked.

"Oh . . ." Manson found a button loose on his shirt, fastidiously plucked it and dropped it into his pocket. "I'd say ten thousand dollars. That's in addition to the six you're holding in the savings bank, of course."

"Good God Almighty," Hillgrin said, and King winced. "And I thought you were a practical man!" To this Manson gestured noncommittally. For a few moments Hillgrin seemed to lose his presence of mind entirely, or perhaps his indignation was mostly for show. He reached under his chair for his hat, sat down in the chair with hat in hand, then rose once more, decisively.

"Come on," he said to King. "Sam has things to do. He's got a bubble pipe under that desk, and he just sits up here by the hour, spinning and weaving."

Manson cracked a grin. "Remember me to Judge Ingram, Counselor."

King stood uncertainly, and Hillgrin, with a hand on his elbow, guided him smoothly toward the door. Halfway there, the lawyer suddenly turned and went back to the corner where Manson sat peacefully, watching them.

"It took me a while to talk Mr. Windom into a conciliatory frame of mind, Sam, and I doubt if I'll be able to do it again."

"Well," Manson grunted, indifferently.

"You questioned the quality of the advice I've been giving him, but I'll tell you for fair I'm going to go right on advising him not to persist in this loaded agreement with Eli."

"Then he'll have to find another tent to do his preaching in."

"He will, Sam, he will, and not for Eli's benefit, either."

209

"You may be out on thin ice there."

"I don't think so. I've been drawing up incorporation papers for Mr. Windom, and I expect to file in a few days."

Manson rose laboriously from his chair and took down coat and hat from a tree wedged between file cabinets. "If you boys aren't in such a tearing hurry to get away after all, I'll walk down with you," he said.

On the way down the stairs to the street, Manson broke his silence. "I don't think you're being fair to your client, advising him to file for incorporation now, while the agreement with the Reverend Mr. Charger is in effect."

"Why?" asked King.

"Because the sole purpose, as I interpret it—as a judge would interpret it—is to illegally break the partnership agreement. I think you'd better stick to dissolution by mutual consent—that is, by an appropriate cash settlement on Mr. Windom's part. It'll save everybody trouble in the long run."

They emerged into the sunlight and Manson adjusted the brim of his old dull-brown felt hat to shield his eyes. He shook hands firmly with both men and said to King, "Good-bye now, Reverend. I'm counting on hearing you preach some night. My car is down this way, boys." And he strode off at a good pace despite the size of his stomach.

King followed Hillgrin dispiritedly back to the lawyer's car.

"Discouraged?" Hillgrin asked, lighting up another cigar.

"Maybe I'd better go back to Florida."

"Sam hopes you'll do something like that. All the talk he was giving out on the way down was to loosen you up, start you worrying. The easiest job he faces is getting the six thousand for Eli. We'll stall as long as we can on that, then back down at the last minute. I would have told you about the savings account sooner, but I thought you had enough on your mind. In the meantime, while Sam is threatening, I'm sure the incorporation will be accomplished. At which time you'll just walk away from the tent and leave it standing. If Eli tries putting another evangelist—even cousin Philemon—into it without your consent we'll get an injunction and close it permanently." He caught King's glance. "Oh, yes, we can do that. And then Sam will take us to court to test the legality of the incorporation."

"What'll happen then?"

"He'll lose," Hillgrin said with a confident air.

18

Cowboy's Day in Court

The General Sessions court judge who was trying Jim Cobb was late in getting to his courtroom—a heavy docket had delayed his lunch, explained the judge's clerk—and so those assembled were obliged to wait more than fifteen minutes in the dry, sunlit room on the third floor of the courthouse.

Cy Hillgrin was not a man to be denied a chance to talk, even when he had heavy going against a collective silence. He held up most of a conversation with the Cobbs' attorney, a swarthy man named Sherlag who had a black mustache that gave him a violent, revolutionary appearance. The courtroom was quite small, with room for only about twenty spectators. Hillgrin and the preacher were on one side, seated behind the State's attorney. Opposite King sat Mrs. Cobb, who wore a plain dark-blue suit with a light-blue turban. She had greeted King with a restrained smile; thereafter she sat sealed off from everyone, motionless, a faint streak of annoyance or resignation across the lucent pink-and-brown skin of her forehead. To her right was her brother, a pale, big-chested man in English-cut sports clothes. He was clearly there only for the sake of Mrs. Cobb; during the quarter-hour wait he never gave the Cowboy so much as a glance.

King would have liked to talk to Mrs. Cobb, to be reassuring in some way, but the situation had him throttled. He slouched on the slippery bench and faced the left-hand windows; there was nothing to see but a blaze of light through the level blinds and presently he began to feel headachy. He shifted his eyes from the windows and studied the judge's clerk, who was earnestly scanning a string of papers from his briefcase. Then, reluctantly, he glanced at Cowboy, whose hair was a golden red in the light.

Cowboy seemed unaffected by the delay. His hands were loosely joined on the table behind which he was sitting and he chewed gum unobtrusively. His Western-style gray suit looked new and with it he wore an ordinary white shirt and a red tie.

Altogether there were nine in the room, but King had sensed another presence on walking in: out of habit he had said a short silent prayer, and then he had met Cowboy's eyes to confirm what he already knew. Satan was there, contemptuous and aggressive, renewing his challenge to the preacher, his bid for an all-out fight. And King had shrunk inside, and slipped with lowered eyes into his seat.

Again he raised his hand and touched the small New Testament in his shirt pocket. The closeness of the Word calmed him. What good would it do to ignore Satan, in the disguise of Cowboy Cobb, now? He had decided on a course, perhaps too hastily—but that course could not be changed.

Doubt returned almost immediately. What if I fail this trial? he thought, chilled to his bones. He recalled Dr. John Matthews, and the man's praise of him for his triumph over the devil of drink that had been dragging poor Mab Shaw to her grave. Yes, he admitted to himself, feeling the grit of exultation in his heart, I licked the devil of drink, with the help of Jesus, with the prayers of a desperate family to back me up. But I'm no figure of valor, that's for sure.

Jim Cobb turned his head in time to catch the preacher smiling at this extravagance. The Cowboy was incurious, but King thought he saw a change in those eyes, a level questioning.

King lowered his head and tightened his shoulders. The devil knew what was up. There was only one sensible way to handle the problem of Cowboy, and the evil that was rooted in him. "Lord be with me," King breathed. He stared at the discolored scars on his palms, shutting out Cy Hillgrin's monologue and everything else in the courtroom. Gradually he felt steadier, he felt better than he had in several days, and he was encouraged to believe that the Lord was indeed taking an active interest in the Cowboy's future.

The court clerk announced the arrival of Judge Aubrey Ingram; they rose, were seated at the nod of the judge, and waited with varying attitudes of expectancy while the clerk had his say. There was no jury; since the facts and evidence of the case were not in dispute, the defense had moved for a trial by Court.

Judge Ingram was an obviously frail man despite the concealing robe. He had about as much hair as a carrot, the nose of a lifelong carouser, and astute black eyes suggesting that if he did drink, hard liquor had never dulled for a moment an exceptional intelligence. He took plenty of time before speaking and looked in turn at each face before him. His eyes lingered on King for a few extra moments; then he experimentally thumbed the stapled sheets of onionskin paper which he'd brought from his chambers.

The proceedings went as rapidly as Hillgrin had predicted. In finding Cowboy guilty as charged, the judge was brief and dry. Sherlag had been forced a time or two to suppress a yawn. Cowboy was composed, alert, and bland as he stood before the judge. But King's hands were sweating and he leaned forward, elbows on the railing in front of him.

"Before passing sentence," the judge said, frowning at his papers, "I would like to remind Counsel that, according to Section 40-2901 of the State Code Annotated, whenever any person has been found guilty of a crime upon a verdict or a plea of guilty, all trial judges in the state having criminal jurisdiction are authorized and empowered to suspend the execution of sentence and place the defendant or defendants on probation—subject to such conditions as the trial judge may deem fit and proper." He looked at both attorneys, who nodded. Then he heaved a sigh and focused on Cowboy; the look was not exactly friendly. Cowboy's own expression was inoffensively pleasant.

"You're twenty-seven, is that right?"

"Yes, sir," said Cowboy.

"Do you work?"

Cowboy looked puzzled.

"Do you have a job?"

"I've got a band."

"I beg your pardon."

Cowboy look slightly irritated. "I've got a band," he said more loudly. "We play a few clubs around town."

"That's not regular employment, is it?"

"We make our bucks."

"But you're not regularly employed."

Cowboy looked to his lawyer for help, and Sherlag shook his head gently.

"No," Cowboy said. "But I belong to the union."

"Have you ever held a steady job?" the judge persisted.

"Your Honor?" Sherlag said, tentatively.

"Not now, Mr. Sherlag." He gazed again at Cowboy, who shrugged and said,

"I'm a musician."

"How many times have you been arrested?"

Again Cowboy turned his head; it was not going the way he had been told it would go. Sherlag raised an eyebrow, indicating that he was to answer all questions civilly and otherwise keep his mouth shut.

"Uh, three times," Cowboy said.

Judge Ingram nodded. "You've been in and out of trouble with the police for the last ten years. You have been arrested for assault, contributing to the delinquency of a minor, and"—the judge stimulated his memory with a glance at the record in front of him—"at one time you had a collection of thirty-seven unanswered summonses for traffic violations. Now you've been convicted for destruction of property. You don't have a very well-developed sense of responsibility, do you, Mr. Cobb?"

"I guess not," Cowboy said.

The judge stared at him until he dropped his eyes slightly. "It's possible that ninety days at the Penal Farm—which is the maximum sentence I can impose in this instance—might serve to revive your neglected sense of responsibility." King saw Cowboy's fingers curl at his sides. Even his lawyer looked a little unhappy, if unruffled.

"It's possible," the judge continued, "but I doubt it. I sincerely doubt that such a sentence would teach you anything. So, although it is my decision that you be sentenced the maximum for your crime of malicious mischief in wantonly destroying the property of another, I am suspending the execution of this sentence by placing you on probation—subject to such conditions as I may choose to name. Counsel will approach the bench."

The two attorneys stepped forward. "As required by law," said Judge Ingram, "I have requested and received a written report of investigation by the probation officer of this county. I'm satisfied by the report on the defendant, James Raymond Cobb, and I don't intend to ask for a mental examination of the defendant. As you know, Mr. Sherlag, all persons released on probation shall be subject to the direct supervision of the county parole officer, and the probationer must report as directed to his officer until such time as he is released from supervision. I trust, Counselor, that you will explain the usual conditions of probation to your client."

"I will, Your Honor."

Cowboy looked relaxed and a little lazy. The judge fixed his eye on him and said, "In the event of violation of any of these terms, or in event you are found guilty of violating the laws of this state, I will issue a warrant for your arrest, revoke the probation, and see to it that you serve out the sentence imposed in my original judgment. Do you understand?"

"Yes, sir."

The judge settled back in his chair. "And now I'd like to acquaint you with my own conditions for your probation." He looked at King, for the second time since coming into the courtroom. Somewhere outside, chimes marked the hour of three. Stripes of sun were falling across the judge's face, and his clerk rose to adjust the blinds.

"From all that I know about you, Mr. Cobb, lack of responsibility is only one cloudy facet of your personality. You have also shown a consistent disregard for the feelings and rights of others. I think I can accurately state that you care for nothing and no one. Would you like to contradict me?"

"No," Cowboy said, complacently.

"There are people who care about you, however, and these people have made every effort to help you find your purpose in life. You come from a good, I might say excellent, and respected family. You have been given numerous opportunities to improve yourself, intellectually and in business, opportunities that other young men would be thankful for—and you have made nothing of your opportunities. Your life thus far has been characterized by indolence, ingratitude, degeneracy, violence, and simple cruelty. There's not a single thing in your record that prompts me to believe you will benefit from this appearance in my court. I do not expect you to express regret for your offense, although I trust its seriousness is as obvious to you as it is to the Court. Quite possibly at least one person could have been killed or permanently injured as a result of your act."

"Your Honor, don't you think—"

"Don't interrupt me, Mr. Sherlag," the judge said. King looked at Mrs. Cobb; she was erect and intent on her grandson, but she seemed to have stopped breathing. His heart ached for her.

Still addressing Cowboy, Judge Ingram continued, "In granting probation in this case it was not my intention to be lenient. I do not intend for you to walk out of this courtroom and resume your former irresponsible life. Fortunately there is one person outside of your immediate family who has taken an interest in you, a person of religious conviction and high moral character. We have thoroughly discussed your situation. He has offered you regular employment at a fair wage, and something which has been entirely lacking in your life: spiritual guidance. Therefore these are the Court's conditions for your probation, Mr. Cobb. Since you have no regular job and no immediate prospects of acquiring one, you are directed to accept the offer of employment which the Reverend Mr. Windom has generously made, and you will remain in his employ for the ninety days of your probation. When not at work, you will be restricted to your residence. You may not be on the streets of this city past eleven P.M. unless you are accompanied by either Mr. Windom or a parole officer."

"Now, Your Honor!" Sherlag cried.

Cowboy's eyes had raked over King's face; he turned quickly to his lawyer. "Can he do that?"

"I have done it, Mr. Cobb. Your period of probation will begin immediately upon the close of this trial. All right, Mr. Sherlag. Let's hear it. And don't take all afternoon."

Sherlag had an incredulous smile on his face. "May I point out to the Court that there is bad blood between these two men?"

"Forget it," Cowboy said in a sulk. "I ain't working for him, forget it."

"That'll do," Judge Ingram said, and his tone was such that Cowboy clammed up and dug at the floor with a tapered boot heel. "I've already satisfied myself that Mr. Windom bears no grudge in this matter; further, I feel that his motives are beyond reproach. He is a duly ordained minister of a recognized church group, idealistic as well as practical, and eminently suited for the serious responsibility he has chosen to assume. I believe you'd do well to reconsider any further objections, Counselor."

With Cowboy eyeing him angrily, Sherlag fetched a heavy breath and said nothing.

"What about my band? What about—"

"Mr. Sherlag, you may wish to have a few minutes with your client immediately following to impress upon him that I mean business. This court is adjourned. Mr. Windom, would you mind waiting for a few minutes after the others have gone?"

Cowboy was ready to have it out with the judge, but Sherlag was too quick for him. With his lawyer on one side of him and Mrs. Cobb on the other, Cowboy left the courtroom, talking in a low, heated voice. His great-uncle trailed woefully after the group. At the door Cowboy looked back and his eyes settled on King, ominously. Then they all went out.

Ingram's clerk beckoned and King joined him in the judge's chambers. The judge had produced a bottle from his desk and was measuring a milky dose of medicine into a half glass of water. "Terrible weather for sinus," he said, sniffling. "Sinus capital of the U.S., here in Clearwater. Mr. Windom, you looked unmercifully cramped on that courtroom bench. Why don't you stretch yourself?"

"Thank you," King said, gratefully; his spine cracked audibly. Judge Ingram looked up at him with a fond smile as he drained the water glass.

"I'm taking quite a chance on you, and I hope you realize it."

"Yes, sir, I do," King said earnestly. "I could have kicked myself after I went home from your house the other night. Left out half of what I meant to say. I thought when you came in today you'd decided trusting Cowboy to me wasn't worth the risk."

"Make no mistake, I had second thoughts. That's a very hostile young man. The success of his probation depends on your ability to handle him. Disregarding the fact that Jim Cobb is a member of one of the city's finest families—his grandmother and I are old friends, by the way, so I suppose I should have excused myself—I would have hated sending him to jail. He'd only get into worse trouble there. If you have any difficulty with Jim, any at all, I want you to get in touch with me immediately. Day or night. You know how to reach me. Frankly, I don't believe you'll have too much influence with him. What, exactly, do you have in mind?"

"I'm just looking forward to having his company for a while," King said evasively. "I'm not planning to lecture him or tell him Bible stories or anything like that—Lord knows which one of us would be bored the most."

"No, I didn't think you had Bible stories in mind," the judge said, and stared curiously at the preacher for a few moments. Then he smiled a hopeful smile. "Just be cautious with him; don't be afraid to holler for help." He put out his hand. "And good luck to you, Mr. Windom."

19

A Visit to Jeremy

Cy Hillgrin was waiting for King outside the courtroom.

"Sherlag and I had a talk with Cowboy," he said.

"What mood is he in?"

"I think we made him realize he's fortunate not to be waiting on the bus to the penal farm right now. Beyond that I can't say how he feels. Sore at you, for one thing." The lawyer shook his head in exasperation. "Boy, why didn't you tell me? You could have knocked me over with a daisy when Aubrey named his conditions for probation. Incidentally, it's rare for him to make such a decision. He must have taken a powerful liking to you."

"Well, I believe Judge Ingram and myself understand each other, and I'm sorry I didn't consult you before I saw him. It was spur-of-the-moment; I didn't stop to think I might be making a fool of myself by calling on the judge. Lucky things worked out." King looked around the marbled corridor. "What happens now? Where did the Cobbs get to?"

"They took the elevator down; we'll meet them outside. I wanted to see you alone before you tackle the Cowboy singlehanded."

"Oh, he'll behave himself, Cy. Anything special you want me to know?"

"I suppose Aubrey urged you to be wise and restrained."

"In so many words."

Hillgrin shrugged. "That's about it, then. From what Molly's told me about Cowboy, I know he's totally unpredictable. When he stops sulking, it may be time to watch the back of your head. I'm doubtful the threat of jail fazed him at all. And he *is* on the books for aggravated assault."

King remembered Molly's warnings, but he shook off the feeling of gloom that lagged after this memory. "Cowboy and me'll hit on an understanding. Let's get going. I want to stop by the hospital to see Jeremy; haven't looked in on her since yesterday morning. But with that free television to gawk at, it's a cinch she hasn't missed company."

They rode down in the elevator with several earnest-looking young men who might have been law clerks, and a sad creature handcuffed to a detective. The Cobbs and their lawyer were waiting outside the courthouse. Cowboy stood apart, smoking and looking off at a building under construction. He didn't turn his head when King approached.

Mrs. Cobb extended her hand to the preacher and her eyes had a maternal warmth in them he hadn't seen before. He was pleased by the firm grip of her hand. "I'm glad it's over," she said. "And I hope you'll come to see me often, whether or not you're with Jim."

King thanked the old lady, tripping over his tongue for one of the few times in his life. Her brother jangled keys nervously in his hand and studied his watch. There was a brief uncomfortable silence, then Hillgrin said to King:

"I'm due in small claims court at four, so we'd better run."

"Cy, I hate to take you out of your way; it's three now. I'll just catch me a bus."

"We'll be glad to drive you wherever you want to go," Cowboy's great-uncle said unenthusiastically.

"Thanks, but I don't—"

Jim Cobb turned, squinted at King, and dropped his cigarette butt on the courthouse steps. "My car's down the street," he said, then looked again at the sky, patiently.

Mrs. Cobb glanced at her grandson, and at Cy Hillgrin. The lawyer smiled encouragingly.

"All right, Jim, why don't you go with Dr. Windom? Will you be home for dinner?"

"I don't know," Cowboy said. His face was a mottled red from the impact of the sun, and sweat had broken out on his forehead, but his eyes looked cool and shaded. "Depends on what time the chief here lets me go. Well . . ." He turned on his heel and ambled off down the courthouse steps, hands in the pockets of his ranch-cut trousers. He seemed self-possessed, uncrowded, uncaring.

King said his good-byes and caught up, falling in beside the Cowboy. After a block and a half of silence, Cowboy paused to light another cigarette. He offered the pack to King, then tucked it away. "Old Aubrey was ready to give me my lumps," he mused. "Good thing you wheeled and dealed."

"I thought you deserved better than pulling time."

There was a wry look on Cowboy's heavy face, but he only nodded. "Car's opposite. How are you planning to use me, Chief?"

King looked into Cowboy's eyes, which were half-hidden by the sun. His gaze was steady, but disguised. The preacher answered, "Until meeting time tonight there'll be plenty of work setting up chairs, stringing lights, and so on. During meeting you can take up the collection. If folks clutter up the aisle or want to climb up on the pulpit to witness without being asked, it'll be your job to show them back to their seats. That's important, because the devil is competition enough while I'm preaching." He wondered if he was addressing Satan at that moment, but here was not a sign of duplicity in the Cowboy's face. "If you run errands for us in your car, Molly'll fix you up with expense money. That's about all I can think of offhand."

"I can count on putting in, say, six hours a day."

"More like seven—weekdays from five to eleven-thirty. And Sunday afternoons. Dollar fifty an hour OK?"

Cowboy nodded. "Since you and the judge are so close, maybe you can fix it up so he'll let me practice with my band and do the Kay-tip show Saturday mornings."

"I'll try my best, Cowboy."

Jim Cobb stretched himself, and his powerful chest swelled. "I was going to say it beats jail," he said, "but we'll have to see about that." He wasn't trying to be funny. He turned abruptly and crossed the street, ignoring the traffic and an angry horn. Watching him, the preacher thought, with a measure of admiration, He makes a lot of room for himself. There was an air of importance about the Cowboy, and he wasn't all bluff. Some men would follow him no matter what. And now King knew why Mrs. Cobb was so anxious for him to believe in her grandson—in the goodness he still couldn't see.

What trouble was the devil planning for Cowboy? It could be that nothing at all would happen, that Cowboy would keep the peace and walk through the ninety days of his custody, amiable and unrepentant. King felt a sense of shame as he caught himself hoping that would be the case. But at least Cowboy had made an effort to outline their relationship. He'd dropped his mock-hillbilly manner, and done some talking. There would be other chances for them to talk—there was always a possibility he could catch the devil napping. King found himself tensing up, and decided not to worry unnecessarily about the Cowboy's plight. He vowed then to stay on his guard against all the evils which the devil could contrive; but he would not try to anticipate them.

Once they were in the Buick, King asked Cowboy to stop by Trinity Hospital.

"How's the girl doing?"

"Still stuck in bed, but the doctor figures she'll be on her feet tomorrow and out by Thursday."

"She's your girl, isn't she?"

"No, I wouldn't say so."

"You know, I never saw her that night. Real lucky I turned off when I did; I'd've run right over her."

"I thought the canvas had got Jeremy, and she was being dragged. Reason I was in such a hurry to cut you off."

Cowboy said, "What would you have done if you'd stopped me?"

"I don't know. If Jeremy *had've* been in that canvas, I probably would've killed you."

"Bare-handed?"

"Wouldn't have needed but bare hands."

"Do any damage with your fists before?"

"Cracked a couple of noses when I was a boy. I'm not the world's greatest fighter."

"I almost killed a man one time in a fight—you probably heard about it."

"What was the fight about, Cowboy?"

"Nothing. I didn't even know him. We were both half-drunk.

221

I had him down and I was just kicking him to death, regular as pumping water. I had a feeling in the back of my head like a hot wire loose."

"Are you sorry for it now?"

"No. I never have been sorry for anything."

"I don't believe that, though." King gripped his knees with his hands. "What you mean is, you've learned not to be sorry, and you can't unlearn."

Cowboy looked amused again, but there was a drab line across his forehead. "Maybe these ninety days won't go as fast as I thought," he said, half to himself, then jammed on the accelerator and beat a city bus through a narrow slot in stalled traffic.

At the hospital he parked at the edge of a cab stand and King got out, feeling mussed and tilted from Cowboy's slam-bang style of driving. He paused in the hotel pharmacy to buy a tin of mixed nuts and they went upstairs to the private room Mrs. Cobb was paying for.

Jeremy's room was bulging with flowers, or so it seemed at first glance; two dozen orange chrysanthemums took up most of the space on the dresser, and their brilliance was reflected in the east-facing window. Jeremy was dozing in an upright position, well buttressed by pillows. The television was loud and weepy.

King tapped on the door. Cowboy hung back, his hands in his pockets. "Company," King said. "What are you up to?"

"Just generally loafing," Jeremy said with a sleepy mouth, then reached for a hairbrush. When she saw Cowboy she blushed, not knowing him, and made sure the bedsheet was tucked up around her chin.

"Don't you ever turn this thing off?" King said, and wheeled the television out of his way.

"King! Look!" As if he hadn't noticed, she pointed at the chrysanthemums with her hairbrush and then went furiously about putting herself in order, throwing glances at Cowboy, who was still partly hidden behind the door. "Mrs. Cobb sent them this morning. I never have seen flowers like that in my life! Pick me one; I just want a flower to hold. . . . Who's that with you?"

"Cowboy," King replied, and selected a blossom for her.

Jeremy's face fell grimly. "Hmm," she said. "Well, tell him to come on in."

King introduced them.

"You can thank your mother for me when you see her, and be sure and tell her I'm coming around myself to say thanks when I'm let out of here."

"It's his grandmother, Jeremy."

"That's right, it is. Go on and find a seat, both of you. What's that you've got, King? Not *more* eating nuts!" To Cowboy she confided, "I've had two canfuls already since I've been in here."

"That's about all she eats," King said with a smile. "Nuts and eggs and black coffee."

"Fresh peas and peaches and tomatoes when I can have them," Jeremy added. And then, with a spark of vanity, "That's good for my complexion. Most girls I see have skin like a muddy creek bank and I know it's because they don't ever eat fresh when they can get boiled or fried." She put down her brush and studied Cowboy more seriously. "What sort of time did you have with the judge?"

"Well, you see Cowboy standing here," King answered, "so it's proof we didn't have too hard a time. Cowboy's on probation, and he's going to be working with us for a while."

"Oh," Jeremy said, with careful emphasis, and thereafter excluded Cowboy from her attentions. Before long he became either bored or disgruntled and wandered out.

"Jeremy," King complained, "you could have been a whole lot nicer."

"I don't know why I should be! He didn't have two words to say to me. His mother—grandmother . . . She's called every day to see how I'm feeling. What was he doing up here, anyway? Did the judge make him come and apologize?"

"Nothing like that. Cowboy's on probation and . . . in a way I'm supposed to keep track of him."

Jeremy picked up a hand mirror and glanced at her shining hair, carefully avoiding looking at the rest of her face, and her bad eye, which seemed to have benefited from the rest she'd been getting. "Why should you have to do it?"

"Jeremy, the whole idea was mine. Cowboy's had a sad life, and not always his fault. It's the devil at work, I'm positive, and I'm sure meaning to help him if I can." He stared down at the silent blue figures on the TV screen.

"He's just bad-tempered and no-account," she said authoritatively. "You won't change him."

"Can't expect you to see what I see," King mumbled.

"How long do you have to keep an eye on him, then?"

"Ninety days. He'll be a big help around the tent. And we could use the extra help, now that Philemon's taken off on his own."

Jeremy's skepticism melted away at mention of the tent. "Have you seen it? Is it here?"

"Should be going up this minute," King said, with a glance at his watch. "I'll be preaching tonight, with luck."

"And I can't go!"

"Plenty of other meetings."

"But tonight's the one I care about!" Jeremy looked as if she were about to jump out of bed, but she quieted down when her back gave a twinge, and slapped her hands dispiritedly against the mattress. King couldn't help smiling. "Well, get on out of here if you're going to make fun of me!" He shrugged and made a move toward the door and her expression changed quickly, to dismay and hurt. Then they both laughed at his bamboozling.

Past this spontaneous expression of intimacy King didn't feel willing or able to go, and by this time Jeremy was especially sensitive to his limits, frustrating as they were to her. Because of her accident, a part of the restraint between them had disappeared immediately and they were on good terms again, as good as before the night he had impulsively made love to her. He hadn't mentioned that night and she wouldn't think of it, for fear of destroying her renewed good luck. So when silence followed their laughter, she filled the space with business, holding the fist-size chrysanthemum one way and then another, trying it in her hair and above her heart. She said, "Eli and Philemon came this morning and stayed an hour. I think Eli misses me, or anyway he's got used to having somebody tidy up after him. Philemon brought that little bunch of posies there." She pointed to a small vase of blue flowers overwhelmed by the mountain of chrysanthemums. "Had on his new preaching suit too." She smiled, partly in irony and partly in understanding. "Needs taking in here and there; I'll do that for him soon's I get back." She paused, and her eyes were shadowy, her mouth looked long and touched with a bare, funny sorrow, like a clown's mouth awaiting a slash of makeup. "Soon's I get back home."

King had already made up his mind that when Jeremy left the hospital she was not going to return to the just-livable and depressing house on the ridge behind the fairgrounds. Where she *was* going he hadn't worked out yet, but as he looked at her he thought of Molly Amos. This seemed like such a fine answer to his worries about Jeremy that he said, without bothering to think it over, "Even if the doctor lets you go Thursday doesn't mean you'll be well. You'll be needing planty of rest for a week or two. If you sprain that back again . . . well, and you need a good bed to sleep in."

"What am I supposed to do, then? And I've got a good bed."

"You've got a mattress on the floor and that's not fit for you, Jeremy. Mrs. Amos will give you a place to stay, long as you need one."

"How do you know?" Jeremy asked promptly. "Did she say so?"

"I didn't ask Molly yet but she won't mind. Don't get set to argue, because I'm leaving, anyhow; I've got plenty of work left to do today."

"I'm not fixing to argue," Jeremy said calmly. "I just want you to understand that no matter what, I *can't* leave Eli. I can't break from him. Maybe I'll limp around for a couple weeks, but he's in worse shape. I never have seen him like he is right today. You know how much it must have hurt him to come all the way to the hospital with Philemon this morning? Eli should be lying here in this bed and not me."

"If he's not going to help himself, then what can you do?"

"I don't know how to do anything but try to be a comfort to him." Jeremy was becoming more and more unhappy, but King didn't know if all her unhappiness was due to Eli's distress, or to her own. "You could do more than me. You could help him if you just wanted to. Give him what he wants."

"Jeremy, now that makes me good and mad. Because—"

"Oh, I know! Don't tell me any more, don't get hot about it. And I'm not aiming to sit here in this pretty room with my grand flowers and be upset over things I can't help, so why don't you leave, and this time I'm serious." She sniffed and held a hand crookedly and protectively to her face. "No, wait! Changed my mind again. This is a happy day. It is, it just *is*, and I'm not spoiling it no matter what. Would you come sit beside me? For a minute, now."

King sat down at the foot of the high bed, casting a glance at the half-opened door. "Jeremy, I'd like to explain about Eli and me. I wanted to buy him out altogether but neither Eli nor his

225

lawyer, that Sam Manson, is willing to be sensible. They want sixteen thousand dollars and the tent besides; I'm not worth that kind of money and don't think I ever will be. So it looks like I'm just going to have to leave Eli sitting with his empty tent and—" He shrugged, watching Jeremy's face become progressively more glum. "Who knows? I don't want to think past tonight if I can help it. But . . . do you understand? If Eli could admit how wrong he is, I'd have some hope."

"Has to be Eli," she said.

"Yes'm."

"You've got your feelings, and I've got mine. I have to go back to him. Because he did take me in, you see, when I didn't have a thing to look forward to but a county home somewhere. So it's settled. And let's don't talk about it any more. You won't have to mention to Molly Amos about my staying with her. I expect I'd rather sleep on a mattress on the floor anyhow." This thrust at Molly annoyed King only slightly, since he didn't know what had prompted it.

He glanced at his watch again. Jeremy nodded forgivingly. "Go on, then, I know you're anxious. Look there. See that telephone? I heard somebody say this room costs thirty dollars a day, and nobody's called me on the telephone yet!" When he didn't seem to get the hint, Jeremy set her teeth against her pride and said, "Would you call me tonight and talk to me before bedtime? I won't sleep until I hear about the meeting, and the new tent. They come around here with medicine about ten but it doesn't make me sleepy for a couple hours, so you could call me at midnight and I'd still be awake."

"Sure, I ought to be free to call by then."

Jeremy turned her head on the pillow so that she wouldn't have to look at him, but she still felt bold, transformed by the strangeness of the hospital room, by his visit. "You know, if you don't want me going back to Eli, there's something you can do. And what that is I won't tell because I've said enough. You'll have to say it, I never will." Then her boldness turned to fright and desolation and she pressed her cheek deep into the pillow, closing her eyes. "And I won't wait forever for you to . . . say it, either."

King could be heedless but he wasn't a fool, and he understood what she had led him to ask. He felt more wretched than the night Jeremy had pushed him off the porch, but at the same time a part of him was cold and still committed to the

226

dead Mary Kate. He said, gloomily, "I'll be sure to talk to you tonight, Jeremy," and went out, closing the heavy door behind him.

20

The Only Way to Preach

Cowboy was in the car, reading a newspaper and eating from a sack of potato chips. "You didn't stay long," he observed.

"Work to do, Cowboy." The preacher's tone was slightly cross. "Want to head on out to the fairgrounds now?"

Cowboy slipped on a pair of wraparound sunglasses and got them under way. His car radio was tuned to Kay-tip. "Care anything about country music?" he asked, in a conversational voice.

King grunted. "Practically raised on it."

"I've been working on a tune. Tell me what you think."

King nodded in a preoccupied way.

" 'Kilgore Posse Blues,' " Cowboy announced, and sang two verses. "What do you think? It sounds better with a banjo, naturally."

"Real professional to my ears," King admitted. "Do much writing?"

"When I'm in the mood." Cowboy gunned his motor at an intersection to attract the attention of a carload of schoolgirls. He gave them a celebrity's grin. "I saw Suzie yesterday. From about here to there." He indicated a lamppost on the corner. "She wouldn't come any closer than that to me." This seemed to strike Cowboy as a jolly joke.

"Then maybe it's a good thing the two of you didn't get married," King said, wondering if Cowboy was baiting him.

"I can get her back when I want her," Cowboy replied, and turned his head to see the preacher's reaction. His eyes were barely visible behind the green glasses. His lip had curled in a

227

knowledgeable half-mocking smile, and King decided if there was one thing he really disliked about Cowboy it was his mouth. He was conscious of muted animosity and he felt both disturbed and defensive. But Cowboy apparently didn't intend to probe the subject of his former girlfriend and restate all the tensions between them. He gave the wheel a casual spin and they surged on through the outflowing traffic.

"What gave you the idea of being a preacher?"

"Wasn't something I picked out for myself, Cowboy."

"Oh, you were called. Tell me about that. Did you have a vision?"

King had legitimate doubts that Cowboy was really interested, but he said calmly, "No, I've just always felt—since I was seven or eight years old— that I was put on this earth to preach. I enjoyed church and Sunday school more than I did regular school. I read the Bible cover to cover when I was nine years old. That's a fact. Knew a lot about what I was reading too. I used to tell Bible stories to anybody'd listen to me. But visions . . . I had my feet on the ground, Cowboy. All I read in the Bible was real and true to me; I didn't have to see angels coming down in clouds of glory to be convinced of my faith."

"I've heard radio preachers talk about some vision or other that saved their life or changed them from hell-raisers into preachers. And you never had a vision?" He sounded disappointed and skeptical.

"I've had . . . experiences that are precious to me. So precious and beautiful that I couldn't describe them. And I've had other experiences . . . well, I just can't say. God grants wonderful and unexpected favors, such as unforgettable sights of Eternity. I know this to be true. And I know there are preachers who twist every dream they have into some sort of Divine vision. I suppose they don't do themselves or others any harm by their zeal."

"So you've had real visions! I'd like to hear about them sometime."

"Why? To make me out a fool? You're convinced of that already."

Again Cowboy turned his head, this time with a quick annoyance. "You said you read the Bible through when you were nine. I wasn't much older than that when I did the same thing. Seventy-two hours straight through; I read until I couldn't see the pages. I had a miserable headache when I was

228

done; I still remember how my head ached. I fell asleep and I dreamed . . ."

"What, Cowboy?"

"Nothing. I dreamed nothing. And when I woke up I couldn't remember what I'd read. I still can't. And I've never opened a Bible since. Don't want to."

"Don't you?"

"No," Cowboy said emphatically. "But I wonder about this: why were we different? Why was it so real for you, and why did I forget so easy? I wonder."

"We might find out, Cowboy," King suggested, a feeling of cautious pleasure in his heart.

"Oh, no, we won't. Because it doesn't make any difference to me now. I only thought I'd tell you, in case you were curious did I have any religion at all."

"I suppose I *was* curious."

"Well," said Cowboy, "there's your answer. And there's no reason I can see for us to talk about it again."

The circular blue top of the new canvas had been raised on six red-and-white striped poles and secured with a complex of steel cross braces and long triple-pegged cables. According to the tent-and-awning-company foreman who accompanied King inside, the new tent was some sixty feet in diameter—big enough to contain a two-ring circus and bleachers for several hundred people.

Workmen were still securing the stays and hadn't begun to install the side panels of canvas. In one quadrant of the tent Age and a crew of Negroes he had recruited were putting together the pulpit and the framework for the small spotlights that would be trained on the preacher during the meetings. King stopped and stared at the durable canvas roof, and he was convinced all over again that this was the only way to preach. He remembered vividly the thrill he'd received upon walking into the old tent only a month ago, the blindness with which he had coveted it. He had had endless reveries about a tent like this one, clean and new; he wondered why he felt so calm now, very nearly unmoved by the fact of possession. Well, it really wasn't his, as Cy Hillgrin had made clear; he wouldn't be there for long unless a miracle happened—unless Eli changed his mind, which amounted to the same thing. So he would do his preaching a day at a time and be thankful for the generosity of the Lord and try not to grow too fond of the tent.

Age stopped work and came over, drying the hollow of his throat with a crumpled paper towel; it was hot under the canvas. He glanced at Cowboy, placing him, and then looked at the preacher, who smiled enigmatically.

"Four-thirty, Age. What chance we'll make it?"

"Hard job is putting up the lights. Might find out we don't have cord enough; this a whole lot more canvas than I thought it would be."

"Just make do with what you have. Better start on the lights now, save the pulpit for last. You're building it right high, don't you think?"

"Plenty of lumber and plenty of head room. I thought would look best for the choir to stand down below the pulpit instead of on it." From his back pocket he pulled a sketch he had made. "This is a wide stairs from the pulpit to the ground. Choir stall on both sides. Down here is a platform raised about a foot and a half off the ground. So you can preach up on the pulpit or right in front of the congregation, whichever suits you."

King studied the drawing. "I'd say it's a fine plan, Age."

Age said, his eyes veiled, "That woman's got even bigger plans. She wants to put down gold carpet all over everything."

"Oh, Mrs. Amos been around today?"

"She was. She'll be back." Age snatched a hammer out of a loop on his carpenter's overalls and returned to work.

"What's the matter with your nigger?" Cowboy asked.

"Nothing I know of."

"There's places where a surly nigger like that wouldn't live five minutes."

"You can call him Age around me, Cowboy. He's about the best friend I've got."

"No offense," said the Cowboy, slipping his sunglasses down over his eyes again. "What does Molly have to do with all this?"

They walked outside, where King dug into a pile of sawdust on a square of canvas. Satisfied that the sawdust was dry and fresh, he moved on and began counting chairs. Cowboy tagged along, waiting to be answered.

"If I'm a success at all, it's Molly's doing. The radio program was her idea. She went out and found friends for me when I needed them most. Men like Martin Handwerker and Cy Hillgrin. If Molly wants to put down gold carpet on the pulpit,

230

then I'm all for it, because I know she has good reasons and she's figured out a way to pay for the carpet without strapping us. She talked the city into fast action about giving us this space for our tent."

He straightened up from his chair count and looked around. They were hard by the fairgrounds, where the carnival people had parked their trailers not long ago. The land was lighted, level, well drained, and within a hundred yards of paved parking. The only drawback, King thought, as he heard the hoot of an air horn, was the nearness of the railroad yards, just half a mile to the east. But the noise of a few freight trains would be only a small distraction. King raised his eyes to the ridge and the deserted-looking house. He wondered if Eli was at the kitchen window, looking at them, at the new tent which had sprung up. What was Eli thinking? Would he come tonight? Maybe, King thought, he should pay Eli a call, invite him to sit on the pulpit. But he soon forgot this idea, and shook his head. Eli wouldn't talk to him at all unless he went abjectly, willing to yield.

A familiar Cadillac was headed their way and the preacher smiled delightedly. He left Cowboy and strode off to greet the new arrivals.

"Mab!" He reached through a window to shake the woman's hand. "It sure is a pleasure to see you. Daniel! How is everybody out your way?"

"Bless you, Preacher, I'm fine; we're all happy in the Lord and dwin fine."

"Come to visit you in your new tent," Daniel put in.

"Ain't it a beautiful sight!" Mab cried. "Let me out of this car; I want to see close up for myself."

King opened the door and helped the woman out of the front seat. Mab was dressed in black, as she had been the night she was redeemed, but today she also wore a fringed black shawl to cover her bare shoulders, a sparkling rope of matinee beads, and a pastel gem on one hand. The soiled, unkempt look had disappeared. Her eyes were clear and her braided hair was as clean as a cloud.

Mab stepped off grandly with King on one side and Daniel on the other. Despite her size, she wasn't blubbery, and she held her head at a proud angle. King wondered what she had been like in her youth, for she was a glamorous woman now.

He pointed out some of the features of the tent as they

approached, and Mab exclaimed over each one. "I don't know how much good it did," she confided, "but when Daniel told me what happened to your old tent, I went down on my knees and prayed."

"Tears running down her cheeks," Daniel said solemnly. "Hurt her some little to be on her knees that way."

"I prayed for a new tent for the preacher that saved my soul. Precious Lord! Did He hear me? Did He grant a wish for an old sinner? Well, it don't matter, but anyhow I prayed if He would be merciful enough to set you up in a *new* tent, then I'd come every night to sing in that tent. Sing for my Lord Jesus! I'm living a new life now, and I'm done with blues! But I kin sing Gospel pretty fair too. That is, if you need me to."

"Bless you, Mab, you're welcome to come sing any time. How about tonight?"

"Sure, I kin sing tonight." She stopped suddenly and turned her head. "Take me over there," she directed, "and let's hear how that piano sounds."

Cowboy had been lounging near the white piano, which was sitting outside on a flooring of planks until the pulpit could be completed.

"Mab Shaw, this is Cowboy Jim Cobb. He's going to work with us for a while."

"How do you do, Cowboy. Are you a preacher?"

"More like a musician," Cowboy said, studying her with unusual attention. "Are you the Mab Shaw who—"

"Only *one* Mab Shaw, Cowboy," King said, aware of his interest. "I expect you've heard some of her records, if you like the blues."

Cowboy nodded. "I own a few sides," he said respectfully to Mab, "that you cut down in Atlanta with Eddie Lang on guitar. They're as rare as a blue-eyed tiger."

"Oh, yes," Mab said, extremely pleased. "I remember that session. I remember Eddie too." For a few moments her eyes were wistful. "That was all some time ago."

"Is it true that you and Mississippi John Hurt cut the old 'C. C. Ryder' in Memphis, back about nineteen and twenty-five? I've heard it was so, but I've never been able to find any such record."

Mab fondled the matinee beads that lay around her broad neck and stared down at the tip of one tiny shoe. "Cinch I don't know," she confessed. "We worked together many a town in those days. Memphis? Yes, Memphis too. But I don't recall if we made a record. Daniel might know. In my *other* life, before I was saved, thanks God, I never throwed nothing away. Daniel spent a lot of time gwin through my old junk back there in L.A."

"Turned up a barrel of records." Daniel shook his head. "But I couldn't tell you all that's in it. One of these days, when the barrel comes, you're welcome to take a look for yourself."

"Find what you want in that barrel, you kin have it," Mab promised.

"Well, it would be worth a lot of money, Mab," Cowboy said.

She waved aside his objection. "That's all right. I know you'd take good care. I don't need old records. I don't need memories. I'm happy, I'm cured of the bottle." She smiled. "Do you play piano, Cowboy?"

"I've fooled around some with it."

"How about Gospel? Play any Gospel? No? Let me tell you, I ain't sung in so long a time I better start with something I *know*. Think you can back me on 'You Are My Sunshine'?"

"There's a guitar in the trunk of my car. I can do better with that."

"Well," said Mab, with a noble wag of her head, "fetch it then. And help this old woman out."

When Cowboy was out of earshot she said, in a more serious voice, "Daniel? Preacher? Is that the boy who went and wrecked the other tent?"

"He's the one, Mab. The judge let him off on probation. I hoped it would do Cowboy good to be around meetings and the Holy Ghost for a while, so he's working for us."

"Is that the boy got serious trouble in him? Or do you think the Lord kin save his soul?"

"Satan is flogging him straight to hell, Mab."

"Then he'll trample down anybody standing in his way, most likely." She looked hopefully at the preacher. "Kin you lick old Satan? You've got the power, I know that. Thank God! I got a lots to tell in meeting, if you're willing. Maybe what I have to say will open up Cowboy's hard heart, praise Jesus."

King shook his head. "Devil won't let him listen. I'm concerned that the devil will turn him against me. Because I *will* stand in his way, and I won't be trampled on without a fight. It means life for Cowboy, and life for me." He finished with his jaw set, and Cowboy gave him a speculative glance when he returned lugging a worn-out guitar case.

"Go ahead and play something *you* like first," Mab urged him, and King noted again that Cowboy was susceptible to her encouragement. He played the guitar skillfully, despite his protestations, and with a Lightnin' Hopkins touch that Mab recognized right away, and applauded.

"You're dwin fine—I like your style."

Thus beknighted, Cowboy worked with Mab on "You Are My Sunshine," which she treated with a distinctive touch of the blues.

The sun had begun to set and a light wind was cooling the air. Daniel had drawn up a chair and his eyes were fond as he watched Mab. King leaned against the upright piano, feeling a rare sense of leisure and peace now that Cowboy was diverted.

It could be, the preacher thought, that Mab would be an inspiration to Cowboy after all; she seemed determined to take him under her wing.

But Cowboy could change in an instant, become as bored as he was now engrossed. And once boredom came, and restlessness, what cruel action would the devil take? Perhaps Mab's tale of suffering and redemption would move Cowboy, but King doubted it. A great shock was needed—a Heaven-sent sign that Cowboy could not ignore. Then the Holy Spirit might be able to enter his heart at last.

It was a quarter to five. King left the little group without a word and went to his pickup truck, which was parked near a screen of wind-ruffled and yellowed poplar trees between the tent grounds and the railroad embankment. There he sat in the cab for the next quarter hour, hands clasped between his knees, listening, as he listened every weekday, to himself on the radio.

21

Inspiration

The idea for the Train came to Molly that same night as she waited at a grade crossing near the fairgrounds for a long freight to clear. The slow-moving string of stock cars and tankers was making her late for the start of the revival, which annoyed her only because of two large lithograph posters lying on the back seat; these she'd hoped to have mounted in front of the new tent before many of the congregation arrived.

An artist for a local advertising agency had designed the posters, basing his portrait of King Windom on Polaroid snapshots which Molly had taken of the preacher in action. The posters showed the rail-thin preacher dynamically in motion, black and white against a flash-fire background of vermilion and gold. Molly thought the lithograph was brilliantly conceived and she had ordered six new ones; she was mulling over a television spot-advertising campaign as the train rolled doggedly by at ten miles an hour, and it had occurred to her that the various posters would be effective for this campaign.

Then she forgot completely about the television commercials as something much more profound and exciting occurred to her. She straightened up behind the wheel of her Volkswagen, staring at the train, at the cross blink of the warning signals.

From Cy Hillgrin Molly had learned about the meeting with Eli Charger's lawyer; she had already predicted to herself what the outcome would be. Hillgrin had stressed the fact that if Eli was to be effectively blocked in his efforts to claim an equal share of offerings from King's revivals, King would have to look for another place to preach. Hillgrin had suggested several, from the expensive city coliseum to the not-so-expensive but hard-to-reach Masonic auditorium. Molly had rejected all of his ideas: why should King stay in Clearwater at all?

The train clattered on while Molly re-evaluated earlier conclusions.

If he didn't stay in Clearwater, then obviously he would have to travel. But an unknown, unsponsored evangelist, unless he was personally wealthy, had little chance of sustaining himself or attracting attention on the road. The example of Harlan Gray came to her mind. Long years of hand-to-mouth before he found himself famous! Of course, King already had what they hoped was a substantial radio audience—in a limited area—and with a little time to work at it Molly was sure that she and Mr. Handwerker could obtain sponsors for the preacher in many small towns and cities. Keep him busy through the winter, and then in the spring . . .

But this was not in keeping with the visions she had of a successful King Windom. No, not one small revival after another, respectable churches and meeting halls, and, worst of all, continued obscurity. It had taken Harlan Gray years to establish himself, to become talked about and gain friends, but since he had broken new ground, Molly reasoned that the way should be much easier for King. He was as gifted a preacher as Gray, and, if he could not match the older evangelist in erudition and sophistication, he surpassed him in excitement, in—to be blunt about it—sex appeal.

Except for Gray, whose revivals were very expensive and prestigious, all other successful evangelists worked the same way: Following a modest advance publicity campaign, they arrived in one city or another, set up shop in an auditorium or unfurled a circus-size tent, and went about their work for one week or ten. And . . . who really cared or took notice? The same faithful who went to revivals as regularly as other people attended movies? The few sensation seekers? Molly already knew how difficult it was to get outstanding press coverage for an evangelist.

But a man like King, who had flair and an unforgettable face, could attract a great deal of attention to himself under the right circumstances, and generate wonderful publicity.

The cattle cars crept by a few feet from the bumper of her Volkswagen; flashes of light from the other side of the tracks revealed the fatted beeves inside, huddled and glum.

If he had a train of his own, Molly thought, slowly crystallizing her inspiration, if his going and coming in every town were an event, if they ventured out of the barbershops and the pool halls and ran from the school playgrounds and lined up under the tin roofs along the sidewalk to see him, and went home talking to each other about the train and the Gospel and the evangelist too, and if in a day he passed through five or six towns and preached, and roared out again on a long silver train, they'd damned well remember, and tell of him, and down the line they'd damned well be waiting, like they used to wait at the crossings for the Presidential candidates.

If he had a train then the people would find a name for it—the Gospel Train, the Glory Train, the Southern Cross Express—never mind which; King Windom and his Train, one hundred fifty towns a month instead of twenty a year! Molly knew small Southern towns, she knew how little ever happened in them to stir the citizens, she was familiar with the ripple of interest that flowed outward from the station when the most insignificant four-car passenger-freight stopped for a spell. How they would come running to see King Windom's Train, twelve or more cars of polished silver and chrome, right down to the wheels, and with—with a thin gold cross up front, seven feet high, a cross to shine in the night! Over a hundred stops a month, and how many people would hear him? A hundred thousand? A million? Who, in fact, would miss King Windom, would dare to miss him or his heralded Train?

Molly was so excited that she couldn't stay inside the tiny car. Outside, the wind tore down her hair and she didn't mind at all. The boxed cattle lumbered by, smelling hot and fouled. Molly reached down for a handful of ballast and tossed it into the wind, then wiped her gritty hand on her skirt. Her self-congratulatory, grave, and silly smile worked gradually ear to ear.

"A train, a train, a train!" she sang, as the iron wheels rolled, and the high caboose slipped by, leaving a lonesome gap in the night. The red lights disappeared, the signal stopped. Behind Molly a baffled spectator to her clownishness gave a tentative tap on his horn. She climbed back into the Volkswagen and drove across the tracks.

Of course, it would all be fantastically expensive, Molly thought in her first calm moments, puffing on a cigarette. But there, right in front of her, was the new tent and what appeared

237

to be a jammed parking lot, proof of prosperity and good fortune, and once luck had begun to flow in golden rivers, all things were possible. Mrs. Cobb could afford to equip King Windom with a dozen railroad trains if she were properly persuaded.

The problem, as Molly saw it, was to get the preacher to understand the values of her inspiration. Molly felt very good about her chances; so far she had done well when it came to influencing King. But she knew her man, and she knew that dramatic ideas, no matter how practical they might be, had a melancholy effect on him. Molly decided then that she would keep her inspiration to herself until she had explored all the possibilities and consequences. It might not be a bad idea, she thought, to get reacquainted with Mrs. Cobb, and talk over everything with the old lady before approaching King.

Molly's thoughts went racing along as she hunted a parking space. Before going to Mrs. Cobb she would put the whole thing on a dollars-and-cents, profit-loss basis. There was no question that the Gospel Train would pay its way once the initial expenses had been recovered.

Molly bounced out of her car and reached for the rolled-up posters on the back seat. That afternoon she had badgered Age about making frameworks for the posters, which she intended to place outside the tent entrance. But he'd put her off, and she'd just barely restrained herself from taking him down a couple of pegs. After all, he was—for reasons Molly didn't understand—the best friend King had. She was momentarily curious about how the two had met, and why King was so respectful of the scarred, aloof Negro man.

Tucking the posters under one arm, Molly hurried toward the tent, which was blazing with light, heaped with shadows and shapes, overflowing with hand-clapping and old-time religion. The bluesy hymn being sung was unfamiliar to Molly, but she made out some of the words after half a dozen repetitions: "The Lord God Almighty done brought me out."

The tent looked filled to capacity, and there was a line of standees inside the entrance. Molly made a place for herself and stared approvingly at the pulpit stage. When she finished with it, it would be attractive as any in a church. Below the stage, members of a Negro church choir in scarlet robes swayed and sang; in their midst, on the dividing stairs, was Mab Shaw, her hair like an angel's wing under the hot lights.

Three hundred pounds if she's an ounce, Molly thought, and where had the Reverend Mr. Handwerker come up with *her?* The pounding spiritual ended and the Negress, light on her feet despite her size, climbed the steps to the stage holding a microphone in her hand, and commanded the congregation with a readying lift of her head. She sang "By and By I Will See Jesus." Her voice wasn't altogether firm and showed an occasional crack, but it was quality despite the flaws, rare old china with a deep imperishable gloss, and Molly was fascinated, nearly spellbound by Mab Shaw's talent.

Molly felt someone move beside her, and she gave way without shifting her eyes from the pulpit. Between hymns she felt restless for another cigarette and decided to take a breather: King would not be preaching for a quarter hour yet. The man to her left blocked her exit, so she glanced up, then smiled politely, without enthusiasm.

"Oh, excuse me, Dr. Matthews."

"Hello, Molly. Going out?" He had to lean toward her to be heard. The night was not warm but his face looked, as it always did to her, slightly sweaty and disconsolately red. She had no use for the physician but she was intrigued by his faithful attendance at the revival meetings. She held up two fingers to her lips, indicating a need to smoke; he nodded and shuffled around so she could reach the tent opening. Then, as if in afterthought, he followed her out under the clear sky.

Matthews lighted Molly's cigarette for her, and Molly, who would just as soon have been alone, thanked him perfunctorily. Her reticence prompted an attack of timid shrugging and pocket-searching on the part of Matthews, and then he said with his wide, glum smile, "She's very good, isn't she?"

"Oh, the woman? Wonderful. I didn't know there was talent like her in this town."

"There's not much talent like Mab Shaw in the world."

"Mab Shaw? Now, I've heard that name. Sure I have; she was very big back in the twenties. Along with Billie Holliday and the like." Molly studied the tent. "Where do you suppose she's been all this time?"

Dr. Matthews explained, and Molly listened with elbow in hand and her cigarette burning away, forgotten, illuminating her clever eyes behind the glasses.

"That's almost too good to be true," she said in an

admonishing tone of voice when the doctor had finished his story. "It sounds like a put-up job. Still, they might go for it down at the paper." Molly held her wristwatch toward the light. "Eight-thirty; plenty of time before the last edition."

Molly squashed her cigarette on the sole of her shoe, then scuffed it under the sawdust. "I'm going to hunt up a telephone. We could possibly make front page, second section with this story. Mab Shaw turning up after all these years! I know the AP will move a couple of paragraphs tonight, and more than likely they'll follow up big in the morning."

"Mind if I go along with you, Molly?"

"I'll only be gone a few minutes; there'll be a telephone in that little grocery store across the tracks. Come along if you feel like it." Molly threaded her way through the parking lot to her Volkswagen and waited impatiently until the doctor had maneuvered into his seat. Once they were racing toward the highway in the little pepperpot car, she felt more charitable and was sorry for her rudeness.

"I've been trying to think of a good publicity break for a week," she explained, "and this is Heaven-sent. Lucky I ran into you tonight, Dr. Matthews. King wouldn't have said a word about Mab; that's the way he is."

"One of the appealing things about our preacher," the doctor murmured.

"Oh, have you met him?"

"We had a long talk a few nights ago—in fact, the night Mab Shaw came."

"Not that it's altogether my business, but what's your interest in King? You haven't left the Church, have you?"

"No, nothing like that." The doctor gripped his seat with both hands as Molly lurched onto the highway ahead of a big tractor trailer; in the deep glare of the truck's headlights his smile was bonelike, unrevealing. "We have . . . common interests. At least I think so."

Molly had no patience with his evasion, and for the moment little interest in learning what King might have in common with a drab failure like Dr. Matthews. She was absorbed in the story about Mab Shaw which she was putting together for one of the rewrite men on the morning paper.

Molly pulled up in front of the store and got out, leaving the motor running. It was an old country commissary with a false front of metal advertising signs—*drink! eat! chew!*—an old thermometer-type gasoline pump that probably had drawn nothing but rust for years, and a porchful of hangdogs, animal and human. Within five minutes she came bounding out and rejoined Dr. Matthews. Her hair was in a worse tangle than before, and she was panting from too many cigarettes, but the look she gave him was a victorious one.

"City editor's sending out a team, and they should be at the tent by nine-thirty. I think they're going to pull a second-section lead on potholes in the city streets for Mab Shaw's sake."

"This story should be a great help to King," Dr. Matthews said indulgently.

"You betcha. A lot of people who don't give a hang about revival meetings will come out just to hear that woman sing. We'll have a full house all week long, barring really lousy weather. And by the time it turns cold—" Molly was aching to tell her plans, but she managed to contain most of her enthusiasm. The Train was so important, so vital, that she was superstitiously afraid to say a word about it until she had thought out every move.

Matthews had filled a pipe, but on the drive back to the tent grounds he held it without firing the tobacco. "What do you know about him, Molly?" he asked suddenly.

"King?" She felt hostile again, as if such a casual question were an invasion of her own privacy. "What do you mean?"

"Do you know much about his family? Where does he come from?"

"Somewhere in South Carolina. And I don't know anything about his family." After this sharp reply Molly's feelings took a different tack; she felt unaccountably and undeservedly lonely. Uncared for. It was true, he hadn't talked much about himself, had volunteered nothing about his life. They'd been together very little except to discuss the business of revivals. When would she see him when he wasn't brooding about some crisis or other, about his insufficiencies? When would King Windom come looking for *her*, instead of the opposite? Molly pulled away from such thoughts, from the doldrums; they had a way of spawning attacks of wrathful self-disgust. Instead she explored for happier memories, those times when she had felt especially close to the preacher. Her loneliness lost its edges.

"King's mother died when he was twelve," Molly said, by

241

way of apology. "He's never said anything about his father; I suppose he's dead too."

Dr. Matthews nodded. "I'm sure King would have mentioned his father if he were still alive. I wonder what sort of woman Mrs. Windom was?"

"I don't know a thing about her. A couple of times I've tried to imagine what she was like. You know the way he looks, tall and raw-boned—well, I saw 'mother' the same way, big and slightly stooped, gouty, sixtyish, face like cast concrete, neck sunburned well down to her chest. I saw her wearing a bonnet or a wide-brimmed straw and a cotton dress with an uneven hem, five inches longer than other women wear their dresses. And I saw her with a spading fork in a tidy little sun-baked garden behind a frame house about seventy years old." Molly was silent as she inched into a parking space. "But I'm sure his mother wasn't anything like that. In fact"—she tugged at her skirt and got out of the car, reaching again for the rolled-up posters in the back seat—"the only thing I know for sure about Mrs. Windom is that she was a medium."

Matthews turned his head sharply. "Would you say that again?"

Molly shrugged. "She was a spiritualist medium. King told me so. We were standing inside the main gate of the fairgrounds and discussing mothers in general, or else I'd been telling him about *mine*, and he came out with that piece of news. Somehow I had the feeling that he'd . . . suffered because of his mother."

The expression on the doctor's face was unexpected; Molly was used to seeing only that lugubrious, gentlemanly smile. The tigerish satisfaction reflected in his eyes put her off balance and she said, almost guiltily, "Or I may be exaggerating. I didn't know him well then, and a deep scowl is his normal response to nearly everything."

Molly struggled with the posters, which were slipping from under her arm, and when she looked up again, Dr. Matthews' face was mild and his eyes unimpressive behind the tinted lenses. He gestured toward the tent.

"Sounds like most of the excitement has died down, Molly. King will be preaching soon. Let's hope there's still standing room. Can I help you with those posters?"

"I'll manage, thanks." They plodded across the parking lot to

242

the spread of fresh sawdust. And Molly was still tingling from the change that had come over Dr. John Matthews.

"What is a medium?" she asked, timidly. "I suppose I should know. It has something to do with ghosts, doesn't it?"

"A medium is a highly susceptible individual, supposedly able to communicate with the dead, or to carry out unusual acts under the influence of spirits. A clairvoyant is someone with preternatural gifts for perceiving all kinds of objects not present to ordinary senses. Yes, ghosts, for instance."

"Well, I was on the right track," Molly said with a short laugh, and the doctor smiled as he ushered her into the crowded tent. They found space in which to stand. King hadn't begun to preach but he was onstage, sitting unobtrusively toward the back with visiting preachers while Mr. Handwerker held forth. Molly studied the shadowed, immobile face, the strong clasped hands, and shivered; then she stared at the ground to keep her emotions from galloping off. Beside her, Dr. Matthews stood alert and silent, but as if he had felt the leap of Molly's desires against his skin, he turned and looked quizzically down at her.

Molly wanted to ask, Could it affect him too? What his mother had? Could that be in him? Yet she hesitated, feeling foolish. Then the singing began again and the doctor's attentions were swept away. Tentatively Molly shifted her eyes to the stage and waited, like the others, for King Windom.

22

Brother Hazelman

Philemon had come early with his friends in order to find choice seats.

Although he had bitterly proclaimed to himself that he would never set foot inside a tent where King Windom was preaching, Philemon was not having too bad a time. It was not for his own sake that he was sitting there, but for Eli's. Eli was too sick to leave his bed, and he would need to know everything that went on in case King Windom tried to cheat him—again—out of his fair share of the offering. Philemon did not understand just why the preacher had turned against his uncle, because Eli explained little of his affairs and Philemon listened badly, but what he did know was that King Windom had caused Eli to suffer terribly, and if Philemon had not been quite able to justify his hatred of the preacher before this, he now had enough reason to give himself considerable peace of mind.

Also he was content to be there because he had good company in Walter and Evelyn Hazelman. The Hazelmans had persuaded Philemon that he would be doing them a service by introducing them to the new evangelist they had been hearing about, although they were sure—as Brother Hazelman had said—that King Windom, however impressive he might sound on the radio, was a long way from the equal of the Heaven-sent boy who had wandered into the midst of their congregation one Sunday afternoon and proceeded to turn the Church of the Apostle's Creed into a modern Pool of Gethsemane with the intensity and brilliance of his preaching, testifying, and devil-scorning.

Philemon was at his best spiritually, having been fortified with one triumph after another at the Hazelman family church, and he was also splendidly turned out in one of the two outfits which he had been able to buy thanks to Cosh, who had mastered the bloodthirsty best of Beersheba County's pit dogs. His sports coat was as pink as a baby's ears, and although it was cut too long for the length of his stubby arms, it had splendid black velvet piping on the lapels and cuffs. His shirt featured French cuffs four inches deep and a tiny collar pinched together under his chin with a gold clasp. He wore black beltless trousers with a metallic sheen and these were pegged down almost to the width of his ankles. The cuffs of his trousers barely fit over a pair of tight boots so beautiful he still did not fully believe they belonged to him.

Several times during the course of the revival he had realigned his feet on the sawdust so he could study the boots from all angles. The nine-inch-high uppers were of soft brushed suede, concord-grape blue in color, with side zippers. They tapered drastically to the toe, like Western boots, and had two-inch heels. Although Cosh had won a lot of money for him, over a hundred dollars, he had not been able to afford such a marvelous pair of boots. They had been a gift of the Hazelmans, in appreciation of the miracles Philemon had wrought in their sin-sick congregation.

As Brother Hazelman had explained it, he was at his wits' end before Philemon showed up, his flock had turned deaf ears to him and to Heaven, and no amount of hellfire preaching on his part could haul them back to Jesus. Why, at least one young girl from his congregation had come to him because she was pregnant, and she had asked not for the Lord's forgiveness but for the name of a friendly and discreet doctor; could there be more positive proof that a church had become mysteriously infected with the many plagues of hell? Brother Hazelman had been ready to admit defeat, to give up his church and retreat to a far city with those few of the faithful who cared to follow him, there try again to form a church body devout enough to withstand the onslaughts of the cloven hoof.

But, just in the nick of time, the moving finger had writ and behold, there was Philemon, and the Church of the Apostle's Creed was now secure. Philemon, in short, had found a home, and a following. Yet his happiness and rejoicing over this long-prayed-for recognition was not complete; he had only to look around the spacious new tent—warmed by the collective body heat of nine hundred or more worshipers and the hundred light bulbs overhead—to taste gall and feel the quicksand of jealousy and insecurity stir in his belly, swallow all the fruits and flowers of his triumph at a gulp, and suck agonizingly at his heart.

Philemon reached down to flick a shred of sawdust from the tip of one of his boots. Walter Hazelman, aware of Philemon's distress, smiled and laid a fatherly hand on his knee. All around them members of the congregation rose and fell—they were as excitable as the sea—and the music drove them through the paces of their passion like a merciless wind. Philemon looked up, at the face of his friend.

Walter Hazelman was in his sixties, a blond barrel-chested man as curried and combed as a prize palomino parade horse. Although Philemon had a full quota of eccentricities when it came to dress, he could not compete with the Reverend Mr. Hazelman, who had had many more years to indulge himself. Brother Hazelman seldom wore a shirt without a thousand frills and ruffles, nor was he ever seen—whether he was preaching, marrying, or burying—in a pair of conventional trousers. Those he wore tonight were styled like a flamenco dancer's: they were of burgundy silk with cloth-covered buttons rising dramatically from ankle to waistband on the left side. He also had on a yellow mess jacket and a silk sash for a cummerbund, salmon pink. Because he had an eye for color, the outlandish outfit harmonized and seemed madly appropriate to the bull-trim, blond and actorish man.

They had created a stir among the other early arrivals, which Philemon had both enjoyed and been embarrassed by. He was proud of his association with Walter Hazelman, who was well known in the city of Clearwater, both on his own and for the large family which he headed. Roughly a third of the members of the Hazelman family were religious figures, like Walter; a third were hillbilly musicians, and a third occupied nooks and crannies of various jails in the South. Most of the incarcerated were also, on the outside, preachers and country musicians.

Walter Hazelman hadn't had much to say during the first hour. Upon sitting, he had inspected the tent with a favoring smile and revealed that he thought it was "Very nice, very nice." The pulpit which Age and his crew had built was also very nice, and so was the Negro choir. Philemon had been hoping that Brother Hazelman would find fault, but after all, he admitted, there was not much to criticize; the quicksand began to heave uncomfortably in his stomach as he looked into Walter Hazelman's serene and remarkably clear blue eyes.

"It makes our tabernacle look small, don't it?" said Hazelman genially, leaning close to speak in Philemon's ear, and Philemon's face clouded at this unblushing admission of inferiority.

Hazelman chuckled and squeezed Philemon's knee more tightly. "The important thing," he went on, "is not *where* you preach at. True? True? But *how* you preach. Does he . . . get . . . *results?* Does he . . . *save?* Does he?"

Philemon cracked a hopeful smile but he said, with downcast eyes, "Oh, he saves. I don't hold that against him."

"Well, never you mind! This tent"—Walter Hazelman cast about—"is very . . . nice. But you'll take your turn, Philemon, you'll take your turn! In a tabernacle like you never have seen before. A tabernacle fit for the kingdom of Heaven in all its glory." Philemon looked at him uncomprehendingly. "It's coming, Brother. Coming soon. After all our years of hard work and prayer. And I think"—he pressed the fingers of one hand to his forehead, prayerfully—"I think I see *you* preaching there!"

This statement gave Philemon quite a jolt, and because there was a faraway look in Walter Hazelman's eyes, he wondered if the man had had a vision. He glanced to his right, where Evelyn Hazelman was sitting on the green velour pillow which she always carried with her because of a painful and unmentionable complaint. She was enjoying herself, stretching her hands upward to the doorstep of Heaven, occasionally letting go with a shrill, satisfied "A–men!" or an emotional "Je–sus" that threatened to rock her off the pillow. She was a small woman with thin hair, eyeglasses, a relentless vacant stare. Five minutes of being watched by Evelyn Hazelman could drive a strong man to insanity, or unnerve a sleeping dog. When she preached, those witless shrieking eyes riveted people to her and she could go on for an hour without varying a decibel in pitch, without making the slightest bit of sense in her rambling sermons. After an evening in church with Sister Evelyn, sin came as a relief.

But to Philemon these two were luminaries. There had been times when he had frankly and gloomily wondered why they took so much pleasure not in his preaching, which was God-inspired and therefore admirable, but in his company, why they had taken him in so eagerly when they had numerous nephews and cousins of their own. Philemon was easily moved to tears and as he gazed down at his boots, the evidence of their regard for him, his eyes watered and he was forced to dry them with a velvet-trimmed cuff of his new coat.

By then the mood of the revival had changed. The lights dimmed and the singing softened. Looking up, Philemon saw the tall preacher approach the front of the pulpit. The metal buttons on the blazer he wore caught the light and shone vividly.

The sight of those buttons, which Philemon willingly took for gold, gave him cause to forget his remorse at being loved, and as the preacher made ready with his Bible open in a shovel-size hand, Philemon thought, Look at him! Either you preached the Gospel of the fiery hell in humble cloth of black, or you preached the remote purities of Heaven in a clean white suit, as Philemon himself did. You didn't read from the Book with a look of wickedness like that of an Indian savage and flaunt gold buttons at your congregation, and all the evils that gold buttons stood for! Lust, greed, the filth of Mammon . . .

"Filth," muttered Philemon, but no one heard or bothered with him. He listened to part of Paul's letter to Timothy but he was not in a reverent frame of mind; instead he studied the preacher avidly. Despite his illustrious company and his fine new clothes, Philemon felt weak and despised and naked, for the preacher was raised above them all, his uplifted eyes were like jewels in the slanted pulpit light. The preacher was the Book and the Faith and all the prophets in one, the preacher was in possession of the sainthood that lived in their beating hearts and he, Philemon, was bereft.

Now he felt the agony of the fool because he had come here, because he had brought his friends in all innocence to meet King Windom. In a glance he saw the eagerness with which Walter Hazelman had received the preacher, he saw the approval in Sister Evelyn's eyes. He slipped without a struggle into the terrible quicksand that had always made life such a hazard for him. Frantically he tried to raise himself.

I'm loved—I'm strong—I'm inspired. I'm blessed.

But what if I'm not?

The answer came back to him from the preacher's high, serious eyes.

"Filth," Philemon thought again, and longed to cry out, to shake the entire congregation from blind devotion to King Windom. Then cold violence composed him. Filth for his theft of Eli and, worst of all, Jeremy. Filth, filth, filth. Unexpectedly violence swung about, striking him a numbing blow. Philemon hung his head in blackness and solitude. After a while words came to him, words to describe his helplessness and his resolve.

You will not.

But Philemon did not yet know what he could do if King Windom smiled and spoke and took the Hazelmans from him too.

23

The Preacher's Touch

Mab found her chance for a heart-to-heart talk with Cowboy
while King was preaching.

She and Daniel had retired to the Cadillac, which was
parked just behind the tent, following Mab's appearance. It
had been hot on the pulpit under the grid of lights, and Mab
was bundled up in a sweater and a light scarf to prevent a chill.
Where they were sitting, in the dark, they could hear King's
sermon without straining, and both were absorbed until Mab,
out of the corner of her eye, saw Cowboy step out of the tent
close by and duck his head to light a cigarette.

Mab cranked down the window and said graciously,
"Cowboy, won't you come and set with us for a little?" They
had known each other only a few hours, but Mab was quite
confident of Cowboy's esteem for her, and she was not timid
about the prospect of speaking her mind.

Cowboy turned his head inquiringly, then ambled toward
the Cadillac. Mab was in the back seat, so he sat up front,
leaving the door open.

"How was I to your ears?" she asked him, as if she were
anxious about her performance. "Right now my throat's tight as
a drum, but with a week of practice . . ."

Cowboy drew on his cigarette, and the red glow gave his
smile an ironic tinge. "Mab, you've had forty years to practice.
And you were ready tonight."

249

"Can't say I'm satisfied," Mab grumbled. "Not that it matters, praise His name, long as folks received the message and the Spirit. Still, I missed having you up there behind me. . . ." Her voice had become as silken as it was likely to get. Cowboy smiled again and said nothing.

Mab sniffed at a scented handkerchief and stared thoughtfully at the back of his head for a few moments. "I'm thirsty," she complained. "Daniel, I could do with a cold soda. Maybe Cowboy will have one with me?"

"No; thank you anyway, Mab."

Daniel glanced into the back seat to confirm the hint of conspiracy in Mab's voice; then he left the car and walked slowly to one of the pronto-pup wagons on the tent ground. Mab and Cowboy listened to the preacher for a few moments, silently; Cowboy's eyes were on the stars.

Mab sighed. "He's a marvelous man, a great man. Great in word *and* deed. Wouldn't you say so, Cowboy?"

"I believe he is, Mab," the Cowboy said obligingly, not as if he were humoring her, but not as if he cared very much for the subject of her enthusiasm, either.

Mab scowled but composed herself and went on, sweetly, "I suppose you already know about what he's done for me, thanks God."

"Well, I heard you had a liquor problem," said Cowboy after another silence.

"Yes, I drank. That was a fault of the devil down deep inside of me. Reckon you know what that's like. Hmm?" Getting no response, she went on, "And little as a week ago I thought I was a goner. What a difference a week can make. Bless him!" The voice of the preacher intruded; Cowboy turned in the seat so he could see Mab as she talked to him.

"When I set eyes on the preacher, devil give a jump in my body. The devil was afraid of him! Sick as I was, I had hope then. I laughed. Ha-ha, devil, here's a man gwin to fix you for good!"

Cowboy flicked his half-smoked cigarette and listened to the fluted turbulence of Mab's breath, all the while smiling edgily. "What did he do, Mab?"

"Cast out the devil and brought me home to Jesus. But he did even more, because he's a great man with the Power of Heaven in him. I was sick, and he healed me."

The car was silent except for the preacher's voice and the

intermittent sounds of insects, dazzled by a light on a pole not far away, thumping against the windshield. Mab sat with her mouth thinned and her head held high, somewhat defiantly, as if she was waiting for Cowboy's derision.

But he said only, "How sick were you, Mab?"

"Sick in ways I can't speak about, because it ain't decent. I wouldn't see no doctor, not me! I knew what the doctor would say. I waited till the devil said it for him. Almost waited too late. But the preacher healed me."

Cowboy said calmly, "I don't think so."

"Do I look sick to you?" Mab demanded.

"Not a bit."

"Well, I tell you I had a sick liver, and it was more than drinking pains. Daniel can assure you I ain't complained for days. I'm a well woman now. But I lived ten years with my sick liver, Cowboy." She trembled a little with indignation, as if his skepticism had prickled her skin. "Where's my sick liver gone? Precious God, it would kill me dead as a doornail to drink down a whole glass of buttermilk before I met the preacher. Know what I had with my supper tonight? *Two* glasses of buttermilk! I can drink it without harm. The preacher's touch made me well, his touch and his Power."

Cowboy cocked his head. "What power are you talking about?"

"Well, it was—it was like I'd been handed over a new body. Mortification was gone. I felt happiness. Beautiful happiness." Her vagueness stifled her, and she fell silent. "I reckon I can't truly describe what happened to me," she said after a long pause, confounded by her inability to express to Cowboy what was perfectly clear in her heart. "I hope you believe me," she said then, "because what I'm telling is the truth. Which I ain't told to another soul, not even Daniel. Not even that Dr. Matthews, who came slipping around saying he was a friend of the preacher's and trying to pump me about the preacher's Power. No, I ain't spoke a word till tonight, since it's nobody's business, but I'm telling *you*, Cowboy, because I know you're in the same fix I was in about a week ago. There's a bad devil in you that's causing all kinds of trouble, and if the devil's not drove out, there's no way to describe what misery he'll bring you to. You're sitting here right now and not in a prison because the preacher spoke up in time to thwart the devil and all his plans for you. I think if you give King Windom half a chance he'll banish that devil for good. He *commanded* the devil to jump out of my throat, and my throat was so sore next day, had all I could do to swallow. I'm telling you!"

"*. . . Many people say to me, Preacher, how can you feel so close to Jesus Christ? Does He talk to you? Do you talk to Him? Beloved, that's exactly what I do! Every day I talk to Jesus on my knees in prayer, and every day He answers me, in the books of Mark, Matthew, Luke, and John . . .*"

"Cowboy," Mab pleaded, "believe in him. Won't you? Follow him, and you won't never have regrets. Ask him to pray with you, to thwart your devil. You've got *so* much talent, and such a good head—I ain't knowed you long but I know that much—with the two of you working together the devil wouldn't stand a Chinaman's chance!"

Cowboy's fingers dug into the back of the seat, but he was otherwise motionless. He didn't look at Mab. When he spoke his voice was dry, different—without an agreeable touch of drawl, or a not-so-agreeable edge of sarcasm. Mab crossed her arms involuntarily as if she'd been struck by a chill.

"I don't hold it against you that you'd lie for him, and about him—"

"Lie!" said Mab, her eyes wide with astonishment.

"And I'm happy you don't take whiskey anymore; if you want to blame your drinking on the devil, that's all right with me, and if you want to give the preacher credit because you're off the bottle, that's all right too. Just don't try to make me believe he's . . . anything. That he has"—bitterness exploded into the Cowboy's voice—"a *power*. Because if I get that idea in my head, I'll have to prove you're wrong."

He ducked and stepped out of the car, then walked away without so much as a good-bye. After a few steps, however, he changed his mind and again approached the car, putting his face in the window. Stray light grazed his eyes, and gave a sad shadow to his often-belligerent mouth. Blood came in a rush to Mab's head, whether from fright or from sympathy she couldn't tell.

"Maybe you and the preacher are right, and there are devils around. The devil is welcome to what's left of me. I think I gave him my soul a long time ago, when I would have given anything to get out of . . . that house."

"You didn't give up your soul," Mab said sternly. "Don't talk such talk."

252

Cowboy shook his head. "Who knows what I gave up, or what's still there, buried in the yard like pennies, rotting behind the furnace like an old rubber ball? Put it this way, then; I gave up *feeling*. That's as much as a soul, or more. Let me tell *you* what life with the devil is like, Mab—"

"I know too well," she breathed.

"Why, Mab, it can be easy! Ummm, easy. No troubles. But, all right. I won't say any more. I just want you to understand why the preacher's not going to have any luck trying to bring me into *his* house—the House of the Lord. I'd die first. I'd kill him." Her breath hissed. "No. Don't you worry, Mab. That won't happen. I'll stay out of his way, do what he tells me to do, and when my time's up I'll just walk off. I won't hurt him for your sake, Mab, because I like you."

As if she'd had a whiff of perdition, Mab covered her face, and when she ventured to look again, Cowboy was gone. Daniel returned a minute or two later, and put a cold soda in her thoughtlessly outstretched hand.

"... *Beloved, it was hot there in Jerusalem, hot as a soybean field in August, and His skin was brown and tough like yours is after a hard summer working in the fields....*"

Mab drank her soda with tears streaming down her face, to Daniel's consternation; but he couldn't get a word out of her the rest of the evening.

24

The Northcutts

It was possible that the story which Molly had promoted about Queen Mab and her association with the preacher had an immediate effect on attendance at the revival, although there was no way to be sure; likely the people who turned out in growing numbers every night through the end of October were attracted for many reasons, among them Mab Shaw. The continuing revival was an excellent one, with nothing sleazy or ill-considered about it. The singing was varied and attractive, the surroundings clean, and the preaching of a quality that brought back some of the faithful many times. Whatever the reasons, the tent was filled every night and on Sunday afternoons; weekends the congregation was so large that three hundred extra chairs were rented and placed outside the tent for latecomers. Fortunately, the nights continued mild and almost rainless, so the sides of the tent could be removed for the benefit of those in the open air.

One night, in an attempt to gauge the effects of the daily broadcasts over Kay-tip, Molly conducted a car-by-car count in the parking lot and discovered that better than half of the cars carried out-of-state license plates; they had come from Mississippi, Arkansas, Missouri, and even Louisiana. To Molly this proved the efficacy of the broadcasts and, as she poked around the fringes of the tent during the sermon, her eyes roving from King Windom to the attentive, pleased—and sometimes distraught—faces turned toward him, she wondered how many would eventually come to see and hear him in the remaining weeks, and from how far? Why did they seek him out? Was it simply curiosity, the chance for an outing, or something much deeper and more mysterious? Did they come because they felt the way Molly herself felt about the preacher? Did they love him? Or was it simply the fact that the people required a god, any god, who would fulfill their need to be amazed?

She was enthralled by this phenomenon which she had set in motion. She never tired of talking to worshipers whom she encountered on the tent grounds; her interest in people, from the ignorant and reticent farmers who arrived with endless families in tow to the flighty girls who giggled among themselves at sight of the preacher, came to life during those nights and was heightened. She spoke to them all about the preacher, relishing their comments, and their awe.

But Molly knew very little of the religious desperations of the poor and unnoticed. And she knew nothing at all of promises which King Windom had once made in innocence and conviction, promises which were still heard from time to time, in out-of-the-way places, in hills and valleys where small congregations met to celebrate the Lord by frenzy and incantation. They were promises which a few in their hardship and suffering were determined he must keep.

The car that came along the back road through the poplars and turned into the tent grounds was a pre-World War Two Dodge, long and hippy with fenders; at least two of those fenders were turning lacy with rust in places. The low-pitched headlights wobbled and the Dodge had a bad front-end shimmy which the driver had to control with the strength of both arms.

The driver brought his car to a stop abruptly, across the tracks of other cars and light trucks parked in disorderly rows behind the tent, and got out right away. He was a tall rural type and he looked nearly done in with fatigue.

With one elbow resting on the counter of the pronto-pup wagon, Cowboy peeled down the wrapper of a candy bar and studied the man and his family with a stare that would have been unbearably rude indoors. They might have been out riding around and decided to take in the tag end of the revival meeting in progress, but Cowboy had a hunch they'd traveled hard, and were far removed from their own home. For one thing, the man had the glaze of sun and the lights of highways in his eyes; then too, there was the anxious way the boy had bolted out of the front seat to raise the hood of the car.

They were father and son; the paleness of their eyes and the kinship of movement told Cowboy that. There were also in the car a young girl of twelve or so, face half-hidden in a thicket of red hair, an older woman whom Cowboy took as the man's wife, and—he lifted his heels from the hard clay in front of the pronto-pup wagon, and stretched his neck unobtrusively—someone lying in the dimness of the back seat, half sunk in pillows and covered over against the chill of the November evening by a quilt.

The boy had lifted his head from the innards of the Dodge and spoken to his father, who looked back deliberately for a long minute, then straight at Cowboy.

Cowboy strolled toward the man, who took a bare step forward to acknowledge his approach and unspoken inquiry. The man wore a pin-stripe silver-gray suit that was long out of style and a white cotton shirt unbuttoned at the throat. They were poor people, Cowboy knew, living the kind of poverty

255

that is common in many parts of the South; yet they seemed uncommonly fearful.

"Howyou," said Cowboy.

"Howyou."

After this greeting Cowboy remained properly silent, offering nothing, until the man could become accustomed to him and speak his mind. Although, technically, the man was the stranger there, Cowboy's dust-soaked boots and stylish rancher's gabardines made him the alien, at least as far as this man's existence went, and so he waited to be accepted, or not.

"There a branch hereabout?" the man asked hoarsely.

"None I know of; but a spigot under the cottonwood there."

The man turned his head carefully, studied the tree and the pipe that came up out of the ground, with a board spillway and a concrete trough below it, and directed his boy to the water. He then bent his attention upon the tent and his chest lifted slowly and grandly. The expression on his hard-water face was capricious: he seemed thankful and about to break into smiles; then dubious and concerned; at last his head dropped as he cast his eyes away from the tent, the rebellious gesture of a child who will not see or hear for fear of unbearable disappointment, and he stood somewhat more rigidly than before until his boy approached with a porcelain pitcher in one hand and a plastic mug in the other, and offered the mug of water to his father.

The boy rubbed at a mosquito bump in the hollow of one temple and his mouth flexed impatiently; he had his look at the tent too, then studied his father and Cowboy as well, with some faint animosity, as if he suspected Cowboy to be all the reason in the world for the watery fatigue and sadness in his daddy's pale-blue eyes.

The boy jerked his head so hard in the direction of the tent that his arm moved too and some of the water from the pitcher spilled down over his wrist. "Is that it?" he demanded.

His father squinted a little. "Ain't ask," he said.

He was a handsome boy, not more than seventeen, blond and filled with a maverick ardor. He knew to let his father do the asking for the family, yet he was also sore enough to ignore this small diplomacy and, after a warning flash of his eyes which the man did not see, blurted out to Cowboy:

"Is this the tent of the Healer?"

Cowboy then understood part of what he had been groping

for since his first glimpse of the family and the makeshift sickbed in the back seat of the Dodge. The devastation that was heavy in the hanging hands of the man almost sickened Cowboy for a moment; the reason for the boy's sullenness and impertinence was now clear, and there welled up in Cowboy the memory of his talk with Mab Shaw not too long ago. He smiled slightly, incredulously, a smile which the boy took as an admission of ignorance.

It seemed as if the three of them had become absorbed in listening to the preacher at the same time. They might have become gradually aware of his voice, as one becomes aware of a radio playing in a neighbor's house, or perhaps the wind had brought his amplified voice to them.

"Reckon that's him?" the boy now asked his father.

"Take the water to the wummun," the man said curtly, sending him on his way with the briefest glance of authority.

Cowboy's eyes followed the boy as the voice from the tent grew less audible. The red-haired girl was outside the car now, straightening her skirt. She had a drink from the pitcher, then passed the pitcher through an open window to the woman inside, who poured a cupful of water and leaned across the seat to lift a blue old head from the shadows and the pillows.

The man had taken a couple of steps toward the tent, but was now motionless. As if musing, he said "It must be him, for they said he was a fair talker. This time the Lord had delivered us to our Healer. Is't him? King Windom a-preachin here?"

Cowboy nodded.

"God's blessing!" the man exclaimed. He beckoned to his son and from a pocket of his suit coat withdrew a folded dollar bill. This he passed wordlessly to the boy, who went along to the pronto-pup wagon.

"Would you join me in the meetin," he said, and Cowboy fell in beside him, intrigued by the sense of family destiny and mystical conviction which the man bore with him, and intensely aware of all the implications spoken aloud in the word "healer."

"Northcutt," the man offered. "Von Northcutt. The boy is Jimmy Alvah."

"Jim Cobb. Cowboy, they call me."

"Mighty pleased, Mr. Cobb."

"Traveled far?"

"We left home in Hokes Bluff Monday last and gone on up to

257

the Sugar Tree Valley in Virginia, but it's morn four year since King Windom was there. Church brother ourn told us to look up Sister Bethel Pettigrew in Nashville. Found out he was on the radio here and come on down. But till this night, mister, it was a spell of drivin for naught. Morn nine hundred mile."

"Enough to wear down any man," Cowboy said.

"Morn nine hundred mile since we started out, and we are whipped," the man acknowledged with a stiff smile. They paused before the back entrance to the tent, a half-rolled flap of canvas, and anxiety seemed to stifle him again. He made a maul of his hands and lowered his forehead in an attitude of prayer. As his head touched his laced fingers, there came from behind them a weak, needle-sharp scream of pain, hardly human at all, and involuntarily Cowboy looked back for the source of the scream. Oh, he thought then, here it comes. But more likely the screams had been coming for days on end while that old car battled the road.

The man's hands shook. "It is my ma," he said. "She is suffern a cancer, and the doctors sent her home for good some little time ago." They both anticipated a second scream, but it did not come. The man thrust his fingers through his graying hair and continued: "Ma never laid down and quit, and I know she is right when she says the cancer is God's measure of a true Christian family. Every night of the week at home we was joined in prayer by brothers and sisters of the church. Yes, we prayed for the guidance of the good Lord God in time of need. We are a family that loves God. All of us down to the youngest honors Him and praises His name. We have never ask for no Miracle. Ma said God would make His Power to move among us if it was His Will/and glory to my God/one night there in meetin she was taken with His Spirit and His Love/spoke out in strange tongues/oh *glory be* to my Lord and my God!"

The suffering of the man never had been more visible than it was during this unexpected rapture, half whispered and half sung. Another scream returned him coldly and apprehensively to the moment. He would not look back, but lowered his head and went on in a different tone: "We never prayed for Him to take hold on that cancer and fling it out her body like He's done for other folks. But Ma spoke to us in her vision/yea surely it was God in His Wisdom and His Power spoke through her lips! 'God has seen fit to rid me of this cancer, and the Miracles of God are in the hands of King Windom.' "

Cowboy stooped to pick a crumpled handbill out of the dust at his feet. He smoothed the paper and passed it to the man, who took it solemnly and stared at the picture of King Windom and the text for so long that Cowboy suspected he wasn't able to read.

"Had your ma ever heard of him? Before she spoke out in meeting that night?"

The man raised his eyes from the handbill. "Ma knowed of him from a nephew ourn, who sometimes passed through the Sugar Tree Valley. But we found that church burned down, and folks was not quick to speak the name of King Windom. One youngern said he perished inside his church, and it were God's Will. Nother said he never perished, but moved way off to Florida; said he'd seen the preacher there himself, big as life on the streets. And so it is we have come this far, Mr. Cobb, with the finger of God to point the way. My ma is sixty-eight year old, but she has grit to spare. She never left off singin and prayin till this day—"

He seemed to lose his courage as well as his voice; a shudder convulsed him, and Cowboy put out a bracing hand. But the man composed himself, throwing off his terror, and said, "I only found Jesus myself year ago, and I tell you I still quake at the knees fore I enter God's House." With that he bent sideways and stepped under the flap and into the tent, and Cowboy followed.

The meeting was nearly over; Cowboy listened for a few minutes, wedged between a man with an infant in the crook of his arm and an extremely fat but unyielding girl. He studied Von Northcutt thoughtfully, then gave King a part of his attention. But his heart was jumping. *The church burned down—folks was not quick to speak the name of King Windom.*

Cowboy shouldered his way outside and gulped fresh air. With a cigarette in his hand, he wandered aimlessly from the tent. A train was passing on the railroad embankment, its lights flickering through the still leaves of the poplar trees. When it had gone, Cowboy heard the sounds of sobbing, and he searched the dark. The red-haired girl was standing not too far away, her face in her hands; she was half-concealed behind a tree. Cowboy listened unwillingly; the sobbing of the girl turned his thoughts back to Von Northcutt and the preacher. He glanced at the well-traveled Dodge and at the boy who leaned like stone against one of the fenders. There was no sound from the old woman lying in the back seat.

Cowboy finished his cigarette, aware of a tingling of excitement and anticipation in his fingers, and watched the people spreading out slowly in all directions from the tent. He let his thoughts loose in the rubble of voices, and his eyes wandered. Within a quarter hour the tent ground was cleared, except for the inevitable stragglers, perhaps those who had stayed behind to accept Christ and be welcomed individually by the preacher. The pronto-pup wagons were clamorously surrounded, with everyone yellow as Chinamen in the unrealistic light. But soon the last couple passed through the film of dust above the road, growing suddenly invisible in the dark just beyond, and the concessionaires locked up.

Cowboy looked quickly at the Dodge, where the boy still leaned, in the same attitude as before. The girl had returned to the front seat and was brushing her hair. Cowboy turned and walked back to the tent, but he didn't enter. On the pulpit King was conferring with several preachers. Von Northcutt was not in sight.

Cowboy scratched at the nape of his neck and waited. Before long the preachers left and King Windom sat tiredly on the piano bench, hands slack below his knees. For several minutes he did not move at all. Cowboy shifted his weight and lifted the tent flap a little higher. This time he saw Von Northcutt, standing gaunt and watchful in the shadows at the back of the tent. Cowboy wondered how long the man had been there, and why he did not now make a move toward King; he had spent nearly two weeks tracking the preacher down, from a word spoken here, or there, on either side of the Appalachians, maintaining a pace that ultimately was only a little ahead of his mother's death. There was no telling what had rooted Northcutt at this moment: it might have been awe, or disappointment at seeing that King Windom was just a man, after all. Perhaps his hope had gone cold now that the confrontation of a name, and a rumor, was possible.

"Pa! Pa!"

The cries of the red-haired girl startled Cowboy, but the momentary confusion he felt in looking for her was mild compared to the preacher's reaction: apparently he had thought he was all alone, and the sound of her voice sent him

260

straight to his feet. The girl flew by Cowboy and into the tent, where she ran almost into the arms of her father.

She backed off a step, tried to speak, found she couldn't and simply pointed eloquently in the direction of the family car. Northcutt sent his daughter off with a hand clapped against her shoulder, shook himself with ashen desperation, and plunged toward King Windom.

"I never thought to come on you so quick," he said to the preacher as he climbed the stairs to the pulpit. "That was my girl hollerin." His lips parted in a beseeching smile. "I believe she meant to say Ma is fixin to die on us. We expectin that since way last Tuesday, any hour almost, and I have been at my wit's end to find you fore it happened. If you are the King Windom who lived in the Sugar Tree Valley, then God be praised we are still in time."

King raked at his hair with the fingers of one hand, and still seemed shocked by the interruption of his reverie. The words "Sugar Tree Valley" seemed to catch him like a blow a second after they were spoken, so that his shoulders lifted protectively, and a hard wary light appeared in his eyes. He didn't speak but backed up and stood firmly against the piano, his eyes level on Northcutt.

"You come from the Sugar Tree Valley?" he asked.

Northcutt's smile faded gradually and unwillingly; he was dismayed by the young preacher's tone and stance. He lowered his eyes, then his gaze swept across the tent and through the unobtrusive Cowboy, and fear seemed to fall on him with the light, clinging touch of a large spider. He raised both hands as if he would gently lift Windom into his mother's presence, as if by some act of strength he wished to make the miracle that was necessary to save her instantly more vivid to himself, and to the preacher.

"Reckon you know—as we have a dyin wummun there—that it's hope for a healin miracle brung us. God Himself give us our hope, Preacher." Voicing this assurance seemed to help him, and he went on, rapidly, "God Himself give us our hope. A vision Ma had of the healin hands of King Windom is all that has kept her with us. We know the miracles you have worked in His name, Preacher. The cancers and tumors you have licked, and the blind eyes made to see. Church brother ourn give us names of folks seen how you laid hold on a boy's twisted back, and made it good as new again . . ."

Northcutt began to ramble ecstatically, becoming more and more descriptive of physical horrors beyond the skill of surgeons, of incurable diseases that had responded only to the supernatural touch of the preacher. Cowboy felt shocked, despite himself.

Northcutt abruptly faltered in his passion; he had talked as if he was trying to please or placate the preacher with a recitation of his triumphs, which seemed as unreal in the telling as the legends of a long-forgotten tribe. Yet King did not look pleased, or proud or properly and devoutly somber; he looked ill. He shook his head many times in protest, and his hands fell weakly to his sides. Cowboy thought that he might turn and run from Northcutt, except for the obstacle of the piano behind him.

The older man seemed panic-stricken by the preacher's reticence and visible unhappiness. His jaw fell, revealing a gleaming gash of false teeth, then his face closed, studiously; he was a man who had been presented with an urgent riddle, just when his competence was strained to breaking by his mother's suffering. His response to the shaking of King Windom's head was to pull names from his memory, names which the preacher knew, or should have known.

Suddenly King's hands swept outward in a violent gesture of denial, and he shouted: "No, no, no! Who are those people? I don't know those people! I'm sorry, I'm sorry your ma is sick! I'm just one of God's preachers! Let me pray for your ma—I can't do more than that. Praying is all. We'll find a hospital to take her in if you—"

Northcutt caught at King's hands, squeezing them in his own as if he were disciplining a recalcitrant child. His smile was heartbreakingly bright.

"Hospital? They done sent us *home* from the hospital, Preacher, and that were two month ago!"

The preacher's face was tense with revulsion and his own panic. He struggled to free his hands, but Northcutt was strong, and nearly out of his head from grief.

"Let go," King pleaded. "You're wrong—what you heard is wrong! It's not me, it's not true!"

Northcutt winced angrily and squeezed the preacher's hands harder, drawing them closer to his own chest until their faces were only inches apart.

"Preacher, it's got to be true—what so many folks have saw with their own eyes has got to be God's truth!"

"Let me go." His voice broke in a sob. "I can't do . . . anything but pray. Take her . . . to town, Brother. Please take your ma to town where they can look after her!"

"It is God's will that you help her," Northcutt said grimly, but the mark of bewilderment was on him. "God has sent you, Preacher, that's what there is to it, and you are charged to save my ma's life—" He tried to continue, though his voice had become an unintelligible rasp, and Cowboy saw it all happening to him in a rush, saw his hands go slack as the knowledge hit him. Somehow, despite his sense of destiny, and his prayers, he had been deceived, wronged, dismissed by God Himself, and his pain was concentrated in a moan that froze Cowboy to the marrow. Smoothly, but with great force, Northcutt smashed the preacher twice across the face with his large open hand, and King dropped to his knees, trying to shield his head with his arms.

"Oh, my God," Northcutt sobbed. He stood over the preacher with one fist held high, but he didn't strike. "Oh, Jesus, oh, Saviour, I can't lose her, I have come a long way, and I can't lose her now."

"Pa," his son called irascibly, "Pa, you come on right now!" and Northcutt turned away, jumped down from the pulpit, and ran outside. In a few moments, recovering from the shock of being hit, King hurried after him.

Cowboy waited long enough to go clumsily through his pockets, looking for a smoke. The hatred which he had felt for King Windom before Northcutt's spasm of violence cooled, but he still felt unable to draw a decent breath. He moved closer to the back lot and the old car, but stayed near the tent, away from the Northcutt family and out of the coils of their tragedy.

The tragedy, surprisingly, seemed not to have happened. The rear door of the Dodge was open, and Northcutt leaned head-in, his big hands braced against the roof, the cuffs of his trousers hiked to mid-calf. His son and his daughter stood behind him, young heads awry, their elbows almost touching, and his wife was sitting in the front seat with her feet solidly on the running board. One hand was fallen like a dead bird in her lap, and the other held a cigarette. Her face had the expression of one who has learned to clutch at, and relish deeply, small pleasures.

"I reckont the end had come, but she is some better now," the woman said matter-of-factly. She drew on her cigarette, and turned her head for a weary, incurious look at her husband's face.

King Windom had approached the car very slowly, touching his cheek perhaps unconsciously where Northcutt had slapped him. At each step he looked unwilling to take another; he struggled obviously against the impulse that was drawing him nearer the sick woman. Northcutt's wife saw him and then the children turned, one at a time. The girl said, shyly, as King went by her: "Pa, it's the preacher," and the boy mumbled, as if in greeting: "Preacher's here," but Northcutt either didn't hear them or was so absorbed by the face of his mother that he could think of nothing else. His wife stepped down from the running board and let the cigarette drop unobtrusively at her feet, where she ground it out.

Some sound caught her attention and she cocked an ear toward the car almost angrily. She had a great sun-stained face and uneven ringlets of copper-colored hair all over her head, and a fierce fallen mouth that broke into an unexpectedly attractive smile.

"Fore God if that wummun ain't got a pair a ears, stricken as she is . . . How there, Preacher, you would be King Windom. We have heard a mighty lot of talk about you, and it were nothin but praise. Folks in there tonight"—she waved a hand toward the tent—"was chock full a your message when they come by us." His looks intrigued her, as they did her daughter; the boy was hunkered down picking bottle caps out of the dirt and flicking them at a tree.

Northcutt lifted his head out of the back seat. " 'Send me the preacher,' " he mumbled. "Ma said, 'Send me the preacher.' "

"First words past her lips in three days," his wife said, pleased. "That's somethin to be thankful for. Preacher, she fetched me a real scare; that's why I sent the girl after you and Northcutt. The old lady couldn't catch her breath. But now she is even talkin again." She paused and stared at her husband, and at the car, frowning. "Reckont this ain't no place to go bout your work, but Northcutt will be back up there next the tent and the two a you likely can lift her outen the back seat."

"Hold on," King Windom said firmly, catching her drift. He seemed more sure of himself with the woman. Northcutt had run through his strength; he was on his feet, but that was all. His wife acted as if she were not unreasonably burdened, and it was likely King realized that her wishes and her tongue ruled the family, at least under ordinary circumstances.

"Listen to me a minute, please. I can't do what you people have come looking for me to do. I can't! I'm no . . . miracle worker!"

The woman's eyes focused rather bleakly on his belt buckle. Northcutt rocked on his heels, and licked at his lips. The children were hard and fast and all ears.

"Yea—oh?" she said, perplexed, and looked straight to his eyes, and then at a point beyond his head where the evening star was still burning, redly. Her face was square and composed. But her patience was chilly, and there was both a challenge and a warning in her voice when she said:

"Go on, Preacher."

"That's the Will of God, as I am standing here," King said unflinchingly. "But I'll comfort that sick woman any way I can, and pray as long as you want me to pray for the end of her suffering."

She remained rigid, as if she were about to come down on him in a temper. But gradually she weakened; the sincerity of his appeal was beyond question, and so was her instinctive liking for him. Still sore with her own passion for a miracle, ironically aware of having stooped to asking for the incredible of a beleaguered God, she shook her head scornfully at herself, at all of them, and lifted her hands in a pronouncement of futility and acceptance.

King smiled timidly at her. Northcutt slowly lowered himself to the running board of the Dodge and sat with his hands clasped riblike beneath his knees. The boy raised up and popped another bottle cap against the trunk of the tree; his aim had been phenomenal right along.

"You are just a young man after all," she said haltingly, looking at length into his face. "I knowed, knowed all along it was wrong, somehow, but he"—the glance she gave her husband was filled with admiration, and then a flashing regret—"he wouldn't be talked outer nothin, he always paid better mind to his ma than anybody, and what can you expect, a dyin old lady, who's to say I'll be any braver when it's my turn; well," and she returned to King, apologetically. "You are a good-lookin young man, any soul with half an eye can see that you are on fire for the Lord. I reckon there is people heard you preachin and took on a little a your fire and give you credit for things you never done atall." King Windom hung his head slightly and was serious and mute. "Which is no fault a yourn, Preacher. We"— she embraced them all with a tiny movement of one pudgy hand—"we are pleased to know you, and pleased that you would go down on your knees in prayer for one of ourn."

"God bless you, Preacher," the girl said primly. Northcutt blindly lifted his head and cried out in a rebuking anger:

"The Lord ain't never heard me one time; death is at my mother's throat, and the Lord—"

"Don't start asayin *that*, mister." his wife warned him, and in her voice was a hint of all the years it had taken to firmly yank him inside the churchly fold; many years would pass before she forgave him this disastrous night. She reached down and took her man by the arm, lifted him from the running board, and led him away.

"It is all right, any time," she told King Windom, and he went immediately to the car, carefully cleared a place for himself on the back seat, and eased in; his long legs remained outside, ankles bent against the clay.

25

Exorcism

The wind ran high, then it subsided; on the rail lines trains came and went, and in between were vast bowls of silence. There was a chill, inside the canvas as well as out. The preacher had put on his old blue sweater, the one frayed at the elbows, and it was adequate protection as long as he moved about. This he managed to do, on one small errand and then another, of cleaning up, or putting aright.

There was nothing in the tent for him now but waiting. He had unplugged all lights but two, which burned unshaded above the pulpit. The tent was not much more than a deserted theater, slightly ominous with empty chairs, a receptacle for his solitary fears, his recriminations, his prayers—his prayers. But he had no more prayers to offer, either in defense or in hope; the last of a lifetime of his prayers had gone into his vigil with a mortally sick woman who had been as light as a wax ornament in his arms. The Northcutts had gratefully accepted his prayers and he had seen them go, perhaps strengthened. He remained behind, stubbornly in possession of his faith, for whatever might come—for more like the Northcutts, if that was the Lord's alternative.

His senses were extraordinarily alive and sharp: the nightshine seemed visible through the weave of the canvas; the earth held voices, omens; the night was well traveled, and dim forces vibrated in the well of his subconscious. They kept him restless, alert, waiting. Perhaps for the unfolding of God's persistent riddle, for his own justification, or final derangement.

King felt both eager and dismayed, reviewing the hour in which the Northcutts had come and gone. Thank God he'd been alone and unobserved—except for Cowboy. Only Cowboy had observed them, and then he had disappeared. How much had he seen, or heard? Where was he now, and what was he thinking? King shuddered and prowled along the pulpit, his forehead hot and agleam with light, eyes masked by shadow. In front of the small altar he studied the brass candlestick, fulcrum of his ministry. It looked frail in the available light, and breakable. Crisis throbbed in the preacher's body; his dry lips moved wordlessly and he frowned. Again he was rooted by the Divine riddle posed by the visit of the Northcutts and the freshening of his past. It could not be an aimless cruelty on the part of the Lord, a negligent demand that his ministry come to an end. No, the Lord had brought them all together, including Cowboy, for a more serious purpose.

Again King shuddered, as omens pressed upon him. Turning, he faced the pit of the tent, sharp with shadows, and excitement ran in his blood, then hardened to ice. He'd heard nothing, but there, in between the rows of chairs, was the shape of an enemy.

He watched in fascination as the dog, which was muscled like a lion, advanced slowly toward the pulpit. The studded collar which King had once used to strangle Philemon's beast was missing; a flicker of his eyes told him that the dog was running free, no one else was in the tent. At least there was nothing human there, he thought, and recoiled. The ice crept to the surface of his skin.

Now the dog was in the light, at the pulpit steps. It looked up at him, close-mouthed. There was blood on the black muzzle; black blood fudged the short hairs on the powerful forelegs. The dog trembled at the preacher's scent; raised teeth glinted in the light.

King reached behind him and picked up the brass candlestick, which he held like a club. Obviously the beast had sampled blood that night, the blood of some heedless field animal.

Yet as King crouched, readying himself for a fight, he was not altogether convinced that the dog he was looking at was real; his mind was filled with reminders of the audacity and cleverness of Satan. He felt a passionate loathing for all the devil figures of hell.

For nearly a minute the dog made no move, but a peculiar moan rose in its throat. King straightened and walked slowly to the edge of the pulpit. The dog stiffened at his approach, hair rising in a slight ruff around its bulging neck, and the moan changed to a warning snarl. The dog was all teeth now; King looked calmly down into its throat. He thrust the candlestick out, holding it at arm's length.

"I'll kill you in God's holy house if I have to," he said. "Hear this! I believe in the Lord God. I believe in His might. My faith's not hurt. Is that what you came to find out, Satan? Then know that nothing can take away my faith; not even God Himself can do it." He trembled, and was silent, staring keenly down at the murderous dog. Unexpectedly, perhaps from strain, his eyes stung with tears. He raised his head toward the top of the tent, and the light cut across his eyes, blinding him for a few moments.

When he glanced down Philemon's dog was no longer there. He thought he saw a bounding shadow near one wall of the tent, and heard the flutter of canvas. He shook his head and sighed almost convulsively, and when he sank down on the edge of the pulpit he felt weak and hollow.

Within a few minutes, as the chill air was cutting into him, a car entered the tent grounds with a roar. Headlights burned dreamlike through the canvas, creating a shadow-lattice of rope. King lifted his head from contemplation of the candlestick, which he held lightly balanced on one knee. The engine died, and the grounds were quiet. Presently a door slammed, and King heard a low oath. His heart jumped. Cowboy. But . . . yes, where else would Satan have gone? And he felt a new releasing of the riddle; the riddle was as close to him, as momentous as his own held breath.

King stared at the back of the tent; a blocky shadow was printed there as Cowboy hesitated between an outside light and the wall of canvas. Then Cowboy came in, still silent. Just inside the tent he stopped once more. A train bore down on them, and when the thundering had fallen to a low pitch, King said in a dry voice:

"You've come this far, don't you want to come the rest of the way?"

He was drunk, judging from the way chairs clattered out of his path. Or was he? King's eyes narrowed; he had seen Cowboy put on an act before, a day when he had been upset, or terrified. Cowboy kept one hand in a pocket of his coat as he came down to the pulpit, but that pocket bulged with more than his hand; King swallowed, feeling his chest expand with tension at this silly-menacing approach. But his expression was unchanged.

"Where have you been?" he asked.

The Cowboy continued at a slow pace until he had cleared the last row of chairs. Then he planted his feet and stood looking up at the preacher, his face flinching against the light, his eyes blurred by an alcoholic film. Despite the temperature of the night air he looked flushed. His breathing was rough and uneven.

"Having myself a goddam good time," he said hoarsely. He gazed here and there in the tent; worry appeared in his eyes.

"No company—they all gone?"

King coughed into his sleeve. "I sent the Northcutts back to Alabama, where they belong. God willing, the old woman will die in her own bed. God willing, their faith is still strong."

Cowboy continued to peer into the dark, and his shoulders twitched, one and then the other. His right hand stayed firmly in the pocket and King's eyes kept returning to it. The left-hand coat pocket was ripped half off as if Cowboy had caught it on the car door handle. King could not yet figure out his mood; instinct told him Cowboy was running wild under his skin, and the shoulder twitches justified that conviction. Yet when

Cowboy looked back at him, a slaphappy, faintly pleased smile was stuck to his face. He said, in a comradely tone:

"Come on, let's get out of here! I know where we can get a good piece this time night. Man, what do you ever do for a *piece*, anyway?" When King did not reply, his smile became sour, and he blinked at the annoying haze in his eyes. "Goddammit, I want to have some *fun!*"

"Is that why you came back here? To take me to a whorehouse?"

Cowboy wrenched his head irritably, then shifted his feet so the light wasn't blazing solidly in his eyes.

"I can't have any goddam fun by myself," he complained. "I *tried!* And goddam it—" His voice was lost as he reached for breath. For several seconds he seemed pitiably confused, then his eyes drifted slowly over the preacher. He was close enough to reach out and jerk the candlestick from King's unyielding hand. He studied the candlestick for a few moments, then turned and hurled it thumpingly against the canvas.

"You don't need *that!*" he cried. "There's two whores—and I happen to know they're not busy tonight—"

"I'm not lying down with any whores, Cowboy. Tonight or ever. Isn't my idea of a good time." King looked where the candlestick had gone. "Now, will you—"

"Giving you a chance!" Cowboy shouted, savagery in his eyes.

"Chance for what?"

"To show me—t-to be a *man*, you— To save face, you fake, you liar, you *nothing!*" His vehemence almost upset him, but he maintained his balance, his face staining red from effort. Once he was steady—and almost as an afterthought—he pulled his right hand from the coat pocket and made a show of the weapon in his fist. A niche of concern appeared between the preacher's brows, but he felt no panic. His eyes sharpened and he said:

"Get control of yourself, Cowboy. Do it now."

Cowboy's face was lined with emotion. "You can get drunk with me, get in bed with a whore, and act like a natural man, and you can"—he raised the muzzle of the olive-drab automatic—"admit it's all a lie: your faith, your miracles—all that is a *damn* lie. You're just a man like anybody else, and you'll—It doesn't make any difference to me if I have to shoot you—"

King was lost in a stare, nerveless as the deaf. His hands flattened slowly, and he reached for his narrow knees, gripping them. He was pale, and for a moment fear appeared in his eyes: the fear of a hounded and misjudged man. He shook his head to clear it, then focused on the Cowboy, reviewing the tension between them, that had nothing much to do with the absurd, deadly gun.

"I don't know just what all Von Northcutt told you about me," King said, "or even if he talked to you. If he did, then he must have used the word 'healer'; I suppose you know what that means. But I'm just as real as you are, Cowboy, there's nothing . . . supernatural about me. My feelings get hurt and my body gets tired and, yes, it aches for a woman's love—love that I had once. But at the same time I *am* different from you, from almost all men, and nothing can change that. If you're going to judge me a hypocrite, and if you think that's a crime calls for killing, then you'd better know a lot more about me than you already know. Sit down; it'll take a few minutes. Sit, because you make me nervous standing there like a gunman, which I reckon you're not." His voice became harsher. "Sit, if you want to learn the meaning of faith. Because I doubt if there's a man alive better able to teach you than me." He thrust up his scarred hands, palms out. The barrier of his hands seemed to intimidate Cowboy, who lowered his head but not the automatic, and then backed off to a chair, where he sat uneasily, still buffeted by the wildness under his skin.

Satisfied, King drew a settling breath and began.

"I vow I can tell you about the Sugar Tree Valley quick enough. A man named Bonner and myself was preaching early one fall in middle Tennessee, around Wartrace. Some people from the Valley heard me one night and right away they offered me a church had been standing empty for want of a preacher. I said no, but they came back, more of them each night, and pleaded. Well, what was I to think? God seemed to have a plan. Bonner was doubtful, said he needed me too, but he was off to California for the winter to lead church revivals; I didn't see where he could use me at all. And the idea of having a church appealed; I longed to settle down after those months on the road." He made a slight gesture with one hand, expressive of his acceptance. "They have hard winters in the Sugar Tree. Snow, ice, and darkness for days on end. The people of my church were poor, and in wintertime they suffer the most. The only place they can forget their miseries is in church. So I generally had a full congregation Wednesday and Friday nights and all day on Sundays. In the beginning they had nothing but praise for my ministry; I can tell you I was happier than I'd been in blows. But after about three weeks the elders came in a body and asked me when I was going to start the healing services."

King got up, and Cowboy jumped slightly, his red eyes straining. "Don't worry," said the preacher, in a soothing voice. He left the pulpit and went hunting for the candlestick. When he had found it he restored it to the altar.

"I explained that the Lord wouldn't heal a sick man just because that man was a churchgoer, and I made it plain I was against laying on hands and giving false hope. But I granted them that prayer for the sick could be a help, I'd seen prayer alone work near miraculous cures, and I proposed to offer healing prayers at every service. They were fair-minded men, and my pledge satisfied them.

"The next few weeks everything went all right. But at each meeting I saw more and more of the sick, and the pitiful old that couldn't do for themselves, and it seemed like my flock wouldn't ever get enough of praying for those sick bodies, and weeping for afflicted loved ones." His expression was lugubrious; moodily he combed his hair with his fingers. "One night in a rapture they carried me down from the pulpit and they were touching me all over as if I was a holy man; they washed my feet clean and then they set me before a woman that was turning to stone. Yes, rapping on the flesh of her arms was like to rap on this chair here." He demonstrated. "I cried as if my heart would break; the rapture had taken hold on me too. The Lord heard me; He sent His Power into my body. I laid on my right hand and the Power flowed through it like water pouring through a pitcher. The woman raised up her head, turned it every which way. She straightened her legs and her joints cracked. She stretched out both arms and her elbows popped like pistol shots. She was flesh again. Men fell down in ecstasy. It was so beautiful."

Cowboy shrugged and straightened. He had been sitting with his body slack, his eyes at a great suspicious distance. They swam to the level of his metallic, shining face, filled first with outrage, then with indecision, and then, again, worry and fearfulness as tension ground slowly to the quick. He passed his left hand clumsily over the barrel of the pistol, and his shoulders firmed. King faced him calmly, hands loose at his sides.

"Well, I lost my hold on them," he went on. "They wanted more healings. Command ye Me, said the Lord, and they commanded, they decreed miracles that came to pass through the instruments of my hands. Each miracle was more of a shock to me, and before long I was worn to nerves and bare bones, walking around somehow, but not really alive."

He came back to sit on the edge of the pulpit, sneaking several looks at Cowboy, meeting the same resistance, and he drew a despairing, whistling breath between his teeth, wondering if his efforts were useless. Cowboy was writhing under the devil's hand, he understood that, but he was barely encouraged by this struggle, for he calculated that before the devil would let go he would raise Cowboy's hand and commit a murder. King's face drew tight with concentration. But if Cowboy came close enough, if he were driven to the last split second of murder, would he be appalled, would he find the strength to throw the devil off?

King clasped his hands; it was more difficult for him to speak now, but his audience of two was waiting in judgment.

"Not long after I came to the Sugar Tree Valley I . . . married a woman named Mary Kate Ransom. Her husband had been killed by a felled tree when she was only twenty-one, leaving her with a year-old child. Mary Kate needed me, I know that; it was hard times for any of them in the Sugar Tree, but for a widow and a mother life was near impossible. Mary Kate saw that I was going wrong. She tried to warn me. I was living for each miracle, never mind all the . . . terrible failures in between. I began to think of myself as a holy man. I neglected my preaching. I neglected the Bible. My faith should have sustained me, but sad enough to say, after each healing my faith was less. I can't explain why."

Cowboy leaned forward and his lips parted, then the shining metal of his face hardened.

"What is it? What did you want to ask me?" Intuition told King, without a sign from Cowboy. "Yes, I must have been afraid. But fear didn't teach me anything." He smiled then, a smile so cruel and devoid of warmth that Cowboy stirred; his mouth crimped slightly as if he were aware of the depth of the preacher's suffering.

"By then Mary Kate's daughter was three years old. That little girl was the apple of my eye. When she came down with pneumonia the doctor told us there was a good chance she might not pull through. He had come late to the house, and he said it would be fatal to move her forty miles to the hospital. We had a few hours' wait to know if the penicillin would take hold and free her lungs. I prayed most of the afternoon, but she didn't improve. Mary Kate had fallen fast asleep, poor girl. I convinced myself that the drugs hadn't worked and that Mary Kate's daughter was going to die. I gathered her up in my overcoat and carried her a mile through a freezing rain to the church. I knew the Lord wouldn't deny me when He'd saved . . . others less worthy. I can't tell you if I was in my right mind. I suppose I had visions of the baby sitting up and laughing, the fever gone from her lungs."

His voice continued, dry and terrible as a curse. "She was dead when the men came into the church to take her from my arms. They didn't horsewhip me the way I deserved. That might have brought me to my senses, late as it was. No, they never touched me, nor spoke a word. They went off with her body and left me alone in the church."

Again Cowboy leaned toward him, with a hint of anxiousness in his eyes, but the large automatic appeared to jump in his hand, begging for attention, and he gazed down it at instead.

"What's the matter? Won't he let you speak?" King's voice was even, unperturbed. "You're in God's holy place, Cowboy. Don't forget that."

"Then—then—"

"Then . . ."

"They burned—the church with—you—inside." Slowly Cowboy lifted his head, his free hand clenching on his knees.

The preacher pressed his own hands together so tightly the knuckles popped. His eyes had clouded from strain, from the unsparing effort to face himself while trying to control his auditors.

"Do you know how hard it is for me to remember that night? I'm thinking of two walls of solid flame, and the rafters blazing crookedly over my head. And smoke—the smoke of raw pitchy pine, suffocating me."

"Couldn't you—run? Go—through a win—window?"

"I stayed on my knees. You see, I didn't want to live." After this declaration of weakness his eyes became colder, as if he had found a core of iron in his self-contempt. He turned his hands over to survey the burn marks. "I've come to believe I set fire to the church myself, with coals I took bare-handed from the stove. But I don't know for sure. Likely I'll never know the exact truth."

"If the —the church burned down, who—got you—out?"

"Oh, it was Age." Silently King pleaded, *Lord, let him speak, let the truth penetrate his heart, let him believe in us.* "When he got there, he never hesitated a second. There was only a chance I would be inside, but he had to see. He pulled me out, and suffered burns doing it. For weeks I was close to the Valley of the Shadow. But God had pity, and turned me back with His own hand. He restored my will to live. He replenished my faith."

King looked back, and his eyes steeled on the candlestick. "Before tonight, before the Northcutts, I wasn't fully brave enough to accept the wrong I'd done." Moving slowly, he let himself down from the pulpit and began to pace, in and out of shadows, wordlessly, and Cowboy followed him with his eyes.

"Men—even preachers who should know better—pay lip service to the Power of God," King said. "But what do they know of God, or His Power?" His eyes searched the tent again, wearily. "The Power He sent through my body to heal the sick is nothing compared to the Power of His love for sinners. What do you see in this tent? I see the bitter faces of the unloved, the unredeemed. Those who pay lip service to the Power, and those who have no knowledge of it. I'm a failure, but I have hope now. I'm convinced the Lord wants me to reach them."

Cowboy heaved himself up from his chair and then stood uncertainly, the pistol down on his hip, staring at the preacher, his face congested still, his eyes dull but not totally without intelligence; his lip curled with every breath, as if he were devouring air. King was no longer sure that he had Cowboy's interest, but he raised his hands slowly, spreading them, as if the threads of reason which inhibited and controlled his listener were fastened to his fingertips, and he said, "The Lord is sending for me to help you, Cowboy. Use my faith. Take hold of my hand and call out. Just one word. *Jesus!* The devil will disappear like he'd never been. Believe me; trust me."

Cowboy shied at the thought, and the inspiration of the devil leaped through him, dreadfully. King braced against the invisible, against the treachery of his own imagination, and held his hands steady, upraised, making a single sound of comfort: *Saviour*. This eminence he pressed upon Cowboy, and felt the writhe of a dismal flesh. Cowboy's head jerked harshly; his eyes fell back in his head and he uttered a curse. King held fast, although he was horrified by the contact he had made.

Cowboy's head lay back, and his eyelids fluttered as if he were in a faint. But his voice was unaffected, and agonizingly cold. "What happened to your wife?"

The new voice was startling. "Is it you, Cowboy?" King asked, and he peered at the closed face. "Dead," he answered. And then, "She died not long after her baby."

"Because of—you?"

The preacher groaned, but held his sanity despite the weight of grief and guilt which the devil had rolled like a stone against him.

"Because of me."

"You killed them," said the remorseless voice.

"God in His mercy, I never knew what I was doing!" The terrible stone weight was crushing his body; he clasped hands in supplication. "Lord God, let me breathe?"

"Now tell me about your faith—"

"As real—as they were real, and precious to me." Suffocation rolled over him in a dark wave. He cried, "Satan!"

"Here."

King forced himself to open his eyes. The voice had been cold, confident, with a hint of contempt. Cowboy's head lolled, as if in a puppet's dance; his own eyes were painted dimly, sightless, beneath the broad weight of his crimson, perspiring brow. The gun in his hand was lifted, aimed rigidly at the preacher. Cowboy's lips parted and, although they didn't move, King heard clearly: "Your faith is false; your God is evil."

His eyes swarmed with lights and visions like those of a drowning man, and in an electric flash of despair he felt his hold on consciousness slipping fatally. "Kill me, then! There's no other way. I won't swear evil against my God." He felt himself toppling, falling from a height into the blank pit of the tent. And as he fell every chair seemed to be filled, the faces of the devout shimmered like the sun. A thousand hands reached out. Tears burned in his eyes at this miraculous sight.

"Praise God!" they sang in thundering voices. "Go, devil!"

From this miltitude strength rained into his body; the breath he had sought came to him in a rush and he staggered upright.

Cowboy's attitude had not changed; the gun in his hand was as steady as it had been, but because of his vision King had no fear of it. He was charged with the wonder of breath, by the unmistakable Presence. He lifted up his hands again and clenched them, powerfully. His eyes glowed with purpose.

"Now," he said, "now, Cowboy! Are you hearing me? Now do you know what I mean by faith? I've earned the right to my faith. I loved them both—but I can live on. Devil? Call on all your powers of hell and take him from us if you can! Because the Lord is saying, 'Jim Cobb, I need your love and your trust. Come to Me!' Hear Him, devil? *Feel* His might! How long do you think you can hide in that poor boy's flesh?"

Cowboy's eyes remained closed, but anxiety rippled beneath his skin. King wanted to close the gap between them, to reach out and fasten his hands on Cowboy's shoulders, then squeeze the devil until he moaned, but the muzzle of the gun pointed at his heart restrained him.

"Cowboy—let go of the gun. It's the only weapon the devil has now. I don't believe he's won. I believe you can still hear me, and act. I believe you'll open your hand and let that gun fall to the ground. And then you'll be free!"

Cowboy's mouth opened wider in pain, and his head bobbled helplessly. It was almost more than King could bear to watch the struggle which Cowboy was having for his life and not be able to help him more. But he continued to talk, keeping his voice low, praising Cowboy for the fight he was waging for possession of his soul. Cowboy's eyes opened unexpectedly and a storm like blood moved into them. His face was set in lines of evil.

"No," King said quietly but urgently, "he hasn't won yet. Don't give up, Cowboy. Don't let him kill me."

A sob came from the boy's throat. He lifted his free hand, biting savagely at the heel of his thumb. His eyes cleared for an instant and he stared imploringly at the preacher. Then a new seizure came. The gun in Cowboy's hand dipped; King caught his breath.

"What's the matter, devil?" he shouted. "Where's your power? We're taking this boy away from you; *Christ* is claiming him. Cowboy—if you can, let yourself go, fall down on your knees. Jesus is waiting."

The gun in Cowboy's hand jumped, and the preacher stiffened at the shock of sound. Fear welled in his mouth like liquid brass, bitter and corrosive. But the bullet had not hit him, and now Cowboy's hand was lower, the muzzle of the .45 dipping toward the sawdust-covered ground.

"Ahhh!" Cowboy moaned, and there was a second shot; sawdust puffed only a few inches from where the preacher was standing. But King held his ground, his face drained of color, his shoulders raised in a hard line. There were dark circles around his eyes, they were black as a raccoon's, but within the circles his eyes were clear, colorless, and cold depthless ice.

"Shoot again," he whispered to the suffering boy. "And again! Use up all the bullets, Cowboy, every one. It's devil's ammunition! Shoot! Get it all out of you, your misery and heartache. Become the child again, the child you need to know."

Blam! King gritted his teeth as the third shot went wild, smashing through the slat back of a wooden chair close to his right hand. There was a banner of gunsmoke in the air between them, and the smell of powder was strong. How many shots? he asked himself, dazed; how many bullets would an Army automatic hold? He stared at Cowboy, locked in his puppet's trance, and at the weaving gun. Again a shot, and again it was wide, missing him.

He fought down an urge to run that came clawing up out of his bowels; the ordeal was almost over, if Cowboy could maintain his perilous control of the weapon in his hand. But with one true shot the devil would have his victory. One shot from that powerful automatic, at a range of only ten feet, would kill.

The preacher could not help himself; his eyes squeezed shut and he flinched appallingly as the fifth shot was fired. But again the slug had taken only sawdust or canvas. When he stole a look he saw that Cowboy's attitude had changed; his head was hanging and the automatic pointed almost straight down, held there, it seemed, by the full strength of his arm.

The sixth shot sent Cowboy reeling backward and he nearly fell. He lifted his wet, exhausted face from the stain of blue smoke in the air and his throat worked.

"Oh, my God!" Cowboy cried, heartrendingly, and instantly the muzzle of the automatic was high against the side of his head. Before King could take a step, the hammer of the .45 tipped back and snapped home.

Cowboy continued to hold the gun to his head, pulling the trigger convulsively, until the preacher reached him and pried the gun from his fingers. King's heart was beating madly. There had been only six bullets, instead of seven! The devil had lost. But—he drew back the slide of the automatic and a brassjacketed cartridge arced to the ground. Throwing the gun aside, he stooped and dug into the sawdust for the cartridge.

So the gun had been fully loaded after all. The marks of the firing pin were obvious on the brass casing, where the hammer had fallen again and again. The bullet was defective in some way; it had failed to fire.

King pocketed the dud cartridge and turned to Cowboy, who was swaying on his feet. Gently he helped Cowboy into a chair, and knelt in front of him. Cowboy's arms circled his neck and he slumped forward, his head on King's shoulder. He smelled foul with sweat. For several minutes he rested, then lifted his head and looked, bewildered, into the preacher's eyes.

"Why didn't I—kill myself?"

"The Lord spared you. I think He must need you, Cowboy."

"But I—I don't know Him. How—what should I—"

"Why don't you say to Him, 'I accept you, Father—Lord.' "

Obediently Cowboy whispered, "I accept you, Lord." He lifted his head another notch, listening. Then he began to tremble. Tears had formed in his eyes, but King couldn't tell if they were tears of thanksgiving or strain.

"How—how should I feel now?"

"Alive."

Cowboy sagged back into the chair, and a frown pressed down on his bloodshot eyes. "Yes. I feel—a life in me." He struggled. "But what life? Whose?"

"Yours, Cowboy. Your life is just beginning again, praise God!" The preacher grinned. "The devil's gone. There's room for love in your heart at last. Love, and faith. Isn't it so?"

Cowboy gaped at him with the eyes of an amnesiac making his first contact with an unfamiliar world. "Love—did you say? I can't—give it a name—right now. But I feel—" He licked his lips. "I just want to think about it. I'm—it's strange. I feel *love*. But who do I love? What? And—" The tears started again, pathetically. "What's going to happen to me now?" At the sight of the grin splitting the preacher's face, Cowboy sobbed aloud.

"I'm only smiling for joy," King assured him, "because I've heard others talk like you. That's right, others, just waking up and discovering their great hunger for God. Discovering that they're inseparable from God. I tell you I'm going to pray tonight, and rejoice in the Lord, because there's been a miracle happen here!"

Cowboy shuddered, as if remembering some of the forces that had driven him to the preacher with a gun in his hand, but King steadied him. Both looked at the .45 automatic which King had hurled aside, the preacher gravely, Cowboy in fear. He cried:

"I came to kill you tonight! I *had* to kill you. I was afraid of the way you talked about God. Accepted god. Accepted—me." He held his head low in his hands. "Is it true then? There are devils; there was one in me." His face was hideous with torment.

"There *was* a devil. Gone now, because you forced him to go."

Cowboy looked up, and King thought of the unfired cartridge in the chamber of the .45. "Because it was the Lord's Will."

Again Cowboy cried out. "But what does He want from me?" And he looked around fearfully.

The preacher calmed him with a touch. "Can't expect to know everything at once," he said, judiciously. "Right now the notion's in my head He only wants us to pray. That's simple enough. Will you get down on your knees with me? Do you have the strength?"

Cowboy nodded and, with some hesitation, kneeled.

"Just pray along with me, Cowboy. Remember that you don't have to utter a word to be heard in prayer. Let yourself think of the greatness of love, and the newness of your soul. Think of Jesus, who died for all of us. Think of His agony on the Cross for the sake of miserable sinners. And then you'll be praying."

Within a few minutes King had spoken in plain words all the relief and happiness in his heart; then the two men continued to kneel side by side, silently, elbows propped on folding chairs, until Cowboy rose to his feet. King remained on his knees, but lifted his eyes questioningly.

First Cowboy bent to pick up the .45, and as his fingers closed on the butt a grimace of dismay crossed his face. But he didn't drop the automatic; instead he mounted the steps to the pulpit and approached the altar, where the candlestick stood in place of a cross. He studied that relic intently.

"Go ahead," King urged, divining Cowboy's thoughts, and Cowboy reached out with his free hand to touch the candlestick. The gun he carried then seemed not to worry him. But he said:

"What if the devil comes back? I prayed with you, but it wasn't all that I thought it would be. I felt myself loving, wanting. But at the same time I felt—rock-bottom, hollow as a skull."

"I know there's a hollow," King replied. "And faith will fill it. But that takes time. You've come a long way already tonight. Just keep the Cross in mind. And, Cowboy, when you feel in need—open up your Bible. Read any of the Psalms. Dwell on the Gospels. Jesus is there on every page, to reassure you. He lived, He was, and because of Him, you live, and will be."

Cowboy turned from the altar. "I'm still afraid, though. It took me over, swallowed me whole—evil, the devil, whatever it is. I bit my tongue until it was raw, but I couldn't control my body. My hand was on fire, but I couldn't let go of the gun." He looked white and ill, and began quaking. "It was terror. It was like being walled inside a dead body filled with viciousness and hate." He drew a fierce breath, then came to King.

"Will He always be with me? Would He let that happen to me again? I'll do anything, anything. Please, give me faith!" The heavy gun thumped on the plank floor of the pulpit. "Can you give me a faith like yours? Don't make me suffer!"

"The nightmare's over, Cowboy," King said firmly, "and you'll find faith now, wherever you look. I promise you that. You're not alone. So many other souls have been wrenched from the devil, and they've all burned with doubt like yourself. Why don't you try to get some rest now?"

"I won't go home," Cowboy said, teetering, his lips compressed. "Too many mistakes are hiding there in that house. I'm not strong enough. No, no, I won't!"

"I'll give you a bed for the night. Won't be needing it myself. You can sleep around the clock if you want to."

"That sounds good." Again Cowboy rubbed his face. A sigh passed his lips and seemed to leave him easier, but King could tell he was nearly all used up, harried to the bone. He'd felt that way himself, far too often. In sympathy he rose to help Cowboy down the steps of the pulpit.

"And tomorrow—you say—wherever I look I'll find faith?"

"With God's help I know you will. But you'll have to be prepared to look in some places where you thought you'd never go again. You'll have to have courage to find faith. It took me years to learn that lesson myself."

The two men went slowly outside, one guiding, the other leaning, and King thought that he never had tasted fresh air or loved the stars before this moment. The past hour in the tent now seemed incredible; his horror at the devil's entrapment of Cowboy, his fear of being killed, all this faded away like a fantasy in the far-reaching night.

Cowboy halted them both and looked behind him at the tent. He trembled, but it wasn't the ugly trembling of a haunted man. He seemed in awe of his escape, but equal to the miracle that had occurred.

Once in the truck, Cowboy said in a sleepy voice, "What did you mean, when you said I'll have to look for faith where I never thought I'd go again? Were you talking about the Bible?"

"The faith you're needing isn't all in the Book, Cowboy. It lies behind you, and ahead of you; sometimes it has to be dug out of what you think is ashes, like my candlestick."

"Where do I go, then? What do I do? Because I know I'm ready; if I wasn't so tired I think I could start tonight. I could search for a faith the equal of yours."

King hesitated, not quite confident enough to freely speak his mind. Maybe tomorrow, he thought, after Cowboy had rested, and was better able to cope with the miseries of his old life. But, no; the preacher reconsidered. He's whipped, nearly fainting on the seat, yet his head is clear, and as for vision, he can see to the stars tonight; his vision and his need are equal to the panic my advice will bring.

"Years ago you married a half-grown girl, Cowboy, and left her with a child. She's survived, I know that from your grandmother; she's raising the child you've never seen with another man's help and love. Could be that's where you begin. Maybe it's cruel of me to suggest that you go see her—cruel for her, I mean. But if you go to her honestly as Jim Cobb, trusting in Christ, then I don't think she'll suffer from your visit. And only our Lord knows how you might be helped."

Cowboy braced himself against the lurching of the truck and said nothing until they had driven into the trailer park. King wondered if he had fallen asleep sitting up in the seat, but

282

when he glanced at Cowboy under a light in the park he saw that Cowboy's head was lifted tensely; King knew that he'd listened. A kind of terror was on him, pure enough to burn out the last traces of the devil's possession. King felt satisfied.

They went into the trailer, where a night light glowed in the kitchen. Age came awake instantly at the suggestion of a stranger and sat up on his couch in the small living room.

"It's only Cowboy," King said with a glance. "He's taking my room for the night, and I reckon he'll sleep late. In fact, he'll be coming and going the next few days, and if we don't have a spare key you might order one made tomorrow."

Age knew without being told that something important had taken place. The light was strong enough for him to see that neither bore the marks of a fight. He said to the preacher:

"Are you all right?"

"Yes," King said. "Go on back to sleep."

Down the hall Cowboy waited politely to be waved onto the bed, which was made up for a change, then he fell as if stoned, his eyes closing quickly. King located a blanket and dropped it over him. He thought that Cowboy had gone instantly to sleep, but as he was leaving, Cowboy said:

"What happened tonight? To the old lady those Northcutts brought? Couldn't you help her?"

"I hope I was able to help her, with prayer."

"But couldn't you heal her? Was she too far gone?"

King glanced in puzzlement at Cowboy's face, but saw no sign of mockery there.

"Cowboy, I can't heal. That's over and done. The Lord withdrew His Power from my body long since."

Cowboy breathed deeply and his eyes closed; his hands, which had been clenched, spread open on the bed. But his face remained taut.

"I thought you understood that," King said.

"Mab told me—that you healed her."

"Oh, no. I couldn't. There was nothing wrong with Mab; it was her soul that was sick."

"Mab told me—she said that she felt your healing Power in her body. She said you cleared up her sick liver. Something like that. Maybe—"

"Mab Shaw was wrong. If her liver was bad, drink made it bad. And if it's healthy now, then that's because she hasn't had a drop of liquor in two weeks' time."

Cowboy's exhaustion was making him restless, overanxious for sleep, and his breathing became labored. "But what if it's true? What if you have the Power?"

"It's the Lord's Power, to give and to take. Once it was given to me and I set myself equal to the Almighty. For that blasphemy I was punished and I almost died. Now I'm trying to make my way again, to be a good preacher and win souls for the Kingdom of Heaven. The Lord would not—" His throat tightened up on him and he paused. "The Lord wouldn't shackle me with His Power again." This last he spoke emphatically but unemotionally. Then a shudder seized him, born of a sensation of corruption and evil, as if the devil had stopped by on his way back to hell and given him a spiteful nudge. He shook his head slowly.

"I have no Power, Cowboy. It's gone, absolutely, and a good thing, because I'm only human clay. The Power to heal was temptation like I'd never known. Maybe there are men on earth who can be grateful for the Power to transform human clay, to drive out sickness and disease—men who have the wisdom and self-control to use their Power and still find peace apart from it. I couldn't be that kind of man. Why don't you sleep now, and if you can"—a note of strain came into his voice—"forget what I had to tell you tonight. I know there are other men like Von Northcutt who still remember what I did there in the Sugar Tree, who remember my crimes, but I hope that they'll find it in their hearts to leave me alone, leave me to preach and find my peace."

He stared mutely at Cowboy's face, at his now motionless body across the narrow bed. After a minute or so he decided that Cowboy had finally fallen asleep and he went out, closing the door.

In the kitchen King took a carton of milk from the refrigerator, being careful not to disturb Age. Before he could drink, fatigue weakened him and he leaned against the sink. He wasn't aware that he'd made a sound but presently Age got up from the couch and turned on the light.

"What have you done?" he asked the preacher.

King lifted his shoulders. "Routed the devil, I hope." He told Age about the family of Northcutts, about their appeal, and then of the strange, hair-raising confrontation with Cowboy and his evil.

Age listened, rubbing his bald scarred head with one hand,

284

and when King had finished he said, "I've thought this before, but I didn't say it. You ought to get away from this part of the country. Where there was one, there'll be a pack of others. All wanting miracles from you. They'll drag you down with their hopes and lynch you in their grief."

"I can handle . . . all that come. I'm ready for them now." He straightened and gulped milk from the carton. Age was doubtful, and his doubt created a viable tension in the air.

"You can preach anywhere, do good for the Lord anywhere. What about California?"

King shrugged, indifferent to California or to the future beyond this night. Age said harshly:

"I'm telling you, it's time to go away."

The unrealized fear in his words caused King to turn a pale, watchful eye on his friend.

"Why? Who can hurt me?" He looked in the direction of the bedroom. "I met the devil tonight. I came within a hair of dying—again." His expression was remote, almost indifferent. "How could I be hurt by the sorrows of a few poor people, if they find their ways to me?"

Age scowled. "I'm trying to say you don't know what might find its way to you, once the fact is known you're living, and preaching the Gospel again. More evil than you can dream of is still breathing in the ground of that Valley."

King gave his friend's words some study and found them unnecessarily forbidding. He swallowed the rest of his milk and stared through the small kitchen window. Then he turned and briefly clasped one of Age's stringy strong arms. But Age was unmoved, and he repeated:

"It would be smart to leave."

"You have a reason," King suggested, after a few moments, and he clasped Age's arm again, hard.

"Just what I've said," Age replied, but his eyes wavered.

If the preacher had been less tired, less preoccupied, he might have noted this and demanded more of Age, but he let his hand drop and smiled thinly. "We'll both feel better by the light of day. I've won a victory tonight, could be the most important of my life. Cowboy still needs my help, all I can give him. He's only made a decision against the devil, he hasn't decided for the Cross yet." He yawned. "Believe I'll spend the rest of the night with my Bible. I'm empty as an old washtub; I crave to fill myself up from the Bible until I'm brimful of praise and thanksgiving. I feel a sermon coming on; tomorrow the people will hear preaching like they've never heard before!"

Age pointed to the couch. "Why don't you lie down there and leave me sit in the tent the rest of the night?"

"No, no, I'm fine, Age—just fine." And he headed for the trailer door in an imitation of briskness that ended with a misstep and a quick laugh. Age started to speak, to protest, then shrugged.

"Go on then. I'll be there myself at daybreak." He turned his head for a last look at the preacher's moonstruck eyes.

The truck motor roared as King drove away. Age scarcely heard it. He sat tensely on the edge of his couch pondering everything that had happened. Soon his thoughts turned, against his will, to the Sugar Tree Valley. He relived the timeless roving life he'd known, and his heart throbbed with a sense of displacement. Then he remembered the coming of the preacher, and the slow growth of his devotion to that unusual and appealing boy.

At the end of an hour he rose, awkward in a vise of irresolution, feeling a need, for one of the few times in his life, to call on someone. From the small table that served as a desk in the living room he picked up a wooden box and opened it. Inside was stationery, given to King on a past birthday by one of Frank Henderson's adoring grandchildren, and three letters from Henderson himself which King hadn't found time to answer.

Age picked up one of the letters carefully, turning the envelope over and over in his hands. He thought of the last conversation which he'd had with the carnival owner, and he felt like a blade in his heart his responsibility for King, which Henderson had so confidently assumed.

He stared at the unreadable words, at the address in Florida to which he could not write. But even if he'd known how to read and write he would have found it impossible to put into words all the trouble he felt, without bringing what might be worse trouble down around their heads.

Of course, he had Henderson's telephone number committed to memory. All he had to do was call and say, It's going to be bad, and Frank would come. Maybe the two of them could convince King that the Sugar Tree Valley was too close, in miles and in years. But on another day, with a clear head, King would want to know why Age was so insistent.

The choice had crystallized and Age, somewhat relieved, went back to his couch to lie and stare at nothing until the pale light of dawn had crossed a third of the sky.

26

Angel of Death

The next to last gunshot had awakened Jeremy and the last one had sent her upright in bed, listening uneasily, for the sound was spread by distance, weakened; on reflection she could not be sure that she'd heard gunshots at all. For several minutes after her waking up, Jeremy heard only the inevitable freight train on the river of rails down the ridge.

She found herself listening not for gunshots but for Eli's breathing, which frequently poured like a torrent of bees across the house to reassure her as she dozed. Not hearing him, not hearing even a watery whisper of breath, she crept forth from the blankets to the cold space of linoleum, upsetting an assortment of half-grown cats, and put a robe on over her cotton pajamas. The glass in the back door was as dark as a mirror. There was pale yellow-blue light in the gas heater near the front door, and this light caught the height of a table, the end of a couch, the rump-shape of Philemon in his slumbers. Beyond, where Eli lay, the dark to her eyes was like a wall, and vaguely frightening.

Jeremy made her way through the house, pausing by a window to look out. She stretched her neck to see the tent down below, a paper lantern with a sliver of candle inside it. On the porch outside the dog lay on a crumpled mat. Holding her robe together, Jeremy went on, through the house, skirting Philemon as he muttered. The light seemed to shift subtly with her progress and she looked down on Eli, a slight man under a mound of bedding, face up and silent.

As if her fears were new to her, Jeremy stood dumfounded for several seconds, her bare feet aching on the cold floor, her heart bumping her breast, then she bent down and put a hand under Eli's head, lifted it slightly from the pillow. At the same time she heard the steady, if soft, hissing of his breath, which must have been there all the time. But she felt quite dizzy from relief and the collapsing-in of apprehension.

With her other hand she rearranged the weight of blankets on his chest, including the electric blanket that lay, intolerably hot to her touch, against his skin. His breathing became a cry, like that of a man dimly seeing a catastrophe before his mind can focus upon it. One of his crippled hands beat its way into the air and Jeremy stepped back, wide-eyed.

"Eli?" she said, and "Eli? Is it a bad dream? It's only me. I came to make sure you—" But she couldn't say, *To make sure you hadn't died.* She felt dull and hot with the afterglow of senseless but unshakable fears that gathered around the house at night, every night, like an unbelievable zoo of stooping, walking birds. "To make sure you were comfortable," she finished, in a whisper, and stared at him as his spasm continued. She wasn't certain that he was awake at all. But he cried out again, weakly.

Jeremy sat down on the edge of the high bed and put her hand lower between his shoulders, to raise him more. His forehead was hot and dry; that didn't alarm her, he thrived on heat.

His flailing stopped.

"The Angel of Death," he gasped.

"What?"

"The Angel of Death was here."

"No, sir," Jeremy said firmly. "You just had a dream." She held him closer to her. He was as rank as an old vegetable, but she didn't mind. "Are you dry? Could you do with a drink of water?"

Eli stared at her. "I know the Angel of Death was close," he said, in a dignified voice, untinged with panic. "He flew over this house. I felt his wings above my head. I wasn't asleep. It wasn't no vision. He was here, but he didn't take me." His breath was snipped like a length of thread, and he gulped to restore it. "It is all right," he said to Jeremy, as if he were taking care of her. "Ain't nothing to be afraid of. I've lived too long to be a scared man when the Angel of Death ruffles my hair."

"You're not going to die," Jeremy said. "Why, that's the dumbest talk I ever heard from you." Tenderly she caressed one of his toad-swollen hands, knowing that the heat had pushed the worst of his pain below the level of her fingertips. "Angel of Death! Eli, you've done better in the last two days than you've done for weeks. One trouble is you shouldn't've worked so hard today. You have to go easy until your strength is up."

"Jeremy, I believe I could stand a glass of water," he replied, obliviously.

She brought it to him and helped him drink.

"Now," he said, when he was through, "I don't want you to worry. It was just the Angel of Death." His voice was tired, and he seemed to be talking to himself. "Probably he won't be back for me any time soon. I know the Lord intends for me to finish all my work. That's months to go—two or three years anyway. I know God in His Heaven will see to it I have the best of my enemies."

"The Lord means for you to live a good many more years, Eli," but she found it hard to talk at all; there were showers of unwanted tears behind her eyes. "Please don't put too much stock in this dream of yours. And you know you don't have enemies. Nobody in this world would harm you."

Eli made several sounds which Jeremy rather incredulously accepted as laughter; she had seldom heard him laugh. His chest shook with this middle-of-the-night laughter. Then he became quiet, and she thought he had drifted into sleep. She was resetting the bedcovers when Eli muttered, "You come to look at me every night."

"How do you know a thing like that?"

"I know."

"Well, hush; and turn your head—you'll be more comfortable that way."

"You come to see if I'm still a-breathing, don't you? Jeremy?"

"Oh, Eli . . ."

"It's all right. It's all right for you to worry over me. It used to get me mad, but I didn't let on. And I don't care now. I'm glad about it. Jeremy, do you know how old I am? I'm seventy-four."

"Oh," she said, "you're not!" But she was shocked. She had always thought of Eli as old, but she had never put his age in terms of years, and suddenly he seemed more vulnerable to her than ever. She pushed a hand gently against her mouth.

"Would you sit down with me again, Jeremy? Before you go back to your own bed."

Jeremy nodded—but of course he couldn't see—and sank down beside Eli, still damming up all the stubborn emotion that threatened her. Fortunately he wanted to talk, and he did, going on and on about his work and himself, and Jeremy's importance to him. She'd never heard Eli flatter before, and gradually she felt better. Then concentration deserted her. Bleakly she thought of the tent, wondering if King was there, and if so, what he was doing at this moment. She would gladly give up an arm to bring King Windom to this house and sit him down with Eli and somehow urge an understanding on them both.

Jeremy yawned; Eli had stopped talking and when she spoke to him quietly he did not respond. She made her way back to her own corner of the house.

Unexpectedly she was blocked by Philemon; she stopped in annoyance, waiting for him to blunder outside and relieve himself from the porch. Instead he seemed to be wide awake. Jeremy could feel his eyes on her.

"What's the matter?" he asked.

"Oh, nothing." And she tried to get by.

"Eli sick?"

"You know he is." Jeremy looked at him in a calculating way. Philemon slept in his trousers for modesty's sake, but she didn't like being so close to him in the dark. "Sometimes," she said, to be talking, "he can't get his breath. But he's an old man, it doesn't mean anything. Doesn't have to mean—" She stopped, wearily, not wanting to give Philemon cause for going on a jag, for rushing over and disturbing Eli and probably scaring him.

But Philemon's reaction wasn't typical. He sniffed and rubbed his head and settled down into a long quiet that puzzled Jeremy. At last she simply pushed him aside, saying, "I want to go lie down now," and he yielded, but remained standing.

Jeremy groped her way around kittens and slipped into bed. The next time she raised her head there was Philemon, partly visible by gaslight, still standing barefoot on the cold floor facing the corner where Eli slept.

Puzzlement lay in her heart for a restless hour, for as long as she was aware of Philemon standing and keeping watch, his mood this once well hidden from her. Almost always she knew what he was thinking, she could sniff his emotions with accuracy. Tonight it was different.

With the morning light she had an hour's wretched sleep, spotted with nightmare. When she awoke, Philemon was sitting hunched at the table with a mug of coffee in his hands, staring in a grim way at the brazen east windows. In his face was the unfamiliar look of a man. Jeremy was both relieved and fascinated. For the first time in a long while she had kind thoughts for her cousin, and she arose willingly to cook him some breakfast eggs.

27

A Bargain at $32,000

Molly had bumped into Cowboy several times at the revival during the first days of his probation and she had found him as usual, cynical to a fault; but behind it all, perhaps a shade more restless and moody. Then her visits to the tent became less frequent. The next two times she dropped by, Cowboy wasn't there. Molly wondered if he had broken his probation in some way; but the preacher only smiled when she mentioned Cowboy and said, with a noticeable gleam of pride or satisfaction, that Cowboy was away visiting someone he had needed to see for a long time.

Thereafter Molly missed several meetings in a row. It was necessary for her to go through the motions of earning a living, and she was busy every spare hour with her plans for the King Windom Gospel Train. She had roughed out the first stages of a four-month tour and prepared a budget which she considered reasonable. Also, she had given in to temptation and secured an ally. The Reverend Mr. Handwerker's unconditional enthusiasm for the whole project was enough to keep Molly in a fiery glow of work and anticipation.

When she did return to the tent, on a raw November night, there was Cowboy again, but with a difference—wide awake and cold sober in a dark-gray rancher's suit, sitting on the pulpit in the midst of other preachers and with a Bible in his hand. Even from where she was standing Molly could see the change in him—the new attitude, the seriousness—and when Cowboy came forward to read the Scripture that preceded King's sermon, Molly nearly fell over.

After the meeting he stayed by King's side for the counseling of the proselytes, watchful but silent. Molly, not wanting to interrupt, waited unseen for Cowboy; she felt shy and confounded by the sight of him. But, after the proselytes were gone, he spent another half hour with the preacher. When Molly was driven to her car by the cold, they were still deep in conversation over opened Bibles.

Finally Cowboy left the tent and walked toward the parking lot. Molly watched him closely: he walked in a moderate hurry, and the old Cowboy had never hurried anywhere. When he was near she cracked open the window and said cheerily, "Hi, Cowboy, come and say hello to your buddy."

He looked up, startled, then offered a preoccupied grin with a hint of dogginess in it; that hadn't changed, Molly thought, and she was absurdly grateful because she still didn't know what to make of the Bible-reading, pulpit-sitting, soul-conscious Jim Cobb. Whatever it was that had got into him, the change was bound to be temporary. But as this thought crossed her mind, Molly remembered how he had sounded reading the Scripture—King Windom, down to the last syllable, the most devastating pause—and she felt a funereal heaviness in her heart.

Cowboy lowered himself into the ill-fitting Volkswagen, hunched his shoulders, savored the heat, and then said, "Hi-yeh, Mollleee. Spare me a cigarette?"

"Sure." Molly went around the pockets of her deer-slayer jacket. He had spoken with a drawl and she could almost smell the beer on his breath. Some of the old mischief crinkled his face. But Molly sensed that it meant nothing. His head was down and she couldn't read him, but it was her opinion that he had assumed a familiar disguise to give himself a little time, or perhaps because he wanted to put her at ease.

"Were you at the meeting tonight?" he muttered as he cupped a match to his cigarette.

Molly shot a glance at the Bible on his knee. "I took it all in," she admitted, in the same cheerful tone of voice. But she was poker-faced.

"Well, what did you think?" he demanded, with an impatient shrug.

"I've never been so astounded in my life, Cowboy," she said truthfully. "Or is it . . . Cowboy anymore?"

He smiled fretfully at that, and scratched his red head. "Sure. I suppose I'll always be Cowboy. It's a showboat name; still I like it better than plain Jim Cobb." He smoked awhile, and was more nervous than before. "There's a lot of showboat left in me, Molly. But, all the same, old Cowboy is gone." He looked up and directly at her for the first time, braced for God knew what kind of sarcasm from his pal Molly.

"Dead?" Molly asked, after a moment.

"I'd say so." He stared at her.

"Hmm. This is quite a turn of events," Molly said graciously, but her tongue felt studded with dry pebbles. She dropped cigarette ash out the partially opened window and bit her lip, not knowing what to say, or what to ask. "Can you tell me what's going on? What happened? To begin with, you . . . got religion, as the old-timers used to say. . . ."

Cowboy shook his head earnestly. "I don't know yet, Molly. I'm still looking for religion. King told me I'd have some problems. But he's not worried, and he doesn't want me to worry. He says the important thing is for me to *want*. To search, and think, and practice faith, no matter how awkward I feel at the beginning."

"Practice faith?" Molly repeated. She couldn't keep her eyes from Cowboy; she was wary of something monstrous, some black comedy he had devised. There had been times in the past when she was afraid of Cowboy, and she felt vaguely afraid now. But either he wasn't aware of her reservations, or he was confident that he could overcome them. He snatched a deep breath and said, "Most people have the idea faith should come like lightning—they think it'll knock them over, and with a hundred-piece orchestra in the background. That's kid stuff, really. King feels that faith is a down-to-earth proposition. A man has to hoe his fields and build his bridges and spend a lot of time in prayer and thought, without being afraid to doubt

293

himself. The day will come when faith and conviction are so strong in his heart a hurricane couldn't blow them away." Cowboy smiled yearningly. "I'm a long way from having that kind of faith. But almost every day I get a little more confidence."

Molly said, "Yes, but I still don't understand. Was it King? How did he persuade you? I had the notion you'd be at each other's throats by now."

"It would be hard for me to explain everything. And to-night . . ." He spread his hands tiredly. "One day I *will* tell it all to you, Molly, that's a promise. I'll say this much: I had a devil inside of me, that was dragging me down to hell. I think I knew the devil was there, but I didn't care enough to fight. King cared, though, and he risked his life to rid me of the devil."

"The devil is gone," Molly said, with a stark frown at this kind of talk from him.

Cowboy was not aware of her frown. "King drove the devil out; when I could breathe again, I asked him for faith." His lip curled. "As if it was something he could just hand to me. But he had patience. He showed me a long road, and said that if I wanted faith badly enough then I might find faith somewhere along that road. Two weeks ago I took my first trip, the one trip I had to take before any other."

He drew on his cigarette and blinked his eyes, and misery settled on his face like a cloud. "You know I was married once, don't you, Molly?"

She remembered the whole disgraceful affair, and her mouth froze in a line of reprobation, which Cowboy acknowledged with a nod.

"Well, I went to visit my—my ex-wife, and my boy. I never had set eyes on him. I didn't know what to expect. No, I think I expected to be spit on. But as God would have it, she'd found faith before me. She'd married a Christian man, and when I came to their door they both seemed to understand what I needed. I stayed in their house, ate their food. I mean I was welcome. I stayed five days—not so I could tell her I was sorry, or to beg forgiveness; I stayed until I felt able to pray. Since then I've prayed a lot."

"How is your—how is she getting along?"

"She's happy, she has a good man to do for. And the boy . . ." Cowboy was silent, wincing. "I'm too busy now to think about the past, and the . . . waste. But I can't help thinking about him.

He's five, big for his age; he can throw a ball hard and straight and swim like a streak."

"Does he know who you are?"

"No, and he shouldn't. We all agreed on that." Cowboy lifted his head and stared at the lighted tent for a while. "Someday I want another chance to have a boy like that. But for the next couple of years I'm going to have all I can do helping King."

Molly, eager to switch the subject from thwarted fatherhood, said, "Our preacher's really been at his best this past week. For a while he had me worried; he looked so thinned-down and nervous I thought he was going to collapse. I'd say the change in you has been marvelous for him."

"Some nights when I hear him preach I'm afraid he'll burn himself out. But he's stronger than any man I've ever met. I feel like straw next to him."

"He's ready now," Molly murmured, half to herself.

"Ready for what, Mol?"

"You love him, don't you?" she asked abruptly.

After a moment's surprise Cowboy said, "Yes, I love him. What are you thinking?"

"Cowboy, can you spare some time tonight? There's something I want to show you."

"Tonight? Molly, I'm—"

"Won't take long. Believe me, it's important, to you and to King."

"What is?"

"I'm not telling; it would spoil the surprise." She straight-armed the gear shift and the little car took off. "Just be prepared to have your eye knocked out."

Cowboy groaned softly, then lapsed into an obedient if gloomy silence.

The Appalachian and Atlantic Railroad yards occupied a dark sink of land on the south side of the city. In the ribbons of light Molly drove across rails and down channels of beheaded freight trains without hesitation, while Cowboy hung onto his seat and gave her increasingly troubled looks.

"Know where we are?" he asked finally. "I used to bum around here when I was a kid, but—"

"Don't worry about a thing." She twisted the wheel sharply and they jounced through a little-used section of the yards, a skid row of obsolete dormitory cars, some long sheds, and a brick roundhouse. From far off a diesel rolled its yellow eye at them and sang a monotonous tune. "Darker than I thought it would be," Molly muttered. "I've never been here at night. Oh, well . . ." The Volkswagen stopped abruptly and Cowboy sprawled forward. "Sorry. This is it!"

He looked around dubiously.

"Come on." Molly got out briskly, took a few steps, then turned and beckoned impatiently to Cowboy. He joined her, grumbling, and they stepped carefully over rusted rails, circling the roundhouse. Cowboy jammed his hands into his pockets to warm them, and kept an uneasy watch.

"This is not the best place to be wandering around after dark."

"I'm not afraid, as long as I'm with . . . you," Molly sang. She was in fine spirits. "Good! There's a light after all." Her face was silver-white as they passed beneath a mercury-vapor lamp standing at the opening of a long passage between two sheds. Molly stopped and reached for Cowboy's arm. She was shivering, ecstatically, as she pointed with her free hand. "The Gospel Train," she announced. "Nearly ready to roll. It just needs cleaning up and a few alterations."

For a minute or more Cowboy did not respond; he stood still, staring at the train that sat in obscurity and abandonment on the poorly lighted siding. He had never seen quite anything like it, except in drawings of so-called Trains of the Future. The line of the quarter mile of coaches was lower, by perhaps eighteen inches, than that of conventional passenger trains. The engine too seemed smaller, compact, yet inexpressibly powerful. It did not have the bell-like, one-eyed prow of other diesels. It had a jet-fighter profile; a raked and out-thrust nose, curving gracefully down and in to the tracks. The engineer's cockpit was set about six feet back from the nose; rising above the roofline, it gave him an unobstructed view in any direction.

"It's beautiful."

"Look at the way the cars fit together—as if the whole train was carved out of a single long bar of aluminum. It looks to be in full flight just standing there with weeds growing around the wheels."

"Built for speed, all right. But . . . what's it doing here?" He had begun to see signs of neglect, the dulled finish, the water stains. "And how long—"

"A Western railroad had the train built ten years ago. There was a lot of fanfare—it was designed to travel as fast as the roadbeds would allow; Chicago to Los Angeles in 39 hours instead of the usual 46. Nearly a hundred ten miles an hour over some long stretches. The train was light and swift, but that was the catch. It was too light for most of the trackage, and when the going got rough, it vibrated like a tuning fork. They tried structural changes, but even then at speeds approaching 75 the passengers were jolted out of their chairs. Finally the road had to give up, take its losses, and sell the train to a commuting line between Chicago and Milwaukee. This line had a road like velvet, and the train could really move between stations, but—" Molly shrugged. "Same story; the train cost them too much money. It couldn't haul enough passengers in the available coaches. The train sat around a siding in Chicago for a few months, then the A&A bought it for practically nothing, and ran excursions for a while in the Smokies until they went out of the passenger business altogether." Molly began walking toward the train, and Cowboy followed slowly. "Since then it's been right here. No takers. A Japanese line was interested for a while, but in some respects the train's power plant is obsolete; the Japanese railroaders decided to develop their own speed demon." Molly paused, indignantly. "Look at that! Dents. Kids, I bet, standing here with rocks in both hands, just trying to see how bad they can hurt it. Half a dozen windows with nothing but plywood in them, and"—she reached out and scraped the side of the diesel with a half dollar—"fly ash or sulphur corrosion, or both, like scabs everywhere. But I hired a metallurgist to go over the train inch by inch. He said that with a good cleaning and a couple of coats of aluminum paint baked on, it would glow like a freshly minted nickel."

Molly swung around, consumed by her itch. "It's for King. With this train he'd cover three states in a month. And crowds, don't you know? He'd be *seen*, Jimbo, he'd be recognized by his train, the way he deserves to be recognized! Sure, he's strong as an ox, but how is he going to keep going night after night in that tent with winter coming on?" Molly shivered as if she had felt a blast of icy wind on her neck, and glared at Cowboy, who was studying the length of the train stonily. "He has to have this train! Otherwise it might be years—otherwise he might never be heard by all those who should hear him. There are a lot of things that could kill King Windom before his time, and discouragement is only one of them."

Cowboy looked at her, startled. "What do you mean, Molly?"

She gritted her teeth. "I mean he's fine, he's strong, but he can be hurt, he can . . . die. I see that in him but of course you wouldn't. That's why I'm in such a damned awful hurry to get this train moving. I've had a cramp in my stomach for two weeks from thinking about it, the hurry, the cost—"

He trembled as if her vision had teeth in him. "How can King preach, hold revivals, on a railroad platform?"

Molly grabbed the Cowboy's arm, then firmly hauled him along the rails toward the center of the train. As they progressed she described, as she saw it, the evolution of King Windom's Gospel Train.

"The baggage car can be used for storing anything up to a full-size tent. We'll turn the mail car into an office, with a complete communications setup, including radiophone. Adjoining that will be a visitors' lounge with a small kitchen and a library. Here we have two chair cars, one of which will be placed at the disposal of choirs traveling with us. You see, we'll pick up an outstanding church choir, carry them with us for a couple of days, then send them home by chartered bus. All these cars will be supervised by hostesses—I see them as well-qualified girls studying for master's degrees in Christian Education. Maybe later we'll be able to work it out so they can get credit for their time on the Train. Now, here's the observation car, which will be turned into a chapel, and I've already consulted with a couple of good church architects about that. On down the line we have four Pullmans for permanent staff. Some of the luxury sleeping units can be combined to make good-sized apartments. King will have his office and study in one of the Pullmans, where he can properly receive anybody, including the President. A possibility I wouldn't rule out! Bringing up the rear, our diner, and then a recreation car with TV, movies, etc. Whew! I'm busting to have a cigarette."

Molly's hair was loose and tangled on her forehead as she dug into her purse. In addition to her cigarette case, she came up with a mimeographed copy of specifications for the Gospel Train, which she handed to Cowboy. He looked at the stiff blue paper binder but there wasn't enough light for him to see the inscription.

"Read that, just read it," Molly muttered euphorically as she fumbled with cigarettes and matches. "It's a fantastic idea. The train is a perfect setting for an evangelist with King's sense of style, his imagination. No one man in a million could make use of a train like this—it would dominate an ordinary man. He'd look foolish or, at best, like some obscenely rich snake-oil peddler."

"Maybe," suggested Cowboy, "it would even make King look foolish."

Molly was offended. "Never! That wouldn't happen. Can't you see it yet?" In her anxiety to make a believer of him, she twisted a cigarette to shreds and had to discard it. "People will come out to gawk at our Train, but they won't laugh, because the Train will say to them a power, a *man* has come. They'll be fascinated by what they see, receptive, ready to listen—and King won't disappoint them. Look there." Again she closed a hand on Cowboy's arm, and turned him toward the domed observation car. "You wanted to know how he could preach from the Train, preach to hundreds or thousands?" She was out of breath once more, but continued in a series of raw gasps. "After the Train is in and the choir has sung, the dome on the chapel car will slide back, revealing the pulpit. Then King will climb the stairs from the chapel and stand up there in full view against the sky. Where ten thousand can see and hear him. Believe me, before too many weeks have gone by a crowd of ten thousand will be commonplace. I know!" Her excitement was exhausting, and she sobbed, mauling his arm with her iron fingers. "Cowboy. *Damn* it. Don't you see?"

He hesitated for so long that she broke away from him and stalked away in despair and anger toward the rear of the train. There she stopped and with a hard effort lighted the cigarette which she badly needed, glancing several times at Cowboy, who stood, motionless, face up to the darkened dome of the luxury train.

"Molly," he called, and she came on the jump.

"How soon?" he asked, and a tremor of anticipation ran through him.

Molly almost bawled with relief. "Three weeks. Working nights and weekends, we can be on our way out of here in three weeks, no more. All the contracts are sitting in my desk—"

"How much will it cost?"

She gulped. "Thirty-two thousand dollars. We must have that much capital. I know it seems like—I know it's—you see, they want ten thousand in advance on the train with a lease agreement; I think I can bully them down to seven-five. Oh, hell, it's all in the brochure, read it for yourself. Thirty-two thousand—maybe the whole thing's just impossible." Her emotions had no sequence, they battered her senselessly, high elation and crushing despair in a growing avalanche.

"I don't think it's impossible. No, not for *him*. Not for King. Molly, we can get the money."

The blood that had been simmering inside her head suddenly reversed its flow, leaving her weak and giddy. "When?" she asked timidly.

"We can get it Monday."

Molly flew at Cowboy and kissed him like a wife. He stepped back in confusion; the kiss had brought out a blush as well as the tomcat that still lived in him. But Molly was oblivious. She capered on the rusty rails and threw a pocketful of pennies at the moon. Then, in a fit of sobriety, she sat down on the cold cinder bank.

"We'll never convince *him*," she groaned. "He'll take one look at the train and walk off in a funk. He won't see the possibilities, he's such a stubborn—"

Cowboy was laughing at her, and her moods. "Molly, we'll convince him!"

"Never!"

"Then we'll shanghai him."

She was up instantly. "Tie him hand and foot!"

They capered in a ring until Cowboy lost his balance and fell. Molly helped him up, with another potent kiss to heal his hurt. Face to face, hushed, they stared intently at each other.

"We'll bring him in the morning," Cowboy said thoughtfully.

"Between the two of us he won't stand a chance!"

"No."

Molly tried to laugh, to caper again, and was disappointed by the hollowness she felt. She then became aware of the tomcat living in Cowboy and her hush changed to gloom.

"Well, like old times, Cowboy," she offered.

He sighed.

Molly looked at him closely in the dark. "Why don't you come up? We'll have a drink together—like old times."

Animal heat was in his face, but he fidgeted.

"I need the comfort," she said softly. "On this . . . night of nights."

He sighed, ruefully. "But it's late, Mol."

"Oh, it is."

"It's too late. Getting on to eternity." His shoulders fell.

Molly felt as if she could cry. "I know," she said, astounded by the cold weight of the truth he'd uttered. She touched him, a tentative, friendly touch. They put their heads together. Then they separated, reluctantly, a trifle awkwardly, and walked the length of the train back to her Volkswagen.

28

Sam Manson's Ultimatum

Contrary to Molly's fears, they did not have much difficulty selling King on the advantages of the Gospel Train.

For one thing, he had been preaching well since the salvation of Cowboy Cobb, he'd been saving other devil-downed souls, and he was in his glory. He thrived on a limited ration of sleep, walked with a bound, and ate like a troop of soldiers. His days were blessed with cold crisp weather; his nights began with a downpour of stars and a whisper of power, and ended in complete triumph of the Spirit and the Heavenly Host. No reasonable man could be pessimistic for long under such circumstances, and not even the painful weeks-old rift with Eli could plunge King into brooding. He was feeling his luck—although he wouldn't have thought to call it that—and he was getting restless, for the fulfillment of old vows and ambitions, for new and more complex tasks should the Lord be willing.

What Molly proposed was unique, and so audacious that it took his breath away. A whole train! And at this point a childhood dream of true opulence reasserted itself; the dream accompanied him like a tour guide on his first hasty exploration of the shunted, dimmed-out train. He had lived close to a railroad back there in South Carolina, had often hitched rides on slow-rumbling freights from the foot of the alley some seven miles to the Pee Dee junction, and back again, and laid awake after ten P.M. on summer nights just to mark the passage of the big Florida-bound Silver Meteor, shriveling from excitement at the sound of the traveling horn, shriveling from envy in his homebound bed. Like so many men, he had never outgrown his love for the enchanted thunder and lightning of streamliners. Although he thought he had traveled his fill in ten years' time, just one look at the dirt-swigged dome of the observation car and the chairless diner was enough to inspire him for another hundred thousand miles.

He had legitimate doubts, and questions. It hurt him to think of taking a nickel from Cowboy and his grandmother, no matter how eager they were to press the money upon him, and the thought of willfully going into debt some thirty thousand dollars was good for an hour's panic, some lusty visceral fish-flops. But Molly had laid her groundwork meticulously, her arguments were sound, and the combined enthusiasm of all around him carried the day. The Gospel Train became the property of the Southern Cross Crusade, Inc., and was pulled off to the railroad shops for a paint job. The gleaming cars were then reassembled on a convenient siding and a horde of decorators, plumbers, electricians, and carpenters swept through.

At King's insistence Molly had a title: she was secretary-treasurer of the little corporation. Molly had unreluctantly quit her job with radio Kay-tip, and once the mail car had been remodeled as an office, she moved in with her staff of two, a young accountant named Haygood and a younger secretary, distant relative to Martin Handwerker, who developed a swooning crush on King the first time he blinked at her. With Cowboy's help they all worked long hours on the coming campaign, in fits of exhilaration and rounds of stimulating argument.

Molly's eyes frequently shone with fatigue and she got as skinny as a rat, but her energies waxed on satisfaction alone. During the day she kept an eye sharp for King, and made good on any excuse to hunt him down and have his opinion, and savor his awe of what was taking shape under the sparkling skies of a warm Christmas season. And one of them would inevitably say, with a quick breath or a nod of pleasure, "Seven more days," or "Five more days," and then their eyes would meet, which had the effect of knocking Molly silly for a good quarter hour—just like Florence, the secretary—and how did he feel, *what* did he feel? She was like a fumbling fortuneteller, alert for significance, for signposts in every hollow of his face, but all she really knew was that in seven days, or five, they would be aboard the Train, together, voyaging, twenty-four hours of every day, and then, surely, if there were miracles in the air, if there existed a God with any measure of justice in his heart, well then—please God—she would at last have her man.

King wrote, in a long-delayed letter to Frank Henderson:

The chapel is my joy. I don't know how much Molly is spending on it (afraid to ask), but she has a knack when it comes to getting talented people to work for her. An art teacher from the university is putting in the windows, which he designed and made himself in his own workshop—he actually makes the glass from scratch! The windows are divided up into odd-size panels, which are etched in black and silver with streaks of gold, depicting such popular scenes as the Agony on the Cross and the Resurrection. A lot of people come down to the Train just to see this man's work—we are attracting a certain amount of attention here in Clearwater already. Inside, the seats have been recovered in a beautiful shade of blue, and the altar, made out of all sorts of expensive wood, is taking shape. Once again the designer is this superb talent from the university. Maybe Molly is getting him for peanuts, who knows. Up top we still don't have a roof over our heads; the dome is being fixed so it can slide open on aluminum rails and a lot of work is going on which will result in my having a pulpit to preach from above the floor of the chapel itself, quite a unique feat of engineering when it's all over and done with. I wonder how much all this is going to cost in the end, but I'm not worrying. So far all of Molly's strategy has been right on the mark; she's certainly a superb businesswoman and I'm lucky to have her on my side at this time. Probably I'm boring you with all this talk about the Train so I'll just close now with much love to Tim and Marsh and Tip and Patty and to you and Mamaw particularly; cross your fingers we'll be seeing you all soon down in Florida, although that part of the itinerary hasn't been worked out yet.

King raised his head from the writing desk and looked over

at Age, who was sitting on the sofa stitching a new reflector carefully to the worn surface of his beloved yellow slicker.

"Getting a letter off to Frank," he said. "Anything I can add for you?"

Age made no response, and King scowled. Age had never talked much, but his silences had never been depressing, either. For over a week he had been distant as an irascible bird; his attitude puzzled and upset the preacher. For some reason Age's petulance had to do with the Gospel Train. His hatred of the Train had once or twice approached violence, but of late he had cooled, and now he displayed only grim indifference. He had visited the Train just once, and he absolutely refused to pitch in and help with the work. King was at a loss to justify his friend's behavior; perhaps it was the idea of more travel that had Age balked. Perhaps he wanted to go home—but the preacher wasn't about to bring that up again; he'd already received one blistering from Age on the touchy subject of retirement.

King dropped his scowl and squared his patience with a sigh. An eye opened upon him like the eye of an octopus, or a stone idol; horrible solemnity glittered in the eye. But Age's face was weak and graying; his upraised arm, trailing a thin black jet of thread, looked like a woman's arm, knobs and bowstrings.

"Anything you want to add to this letter?" King repeated.

Age put down his needle and thread and his snakelike fingers went skillfully along the surface of the slicker, nobbling at the brilliant junk. His face was hard and thoughtful. Unexpectedly his whole hand trembled, leaped into a claw; his eyes shrank from this phenomenon and cursed silently. King looked on, with a curious emotion close to mortification. But Age was quickly himself, and he began to sew again, painstakingly.

"I can't think of a thing," he said.

On the Sunday before the departure of the Gospel Train, a rain-plagued Sunday with a wind like a bone saw, King crawled out from under one of the coaches with a pipe fitter's wrench in his hand in time to see a man sheltered by a vast umbrella alighting from a taxi that had pulled up alongside the Train. Visitors to the Train were common enough, particularly on outing afternoons, and King paid little attention to them unless they got in the way of the workmen. But this visitor gave him pause and a worrisome jab at the heart. He arose from the soggy ballast, hung the wrench from a loop of his overalls, and loped along through the dismal rain.

"Mr. Manson!"

Eli's lawyer turned and smiled from under the umbrella. "Just the man I was looking for."

The preacher, who had not seen Manson since the day of Cowboy's hearing, eyed the paunchy lawyer glumly as he paid off his cabby. The incorporation proceedings had taken place without even a whisper of discontent from Manson's office, according to Cy Hillgrin. With the Gospel Train less than a hundred hours away from formal dedication, what could the lawyer want with him now? The day seemed blacker and wetter than it had only a few moments before.

The taxi drove off and Manson turned for a searching look at the length of the Gospel Train. His tough, tolerant eyes rippled with appreciation. "The stories in the papers don't do justice to what you have here. This is a magnificent sight, Reverend. I've been meaning to see it all for myself."

"Picked a poor day," King said with an unsuccessful grin.

Manson said something about the irregularities of life in the legal profession. "You've got your work clothes on and I don't want you feeling obliged to show me around."

"Oh, I'm not much of a help to anybody. I'd be proud to show you our Train, Counselor."

Manson nodded and graciously handed him the big umbrella. He was wearing his law-dog brown fedora, pulled down low on his youthful, permanently tanned face, which contrasted oddly with the elderly balloon of his body inside a clear plastic rain slicker.

King plodded hopefully toward the front of the Train, and as they passed the solitary window of the former mail car, he looked up and caught Molly's eye, signaling to her that something dire was in the wind.

In a twinkling Molly was walking beside them in a Red Riding Hood rain outfit. Manson acknowledged his introduction to her with a pleasant nod but he seemed to have eyes only for the Train. King pointed out where a slim gold cross would be mounted on the front of the locomotive, then led them aboard. Molly smoked a rain-dilapidated cigarette and kept her silence. The preacher ran on and on about the beauties and high purpose of the Train as they passed from car to car,

305

but all the while he was in a stew, trying to guess the real meaning of Manson's call.

When they reached the club car, they settled down in swivel chairs overlooking the bleak railroad yards while Molly went after a clutch of soft drinks. Manson fished for a stick of gum, unwrapped it, and munched contentedly as he took in the view. King was reminded of that uneasy day in the lawyer's office. He felt helpless and miserable in his smelly overalls and got up to pace, hoping to throw off his sense of entrapment.

"Tell me something about your trip," Manson suggested, but Molly had returned, and as she handed him a 7-Up she said curtly:

"You probably know all about it already, down to the last penny we should be grossing. Do you want to go ahead and tell us what you're up to, or do we wait till Cy comes?"

"Oh, is Cy coming?" Manson asked, looking pleased.

Molly stood over him with her hands on her hips. "I had my girl call him as soon as I set eyes on you. I expect he'll be along promptly."

Manson said, "No, he won't. He's off fishing for the weekend." He plugged away at the 7-Up and smiled benignly at them. "Chirrun, I thought it would be a good idea for us to have a last talk, an informal exchange of views, which wouldn't be easy if there were *two* lawyers present. Since you know how lawyers like to monopolize conversations."

Molly screwed up her face to show that she wasn't intimidated by his folksiness. King stood by numbly.

"Yes, I'm impressed beyond words by what you all have accomplished here," the lawyer said, waving his bottle of pop.

"Get to it," Molly said threateningly.

"Gladly." His eyes changed then; they glittered like a salt flat in a hot sun. "This excellent Train will not move a mile unless the Reverend Eli Charger is aboard it—in his rightful place, sharing the glories and benefits of the great religious crusade which you've planned. Sharing them on an equal basis with Mr. Windom."

Disturbed as King was, he could still marvel at Molly's reaction. Her body arched slightly, drawing back, and there was a flat sick look on her face. But her eyes were nailed on the lawyer and she said evenly, "Eli Charger doesn't have a legitimate claim on the—the glories and benefits of the Southern Cross Crusade. If he did—"

Manson brushed aside her objections. "Why don't you leave the question of . . . legitimacy to those qualified to pass on it?" He pressed back into the comfortable curve of the swivel chair and crossed his stubby legs. "For instance, a man like Judge Neely Stratton, who has been mightily impressed by my petition on behalf of the Reverend Mr. Charger—so impressed that he's issuing an injunction against removal of this Train from the city of Clearwater until such time as I can prepare my case against the so-called Southern Cross Crusade."

"Injunction," Molly said hollowly.

"I expect to have it by nine o'clock in the morning." Manson patted his knee. "Of course, you all could leave in the meanwhile . . ." He glanced inquiringly at the stricken preacher, then shrugged.

"So you're getting an injunction."

Manson tilted his head back and polished off the last of his soda pop.

Molly's fingers curled. "Why didn't you get your injunction sooner, you fat—"

"Molly!"

Manson's eyes narrowed, then he surveyed her understandingly. "That's not a bad question." He liked the question so well that he rephrased it for them. "Why didn't I stop you four weeks ago, before the incorporation became a fact? In spite of what my friend Cy likes to think, I could have done just that. But . . ."

He looked at King, who had paled considerably, and when he spoke again he addressed himself warmly to the preacher. "I was so taken with you, Reverend, during our get-together in my office, that I made a point of stopping by the tent the very next night. My Lord, what a talent you have! I've been meaning to congratulate you for some time now. If I had a seventh of your personal appeal and your persuasiveness, I might have been a big-name trial lawyer instead of—well, that's no never mind. I believed, as every soul in that revival tent surely believed upon hearing you preach, that you were a man with fate on his side—that you were bound to say important words, do important deeds, and become a famous man in our time."

King knew that the lawyer was sincere and that he had been paid a walloping compliment by a man of judgment, which only made him feel worse, and blackly hostile.

Manson paused, then continued with a golden smile.

"Although I was doing a little preaching myself at the time—preaching *reconciliation*, that is, to both you and Mr. Charger—I doubted that would happen. Because you were a young man, you see, all afire and dedicated in the way only a young man can be, and the Reverend Mr. Charger was old, settled, with no great hunger to satisfy in the service of the Lord. No, sad to say, I didn't see any prospect of a friendly reconciliation, and of course as a conscientious man I had my client's interests to protect."

King cried out, "I've been stuffing Eli's purse for the last month now; isn't that enough for him?"

Manson went on as if he hadn't been interrupted. "But your words, your . . . *passion*, touched me to the quick there in the tent, and I thought what a terrible thing it would be to cause you so much grief and discouragement at such a crucial time in your career." Molly said something bitter and unladylike. "Why, I asked myself, should I clip his wings when he's just beginning to soar? I managed to convince Mr. Charger that it would be a shame—it would be *cruelty*—to confine you with a lot of legal fencing, to embitter you with judgments and due processes at a time when there's a crying need for men of your vision and spirit in this world." Manson finished with a triumphant gasp for breath. He reached for a handkerchief to mop his sticky brow; the muggy atmosphere in the car had them all twitching. The bark of his smile sailed confidently on.

Molly reared once again, but this time she merely looked thoughtful. "Well, Cy told me you were slick as a pussycat's ass. So you held back, waiting to see what kind of fortune King was going to make for himself?" She shot a look the length of the dim club car, her jaw bunched, as if she were hoping for the sudden appearance of King's lawyer. Apparently she decided that in Hillgrin's absence nothing much could be lost by speaking her mind.

"That old fool Charger isn't going to put a foot on my—on this Train. You hear? We'll drive it into the river first!"

Manson laughed and King reached out, latching on to Molly's shoulder, probably just in time to prevent her from sinking her nails into the lawyer's cheek.

"What do you want us to do?" King asked, clearing his throat. "I mean, we have to be out of here Thursday noon at the latest, or else—"

"Don't tell him anything he doesn't need to know," Molly said savagely, tearing away from his grasp.

"Molly, sit down. I mean, sit *down*. I've got to find out—"

"I know your problems," Manson said, and hitched a thumb at Molly. "I know as much about your finances as *you* do, Mrs. Amos. You've done a lot of spending the past three weeks and you're going to have a lot of recouping to do right away, or else." To King he said, "Has she told you what it costs to operate a full-size train for even twenty-four hours? There's a good reason why the railroads are closing down their passenger services: they run millions in the red every year." He stressed the "millions" softly and waited until the shock hit home and King's gaze shifted uncertainly to Molly; then he leaned forward and planted his feet solidly on the floor.

"But this Train won't turn a wheel until and unless I say it can. You'd better understand that, then we can get down to serious talk." He divined a flicker of cunning in Molly's eyes and said smoothly, "You all may wait for young Cy if you want to—but then just try getting hold of me. I guarantee you'll waste *weeks* trying. I'm here this afternoon to talk a deal. I intend to walk out of here in a half hour with everything settled—and then your Train can leave on Thursday just the way you planned. With everybody on board who belongs on board."

"I'll get dynamite," Molly vowed in a voice thick with hatred and frustration. "I'll blow this Train through the moon and I'd like to see you stop me with an injunction."

Manson, deciding she was in an unbusinesslike mood, switched his attention to King.

"What do you want us to do?" King repeated. The soft cascade of rain on the roof seemed to roar in his ears. All the joy of possession and anticipation had drained out of him and, as he looked around the luxurious shadowy car, he felt as if he were sitting instead inside a live bomb.

"Very good," Manson said contentedly. "All I want is full participation by the Reverend Mr. Charger in the affairs of the Southern Cross Crusade, Inc. His salary will be fifteen thousand a year." He hesitated. "Also it'll be his pleasure to name three members of the new board of governors."

"In other words," Molly said, "good old Eli will control the policy of the Southern Cross Crusade."

"You could be in worse hands."

Molly accepted this conclusion, or indignity, with an

unblinking venomous stare. The bomb ticked away alarmingly inside King's head, and he crushed his grease-marked hands together. Manson watched the preacher's face with a bird dog's concentration, his eyes unnervingly neutral.

King said, in a stifled voice, "Molly?"

His plea roused her. She turned her head and frowned, then faced Manson. She was still wild; she seemed—in her peculiar fashion, while under stress—to have aged twenty years, but she said calmly, "That's it? The deal? No ups, no extras?"

Manson spread his hands, a priestly gesture.

"We all go to work for Eli tomorrow morning. A sick, obsessed, unprincipled old man who hated King in every cell of his body. Who hates him the way you do, Manson!"

"That's a remarkable thing to say." The lawyer's voice gently mocked her, but for a few moments his eyes lost some of their clarity and authority, they were dimmed in a wilderness of frost.

Molly leaped to her feet and struck again. "I say you hate him and you've told why. You're a bloated worm, Manson; there's nothing about you that lives except your slick brain, and King . . . *blazes!* He's vital, he has a powerful life force. He lives where tenderness is, he can gather souls in his arms like the Good Shepherd. All you can do is paralyze them and suck them dry—worm!"

Manson, who had been called everything in his time, laughed. "You're a remarkable woman." But her antagonism was as caustic and shriveling as a rain of pitch, so the lawyer tilted his hapless body forward in the streamlined swivel chair and, cutting his eyes past Molly, he said to King, "I'm not giving you any more time, Reverend. I'm tired of evasions and temporizing! I've told you what I want you to do and I expect you to do it. Otherwise I can promise you'll be preaching the rest of your days from the tail gate of a wagon or down alleys a self-respecting bum wouldn't sleep in!" His voice was harsh, and King murmured a protest. But the bomb was ticking relentlessly, and he had no protection.

Molly, not to be denied, clutched at Manson to get his attention. "Your magic word doesn't panic us; we'll get your injunction set aside. One way or another! Now, you're not welcome here, and you'd better—"

His face stiff with outrage at being touched, Manson flapped his arm, shaking her off. Whether King saw, or thought he saw,

Manson threaten Molly with his fist is unimportant, because the bomb had exploded like a red thundercloud in his head. He rose with a roar from his seat, six feet five of avenging angel, and his hands shot toward the flabbergasted lawyer.

Instead of seizing Manson and hurling him the length of the car, King fastened his hands on the arms of the chrome-plated, leather-covered chair and heaved. Manson, imprisoned by King's arms, stared up at the preacher helplessly and a little fearfully. King's face swelled dark with blood and the swivel chair, with Manson riding it, suddenly snapped off its pedestal. King gasped, turned, and casually dumped the chair. Manson, from his seat on the floor, continued to stare unbelievingly.

"You heard Molly," King grunted, flexing his hands.

The lawyer struggled speechlessly to his feet, looking pale and grim as a stitch, seized his hat from a table, and hastened the length of the car. They both saw him through the windows, jogging awkwardly through the downpour.

"Worm," Molly chortled, and collapsed in a rack of laughter, holding her side. But King was aghast.

"Molly, we're in trouble!"

That sobered her. "Come on," she said, and leading him by the hand, went racing through the Train to the office.

Florence, the secretary, looked up worriedly as they entered the fluorescent cave.

"I tried to reach Mr. Hillgrin, but he's—"

"Fishing, I know," Molly snapped. "Florence, you can go home now; King and I have some things to discuss."

"I left word that he should call you the minute he gets in."

"When will that be?"

"He's expected around midnight." Florence got up, covered her typewriter, and with many a dovelike glance at the oblivious preacher, she slowly buttoned up her raincoat and went sadly out into the wet.

Molly, too shaken to go to the bother of lighting a cigarette, sat down and rested her head on her arms. King distractedly paced the neatly furnished office. By and by Molly pounded her fist on the desk top.

"Cy *must* have seen this coming. He'd better have an angle."

"What can we do in the meantime?"

"Nothing, nothing . . ." They looked starkly at each other. King was touched by the blighted expression on her lemur's face. He sat comfortingly near on the edge of the desk.

"Maybe we're finished," Molly said, almost relishing doom and gloom.

"Molly, don't give in like that."

"Well, what else? I'm worn out. I tell you I'm up to here!" She hid her face once more. "I could have held out to Thursday somehow, but now this . . ." A suggestion of tears clouded her voice.

King squirmed in sympathy and embarrassment and finally reached out to touch her cold nervous hand. "Molly, why don't you go home and—"

She asked in a muffled voice, "Would you come with me?"

"I don't know, I still have a lot of work—"

She raised up and looked furiously at him. "I've had enough and so have you, admit it!" Then she softened. "Let's be smart and get out of this—this aluminum tomb for a while." Her eyes were fresh and wistful. "At my place you can have a hot soak while I'm in the kitchen—"

"You want to cook for me?" King said, a strange distress in the pit of his stomach.

"Sure, sure, why not; I'm no slouch with the pots and pans." The prospect of entertaining him for the evening was a valuable tonic for Molly. "Oh, we've got trouble, all right!" she said lightheartedly. "We've got so many troubles, if we stick around here another minute we'll be clawing at the walls. Come on, let's save our sanity, let's live like *normal* people for a few hours! Cy can reach us at my place when he gets in."

Her enthusiasm gladdened King; he had to admit that he had begun gritting his teeth at all the tensions involved in getting the Gospel Train ready to roll. Their mutual embattlement became a bond as solid as kinship. New oxygen flowed into his blood. Cy Hillgrin would surely think of a way out of their predicament, and in the meantime . . . well, they might as well relax.

"Molly, let's go!" He thoughtlessly shook her like a pup.

But she had already seen the approval of her in his eyes, and that made every galling minute spent with Sam Manson seem like a fair price for what was to come.

29

Archangel Temple of the Healing Grace

While Molly and King were recovering from the shock of the lawyer's visit, rallying their hopes and doing their best to assure each other that Cy Hillgrin did indeed have the means to get the Gospel Train rolling on time—although he hadn't bothered to tell them that there might be the slightest hitch in plans—Philemon was going nearly out of his mind with anxiety and despair, and the surprising cause of it all was a demure blond slip of a girl named Rose.

His day had started right enough at six o'clock that morning with a drive—in the bosom of his adopted family—to the Skullbone Community near Clearwater, which was both the point of origin and a retreat for the large Hazelman family. It was time, as Brother Hazelman had reiterated along the way, to put a lock on their mission in the city for a few days. He for one was worn out, they had reached a temporary stalemate with the devil, not gaining ground but not losing either, and it seemed to be the proper time for all to rejuvenate their faith in a peaceful country setting. Every Hazelman who could possibly be contacted had been invited to Skullbone—here Brother Hazelman paused to paint a full portrait of charming country cottages, towering shade trees, immense skies, and a beautiful lake for Philemon's enjoyment—to participate in a thigh-whacking, soul-shaking brush-arbor meeting that would last all day and into the night, until every soul on hand was prostrate with joy in the presence of the Holy Ghost.

Philemon was so excited about the meeting, and about his own eminence in this remarkable family group, that they were forced to stop, solely for his benefit, at two filling stations during the fifty-mile drive. Sister Hazelman had her revenge for the delay by shrieking with laughter as each time he tried to slip unobtrusively into the toilet, thus conveying without words to all those within hearing distance that Philemon was either some kind of incompetent or had a terrible case of the trots; but even Sister Evelyn couldn't provoke him on this extraordinary morning as easily as she often did.

Some of Philemon's enthusiasm began to drain into the slopping quicksand that lay in his belly once they reached the scene of his expected triumph. The little village of Skullbone lived like a fungus at the edge of a cypress-choked, mist-covered bayou down a stretch of jarring road. The threat of rain and the cold emphasized the hangout look of the place, but Brother Hazelman was all smiles as they rolled through, and he said, with a glance at his watch, "Everybody must be at the church ground already." Philemon held two of his back teeth in place with his tongue and said nothing. They crossed several arms of the bayou on old wooden bridges. Above the thunder of loose timbers grew another sound, the yapping, bugling, and screaming of a pack of hunting dogs.

Soon the church ground appeared through a tangle of forest and ground mist. It was a high spit of land hemmed by the bayou on three sides, and contained three buildings, one with a squat church steeple holding a fat rust-red bell. Behind the buildings there was a small graveyard with a wire fence around it, and immediately behind that a black hole in the forest alive with writhing arms of mist. The whole atmosphere, scored by the cries of a dozen dogs splashing in the murky bayou water, gave Philemon the willies.

"They started the coon-on-a-log contest already!" Sister Evelyn said indignantly, and scrambled out of the front seat almost before the car was stopped.

"Smell that air!" Hazelman exulted, getting out himself, and Philemon obediently sniffed, finding the air of Skullbone at least agreeable. The sun had been cruising visibly through the overcast; now it shone brilliantly, for the first time, in sublime infinite shafts through the ranks of tall trees, lighting the bayou below where a good-sized raccoon squatted on a ten-foot length of log in the middle of the water, surrounded by splashing, lunging dogs.

Philemon's eyes shifted. "Is that the church?" he inquired. Brother Hazelman nodded. He was done up magnificently in purple and gold this day, with a velvet officers'-style cape around his shoulders. "That's where you'll strut your stuff for the Lord," he said, not paying attention to Philemon at all. "And I know you're impatient to light into the devil. But there's plenty more people to come yet." Indeed, another carload had just arrived, and Brother Hazelman went striding off to greet them. Philemon waited by the Cadillac to be spoken to, to be summoned; but Hazelman went on down to the water to join the others and Philemon could only tag after them.

He loved nothing better than a savvy coon matched against an indomitable hound and he soon forgot his uneasiness at being a stranger in the midst of many, and concentrated on the action. One of the dogs was lying in a quivering heap on the shore with his nose half-ripped away, but seven others were still after the coon, who was quiet and concentrating, waiting with his formidable claws for another of the hounds to make a mistake. More hounds, securely tied on the shore, were causing most of the uproar. Nearby stood a station wagon with caged coons looking darkly out at the proceedings, waiting their turn on the log, which was barely thick enough to be defensible.

A lemon-spotted hound, swimming desperately, had managed to lift himself chest high on the butt end of the log and, with distended eyes, was attempting to shimmy down far enough to get his licks at the vulnerable back of the coon. But the log tipped and he sprawled back into the water, to the loud chagrin of his owner.

"Come on, Blackjack, sling his ay-yuss off that log!"

Money was changing hands and Philemon wished for a moment that Cosh was along; but his dog was no good for this type of thing.

"Geet him, boy, go geeettt that coon!"

One of the dogs suddenly turned tail and began paddling desperately back to shore. A few feet out he floundered, and a long-haired boy rushed into the water with an oath to rescue him.

Another hound, that looked like a blue tick to Philemon, got a paw on the log and leaped snapping for the raccoon's spine.

315

He missed, and the coon also missed the dog's exposed throat by a hair. But the coon was off balance for an instant and another hound surged in, forcing him back to the middle of the log. At once two dogs began rocking the log from either end. The coon held on nimbly but he was unable to keep his tail under him. A long-limbed Labrador found extra strength somewhere, or perhaps discovered a submerged windfall that gave him a foothold and a springboard. He flew accurately at the striped tail, fastened on it, and in the same motion gave a twitch that sent the coon hurtling into the water. The shore-bound dogs went crazy. There was a great boiling in the water, and everyone strained to see the finish. But there was nothing to see; the coon had vanished and so had one of the dogs. The remaining five milled around in the water for a couple of minutes, then struggled home.

The ensuing lengthy argument over whose hound had accomplished what ended with the owner of the drowned dog being paid off. By that time it was midmorning and the church ground was teeming. Philemon felt lonelier than ever—he had scarcely been spoken to since arriving—but he consoled himself with the fact that all eyes would be turned to him before long, in fear and admiration. The greatest sermon he'd ever preached was now brawling in his mind; his heart swelled with massive impatience. But the intermittent sun climbed higher, and there were two more "contests" between raccoon and dog, and other games for the younger set. Once Philemon made his way through the press to stand at Brother Hazelman's elbow, and there, after failing to gain attention by the fact of his presence, inquired when it would be time for church.

Brother Hazelman gazed at him distractedly. "Not yet, Philemon, not yet," was all he had to say, in a tone of voice that hurt, and he returned his full attention to the sport at hand.

Around noon the rusty old bell in the steeple came to life and Philemon's heart leaped. Now would come the hours of praying, hymning, and testifying that Brother Hazelman had promised. Now that they all had had a good time and were in a proper frame of mind for Jesus. Now would come . . . miracles! For he, Philemon, was determined that before the day ended they would be, to the merest child, struck dumb by his contempt for the devil, by his challenge and mastery of the fearful diseases that racked their bodies. He had in fact looked around several times that morning for the crippled and infirm,

316

prepared to give words of comfort on the spot, but they were almost to a man an uncommonly hardy-looking bunch of country people. Yet he had confidence that when the time came the Lord would reveal sickness for him to heal. They might look healthy to the unobservant, but Philemon sensed the dark rotting of cancer, the burgeoning of tumor. . . . Oh, God bless you! he had thought passionately. Go on, have a good time, and forget your suffering and your wretchedness for a little while! And when it's all too much to bear, then come to me.

His enthusiasm was running so high that he was the first one into the little church, which was dark at noonday, smelled of the swamp, and trembled mightily with each stroke of the bell overhead. He picked a chair on the pulpit and sat down to compose himself for the holy ordeal ahead. But ten minutes went by and not another soul entered. He looked up from his edgy meditation. The church remained dark. Next door there was a hubbub and so he descended from the pulpit and went out.

They were all having lunch, helping themselves from a vast spread of meats, vegetables, and breads. Brother Hazelman had taken his place at the head of a horseshoe of picnic tables that filled the one-room school building. As soon as most had served themselves and were seated, he banged away with a hammer on a piece of old iron to secure quiet for the blessing. Philemon, who had no appetite for meat or drink and felt nearly sickened by the rich odors, was caught standing near the door, looking lonesomely on.

He bowed his head in the ensuing silence and tried to concentrate properly on Brother Hazelman's prayer. Outside a car door popped. The schoolhouse door was ajar to let in a little air and Philemon peered out. He couldn't see anyone but by and by he heard light footsteps on the plank porch, and urgent breathing. Automatically he stepped aside.

From the corner of his eye he saw an outstretched hand, a feathery blond head, deep-set gray eyes, and a nugget chin. She seemed to reach for him as she came through the door; Philemon recoiled but with a sigh her eyes closed and she dropped into his arms. She weighed next to nothing. Philemon stared unbelievingly at the burden he had acquired and then lifted his reddening face. But no one in the room was looking and Brother Hazelman droned on.

The blond girl's eyelids fluttered. With a second glance he

could tell she was not really young, more than thirty perhaps. She was dressed in a blue skirt that had a thousand creases and a gray sweater the color of the eyes he'd glimpsed. His own eyes strayed to the length of her pallid throat, to the prominence of a collarbone and—deeper still within the V of her frayed blouse —a scant milk-bubble breast and wisp of brassiere. She smelled, disconcertingly, of peanuts and popcorn, like the lobby of a third-run movie house, and this reminded him somehow of another girl whom he had once loved, beyond all reason, when he was twelve. He almost dropped her then and there. But her eyes had opened; she was looking at him. The faintness was gone from her eyes and new light had appeared in them, like distant rainbows.

"I am just fine now," she breathed. "It was the excitement of coming home." Philemon felt life astir in her thin body but he witlessly held on. It occurred to him that Brother Hazelman was no longer preaching and that the silence in the room had become like death. This time he was afraid to look.

The girl twisted free of him, eagerly, as if he were some sort of vine she had become caught up in, and ran on her sparrow's legs across the floor crying, "Daddy, Daddy! Mommy? Where's Mommy?" Brother Hazelman had risen from his place at the table; his eyes were big and moist and his false teeth shone in a gape of surprise. But it was his wife who spoke first.

"Little Rose! It's our daughter!" She tried to get around from behind the tables and a welter of folks but her way was blocked. "Oh, hallelujah!" she shrieked, and ducked under one of the tables, proceeding on all fours. Unfortunately she came up too soon and brained herself on a cross brace. She sat on the floor rubbing her head and saying, "Lord-d God, cured of the leprosy! Home at last! Lord-d God, somebody help me up out of here!" But Little Rose and her daddy had met in a fervent embrace across one of the tables; nearby, everybody else was leaping up and down from joy at seeing Rose home again and there was quite a bit of commotion, so for a while Evelyn went unnoticed except by Philemon, who couldn't keep his eyes off her; he felt almost as stunned as if he had run into that cross brace himself.

Eventually Evelyn and her daughter were restored to each other, and Little Rose, who after her spell of faintness was more composed than anyone else there, made her rounds of the family circle to be welcomed. Walter Hazelman was red-faced and dripping unashamed tears. He roared and laughed and wept until his preposterously blond hair was hanging in his face, then levered Rose into a place at the table beside him and banged on his hunk of iron for order. Philemon had not budged from his spot near the door; a presentiment of disaster had flown in and picked his heart clean.

When he had every ear Brother Hazelman began. "The Lord will surely forgive us interrupting grace the way we did. In just a minute I'm going to offer up another prayer of thanksgiving for the safe return of Little Rose, whom we'd all given up for—for dead, these past three years." He almost lost his voice and cast a fond glance at the crown of his daughter's head. She was sitting with her hands folded beside the plate that someone had heaped with food for her and her eyes were downcast, but she smiled, somewhat painfully, at his words. "This is a day of—of joyfulness and homecoming, a day to celebrate the Lord; it's no time to speak of suffering and other terrible things. Later, when we all go over to the church, I know Little Rose will tell us all about her miraculous release from the ravages of leprosy"—"Ohhhh, beautiful Jesus," moaned Sister Evelyn reverently, and there was a spate of amens—"but right now we're just going to sit here with our heads bowed and be thankful that the good Lord chose to return Little Rose to the loving arms of her family on this special day. Let us all pray! Ohh, Heavenly Father, we *thank* you for your infinite mercy . . ."

Philemon, who had bowed his head once more over his barren breast, felt something stroke lightly against his forehead like the shadow of a bee and he looked up to discover Rose Hazelman sitting unbowed herself at the table with her eyes gravely, nervelessly, upon him. He was so startled he dipped his head immediately, but he could still feel her studying him.

He was distraught with jealousy and agonized by the memory of how she had settled trustingly into his arms, and at the first opportunity he slipped out of the hall and wandered for an hour on the grounds, not knowing whether to fly or to stay. In the end it was Rose's eyes—inquiring, wondering—that persuaded him, along with the hoarse banging of the church bell, to remain.

It was not his intention, after having been ignored all morning, to go directly to the pulpit and take his rightful place; he had visions of standing in humble readiness at the back of the church until Brother Hazelman missed and contritely called for him. But, as he was shuffling into the church with the others, a hand clapped down on his shoulder and someone said in his ear, "Preaching for us today, Brother Philemon?" A woman also smiled commendingly at him.

Recognized at last; Philemon felt he had no choice, so up he went, and Hazelman, smiling, said, "Welcome, Philemon," as if he had just set foot on the place. "Did you introduce yourself to our daughter Rose?"

Philemon shook his head, and his eyes shifted to the blond girl, still holding court with her relatives. He had never seen a leper or a former leper, but he was aware from the Bible and a dozen Biblical movies what a disfiguring disease leprosy could be.

Brother Hazelman seemed to know perfectly well what he was thinking. "Not a mark on her, praise God! A year ago she wouldn't let us come to see her. It was that bad! Rose wanted to die. But then she gathered all her courage and left that leper place, and went away up on the mountain to pray for a cure. Jesus heard her! He descended from His seat beside the throne of Heaven and cradled her in His arms—"

Philemon stared in wonder and dread at Little Rose. "Where'd she come by her leprosy?"

"It was in Africa, years ago, where she served the Lord as a missionary to the black heathen of the jungles. Now she's cured! And she has the Power of Jesus in her own body! Jesus said to her, to my daughter and my only child, 'You must preach the good news of the Gospels, put courage in sick hearts and health in sick bodies.' "

Little Rose lifted her head as if her father had called and after a moment's hesitation she ran to his embrace. Most of the congregation was there and they were ready to hear the Miracle; they shouted and clapped and waved their hands ecstatically. Brother Hazelman left Rose and waded into their midst, chanting, "Say amen! Sayyyyy-y amen!" Women groaned with pleasure and children gasped and suddenly, spontaneously, all began to sing "By and By I Will See Jesus."

Their emotion went through Philemon like a thunderbolt. He and Rose were face to face and for an instant he saw something that puzzled him: a fear to match his own fear. They were alone, out of touch with the others. Rose lifted a hand to her throat and smiled shyly.

320

Philemon blurted, "Is it true? Did you see the Lord Jesus? Did He touch you and say your name? Did He?"

Rose looked blankly at the fired-up congregation, then took a deep breath; her eyes began to glow.

"Did He hold you in His arms?" Philemon sobbed. "Girl—"

Her eyes passed over him, startled. Then she reached out, catching his right hand. "Don't worry," she said kindly. "He loves you too. Believe in Him."

For a few moments Philemon thought he was going to faint. Then he snatched his hand away, stumbled, spied a doorway off the pulpit, and ran through it. Groaning aloud, he fled to the shores of the bayou, where the dogs leaped and roared at his approach. He fell face down at the water and thrust his offended hand in.

Long after numbness from the cold water had gone past his elbow, he continued to hold his hand under. Singing drifted to him, followed by the high-pitched voice of Little Rose, her words indistinguishable. At midafternoon, when the bayou had grown dark and a teasing rain had started to fall, the sort of frenzy which Philemon had hoped to inspire began in the church. He pulled himself up from the wet ground and walked slowly uphill. A woman wandered out of the church, mumbling and crying, her skirt thrown up over her head. Philemon veered away from the threat of human contact and made his way to the edge of the graveyard, where he could no longer hear anything.

He was not seeking shelter; he wanted the rain and the cold whispering air. He was fit company only for worms, ghosts, and depleted dreams; on a bench inside the graveyard he waited for his sadness and the rain to melt him into laden earth.

In the last light of day Little Rose approached, her head in a scarf, her bare arms dripping with rain. She stopped near him, walled out by his misery.

"Why did you run?"

He lifted his matted head.

"Did I do something?" she wanted to know.

Philemon closed his eyes.

"I was intended to preach today," he said, with a bronchial gasp. His tone invited silence. Little Rose crossed her arms over her thin breast.

"We all love you here, Philemon. Daddy's told me what a comfort you've been. He wants to see you now."

"I won't never preach again."

"Yes, you will," she said severely. "If you don't die of pneumonia first. Come on, there's hot soup and coffee in the house. And Daddy really does want to talk to you. I'm going before I get soaked."

Halfway to the house she stopped and cast a look back: he was coming and so she waited; wordlessly they entered the house together. Inside the door Rose took off her shoes and Philemon did the same. She pointed the way and he limped down a musty hallway into a study nearly bare of furniture. There he waited incuriously to be recognized.

Soon Brother Hazelman glanced up from a desk littered with blueprints. "There you are. Rose!" She appeared with a couple of towels and when Philemon blotted halfheartedly at himself with one of them, she seized his head and gave him a harsh but not unfriendly rubbing. A pair of trousers and a clean shirt had also turned up. Soon Philemon was slumped in a wicker chair near the desk drinking coffee and the dangerous hot spot in his chest had shrunk to the size of a half dollar, although he still wheezed and spoke in a hoarse whisper, if he spoke at all.

When Rose had returned for good and slipped into a chair opposite Philemon, Brother Hazelman awoke from long contemplation of his blueprints and smiled comfortingly at them both. Thereafter he devoted most of his attention to Philemon, with a look of utmost seriousness in his eye.

"You know that we have taken you in and loved you just the same as if you were our own son."

Philemon nodded.

"And there will always be a place for you in our family."

These were forceful words of encouragement, and Philemon responded by looking a little less resentful and downcast.

Walter Hazelman thoughtfully tapped the desk with a pencil. "Now that Rose has returned we are bound to make room for her. She's a preacher of the Gospel too and after her miraculous experience in the wilderness she's aching to get into the thick of the fight with Satan."

"Yes, Lord," Rose said softly.

Philemon, feeling pinned by Brother Hazelman's inquiring eyes, said, almost guiltily, "I won't never preach again." His fingers dug at the wicker chair.

"Philemon," Walter Hazelman crooned, "that's not what I expect out of you! A little disappointment's not going to stand in the way of your great zeal for the Word of God! You'll preach! You'll save! I promise that! We mean to see to it you get your chance . . . hmmm, somehow."

His last words settled into a hush. Philemon dared to raise his eyes, but even the soft lamplight hurt them. He felt so lightheaded he was afraid he might drift out of the rickety chair. The blueprints, which had turned an odd color from age, crackled under Hazelman's strong hands. He stroked them like a father stroking the hand of a favorite child.

"Do you know what these are?" he asked suddenly.

"No."

"They are all that's left of a great vision—a vision of the Archangel Temple of the Healing Grace." For an instant pain shrouded the clarity of his blue eyes. "Years ago when I was just another young disciple on the road selling Bibles and preaching at doorsteps, nearly worn out with my travels and with a sense that the devil was traveling faster than I could hope to go, I dropped under a big shade tree one hot afternoon and closed my eyes for a few minutes of rest. When I opened my eyes again, lo, there was an angel of the Lord sitting in the tree above my head.

"I don't want to tell you all about my vision now. The upshot was that this angel, whose name was Langis as I recall—or was it—" Brother Hazelman scratched his jaw meditatively. "No, that's right, it was the angel Langis, and he commanded me to build a great healing church right there beside the road. But I was full of skepticism in those days—beans and vinegar too. I looked around and saw a prosperous farm, and I demanded of the angel how I could afford even to buy that land, much less build a church. Oh, my faith was as frail as your faith is this minute! But the angel Langis was patient with me and told me to cross over the road and stand well out of the way. I did so, and as I was standing by, a great storm built up in the heavens and swooped down on that rich farm, whirling it to smithereens in a minute. Fortunately there were no people about, and not a single animal was even ruffled by the mighty wind. Thereafter the farm stood abandoned, and, in time, thanks to my hard work and the blessing of the Lord, I was able to buy that land, and to commission plans for the church."

Philemon waited a decent interval to find out what had happened next, after such a likely start, but there was a lost look in

Brother Hazelman's eyes and so he had to inquire why the church remained unbuilt.

"Oh, it was one thing and then another," Brother Hazelman said testily. "You know how it is when the devil gets his back up. But despite all the disappointment, there are still days when I hope that I may yet build my tabernacle." He tossed a sigh, fished around, and came up with a schematic drawing which he passed to Philemon.

"Of course I'm too old now," he reflected, "to give proper attention to a great healing church. That would be for a younger, ambitious man like yourself."

Philemon avidly studied the drawing of the tabernacle which the angel Langis had asked for. It was monolithic, with fortress windows, great entrance doors, and three prominent crosses across the rather cheerless stone façade. His head was still reeling from Brother Hazelman's suggestion that he could be the man to hold forth in such a magnificent church when Hazelman leaned forward to provide him with another exhibit, a murky photograph of a foundation and steel skeleton standing in a field.

"Yea, that's all there is of the Archangel Temple," he admitted. "Over the years most of the money I've saved to complete it has been eaten up by taxes and by"—Hazelman glanced fondly at his daughter—"other unlooked-for expenses. Still, I *have* been able to accumulate enough for a fresh start, provided . . ." His voice faded and his eyes glazed. He looked down wretchedly, letting the pages of the blueprints slip through his fingers.

"Daddy . . ." Rose said, in a heart-twisting tone.

"No, Little Rose," Brother Hazelman said gently. "It's all a dream after all. I'm going to fail, and I know it. I'm just a poor man and only the poor know my name. I never have learned to flatter the rich and increase their charity for my sake." Slowly but decisively he began to roll the blueprints, and his shoulders slumped. "Better for me to forget my vows and face the displeasure of the Almighty than to break my heart trying to do the impossible."

"Oh, Daddy, no—"

"What chance do I have of building a great church?" The hope of only a few moments ago seemed to have leaked from him like air from a punctured balloon.

Philemon watched the rolling of the blueprints and

swallowed nervously. "Why," he croaked, and Hazelman acknowledged him with a sad eye, "why can't you just raise the walls, and put a roof on, and move in? I bet a lot of folks would come, and lend a hand too."

Brother Hazelman smiled benevolently but shook his head. "That's a thoughtful suggestion, Philemon. But even walls and a roof—a plain tarpaper roof to keep the rain out, mind you, not the beautiful slate called for in the plans—would cost twice again the money I've scrimped and put away in all the years since Rose was a young girl." Philemon sought to speak again but Hazelman raised his hand. His smile was still monument-sized, but his voice sounded perilously strained. "Now don't make me feel bad. It just can't be done. I've decided here and now."

"But with enough money . . ." Philemon said urgently.

"More money?" Hazelman dejectedly turned off the smile, shrugged in a mean sort of way, and reached for a fat rubber band to secure the water-stained old blueprints.

Philemon drew a harsh breath that aggravated the hot spot in his chest and the dark periphery of the room threatened to swallow him. The face of Brother Hazelman appeared to drift toward that darkness, away from the desk lamp; he was drifting beyond recall and Philemon panicked. "I could help you," he shouted—it seemed to him that he shouted—and in good time Brother Hazelman returned to sharp focus.

"How could you help *me*, Philemon? It's you *we* want to help, to find a place for."

"If I could get some money, th-then we could go ahead and build some more on the Archangel Temple of the Holy Spirit—"

"Of the Healing Grace. Hmmm, but . . . Philemon, we're all . . . *poor* here. I know you've come by money hard in *your* life."

"Yes, I have. But I swear I"—he fired a look at Little Rose, who was inscrutable—"can get . . . some . . . m-money."

"Bless you, son." Hazelman picked up his pencil and consulted it like an oracle. "How much do you think you could get?"

Straining his imagination to the full, reaching deep for a figure that would stun his friend to a reverent appreaciation of his seriousness, Philemon said wildly, "A thousand dollars!"

Brother Hazelman laughed, then coughed into his fist. At last he said with a negligent kindness, "I know you mean well, and I'll always be grateful, son."

Philemon stared at him, shattered.

The pencil danced along the desk and rolled off. "Philemon, I know a thousand dollars seems like a lot of money to you. But it isn't. Let me explain. The Archangel Temple of the Healing Grace was meant to be a *great* center of worship, not just another country meeting house. You've seen the pictures. A thousand dollars wouldn't go very far. We need walls and a roof, yea, but also we have to have windows, doors, a floor to stand on. Lights to see by. Chairs to sit in. Those are *necessities*. No, no; God love you—but it's hopeless."

"Please," said Philemon. "Let me help you! I'll get"— his voice fell to a frightened whisper—"more money."

For a very long time Brother Hazelman said nothing. Then, with his eyes glazed once again, he pulled the faded photograph of the uncompleted building toward him and stared at it. "Yea," he said faintly. "The Archangel Temple *must* be completed. And if you could do it, Philemon—"

"Oh, I want to!"

"*If* you could do it. But—" He started to shake his head at the absurdity of the idea, then brightened. "Of course, you have friends who might help you raise . . . five thousand dollars, at the least."

"Five thous—"

"I know your uncle would be generous and give you a hand with the money. And then there's the Reverend Mr. Windom. We've all been praying hard for his success and good fortune, and it looks like good fortune has certainly come his way."

"I don't think he—"

Brother Hazelman gazed keenly into Philemon's eyes. "God bless you, son! I think five thousand *would* be enough! Oh, my! What a miracle! *Praise* His name! I believe that with such a contribution from you, combined with my own small savings, by spring at the latest you could be ministering to a thousand suffering seekers in the Archangel Temple of the Holy Anointment."

"The Healing Grace," Little Rose amended, but she wasn't heard. Brother Hazelman bolted from behind the desk and fell to his knees in front of Philemon, who stared down at him, eyes dulled, pinpointed with shock.

"Pray with me, Philemon! Join hands with me, kneel down

326

beside me here on the floor and say Thank you, God! We're going to build a tabernacle! What do you know! Lord, at long last we're going to raise that cash we need to do you honor and fulfill the vows— *What the devil's wrong with you?*"

This last was directed at Philemon, who had suddenly jerked up out of the wicker chair, inadvertently kicking Brother Hazelman just as he was in the act of prostrating himself on the dingy floor.

"Sick," Philemon muttered, clutching his stomach, and he made for the door.

Little Rose sprang to him and skillfully guided him down the hall and into the bathroom before the inevitable moment. Thoughtfully she closed the door on Philemon's agony, lingered in the hall for a few moments to straighten the sweater Philemon had stretched, then went back into her daddy's study, resumed her seat, and crossed her thin legs. Brother Hazelman had turned on the overhead light and was brushing lint off his cape with a small clothes brush. Outside, rain beat at the windows and Rose shuddered from the cold.

"Where did you find that dumbbell?" she asked.

Brother Hazelman completed his brushing before he replied. "He came into the church one Sunday dying to testify, and he did all right. Stirred up the congregation. They took to Philemon, so I let him stay. But it was like feeding a stray dog one time."

"I'll get rid of him if you can't do it."

"No need. I think I made it plain if he wants to preach with us and enjoy the fruits of our family he'll have to pay his way."

Rose smiled scornfully. "You're wasting your time with these stupid blueprints. He'll never come up with a dime."

Brother Hazelman smiled back. "Little Rose, I wouldn't be too sure about that."

Rose held up the picture which Hazelman had used to mesmerize Philemon. "That place is as ugly as a jailhouse," she said irritably. "You could have picked a prettier-looking church to tempt him with." She threw the picture down and put a hand over her eyes, slumping in the chair. "Three years and four months," she said, her mouth set in a line of terrible grief. "Daddy, I feel like old squirrel meat; that's not a word of a lie."

"I hope you managed to be of some comfort to the poor souls you were in there with," he said.

Rose wept bitter tears. Her daddy came to hold her head.

"Rose, Rose, did you have to try a bank?"

"Daddy, I swear-r to you I didn't know what Jimmy was thinking about that day! I just sat there in the car reading my magazine and the next thing I knew there were cops standing all around pointing shotguns at my head."

"I never did like that Jimmy, Rose."

"Oh, Daddy, I have had the can tied to my tail! I hope Jimmy's rotting where *he* is, that's all I hope!"

"There, there, Little Rose."

She snuffled into a handkerchief and dried her mouse-gray eyes. When she was feeling all right again, she stood. "I'm going back to town and get some bright lights in my eyes if it *is* Sunday night."

"Fine, fine, you do that. Also do me a favor and take you-know-who along. I think he's picked up a touch of the flu and I don't want to be all night mopping the floor after him."

Rose whistled unhappily. "He gets out at the first bus stop."

"And, Little Rose—sweetheart. Work on him just a bit. Make him feel, you know, wanted. All he really craves in life is respect and a soft shoulder to prop his head on. He's not such a smart boy to look at him, but I know he'll come through. I've felt in my prayers that if we're halfway decent to Philemon we'll reap a rich harvest." He added, with a faint whine, "Rose, the family hasn't been doing too good lately."

"You're telling me," Rose said, and went out into the hall to collect the bedraggled Philemon as he emerged from the bathroom.

30

Molly's Big Night

The couch in Molly's living room was not large enough for a man of King's dimensions to stretch out, and the wry position he had assumed, flat on his back, precluded any sort of restful sleep. So, following a stupefyingly heavy meal, he dozed, and was plagued. When the telephone rang somewhere in the apartment it was no more than a tickling, a gadfly; he was far away in the bedroom of his father's house, listening to another bell, as persistent as a gossipy woman.

His dreams were remote but vividly colored and heavily populated, reflections in water, glass, and hot automobile metal on a summer's day: he dreamed of childhood friends. What child does not enjoy a certain amount of threat, mystery, and terror in his life? Dark cellars, thick woods, marshes, odd-looking recluses—all these had preoccupied his friends at one time or another, but he was indifferent to vicarious terrors. Perhaps he might have been indifferent even if his home life was ordinary, his parents like anyone else's. Fortunately he had not been a timid and conventionally fearful child, else he might easily have been driven insane during the twelve difficult years he lived with his mother.

His dreams were of bells, and of the morbidity and fascinating cruelty of children. Large as he was, they sometimes had made casual fun of him, in the way that they made fun of Estes Pratt, whose father was a tombstone cutter and displayed his handiwork on the front lawn of their house. Who's buried in your yard, Estes? they said. Is your mother crazy, King? Not crazy. Who rings all those bells then? Nobody rings them, he said. Ghosts ring them. That's a lie, they said. Ghosts can't ring bells.

He'd flattened a nose or two in retaliation, but how could he explain, or defend, what he heard? How could he describe waking from a healthy sleep to hear one of the bells and feel his bladder letting go at the same time; how could he describe the shame and fear and disgust of lying motionless in his soaked bed, not daring to lift his head and look around his room, made strange by the light of the moon and the shadows of the catalpa tree on one wall.

Nothing and nobody rang the bells.

But one was ringing just the same—this time it was the dinner bell in the kitchen, which made a dunning, red-faced, manly sound—and tears wormed slowly down his cheeks as he listened to his father shouting. His father always shouted, Come back to this bed, and he always damned her, but he always stayed behind when she went below. Was he afraid, didn't he trust God to protect him from evil? . . .

King lurched up from Molly's sofa, a stabbing pain in his back. He breathed raspingly through his mouth. His eyes peeped open. The living room was darkened, except for a veil of light in one corner. Rain rattled the windows, then subsided. He turned his head carefully. Molly stared back at him from the chair in which she was sitting.

"Are you all right?" she asked. "What's the matter?"

"The bells," he gasped.

"Bells? Oh, you heard the telephone." He lifted his head inquiringly. "It wasn't Cy, though."

"I heard . . . shouting."

"My neighbors in the flat downstairs. Their Sunday-night wingding. But I think they made up and went out."

He studied Molly for several uneasy seconds before realizing she wasn't dressed. Her feet were tucked under her in the chair and she wore a pink peignoir. She was decently covered but still, he thought, she wasn't dressed, and this dismayed him, like the discovery of a spider in his shoe. There was a drink in Molly's hand. She looked relaxed; as he stared, her head nodded loosely, but then she straightened up.

"I've been watching you sleep."

"What time is it?"

"Who knows? You sleep as if—if you're in chains. It's a theatrical experience just watching you sleep. My captive wild man." She scooted off the cushiony chair and came sedately toward him in a sighing of material. King leaned back as she sat beside him. "Why are you crying?" Molly asked, and with the edge of her palm scooped tears from his cheeks. He hadn't been aware of them.

King grimaced. "I was crying in my dream. I dreamed I was twelve years old, or younger." he tried nicely to duck her hand but she kept stroking his cheeks and finally he just hung his head and submitted. It wasn't such a bad feeling.

"Molly—"

"Why did you dream about bells?"

"I don't know; but I have dreamed about them plenty often and I suppose it's one reason I'd rather sit up all night than—" His tongue was painfully dry, but the odor of Molly's whiskey and soda set it in motion again. "Back there in South Carolina my house was filled with bells, each with its own sound; got so as I grew older and learned more about what was going on around me, I could tell, when the bells rang at night, where the sound was coming from. There was a big brass bell in the kitchen, Swiss bells in the parlor, and those tiny decorative bells of copper, iron, or silver on shelves and whatnots everywhere on the first floor. Each of the—the spirits my mother claimed to recognize had his own bell."

Molly nodded thoughtfully. "You told me she was a medium. I've never forgotten that." She sipped her drink, her free hand resting on his shoulder.

"Molly . . . do you suppose I—I could have one of those?"

"I thought you didn't drink."

"I don't," King said, clenching his hands. "But one time won't do harm and I've always heard whiskey's a great comfort when you're feeling unsettled."

Molly promptly got up and went into the kitchen to fix his drink. He looked after her until she reached the kitchen doorway, where the light showed him the shape of her legs all the way to her waist; then he twisted his head sharply and stared at the dark windows astream with rain, and a solitary street light below.

When she returned he accepted the offered drink blindly and took a satisfying slug, which neither fazed nor appealed to him. Thereafter he drank doggedly with Molly by his side and he told her, in fits and starts but quite willingly, about his mother, while a sense of peace settled in his breast. Molly was good company and Molly for once was a listener; her hovering face and discreet touch slowly became as necessary to him as the drafts of bourbon from his tall glass.

As a rule, he told Molly, many weeks would go by and the bells would be silent, except when disturbed at dusting. During those blissful weeks he came in from play or school to find the house smelling of fresh flowers and spring air, or of winter logs blazing in the fireplace. His mother would be here and there in the gleaming rooms, moving effortlessly as if her bones were as slender and light as a bird's. She had a dozen projects to keep her busy: she tended an herb garden or made feather hats which sold for good prices in a local store, or rendered pen-and-ink sketches for Christmas cards. She was always companionable and witty when she felt well, and King could count on a slice of fresh-baked orange or German chocolate cake. He would look up from his plate to the tiny chatting woman busy at the sink and wonderingly think, Mother, and then, as he thawed over a period of days, he would feel at ease with her once more. He would allow his mother to be kind to him, and if the weeks stretched on without incident, he would laboriously resume the responsibility of love for her. But all the good weeks went like a shot, he said, and the bad ones lasted an age.

She would lose first her wit, then her tongue, and then her will to keep busy, and grayness crept into her face like a pinching frost. The house also became gray and cheerless and soon King's personal untidiness spread from his room to every corner; the black iron cookstove gathered the grease of his father's shift-for-yourself breakfasts and was cold the rest of the time. His mother's behavior during the three or four sad weeks varied little. She clung to her bed, complaining of various pains but rejecting doctors. When she felt like sitting up she spent days walled in her own books, a trunkload of occult rarities, reading until her eyes were as black as doom.

Next came spells of forgetfulness, and of wanderings. During her long absences from the house she did not remember where she had been or what she had seen. Neighbors sometimes passed her and reported that she talked to herself in two distinctly different voices. For by the time she began to wander, she had given herself over to the spirit world, and they could expect the bells to begin in the house during the early hours of the morning. They rang churlishly, urgently, imperiously, sometimes half a dozen times a night.

After the cycle of the bells, lasting only a few days, his mother's eyes lost their look of melancholy horror, her cheeks bloomed, she smiled and combed her hair and with great energy she set about putting the house in fine order once more. Never during the good weeks did she mention the bells or their purpose, and she never spoke of what she had seen or heard when summoned from her bed.

"Your poor mother," Molly remarked when he was done. "What a terrible life she must have had."

"Yes, and I know that now—I know it so well! But I didn't know then, I didn't feel a proper sympathy for her." King wrung his hands and Molly crept protectively closer to him. "I—Molly—God forgive me—I defiled my mother on her deathbed!"

"Hush," Molly said, taking his overheated face between her hands. King was half-lying on the sofa, his feet braced against the floor, his head sunk in one of the primrose pillows. He stared up at her distractedly. "Yes I did! Don't you want to hear? She was dying in bed of an infection and I wasn't even allowed to go upstairs. But I went anyhow, through the window, with a sack of manure I'd stolen from a barnyard. I smeared that manure all over her walls while she lay there delirious with pain, and then snuck off like a thief. That's how much I thought of my mother then! And I've been so ashamed—"

"It's all right," Molly insisted. "I know your mother would forgive you. You couldn't help yourself at that age. Sweet, don't be upset." She stilled his tentative threshings with the weight of her own body, and his hands became enmeshed in the cloudlike chiffon. Slowly they sank to the firm muscle of a straining thigh, the lift of a ribcage beneath her throbbing heart.

"Lord above," King said tonelessly.

Tenderly Molly offered her gleaming breasts to his lips, and he kissed them through the film of the gown. Then he shifted his eyes nervously about the room. Then he kissed her face and held her body fervently while Molly nearly swooned with joy. But it was all too awkward for comfort and so she backed off his lap, pulling intensely at his hand. His face had a dismal pallor but he came.

In the dining room Molly paused to shed the peignoir and King's eyes followed the drift of the material to the floor. Molly returned to him and rubbed like a cat against his side. He was wooden, but he clutched at her. She danced backward, pulling him on.

But at the bedroom King stopped abruptly.

She looked back, baffled. "What's srong?"

"Molly, that's the doorway to hell!"

"Come, now!"

"No, I . . . can't go in there with you! My wife—"

Molly felt as if she were standing up to her armpits in a snowbank. "Your wife?" she almost screamed. "*What* wife?"

"I had a wife—her memory—she's under the ground now— I've never laid a single flower on her precious grave! And I—I can't go in that bed with you, Molly."

"But you want to!"

He shook his head earnestly. "Molly, I don't know about that."

"I love you!"

"Don't say that," King pleaded, and backed up a step. "Let me fetch your—your wraparound thing for you."

She tore at her shortie nightgown and flung it off her head, which left her stark naked with hair standing on end. "Come here. Come here quick before—what are you doing to me, sweet?"

Afraid that she was going to make a lunge for him, King held up both hands placatingly. "All right! Molly, will you p-please not come over here? Just go, get into bed."

"Are you coming too?" she asked, cunning and afraid.

"Yes."

"You mean that?" Molly burst into tears. "I'm crazy about you! All I want is your love! Don't I deserve *that* much in this lousy world?"

"Molly, where's the bathroom?"

She blinked her eyes and sniffed wetly. "Bath—? Ohhh, sure. It's d-down the hall. First of the three doors."

He remembered now; what he didn't remember was which of the other two doors would let him out of the flat. He began edging toward the hall.

"Molly, you promised you'd get into bed."

"I'll wait here for you. Oh God oh God."

"Cover up," he said over his shoulder.

"Yes, yes, I'm waiting for you!"

Stepping into the hall, King ignored the first door, a vague white rectangle in the dark, and, after a few moments' scalding indecision, he seized the knob of the middle door and yanked. Behind him Molly wailed at a premonition of treachery. King hastily shut the door behind him.

He did not find a flight of stairs leading to the street; instead he found that he had trapped himself in a narrow closet. Molly slammed furiously against the door. Grimly he held the knob fast to keep her from turning it, groped, discovered a key and locked the door.

"Come out!" Molly cried. "Why are you trying to run away?"

King tasted bile from his stomach and sank to the floor, his back braced against the door. She hammered with her fists, and he could feel the blows through the thin panels.

"Leave me alone!" he said, groaning. "Molly, I won't defile you!"

"Come out, come out, come out!"

"Please be reasonable, Molly."

"Oh God oh God."

"Molly, I respect you—if you give me your word you won't
—if you'll go put your clothes on—I don't mean that thing
you've been wearing—"

"I love you!"

He held his head and groaned again.

Molly, crouching outside with her ear pressed to the door,
shivered, then in a fit of anger and frustration again beat her
already bruised palm against the wood. She paused for breath
and listened. His silence drove her to a frenzy. She tipped back
her head and howled:

"*Are you coming out of there!*"

Continued silence mortified and frightened her, but,
perversely, increased her sexual desire nearly beyond endurance. She raked at a naked thigh, scratching herself.

"You bastard!"

There was no response.

"Come . . . outtttttt . . . of there!"

Molly scrambled to her feet, whirled, ran into the kitchen,
and returned with a long icepick. Kneeling, she put her eye to
the keyhole, which yielded no light from the small window at
the end of the tapering closet. With her tongue between her
teeth she pried into the keyhole with the icepick and forced out
the skeleton key. Dizzily she pressed her flushed face against
the door and waited for strength to return. As soon as she was
able, she began fishing beneath the door with the icepick for
the fallen key. Several times she almost had it. Then, search as
she would, Molly could no longer feel the key with the point of
the pick.

"Did you take it?" she hissed. "Better give it to me! If you
don't . . . I'm going to break the door! I'll break it down with a
hammer! Give me that *key!*"

She drew back from the door, eyes big with hatred and
longing.

The key skidded through the crack and bounced off the
baseboard across the hall. Eagerly Molly went for it, and when
she had it in her hands tears of relief flowed down her cheeks.

"Don't you worry," she sobbed. "I'm going to get you out.
Then I want you to come to bed, because it's late. Don't worry!
I'm happy just to have your arms around me. That's all I need."
She jabbed the key into the lock and wrestled with it. The door

sprang open at last. Molly staggered into the closet. The light was on. She peered around unbelievingly.

"King?"

Cold air poured over her body. She rushed to the open window where rain was dripping on the sill. The window was barely wide enough for her to lean out. Below was a concrete driveway, a drop of more than twenty feet from the high window. She pulled in her head and searched the closet suspiciously. But he could not have hidden from her. He had gone through the window, risking broken bones in his anxiety to escape.

Again Molly looked out. The house next door was dark; the street, as much as she could see, was deserted. She fell away from the window, dripping wet from head to toe.

"All I really wanted," Molly began in an anguished voice, "was . . ." She became utterly, powerfully still for a few moments, her head lifted in contemplation. Then the icepick flashed upward and poised over her heart.

The telephone rang.

At the fifth ring Molly awakened and began to breathe again. The matter of the icepick seemed as inconsequential as life itself, as an open window with rain dripping in. She put the icepick aside, closed the window, walked out of the closet, and stopped in the dining room to answer the phone.

"Molly, this is Cy."

"Oh," said Molly. "Cy." She thought for several seconds. "Cy, Manson says he's going to get an injunction to stop the Gospel Train until he can test our incorporation in court."

"Yes, I know about that. I didn't bring it up because I didn't want to worry you."

"Well, what can you do about it, Cy?"

He laughed. "We'll get the injunction set aside, of course. Molly, that might take some time."

"How much time?"

"I wouldn't want to go out on a limb at this point."

"He's going to beat us, isn't he?"

"Molly, I wouldn't say—"

"Thanks for calling, Cy," Molly murmured, and cradled the receiver. She went into the bathroom, toweled until she was dry, painted with iodine the scratches she had inflicted on herself, combed her hair, pulled on a fresh nightie, and in the blackness of her bedroom tucked herself beneath the cold covers.

"All I really wanted," she said to the ceiling, "was to hold you in my arms for a little while. I don't know what happened. I didn't mean to be cheap and stupid. I never have meant to be anything like that. Please believe me."

Then she cried until her heart felt as dark and empty as a sealed cave beneath the earth.

31

Legacy

Jeremy heard a bumping in the night and at first thought it was Eli up and about, looking, half-frozen, for the bathroom. She lifted her head into the cold air of the little house but saw nothing clearly except the steady flame of the gas heater, which threw a glazed pallor over the piled bed where Eli had been spending the greater part of his days and nights. She listened expertly for his breathing and heard it, separate from the hiss of the gas flame.

She settled down with a shudder into her warm bedding, then picked up the unusual sound again, the bumping, like somebody or something on the porch. Philemon, or Philemon's dog—but Philemon didn't come in, and the dog always made its rounds silently. Jeremy began to worry. Then, because of her practical nature, she got up almost immediately and went to the nearest window to resolve her worry, carrying along the iron fry pan which she always kept close at hand during the night.

The day's rain had moved on, leaving the sky clear and with a three-quarter moon to light the clay yard and the broad space of the porch. Someone was sitting on the porch steps in an attitude of thorough dejection or drunkenness and Jeremy got quite a fright when she realized it wasn't Philemon. Then she recognized the preacher, instinctively raised a hand to tap on the glass, reconsidered and went outside as noiselessly as possible, protected by her ankle-length flannel robe. The night was piercing but windless and not too damp.

King looked up as she opened the door. "Oh, Jeremy," he said, as blandly as if they had met at a bus stop.

"What are you doing here?"

He grinned foolishly at her. "Nowhere else to take myself, reckon."

"Come inside the house then."

"No," he said, still grinning. "I don't want to disturb old Eli."

This reply, and his odd grin, rubbed Jeremy the wrong way and she said in an annoyed tone, "You just want to sit out here in the cold air in the middle of the night and not disturb anybody." She looked for Philemon's dog in his accustomed place but of course he was off prowling or else there would have been a terrible row when King showed up. She stuck by the door, wondering what came next.

King stopped grinning but his chin sunk down on his chest.

"What's wrong?" Jeremy demanded, suddenly alarmed. "What's happened to you?"

His silence was long and then he said brokenly, "Oh, Jeremy—this is a poor place, a poor time! I don't have a groat's worth of sense tonight. I'll come back later when . . ." He grasped a porch rail and hauled himself to his feet, but before he could step down to the watery clay yard, Jeremy seized him from behind by the elastic band of his windbreaker.

"You can't go anywhere until you talk to me!" She was dimly amazed by her strength and her sense of crisis; she imagined that the world was about to fall off its axis, just as Eli always had said it would do. For a week she'd been in a state of nerves over the departure of the Gospel Train; she hadn't really expected to see the preacher again, or expected the decency of a sincere good-bye, God bless you. So she held him determinedly until he turned to look at her, an expression of guilt and woe on his face.

With a shrug he accepted her determination to keep him there and simply sat down again, hugging his knees like a boardwalk philosopher in a country town. He began talking, in a low-voiced rambling way, of the journeys behind, and the journeys ahead, an apprehension of tigers and pitfalls behind every word; Jeremy, beside him, listened inattentively. She was

338

freezing, but his cheerless monologue had provided a spell for both of them and she wouldn't have thought to coax him into the house, where it was reasonably comfortable. Besides, she had a hard notion of what he'd really come to say, and this notion was enough to make a fool of her without her caring the slightest.

He talked of the loyalty and goodness of those who had helped and were helping him; he mentioned Molly Amos half a dozen times and each time Jeremy bit her tongue and nodded stonily, thinking that his praise of the woman was a shade too reverent. Yet he managed to imply, with the greatest difficulty, that he didn't understand the heart or mind of any woman, and this could well be his chief failing in life.

He had paused, and Jeremy realized that he was waiting for confirmation of his shortcomings, or at least a word of encouragement. She thought, Your failure is holding back. She said sharply, "God only knows what's in a woman's heart. He put the circus there, and I'll bet He's still kicking Himself."

King looked uncomprehendingly at her. "Jeremy, I've prayed tonight, until my breath was boiling in my throat. An hour ago I hated this earth, flesh and bone. The muck of these fields dragged at my boots and I was afraid of sinking. . . ." He stared down at his mud-splashed Levis. "But all along I knew what God intended. It's part of God's plan that I—for the life of me I don't understand—but I do feel that God has always intended me to have a wife." He clenched his fists on his knees, and his face was grave. "Sometimes I hate the earth—and the way of my own blood. But the earth has a cleanness I'm craving, that only a wife can give. The earth gives up pure blossoms and a wife, a child."

Jeremy, looking at his carved face in the light of the three-quarter moon, felt close to tears and a black disappointment. "Why don't you just say you love?" she complained, then rose and walked to the other end of the porch.

"Jeremy," he asked, after a long while, "how can I see you there?"

She shivered. "When will it be? Will I go on the Train?"

"It's such a poor place for a woman."

"But will I go? Don't you want me to go?"

He got up with his back to a post and hung there for a few moments, sadly. "Sure you'll go."

339

"You have to want me," Jeremy warned, her teeth locked. "I *won't* be poor that way."

She heard him coming the length of the porch and was dazed by the force of his hand on her shoulder.

"And will we have a house someday?" she said desperately.

"Jeremy, I promise you a fine big house."

"Because I've wanted that, you see. A house with four or five rooms. And a big separate kitchen. With a walk-in pantry. And jars! Just thousands of jars to put things in. Dried beans and rice and . . . birds' eggs and seashells if I feel like it." She shook her head slowly. "I know I never will get enough jars to put things in." She wept brokenly and turned against his breast.

The front door scraped loudly and Jeremy, frightened, looked out from King's arms. She'd had a few moments' peace, and now here was Eli to contend with.

"Get your things and get out of my house," the old prophet said venomously.

"Let me talk to him," Jeremy whispered, and King let her go. She walked down the porch. "Eli, King and me are going to come inside for a little while. We——"

He was blue and shaking, holding to the edge of the door to stay upright. "My enemy," he said, "come to kill me in my bed!"

"Oh, Eli . . ."

"Where's Philemon? Where's his dog? God in Heaven, Philemon!"

"Eli, you'll hurt yourself screaming like that."

Jeremy tried to put her arms around him, to hold him up; he spat in her face. She fell back, shocked to silence.

The porch trembled as if buffalo were stampeding on it. "There's no need for you to do that to Jeremy!" King shouted.

Jeremy came to her senses just in time to head him off. With all her strength she shoved King to the steps. He glared in anger over her shoulder, but did not resist.

"Oh, no," she groaned, "go away, just tonight, go away! I'll talk to him."

"You're not going to live around this old fool another——"

Eli, muttering with rage, fell down inside the door. "God protect me; O Lord, I weep! Where's the gun? My enemy would slay me in my sleep, Lord! Please put that shotgun in my hands."

340

"He's gone crazy," King observed, prying himself out of Jeremy's grasp.

Inside Eli arose like Lazarus, wailing, and they had a glimpse of his gray-white head and frantic hands. Then there was a thump and a clatter as he fell again.

"Smack over the gas heater," Jeremy said glumly. "Let's don't just let him lie there and burn up."

She switched on the light inside the door. Eli was sitting on the floor in a sag of long johns, his eyes wet with tears. He had knocked the cover off the heater but there was no serious damage.

"Call my lawyer," he said almost incoherently. "I want to talk to him!"

Jeremy held King at the door with a look and kneeled beside Eli. This time she allowed her to touch him. His mouth opened and shut but he couldn't speak; the tears flowed faster. He tried to find a hold on Jeremy but his hands were useless. King, watching, realized that Eli was deeply humiliated by his condition. He saw himself through Eli's eyes: double-dealer, thief, lecher, sneaking around in the middle of the night to steal Jeremy away. He felt an acute gnawing pain in his middle and lowered his eyes. He thought of the Indian-summer afternoon when he had first climbed the porch steps with a feeling of excitement and anticipation. He had considered himself superior to Eli, and all that was Eli's; now he was surely paying for his smugness!

Without causing strain to either of them, Jeremy assisted Eli to his bed and eased him into it. Her eyes were remote but there was a faint smile on her lips and she talked to him pleasantly. She fetched a cold cloth for his eyes and arranged the bedding so that there wouldn't be undue pressure on any of Eli's arthritic joints. When he was bathed and cooled and somewhat calmed, she held his head while he swallowed a dose of aspirin. King worshiped her at that moment; he would have gone down on his knees to tell her so. But when she came toward him, preoccupied, severe, all he could do was scowl.

"Suppose he's hurt?"

"Sick as he is, who could tell? . . . No, I don't think he's hurt. Just all used up. It's going to be a hard night." She searched his face and looked bleak. Her bad eye was a fright. "If my heart doesn't stop beating like this I'm going to go crazy! Say something to me."

341

"Jeremy, I need you."

She slammed against him, her chin hurting his stomach. "Tomorrow you won't. But that's all right. I heard you say it. I'll never forget."

"Jeremy, with all my heart, I—"

"Go away now, I can't have you around! Eli's half under and I don't want him getting excited again." She straightened and pushed him toward the porch. King saw how distraught she was and cut off a protest.

"I'll come back in the morning."

"Yes, yes," Jeremy said, half fearfully.

"Thursday you'll be on the Train with me, with us, It'll work out, Jeremy." He raised his voice. "Jeremy, in my heart—"

She closed her eyes tightly, gave her head a desperate shake, and shut the door on King, barely missing an outstretched hand. "Good-bye, good-bye," she whispered, laying her cheek against the glass in the door. When she looked out through the haze her breath had made on the pane, she saw him for an instant poised in a cat's-eye circle of moonlight on the edge of wet shimmering clay, his head turned toward the house. Then he vanished, leaving footprints.

Jeremy squeezed out breath with a hand against her breast, feeling enchanted, feeling dumb. Absently she pulled the hood over the gas heater and went back to her pallet, there sat crosslegged staring about the house until her eyes burned. Eli lay motionless but she felt he was awake, she felt his silent opprobrium. But Eli, she wanted to say, what can I do? Misery shook her like a leaf. She was down to a minimum of self-esteem, a scattering of wit. But I love him, Eli. The worst he has to offer is more than I ever dreamed. Eli's unspoken malevolence stung her between the eyes. Jeremy burrowed into the covers in hope of respite. She found running room in a sunny dream pasture. But there a maniacal dog devoured a helpless lamb, and a dwindled Eli was drowning in a deep well while she leaned toward the water with a tiny bailing cup.

She awoke to find the lights out; her mouth was dry and her head was afloat. In the darkness she heard ragged breathing, a terse cough. She stood and in the light of the gas heater saw Philemon huddled on the couch. Jeremy was thoroughly disoriented, and she felt a sudden pinching fear.

"Philemon?" she whispered.

He coughed. "What?"

Jeremy moved closer. "I thought you were staying the night with those Hazelmans."

He turned over on the couch so that his back was to her. "I changed my mind," he said hoarsely.

"Don't you feel good?" When he didn't reply, she put a hand on his forehead. "That makes two of you," she said resignedly. "Well, keep warm."

"Let me alone!" he sobbed.

Puzzled, Jeremy backed off, then turned her attention to Eli. For several moments she listened for his breathing. He was still lying face up with one hand free of the covers. She could make out the line of his nose and, as she continued to stare at his face, a slick of drugged eye became visible. Jeremy approached the bed.

"Eli?"

She hesitated, waiting for the thread of his breath. But frequently she had not been able to hear it at all until she dropped to her knees and held her ear to his opened mouth.

"Philemon!"

Philemon jumped as if bitten. "Don't you have any sense, yelling like that?"

"He's dead!"

He rolled off the couch and came up behind her. Jeremy was moaning with fear. Philemon stared over her shoulder. Irritably he snapped, "Eli's all right, he just sleeps that way."

Jeremy grasped Eli's hand and then his shoulders. She put her ear again to his mouth. Then she snatched at the electric blanket and listened for his heartbeat. She began to shake him urgently.

"Wake up! Eli, quit! Wake up and breathe right, Eli, *you hear me?*"

Philemon's scalp prickled, and he forgot about the flu burning in his chest. "Let me." He prodded the stiffened old man.

Jeremy jumped to her feet. "King'll help us. He was outside just a minute ago. If I hurry I can catch him!"

Philemon continued to wrestle with the inert Eli.

"You stay here with Eli! Talk to him, he'll hear you!" Her voice broke hysterically. "I've got to run after King!"

"There's nobody—" Philemon began, but Jeremy was at the door. He let Eli fall back and stood in confusion, clutching his aching head. "Jeremy—" he said, and started after her. A wave

343

of nausea sloshed through him. He looked back at the bed and was genuinely frightened for the first time. Turning on all the lights in the house helped calm him; but Eli was still motionless, no life evident in that sliver of eye.

"Eli," Philemon said, shuddering. "Eli, get up, please." His spoken words mocked him. His throat wouldn't let him swallow. He stumbled nearer the bed. "I don't feel good," he complained in a whisper. In the next instant he became utterly convinced that the old man had died.

Philemon collapsed in a sobbing heap, but fever had sapped him too thoroughly for a lengthy bout of grief. Lifting his head, he contemplated the figure of Eli, and his own fate. He longed for a telephone to call Brother Hazelman, and glowed with the imagined comfort this man would bring in a tragic hour. Then he became uneasy, remembering much of the disaster his day had been, realizing the extent of his dilemma.

"Eli, where can I get five thousand dollars now?" he cried bitterly.

Somehow he had managed to delude himself that Eli would open his purse and give him a part of the money which he so badly needed for Brother Hazelman's sake. But now that Eli was dead, he realized how stupid he'd been to think that his uncle would spend a dime on him if he could help it. After a few moments of apathy, rage bubbled in him, and he stared in frustration at Eli's seamed face.

That was when he thought of the canvas wallet which Eli kept beneath the thin mattresses of his bed. The last time Philemon had seen the wallet, opened, it had contained several thick packages of old bills. Ten days, no, two weeks ago. Philemon's head hurt him so that he could scarcely think. At the end of every month Eli bought a money order with the bulk of those dollars and sent it off to the Crenshaw Colony in Montana. Somehow Philemon couldn't recall if Eli had made the usual money-order purchase at the end of November. It occurred to him that Eli had been too sick to spend even an hour away from his bed. And as usual he hadn't trusted Philemon to get the money order.

Cautiously Philemon reached between the mattresses and withdrew the dull brown wallet. His hands trembled at the impression of money inside. He closed his eyes for a few seconds to steady himself, then unzipped the wallet. He withdrew a handful of bills, wincing at the stench of old

344

money, enough to make him sick to his stomach all over again. He held the wallet carefully away from his nose, and again dipped eagerly inside.

A dry hand seized Philemon's wrist and he almost leaped out of his skin. He looked up, straight into Eli's vengeful eyes. Philemon froze in horror, and the bills slipped from his hand. He tried to speak, to explain, but all he could think of was that Eli had come back from the dead to punish his thievery.

"What are you doing with my money?" Eli whispered.

Philemon rose screaming, pulling his hand away.

Eli sought to rise, sighing with pain. "Hyena!" he said scornfully. "Eating at my entrails! God strike you dead!"

"I'm putting it all back!" Philemon dropped to his knees, snatching at the bills, tearing some. Eli aimed a blow at his skull but Philemon ducked it by falling back. Then he lunged, still on his knees, for the bed, and pushed Eli down. He held his uncle against the bed and stared into his webbed eyes. Despite his handicaps old Eli struggled. Philemon began to use all his strength. He set his teeth and his eyes bulged. A look of fear crossed Eli's face; he squalled.

"Don't get me mad, Eli," Philemon warned curtly.

"Help!"

This cry of terror sent Philemon into a rage. He made a fist and pounded on his uncle's chest. "Said stop it!" With his free hand he pulled the electric blanket over Eli's head. Grasping the blanket on either side, he pinned Eli's head to the pillow. Eli threshed and fouled himself; Philemon held the blanket more tightly. Eli's shrieks, muffled as they were, ate into his heart, but his hands continued to do their work, until sweat rolled down his cheeks from the blanket's heat. At last he sat up, his back aching. His hands were poised above the lump in the blanket: if Eli had arisen from the dead before, he could again. Philemon was excessively hot and his white hands trembled, but he wasn't sick anymore; all the sickness had burned out of his breast. He felt resigned and melancholy; if Eli kept popping up, well, then he would just have to keep putting him down, and that might go on forever.

But, hopefully, he felt no sense of threat. Curiously he stroked the body beneath the hot blanket and concluded that Eli was gone for good.

Having accepted this, Philemon got up and went to the kitchen, where he drank water from the tap. It was a long way back to the bed for him because his body seemed all out of whack, ready to fly into convulsions if he didn't take genuine care with each step, each breath of air. He sat on the edge of the bed, one eye on Eli, one eye on the spilled money. After a while he began to gather the money, which he stowed to the last dollar in the canvas wallet.

"I'm putting it all back," he said aloud, and was startled, as if someone else had spoken behind him. He replaced the wallet between the mattresses. Then he unplugged the electric blanket because it was uncomfortably hot to sit on, and waited with folded arms for Jeremy, or anybody else, to come.

PART TWO

THE TRAIN

32

Wedding Announcement

The golden helicopter flashed down from a blue-white sky, at first without a sound; then the wind turned around and Molly, along with the others gathered at the railroad siding, heard the 'copter. Molly looked up, flinching, despite her sunglasses, at the brilliance of the winter day.

"That would be the Governor," she said, and her heart pounded with delight. She glanced up and down the street that ran parallel to the railroad siding, then plucked at the antique watch pinned to her wool suit. "I'm too nervous to open this; what time is it getting to be, Charley?"

"Five after twelve." The photographer shifted his heavy camera pack around on his hip and stared at the helicopter. "I wonder if the Governor's flying it himself today? Last time he took the controls he almost beheaded a group of nuns at an orphans' picnic."

Molly giggled at this absurdity. After four days and nights of work she was occasionally chuckleheaded, dead for sleep, sore in unlikely recesses of the body. Her headlong labors had been interrupted only by a quick visit, for King's sake, to the funeral service for the man who'd made it all possible by his timely departure to a better life and a suitable reward. Molly had even shed a charitable tear, despite herself, forgetting the agony which old Eli had indirectly caused her.

But the unpleasantness was done with at last, and they were, hopefully, free to go. Again she scanned the street, tense and frowning, then looked out over the heads of the crowd assembled for the dedication, on the chance that King might have come by a roundabout way.

" '. . . I'm going to take a trip on that great Gos-pell train . . .' "

At one end of the platform Cowboy Jim Cobb's hillbilly musicians had for the past half hour been earnestly entertaining them all with their sacred songs and recitations—but without Cowboy himself, whose absence was as inexplicable as King's. She caught the Reverend Mr. Handwerker's eye; knowing her mind, he smiled and shrugged. Mab Shaw and her husband were sitting nearby, drinking hot coffee, and Molly was tempted to ask Mab. But that was foolish, she wasn't thinking. If she started asking everybody where King might be, her question not only would make her look bad, less than a model of efficiency, it might serve to disturb the fine mood of the dedication.

So Molly busied herself by checking over the deployment of the press and television crews. Thanks to the Governor's announced presence, all the TV stations in town were giving the Gospel Train the sort of coverage they usually reserved for major calamities. Molly had been burning up the wires to New York and had talked her old boss at the network into using a minute and a half of film on the six-thirty nationwide news. It would be priceless publicity—and she reminded herself to double-check with New York once the Train was rolling. The cameramen had already filmed the inside of the Train and now, as the helicopter maneuvered in the wind for a landing, they settled down to work once more.

Shivering in the forty-five-degree weather, Molly moved down the platform to keep Cowboy's grandmother company for a few moments.

"I can't thank you enough, Mrs. Cobb, for your help in getting the Governor here," she said graciously to their patron.

"Not at all; Foots loves this sort of activity. All I did was mention it to him." Mrs. Cobb was dressed to the ears in a bulky lamb coat, and she kept her legs warm with a stadium blanket. Molly envied the woman her serenity and her splendor of years; probably, she thought, by the time she reached Mrs. Cobb's age she would be ground down to a ratty bone. Molly hugged herself and decided to ask:

"I wonder where Jim could be?"

"He was out of the house at the crack of dawn." She tilted her head. "Oh, Molly, I forgot to tell you, Foots has someone with him. . . ."

"The more the merrier," Molly said absently. The nearness of the helicopter made conversation difficult. The 'copter hovered, dipped, turned, then landed in a cinder space between railroad tracks. Mr. Handwerker was close by, his clothes whipping fiercely. Two yellow buses had also arrived with a church choir, and the confusion severely strained Molly's patience. Wrathfully she considered King's lateness.

The door of the six-passenger helicopter opened and out stepped Governor Ewell "Foots" Henderson, six feet seven to the crown of his eggshell-white Stetson. Following close behind was another tall, broad-shouldered gentleman, who wore no hat or topcoat despite the cold.

Molly, who was trying discreetly to put her hair in order with an assortment of pins, stopped and gaped at the good honest Scots face, deep-socketed gray eyes, familiar resolute jaw.

"It can't be! Not Harlan Gray!"

"Molly, I frankly forgot—"

In her excitement she seized Mrs. Cobb's thin shoulder. "How did you swing *this?*"

The old lady smiled. "He and Foots have been close friends for years. It just happened that Dr. Gray was visiting at the mansion for a couple of days. . . ."

Molly felt more windblown and giddy than ever. "Harlan Gray. Oh, this *makes* us! He's here—I mean, tonight he'll be seen on the network with King; actually it's an endorsement of King." Short of breath, she swung around to the street. "I can't see so well," she complained, squinting at the glare. "Isn't that Cowboy's Buick coming?" Without waiting for a reply, she dashed off the platform and picked her way over the rails to greet the Governor and his party.

"How do you do. I am Mr. Windom's assistant, Mrs. Amos . . ."

After introductions, they all paused for a look at the glittering Train, like tourists in front of a renowned cathedral.

"Certainly impressive," Harlan Gray said, in that famous voice, and with that famous smile, and Molly had eyes for no one else.

351

"This is such an honor, Dr. Gray! I thought you were in—in—"

"Buenos Aires. We closed out our crusade there just four days ago, Mrs. Amos."

Molly gulped. "I hope your crusade was—"

"We were all encouraged by the wonderful response we received in Dr. Santos' country." Gray nodded to a swarthy man on his left, then his keen eyes returned to the Train. Molly watched his reaction closely. "Wonderful," he murmured; she gloried in his honest praise. "Imaginative! I know the Reverend Mr. Windom is going to do outstanding work for the Lord with his Train." The evangelist turned his melting smile on Molly again. "You know, I wish I'd thought of it. Will we be able to have a look inside?"

"Oh, yes. There'll be a short dedication and a blessing of the Train beforehand, and . . . if you could say a few words . . ."

"I'd be more than happy to, Mrs. Amos."

"Thank you," she said, thoroughly under the spell of this marvelous man. "Then we'll have open house before we leave. Refreshments and a guided tour. This way to the platform, gentlemen, Governor Henderson, Dr. Santos. *So* nice to have you with us. I—" She laughed. "I'm sorry to say I don't know what's keeping our preacher, but I'm sure—"

Molly, not looking where she was walking, stumbled, and Harlan Gray caught her. Embarrassed, laughing again, she turned her head and looked right at King.

Apparently he'd just arrived. He was standing about thirty feet away by the steps to the platform, cheek and jowl with Cowboy and the late Reverend Mr. Charger's niece—Molly found the name elusive—Geraldine. No, more like—

"Excuse me," she panted, and went after the preacher. King met Molly halfway, with a strained smile. "Sorry to be so late." He stared over her shoulder in wonder and awe.

"Oh, it's him, all right!"

"Merciful Lord," King breathed, as the Governor's party caught up to him.

"May I present . . ."

"Dr. Gray, I've always looked forward to this . . ."

"Entirely my pleasure . . ."

The television cameramen were all around, and the potent lights created a webbed glare inside Molly's head.

"Oh, Governor . . ."

"This way, Dr. Gray . . ."

Molly stepped out of the limelight gracefully, feeling choked with triumph. Her eyes wandered over the good-sized crowd. Jeremy! she thought suddenly. That was the girl's name. They had barely spoken at the funeral, but what could one say about an old bastard like Eli? Poor kid with a walleye, but otherwise not bad-looking. She was wearing a very common red cloth coat with a white orchid corsage. Molly wondered idly if King had bought the corsage for her. Extravagant of him. She watched Jeremy climb the platform steps by herself and then look around, lost and uncertain. Molly felt uneasy. Was King taking her along?

After a moment's deliberation she shrugged. Well, what difference? They'd find something for Jeremy to do, and bunk her with the other girls.

Molly decided that Cowboy and Mr. Handwerker could get the dedication rolling without any more assistance from her. She would climb aboard, give the hostesses a last-minute talk, inspect the buffet, then sit down in the recreation car, shoeless, with a handful of aspirin and a 7-Up, and watch the proceedings from there. Hopefully her head would then quit tottering around, an old rum pot without its bottle. Molly sighed, finding the fulfillment of a dream a small sweet moment, like the discovery of new life.

"Molly!"

At the sound of King's voice she almost went back. She was tired, though; she decided that whatever he wanted could wait. But a black shudder teased Molly's shoulders. On Monday, with the leavings of her pride, she had faced him prepared for any blow, but he hadn't mentioned her disgrace. There'd been no hint of censure in his eyes. Of course, the death of Eli had stunned him, it occupied him fully. She'd made the decision to go ahead with the Train on schedule, summoned strong arguments and prevailed. King had taken on the responsibility of the funeral, and left her alone.

Again Molly felt the shudder, rising like a mad grin from some sink of the soul. Yet four days had passed. She could allow herself to think, guardedly, of her disgrace, her ruinous appetite. She could breathe freely of the unscorched, unswarming air. He would forget, he would forgive her—if forgiving was necessary! Because if King was life to her, what was she to him? There was a lodestone of comfort concealed

353

within this mystery, and Molly pressed it lovingly against her heart.

She climbed quickly aboard the Train, throwing a last look back over one shoulder. Thus absorbed, she bumped into Age, who had boarded from the other side.

He went to his knees to keep from spilling the contents of a cardboard box. Molly looked past him at Cowboy's red Buick, which stood below with its trunk open.

"Sorry, didn't see you," she said, noting his pin-stripe suit and polka-dot tie. "Did you drive over with King?"

"Yes," Age said sullenly.

Molly peered at the box. "Dresses? Oh, those belong to Gerald—I mean Jeremy. Let me get my secretary: we'll go down the list and see which one of the kids doesn't have a roommate. If you don't mind waiting a minute or two."

Her eyes still smarted from the sun and the cold. But even if she had been able to focus on Age she might have missed first the look of puzzlement and then the flash of velvet meanness that appeared in his eyes.

"Don't you think I ought to put them in King's apartment?" he said.

"Just wait here," Molly replied with a touch of animosity; then she whirled from the heavy door which she'd been in the act of opening, and her breath wheezed in her throat.

"What do you mean?" Molly said, and the next time she said it she showed her teeth in a horrid way.

Age was silent.

"Filthy nigger, *what are you saying!*"

Her words hit his face like barbs and pulled it apart. He tensed on his knees and for an instant was as animal as she. Then his shoulders eased into a slump. "I'm saying your goose is cooked, lady."

Molly wrenched off her sunglasses and showed him her naked eyes.

Age nodded. "At ten this morning down in Mississippi— where she is just old enough to be married without anybody's permission." His jaw clipped shut, then he said, more softly, "Could be they should have asked *yours.*"

Molly kicked so hard at his face that her shoe flew off but Age rolled lightly aside. She came at him with her flat handbag and, smiling sternly, he jumped off the Train. The box of dresses and

354

personal things tumbled down, striking his shoulder. He looked up at Molly's dead-white face in the vestibule.

"You can tell them both: if I catch her on this Train, I'll *kill* her!"

Age tilted his scarred head to one side, sadly. "It isn't any use."

Over on the other side of the tracks the red-robed choir sang magnificently, and Molly's shriek against the wind was probably unheard by a soul except Age. It was enough to thoroughly chill his satisfaction and temper his ardent dislike of the woman. He waited somewhat apprehensively for whatever was to follow—but Molly turned away, yanked open the dining-car door, and fled toward the rear of the Train, toward the sleepers, and sanctuary. Age had a taste of acid in his mouth. He spat and scowled at the silver behemoth before him and then, because there was nothing else he could do short of desertion, he resumed unloading the Cowboy's car.

Sitting on the platform with King on one side of her and a whole host of celebrities on the other, Jeremy stared at her clenched gloved hands while she listened to snatches of the Governor's speech and wondered, drearily, if she was going to lose her mind.

Not that the wedding had gone badly; it had been a marvel to her, surpassing anything she might have imagined if she'd dared to dwell on it. Had King arranged the wedding himself?—the golden solitude of the country chapel, banked with white flowers, the organist, the unseen vocalist who had, time after time, brought fresh tears to Jeremy's eyes as she stood before the altar. It had been almost more than she could stand, and even during the ceremony she had felt with a stony certainty that she could never be enough of a wife to King to make up for this kindness.

Jeremy bit her lip and forced herself to look up. Cowboy's head was turned toward her, but because of his black glasses she couldn't tell if he was watching her. Jeremy did not, however, like the set of his mouth: she was sure he didn't like her. For an instant she pressed her hands against her ears, which were fiery from cold. She shuddered. She was not prepared for any of this—the crowd, the eyes, the inquiries. Jeremy risked a glance at King; his chin was lifted, his eyes narrowed, he was miles away, unreachable. Am I your wife, your wife? Jeremy thought, panic-stricken. She raced back to the safety of the little chapel, recovered the face of the wispy minister who had sensed her fears, her feelings of wickedness and guilt at marrying so soon after Eli was in the ground, and who had calmed her with a sensible word, a fragile smile, and an assurance of everlasting peace in his eyes.

Where *was* the peace he had assumed she would feel? Oh, Eli! The cry was a cold iron weight in her throat. If I had turned King away, would you be living now?

Blinking mightily to keep back her tears, Jeremy looked the other way along the chairs, past the bowed head of the famous Harlan Gray to the massive white-haired Mab Shaw. Here too was another of King's friends who had been, like as not, taken aback by his sudden marriage—but here Jeremy discovered a fond smile, meant just for her. In confusion she could not smile back; she jerked her head around and looked out into the crowd.

There she discovered a familiar face, Philemon's, and she could not have been more shocked if she'd seen Eli hale and hearty. She stared at Philemon, who was bundled up in a floppy old Army coat, and at last his eyes met hers. He looked every particle as wretched as she felt, and her heart opened to him. He shuffled his feet and planted his hands in his pockets and thereafter gazed at the ground until the closing hymn had been sung by the blue-lipped choir.

Mr. Handwerker urged everyone present to make for the Train and help themselves to hot drinks and sandwiches; there was a great stirring on the platform and Jeremy found herself alone. Tentatively she waited for a sign from King, but he was surrounded. She felt the sting of his absence again. He'd scarcely said a dozen words to her since the wedding kiss. Of course she knew that he had a head full of problems; this was an important day for him. Jeremy decided to slip away and speak to Philemon once more, but when she looked he was gone.

"Jeremy?"

She turned quickly. No wonder she hadn't seen him—he was behind the platform, in the shade, gazing up at her. Jeremy motioned for him to join her but he shook his head with a meaningful look at King and the others.

"You come down."

"Is everything all right?" she asked as soon as she had joined him.

He snuffled; his nose was running in the cold. "Jeremy, I sold my car." He pulled a small wad of bills from one of the pockets of the swashbuckling trench coat. "Here" he said, pressing the money into her hands. "They give me forty-five dollars. You take it. You might need some money on your trip."

"Oh, Philemon——" She was almost positive now she was going to have some sort of fit before the day was over. "Philemon, it's *your* money. I know you don't have any. I want you to keep it." She thought of the money Eli'd stashed away between his mattresses. It was locked up in that lawyer's office now, along with the copy of the will Eli had scrawled out months ago, leaving everything he had to the Crenshaw group. Rightfully that money should have been Philemon's; it might have given him some sort of decent start after so many years of dependence on Eli. Jeremy tried to give the forty-five dollars back to him, but he resisted.

"No, no, it's for you," he said. "I don't need nothing."

"Philemon, where are you going? Will you live with the Hazelmans?"

He hung his head. "They don't have room for me."

"What?" Jeremy said, outraged.

He wiped his nose with a finger.

"Why, I think that's rotten!" She did not know what else to say to him. Philemon wasn't going to take the money back, she knew that, it was his gift, and if he starved to death he wouldn't say a word for pride. But here he was, winter coming on and not a decent coat to his name. Jeremy suddenly realized with a stab of anxiety that he *might* starve at that, if those blasted Hazelmans wouldn't take him in hand. After all, what could he do? He'd never held a job in his life, didn't know gee from haw, actually. Philemon hunched his shoulders and looked morosely at her.

"I'd better go."

"No, wait." Jeremy stared at the Train, busy now with the sight-seers and free loaders. She had an idea and she seized it recklessly.

"Why don't you come on with us, Philemon?"

He licked his lips and tugged at a ragged cuff; but Jeremy didn't miss the gleam in his eye.

"Nobody'd want me to."

"Lord knows there's plenty you could do to help King. Why, look at the size of that thing." She waved a hand toward the Train. "You'd earn your keep, all right."

"He wouldn't let me come," Philemon asserted.

"Just let me talk to him—and you wait around, hear?"

"OK . . . Jeremy!" he called, as she dashed off.

"What?"

"There's Cosh too—I tied him over yonder."

"You still got that brute? Never mind, there's probably a place in the baggage car he can live." Jeremy wheeled and again made for the Train. At least for the moment she felt purposeful, and providing a roof over Philemon's head would go a long way toward quieting some of the guilty feelings that were making a misery of her stomach. Probably, she thought, hurrying, probably it wasn't her fault Eli had died—or else the Lord would have found appropriate means to punish her as she deserved, instead of allowing her a beautiful wedding and a brand-new life.

Philemon rubbed at an ear, watching her go. His lips went in and out, and he looked with wide-eyed interest at the Train. Eventually the sight caused his heart to tremble. For several minutes he was absorbed by the faces he saw through the coach windows. He had hunger pangs, and eased them with a stick of cinnamon gum. Then he wandered away, unburdened, whistling for his dog.

33

The Point of a Pin

Along the main line in Mississippi, the Gospel Train slowed for a crossing obstruction in a hamlet and then speeded up again; this vibrating acceleration was felt by Molly, who for some time had had her ear to the carpeted floor of the room. It was just enough of a change to bring her slowly up from a narcotic fathom of sleep, through tones of black and gray, to the orange eye of the late-afternoon sun that nearly filled the thickness of glass in the bedroom window of her apartment. She sucked at air, inhaled needles, and fell back, hands against her face.

"Molly—Molly—"

"Go away."

"I need to talk to you."

"Go away, I'm sick!"

"It's me, Cowboy. Open the door."

Molly stiffened; then she rolled over and raised herself. Absently she made a one-handed search of the carpet for her glasses. Not finding them, she stood against the motion of the Train and looked out at the passing landscape, which was flat and brown and blurred. Her stomach tucked and tilted. She lunged at the door and snapped the lock back.

"Where am I going? Get me off of here!"

"Molly, what's happened to you?"

"I tell you I want *off this Train!*" She seized him by the ribs and hauled him through the door. Her lip quivered in a low-down way. One of her uncovered eyes was turned in, pathetically, and her face was like suet.

"You knew," she sobbed. "You knew what he was planning and you didn't tell me!"

"My Lord, Molly, you're not going all to pieces just because King—"

With a witch's wrath and a smart hard fist Molly hooked him above the belt. Cowboy puffed, as much from surprise as from hurt. Defensively he seized Molly and threw her down. Grief flattened her against the carpet. She was wearing only a fancy pink slip, with stains from water—or something worse—on it.

Once he got his breath back Cowboy felt badly about her tears. He had counted on Molly being sore about King's marriage, but this was something else, catastrophic: she was in pain, and he was unhappily reminded of his own pain of vacancy in the days following his ordeal with the devil.

"Molly, King never said a word. I didn't know until five this morning. He got me up out of bed to go with him. I asked him where and he just grinned at me and said, 'Well, to hell, most like.'" Cowboy scratched his red head. "I suppose he was kidding."

"He couldn't love her. I know he couldn't. *Why?*" After this last outburst Molly quieted down except for her desperate

359

breathing. Then her breath too seemed to stop altogether and her face hardened to white marble. "Because it's his way of telling me what he thinks. He couldn't just come out and say, Molly, you *disgust* me! Molly, you're a whore! Molly, I wouldn't touch you! No! He had to marry that—"

"She's not a bad kid, Molly," Cowboy murmured.

Molly sat up, made a determined effort to reach her opened suitcase, and fell back in a state of semi-shock, clutching an empty pill bottle in her hand.

Cowboy was startled. "How many of those did you take?"

"Not enough." She coughed. "Don't worry. I heaved them all up, that's why I'm like this now. I'm jumping out of my skin, Cowboy! Where's the next stop? Oh, when does this Train stop?"

Cowboy studied the land outside. "We're probably getting close to Oslo now."

"Where?"

"Oslo, Mississippi. You remember."

Molly nodded, bleakly. She was holding one of the chairs by the window to stay upright. "I chose that little town—carefully. Oh, how they'll turn out for a look at King Windom!" She reacted to the taste of his name as if she'd poisoned herself. "You'll have to help me—I'm too weak. Just get me off the Train—but I don't want anybody to see me!— and put me in a cab. I'll get back to Clearwater all right."

"Molly, no."

"What do you mean?"

"The Southern Cross Crusade will be a total loss without you, Molly. A disaster."

Molly lowered her tangled head to the seat. "I've set it up too well," she said. "Everything will work the way it should. Nothing could stop the Gospel Train short of—Help me!"

Cowboy braced himself against the door as the Train hit a rough stretch of trackage. "Wait until tomorrow. Let me get a porter in here to make up your bed. You can sleep awhile, Molly, then, in the morning, if you still feel like leaving . . ."

She looked at him pleadingly. "Cowboy, don't you understand? You know me as well as any man; we had our good times together—"

Cowboy said grimly, "Now look, Molly, that's all over and done with—"

"Listen, listen! Understand what's happened to me! My

360

whole life was built hour by frightening hour for this day, this man! Oh, Cowboy, I can't stand what he's done to me! I have to quit this Train. It'll be somebody's blood if I don't get away! Please help me!"

Cowboy lighted a cigarette for himself and stared in frustration at Molly's sprawled body. Most of her suffering seemed real to him, and he pitied her. He knew that she could wring honest suffering out of her system gradually, like a heavy smoke. But the odd tone that had accompanied her threat of bloodletting disturbed him greatly.

He felt the Train slowing, and the outbuildings of the town slipped into view.

"Are we there?"

"Whose blood, Molly?"

She looked at him, perplexed.

"You wouldn't try some dumb thing to get back at King, would you?"

"I don't know . . . I don't know!"

Cowboy put his cigarette out in one of the armchair ashtrays and reached over her to pull down the shade, blotting the sun. "We're coming in, Molly. But I don't want you to get off here. Now, don't be upset. I want to talk to you again, later, after we leave Oslo. After you've rested. Then if you still want to leave us, I'll see to it the Train stops at the first crossroads. I'll drive you to Clearwater myself. Is that a deal, Molly?"

"Don't . . . make it too long."

He touched her shoulder reassuringly before going out. "I'll tell Sihugo to be listening for your bell in case you need anything. Otherwise nobody'll bother you."

She sobbed extravagantly. "You're the only friend I've got here! You can get me out. But quick, I'm being cooked to jelly in this pot!"

In the corridor outside, Cowboy, feeling jelly-like himself, got his breath back. He looked up the porter, then went at a clip through the Train. The choir was making ready under the watchful eye of Mr. Handwerker. They were now proceeding slowly into the center of town; Cowboy saw crowds and felt a cramped sense of victory, although his mind was filled with other matters.

He entered the chapel and spied King on his knees before the altar. At first he thought the preacher was alone, but then he

361

saw Jeremy midway in the chapel, sitting with her hands folded in her lap and her eyes soberly on her husband.

Cowboy whispered to her, "I need to talk to King alone if you don't mind, Jeremy."

She looked at him in an unfriendly way, then gathered up her red coat and walked quickly out. Cowboy had no time to puzzle out her mood; he joined King at the altar and kneeled himself for a few moments' meditation. But he was frustrated in his desire for an orderly mind.

The Train jolted softly to a stop. Presently they both heard the members of the choir singing gloriously as they left the Train one by one to stand on the station platform. The sun was setting and there was a fine glow inside the chapel.

King rose with a heavy breath and looked at Cowboy.

"Did you see her?"

Cowboy nodded.

King shifted his shoulders uneasily. "How is she?"

"Molly's in terrible shape; I'm worried."

"She hates me," the preacher said flatly. "I meant to do it right, Cowboy! To talk to Molly and introduce her to Jeremy. I—but so much happened all at once today. I didn't have the chance." He bent his Bible like a saw. "Once this is over with I'll go see her."

"That won't do; better leave Molly to me."

"Cowboy, I never meant to hurt her! Can't Molly understand that?"

The Cowboy said nothing.

After a while King said darkly, "All right, speak your mind, please."

"You could have just brought Jeremy along—let everybody get used to her, Molly included. Then you could have had a long talk with Molly, let her down easy. Then married Jeremy if you'd wanted to."

"That's good advice from *you*, Cowboy," King said with an edge in his voice, and Cowboy tensed.

"Because I know how it is, you mean—to let a woman down hard."

The preacher lowered his eyes.

"Jeremy wouldn't have come any other way. I know her, she just wouldn't have come. No, I—had to have her with me on this trip; now what more do I need to explain?"

Cowboy, still feeling humiliated, swallowed and said,

"Nothing." But then he trembled. "It's Molly who made this Train—never mind who spent the money on it! And if the Train is going to mean anything, if it's going to work for the Lord, then it'll be Molly's inspiration that makes it work. Without her—"

"We won't be without her," King said, so curtly that again Cowboy trembled; he could not begin to understand King's anger and arrogance. For the moment their friendship was balanced on the point of a pin.

Mr. Handwerker entered with Mab Shaw. "Gentlemen." King looked at them, hollowed-eyed, and nodded. The two men walked up the curve of stairs to the pulpit beneath the dome. Cowboy stared upward. A tiny motor made a whirring sound as Handwerker activated the sliding dome.

Mab had lingered for a last look at the words she was preparing to sing. "It's a glorious day, Cowboy."

"Yes, it is, Mab."

"I'm sorry your grandmama couldn't ride along. But I know she is proud of you tonight."

"I hope that's true, Mab," Cowboy said, feeling badly in need of tears. "Well, up you go." And he helped her to climb the stairs. Cold air swirled down. Cowboy heard the choir more distinctly and saw early-evening stars. Once Mab was in her place there was a click and the entire pulpit lifted.

From his coat pocket Cowboy took a length of blue ribbon with KW stamped on it in silver; this he pinned to his lapel and went outside to view the services. Charley, the cameraman whom Molly had hired to film a color documentary of the Gospel Train for showing to church and civic groups, had placed himself atop one of the forward cars. His brilliant lights seemed to be everywhere under the deepening sky. The scene was magical; it jolted the pulse.

Of course Cowboy had expected a good turnout—they'd done their advance work carefully. But this crowd went beyond expectations. The business district of Oslo, Mississippi, was divided in two by a wide railroad embankment. The Train stood right in the middle of town by the station, and it was almost entirely surrounded by people, to the limits of the restraining ropes. They were all over the sidewalks, and on the roofs of the buildings. The two main streets were jammed with cars; before stepping down, Cowboy shot a look at the highway, and saw long lines of late-comers. Overhead the sky was a gun-metal blue; above fragments of trees, the knobbed water tower was golden in the final rays of the sun. The courthouse clock struck five-fifteen.

Mab was singing "We've come a mighty long way," and although her voice wasn't ideal for open-air concerts, she could be heard clearly thanks to the excellent sound system which Cowboy had helped rig. The crowd was well behaved; he saw more than twenty young men and women with the KW ribbons acting as stewards. Cowboy reckoned if they were going to draw such crowds elsewhere they would need more local assistance, and he made a note of it.

He hopped down from the coach and walked all the way around the Train, shielding his eyes from the Hollywood lights. When he came to the Pullman in which Molly had her apartment, he looked up at the proper window and saw that the shade was still drawn. Then he retraced his steps to the headquarters of the Gospel Train.

It was a busy place, and Florence looked at him despairingly.

"Two long-distance calls for Mrs. Amos—television stations in Chicago and Los Angeles."

"Wanting film?"

"I think so."

"Call back when you have time and tell them we'll supply as much film as they need by air express tomorrow."

The conductor of the Train, a hunched and bespectacled man named Grimsley, signaled Cowboy. "Look at those tracks! This is a sight more'n we bargained for; the stationmaster is fit to be tied."

"Why?"

"The Gulfshores Limited is due at six-twenty. That train never stops here but it will be forced to do so tonight."

"The meeting should be over by five-fifty."

Grimsley snorted. "Those people won't leave until this Train is out of sight. Probably five thousand out there, and they're all over the northbound tracks. As long as the Train stays they'll swarm around like ants at a picnic."

"Florence, what's on King's schedule?"

"He's having dinner with some of the local ministers in his study after the counseling of the proselytes."

Cowboy thought over alternatives. "Let's take the Gospel Train out of town, then, and pull off at the nearest siding. We don't want to start making trouble for the towns or the railroads."

The conductor slipped his watch into a vest pocket. "One thing more. My boys are plenty worried about that dog in the baggage car."

"Why, is he loose?"

"No, but he's a mean one. My boys won't go in to use the toilet nor anything else. I'll have to notify the union——"

"King said OK to the dog, so that's how it is. In the morning we'll buy a kennel."

"That should be satisfactory," said Grimsley, and he picked up the receiver of the intertrain telephone.

"I can't keep up with everything I'm supposed to do," Florence complained. "I need to talk to Molly."

"She's not feeling too good right now."

"I can guess *why*."

"No, you can't. Tomorrow morning's soon enough, isn't it, Flo?"

"Well . . . I just need some help, that's all."

"Sure you do," Cowboy said, deciding then that she had the itch of a troublemaker.

It was not his place to fire her, but he decided to leave a note where Molly would see it—if and when she came back to work. She might be persuaded to get rid of Flo and put in a call to Clearwater or New Orleans for two matronly executive secretaries, one for King and one for her. If the Gospel Train continued to make such a hit they'd easily be able to afford added expenses. He was sure Molly would agree. . . .

By six-thirty the Train had been pulled to a siding five miles down the line and nearly everyone was at dinner. Cowboy could no longer keep the problem of Molly at the back of his mind; in the silence of the office he seemed to hear her weeping, and so he returned to the tenth coach. There he entered his own quarters long enough to unpack a bottle of whiskey which he'd included at the last minute, mostly for a psychological advantage in case an old thirst returned late at night.

He hesitated before Molly's door, listening, then let himself in. It was dark in the apartment bedroom, but here was a thin edge of light beneath the window shade. Soon he saw that the bed was down and that Molly was in it, covered by a sheet. He whispered to her, but there was no response.

Cowboy went into the annex, guided by a night light, a

green disk on the wall that revealed his shadowy face in the mirror; it gave him the shudders. "Like old times," he thought bitterly, "just you and me, Molly." He returned to the room with a glass and made himself comfortable in an armchair.

Thirty minutes into his bottle, he thought, O Lord, am I opening all the locked doors and windows and inviting the devil in? Is it his evil judgment I'm clinging to now, or is it somehow right? Lord, would my act offend you so very much? Tell me if it's really evil, let me feel your anger in my heart. . . . But he felt no more than a passing melancholy. She had to be calmed, that was all; what might come after he couldn't say.

A too generous slug of whiskey seared his throat and he coughed quietly. Molly stirred and sat up in bed. "Who's that?" she said, in a frightened voice. "Cowboy!"

"I'm here, Molly."

"It's dark."

Cowboy got up and leaned over her, raising the shade halfway.

"Are we getting off soon? Am I going back?"

"Yes." He stood over her with a clean glass and the bottle in hand. "If it's what you want."

"I smell whiskey—are you back on that stuff?"

"I've been having a drink," he admitted. "It's been a rough one today."

Molly lay back, her bare arms crossed on her forehead.

"Could you stand a drink yourself, Mol?"

"I've never ached like this; I'm so sore and tired from . . . hating him!"

Cowboy sat down on the side of the bed and poured a small share of the whiskey. He held the glass close to her nose until she had the strength and determination to take and drink it. Then she stared out the window, at the half-sky and the Delta land, sweetened by winter moonlight, tranquil and lonely. A pond glittered like an eye fallen from space.

"In the morning I'll go," she said, after a long contemplation.

He poured more whiskey into the glass, and she sat up to drink it. When he thought the time was right, he lay down on the narrow bed, barely touching Molly at the hip. She looked at him, then turned her face to the window again. Thereafter she did most of the drinking, making no sound except to swallow.

"Cowboy, you're the best friend I've ever had."

"You've always been good to me, Molly."

"If you hadn't been here—if I couldn't have counted on you —I think I would've . . . used a razor blade on myself."

He sat up beside her and put an arm lightly around her shoulders; Molly broke down as if she'd been slapped. "How will I make it to morning? How will I live through tomorrow? I'm stuck here, isn't that so, because I loved him! No matter what, I'm stuck!"

In a convulsion of sympathy he tightened both arms around her and pressed her head against his shoulder. Molly was rigid, but she didn't try to pull away. Her breath burned his neck. He petted her, hip and thigh and breast, and she softened, ever so slowly. At last Cowboy lowered her head to the pillow and bent to kiss her. But Molly turned quickly aside.

"No, don't do that!" She leaped and seized a hand with her sharp teeth and ground into it. Cowboy nearly fainted but he bore the pain without trying to free himself, as if it was his due.

"Oh, Molly, my hand!"

She loosened her bite. "Don't be tender—don't be kind to me at all! I don't want to die in a county place in a nice white jacket with buckles at the back because you were kind to me."

Cowboy sucked in his breath, holding the numbed and nearly paralyzed hand protectively against his side. "My God, my God," he said, in a tone of chilling despair.

"Once you had rough ways, Cowboy; make me remember!"

Eyes starkly open, Molly settled back.

34

A Certain Amount of Peace

After midnight King left his study, where he'd spent most of the evening with Martin Handwerker analyzing the first success of the Southern Cross Crusade, and entered his apartment in coach ten. The lights were low and the covers of the bed were neatly turned down, but there was no sign of Jeremy.

He went out again immediately, passed through the other Pullmans, and came to the recreation car without seeing a soul. Apparently after a grueling day no one was up and about. Most of the trainmen, he knew, had departed for a hotel in town, one feature of a complicated deal which Molly had negotiated with the various Brotherhoods, involving multiple crews and feats of scheduling.

The preacher began to worry; where could Jeremy have gone so late at night? She was a shy one and he doubted that she'd made any friends among the several hostesses. Even if she had, those girls were under Mab's watchful eye—and Mab wouldn't allow them to visit or be visited in their rooms past eleven.

He retraced his steps to see if there was activity in the chair cars, but he found only a couple of sleepless faces. Most of the fifty members of the Bethesda Terrace Baptist Church choir were bedded down in their coach, apparently snug under blue woolen blankets. The chapel was empty, and so was the visitors' lounge, but on the darkroom door King found a note proclaiming that Charley the photographer was working late, and that anyone foolish enough to use a passkey on the door would probably ruin a hundred feet of valuable color film. King smiled and went on. The traveling darkroom had been Charley's idea, to facilitate his work, and he'd installed most of his own equipment. Molly had decided that for the first couple of weeks they would send out film to television stations requesting it, gambling that the additional publicity would justify the expense. In a way it was a small gamble, compared to all the others Molly was taking. But King had never doubted her business sense, and as for her ability to organize, to proceed from the wishful to the actual—well, the proof was everywhere. The proof had been a heart-stopping crowd of five thousand waiting by the railroad tracks in Oslo for a glimpse of the Gospel Train; the proof had been in the care and feeding of about one hundred forty people in a fourteen-car train without a single word of complaint or protest being heard. Of course, there'd be problems once the novel became commonplace, but Molly was prepared for almost anything. The smallest fetch-and-carry assignments were all clearly posted on large colorful peg boards in each of the cars, and on a master board in the office, the schedule for the next two weeks, broken down to the quarter hour, was continually being plotted and revised. Opposite this board there was a route map and below it a "city

368

book" in which all information about forthcoming crusades was recorded. Every staff member had a page in a loose-leaf notebook on Molly's desk. Those mistakes which Molly had made were in the name of economy; they would need another ten hostesses before long, and a full-time supervisor for them.

Thinking about all this, about the notes he had made in consultation with the observant Mr. Handwerker, King felt low and desperate. Because of Molly's tantrum upon receiving the news of his marriage—he was afraid everybody on the Train knew about it—he realized that chances were slim they would ever be able to work together again. This was the real tragedy, as King saw it: Cowboy had pointed out in his anger that the Gospel Train was really Molly's success—how true that was! And she was missing the pleasure of her success.

The preacher blamed himself completely for Molly's troubles. Somehow he'd led her to think that he loved her—an old curse revived—and his subsequent actions in her own home . . . But it was impossible for him to go beyond this point in his thinking without becoming physically ill, to dwell on what he'd tried to do to poor Molly, with the devil's connivance. There had been dark and evil times in his life, but nothing to stack up with that midnight hour on Molly's sofa. Now she lay in misery, victimized, and what could he do without—as Cowboy had said—making her misery worse? He might only stir up more trouble, for all around them to observe.

King rubbed his tired eyes. The gates were open, and worry was boiling in. Maybe Cowboy would be able to talk Molly out of her mood. Most likely there was no way she could be stopped from creating a terrible and demoralizing scene. He was sure of only one thing—a fortune had been spent on the Gospel Train, and its continued success depended entirely upon Molly's good will.

He shuddered. But if she could forgive him, then perhaps she might be willing to just leave, quietly. King vowed to pray on his knees for a hundred hours for Molly's peace of mind, if only she would try to forgive him.

The morning would tell. He looked toward it with dread, helpless—and in this frame of mind he continued in search of Jeremy, whom he hadn't seen since five that afternoon.

He came to the office and found the night watchman, a Burns guard named Beggs, on duty. Beggs said that Jeremy hadn't stopped by, and he offered the preacher a cup of coffee. Rather than feed the man's curiosity by hanging around, King proceeded to the baggage car, where a work light burned. In the distance Philemon's dog came up from the floor like a dusty yellow wraith and King stopped dead until he spotted the lightweight chain attached to the dog's collar.

Philemon himself walked out of the crew's toilet, zipping his trousers. He glanced at Cosh, who was making threatening sounds, and then at the preacher.

"He won't give you no trouble," Philemon said confidently.

"What are you doing up here?"

"I just had Cosh out for a walk. What kind of law is there against that?" Philemon sat down on the floor and looked over his knees at the preacher. He smiled snidely. "Up kind of late."

"May be," King muttered.

"Looking for somebody?"

He felt like snatching Philemon off the seat of his pants and giving him a pounding, but he managed to check the impulse, wondering why he'd let Jeremy talk him into bringing this no-good along. Then he sighed; such hostile second thoughts were only one indication of the kind of lackluster Christian he'd been for much too long a time.

Philemon fingered the dog's chain and smiled again. "I own an extra chain I can give you the borrow of—if you know of any use you might have for it."

King flexed his hands. "Have you seen Jeremy?"

Philemon prolonged his enjoyment of the moment as long as he could, and then he nodded.

"She's outside. Walking down the tracks last I saw of her."

King jerked the door open. "You'd better go back to your room where you belong." Philemon called something after him but he'd already jumped down from the Train. He walked past the diesel sections, throbbing faintly on low power—they would run through the night, and for many days to come, until the Train stopped for an extended period. After a quick look down the other side of the Train, he began to stride along the single track to the point where it curved off to join the mainline.

Once his eyes became used to the dark he could see the rails sharp in the moonlight for a hundred yards—and, near the green star of a semaphore, a solitary figure walking in a ground swell of mist.

"Jeremy!" He increased his pace and then broke into a run.

Catching up to her, he complained, "You scared the fool out of me, being gone like that."

"I'm sorry," she said indifferently. King took her arm, but she held back, looking off at the fields, at a witches' warp of creek water. Once he found his breath, he quit tugging at her and they stood apart on the crossties, silent. He was baffled.

"What are you doing out here?"

"I had to get some air, that's all."

"Don't you know there're bums—"

She smiled vaguely. "I've lived around bums most of my life; they don't throw a scare into me."

"Jeremy, you talk like a—"

She turned her eyes on him. "What?"

He shrugged. "Just come on with me now."

Instead Jeremy took another step away. She was wearing a sweater and a skirt, and her slender legs were as white as the mist lying along the ditch nearby. "Like a fool," she murmured, half to herself. "Well, I'll tell you what I was thinking of. Running down these rails until I hit the sun."

"Why?" And then he had an uncomfortable attack of tenderness mixed with self-censure, remembering that it was their wedding night. "Oh, I know it's going to be hard getting used to the idea of—but, Jeremy, there are two rooms in that apartment, and—"

She was shivering, and trying not to reveal it. "I'm not smart at all, but I know enough not to be afraid of my husband. Because I chose you, a long time before you chose me; because I know the man you are; because I love you."

"Then why won't you come with me?"

She hung her head. "No reason. It's a cinch standing here won't get me anywhere; I'll never figure out how far those rails go, and where they end."

"I warned you before that the Train was a poor place for a woman."

"Oh, I'll get used to your Gospel Train. Seeing new places is a magic thing for me. But I'll always be afraid of it too. I can't tell you why; I don't understand myself yet."

King reached out for Jeremy and gathered her in, and she lifted her face willingly to be kissed. Then she said in a dazed way. "That's one thing I *won't* get used to: your wanting me—then not wanting me."

"All the days won't be like this one was, Jeremy. And I'll be wanting you always, no matter what."

"Always," she said, one eye alight with pleasure, one eye woeful and withdrawn. She stiffened to ward off a fit of shuddering. "Let's go back then. Promise you'll stay with me all night long? Even if you can't sleep, you won't go wandering off?"

"You're the one who's done all the wandering so far," King said with a smile, and he put her down to walk beside him to the Train.

In her room Jeremy changed into nightclothes and spent several minutes brushing her hair to calm herself. But just as she went to join him, something occurred to her, so when King looked up, Jeremy had a stricken expression.

"I don't have anything pretty to wear for you. Just this old robe, that never fit right anyway."

"There'll be time for us to go shopping in New Orleans. I looked at the schedule."

Jeremy sat down beside him on the low bed. "Shopping in New Orleans!" she repeated, dazzled. "Will you go with me? Because I don't want to buy a thing that won't please you."

"Sure I'll go, Jeremy." He held back the bed covers for her and she lay down. They stared at each other for a few moments, and then he leaned over to kiss her lightly on the lips.

"That's a big smile," he said.

"Because I feel safe now."

"Well . . . I'll get out of this coat and tie. I've been strangling half the night."

"Just one minute." She caught his wrist. "I swore I wouldn't ever beg, but . . . you do love me?"

He nodded; yet it was the look he had that reassured her the most.

"And it doesn't bother you?" she asked, timidly.

"*What* bother me?"

She cupped a hand around her dismal eye.

King grabbed the hand. "Jeremy!"

"Because if you don't think I'm a freak, then it doesn't matter what anybody else thinks. Then I can face them all and never have to wonder why you married me!"

He snatched her up from the bed and held her so tightly that her back popped and her head whirled from lack of air. Sobs came from him, and at first she found them frightening, but then she understood. With her hands she soothed him, and, sooner than she could have hoped, she felt in her breast the peace and contentment which had seemed to be a promise of the marriage ceremony that morning. She loved; quickly and satisfyingly she became his wife.

With him at last, she slept.

Dawn was visible across the sky like a silver fish in dark water when the new day began for Cowboy.

He hadn't unpacked the night before, so he was ready to go without serious difficulty. The hand Molly had bitten into was stiff and sore, unusable, but it wasn't throbbing, which was a good sign. He'd cleaned it with whiskey and applied a burn cream he always carried in his shaving kit and wrapped the hand in a clean handkerchief. All in all it was in much better shape than his conscience.

He made room beside his shirts for his Bible and closed the suitcase. It was still early but he decided to leave the Train anyway and wait by the side of the road. There was a bare chance that if he didn't go now he might meet someone, be forced to stand and pass the time of morning, and he felt too dolorous for talking.

The cold air and a hint of bronze light in the sky cheered him slightly as he lugged his suitcase to the edge of the hard road that ran along the spur track. There were lighted windows in a field. He drew a breath and waited, sitting on the suitcase, sick with his sense of sin, yet hopeful that he could again be worthy of the Cross and the shed blood, that he could find a way to justify himself as a man and a Christian.

From far down the road he heard a racket and the bobbing headlight of a motorcycle appeared. Cowboy stared, then reluctantly got to his feet as the sickle sped toward him. It slowed with a popping of the exhaust and fishtailed to a stop.

King swung out of the saddle, looking calm and happy. He was dressed in his old blue sweater and a pair of Levis with grease slicks ironed in.

"Where you off?" he asked, lifting a pair of goggles.

"I'm on the road for the next six weeks; advance man in Georgia and the Carolinas."

"That's right." The preacher stretched and yawned, his breath steaming. "Judd late?"

"No, I'm early."

King smiled at him, accepting his curtness with grace. He rummaged in a saddlebag thrown across the back fender of the sickle and came up with a large candy bar. Cowboy shook his head, refusing part of the candy. King peeled down the wrapper and began wolfing his breakfast. "Must have carried myself twelve, fifteen miles down that road," he muttered. "Started out just before the moon set. It was a beautiful sight." He licked his fingers, and threw the candy wrapper into the weeds. Then he studied Cowboy benignly.

"I'm sorry about yesterday afternoon."

Cowboy shook his head again, in a weary way.

"Molly all right now?" King asked, without a great deal of curiosity.

"I don't know; I don't know what she feels, or what she's thinking."

King glanced at the long line of the Train, coming into detail as the night wore away. His look conveyed the impression that nothing could go wrong with this day, or his destiny.

Cowboy's attention was drawn to the road. There were headlights from the direction of the highway, but the approaching car was indistinct. Nevertheless, he picked up his suitcase in his left hand. As he did so the coat he carried over his right arm shifted. King shot a look at the bandage.

Cowboy grinned wretchedly. "That? Oh, nothing; I slept on it wrong."

King nodded just as if he were making sense and waited with his hands in his back pockets for the car to overtake them. It was Mrs. Cobb's man Judd driving the red Buick; King helped Cowboy with his suitcase and stood clear.

"Well, take care of yourself, Hoss."

"See you in Jacksonville, then." The car door thudded and Judd drove off. But Cowboy stopped him almost immediately. They backed up to where King was standing, looking puzzled. Cowboy rolled the window down halfway; his face showed the state of his nerves.

"Watch out for her—I mean it."

"I'm praying hard for Molly, Cowboy," the preacher replied.

For a moment Cowboy looked wild around the eyes, but then he lowered his head tiredly. There had been nothing fatuous in King's tone; his self-possession was formidable, reassuring. Maybe, Cowboy thought, there was no reason to be afraid, because he had absorbed nearly all of Molly's personal demon into his own body. Maybe the only real agony that lay ahead would be his own, as he struggled to make peace with the Christ whom he loved and needed.

Their eyes met again for an instant. "So long," Cowboy said, acquiring a smile. They drove east and King watched until the car was only a traveling shadow with a lantern of sun where the rear window would be. He wheeled his sickle down the bank toward the silver Train, the dawn behind him like the sleeping nudge of Jeremy's hand.

The windows of the Train were still dark; he counted on returning to the apartment and slipping down beside his bride to read or doze an hour before the crews came and the breakfast knock sounded on their door. With plenty of muscle he heaved the motorcycle into the vestibule of the tenth car and left it there, then paused to catch his breath before entering the Pullman.

He had made only a moderate racket getting the motorcycle aboard and the nylon carpet in the passageway softened his footsteps; still, he wasn't being all that considerate of the sleepers, and afterward he wondered why the wide-awake Molly hadn't heard him long before he appeared in the car. But he saw her, in her nightclothes, head bent urgently to the door of one of the apartments, seconds before she became aware of him.

He stopped short in surprise, and the surprise turned to shock as he realized that it was the door to his apartment Molly was interested in. There was light enough in the passageway, and he could not have been mistaken. He had no way of knowing what she was up to, but her stillness seemed sinister to him. Perhaps he heard an echo of Cowboy's cryptic warning. Blood crashed in his ears.

"Molly!"

She snapped back from the door, her hair seeming to stand on end. Her eyes were blank with fright behind the tinted lenses of her glasses. Her breath rasped and she shuddered as if she were about to have a stroke. Then she ran, in a puff of white gown, her bare feet flashing on the dull red carpet. Before the preacher could draw a second breath, she had disappeared around the bend in the passageway, and he heard the door bang.

King bit his lip and followed. But his door was slightly ajar and he changed his mind about chasing Molly and coming to an understanding, violent or not. He hadn't bothered to lock the door an hour earlier when he'd gone for a jaunt, and now he regretted this lapse. Apprehensively he entered the apartment, but all was just as it had been. Jeremy slumbered with a hand poised quizzically at her lovely brow. King prowled here and there, lifting shades to let in the morning light. Had Molly entered their rooms while he was out, had she stood where he was standing now, looking down at his wife? Or had he interrupted her just as she was opening the door? He sat down, brooding. By some neglect on his part the door might have come unlatched. Molly, passing through the car, might have noticed the opened door and paused just long enough to close it.

King stripped and put on his pajamas, thinking patiently, Yes, that must have been the way it was.

He knew that it was the only answer he could live with.

Making himself comfortable beside Jeremy, he opened his copy of Halley and began to prepare his mind for the long days ahead. Gradually the hard knot of outrage in his throat loosened.

35

Dr. Matthews Comes Aboard

That evening Molly made her first appearance aboard the Train. She entered the dining car just after the blessing had been asked and looked calmly around at the crowded tables. For a few moments she went unnoticed; then Mr. Handwerker glanced away from the elderly couple with whom he was in conversation and saw her.

"There's Molly. She must be feeling a hundred percent better."

King, who had his back to her, looked around guardedly.

Molly smiled and came toward them. To his eyes she at least looked a hundred percent better: her dress was a luxurious but tasteful brocade, her hair was admirably fixed, and there was color in her cheeks. There was no evidence of the harridan he'd encountered outside his suite at the break of day.

The fiction that King had decided upon the day before and spread around with Cowboy's help was that Molly had taken to her bed with a sinus headache, so he waited tensely to hear what she had to say for herself. Molly, however, offered no comment on her absence. Mr. Handwerker introduced her to their guests. Molly spoke courteously to each, then her attention shifted to Jeremy, who was seated at King's right hand.

"Oh, I forgot that you two—Molly, Mrs. Amos, this is my wife, Jeremy."

"Yes, I've heard about you," Molly said with her patient smile. "And congratulations," she said to King, giving his arm an intimate squeeze. But her eyes were, so briefly, a wilderness. A chair was brought for her and she sat down at the end of the table.

With his appetite depressed, King had little to do but try to puzzle out Molly's plan of attack. Not until after a quarter hour passed did he begin believing that she'd really straightened out, that she was making a willing effort to accept his marriage. Even so he studied Molly as closely as he dared, alert for a sign of trouble, for sudden cracks in her light armor. He discovered only that she was still quite pale beneath the coloring she'd given herself, that her nerves were still undependable, and that by raw effort she continued to sit there, pleasant and informative and alert, not knowing how many people might be laughing behind her back. Her determination to be good won him over; he was sympathetic and anxious to be helpful.

Perhaps Molly knew; toward the close of the dinner hour she looked frankly into his eyes for the first time.

"Well, Molly," he said, smiling, "so far it looks good."

She didn't understand him.

"For the Southern Cross Crusade, I mean."

Molly laughed then, a little rackingly. "Luck to us," she said, lifting a glass of grapefruit juice she hadn't touched before. The jovial Mr. Handwerker took up the toast and they all joined in, with water glasses and coffee cups. Molly looked at each face in turn; her own face was sweet in repose. "Luck to all of us." And again her eyes became a wilderness, a fine and private place, with all its dangers finely in balance.

She excused herself shortly after, expressing mock despair at the amount of work that surely had piled up on her desk.

The men rose dutifully.

Then just as she was leaving, Molly did an odd, unexpected, and tender thing. She leaned behind King and kissed Jeremy lightly on the cheek.

"I want you to be sure and come see me."

Jeremy's eyelids fluttered in surprise.

"What a lovely person," said one of the older women at the table when Molly was out of hearing.

Mr. Handwerker attacked the remains of a cherry tart.

"Molly's a genius. We'd be lost without her." He winked at the preacher.

"Hmmm," said King. "What would you gentlemen and ladies like to see first? The chapel? Or should we just start with the recreation car and work our way forward?"

Dr. John Matthews met the Gospel Train in Ville Fourche, Louisiana, when it was five days out of Clearwater.

He parked the old pickup truck, which he'd driven from his farm twenty-five miles to the south, alongside the Missouri Pacific freight depot, and walked a block in the midmorning sun to join a small shirt-sleeve crowd at the siding. In a rancher's straw and a pair of gray twill work pants, he was not at all distinguishable from the majority of men there. He found standing room in the shade of a magnolia tree and looked over the Train, which he'd seen once before, in its previously drab and neglected condition.

He found the sermon interesting and gave it careful attention while noting that the preacher didn't spare himself, despite the heat and size of the congregation. He also heard a rasp in King's voice and his professional mind worried slightly over it.

Twice Matthews removed his hat to wipe his streaming forehead with a handkerchief. When the sermon was over he went along with the majority to a refreshment stand operated by a local church group. As he stood sipping from his cup of lemonade, a thin Negro whom he didn't immediately recognize came up to him.

"Are you Dr. Matthews?"

He nodded agreeably.

"King said he thought so, and he'd like to visit with you aboard if you've got the time."

"Oh, I have the time. You're Age, aren't you?"

"Yes," said Age. "Would you follow me, Doctor?"

Matthews tagged along, studying Age as he studied everything around him, with an unprejudiced eye. He decided that Age spoke curtly and walked aloof not because he was an angry man, or a mistreated one, but because he brooded, and forgot the world, like a child forgets an untied and flopping shoelace. Yet he wasn't brooding about himself, some personal quandary. Dr. Matthews said:

"Has it been going well, Age?"

"There been crowds. More people than anyone here thought."

"Is he happy? He looked in good health."

"I think his health is good," Age commented as he stood by to let the doctor climb aboard.

Matthews smiled and fondled his reddened nose with his fingers and gave up asking questions. Age took him to the preacher's study.

Jeremy was there; Matthews bowed slightly as soon as he set eyes on her, and his normally diffident smile became quizzical.

"Dr. Matthews, I'd like for you to meet my wife," King said heartily, rising.

The doctor greeted Jeremy with great pleasure and his best wishes, finding her fresh and likable and as shy as himself, and determined not to show it; he congratulated the preacher. "What a wonderful surprise! I'm sorry to have been out of touch."

"Where did you come from, Doctor?"

"Oh, the farm. I've been here in Louisiana for the past month."

King nodded. "I thought it was you standing under that tree; then after you took off your hat I was sure."

Matthews cast an eye around King's study. The walls were paneled in an apple-green wood, there were two saffron-yellow sofas in the Spanish manner with an elegant woven-top coffee table between them, and ample bookshelves.

The preacher laughed hoarsely. "It's too good for me—Molly went absolutely haywire in here. But I'm happy to have a place to work, where I can ramble into a tape recorder and not drive

Jeremy to distraction. Also I don't keep her awake half the night with my blasted insomnia."

Jeremy smiled serenely and Matthews missed nothing that was implicit in her smile. He thought that despite her years she was feminine and loving and perceptive, and most probably a match for the preacher. He liked her very much, and regretted the strabismic eye.

At Jeremy's urging he sat down on one of the sofas, his straw hat on his knee. She went into the kitchen annex to heat a pot of coffee and Matthews said, in response to a question from King:

"Just loafing, I'd say. I gave over those few patients I had to doctors more interested in the practice of medicine than I, and retired, unofficially. In the spring I may turn full-time farmer. Right now I'm doing some writing and collecting my thoughts."

King leaned back. "Same subject occupies you, Dr. Matthews?"

"Same subject."

"Well . . ." King dropped his eyes. "I wish we could have more time together."

"What's your itinerary?"

"Hammond and Slidell today, New Orleans overnight. Florida by Christmas." He smiled wryly. "Molly plans to keep us on the move."

"Voice holding out?"

King cleared his throat several times. "Not so well."

"You might send out for some slippery elm throat lozenges. They'll do as much good as sprays or gargles, if not more."

"I'll sure give them a try, Doctor."

They had their coffee and talked of the Train. King was restless, as if the results of the brief crusade in Ville Fourche had not compensated for the call on his nervous system. Jeremy watched his every move without seeming to. When he got up to pace, he always returned to touch her hair, her cheek, or the back of her hand.

A telephone rang and King jumped to answer it.

"What? Oh, yes—five minutes." To Matthews he said apologetically, "I'm afraid we're ready to pull out."

The doctor smiled broadly. "Take me with you," he said.

King looked at him uncertainly.

"If you have the space, I mean. I can pay my own way; besides, you might have need of a doctor, even one like me, with so many people aboard. Sooner or later there'll be a

380

sprained ankle, an upset stomach, or . . . a sore throat." He lifted his shoulders. "Who knows? . . . I'm assuming, of course, you don't have a doctor on board already. That Molly doesn't miss a trick."

"She did hire a registered nurse in Clearwater. At the last minute there was a mixup, the nurse couldn't make it, so there's no one on board who has even first-aid training. But, Dr. Matthews, forgive me, what a waste of your time! A man like you—"

The doctor shook his head sadly. "You'd be doing me a favor. The truth is I was getting a little seedy down on the farm, with only old Babineux and his wife for company. This would be an adventure for me; I'd love every minute."

"It sure would be a break for us to have you along." King glanced at his watch. "What about clothes? What about your truck? You said you drove—"

"I'll get a wire off to Babineux. He's used to my strange habits and sudden flights; he'll tie up all the loose ends. I can pick up a medical bag and supplies in New Orleans tomorrow morning. What do you say? Want to talk it over with Molly?"

The preacher hesitated for a moment, frowned, then stuck out his hand. "Shoot, no; Molly will be tickled to have you with us! Doctor, welcome to the Gospel Train. I just hope you don't regret your impulse a month or two from now."

Matthews shook the hand gravely. "I think it's going to be very stimulating," he said. But it was not quite true, for all the evidence of unpreparedness, that he was acting on a whim.

36

A Handful of Change

The train became for Age a natural enemy, although there was nothing about it that seemed immediately perilous, like something alive and worthy to be shot: a wolf or a wild boar cranky with shoats. Rather, he found its jolts and writhings a disaster for his bones, its trumpeting horn a soul-flattener. He discovered in the confinement of the Train trouble he'd never known before, and that trouble was called boredom.

His boredom was pervasive: he felt under wraps and frightened by a loss of power; boredom pinched his throat and tarred his wits, and at its worst it seemed inevitable and queerly reasonable, like a human superstition. He fought, but there was no job of work for Age, no wall for his handyman's skills: Molly's Train functioned beautifully without his help.

Nor could he occupy himself with the menial work he'd done for years, the picking-up after King; all that was now Jeremy's right and privilege. He did not resent Jeremy, in fact she could delight him, but his delight in her did not make him feel less like a cloudy ghost in a forgotten well during the long nights he spent in his quarters. King called infrequently; the preacher was kind but preoccupied. Age tended his recent aches and obscure stresses and kept to himself.

There was one other aboard the Train whose situation resembled Age's, but a common bond was impossible. Age was very much aware of Philemon, who apparently had solved the problem of making himself useful. Although Age had never sought entertainment and had rarely enjoyed another man's folly, idleness was an itch and a curse and brought the red moonlight to a man's eyes, so Age was able to forget his boredom only on those occasions when Philemon was at work, collecting money for the Southern Cross Crusade, and at the same time lining his own pockets with a part of that collection.

Age had learned by accident that Philemon was a thief, since Philemon never stole a nickel by daylight. He was also, despite his nervousness and his pudgy hands, a pretty good thief. It occurred to Age as he observed Philemon on successive nights that Philemon had given stealing a great deal of consideration; he did not steal willy-nilly, for chewing-gum money. But he wasn't greedy either, and Age decided that he must have some long-term plan in mind.

His fascination with the thief grew as King Windom's Gospel Train left the humid Gulf Coast behind and traveled through the narrow corridor of upper Florida. This was very near to home ground, or what had been home during the five years King had worked and lived with the carnival, and Age's spirits were lifted at the first sight of fishing water and white birds, unexpected rivers that were as dark and twisted as life blood. He felt tension in the flat piney land, a sense of imminent sea and giant wind; it set his teeth pleasantly on edge. And the red moonlight glowed in his eyes, the joys of the hunt racked his breast.

Yet he knew what he hunted was a poor beast, a scared galoot unlikely to be dangerous; he didn't want what he hunted, but there was the tension of still water and steaming cloud in his mind, and, sometimes, the cry of a bull alligator near the sidings at night. At the twilight stops, where the largest crowds gathered, he left the Train and stalked Philemon under the red-and-black windswept skies and, from a distance, watched him steal—how much? Ten dollars a night? Age wasn't sure. Perhaps a dozen times during the collection period while he worked his way through the crowd with a woven basket in his left hand Philemon had the opportunity to dip into the basket and palm a couple of dollars, some silver, or, if his fingers were unsteady, nothing. There was little chance that anyone would see him taking the money, because King Windom had enchanted the eye of the people. Philemon was courteous, he bumped into no one, he wore the KW ribbon that all the stewards and Train personnel wore; he was one of the more anonymous members of the Windom team. Age had been looking out a window of the deserted recreation car one evening and had happened to notice Philemon working his way along the edge of a crowded station platform, just inside the restraining rope which was necessary to keep people away from the Train and perhaps from under the wheels. Philemon had been almost directly opposite Age when he took a swipe at the basket. For an instant Age saw his fist cluttered with silver. Then Philemon reached for a handkerchief to mop his forehead; he could almost hear the coins clinking in Philemon's coat pocket. That had drawn a smile from Age and prodded his curiosity.

It began to bother Age eventually; how much was he getting away with? The potential was thousands of dollars over a period of months; where had he chosen to hide such a sum? A Pullman bedroom offered few places of concealment. If Philemon had thought out this matter of stealing, then surely he had devoted considerable study to his hiding place. Because they lived only a couple of doors apart and because he'd been keeping tabs on Philemon, Age knew his habits. Always the first into the dining car, and the first to leave; seldom in his room except to sleep. He seemed to prefer riding in the baggage car with his dog. When the Train was stopped he liked to get off and walk the dog up and down the tracks and sometimes he let the brute off the chain, if there was an empty field handy.

The Gospel Train cut back and forth through northern Florida and stopped in Ocala on a Friday night. Molly had heeded pleas from several local ministers and scheduled King for a night revival at the high-school stadium. Usually he preached only three times a day, but the sponsoring ministers had promised a crowd of at least eight thousand, and King, despite a hard day under a dizzying sun, was excited by the prospect.

Shortly after dinner, buses rolled up to the siding and the Gospel Train staff boarded for the ride to the stadium. Age watched them go, Philemon among them. He settled down in the recreation car to catch the news of the day on television. When it was fully dark outside, he rose, walked through the Train to his room, paused there just long enough to take a wrench from his toolbox. Then he boldly entered Philemon's quarters.

There was an odor of shaving lotion in the air, but otherwise nothing personal to focus upon. Philemon read nothing save his Bible; he didn't write letters, smoke, or drink. His shaving gear took up the small shelf above the lavatory. His few clothes were in the closet, and so was his old Winchester 97 with the thirty-inch full choke, one of the finest and most popular sporting guns ever made.

Age drew a half glass of water from the tap, then thoughtfully and slowly poured it on the floor beneath the basin. He watched as the water ran out into the room. Then he began looking, first in the pockets of Philemon's clothes, then in the bedding of the upper berth, then in the seats, and under them. He searched the carpet inch by inch with sensitive fingers. Finally he took the shotgun from the closet, admired it, squinted into the barrel and examined the shell chamber. The stock was solid.

Then the tension he had felt this close to the heart of Philemon's secret left him all at once: the theft of a few dollars from a collection basket seemed mean and inconsequential, and his own interest inexcusable. What did he want from Philemon, what did he expect? He felt annoyed with himself for being there. Of course Philemon kept the money close to his own body, and that was all there was to it.

While he was thinking these thoughts, the door suddenly opened, catching him by surprise. He looked up into Philemon's angry eyes.

"What are you doing in my room, nigger?"

Age stared at him for several seconds, unable to speak. Then he simply turned and pointed at the water seeping out of the closet-size bathroom.

"Conductor noticed water dripping down under this car. I fixed the pipe, but he told me to see if any of the rooms was flooded."

Philemon glanced at the water, then at the wrench in Age's hand.

"You don't look like you crawled around under no car tonight."

"Don't I?" retorted Age.

"No." Philemon was more pale than usual, and it appeared that part or all of the huge meal he had tucked away in the diner earlier had disagreed with him. But the anger was still in his eyes, and he wasn't backing off from Age.

"What did you want with my shotgun?"

"What shotgun?" Age said, puzzled, for he had put the gun back in the closet.

Philemon rubbed his stomach. "I seen you through the window. Seen you looking it over."

Age glanced at the window, and wondered why he hadn't lowered the shade. He faced Philemon once more and shrugged, his face a blank.

Philemon fired off a belch which crossed his eyes. He went around Age and sat down on the seat and hung his head.

"Feel bad?" Age asked dispassionately.

"You'd better get out of here."

Age hesitated, then walked to the door. Philemon, who was holding his head, glanced at him. Philemon looked mad and sick and red-eyed.

"Don't let me catch you in my room again."

"OK," Age said.

Philemon lurched up and made for the lavatory. He grabbed it with both hands, spreading his feet like a socked steer. Age winced and closed the door on him. Down the corridor, he lifted the heavy wrench and studied it; his forearm trembled. Tension had returned; it ran like a sharp wire into his heart. He knew what he was after, now that he had clumsily posted suspicion in Philemon's mind.

Age waited in his room, with the door partially opened; and it was an easy period of waiting. He sat with his long hands draped between his knees, his head up at a graceful angle, his eyes half-closed. He pondered that way, like a mystic. What he wanted was a flesh-and-blood enemy, to keep his senses alive. He wanted Philemon afraid and hating him—yet he cared nothing for trapping his thief, or exposing him.

In some way, he knew, he would pay for his hounding of Philemon. Despite his ragged nerves, his ignorance, Philemon was a man, a strong man. . . . Age's eyes opened, and he tasted salt on his tongue. There was a narrow cramp in his stomach, and he lost his breath momentarily. Yes, that was what he wanted most of all: he wanted violence.

This irrational desire almost panicked him. He'd never fought with another man. Those years when he hadn't lived alone, he'd shared a house in comparative peace with two women and with King Windom. He looked like a savage with the scars on his head, but even in the wilderness he'd had in him a center of calm, an understanding for the harsh reasonableness of nature.

Now he was losing control. He faced a part of the truth: he was old. From the self-possession of youth he was stumbling into a dotage. Age looked down into the small fire of truth he had kindled, aware of omens. He was old, and no longer free, and more afraid than poor Philemon could ever be. The fire blazed. He saw clearly the end of his life; only the means of his death was obscure.

Almost an hour passed before he heard Philemon stirring, two doors down. As soon as Philemon had gone, Age arose, took from his closet the yellow slicker with its galaxy of pebbled eyes, and got down from the Train. He stood between the tracks in the warm night. The moon was visible behind a thin shell of cloud, like a chick in a candled egg. A freight train bore down on him one track over, leaving in the air a fume of hot metal and engine oil. He waited for Philemon, his eyes on the baggage car.

Soon Philemon got off with his dog, who pawed the air and fought the leash. The dog was not aware of Age, but Philemon saw him right away. He gave Cosh more chain and they scrambled up the tracks, past the engine of the Gospel Train. When they were nearly out of sight Age walked slowly in the direction they had gone. Once he stopped and looked back at the silver Train and the golden cross, which pulled light to it from odd corners of the freight yard.

The dog burst out of the gloom, gasping for air. Philemon ran down the length of chain, gathering it all in. Age stood his ground, despite the nearness of the dog, and the jaws powerful enough to snap his thin leg.

"Here you are again," Philemon said, his chest heaving; and he sounded unconcerned.

"Out for a walk."

"On the lookout for me, you mean."

Age said nothing, but he was a little surprised by Philemon's jauntiness. He observed the trembling dog, ventured a half step, and was rewarded with a snarl. He looked up, calmly, into Philemon's eyes. Perhaps Philemon wasn't suspicious of him after all.

Philemon mopped his brow with a cuff of his shirt. "Why do you want to wear that fool raincoat around on a hot night like this?"

"I like it."

Philemon lowered his arm slowly, staring at Age. He looked amused, then cunning.

"Find what you want in my room?"

"I went there to look for a leak," Age said patiently. But his heart suddenly pounded.

"Ahhhh," Philemon said, disgusted. However, his good humor returned almost at once; Age couldn't understand why.

"What was there to find?"

The question was too pointed, and it gave Philemon pause. The two men exchanged looks. Age suddenly felt lonely and unsure of himself. There was nothing in Philemon's expression to tell him so, but Age decided that he had underestimated this boy—underestimated his resources, or his desperation, or perhaps his sanity.

Philemon said, as if he'd just had a beautiful inspiration, "Nigger, how would you like to make five dollars a week?"

"I don't know," Age said.

Philemon looked disgusted again, and incredulous. "You don't know how you'd like to make five dollars?"

"What would I have to do?"

That was more like it: Philemon seemed satisfied. "I guess you could work for me; help with my dog."

Age reflected. "I don't like your dog," he said at last. "I wouldn't want to be around him."

"That's right; Cosh almost chewed you up once."

Revulsion caused Age's shoulders to flex, but Philemon couldn't see it. "He had a go at me. No, thanks. I don't care about the five dollars."

Philemon lengthened the chain and his dog scrabbled eagerly. When he looked up, all the suspicion that Age had expected was now evident in his eyes. Age knew what had happened: he'd turned down the indirect bribe, which Philemon had confidently expected him to take. Now Philemon was confused and worried. His previous mood had been, not a fake, but a delusion, based on some thin evidence of safety he'd discovered. If there was no money to be found (and he'd hidden it cleverly), then who could name him a thief? Age could; and King Windom's man would be listened to. Maybe they'd kick Philemon off the Train, even if they didn't have proof he'd stolen. Furiously Philemon said:

"So you don't want my five dollars; what do you want around me, nigger?"

Age drew a slow breath, then smiled, a tight-lipped but tolerant smile.

"Nothing."

Philemon's confusion grew; his face was swollen with it, as another man's might be swollen with the sting of bees. "Then stay clean away from me—hear? Because if you don't . . ." He dropped his hands and Age thought Philemon was going to jump the dog at him; he made ready to run. Philemon wasn't playing, though, or faking threats. He was on to Age but he had to steal, no matter what—an intolerable squeeze for someone of his nervous capacities. Age had a glimpse of how bad it was for him; Philemon suddenly shouted:

"Stay away! And keep your mouth shut! Cosh can eat up a skinny nigger faster that I can say scat! And I'll let him do it! I'll sic him on you if it'll keep your mouth shut!"

"My mouth's shut," Age managed to say, then he retreated, feeling shocked and revolted by his own behavior, by the writhing of damnation in his flesh. The night depressed him; the golden cross obstructed his eye.

"Stay away, stay away!" Philemon cried after him, hysteria in his voice.

37

Jeremy Accepts an Invitation

After midnight Jeremy grew tired of her book, and tired of waiting for her husband, who was somewhere in town talking theology and revivals with a circle of churchmen. She was lonely and in the mood for companionship, but too timid to wake anybody up or otherwise impose at such an hour.

There was a milk-dispensing machine in the recreation car, and Jeremy decided to kill some time with a late snack, although she had found that she was getting unexpectedly full in breast and hip since her marriage. The only feature of the Gospel Train that enthused her was the quantity of fresh milk at all meals, and, not knowing better, she attributed the new maturity of her body to all that milk she was drinking. But in a day or so they'd reach Miami, and King had promised to take her ocean swimming right away. If she got a little fat in the meantime, she'd surely lose weight out in that hot sun.

Jeremy got up and put on a stylish black-and-white print dress, one of the few things she'd bought in New Orleans that she was really sure she liked, and went to the recreation car. She sat in one of the swivel chairs looking out at the cheerless rail yard while she sipped her milk through a straw and felt less lonely, just for being up and out of the small and restricting apartment.

He would come, she thought; perhaps in ten minutes, or half an hour. Then they would have the remainder of the night together. Jeremy had learned to be as sleepless as he, to stay wide awake until after dawn, because only in the late hours could King be totally free, could he spare himself. This was the time he soaked and scrubbed and sang half-remembered songs, jittered with excitement, boasted outrageously, cried with restraint over kindnesses along the way, and picked fights with Jeremy simply to see her fire up, and shudder with asperity, and forgive him with a glare. He could also lie silently in her arms—only to leap up and haul both wife and motorcycle from the Train, go dashing around in the dark scaring her to tears until the sun rose on her tangled hair and bloodless lips and eager eyes. Sometimes, then, he calmed down, and was totally hers. But usually, Jeremy thought with regret, this happened when there was such a short time left. Afterward she'd scarcely see him the whole day, for his energy was as important to the Gospel Train as the energy of the diesel combine up front. By his presence King Windom made the whole nebulous idea of a "crusade" seem sharply real.

Jeremy finished her milk. In the quiet of the recreation car she thought more deeply about being a wife. Already she had accepted the condition that she would never know what it was like to be married to an ordinary man, like all the men of her experience before King Windom. She was sure that she would have known just how to take care of an ordinary man—a farmer, laborer, or country preacher. But here, on this Train, there was nothing she could do for her husband. Only by reversing her days and nights could she net him, like some enormous, fateful, supercharged dragonfly, and claim his attention for an hour or more. This limitation hurt, and so did the knowledge that many people were making demands on him. He gave time to all; probably he couldn't refuse a solitary soul.

Jeremy was upset by his generosity and intolerant of his patience with others, but she hadn't spoken out yet. The marriage was too new, and like many brides she was very much afraid that the wrong word could shatter it forever. But already she had a notion that there would come a time when, for the sake of a really good marriage, she'd have to make her own demands. She'd need tact, and calm, and self-assurance. Until she found this balance within herself she could only hope to catch her breath, please him, and try not to mind the swarming Train and the deadly nuisance of celebrity.

Restless, big-eyed, and filled with a sense of responsibility, Jeremy left the Train for a breath of air. As she walked slowly along the tracks she was alert for King's return, but no one came and no one left.

A light was burning in the office. Jeremy studied the right-side window and wondered if Mrs. Amos was working late. Most likely; the few times Jeremy had seen her she'd been busy. And . . . not sick, but not looking too strong, either. She never seemed to be at dinner. Jeremy was sympathetic. She remembered Molly's quick kiss on the cheek, and her invitation. Still, if she was working tonight . . . Jeremy shrugged and boarded the Train. She'd just have a look-in. If Mrs. Amos didn't want to be bothered, then she would duck right out.

Molly was sitting at the gray steel desk in her end of the office, writing; the cone of a suspension lamp was pulled close to her bent head. She seemed not to realize that someone had come in. Jeremy looked at her politely. Molly's hair had collapsed for the night, and there was a granite-like block of cigarette smoke around the desk. Jeremy decided that she would have to be bold and announce herself.

"Mrs. Amos, is there anything I can do for you?"

"What?" Molly turned her head like a turtle. Her eyes looked odd until she blinked Jeremy into focus. "What is it?" she asked again.

I—I thought—" Jeremy, feeling instantly unwelcome, lost her presence of mind. "I was up, and—" She cast around the office, which she'd never seen, and smiled. "Didn't think you'd mind if I came in." She lifted her hands helplessly. "Isn't there a—a scrapbook, or something?"

Molly continued to stare at Jeremy, and her face looked dull and old and marred, like pewter. She took off her glasses and rubbed her eyes in a tender agony.

"I don't mind," she said, following a long silence. "We have a scrapbook and a letter book. They're—" She pushed back her chair. "Here, I'll get them for you."

Jeremy sighed, feeling better about having intruded. She followed Molly to a long workbench with a number of ledgers and books upon it. Molly laid her hand on the red leather cover of the largest book, which was stamped in gold: THE SOUTHERN CROSS CRUSADE.

"In this one we paste all the legitimate publicity—not our own news releases. Five pages filled so far." Molly coughed and waited for a breath, then opened the book and switched on a miniature lamp. "We should use a dozen scrapbooks in a year, if my projections about the popularity of the Gospel Train are good."

"A dozen scrapbooks," Jeremy said. "My!"

Molly smiled bleakly. "And this one is the letter book. Just a sampling, actually, a cross section of opinion, some thank-yous, a few criticisms. None of the crank letters—" She hesitated. "I keep a separate file nobody'll ever see."

"Crank letters?"

"I'll-kill-you, you-rotten-spawn-of-the-devil-type letters."

Jeremy was appalled. "King gets those?"

"Only one so far—but then he's barely known, barely exposed to—to all the deranged minds who are attracted by luminaries." Molly ventured a look at Jeremy, for the first time since she'd come in; her gaze became fixed, as if here was a phenomenon she couldn't bring herself to believe. A vein of tension pumped in the hollow of a temple, then subsided. Jeremy was reading a clipping from a Mobile paper, and she was oblivious.

Molly coughed again, and clutched gently at her raw throat. Her eyes began to burn brightly in the pewter face. "Speaking of publicity, I haven't told anybody yet, the telegram just came tonight . . ."

Jeremy looked curiously at her.

Molly smiled fiercely, holding Jeremy's attention, holding her own secret in check. But it all burst out of her quickly enough.

"The telegram was from *Life* magazine."

"No!" Jeremy said, thrilled.

"They're going to do a full-dress feature on King, and the Train. Six or eight pages, color shots, everything. Maybe"—Molly was improvising now, desperate to prolong the ecstasy of the moment—"maybe if there's a lull in some of the little crises around the world, King will make the cover."

"*Life* magazine!" Their eyes met. Unexpectedly, they were intimates. "Won't he be bowled over when he hears the news!"

Molly shook her head hopelessly. She had cherished her news for the past four hours, and, in the telling, everything seemed to be wrong—her triumph had a blackness to it. She thought she was going to cry, and laughter was tearing at her throat. Her face had taken on color and her eyes were clearer, but at the same time she was terribly upset. She had badly needed some pleasure, after days of steeling herself against the slightest shock of memory; but she couldn't handle her emotion.

"I didn't have to work for it, either," Molly gasped. "It was all their idea. They'll be down in two weeks, b-before we leave Florida—let me read you the telegram—" Molly turned away, nerves failing, and wiped at her watery eyes. Her vision was dimmer than it ordinarily was. She struck a swivel chair and fell over it.

"Oh, Mrs. Amos!" Quickly Jeremy tried to help her up.

Molly turned on her side, face gray again. "Don't!" she begged, shrinking from Jeremy's hands. "I'm not hurt!" She sobbed and sobbed. "I f-fell over a chair, that's all. I'm all right." She tried to get up by herself, but she was trembling too violently. Jeremy stood by, frightened.

"Please let me help you."

Molly, on elbows and knees, dug her fingers savagely into the tough carpet. Slowly the storm of her nerves passed, leaving behind occasional rattling sobs, flashes of pain. This time she didn't seem to feel, or to mind, Jeremy's touch. There was a small couch near the desk. Jeremy guided her to it. Molly's head hung loosely.

"Is there something I can get for you? What would you like?"

"Like for you to go away," Molly replied inaudibly.

"What?"

"This had to happen, didn't it, just h-h-had to happen,

bigger fool of myself—God, are you trying to *kill* me? How much can I stand?"

"Mrs. Amos—"

Molly reacted to the sound of her name. Her chin came up. There was a fiery streak across one ashen cheekbone, and her little cat teeth were sharply exposed. She breathed through her mouth and looked at Jeremy with difficulty. Her jaws worked and her teeth grated side to side.

Jeremy smiled, tentatively, but she felt uneasy.

"If you're smart, you'll get out of here," Molly said, speaking more distinctly, but in a low rapid voice. "Yes, I'll let you go, because—my fault for letting you come in, letting you stay. So walk out. And nothing more'll be said. But you'd better hurry!"

"Don't you want to go to bed, though?" Jeremy suggested, laying a hand on Molly's sleeve.

Molly shuddered once more with an emotion that seemed to leave her ripped and cold and dead. Only her eyes lived; they appraised Jeremy.

"All right," Molly said, after a baleful silence. "Stay."

"If I can help—"

"You rat. You terrible crud. You twat!"

Jeremy was dumfounded.

"So you took him away from me. All right. . . . What's the matter, didn't you know? Didn't anybody whisper in your sweet ear? King was *mine*. I loved him. You walleyed pig. I was all set to have him too. All I needed was a little time and patience! I thought we'd be married on the Train." A dreadful smile leaped across her face. "But you married him instead." She leaned closer, urgently. "How?"

It occurred to Jeremy that she must get up, with all possible dignity, turn and walk quickly out of the car. Then she could pretend, to herself if not to Molly, that she hadn't heard a word, that she hadn't seen the obvious, the patterns of hatred in Molly's face. But shock was working on her, swiftly, numbing her reflexes with skillful hammer taps. Something began beating in her mind like the black wings of a terrified bird. When she finally made a move Molly hooked her arm.

"I'm asking you: *how?*" Molly repeated, serious and intent. "Did you get him into bed with you? But making love is worse than hell—that's what he thinks, you know." Again Molly leaned; her eyes became anguished. Her head drooped. "Maybe you'd better go," she muttered. "Oh, good Lord, get out of here." But she continued to hold tightly to Jeremy's wrist.

"Yes, ma'am," Jeremy said hopefully. She slid to the end of the couch, eyeing Molly incredulously. This woman, and King, she thought; she tasted rotten apples in her mouth. "If you'll just let—"

Instead of letting go, Molly's fingers dug into her wrist. But Molly wasn't trying consciously to hurt her; all of her ill will was centered on an image of King Windom.

"Let him have his *Life* magazine," Molly said thickly. "I want him to be famous. I want his name on every tongue. That's what I planned. Then when he's famous enough, when he has all his glory, then I'll fix him."

Jeremy squirmed. "I'm sorry!" she cried. "I'm sorry; what can I do? Please leave King alone!"

"Leave him alone?" Molly sneered. "I'm going to kill him. No—come within an inch of killing him. A bare inch. I don't know how yet—but I'll find a way. Depend on Molly." She looked strangely lecherous as she stared at Jeremy. "Go ahead and tell him. Won't do any good, he won't believe you. We've made up, we're friends. He's anxious to stay friends. I'm sweet as a peach around him. He'll hate you for bad-mouthing me." Molly's eyes flashed, then she coughed painfully. Her grip on Jeremy loosened; she slumped. "All right, you cheap poke-bottom."

Jeremy got up and made her way rigidly to the other end of the car. But for some reason she couldn't solve the simple mechanics of opening the door. She felt ridiculous. She leaned against the wall in a kind of trance, holding her head.

Molly secured a cigarette from the desk and stood smoking, elbow propped in hand. She studied Jeremy darkly, then she became puzzled. "I thought you were leaving." Jeremy didn't budge. Molly felt slightly worried. Was she putting on an act? She looked on the verge of a falling-down fit. But with that bad eye who could tell? Molly's own mood was somewhat improved now that she had purged herself. She went to open the door for Jeremy. The girl's face was drained. She drew back slightly at Molly's approach.

"Don't you touch me—again!"

"I don't want to touch you."

"I know how to kill snakes," Jeremy said, with a raised lip. "Chop off their heads!"

"What?" Molly looked into the girl's clear eye, which was

unfathomable. She squared her shoulders and forced open the stuck door. Jeremy was motionless. "Do I have to push you out?" Then Molly's heart stirred. "Look," she began, "I don't . . ." and she faltered. "I don't have anything against you. If it hadn't've been you—what I mean is, I don't hate you no matter how I sounded. Is that any help? I—" Molly gave up; she felt chilled. Impulsively she raised her hand in a gesture of conciliation. Jeremy's lip curled again, loathingly. Suddenly she cut and ran, wide-eyed, through the doorway.

Molly, silenced at last, looked after her bitterly. She barely understood the last-minute desire she'd had to keep the girl with her. It wasn't because she was afraid of the stories Jeremy might tell. No, Molly was confident that Jeremy wouldn't be able to say a word.

On her tongue was an aftertaste of the poison that had been stirred up by her fall. Before that spell of vindictiveness she'd truly only wanted a talk, she'd wanted to seek the heart of Jeremy, to pry deep and discover why King had chosen this child for his wife. She sensed that there had been more than one reason. She'd driven him away, yes; but he'd wanted Jeremy even before that night. Why, why, why?

In the empty railroad car Molly's curiosity raged, but there was no longer any way to satisfy it. Eventually she was left with her disinterred threats. For the first time in days Molly wondered if she had the courage to carry them out.

38

The Healing

MIAMI.

Dr. John Matthews stopped writing in his logbook about eleven o'clock, long enough to make another brandy and soda—his fourth of the night, he reminded himself with an insistent cheerfulness—and to have a look out the window of his comfortable drawing room. The black rainstorm which had followed them into the area was still hammering at the Gospel Train, and he could tell very little about his surroundings. He'd seen a few lights, a distant beacon, and what looked like an endless expanse of concrete, submerged a half inch or so in the rain, and he'd decided they were parked either at an abandoned airfield or in an unused corner of an operating field.

Here, a few days after Christmas, King would begin his first extended crusade since leaving Tennessee. The doctor had heard Molly discussing the Miami crusade at dinner, and he knew that she confidently expected an attendance of more than one hundred fifty thousand for the two-week stand. Although she hadn't said so, it was obvious that she planned to spend heavily in Miami.

Charley the photographer had already compiled a series of television announcements—Molly's word for commercials—in color. Dr. Matthews had seen them the night before, at a pep-rally-style screening in the recreation car. Most of the film clips opened with a panoramic shot of the beautiful Train racing along against a spectacular twilight sky, then cut to a filtered, full-screen head-on shot of the engine and the gold cross as the Train pulled into a mobbed station. After that the clips varied in content: there were crowd scenes, emphasizing the faces of earnest young people, mood shots, all of excellent quality, and there was a lot of King: arm in arm with Harlan Gray, preaching from the Gospel Train pulpit, counseling seekers in the chapel. In all his appearances King was serious, composed, literate, and incisive—there were no attempts at stock-revival dramatics. The presence of the Train created all the drama necessary.

If the weather turned good, Dr. Matthews thought, even Molly might be surprised by the numbers attracted to the Southern Cross Crusade. After all, this was their first revival in a large city. He smiled wonderingly. What King had already accomplished was remarkable for a preacher whom he'd seen jousting with the devil, a makeshift firebrand in one hand, only a matter of weeks ago. Of course, you could say the achievement was all Molly's, and not be far wrong. . . .

Dr. Matthews discovered, once he reached the bottom of his glass, that he was pleasantly tight. He was not a man who particularly enjoyed the taste of liquor, and often even a moderate amount gave him trouble physically. But liquor is adequate protection for the man who finds contact with people difficult, and in Matthews' case it provided a bonus—judicious drinking sharpened his intellect, and increased his capacity for work.

He rubbed his reddened nose tenderly and bent to study the pages of the loose-leaf notebook in his lap.

The knock on the door came shortly after the end of the rain. Matthews looked up, startled, and saw by his watch that two hours had passed. In his absorption with his subject, he'd been totally unaware of time.

Stiffly he got to his feet, looked around for shoes, then padded to the door without them. King stood outside, in pajamas, robe, and slippers.

"Doctor, can you come?"

Matthews blinked; there was suffering in the preacher's face. "What's wrong? Are you ill?"

"No. Jeremy . . ." King raised his hands helplessly.

"Let me get my bag." He asked no questions, but followed King immediately to his apartment in coach ten. Outside, the sky was clearing. A fat-bellied military plane droned low, its flashing lights reflected in the water still standing in patches on the old runways.

Jeremy lay on her side in bed, hands covering her face. She was trembling with soundless sobs.

With a glance at the preacher, Matthews sat down on the edge of the bed and spoke to Jeremy.

"Can you tell me what the trouble is?"

Jeremy stiffened and went on weeping. The doctor bit his lip anxiously, then grasped one of Jeremy's wrists and slowly pulled her hand away from her face.

"Don't look at me—I'm afraid for you to look at me!"

"I'm afraid for you to look at *me*," Matthews replied, studying the part of her face he had exposed. She was flushed, but probably not from fever. He felt a puckering at the nape of his neck. "Jeremy, is it your bad eye? Please, let me help you—can't you see?"

Her resistance lessened. She turned on her back, still protecting the left side of her face. She wiped tears from her good eye and looked at him; she was frightened, he saw, but behind her fear there was something else, perhaps some extraordinary joy. She breathed in quick bursts through her lips.

"I woke up, and it was—was dark outside. I saw my face in

the window glass. I saw—" Her mouth contorted; she looked wildly for King. "Is it true? Did it happen? Did a miracle happen?"

Matthews felt the preacher behind him. "Jeremy," King said in a low voice, "show Dr. Matthews your eye."

The doctor drew her hand gently down. Jeremy's eyes were tightly shut.

"Please, Lord, let it be true!"

"It's true, Jeremy," King whispered.

With a long shudder Jeremy timidly opened her eyes and gazed up at their faces. "Do I look—" she said. "*How* do I look?"

"Beautiful, Jeremy," Matthews said after a moment. "Your eye is perfect. Don't believe me? Here, I'll show you." He reached into the medical bag at his foot and withdrew a steel-backed mirror, which he held a few inches above her face. Jeremy stared and stared. The doctor glanced over his shoulder for King's reaction; but the preacher had turned away.

Jeremy raised a cautious hand.

"Go ahead—touch your eye if you want to. It's as real and beautiful as the other one is." Matthews spoke placidly, with a smile, but he was in knots. "Do you mind if I have a closer look—with this gadget?" He held up an ophthalmoscope. "King, could we have more light here?"

He spent several minutes studying the interior of Jeremy's eyes. He was not an authority, but he thought he knew a normal eye when he saw one. He bitterly regretted not having looked at the left eye before this, so he would have had some knowledge of its condition.

All the while he examined Jeremy he was talking to her, asking questions, trying to keep her diverted, and calm. He'd taken her pulse and found it drastically high. He was afraid that the sudden release of trauma in one part of the body might be the signal for a serious, psychosomatic disorder somewhere else. But, although he wanted to get this over with, he felt compelled to ask:

"How much vision did you have in your left eye, Jeremy? Before tonight?"

"I couldn't see at all."

"Were you blind?"

"I don't mean that. I could tell day from night, and

sometimes see bright colors. But no faces. Two years ago I could make out faces around me."

"Bright colors," the doctor said solemnly. "How about this nose of mine? Would you say it was beet red, or just ordinary sunburn red?"

Jeremy smiled halfheartedly; she was becoming restless again.

"Are you in pain?" She shook her head. "Now be honest with the sawbones; tell me what's on your mind."

"I don't deserve . . . a miracle like this! I don't deserve for God to be so good to me!" Tensely she lifted her head from the pillow. "King!"

Matthews gave way to the preacher; King held his wife tightly in his arms. "Jeremy, accept the Lord's gift and bless His precious name!" The doctor retired to a corner of the room and with an unsteady hand fished in his pockets for his seldom-smoked pipe. King looked more disturbed than Jeremy by the—Matthews hesitated, then gave it the name it deserved—the miracle. His lips trembled woefully in prayer; his face was still gouged and nicked by suffering; his eyes were ghastly pink, like flares. Matthews chewed fitfully on the pipe stem, letting King run on. But his prayer was nothing more than jargon; from the expression on Jeremy's face the words simply burned in the flat of her mind like clumps of phosphorus, illuminating, but grotesquely.

He searched his medical bag for a sedative, found one that would allow Jeremy to sleep soundly without wringing her out, filled a paper cup with water, and approached the bed. King looked up, startled, at the weight of the doctor's hand on his shoulder.

"Better let me give her this." He slipped a hand behind Jeremy's head, popped two tablets onto her tongue, and held the cup so she could drink. The bitterness of the sedative seemed to be a relief to her.

"What will that do?"

"Make you sleep. You'll be as bright and fussy as a terrier in the morning."

"I don't want to sleep; I'm afraid when I wake up—"

"King will be right here."

"Yes . . ." Jeremy said, and she savored the anticipation of that moment. Her lips curled in an unconscious smile. "And it was a true miracle, wasn't it, King? God won't just change His mind?"

"You can trust in Him."

"Thank you," she breathed, and then, with loving conviction, "thank you for bringing this miracle to me."

King hunched his shoulders. "Jeremy, it was God's gift, not mine."

"But I know better." Her eyelids drifted shut. "How long before I . . . go to sleep?"

"Any time now." Matthews closed up his bag. "Come see me," he said to King. "If you're able."

The preacher looked at him wordlessly, then shifted his eyes to Jeremy. He was holding fast to one of her hands, chafing the wrist gently.

In his own apartment the doctor poured out two glasses of brandy, all that was left in the bottle. Then he sat beside the rain-beaded window with the homely looking-in mask of his face for company, and watched the beacon in the distance. His thoughts flashed too, from revelation to revelation, and to the beauty of a child restored. He couldn't help himself, his shoulders quaked. He seared his tongue with brandy and grew taut with accustomed scorn, but his manly defenses were of little help, so he gave in and snuffled into the back of his hand, joyously, like an old-timer sitting in a park, watching a summer's-day celebration of his nearly forgotten youth. He drank all of his brandy; the other glass went untouched. Finally, as he was nodding and yawning, with passion, mystery, and a holy warmth in his mind, he heard King at the door and jumped, slow-witted, to answer it.

The preacher still looked sore and wretched, pursued by fatigue; he bumped the jamb hard with his shoulder on the way in.

"Jeremy finally went under. I couldn't bring myself to leave her side until—" He looked around, slow to see. His murky eyes came up to the level of Matthews' face. Reluctance showed in those eyes, and alarm.

The doctor thrust the brandy into King's hands. "Drink it. No, I'm serious; think of it as medicine if you have to."

"Thank y' lot," King muttered, then belted the brandy down with a casual bend of the wrist. He hawked and cleared his throat, rocked a little, and smacked his lips in a satisfied way. "Poor little babe!" he said then. "That angel! We never asked the Lord to heal her poor eye—no, and she wouldn't have wasted sympathy on herself." He clasped his hands, perhaps prayerfully. "But He knew how much it hurt my babe to have that eye wasting away in her head—He knew how she suffered, and blamed herself for sin. Sin! A sinner! It's that damned Philemon who was the sinner; if not for him she wouldn't have hurt herself in the first place." His prayerful hands became cocked fists, and the cold look of a fighting man erased some of the tiredness in his face.

Matthews, who had made a point of becoming acquainted with nearly everyone on the Train, knew that Jeremy and Philemon were related, and he knew of their former loyalty toward, and their dependence upon, old Eli the Prophet. Apparently Jeremy had had serious difficulties with her cousin at one time; the doctor wouldn't have suspected it. In his conversations with the often garrulous Philemon he'd detected no antagonism for Jeremy. He wanted to hear this story, and he wanted to hear so much more from King that his head ached from excitement. All of the preacher's history was on the tip of his tongue tonight. Matthews realized that he longed for a confidant; the healing of Jeremy had opened him up. But King was in a mood for threshing about, for clawing at himself until he found just the right expression of thanksgiving and exultation, and—Matthews thought—if he himself wasn't careful, if he chose the wrong words, if he was sly instead of bold, or too bold and demanding, he would shut the preacher up forever. He would never have another glimpse of the marvelous power which had cleansed Jeremy's eye and strengthened it in an instant, at a touch.

"I thought probably the eye had been accidentally damaged," the doctor said, wanting to turn King's attention back to Jeremy. "From what she told me about the vision she had left—light and color perception—it seemed likely that the optic nerve wasn't damaged. Did the trouble start with a blow on the head?" King nodded; he was still standing in the center of the room with his fists clenched, a faraway look in his eye.

Matthews sat down by the window and took off his tinted glasses, which gave his face an unexpected openness, a guileless charm. He rubbed his forehead and smiled. "When I was interning—all those long years ago—I examined a young man who'd been gored in the head by a bull twelve years before. His eye, when I saw it, looked much like Jeremy's

402

damaged eye, but I believe there was less color in the iris. Two of the extrinsic muscles had been nearly severed by the goring, and, although the muscles had grown back together, they were extremely weak. This weakness caused the eyeball to be pulled out of shape by the stronger muscles—Why don't you sit down here, I'll try to sketch it for you." He lifted his logbook from the other seat and made room for the preacher; King sat gingerly on the front of the seat, long hands dangling.

Matthews took out a piece of scratch paper and explained with a schematic drawing what he was talking about. "I don't know if I have all the muscles hooked up in the right places, but this is the idea." He was deliberately taking his time, attempting to absorb King with medical minutiae; he hoped that if he offered a sound explanation of Jeremy's eye trouble, and pointed out just what had taken place in that instant of healing, King would find it easier to answer some of the potent questions that were crowded in the back of the doctor's mind.

"When the muscles pull at odds, the result not only is severe eyestrain—which may be painless—but also, over a period of time, actual physical damage." The doctor drew a cloud on the lens of the schematic eye. "Cataracts, for instance. The young man I was telling you about had something similar to a cataract—the exudation in the anterior chamber between the cornea and the iris, right about here, was beginning to harden, cutting off his sight. If he'd gone a few more years without treatment, and surgery, the pupil would have collapsed, shutting out all light from the retina. And he would have been totally blind in that eye." Matthews put his pencil aside. "Going on the evidence I have, I think this was Jeremy's trouble. The deterioration was so gradual that she was mostly unaware of it. And of course, she was never in pain."

"Thank God," King said. "Thank God for that!" And his eyes were clearer, he had a strength in him which he hadn't had upon entering the doctor's quarters.

"You should feel proud that you were able to help her."

"I am! Proud, and so grateful to the Lord my God." He twisted his hands together suddenly, but not in agony, the doctor thought; no, it was the still untapped strength in him. This man could uproot a stout tree tonight, he could reach into hell for the devil and drag him from his brimstone ground like a wriggling earthworm; he could gently touch a sleeping girl with those hands, and undo a terrible injury.

"Why?" the doctor asked quietly. "Why did it happen tonight? Do you know why the Power was yours to call—have you ever known just when it would be there?"

King winced and sat back in the seat, his eyes half-focused on the curved ceiling of the room. He started to speak and made only a dry sound; his throat muscles jumped. He lowered his eyes and looked at Matthews, doubtfully. He set his jaw and appeared ready to lunge for the door. The doctor watched him keenly, a long line of sympathy tugging at one corner of his mouth. He felt calm, wide awake, receptive. Some of his calm was transmitted, and King, whose throat was still locked by the caution of many years, became easier in his seat. He seemed to realize that Matthews had been certain of his extraordinary power all along, but had had either the generosity or the insight to wait for King to accept him fully. His hands opened, rested on his knees. He studied the face of Dr. Matthews. There was nothing morbid about the doctor's interest in the magnificent arts of God; he was a gracious, intelligent man with a touch of obsession, and he desired to hurt no one.

"I've known for weeks that I had the Power at my fingertips," King said, but even though most of his reluctance had gone he still spoke in a shadow voice, his words were elusive, and Matthews was forced to lean forward unobtrusively to hear every word. "Not because I had any special desire to heal—someone, anyone. No, healing was far from my mind, I swear. I just knew that God had, for His own dear and inscrutable reasons, taken the curse from my thoughts, redeemed me from my guilt, and allowed His strength and goodness to flow like a warm bath through my flesh. That was strange, different: in the years since the Sugar Tree Valley when I felt the Power, it was always as a cramp or convulsion." He looked closely at his hands, and Matthews was struck, as he had been on other occasions, by the ferocious scars.

"Death by electrocution," King went on, "must be a horrible experience, a tearing-apart and breaking-down into filthy blackness, an unspeakable thing to happen to living flesh. But there's a worse experience, Dr. Matthews, and I say it's worse because I've *lived* through it: I'm talking about God's Power at full flood in the body of a worthless sinner, astream in flesh that can't reject the Power or abide it. Imagine the impact of God's Power against a sick remorseful soul, sickened from the wrong use of that Power! I thought my heart would stop beating—I prayed for it to happen. I thought my eyes would burst in their sockets. The experience was so awful that I had to lie to myself, I had to shout against the howling in my head that it wasn't the Power at all—it was only a wish to die, a monstrous thing of the mind gone crazy in my flesh. That was the lie I told myself, and I was satisfied."

For a few moments anxiety wea‿ ‿ned him, and his head fell back. He trembled with every breath.

"How do you feel now?" the doctor asked him, wondering what had happened to the two ounces of brandy the preacher had swallowed; probably it had turned into an unnoticeable vapor in the flash fire of his bloodstream.

"I'm fine," the preacher asserted. "A month ago I would have cried out, Lord, what have You done to me? But now I want to sing a worshiping song. I'd like to sing of Jeremy, beautiful now, the way she deserves to be. I want to embrace my God and say to Him, Look what we've wrought together!" He struggled upright, his expression beatific. "Isn't it strange what victory means to a human heart?"

Matthews smiled. "I'd put it this way: the heart thrives on a great victory, as long as the commonplace has kept it alive, some small glint of beauty that won't be ignored, or forbidden. You never wanted to die, or He didn't want you to— What's wrong?"

"I think I should be ashamed; did you hear what I said? 'What we've wrought together!' "

"He won't object because you want to soar—to feel the heat of His love a little more strongly than you can with your feet on the earth." Matthews felt a tugging of impatience in his mind; he was afraid that King might get away from him yet, before he had a chance to learn it all, to see where the hints of shattering guilt and abuses of God's Power would take them.

"Could I ask something more about Jeremy?" King gave his attention, but he was restive. "She said that she awoke, and saw her face in the mirror of the window. Was she asleep, then, when you . . . transformed her with the healing Power?"

King nodded.

"What prompted you?"

The preacher, with his lips compressed, thought it over. "Jeremy had been feeling bad the past two days. I couldn't find out what was deviling her. It wasn't something I'd done, I'm sure of that, because she let me hold her like always—I can't come close when she's really peeved at me. But she didn't have an appetite and she stuck to our rooms. When I came in tonight from taping my radio program she was already in bed asleep. I took my shower and sat down with a parts catalogue—needing a new drive chain for my motor. A little while after that Jeremy commenced having a nightmare. And it must have been a bad one. I got up to see if I could do her any good. I reached down to straighten the bed covers and then I felt the Power in my hands, but it wasn't overwhelming. I just knew I had to lay my hands against the left side of her head, like this." He demonstrated, with one hand overlapping the other. "That's all I did—it couldn't have been for more than three or four seconds. Both my hands trembled, and I felt the—the muscles of my right forearm contract, and it was over and done with. Jeremy didn't wake up, but she was peaceful. To tell the truth, Doctor, I didn't know what I had done. I was puzzled; the Power had been strong, but gentle too. I didn't give a thought to her poor eye. Right away I felt tired; I lay down beside her, and I expect I dozed off. Next thing I knew Jeremy was shaking me and—and sobbing, saying a miracle had come to pass."

"This wasn't a new experience for you. But when I opened the door tonight you looked . . . shocked; you were suffering."

"For a good reason," King said, his expression grim. He gazed out the window, preoccupied but in control of himself. "Yes, I was shocked," he muttered under his breath. "Because I couldn't believe—" Abruptly he spoke up. "Doctor, forgive me, but I'm wondering how far I can trust you."

"With what?"

"With my life."

Matthews waited, knowing that he would have to give a difficult and perhaps unsatisfactory answer. But King was in no hurry; he'd made a decision. Depending on what the doctor had to say he would either rise, shake hands politely, and take his leave, or he would stay and strip himself unsparingly.

"I have the deepest respect for you, and for your work," Matthews told him when he had his thoughts in order. "I'm attracted to you because—as I said the first time we met—you're a figure of valor, and my own life is, has been, a waste. The idea of being responsible for your life in any sense—even a medical one—causes anguish. While I practiced medicine I was directly responsible, many times, for the lives of others, and I always felt inadequate. I feel inadequate now." He paused; King's

406

eyes were on him inquiringly, but the preacher's expression gave no indication of his feelings. Matthews looked again at Kings's hands.

"I want to be important to you in some way. You must know that's why I came aboard the Gospel Train in the first place. And that's why I began this logbook." He handed the heavy black book over to King, and with a nod of his head encouraged the preacher to leaf through the neatly written pages. "It's about you, and the Southern Cross Crusade. There's not much so far. I began it with few certainties. I knew only that you were an extraordinary man, capable of both profound reflection and meaningful action. Although you didn't encourage me, I held fast to my belief that you had a rare and great talent for healing; for the best of reasons you chose not to use your Power, or admit to it. I felt that your reticence might have had its beginnings in tragedy of some sort."

King didn't reply immediately; he was reading. When he had closed the book and passed it back to Matthews he said only, "Interesting. You write real well, Doctor."

"But does it please you?"

"I don't know."

Matthews smiled. "I'm ready to leave the Train whenever you say."

"No. You've been entirely honest with me. I wouldn't want you to go." He made himself more comfortable, extending his legs and crossing his bare ankles. "I'm sorry I had to question your good faith; call it a quirk of my mind. I realize your interest in me and the Power isn't—hmmmm, what's the word?—meretricious. After all, you've had a taste of it yourself. I'll tell you whatever you'd like to know about me, and answer all questions."

By the time he had finished talking it was nearly dawn. Despite three pain-killing tablets, Dr. Matthews' head ached dully, and King's voice was a croak. Once during the preacher's long and heartbreaking reconstruction of his life in the Sugar Tree Valley both men had been moved to tears. The doctor was gratified by the extent of King's belief in him, and enormously excited by what he had heard. He faced several more hours of getting it all on paper, but he'd never felt more eager to work.

King moved around the sizable room at a listless pace, building air castles with one motion of his hands, then collapsing them with another. He was still keyed up; his thoughts flashed almost too fast to be expressed.

"Now I have a question, Doctor, one question: what good will it do? What difference will your book make if and when it's read a hundred years from now? Men believe what they want to believe. God's Power is a holy mystery; can you explain it? Can I? You know more about me than any living man. I told Jim Cobb that the Power was gone, and I believed it myself at the time. Now you can see that I wasn't exaggerating when I said I was putting my life in your hands. But what light have we shed on the Divine Power of healing? I'm nothing, a cipher, a vessel; God has used me. Is there anything else to say?"

"No; not if God is first, last, and always the source of healing Power. But what if the Power is independent of God's Will?"

King stopped and peered at him, unhappily. "Impossible." He yawned. Matthews realized that he was eager to go. "What time do you have there? Four-thirty? Well . . . we've covered everything, far as I know." He turned an expectant eye on the doctor.

"Enough for one night," Matthews agreed. He tapped the cover of his book with a fist. "But what about the future? The Power is yours, God-given, God-restored, however you'd put it. What do you intend to do with the Power? Others like the Northcutts may come. Men who've heard of you, and who need you."

"I won't see them," King said flatly, and the skin around his mouth was white. "I won't have to—this Train travels fast. It can travel faster than all the rumors Satan might whisper about me. I won't misuse God's Power again. I think I would—I would surely lie down beneath the wheels of the Gospel Train and die rather than lay my hands on another sick body." He was tense with dread at the thought.

"There's Jeremy, though."

"Yes; I'll have to tell Jeremy about the Power, and Age will know what's happened. But no one else needs to know." He pondered for a few moments, eyes closed. "We're spending Christmas with close friends of mine from over by Fort Myers. Frank and a couple of the kids are driving down early, around six, to pick us up. None of them know Jeremy, they've never seen her. With your help, Doctor, I reckon we can get away without anybody from the Train noticing us. Then when we come back—Saturday, that'll be—Jeremy will have her eye bandaged and we'll say that she had an operation during the holidays." He fell silent, then looked uncertainly at the doctor, who gave a contemplative nod.

"It's a plausible story, and I'll help you in any way I can." Matthews stood, the logbook under his arm. He gave King a professional sizing up. "How do you feel now?"

"Like I've missed another night's sleep," the preacher said dully. "I'll snap back—I always do."

"I'd like to check you over, quickly, before—"

King shied visibly at the suggestion, and shook his head.

"I can prescribe for you, then. A muscle relaxant, or a couple of mild sleeping capsules."

"No, no, I'm not much for popping pills." His smile was strained. "Not counting those slippery elm throat lozenges, which are a godsend, I don't reckon I've chewed so much as an aspirin in the last twenty years." He straightened his shoulders and glowed with physical pride. "Few hours from now I'll be with people I love, and I'll be having a high old time. Nothing pleases me like sitting in the end of a boat going after bonito with light tackle. They're medium-size fighting fish, Doctor, not fit to eat, but a certain thrill to catch." He wet his parched lips with a cup of water and rubbed his throat. "If you'll stop around . . . I'd like for you to meet Frank, and Jeremy will want to say good-bye."

"I'll be sure to."

"Hope you won't get lonely over the holidays; nearly everybody is taking off for somewhere."

"It's been several years since I felt any nostalgia at Christmas time. I have more than enough work to keep me occupied."

When King was gone, Matthews sat down again by the window, favoring a weakness low in his back. Dawn was coming; the storm sky had been broken and rutted by the machinery of heaven, and the airfield looked like a sky in itself, evenly glazed by a thin pink light. It was a curious inversion, and the doctor felt lightheaded, pleasantly insensible. He closed his eyes gratefully; he was just conscious of the weight of the black book against his side.

Yes, he'd told King the truth, there'd be no time for loneliness. He would need a full week to get the preacher's story into the book, to record his own observations and suppositions. Then—would that be all? he wondered. Would the logbook end abruptly, inconclusively? For King's sake it must. He could not live in peace with his unearthly healing Power, and so he had to deny it, suppress it. All of the doctor's sympathies were with King and his decision, but still he felt a sharp regret. The Power would be wasted; perhaps, unused, it would simply disappear.

It distressed him to think that he would not have the opportunity for further, repeated observations of healing phenomena, the opportunity to keep accurate records of King's psychological and physical reactions. He would have ordered expensive equipment in a minute to keep such priceless records, including electroencephalograms—"EEGs." Several times during King's monologue he had even had excited thoughts about hiring an assistant—but there were limits to the preacher's tolerance. Even if he were prepared to heal again—carefully, judiciously—he would never consent to lengthy physical examinations each time.

All this was wishful thinking, Matthews reminded himself. The decision had been made: it was irrevocable.

But as he rested, a possible dilemma occurred to him. There are few authentically great and gifted men; had any of them been able to resist involvement with the less fortunate who seek their wisdom, their experience and advice? A man with great healing Power, like King Windom, was nearly unique. Because of his gift he could restore life to a dying man. How many of the afflicted, once King's name and an insinuation of his Power had fallen upon their ears, would rest a single moment until they had clawed or beaten their way to his side? The more he tried to avoid them, the more desperate such people would become.

Dr. Matthews held the book in his hands, and for the first time he fully realized what he was about to do. To many men the contents of his book would be more valuable than a title to the earth.

He shuddered, and drew a long breath. Then, taking out his fountain pen, he turned to a fresh ruled sheet of paper and began unhesitatingly to write.

39

Sanibel

In a very short time after she'd been introduced into the Henderson family group, Jeremy was knee-deep in children, all of them angling for her exclusive attention. Before midday she'd been coaxed into the first swimsuit she had ever worn and she was out on the long pier by the trailer village inspecting and praising the various handcrafted sailboats of the young clan, faced with the impossible task of selecting one for her first voyage down the wide Caloosahatchee. King watched all this activity with a proud indulgence, then left her in the hands of the kids and went off to fish with Frank Henderson, his brother Averill, and Age.

Jeremy's skin apparently was indestructible. After a half day under a sun that would have crisped the average female, she was a suspicious but painless red. Then, overnight, she turned a marvelous rum brown. By sundown of her second day Jeremy had forgotten all self-consciousness at revealing a major part of her body in the skimpy tropical-weather dress everyone seemed to favor. King approved; that was enough for her. The Gospel Train and the punishing cycle of revivals seemed far away indeed.

The eight children of the brothers ranged from ages six to fifteen, and they were of a kind—versatile, self-sufficient, shrewd, and eminently manageable. She quickly learned them well enough to speak to each in a separate, special way. She had no favorites and didn't play favorites, but little Coral Henderson, with her pale-blond thatch and wahine warmth, seemed to have a rare knack for snuggling in next to the heart, and her brother Tim, a dark-eyed and manly fourteen, treated Jeremy with unusual courtesy and remarkable patience, considering that she possessed none of the skills that were second nature to him; she couldn't even swim.

More than once Jeremy felt with a twinge that she should spend more time with the older members of the family, so she dutifully dropped around to the trailer kitchens, intending to scrub pans and make small talk. But the children's conspiracy was relentless and one or another of them always appeared to haul her off.

"Now where is she?" King asked more than once, having just missed his wife, and they always said the same thing:

"Let Jeremy have her fun."

Christmas Eve morning the family loaded themselves, two dogs, and several dozen presents into their station wagons and made the trip across the causeway to the lodge on Sanibel Island. There was a crisp wind to swell the gray-green sea, and once they were there the children went hurtling and yelping into the low surf with hardly a pause. Jeremy helped store provisions in the pantry, was taken on a tour of the spacious lodge, and then went wandering off by herself in a happy daze, the Gulf wind tangling her hair, the white sand of the beach warm on her bare feet and ankles. Some of the children clamored from the water below, wanting her to come in for a swimming lesson—it had become a group project—but she shook her head and sank down, face to the sky, smiling, feeling as if she were in a dream.

A touch on the shoulder caused her to look up quickly.

"Oh . . . I thought it was King."

Frank Henderson shook his head. "He and Averill are arguing about who runs over to the marina for the cruiser. I decided to have my one smoke of the day and Lil ran me out of the lodge." He held up an evil-looking green cigar and winked. "Care to take a walk with me, Jeremy? I solemnly promise to stay downwind."

Frank helped her to her feet and they set off at a leisurely pace down the beach. He paused three times to shield his cigar from the wind while he got it started, then puffed away contentedly. He was wearing the same costume King favored—rumpled Bermuda shorts, a chopped-up cotton jersey, and aviator's sunglasses. Jeremy didn't mind the smoke and she was flattered that this man, whom King revered, had made a point of inviting her along.

"Well," Frank said, when they were around a bend from the lodge, "any complaints about that big old boy you're married to? I've still got the better part of two days to straighten him out; just say the word."

"Oh, I reckon he'll do the way he is." She grinned. "But I'll be sure to tell him about your offer the next time we get to disagreeing." As she looked at Henderson, it seemed odd to think that King's own parents were dead, and that he had known these people for only a few years: she could not have chosen a better father for him than this man. Jeremy wondered how they had met. Neither she nor King talked about their lives. Jeremy had little to talk about except poverty, the life of a kettle cousin, and King was just close-mouthed. . . . A shudder raked across her shoulders.

Frank saw the look on her face. He pretended to be short of breath and pointed the way to a length of driftwood. They sat down together on the bleached wood, within a few yards of the sea.

"Looked as if you had something on your mind," Frank observed during a lull in the wind.

"Nothing much. But I was wondering . . . King never has said how you two got together."

"Oh, he hasn't?" Out to sea a tanker had come into view, so low in the water it seemed to be half-sunk. He stared at it for a few moments, a forgotten smile on his face. "About five years ago he had a little country church, but his heart wasn't in that kind of preaching. He wanted to be an evangelist. Of course, you know all that. But he decided he couldn't make his start on a shoestring, so one day he—he and Age together, they showed up at the carnival ground, we were playing somewhere in east Tennessee at the time, and asked for a job. It happened I needed a couple of extra men. So . . ."

"That's the same as he told Eli the first time they met." Jeremy frowned. "Do you know how he burned his hands?"

"Burned . . . Oh, I recall he and Age were working on a piece of machinery one time and there was a flash fire, some grease caught accidentally."

Jeremy nodded, but her mind was far away; she seemed to

hear another voice behind the wind. "He told me it was live coals, though. I probably don't remember correctly. The night he went to work for Eli I took him a couple of fried egg sandwiches and hot coffee, and we talked. King said that he had burned himself for . . . atonement. And he said—let me remember now . . ." She lowered her head for a few moments, concentrating. "He said that he never had questioned the Will of God, no matter what. He said God's Will is powerful enough to bring down whole nations, and sometimes it's . . . like a wraith, invisible as air. And sometimes men mistake the Will of God, so they suffer." She looked soberly at Frank Henderson. "He also said, 'Once God condemned me, then He let me live. I'll never rest until I know the reason why.' Do you know what he meant by that, Mr. Henderson?"

"I'm . . . afraid I don't, Jeremy."

"But it was just a fire in a motor that burned him, that's all."

"Yes."

Jeremy laughed. "Well, you must think I'm making a fuss over nothing. He never hurt himself on purpose, that you know of? Not for atonement, or for any reason."

"He's not that kind of person, Jeremy." Frank grasped her hand to reassure her. "Why the dark thoughts?"

"I suppose I . . . nearly go crazy at times, worrying that something might happen to him. I suppose I hate that Train." She laughed again, nervously. It was the first time she'd been able to express her true feelings so bluntly. "I'll just be real happy when we're off it, and settled down. I do enjoy traveling, but . . ." She stomped a pit in the damp sand with her heel. An iron band was tightening around her heart. She longed to tell Frank Henderson about the healing of her eye, and King's desire—no, it was almost an anxiety—to diminish the miracle he'd wrought, to keep it a secret from everyone. But surely he could trust this man, who loved him. Jeremy felt unbearably confused. King had treated the miracle as if it were an evil thing, and although he'd spoken of God's merciful Power of healing, he'd said no more, he had resented her questions and her curiosity. Couldn't he trust her either?"

Frank gave her hand a squeeze and she straightened up guiltily.

"Jeremy, is there any reason at all why you think—Has there been some sort of trouble aboard the Train that King hasn't told me about?"

She shook her head emphatically. "No, everything's fine. He—he works too hard, is all."

Frank peeled a flake of tobacco from his lip. "He always has. That's why I'm so happy he has you now, Jeremy. He loves you very much and with good reason—you're a beautiful and thoughtful young lady."

Jeremy, who was not used to praise, felt her eyes stinging. "Thank you," she murmured.

They heard a holler from up the beach and turned to see King plodding toward them.

"First time I've had you to myself for a few minutes . . ." Frank grumbled; then he caught Jeremy's eye again. "I wanted to know if there was trouble brewing somewhere because of Age's attitude. He's like a different man altogether, Jeremy; yesterday I fished four hours in the same boat with Age and I swear I didn't know him at all. Bitterness has marked him, and something else I couldn't give a name to. Resignation? Defeat? Whatever's biting at his bones may be a simple thing. But I can't help—" In sudden exasperation he almost hurled his half-smoked cigar away. "I'm getting old, raving on like this. Age has his moods, like any normal man, and who am I to think—" He checked himself and with one hand jauntily lifted the girl to her feet. Side by side in the sand they were of the same height.

Frank sensed a tremor in Jeremy, as if she was eager to run to her husband. But he held her back momentarily.

"If that Train begins to get on your nerves real bad," he said sternly, "well, then, tell that big old boy to put you on an airplane and you come on home here—for as long as you'd like to stay."

"Yes, yes, I will!" Jeremy said, her eyes bright and amazed, then she hugged him so enthusiastically that he dropped his cigar into the sand.

"Jeremy! How about a picnic? There's a little island up the Sound I want to show you . . ."

"Coming!" Jeremy hollered. She pulled back for a long thankful look at Frank's face and dashed off, flinging up sand with each step. King caught her on the fly and whirled her around. Frank waved to them both and refused a share of the picnic lunch at the top of his voice. He set his shoulders, feeling a quick sadness, then peace. He also felt very pleased with himself, just as if he'd discovered Jeremy there on the deserted beach, as if he had watched her grow, from babe to sprite to woman, in the batting of an eye, and had this instant turned her loose in the world.

He left his cigar for curious sandpipers and diligent crabs to pull apart and began slowly to gather driftwood for the towering bonfire they would all build on the beach that night, the traditional bonfire. Even the older kids knew that without this night-long beacon Santa Claus wouldn't be able to find his way across the dark Gulf of Mexico to their lodge on the shore.

40

The Logbook

Molly found that Christmas afternoon was a bad time to run out of liquor; not being able to obtain a drink easily made her want one all the more. She was faced with the choice of doing without or getting decently dressed, leaving the Train, and taking a cab to the nearest cocktail lounge, where, no doubt, she would be the lone customer on a fine if somewhat sultry afternoon. She was repulsed by the image of celebrating her Christmas in such a conspicuously lonely way. Besides, she hated bars; the best of them were saturated with odors that set her delicate nose to twitching.

It occurred to Molly that cooking sherry or sauterne would make an adequate substitute for her preferred brand of whiskey, so she picked up a set of the right keys in the office and walked back through the deserted and stuffy Gospel Train to the diner, where she prowled with rapidly lessening enthusiasm through the kitchen stores. She discovered not so much as a thimbleful of wine and finally gave up, feeling annoyed with her restiveness. Well, perhaps a good steak house on Miami Beach would do. The trio of magazine staffers were coming aboard the Train about 8 P.M. for a preliminary briefing, but there was plenty of time if she really wanted to make the effort. Of course, there was the problem of being alone. . . .

Molly had a brainstorm. What about John Matthews? He'd scarcely stuck his nose out of his apartment in three days' time. Probably he would jump at the chance of an evening out. And he was company, of a sort.

Molly returned briskly to coach twelve and knocked on the doctor's door, but there was no response. She frowned, wondering if he could be asleep. Repeated knockings confirmed that he had left the Train. Molly shrugged and got off herself, partly for the fresh air and partly to look again for flaws in her plans for the revival.

Wooden bleachers, capable of holding more than seven thousand people, had been set up on the runway of the old Navy field, facing the Gospel Train. In addition there was plenty of good standing room, and Molly had spent the past hour going through stacks of confirmations from church groups who were coming by bus from as far away as Lakeland during the ten days of the crusade. Notices in several south Florida newspapers that a team from *Life* magazine would be on hand to photograph the proceedings had created even more interest in the Gospel Train and in King Windom. Molly had briefly considered hiring the Orange Bowl for a couple of nights and she had made inquiries, but there was too much football this time of the year. Besides, a throng of ten thousand at the Gospel Train siding would be impressive, spectacular; the same ten thousand in the Orange Bowl would cause no comment; the stadium was just too big. A year from now they would come back, and—she'd bet her life on it—they would fill the Orange Bowl to capacity. Had Harlan Gray pulled off such a feat? Molly doubted it.

Sitting high in the bleachers with the sun at her back, looking out over a freeway and a complex of pastel houses with blazing white tile roofs, Molly was struck by the fact that her thoughts of King caused no emotion; he simply existed for her, as the Train existed. Would all that change when she saw him again? Would she lapse into brooding, and sicken with the need to drag him down, to be revenged for his horrible contempt of her? Molly sensed the truth, and she lifted her head to stare raptly at the Gospel Train, which she had made, which was hers; the beautiful Train had become more important than anything else in her life. Molly ground her teeth together. Hurt him! It would be an easy thing, as she had threatened, to come within a bare inch of killing King Windom, merely by destroying his pride. She was filled with the most amazing plots and treacheries, and she would not have hesitated to sacrifice her own pride (the little he had left her with) to see him humiliated beyond endurance, and perhaps jailed. But if King suffered and fell from grace, the Gospel Train would quickly roll to a stop, sit once again silent and dark, forgotten, in some city's railroad yard. This thought frankly terrified Molly, and she badly wanted a relaxing jolt of whiskey.

She remembered then, belatedly, that Dr. Matthews was, and always had been, a consistent boozer; without a doubt there were three or four kinds of liquor sitting on the shelf of a closet in his quarters. He wouldn't miss a couple of ounces. His door was locked, but Molly had the master keys to every room on the Train stashed in her office safe.

As it turned out she was right about the doctor's private hoard, and although he was low on blended, he had a nearly full bottle of cognac, which Molly dearly loved. She wandered around the sitting room with the bottle in one hand and a bathroom glass in the other, dreamily inhaling the cognac. The setting sun gave a glow to the room like a lazy wood fire on a hearth. Molly sat down and her thoughts scratched and licked about, catlike. Opposite her was a writing board with an old-fashioned pen and a bottle of ink on it, and a black-covered notebook. Idly she picked up the notebook and thumbed through it, her eyes unfocused. Then she began reading. And looked up, sharply, staring. And gave her shoulders a shake and turned to page one.

Forty-five minutes later, when Molly heard Matthews enter the coach, she was still reading. The door to his room was open and Molly saw no reason to stir herself. A cigarette had burned close to her fingers and she reached out absently to drop the remains in the glass she had been drinking from. When he appeared in the doorway Molly looked up with a faint smile.

"Caught me red-handed."

His reaction was surprising. He lunged toward her and snatched the book from her lap. Molly had never seen him angry before; she hadn't known he could get angry.

"This is my room, Mrs. Amos! *My* room. You don't have any right to be here. These are *my* personal things. Who do you think you are, snooping around?"

"Snooping?" Molly said, wounded to the quick. "Who's

snooping?" He was holding the book as if he were going to smash it down on her head. His face was deeply flushed. Molly squared her shoulders.

"Look, *Doctor*," she said, her voice a little hard and her tone haughty, "I desperately wanted a drink to take the edge off a long day and I knew you kept a bottle or two around. I'll pay you back for what I drank. There's the bottle; you can see I—"

"How long have you been in here?" he demanded. He looked at the drinking glass, which contained half a dozen butts. The cords of his neck stood out and Molly felt slightly unsure of herself in the face of all this wrath.

"That door was locked, and you broke in here," he said accusingly.

"I did not break in, I had—All right, I'm sorry. Just calm down, Dr. Matthews."

"You get out of my room!"

"Look, don't threaten me. You're on this Train by my sufferance, you know. I can have you put off just any time."

He moved a step closer. "We'll see what King has to say about that."

Molly's eyes were drawn to the black book.

"Speaking of our preacher, maybe you and I better have a talk," she said, forgetting their argument.

Dr. Matthews glared a moment or two longer, then turned and went into the next room, banging the door behind him.

Molly let go a sigh and lit another cigarette. The evening sky was a pretty sight and she gave it her attention, but the fingers of her left hand jumped and curled on the chair arm.

Eventually the doctor came out, quietly, and his face was a less frenzied color. He was not surprised to find Molly still enjoying his hospitality. He cleared a space on the seat opposite her and sat down, clutching his book. He looked at her unforgivingly.

"How much did you read?"

"All of it. Twice." She hesitated, groping for a suitable expression of her feelings. "And it's incredible. If I didn't know him so well I'd say it was a lie, a horrid sick fantasy. But he doesn't know how to lie, and mentally he's—" She grimaced. "He *is* all right mentally? I mean—"

Matthews nodded. "He's perfectly sane, Molly."

"That I would say is remarkable, under the circumstances." She was plainly relieved, but there was more on her mind.

"Could all of these cases of—of religious healing be genuine? I'm not questioning King's truthfulness now, only his judgment. According to what you've written, most of the healings took place under extremely emotional conditions; there was weeping, wailing, and mass confusion."

"King's admitted that he failed many times, that he failed often. The cases I've detailed are the ones he was most sure about. He returned to those people week after week. He found no evidence that they had been misleading, or misled, about the seriousness of their afflictions. A good many had medical treatment prior to seeking King's help."

"The lady with the twisted spine—that was a shocker. You wonder how many there are like her, hopelessly, unmentionably ill or injured, hidden away in back bedrooms somewhere. Pardon me, Doctor, but your book has given me the jimjams. I almost rifled your medical bag for the smelling salts before I was through reading the first time."

Matthews offered a very faint smile of sympathy and rose to hunt for his pipe. He seemed to have recovered most of his self-possession. "I don't know who is to blame, Molly, because you've had access to highly confidential information about a . . . patient of mine. I shouldn't have left the book lying around even behind a locked door, so I'll share the blame." He looked briefly pained. "I'm sorry I called you a snoop. I lost my temper. I didn't think that was possible anymore."

"Oh, don't worry about it, Dr. Matthews. Say, as long as I've already opened the brandy . . ."

Matthews found two clean glasses and Molly poured. He sat down again. There were new hard lines in his face that she rather admired, and when he spoke she was soberly attentive.

"King has placed a great deal of trust in me, and given me his friendship. Inadvertently I've betrayed him. I hope nothing will come of my betrayal."

Molly sipped her cognac. "You don't have anything to worry about, Doctor."

"Because if anything does come of it, I'll blame you. Don't take my words lightly. I'll look for you, Molly, with a good stout paddle in my hand. I might not appear to be, but I'm strong for my age. In my time I've treated fraternity boys who were worked over enthusiastically with a single paddle, and I know how utterly miserable one can feel for weeks afterward, without having any serious injury to show for the ordeal."

Molly blinked and felt no urge to comment on this soft-spoken warning. "If you'll look at it a different way, it's good thing I found out about his—his Power. Beginning Thursday King will have a lot of reporters around him, including a very astute and thorough gentleman from *Life*. I plan to moderate King's press conferences, of course, and tonight I'm going to put together a sizable mimeographed biography I've been working on. I hope the biography will satisfy all questioners. If anyone wants to pry just on the chance of coming up with something dirty, I think I'm equipped now to handle that situation without raising suspicions. I can be remarkably bland and persuasive when I want to be."

"I know you can."

Her tone changed. "I'm going to be very careful with the press from now on because of what even a few suspicions can do to King. He's being watched and I hope approved because he's a damned fine preacher, earnest and inspirational, with just enough rough edges. If word gets around that King is or has been a faith healer, we'll lose our best audience, the square-in-the-middle Baptists, Methodists, and Presbyterians. They'll put him down along with the seedy ghetto types—anything for a buck: black magic and resurrections—and they'll stay away forever. If they do, then so much for what we're trying to build."

Dr. Matthews raised his glass until the liquor in it caught the light. She couldn't tell what he was thinking. Then he put down a lump of the cognac and his eyes softened. "I think we both appreciate the danger in King's situation, particularly when there are many people living who will never forget his name or what he . . . tried to do for them. I feel better about . . . sharing it all with you. I know there are reasons why you might be feeling a great deal of resentment toward King. I'm not interested in discussing the sources of your resentment. I only hope you'll be able to keep your feelings in check."

"Why, of course," Molly said, but there was an unpleasant taste in her mouth which even the mellow cognac couldn't neutralize.

Late that night as she typed the biography, Molly found it difficult to concentrate on anything but King's life in the Sugar Tree Valley, of which she had not written a word. Earlier she had looked for the Valley on a road atlas, but it was not listed.

King hadn't been specific about the location, according to Dr. Matthews' logbook. The Valley was somewhere in western Virginia, in that ragged blade of land thrust between the states of Kentucky and Tennessee. Ridge country. The Appalachian Mountains began a little to the north. She had a hazy picture in mind: bad roads and lonely cabins, settlements in the flats, low skies and, this time of year, torturous weather—wind-driven rain and snow and the hills black as coffins. Here he'd lived a long winter and discovered a monstrous art. How had the people looked at King Windom then—with love and thanksgiving? Had they seen an angel in him, a light of Heaven? Or had he driven some of them half mad because he was only half successful, because he failed more men than he healed?

Molly rested her sore head. What had King's wife thought of him? Mary Kate Ransom had suffered most for his failures—even more than the preacher himself. Perhaps she would have lost her child anyway. If I had been his wife, Molly thought, I would have forgiven him. But he should have gone back to her, as soon as he was able. If he had returned in two months, or three, would Mary Kate Ransom have died?

And what had Mary Kate been like? Molly dragged herself up and brewed a pot of coffee. Was she dark or fair, was she thin or plump or prematurely gnarled as some country women are? Had the preacher really loved her? Molly was intrigued by this line of speculation. If he had loved Mary Kate, she decided, then he would have risked anything to get back to the Sugar Tree Valley, once he recovered his senses.

Molly felt despondent as she drank her coffee, and despite the fact that she knew nothing of Mary Kate a strong feeling of kinship possessed her. Had Mary Kate died as Molly had thought she herself was going to die—of King Windom's indifference? Only Age knew for sure what had happened to Mary Kate during those months in the Valley after the preacher's disappearance. And he had reported very little, if King's memory was accurate. Perhaps there was nothing to tell. But Molly wasn't so sure.

She went to bed after two sleeping capsules designed to nail her head to the pillow, but her dreams gave her no peace and right after dawn she awoke with the world looking queer and yellow; Mary Kate was still on Molly's mind, and she continued to be for several more days.

Around ten o'clock on Thursday morning, when the Train

had come to life with everyone returning from the Christmas break, Molly sent for Age and received him somewhat anxiously at her desk in the office.

"I've been working on a biography of King," she told him, "and I want it ready for mimeographing at noon. I've decided not to mention his marriage to Mary Kate Ransom because . . . well, it only lasted a few months and ended tragically, and it might inspire more questions than King cares to answer." She was watching Age closely and, to her disappointment, he failed to show the slightest flicker of caution. He simply stared at her with a dislike he wasn't troubling to hide. Molly already felt tense because of a drug hangover and she had to bite down on her tongue to keep from telling him off. But she said pleasantly, "King told me about Mary Kate, of course, a few days before we left Clearwater. But he didn't say anything about her death, except that it happened quickly. I gathered it was . . . pneumonia, something like that."

She paused, wondering how much she could risk saying. "I don't want to bother King today, he has enough to cope with. I thought you could tell me about Mary Kate. When she died, and of what; where she's buried."

Age was silent for so long that Molly almost lost her temper. But then he shifted in his seat, and took his eyes from her face. "It was pneumonia. I can't remember just when she died. Late in the winter, about six years ago. She's buried in the churchyard."

Molly nodded. "The churchyard there in the Sugar Tree Valley."

"That's what I mean." Age stood up. "I've got work setting up the portable toilets if you're through with me."

"What did she look like?" Molly asked quickly.

He gazed knowingly at her and almost smiled. "Her hair was long and thick. Black in color. And she had bright-blue eyes. Her nose was too thin, but even so she was a pretty woman."

"Many of her family still living?"

"I never knew of any other Ransoms."

"Oh," Molly said lightly, "I thought you might have talked to some of her family when you went back."

"I was back one day, and I didn't talk to a soul. . . ." Gloom gathered in his velvet eyes, and he looked at Molly in a new way, and blinked once. His face became hard as ebony.

"Then how do you know what she died of, Age? If you only went back one day . . . if you didn't talk to a soul?"

She had taken a chance, and said too much. But Molly was convinced she had Age trapped.

"I *heard* talk," he said. He hesitated too long before speaking, however, and knew it.

Molly hit at this weakness with all her sharp teeth showing. "I'm beginning to wonder what you heard—what you saw. What lies you may be telling!"

Age took a step back, softly, and began to turn, his expression bitter. Then he stopped and stiffened. "*I'm* beginning to wonder," he said, "why King puts up with you—why any of us do."

"You *are* lying about something—aren't you? Speak up, nigger!"

His hands trembled as if he longed to reach for her, and Molly, fascinated, stared at him. But Age controlled himself so effortlessly that no one working in the office would have noticed, if he had taken time to look up, that anything unusual was going on.

"No," Age said deliberately, "I don't lie." He picked up his soiled and spotted felt hat from the top of a filing cabinet, squared it on his welted head, and walked leisurely to the door.

Molly leaned back in her chair, and excitement struck horridly in the pit of her stomach like the blurred head of a viper.

41

A Job for Philemon

On the twenty-seventh day of January, Cowboy arrived in Jacksonville and took a cab from the airport to the Gospel Train. His driver seemed to know exactly where the Train was without being told, an indication that the one-day Jacksonville crusade had attracted quite a lot of notice. The cabby had his say about evangelists. They were all frauds, they bled poor people and lived in penthouses. Hadn't he read in the paper just the other day about this evangelist in Texas who had a speedboat and six wives? Cowboy agreed in monosyllables with everything the cabby had to say and the conversation soon ended.

The afternoon portion of the crusade was in progress and a light rain was falling. Despite the rain and the gloomy tone of the day, Cowboy observed that the crowd numbered around three thousand. Some of the people had found shelter under a big canvas provided by a local caterer and many had umbrellas, but the rest seemed content to stand in the open with water dripping down the back of their necks. King was almost as wet as they, although Martin Handwerker was doing his best to keep an umbrella over the preacher's head.

Cowboy paused to look the crowd over more thoroughly. It was after four and there was a big group of school children on hand. Not so many Negroes, however, and Cowboy wondered why. Perhaps because the Negroes preferred a different kind of revival, the kind King had given them under the old canvas back in Tennessee.

In his compartment Cowboy found a gift wrapped in gold paper with a card saying: *"Welcome back! King and Jeremy."* Smiling, touched by their good wishes, Cowboy uncovered a large and lavish Schofield Bible, a limited edition put out by a printer who loved his craft, with a fine leather binding and parchment-like paper with a life expectancy of several hundred years.

Cowboy got his boots off and sat down in the semidarkness to leaf through this treasure. But before he had turned a dozen pages he fell asleep.

He awoke at the sound of King entering his room.

"Hello there, Hoss! Go on with your resting; didn't mean to wake you up."

"No, no, good to see you." Cowboy arose, rubbing his eyes. They shook hands, grinning.

King stepped back for a squint-eyed look. "What's different about you?"

"Well, I'm nineteen pounds lighter as of this morning. Down to two ten. My clothes sort of hang on me." He patted himself at the belt line.

"Did you cover those Carolinas on foot?"

"Nothing like that; I made up my mind it was time to lose weight. Now that I don't knock down a couple of quarts of beer a day it isn't too tough."

King nodded. Cowboy was still far from lean, but his face was much thinner and his double chin had nearly disappeared; no more hawg jaw for Cowboy.

"How's Molly? We talked long distance several times, but she was all business."

"Fine, fine," King said, dismissing Molly.

"How was Miami?"

"One hundred thirty-nine thousand people in two weeks," King said promptly. "Twenty-six hundred Decisions—I'm not including those who came to me at odd hours of the day and night. And I must have talked personally to another two hundred souls on the telephone."

He sat down and his good-natured look disappeared. "Cowboy, I wish I could tell you some of the sad things I heard. I wanted to rush out and find each one of those fearful people and pray with them until they accepted Jesus as their Lord and Saviour. But it wasn't possible; even if I could have lasted without a single hour of sleep I couldn't have accomplished all I wanted. A few nights ago I pleaded, I begged Molly with tears in my eyes to let us stay in Miami."

"It's the same everywhere; you're needed just as much in Jacksonville. Or Kings Mountain. Or Tuscaloosa. Fine, hard-working people are sponsoring us there and in fifty other cities I visited. The pastors I've talked to are going all out to spread the word that King Windom is on his way."

"If I had more time . . . Cowboy, do you know how I feel? I'm overjoyed that so many are coming to hear the Word. . . . This afternoon, in such weather—incredible! Then again I'm so scared my teeth chatter. Is it really working, is all this worthwhile? I think, Three thousand brand-new, blood-washed lambs in Miami, three thousand in the fold. And he's proud—oh, the pride he feels!"

Cowboy scratched his head; he'd never heard King refer to himself in the third person. Or was the preacher talking about the Lord?

King scowled. He continued to talk, a glaze in his eyes, just as if Cowboy wasn't in the room. "But what has he done to feel so proud? What of the thousands who will never know the bliss of laying their hands in the nail-scarred hand? For one new Christian there must be thirty doomed souls in that city, doomed not so much because of their terrible sins but because they never will be reached. And he—he feels so helpless. Cowboy!"

The Cowboy gave a jump. King's mood had changed, he had passed from dire emotion to a smile in an instant, and he now seemed perfectly at ease. Cowboy smiled back, but he was perplexed by the way his friend had talked about himself, in so detached a manner.

"Did you like it?" King asked.

"What? Oh, the—the Schofield Bible. Just having a beautiful book like that around is going to make a better Christian out of me. Thank you both, very sincerely."

King yawned and sprawled out, hands comfortably folded on his chest. "Jeremy shopped for it herself. By the way, while we were in Fort Myers for the Christmas holidays Jeremy went into the hospital there for a little operation."

"Good Lord. Molly didn't say a word to me about that!"

"Nothing serious. Dr. Matthews suggested the whole thing. You haven't met him; he's a friend from back there in Clearwater and he's going to be traveling awhile with us. Anyway, it was a simple operation, and the upshot is Jeremy's eye is fixed up good as new."

"That's wonderful to hear. You had me real worried." Cowboy fondly picked up the Bible they had given him. "I had some news, but it doesn't seem like much now."

King cocked his head. "Come on, let's hear it."

"I could hardly wait to get back and tell you—but I'm not so sure of myself as I was." Cowboy paused to chase the worst of his misgivings, then said flatly, "I want to preach." He shied a glance at King, but the preacher's face was impassive. "It isn't just a half-baked idea," Cowboy stumbled on, "believe me. I haven't thought about much else for the past three weeks. And I've never felt so on edge, so impatient to make it all come true. When the idea first hit me I was surprised, then shocked. I knew of a hundred good reasons why it was impossible—but those reasons seemed to melt away in my head, they didn't stick at all, and finally I had to admit that, impossible or not, there's nothing I want more out of life than a chance to preach." He sucked in a breath and hunched his shoulders, waiting for King's criticism, or an oblique expression of disapproval.

King said, with the same flinty face, "You'll be a fine preacher, Cowboy. It's what I would have wanted for you—but of course you had to make your choice without any help from me."

"You mean it?"

"Why, sure—" Cowboy swung at him, and King toppled over, surprised. "Hey what for?"

"You had me hanging by my insides, that's what for! Good old Chief! Never crack a smile, you—" He was about to take another poke at King's shoulder but he stopped, his fist in mid-air. "I'll never do it," he said dispiritedly. "I'll never make the grade. I can't preach; what in the name of the Lord am I thinking about?"

"So far so good," King said dryly. "Those are almost the same words I said to myself fifteen years ago. Mind if I get up? Thank you. Now you know you want to preach, what will it be for you? College, a seminary, then a church somewhere?"

"I don't even belong to a church yet; I'm as homeless a Christian as you'd hope to see. But"—Cowboy looked at him gravely—"if I can do it, *if* the Lord is going to tolerate this—this obsession of mine, I think I'd like to finish college. That's the first thing, provided I can find one that will take a chance on me after what I pulled my last time around. Then . . . I'll give seminary a lot of hard thought. But in the meantime, I hope I'll still be working with the Southern Cross Crusade, finding out what it means to be an evangelist."

"You'll have plenty of opportunity to find out. And just as soon as you think you're ready, Cowboy, I'll give over my own pulpit to you."

"When I'm ready," Cowboy said, hopelessly.

"That may be sooner than either one of us thinks," King said, as if it was a promise.

After dinner, which he wasn't able to eat, Philemon returned to his room, half-paralyzed by the implications of Molly's command that he join her in the office of the Gospel Train at seven o'clock.

His primary impulse was to pack up, while almost everyone was still in the dining car, and get. He was dragging his dime-store suitcase out of the tiny closet when it hit him that if Molly had solid proof he was a thief, she likely was prepared for any sudden moves on his part. His paralysis became worse at the thought but he took himself over to the window and lifted the shade a scant inch. Kneeling, he was about to peer out when he remembered the light behind him. He staggered up, muttering fearfully under his breath, and put out the light. Then he had his look around. He didn't see the pack of police cars he'd fully expected, but—Philemon caught his breath, and it burst like a hot bubble in his throat—a suspicious-looking man in a light-colored trench coat was walking slowly beside the Train, coming his way, studying the convex coaches with unusual attention. Philemon dropped the shade and moaned softly, wiping at a sweat-greased cheek with one hand. If he'd trusted his legs to carry him, he would have run that moment to Jeremy, and fallen at her feet to beg for her help. But he knew she'd gone into town with King for a civic dinner. By the time she returned to the Train, it was bound to be all over.

Having spent a little time in the jailhouse at the age of fourteen for the venerable crime of chicken-stealing, Philemon well knew the scope of his future, once Molly was through with him. The prospect of facing her was even worse than the remembered misery of jail, because he had feared Molly and dreaded the sight of her since he'd been on the Train. One more reason why her brusque request for a meeting had dropped on his head like a thunderbolt—they were the first words she'd ever spoken to him.

There was no way to shine a hopeful light on his predicament. He was in awful trouble. He'd seen the proof with his own eyes—the detective prowling the length of the Gospel Train, alert for a breakout.

Philemon's panic was nearly insupportable. Luckily for him he was able to concentrate on the source of his present difficulty, the thrice-cursed and abominable nigger who seemed to watch his every move with calculating eyes, who smirked from the darkness and faded, black into black, whenever Philemon ventured near. That dog-meat nigger! The day would come . . . He trembled, and ground his teeth, and murderous sweat stood out on his forehead—the air-conditioner in the coach was only half-effective because of high humidity outside.

His fury slowly burned into an ashlike calm, and, curiously, he began to analyze the situation, to grasp its proportions. So they thought he was a thief; could they prove it? No one had seen him take money, he was sure of that, no one since the nigger. Who had eyes to see in the dark, in the thick of a crowd? Philemon regained his feet and turned the light back on. He looked at his face in the lavatory mirror and saw the uneasiness registered there. Then he delivered his final reassurance: no one, not even the nigger, could turn up the money. Without it they had nothing on him. Mrs. Amos could not shake him, no matter what, because the money was safely tucked away.

Therefore it could not hurt him to keep his appointment with her.

Philemon steadied himself further by washing his face carefully in cold water. Then, knowing it must be past seven, he hastened to the front of the Train.

The sight of Molly almost cost him his headlong confidence, but she looked up without asperity.

"I was beginning to think you were lost."

Philemon glanced from Molly to the man seated at the end of the couch by her desk. He was middle-aged, with slicked red hair, a four-cornered face, freckles, three-cornered gray eyes. It was not a hard face, and the man returned his look casually. But Philemon stiffened, just as if the man still wore a dripping trench coat. He felt his secrets flocking into the open, raucously, advertising themselves like so many blackbirds on a bush.

Molly misinterpreted his stiffness. "Oh . . . this is Mr. Gilmer, from Atlanta, Georgia. Philemon . . . ah, what is your last name?"

"Love."

Mr. Gilmer from Atlanta nodded, but failed to offer his hand.

"Why don't you take a seat here?" Molly pointed to a handy chair. "This won't take long." She smiled, and seemed nervous. Philemon couldn't imagine why she should be, but he found that by watching her restless bony hands he was better able to keep his wits about him as he perched on the edge of the chair.

"You're one of the stewards, aren't you? Under Mr. Handwerker?"

"Yes, ma'am."

"How much do we pay you?"

Philemon's mouth promptly dried up. He looked again at Gilmer, whose hooded eyes seemed capable of boring through to the soul.

"Room and board, and free laundry, and . . . fifteen dollars a week."

430

"That isn't much, is it?" Molly remarked; she looked genuinely sorry. Philemon drew himself up a little straighter, thinking, What goes on here? And he stared at her fidgeting hands.

"Mr. Gilmer is a private detective," Molly went on. "He's going to do some work for me soon. We've talked it over the past couple of days, and I think we agree that he'll need some help on his assignment." Gilmer nodded in a glum way, maintaining his silence.

"You want me to help him?" Philemon asked, getting ahead of Molly.

As if she had just noticed how antic they were, Molly folded her hands. "Yes. You see, I'm trying to find out about someone—a woman. She died almost six years ago, in a little valley up in western Virginia. It may take several days just to find her grave. And as for friends and relatives . . ." Molly took off her glasses to give her eyes a rest. After nearly four weeks in Florida her skin had no more color to it than the fluorescent light burning overhead. "Mr. Gilmer was born in the Cumberlands, and he knows about mountain people. They don't talk easily to strangers, and not at all to policemen. He'd get nowhere in the Sugar Tree Valley, asking questions about the woman."

"What woman?" Philemon asked, startled by his rashness.

"Hmm? Her name is—was—Mary Kate Ransom. As I was saying, Mr. Gilmer wouldn't get much cooperation on his own. That's why I'd like for you to go with him, Philemon. The people in the Sugar Tree Valley will listen when you ask about Mary Kate Ransom, because . . . well, you can talk their language. You won't look out of place. And if you have a good story to explain your curiosity, if you claim to be a close relative . . . Where were you born, by the way?"

"Ogdenburg, Kentucky. That's in Jessamine County. Near Lexington."

"Fine. The story will be—the first few days at any rate—that Mary Kate Ransom is wanted at the bedside of a dying aunt in Jessamine County, and you'll hint that a small legacy is involved. Two things even mountain people will accept without question are death and a proper sum of money, not too much to tax their imaginations. Once you encounter actual relatives of Mary Kate Ransom, the story will have to be changed, and"—she cast a meaningful look at the private

431

detective—"Mr. Gilmer will give you whatever instructions you need, as he sees fit. Now what do you say, Philemon?"

Philemon wondered why she was so interested in a woman dead six years, but that was not his business. If she wanted him to go off with the detective somewhere and poke around, that was OK with him, just so it didn't take too long. He nodded.

"Good. Of course, I'm going to pay you more money for this job." Philemon smiled tenderly. Molly studied him for a few seconds, then she said with a touch of grandeur in her voice, "How does fifty dollars a week sound?"

"Yes, ma'am." Fifty dollars a week! He was beginning to feel just a little contemptuous of Molly, because she certainly threw money away on wild goose chases. If he was to be paid fifty a week, how much was the detective getting? Philemon felt a moment's caution. Was she tricking him in some way? Had she told him the whole story? He looked to her hands for information. They were jittery again. Philemon raised his eyes to Molly's. It wasn't just nervousness; down inside she was afraid of something. The knowledge that Molly Amos could be afraid warmed him.

"You may be gone two weeks, or four," Molly said. "Or longer. Mr. Gilmer will take care of your expenses while—"

"That long? I can't go for that long."

"Why not?" Molly said harshly.

"My dog . . ."

"Oh. Don't worry, Philemon, I'll see that he gets the best of care. Our comptroller is a dog fancier; you can introduce him to your dog before you leave and I'm sure Haygood will get along fine with him. Anything else?"

He could think of nothing. Despite the promise of fifty dollars a week he felt obscurely trapped. One good thing, though; that private detective wasn't a talker. After ten years with old Eli, Philemon didn't think he could stand being closed up for any length of time with a talker. Thoughts of Eli gave him an unexpected jolt and he looked quickly at Gilmer. But the man was ignoring him. He had his job to do and he wasn't really interested in Philemon, or anything Philemon might have done. Philemon scratched the back of his neck and shrugged.

Molly peered at the clock on her desk.

"Can you be ready to leave in an hour?"

"Sooner if you want me to."

"Just be here in the office at eight-thirty, packed and ready to go. One more thing. I don't want you saying a word about this to anyone, is that clear?"

The congregation for that evening's meeting was already forming under the caterer's tent outside when Philemon returned to his compartment. He stuffed his suitcase in a hurry, then remembered that he had given two of his three shirts to Jeremy for darning the day before. He went into the next Pullman to see if Jeremy had returned from town. She was in the Windom apartment, all right, but she hadn't darned the shirts.

"Philemon, I'm real sorry. I'll get to it right now."

"No," he said, "I can't wait."

"What's the big hurry?"

"Mrs. Amos is sending me up north to do a job for her."

"She is?" Jeremy looked dubious. "What kind of job?"

"I can't say; but I'll be gone a month. And I'm getting paid fifty dollars a week."

"Oh, fifty dollars a week. For what?"

"What did you do with my shirts, Jeremy?"

"I'll bring them." When she returned from the other room with the shirts on hangers, she said, "I'll be happy to touch these up for you with the iron if you'll wait."

"They look all right." He fidgeted; he thought he was used to the eye that had been fixed by surgery, to the new beauty that lay in her face, but sometimes when he looked at her he felt as numb as if a mule had kicked him, and unsettled, and for no reason at all, displeased.

"Are you traveling by yourself to wherever it is you're going?" Jeremy prodded.

"No, another man'll be with me."

"Unh-hunh." Philemon did not stand excitement well, and he appeared queasy to her eyes. Jeremy got furious waiting for him to tell her all about it, because clearly he was dying to. Finally she thrust the shirts at him and waved toward the door with her free hand, saying, "Go on, good-bye!"

Philemon hesitated. "I might not be away a whole month, though."

"Is that so? Tell me about it sometime." She gave him a hard push. Philemon looked crestfallen.

"Say," he said, as he was going out the door, "do you know

where the Sugar Tree Valley is?" He tried to sound casual about giving information which Mrs. Amos had warned him was privileged.

Jeremy had her back to him. "The which?"

"The Sugar—"

She whirled. "Is that where you're off to?"

Jeremy looked so startled and interested that he mumbled, "I only wondered if you'd heard—"

"I've heard of it. Philemon!"

Her tone stopped him in his tracks.

"Why are you going there?"

"To see about a woman," he said reluctantly.

"What woman?"

"If I don't get done packing—"

"Listen to me, Philemon." She had a dangerous eye on him. "There's plenty I've done for you since we've been knowing each other, and all I'm asking is a simple question. Believe me, you'd better answer it!"

Weighing Jeremy's demand against Molly's warning, Philemon wondered what harm it could do if he told her.

"It's just some woman who's been dead six years. Her name was Mary Kate Ransom. Mrs. Amos wanted to know—I don't remember she said what it is she wants to know. She probably told Gilmer—he's the one I'm traveling with. Jeremy, I'm gettin, right now."

He glanced over his shoulder. Jeremy looked puzzled; she was biting at a knuckle.

"That was all of it, you swear?"

"Sure," he said, in a surly voice, and plodded on down the corridor with his shirts. It had been no fun telling her, and he was sorry he hadn't kept quiet. If he'd just left the Train and let her discover he was gone, then she'd really have been anxious and filled with questions when he returned.

Jeremy went back into the apartment and closed the door. Perhaps she might have wrung more information out of her cousin, but she doubted it. Jeremy found it difficult to believe that Mrs. Amos was depending on Philemon for anything. But, then, he wasn't going alone. He couldn't possibly get into trouble.

She sat down, still biting the knuckle, dimly aware of the sound of a crowd gathering outside her window, filling up the parking lot of the factory the Train had parked beside. It

434

seemed queer to Jeremy that Mrs. Amos would be interested in the Sugar Tree Valley, and some woman who had died six years ago. She peered closely at the shadows which Philemon had left with her, and suddenly understood. It was King who was interested, not Mrs. Amos. After all, he'd lived in the Valley. Perhaps the woman had been a friend, had helped him while he was establishing his ministry, and now that he could afford to do so, he wanted to repay the kindness by seeking out her family, making sure they were all well provided for.

This reasonable explanation satisfied Jeremy completely. She halfway thought about mentioning Mary Kate Ransom to him later on, but long before she saw King that night other matters had claimed her attention and she completely forgot about it.

42

The Burning Bus

Harsh weather from the north greeted the Gospel Train as it toiled through the outlands of the Okefenokee Swamp on the Florida-Georgia border. In the hour since they'd left Jacksonville the temperature had dropped nearly fifteen degrees. A wind that hurled sledges of rain against the coach windows was gusting up to forty-five miles an hour, and those still awake could feel the lightweight Train rocking uneasily through the rough winds.

Cowboy scrubbed one of the misted windows in his apartment and, looking out, estimated that the Train was making about fifty miles an hour, but it was difficult to tell. There were no points of reference beyond the tracks, no nearby highways, no town lights. He had the disquieting notion they were traveling in a void as depthless as outer space until something thumped against the Pullman by his window, scaring him thoroughly. A big branch torn from a pine tree, he thought.

He kept his face to the cold window, looking ahead, and saw

the will-o'-the-wisp lights of the engine as the Train took a curve. He caught a glimpse of whipsawed trees and the slashing rain and shivered, wondering how much swamp they had to cross.

He was tired but not sleepy, so he put on his boots and went looking for someone to talk to. It was after one a.m. and he didn't feel free to knock on any doors, but there was nothing going on in the coaches either, the church choir they had boarded in Jacksonville for a two-day jaunt was tucked away under low lights. He decided it might be worthwhile to visit the cab of the engine and have a closer look at what was going on outside.

The yellow dog of Philemon's stirred and growled in his kennel as Cowboy passed through the baggage car; fascinated, he paused to study the monster. Sudden deceleration almost threw him against the front wall of the car. He continued on through the long, brightly lighted engine passages, where turbine energy hummed at him as the Train gained traction. They had speeded up again. He entered the locomotive and climbed the steps to the cab.

It was his first time there while the Train was in motion; his eyes jumped from the array of dials on the instrument panel to the night churning madly around his head, and back to the two men who were responsible for guiding the multimillion-dollar Train along the rain-silvered rails, which seemed incredibly insubstantial from such a height.

The fireman, who was leaning forward in his leather-covered pedestal chair to catch the white warning markers that flashed into view along the right of way, called out an indicated speed to the engineer and turned his head, having caught Cowboy's reflection in the slant of glass above his head.

"OK if I stick around?"

The fireman shrugged and pointed to a third armchair, located between but slightly behind his and the engineer's. Cowboy decided to remain standing and gave all his attention to the storm. On either side of the double line of tracks tall pines swayed and dipped; the air was filled with debris, part of which stuck from time to time to the front windows. The big wipers patiently removed it all and the Gospel Train moved effortlessly across a long trestle. An ear-splitting hiss from the air brakes almost caused Cowboy to go through the roof. For a few moments he watched with interest while the engineer

436

worked, then sat down beside him. The engineer was keeping his eyes peeled for trouble and he merely grunted the first time Cowboy spoke to him.

"What's that?" Cowboy asked eventually, leaning forward.

"Say what?"

"I thought I saw a light."

"House, more'n likely."

"People live out in the middle of this?"

The engineer grinned but didn't take his eyes from the tracks. "Surely do. It takes a certain breed a man, though."

"How far are we from a town?"

"Oh, reckon fifteen miles. Depends on what you mean by town. They's two, three settlements along the road twixt Breedlove and Tallie."

"What road?"

"It's close by, but you can't see it this time the naught. Just a little blacktop path, actually. Cuts across the line two, three times. Only road that crosses the Okefenokee anywheres. Of course, we're on right solid ground this far south. Ground gets real loose and a-shaky another five miles on up above the state line."

"Is that the Suwannee River?" Cowboy asked, as the Train pounded across a wide black stream.

"No, we ain't nowheres near the Suwannee yet. I'll point her out to you—got to look quick or you won't see her atall."

The engineer, it turned out, had been hunting the Okefenokee since boyhood, and they discussed the local wildlife until Cowboy was nodding, lulled by the flailing rain, the warmth of the sealed cab, and the faint vibration of the diesels that penetrated the soles of his feet and tingled at the base of his spine.

"Them's flares," the engineer said abruptly, and he leaned closer to a side window.

"What?"

"That glow there through the trees? Railroad flares. Say, Claude—" The fireman looked up from the side of the road. As he did so, a flare burst above a stand of live oak about a thousand yards off and to the left, then quickly vanished in the wind. The engineer had, in the space of thirty seconds, reduced his speed by half, and now he sounded his horn several times. "Some kind emergency," he muttered. "Now, what's south-bound this time the naught?"

"Freight," the fireman said, consulting a clipboard. "We was to pass it two miles on back."

"Reckon it's the tracks."

"Washout?" suggested Cowboy.

"No stream hereabout big enough to wash over its banks even in weather like this is. My guess is there's a big tree fallen down. Maybe they hit it. We'll see in just a minute. They must a seen me comin by now. Wonder why they don't sound their whistle?"

"Wind prevents us hearing," the fireman observed.

"I sure's hell hope they didn't go off the tracks. Lord God, it'd be daybreak fore they'd get the derrick up here from Jax."

The Train had passed into a cypress forest so impenetrable that even the long-range headlamp beam turned to a white-hot smoke beneath the trees as the tracks curved gently toward a meeting with the stalled train. The windshield wipers worked in great arcs, but the rain was so heavy it was a strain to see anything outside. The engineer cursed.

"That another flare gone up? Better slow her down a notch; it might be a bust track after all." The air brakes screamed. "Oh, oh, now look there. There she sits. And what's that a-burnin?" He moaned suddenly, a chilling sound. "God damn this rain! What's that off the left? A truck? Chrastalmighty, they hit a truck on the crossin." He cranked the little side window and stuck his head out in the rain. "No, it ain't that atall!"

Now Cowboy could see the yellow rose of flame low to the ground and about two hundred yards ahead. The revolving lamp of the diesel in front of them was throwing a glaze against their windows. He clenched his hands, feeling slightly horrified as they approached the scene of the accident. Rain from the open window jumped in and struck his eyes.

The engineer pulled his head back in and dried his face on his sleeve. His eyes in the light of the cab were pale and shocked.

"It ain't a truck they hit—I seen it. Burnin like a son of a bitch, but I made out what it was. They hit a school bus!"

Cowboy felt as if he'd been kicked in the heart. The fireman groaned.

"Let's don't get no closer—I don't want to look at it!"

"Shut up," the engineer said, and leaned out the window again.

"A school bus, this long after midnight?" Cowboy said.

"Yes, but it weren't empty. Jesus wept! I see . . . people. Runnin around. Layin down like dead. Throwed all over the place. My God, that fire's gutted the bus; gas tank must have went! They must have all got out, though." His voice broke. "Oh, if they didn't all get out they're goners!" He shook his dripping head and closed the window. "Claude, ring back and get the crew on their feet," he said more quietly. "Maybe there's something we can do yet." To Cowboy he said, "Doctor aboard?"

Cowboy nodded.

"Well?" the engineer said harshly.

Cowboy shook himself from the dreadful lethargy that was binding his hands and feet. "I'll get him."

"Bound to be some hurt if not killed. Need a place to put them all. Need plenty of warm covers."

"How far to a hospital?"

"Nearest by road is at Nora. They wouldn't have no staff for something like this. Valdosta's got a big hospital. Flat out, this Train'll make Valdosta in under a hour."

Cowboy got out of there and ran to the baggage car; there he encountered one of the senior conductors. The man was only half-dressed. He was stockpiling flares, lanterns, crowbars. Philemon's dog was about to tear his kennel apart. The old conductor, having seen for himself what was happening, didn't waste time questioning Cowboy.

"Maybe one or two of those choir members had Civil Defense or Red Cross training. If we're lucky. Have all the ones who won't be any use move into one coach and tell them to *stay on the Train*. I think the doctor had best set up his emergency room in the lounge, but we'll need a couple of coaches for the injured. There'll be shock cases. They'll need stretch-out room and plenty of blankets."

"How about taking up some of the seats in coach seven?"

"Don't have the proper tools."

"I know a man who has the proper tools," Cowboy said.

"See to it, then. I want all my crew up front right away if you happen to find any of them milling around." The Train braked to a stop, and rain crackled on the roof of the baggage car. The conductor hauled on a rain slicker. "Help's going to be a long time reaching us out here," he grumbled.

"Engineer said Valdosta's close."

"Good thought. Ring the Valdosta yardmaster; he'll do all the necessary phoning for you. Number's posted by the radio-telephone there in the office." He went by Cowboy with a pocketful of flares, swinging a lantern, spat in front of the dog's cage, and pulled open one of the baggage-car doors. Cowboy looked out briefly, at the hard rain and a violent sky lit up by the unquenchable fire. He heard a few stifled shouts above the wind. Except for the pink flare bubbles, the deeper glow of flames, there was no specific indication of disaster. Maybe they had all got out before the collision, Cowboy thought. The bus might have been stalled on the tracks for half an hour before the freight came. But he remembered the horror in the engineer's face, so he turned and started urgently on his rounds.

In less than two minutes after the Gospel Train had come to a stop, his call to Valdosta was completed. He entered the seventh coach and was astonished to find that the lights were still low; only a few people had been awakened by the stop. They were staring out the windows, trying to make sense of what had happened.

Cowboy selected two of the non-sleepers who looked as if they could be relied upon to keep their heads and told them flatly what had happened, so far as he knew.

"My name's Lukens," one of the men said promptly. "I'm a lieutenant colonel in the Army Reserve. If it's all right with you I'll get my people organized for this thing. We have at least two RN's in the choir."

Cowboy explained what was to be done and left the colonel. The Gospel Train was coming awake, its passengers prompted by some hidden alarm, a common intimation of danger. Age was already out of his room, wearing his yellow slicker with the hundred eyes. Cowboy sent him back for his tool chest and rapped on Dr. Matthews' door.

"Yes . . . what is it?" Matthews looked out blearily, fumbling with his glasses.

"There's been a wreck on the line."

Matthews stared at him. "I've been awake; I didn't feel anything."

"A southbound freight hit a school bus. We're setting up an emergency hospital in the visitors' lounge. You'll have at least two nurses to give you a hand." He smelled the mash on the doctor's breath and wondered if the man was competent, but Matthews rubbed his neck hard and braced himself in the doorway. "I'll be right there, as soon as I . . . put on a shirt. Is it raining hard?"

"Yes."

"How . . . bad . . .?"

"I haven't gone out to see."

"Well . . . I'll need all the first-aid supplies on the train. And clean cloths. A good hospital nurse will know what I want. Where's King?"

"In his bedroom, I expect. I'll get him up."

But only Jeremy was in the apartment. She pointed to a window as Cowboy entered.

"He went out, less than a minute ago. What's wrong?"

"Crossing accident." Jeremy looked at him, blankly, and then her lip curled.

"Is anybody . . . ?" She swallowed, then said, "I'll get dressed."

"Wake Molly, will you?" Cowboy called over his shoulder as he was leaving.

"Where are you going?"

"To find out how bad it is."

Once outside, Cowboy was drenched and chilled before he'd taken a dozen steps. He was astonished by the force of the wind, which he thought he had appreciated from inside the Train. This wind was an instrument of a world with a black, boisterous sense of humor. It was a mousetrapping wind, that would pry and explore and find the secret weaknesses of an old house and rip it apart. The wind had a way of making him feel puny, badly articulated; it made each of his steps a ponderous uncertainty while the rain cross-whipped his eyes.

A boy struggled toward him out of the wind and darkness, not running but hurrying for all he was worth. There was something fearful in his haste; Cowboy seized an arm. The boy's head flashed up. His face was gray-green, his eyes intoxicated with horror. He wasn't big but he fought hard, kicking with one foot and then another.

"Mister, please let me alone! My ma'll kill me if I don't get home!"

"Climb aboard the Train!" Cowboy shouted. "We'll take care of you!"

The boy didn't or couldn't understand; he fought free of Cowboy's grip and staggered away. The Cowboy started after him but he thought, He isn't hurt, he's one of the lucky ones, and how far can he go in this storm? He continued on, between the tracks, his way lighted by spillover from the windows of the Gospel Train, by the headlamps of the two trains, which were parked only a couple of hundred feet apart. In this rain-swept arena of powerful floodlights men were gathered, faces reddened by dolorous flares. King Windom was the dominant figure. The others were trainmen. One of them, in sodden overalls, was describing, with precise gestures, how the accident had looked to him. His voice was steady, but his lacerated face looked grief-stricken.

". . . No tellin how long they'd been settin there on the track, not a single light showin. Just settin in the black dark, waitin for God knows what. Maybe one of em was under the hood, checkin for the trouble; I couldn't tell you. All I know is they heard us or seen us even with all the rain because about the time we spotted that yeller bus they was leapin out doors and winders and a couple of kids came diggin up the track awavin us to stop, but, hell, man . . ." He paused, and looked grimly around at his audience. "I'm askin you what chance did we have, with twenty carloads a heavy machinery back there, and the rails like they was greased; what chance to get stopped in six hundred feet? Henry and me couldn't do a thing but pray they all got out, and pray that them kids was already out would have the wits to stand clear, and pray we wouldn't burn up ourselves if the gas tank of the bus exploded." He wiped his sorrowful red face. "Two seconds before we rammed it we could see they wouldn't . . . all get out; some was still inside. And just when we hit, there was one at the front door about to jump. I saw him lookin straight up at us. Lord! And that bus, it was years old, must have been a bucket of rust, cause it broke half in two stead of pilin up ahead of us on the track. Only thing saved me and Henry from roastin. I seen that kid, the one I was tellin about in the doorway, just fallin through the air like a rocket, all aburnin; and there was more screamin than I ever care to hear in my life again; and finally we stopped. I got down quick and I—I looked for that kid what was on fire. But I didn't see him nowheres."

"Did anybody get out of the bus after you hit it?" King asked.

The trainman looked angry enough to throttle him. "Git out? Mister, you have a look! And them flames was twice as hot five minutes ago! I couldn't git close enough to see who or what

442

was inside. One little girl said they was at least six more left in there when we hit, but I don't know; she was cryin so I didn't understand half a what she told me. Look at them poor children! Whoever was drivin that bus ought to go to prison. I'll stand up and swear that in court. It was a criminal act. . . ." He licked his lips and dropped his head and clenched a vengeful fist in front of his nose.

"We'll take care of the children," King promised. "And we've got a doctor aboard." He placed a hand on the man's shoulder. "Will you be able to help us?"

"Sure, sure—just as soon as I see to Henry. He's an old man, only a year off from retirement. He's still a-settin up there in the cab, his hand on the brake; I got to git him on his feet somehow. Convince him he weren't at fault. . . ."

Others, including women, had come from the Gospel Train. King turned to them, raising his voice. "We need all the help you can give us! Did you bring blankets? . . . Good, but we'll be able to use a dozen more. The children are scattered along the tracks for two hundred yards. Take all those who can walk back to the Train. If you find an injured child, stay with him but don't try to move him. We'll get to you. Cowboy?"

The preacher loped off, seeming not to notice the barrier of the wind. He had an electric torch in his hand with a barrel two feet long, and as soon as they were beyond the periphery of the train lights he switched it on, playing the beam across the mire. At each step they had to struggle up from the earth. Cowboy was wearing boots and the going was easier for him.

He paused to study the bashed-in front of the diesel engine on the freight. The rain was angled away from his face and he could see better now; he had a clearer idea of just how awful the wreck had been. The front end of the bus was blocking the northbound tracks some twenty yards back of the engine. Although it looked as if three sticks of dynamite had exploded under the hood, the remnant was still recognizable as part of a yellow school bus. The folding front door was hanging by a hinge, and the big red STOP sign under the driver's window was flapping in the wind. One of the warning flashers above the whitely crushed windshield appeared to be glowing, eerily, but it was only a reflection from a flare. Cowboy could make out part of the lettering on the body: TA LIE SCHO DISTRIC. His eyes shifted to a twisted window frame, a flag of white like a torn shirt.

443

There was little that was recognizable about the other half of the bus, which lay in the mud on the opposite side of the tracks. Cowboy saw an axle, a fender, a hollow lump of roof with flame in it, like an exotic potted plant. There was shredded and twisted steel, seats, other unknown hunks of metal up the tracks to the crossing. And there were bodies, dark isolated forms scattered in the rain. It was impossible to say who was dead and who was living until they were within a dozen feet of the burning wreck.

Perhaps ten boys and girls, ranging in age from twelve to seventeen, were gathered there. Only one was standing. Two others were on their knees, whispering, as if in prayer. A girl moaned, "I got out. I got out. I got out." Cowboy slipped down on one knee to speak to a boy who was trying to keep warm by clutching a girl's cloth coat against his chest. His face was mauled and peculiarly scratched. His eyelids twitched and jerked, like those of a sleeper having a nightmare. He didn't respond to Cowboy's voice.

A couple of heads turned slowly as King's flashlight went from face to face. They were quiet, rain-streaked faces. Eyes squinted at the light, but the faces were reserved, dubious, and more than one was uncaring. They were not minding the wind, or the rain, or the faint city-dump odor of the thing that had burned.

"Is anybody hurt," King yelled.

Nobody answered; then the boy who was standing walked toward them, listing in the mud. He had a pair of basketball shoes slung over one shoulder. He was holding his right forearm with his left hand.

"I guess I am," he said, when he was close. "I got a lump like a egg on my arm. Fell on it getting out of the bus. Have you seen my girl?"

"Doctor on our Train will take care of you. Hey! Come on! All of you! Come on to the Train!"

"Is everybody all right?" He was a good-looking boy, with a serious face. "I didn't look to see. I was scared, I guess. I just took off runnin. I heard it, though." He leaned against Cowboy. "I don't know why this had to happen; we won tonight. Where's my girl, please?"

"I don't know; what's her name?"

"Mary Lou," said the garrulous boy. He seemed anxious to go on talking, but he couldn't force another word. He looked

444

apologetically at Cowboy; it was a sweet look but the boy was trembling pitifully.

While King rounded up the others and coaxed them to follow, Cowboy half-carried the boy with the broken arm to the Train, where other hands helped him aboard.

By that time there was a crowd of children on the tracks waiting for directions, waiting while the injured were taken into the coaches. Cowboy was struck by the behavior of this larger group; again not a suggestion of panic or even impatience, although all were as wet and mud-miserable as he was. They seemed willing to stand, uncomplaining, until the effects of exhaustion and exposure sent them sprawling. He joined them, studying faces. Many were cut and bruised. Had they been cut in jumping from the doomed bus, or—a worse thought occurred to Cowboy—had they fought each other for the exits, had they trampled and butted and clawed and ultimately escaped, leaving behind the weakest to die? Impossible, he thought, these children . . . But some of them had surely been asleep, and had awakened to screams, with the light of the freight train as blinding as the sun in their eyes. A misstep caused him to bump into one of the girls. She shifted her feet and smiled at him, emptily, and fixed her eyes on a coach window. There was mud, or a dark bruise, on her forehead. At the sight of it Cowboy felt dismayed, enraged. Could any of them remember accurately what had happened? Were they thinking now of those who hadn't escaped? Did they care?

He looked away, shuddering. The rain had slowed. Two girls were running between the tracks, headed toward him. They were blond and looked like sisters; the oldest grabbed Cowboy's arm.

"Are you a preacher?" she gasped. "Someun said there's a preacher on this train!"

"Yes; what do you want him for?"

"Our brother Joe is fixin to die; said the little one, "and we want the preacher to pray over him!"

"If he don't mind," the oldest said politely.

Cowboy stared at her. "Wait here." He searched for King, and found him handing out hot coffee to the children already blanket-wrapped and seated inside the coach.

They joined the blond sisters, who took off through a hollow of the wind. The bad footing didn't seem to bother the girls;

when one slipped she rebounded immediately, casually, and ran on. Both men had trouble matching the pace of the girls and Cowboy thought that their endurance was incredible. How had they kept going, when so many others had given up? But they had a brother, who needed them; maybe it was reason enough for their endurance and courage.

The girls stayed with the tracks past the middle of the long freight train, where the blacktop road came into sight. The demolished half of the school bus, with a few flames still visible, lay twenty yards south of the road. There were low places on either side of the blacktop, partly flooded, and, on higher ground, beyond the water, stands of pine could be seen, thinned out by loggers or by previous storms. The oldest girl led the way across the road. Her sister had picked up a rock and was limping badly. Cowboy scooped her up in his arms.

"Sneakers all wore out," she explained. "But y' don't have to carry me; foot's just bruised."

"How did you get out of the bus?" Cowboy asked. "Do you remember?"

"Sure I remember. Rita and me both squeezed out the winder. There was too many kids in the aisle screamin their heads off; they should've gone out the winders like we did. Rita's big and she didn't have no trouble, except I had to give her a push and she bloodied her head somehow. Probably fell on it. Maybe you can tell me, was there any on there didn't get off in time except for Joe? I fell in the ditch and didn't see what happened."

"I think everybody made it," Cowboy lied.

"That makes poor old Joe the unlucky one. He should've been sittin with us; Rita would've seen to it he got off. Ma's goin to lose her mind when she hears about Joe. We had a older brother fall off a tractor into a disk and was killed about two years ago; Joe's the only boy at home now."

"What's your name?" Cowboy asked. He knew she couldn't be more than twelve.

"Dawn," said the girl. "Dawn Mabry. Are you sure you're not tired out carryin me?"

"I'm just fine." King was leading the way now, down from the road and into the trees. His light revealed a third girl, crouched over the body of Joe Mabry, who lay beside a windfall, protected in some measure from the wind and rain.

"That's Edna, Joe's girl. If I know old Joe, he was lettin

446

everybody off the bus ahead of him." Her voice weakened. "I hope he didn't die yet. But I wouldn't want Ma to see him neither, lookin the way he does, hardly a stitch a clothes on his body." Dawn gulped for air. "Put me down now, please." She ran to her brother's side. "How's he, Edna?"

"I don't know; I tried to keep him covered." She straightened and wept, hands over her face. "Help me pray for him!"

King turned his light on the boy's face. One look was enough for Cowboy. About half of Joe Mabry's face was deeply seared, a purplish-red color. His lips were puffed and one eye was sealed shut. Had he protected the rest of his face with an arm, or a hand? Mercifully King lowered his electric torch. Cowboy glanced toward the railroad line. They were at least two hundred feet from the right of way. Apparently Joe had crawled some distance, through the water, into the woods. It was almost beyond belief that he could have traveled at all without help. Except for the untouched half of his face, he was literally burned from head to toe, and, as his little sister had observed, his clothes were no more than patches and scraps glued by fire to his body. The gas tank must have exploded right at his feet as the bus hurtled from the tracks.

Without saying a word, King thrust the torch into Rita's hands and carefully picked up the burned body.

"Is he dead?" Rita asked, timidly.

"Light the way," said the preacher. "And let's be quick."

Cowboy went last, helping Dawn Mabry. He kept a hand out for Edna, who wandered in a dream and cried aloud, hopelessly.

"Ah, Edna," little Dawn said soothingly. "The Lord's lookin after Joe real good. Please don't suffer, Edna."

The conductor met them at the Train. He looked sharply at Joe Mabry and said, "Four more? I think we've got them all. Twelve hurt, and several in shock I don't like the looks of. We'd better start for Valdosta."

King nodded and continued on his way.

"Where are you taking him?" Cowboy asked.

"To the chapel."

"Dr. Matthews—"

"Get him if you want. But it's too late now."

Cowboy hesitated; the girls followed King.

"You climbing aboard?" said the conductor.

Cowboy swung up the steps into the vestibule and entered

447

the lounge car, where Molly fed home-town royalty and reporters. Dr. Matthews and one of the nurses from the choir were sweating over a youngster with a nasty-looking scalp wound. Cowboy didn't interrupt but looked around for a place to sit. Someone handed him hot coffee, which spilled. Someone else broke a tube of ammonia under his nose and his head snapped back. He offered no objections as his soaked shirt was unbuttoned and removed. He hadn't realized how cold he was until he felt a dry blanket next to his skin. Then his teeth began to chatter outrageously. More hot coffee gradually stopped the chill. He looked around, tears obscuring his vision. The tears were prompted by no particular emotion, but he couldn't stop them.

"How do you feel?" Dr. Matthews asked him.

"All right." Cowboy was aware that the Train was moving, and he made a real effort to sit straight in his chair. Matthews offered a towel. "Better give your head a rub; if you want to lie down I'll have somebody take you back to your rooms."

Cowboy shook his head at the suggestion. He accepted the towel and dried his hair slowly, peering around the lounge as he did so. He recognized Jeremy, who was making a bed for the boy with the scalp wound. It was quiet inside the Gospel Train, blessedly quiet, but his ears still rang from the wind.

"I have to look at the shock cases in the next coach," the doctor said. "If you feel like fainting, put your head between your knees."

"What if that doesn't work?"

Matthews smiled tiredly. "Well, you won't have so far to fall."

Cowboy nodded and closed his aching eyes. The scratchy blanket was comforting, and he wanted very much to sleep, but he remembered King.

"Doctor, King brought a badly burned boy with him."

"I haven't seen our preacher at all. Where—"

"He carried the boy to the chapel. How long have I been sitting here?" Cowboy stood, finding his knees undependable. He braced himself against the chair. "We'd better have a look—but I think the boy was dead."

Matthews picked up his bag and led the way. Most of the refugees from the wreck were in the first coach, many of them lying down in the available space; he and Cowboy had to step carefully over the children.

The doctor paused for a few words with one of the nurses. They glanced at a boy whose skin was a strange blue-gray shade, who seemed not to breathe at all. When they left the coach Matthews said worriedly, "That one had convulsions when he was brought aboard. He's in very bad shape. We're trying to keep a close eye on all the children, even the ones who look normal. Shock could carry them off in a matter of minutes, without warning. And there's little we could do."

They entered the chapel, which was almost dark; the only light was focused on the antique candlestick and the altar. Rain poured down on the glass of the dome overhead. Above the noise of the rain they could hear King praying. The preacher and the three girls were on their knees by the pulpit, the body of Joe Mabry in front of them.

After a few moments' hesitation Matthews made his way down the aisle of the swaying car; Cowboy stayed where he was.

Apparently King heard the doctor. He ended his prayer and looked up.

"Is there anything I can do?"

"I don't know," King said. One by one he helped the girls to their feet. They stood back, out of the way, holding onto each other for balance as the Gospel Train rushed on.

"But he's all right now," one of them whispered. "Didn't Jesus—?"

And King said, "Hush. Your brother is all right. I want the doctor to see him."

"Would you get the lights, Cowboy?"

Cowboy did so, then walked slowly down the aisle, studying the girls. They looked heartbreakingly wan but peaceful too, even Edna, who'd been edging toward a nervous collapse not long ago. Joe Mabry was covered with a clean blanket, and his face was hidden by the kneeling doctor. Cowboy's foot struck something in the aisle and he bent to pick it up. It was a burnt piece of cloth with a button attached. The red-and-blue plaid of the material was still visible. He held the patch of cloth out to the preacher, who examined it, then looked calmly into Cowboy's eyes.

"I know you're as thankful as I am the Lord has seen fit to spare the life of Joe Mabry."

Cowboy was so startled that all of his upper body shook in a spasm. He dropped the burned cloth and stepped forward to

449

stare over Matthews' shoulder. The doctor had pulled the blanket down to the waist of the naked boy. He took his stethoscope from his bag and listened to the beating heart. Joe Mabry stirred at the touch of the cold metal on his breast; he sighed peacefully in his sleep and the fingers of his right hand curled.

There was not a mark on him that Cowboy could see, except for a few freckles on his muscular shoulders, and two moles over his right-side ribs. Cowboy reached down and pulled the blanket to the boy's feet. He touched the feet lightly with his fingertips as if to be reassured that they were of flesh.

"It isn't him," Cowboy said angrily. "The boy I saw was—"

"God give Joe back to us, mister," Dawn Mabry said, in a voice to comfort him. "Believe in His miracles, won't you, please? The preacher laid his hands on Joe and the blisters went away. God heals the ones He loves, it's in the Bible—"

Cowboy said to King, "You told me the Power was gone!"

"I didn't lie—I thought it was. But what difference? Just look at the boy."

Cowboy looked again, obediently; and his skin crawled. "Was he dead, though? Was he already dead when you . . .?"

King was puzzled by the light in Cowboy's eyes. He said, simply, with a glance at Matthews, who was taking it all in, "What I did I couldn't help."

"But he *was* dead." That word seemed to weigh unbearably on Cowboy's mind; he struggled to throw it off. The enraged light went out of his eyes abruptly, leaving him blind and frantic. "Let me get out of here," he murmured, lunging, shedding his blanket. His groping hands glanced off King, then returned to batter him as if he were a door. King stepped aside; Cowboy ran down the aisle of the chapel, losing his balance again and again as he bucked the momentum of the speeding Train.

Dr. Matthews stepped back, blocking the aisle for King, who looked at him protestingly.

"He thinks I've—that what was done is an evil thing!"

"Let him rest. Let him sit with it. If he needs help sleeping later on, I'll see that he sleeps."

"Will he ever understand?"

"No more than you or I do. But he'll understand enough."

43

Molly's Grand Strategy

There was no revival in Valdosta the next day, which was just as well, since the norther left behind a certain amount of ice and twenty-degree temperatures, two factors which will clear the streets of any deep-South town as efficiently as a plague.

Telegrams arrived throughout the day from a hundred sources, including the Governor's office, praising the resourcefulness of the staff and crew of the Gospel Train. Prompt action in getting the victims to a hospital had undoubtedly prevented more deaths, according to attending physicians. For hours, until the wintry sun was high, there was little chance for sleep aboard the Train as relatives and friends of the luckier children arrived over slippery roads to take them home. Investigators from the state, the railroad, and insurance companies swarmed in, and there were a few lawyers, looking for clients. Newsmen from south Georgia papers and radio stations followed Molly around recording interviews.

By early afternoon there was a general letdown aboard the Train; the atmosphere in the coaches was subdued, even depressing. Molly reluctantly canceled a late-afternoon stop at Waycross and decided they should leave for the next city on their itinerary, which was Savannah, about eight. In the meantime they were all on their own. The staff members could retire in comparative privacy, snooze, do a wash in the laundry, or take long hot baths—this was a luxury, since showering was strictly limited at other times. There were two shower rooms in addition to shower annexes in the apartments, but only so much water could be carried in the Pullman tanks, for all purposes. Molly had arranged for the tanks to be refilled continually while they were in the station.

The sixty-two members of the choir were not as well off. They had the use of all facilities but not much chance for privacy, and sleeping was difficult hard by a busy railroad yard. A very few of them, freezing in light sweaters, went downtown, and came quickly back again, because downtown Valdosta offered few chances for amusement. For the most part they passed the time with gossip, and what they gossiped about was the miracle-working of King Windom.

About three that afternoon in his compartment, Cowboy began playing the banjo, but he found that a banjo wasn't suited to his mood, so he soon switched to his splintery old guitar, which was just right for the sounds he wanted to hear. First he sang of deep regret and sadness, songs of the October wind and the footloose. There was grit in his heart but a sweetness to his voice: he sang "The Last Thing on My Mind" and "He Was a Friend of Mine" and "Five Hundred Miles." And as he was singing these, a taste for the hard blues grew sharp on his tongue. He sang Leadbelly and Blind Lemon and Fred McDowell while the strings chugged, throbbed, and gave out high-tension wails.

Mab Shaw heard him, heard the bone-in-the-throat harshness, and came as if she'd been summoned to nudge open his door and stand listening until he beckoned her in with his eyes, not pausing, not giving his strong grasping fingers a rest. There was an anxious sweat on his forehead. Mab's lips pursed in sympathy at the guttural sounds as if each was a knife she had felt many times in her own breast. He sang, finally, "The House of the Rising Sun," strings popping, his voice flat and nasal and slurring. Mab nodded and clenched her hands; she no longer sang the blues, she could not bring herself to do so, but her lips moved and she whispered in a ghostly voice snatches of the terrible death song of a prostitute.

At the last limping, dwindling chord there were tears in her eyes, tears of pain because he was in pain, he had finished with aching wrists and cramped fingers and devastated eyes.

They said nothing to each other and Mab went as she had come, helplessly.

At dusk Molly went out by herself and walked three blocks to the center of town, looking for a restaurant in which to have dinner. A menagerie of worries large and trivial followed at her heels. She'd come fresh from an argument with Haygood, the comptroller, over the food budget ("As pleasant as that might be, we just can't operate like a luxury hotel, Molly") and from a long-distance telephone conference with two irate parents about one of the hostesses, who had suddenly packed her bags and taken off without a word to anybody about her destination (She *is* of age, Mrs. Tanner, and if a girl wants to leave we can't stop her; shall I put you in touch with the local police?").

A place called the Ranchhouse appeared likely to have decent steaks and a booth where she could enjoy an undisturbed hour, so Molly ducked inside. As soon as she was seated she ordered dinner without a look at the menu, then unfolded the two newspapers she'd bought. The Jacksonville paper had given the crossing accident almost as much space as the local one; Molly read both accounts eagerly, then settled back to light a cigarette. She was somewhat comforted to know that neither paper had said anything about King Windom's miracle of healing. Their stories, however, had been written hurriedly, against deadlines. Six children and the bus driver were dead, but forty-one were safe.

Molly was confident that she had bumped all reporters off the Train before rumors of the miracle had begun to sprout like so many obnoxious weeds. She'd done her best in an ungovernable situation—there'd been confusion everywhere, tearful scenes, rejoicing, picture-taking. Molly had been tempted to ban the press altogether, but she'd come to her senses and realized such a ban was unenforceable, so she'd compromised by handling the reporters herself, almost leading them around by the nose. She had also rather desperately insisted to King that he make himself unavailable, until further notice, in his study.

Looking back, Molly could see that keeping the preacher out of sight most of the day had given the gossip-mongers something real to talk about, but at the moment King and Jeremy were having dinner with fifty others; Molly had a hunch that even those who had most avidly accepted the tales of a great healing miracle were having trouble believing what they'd heard while King sat there in plain view forking in the cutlets and chatting with his teen-age wife, happy and unburdened—at least Molly hoped he would be, for he'd been sober and preoccupied much earlier that day.

Molly had heard about the miracle from John Matthews, who'd seen to it that the Mabry children and the girlfriend were off the Train and on their way to a small private hospital by taxi almost as soon as the wheels stopped turning. The doctor had agreed it would be best if he stuck close to the children until all were thoroughly examined and the parents had come to take them home. After that it wouldn't matter what they had to say.

Molly had accepted the miracle grudgingly; in the end she'd reasoned that five people, including the old Cowboy, could not have been out of their minds for the better part of an hour. And as for mass hysteria, well, she didn't know anything about mass hysteria and probably nobody else did either. A quick meeting with King had been necessary; she hadn't bungled it, fortunately, given away the fact that she knew about the doctor's logbook. King had admitted that he wanted time to get a few things straight in his mind, and he had cooperated.

Thinking about the gossip—who could have known, who could have started it?—Molly had a sudden case of the jitters in the steamy restaurant. Had she been wrong not to move the Train out of town immediately? If she'd kept them all too busy to think, the rumor might not have found its voice.

She hoped that the subfreezing weather—and it was getting colder by the hour—would isolate the Train just as if it were back in the swamp. But a reporter getting a late start, or looking for something new to write, *might* happen around. Molly slugged down some hot coffee to calm herself. Or one of the choir members might trudge out to a telephone and try to sell the story for a few dollars. Well, suppose that happened. No editor would print such a story without checking, and eventually he'd have to check with Molly.

She smiled and felt better. She'd done her best, and in two more hours the Train would be gone. The gossip would die hard, but it would die, with distance.

Her steak came, and Molly ate with great enjoyment. Thanks to Dr. Matthews' keeping a cool head, they would be all right. The Mabry children could have ruined them—but the doctor had kept them all under wraps. By now that whole outfit would be back in the swamps, praising God and King Windom around a potbellied stove.

Molly chuckled at the thought and called for more coffee and a piece of egg custard pie.

Age knocked twice on the door to King's apartment before he heard Jeremy telling him to come in.

"No, he isn't here. In his study, I guess."

"I couldn't raise him."

"Let me try," she said thoughtfully, and went out. "Why do you want him, Age?" she asked over her shoulder as they walked from Pullman to Pullman.

"Some people here, from down around the swamp. Children who were in the wreck. Joe Mabry and his folks."

Jeremy stopped. "I thought—"

"The doctor couldn't keep them away. The Mabrys said they would wait to see the preacher, no matter how much time it took. Said if they couldn't see him here, then they'd drive on to Savannah."

"It's cold, and I'll bet they're not dressed very warm."

"I told them they could come aboard. But they won't, not unless King does the asking."

"Well, all right." And Jeremy went on to the preacher's study. She couldn't raise him either, but she kept trying. Then the door cracked open. "Oh, hello, Jeremy, Age. Come in."

A single lamp provided light at one end of the study. The spools of his tape recorder were turning. Beside the machine on the desk was a small Bible Jeremy hadn't seen before; there was a large skeleton key atop the Bible, with a length of string tied to it. King put all these things away in a drawer as soon as they entered. She noticed that his hands trembled, but otherwise he seemed composed.

Age explained that the Mabry family was present, and King listened, nodding, as if he had expected their visit.

"I'll see them," he told Age. "But not here; in the chapel." He looked at each of their faces. "It's all right," he said. "They need to be told that what happened wasn't a mistake—that God won't name a price for His generosity. You can understand how they must feel. They're Christian people and all their lives they've paid lip service to miracles, because the teachings of the Gospels demand it; but they don't know what to make of a

455

living, breathing miracle right there in the family. It's up to me to explain God's Power, and affirm it."

When Molly returned from dinner about twenty past seven, the large Mabry clan was leaving the Train. There were numerous children, and several old ones almost too feeble to walk. Molly had no way of knowing who they were, but when she saw Dr. Matthews at the edge of the crowd she made a quick guess, and pulled him aside.

"What are these people doing here?"

The doctor smiled vaguely. "Molly, they're here because I had no means to keep them away." He was unsteady on his feet and she thought he might be drunk, which disgusted her; then she realized he probably hadn't closed his eyes for the better part of two days.

"Don't worry," he said, rubbing his boiled-lobster nose. "They're all going home. They only wanted to look in his eyes, and hear his voice, and feel his touch. King has satisfied them. They can take the boy home now, with no sense of guilt because he's alive."

Molly eyed the family group. "Which one is Joe Mabry?" she asked, smitten by curiosity.

"The tall young man in the red suburban coat."

"I see him." There was a mist of light from the Train, but not enough for Molly to have a close look at Joe's face. "How does he feel about all this? Have you talked to him?"

"Oh, yes." Matthews sagged against her and Molly righted him with both hands. He smiled gratefully and apologetically. There were tears on his cheeks, from the cold or from exhaustion. "I questioned Joe for an hour this morning, after he was awake and had had some breakfast. I was the first one he talked to. He remembered very little about the accident. He didn't know how he managed to get off the school bus. I hated doing it, but I had to tell him he'd been burned. I had to prepare him as best I could for what was to come, when he saw his sisters and his mother. I made him go back and think it through, the last few minutes before the collision. It was terrifying for him; he wept. His body was literally on fire again. His skin was hot to the touch. If I could have taken his temperature just then I probably would have found it was over one hundred and five."

"Good Lord. And he's up and around tonight?"

456

"With the help of a nurse I packed him in ice in a bathtub and broke the fever. Physically he's sound. But he's a badly bewildered boy. He has an ordeal ahead which I'm not sure a saint could survive. I'm sorry for Joe Mabry." He teetered on his heels and his eyes looked bulbous behind the glasses he wore. "Am I right?" he demanded of Molly.

"I wouldn't know," she said curtly. "I don't care about Joe Mabry."

He smiled, hatefully. "No, of course you wouldn't be interested in his fate—but think about it for a moment. What are the choices for Joe Mabry? Will he grow up to be a humble man? Will he rebel against God's self-interest? Will he be driven to throw his life away? Oh, I wish I could stay close to Joe Mabry for the next few months—"

"You'd trade lives with any man, and I don't blame you," Molly said, not intending to be cruel. Probably he didn't hear her; the tide of fatigue in his mind was throwing his thoughts together like heavy stones. "You think too much. It's worse for you than rum and brandy. Why don't you lie down, Doctor?"

"Yes, I'll do that," he said in a dull voice, wiping his streaming cheeks. "I'll just say good-bye to them. . . ." He started off then turned abruptly back to Molly. "You'll want to see King; I left him in the chapel."

"Better get yourself aboard quickly, Doctor. We're leaving at eight."

Matthews grinned and wagged his head. "Wouldn't want to be left behind," he said to her.

When Molly entered the chapel, King was coming down the stairs from the dome. She knew he'd been up there in the dark looking down on the departing Mabrys. Thinking what? she wondered, with a perplexing uneasiness. The preacher's face was a blank, but he smiled readily when he saw Molly.

"Missed you at dinner."

"I was stir crazy," she admitted, pulling off her gloves and coat. "I had to get off by myself for a while."

King nodded. "I'm going to slip away when we reach Savannah. Take a long ride on my motor, cold weather or no. Maybe Jeremy will come along. There's a little fishing village I'd like to visit again if I can find my way. . . . Molly, why don't you sit down?"

Molly knew then he had plenty on his mind, and her eyes

turned a shade darker. She laughed suddenly. "You know, we're going to get away with it! Once the Gospel Train, and the Mabrys, have gone their separate ways. They can shout about the miracle as loud as they want to on their own stamping ground—who'll listen? It'll just be country people kicking up a ruckus in a pine-board church. You don't have a thing to worry about."

He reacted to her outburst with a grimness that was stifling. Molly scrabbled in her purse, not needing anything but a little time. "Isn't that the way you see it?" she said.

"Molly . . . I want it understood that I'm in no way ashamed of—or upset because God ordained a miracle of healing through the instrument of my body. I've had the pleasure of talking to and praying with Joe and his family, and I was moved to tears—we all were—by the presence of the Holy Spirit here in this chapel. I wasn't too sure about facing them, I was afraid of their questions and of skepticism, but, Molly, the faith those fine people have! Even Joe, who is just a boy after all—and six of his friends died in that wreck." King groped to reassure himself about Joe Mabry. "Joe will come through, if his own preacher down there is a wise and tactful man."

Molly, barely breathing, looked at him worriedly. "What else do you want me to understand?"

"I'm going to be known as a healer, Molly. It's inevitable. Because of Joe Mabry, God's great plan is perfectly clear to me—"

Molly's purse fell from her lap. "Didn't I say— It hasn't leaked out—there wasn't a word in the papers!"

"The papers," he retorted, softly scornful. "Molly, the afflicted will know about me. They are the ones God will tell—and somehow they'll seek me out." His voice was very dry. "Believe what I'm telling you, because I've been through it before. A week from now they'll be at every crossing, waiting. And God give me courage to do what is right and fair. God help me to heal with reverence, and fail with grace. Blessed be His name. I have accepted His Will."

"You've gone crazy!"

"Can't we talk, Molly? It's important that you—"

"We can talk when you start making sense. What do you mean, heal with reverence? You bloody fool!"

King said patiently, "I know you'll need time to arrange it, but I'd like to have a tent at each stop, near the train, where the

458

sick can find shelter. I'll receive as many as I can here in the chapel. But some won't be strong enough to walk aboard the train. So a tent would—"

"No!"

He looked down at her, unhappily. "Let's don't fight, Molly."

"I'm not fighting with you. I'm telling you it's out of the question! You're not going to turn this train into a traveling leper colony. What do you think will happen to the Southern Cross Crusade if every station platform is cluttered with hospital cases? All the decent people will stay home. The good middle-class pastors we depend on won't touch you; they won't even acknowledge your presence in their towns! We'll go broke in a month."

"You're exaggerating."

"After the torture I've put myself through for your sake, you come up with this scheme!" Tears formed in Molly's eyes. Still sitting down, she kicked at him, one foot and then the other. The indignity pained him more than the kicks. He backed out of the way. Molly sobbed. "God damn you!" She lurched to her feet and tried to kick him again. "Why do you think I've worked so hard? Do you want to lose all the respect you've won? Do you want to be looked on as a freak?"

King grappled with her and suffered more kicks. He shook her until her glasses flew off and her face was a blur.

"Stop!" Molly cried at last, and fell back, gasping, into a chair. The preacher retreated, hands clenched, and sat on the edge of the pulpit. Safely apart, they glared at each other.

Molly's mood reversed then, because it had to; she was aware that she would only defeat herself by violence. But what argument could change his mind? She was panicky; she had seen him this way a time or two. He looked normal to the eye, he spoke clearly, but his thoughts were locked to a wheel, he was in a mild state of shock, religious shock.

When Molly thought she could trust her voice, she said, "I didn't get around to telling you yesterday. I talked for half an hour to the—the chairman of the Southland Ministerial Association. That's in California—Los Angeles mostly. They're thinking about a week at either the Sports Arena or the baseball stadium in Chavez Ravine for you. That could mean a minimum of—of seventeen thousand people a night depending on the location. Dr. Lundgren's very enthused about you. I think what really set the SMA up was the fact that *Life* will

459

feature your story the first week in April, right at the beginning of the California crusade." Molly took out a handkerchief and blotted her cheeks, then reached for her glasses. "I'm sorry I kicked you. I'm sorry I God-damned you. I know you haven't had an easy time today. I think we can . . . discuss our problem now, and decide what to do—"

"Molly, I know what I'm going to do."

She winced, as if she couldn't believe her ears; he'd paid no attention to her at all.

"I can't understand why God would put His trust in me again. But He has. He intends for me to use my healing Power." The preacher's expression was hard, his eyes unkind, as if he could never forgive having been kicked like a schoolboy. "There's nothing to discuss, really. I'll go on preaching as I have done, wherever we go. But I'll also spend as much time as I possibly can praying with the sick for their recovery. Laying on hands where God directs me."

Molly's eyes flashed with fear. "You'll kill yourself; there isn't time enough now for all you want to do."

"Still I couldn't rest if I knowingly defied the Will of God. Whatever happens, I'm certain He'll be with me." King grasped his knees and lowered his head wearily, as if in judgment on his avowed certainty.

"All right," Molly said, casting about for a temporary compromise. "If you have to use your—your Power, don't make it known. Go out at night, visit the sick in their homes. That would be satisfactory, don't you think? That way you could choose: see only those you wanted to see. We could arrange your visits ahead of time; then there wouldn't be . . . bad publicity."

"I'm not looking for good publicity or bad publicity; I only mean to fulfill an obligation I—I'm not privileged to understand." He looked up, looked to Molly for sympathy. "Your suggestion is . . . thoughtful."

"It would work out," she said, gaining hope.

He smiled a rueful smile. "No, it wouldn't, don't you see? It's just another way of denying the Lord—choosing this one, or that one, going out only at night, pretending by day that I don't have the Power for the benefit of people with little faith and no tolerance. Those who need my help will come here, Molly, to the Train, because the Gospel Train is a part of God's Power."

"The Gospel Train is . . . all I've ever had to give you," Molly said in an anguished voice. "And you want to destroy it!"

"No, Molly, believe me—"

She groaned as if a needle had pierced her eye, fought against the chair, then laid her head back, looking still and shocked. "What makes you so certain word will get around? Tomorrow we'll be in South Carolina; Texas, three weeks from now."

King stepped up on the pulpit, turning his back on Molly. He lifted the candlestick from the altar and held it reverently to his lips. He seemed unwilling to utter another word.

"How will you be found out? Tell me!"

"I spent the afternoon making tapes, Molly, for those stations that carry my broadcast. I made an appeal to all the shut-ins who could hear my voice—the crippled, the incurable, the lost. I asked them to come to all the places where the train will stop in the next month. Age took the tapes to the post office a few hours ago, and mailed them for me."

Molly said savagely, "I'll get the tapes back. I'll see that they're burned or erased!" She left her chair and advanced on the preacher; he turned indifferent eyes to her. "And as for the human wreckage you care so deeply about—I'll hire a hundred men if I have to, but I'll keep those people away from you."

"I won't stop asking them to come."

"By tomorrow evening there won't be a station left to carry your message!"

"It's too late. You can't make me a prisoner on this Train, and you can't stop my voice from being heard. What time is it now? Seven-thirty? Eight? I'm talking right now over that big station in Mexico—the one that reaches from South Carolina to Texas and beyond, Molly. I changed tonight's program by telephone."

"Why? Why couldn't you have waited and talked to me?" Molly knew the truth immediately, without a word from him. Again she groaned, hopelessly. "My God, my God, what am I going to do now?" She turned and walked down from the pulpit and stood by a window. It was a quiet time of the evening. She looked down the rails at the old station, the windows of which were steamed up. They were on a main line of the Southern Railroad and she knew there would be a passenger train along sooner or later to take her . . . somewhere.

"I'm leaving then; do what you like. Get by without me, if you can!"

461

She waited a few moments for him to speak, but he was looking at the candlestick again, his eyes remote. Molly trembled, and her throat felt hot. But she had committed herself; to continue standing there was humiliating and purposeless. She started down the aisle, and then, as if she were naked in front of a hundred unfriendly people, Molly ran for her life.

She was sitting in her room beside a half-packed suitcase, suffocating with sobs, when he burst in without knocking.

"Please don't leave, Molly. I need you. I can't go back to a tent by the side of the road, to being alone, no matter what the Lord would have me do."

Molly wouldn't look up, admit to him or to herself that she cared he had come.

"I'm not crazy, Molly!" King said, emotionally. "Believe me I'm not!"

"I wanted so much for you," she cried. "You've beaten me. Can't you let me alone now?"

Abjectly he fumbled for her hand. She struck halfheartedly at him, and collapsed.

"Tell me you'll stay. . . ."

Long after it could really matter, he held her in his arms.

"Yes," Molly said, in a voice from the other side of the moon. "I'll stay."

44

Mary Kate Ransom

The little city of Teal, West Virginia, is situated at the back door of the Appalachians. It has sizable hills—which in the winter doldrums look like the teeth of a snuff-taker—a streaky river, a railroad branch, marginal industry based on coal and transportation. From the southwest Teal is reached by a state road that winds, dangerously at times, through coal-mining hamlets, where the veins are giving out day by day, and passing through them it is hard not to feel that in each a funeral has just ended, a funeral for the human spirit. By contrast you come over a succession of ridges like steps in the sky and there is Teal below, and you want to slow down, to go back or otherwise avoid direct contact, because it is a mean-looking place, old and gone a little mad with neglect: here the funeral might be yours. But look a little closer, for the iron steeples of the Catholic church and the Lutheran church promise a certain tranquillity. The hills are nicely paved with a still-white snowfall, beginning to soften in the unusual warm spell, and though a man knows the weather is apt to turn around and grow twice as harsh, still it is pleasant to think of spring near the midpoint in March, with the sky so blue and cloud shadows racing everywhere, mysterious as eternity.

Philemon, whose breakfast had poisoned him, said with a taste of brass in his mouth, "I got to stop."

Gilmer pulled in at the first service station and Philemon made tracks into the men's room. A few minutes later he reappeared, squinting at the bright sun, still looking miserable. But he'd eaten half a roll of stomach mints and he cherished the hope they might do some good, for once. In fact, he managed a tiny acrid belch as he trudged back to the car. Once in the car he could loosen his belt again. He thought, for the hundredth time, of seeing a doctor. But Gilmer wouldn't listen. The private detective wanted only to keep moving. He couldn't have cared less if Philemon died of a busted belly or a blocked intestine. He cared about nothing except finishing the job.

Gilmer was getting directions from the owner of the station and making notes in the little book he carried. Philemon drank some water and then wandered to the car and stood leaning against it, disconsolately, watching the coal trucks roar by on the state road. He looked with loathing at the city they were about to enter. He had only a vague idea of where they were. Somewhere in the south of West Virginia. He knew where they'd been the past six weeks: all over hell's half acre. Ohio, Virginia, Tennessee, Kentucky, West Virginia. They'd slept in hotel rooms that were glacially cold or unbearably steam-heated, and eaten wherever they could find meals. Sometimes a whole day passed and they didn't eat, and that was the trouble with his stomach. Too much food at one time, or none at all. Gilmer always watched him load his plate with a cynical smile, but said nothing. Probably he hadn't said ten words a day to Philemon, on matters other than business. Ate like a cat himself, and with care: always wanted to see the hamburger meat before it was fried, then cut it up into little pieces on his plate. No salt, no mustard, nothing. Sipped lukewarm milk. That was what he lived on. And at night, in the rooms they had to share, he sat down with his deck of fortunetelling cards and dealt them out endlessly. Or he cleaned his hand gun. If the town was big enough he occasionally went out to a bar, and maybe, Philemon suspected, a whorehouse, then returned to sit looking out the window, sometimes until three in the morning, while Philemon muttered in bed, shivered or baked, or locked himself in the bathroom trying to force cooperation from his reluctant gut.

Gilmer finished marking a road map and turned his eyes, which were like wet gray paint, on Philemon. "Ready to go?"

"Guess so," Philemon replied, his voice surly; he had long since given up hiding his dislike of the man he'd been cooped up with for over a month. But he'd flared up only once, over some petty annoyance in the depths of one of those forsaken small-town hotels Gilmer invariably chose. He'd given the detective a little too much lip and wound up on the floor holding that lip—split by the hard-shell back of Gilmer's hand—his mouth trickling blood. After that Philemon had cautiously discovered just how much resentment he could express without risking another belt in the chops.

He hated Gilmer because he was afraid, and he hated Gilmer for reasons more difficult to articulate. Perhaps it was the way he had been hit, cruelly but indifferently. If Gilmer was aware of Philemon's anger, or resentment, or boredom, he gave no sign. Philemon barely existed for the detective, and, as the days had passed, this fact wound like a shroud around Philemon's already troubled soul. He urgently needed to prove—to himself as well as to Gilmer—that he did, indeed, have a life, that he existed. The more he ached to acquaint the detective with the reality of his life, the less he was able to talk, even to think. Consequently his mental life and his dream life began to give him anguish equal to that of his mistreated stomach. He lost touch with the fantasies of an incomparable future, which had consoled him many a bleak night since Brother Hazelman had tactfully told him to go forth and seek his fortune. Instead he dwelled more and more on the one really significant act of his life, the murder of old Eli the Prophet.

Not for a single moment did Philemon ever admit to himself that he had actually done in a living soul, but somewhere in the snarls of his subconscious mind the truth glowed inescapably, and gave light to a great many horrors that paraded in nightmares which even the stolid Gilmer must have noted as hair-raising.

Because the detective had cut him off, denied him any sense of importance, Philemon could no longer boast with assurance about the future. (I'm a preacher, he'd said once, and Gilmer, looking at him, had doubted it; and Philemon had let the doubting lie and now he could no longer speak of being a preacher, because he himself did not believe it.) Instead he was often strangling to speak of that one crucial hour with Eli, who had wandered restlessly from the prison yard of the dead, only to be thrust firmly back where he belonged by Philemon's unflinching determination. Surely this had been a brave thing to do, his only bravery, and the detective would admire him for it.

But at other times Philemon wondered. Gilmer, in his way, was much like Eli. Eli had never wanted him to be a person, or to have a life. And so there were days when Philemon was so suspicious of the man he rode with that he considered running away at the first opportunity, forgetting all of the future that had become a blind spot in his thoughts. At times his fear of Gilmer had taken new turns. One night he had seen the square face of the detective become almost supernaturally sinister above his fortunetelling cards, and this sight had scared Philemon badly. He easily imagined himself as a captive. They were together almost constantly, except for those rare times when Gilmer went out of an evening to relieve himself.

Suppose, thought Philemon, there was no Mary Kate Ransom, and never had been. Suppose they were in these mountains for another reason and suppose . . . he was being taken somewhere by Gilmer. But where, and why? Philemon had no answers, but the face of Eli had been in his mind for a long time after that glimpse of the stranger who was Gilmer, and in every desolate town he looked with dread for Eli, returned once again, and vengeful.

465

This was a new day, however, almost springlike if the banks of glistening snow could be ignored, and Philemon had largely forgotten his recent terrors. He was reconciled to going on this way forever, or at least until his stomach burst and left him dead. Death, he thought, with a sad lifting of his eyes toward heaven, would be a relief—and it might be the only way he would see the last of Gilmer.

They drove into the city and down a precipitous hill; the gutters of the street were running full with the melt-off from the slopes. The glare of white snow and brisk water hurt Philemon's eyes and he closed them; he was not at all curious about where they were going, or what would happen when they got there. He knew what would happen.

"There's two places here in town," Gilmer said as they drove, and his attempt to make conversation was so unexpected Philemon looked up.

"Make no difference," he grunted. Then he said, "She's bound to be dead," and he had said the same thing at least a dozen times in the past week, without getting a response from Gilmer. But this time, after a gap of a few seconds, the detective turned his head slightly.

"She ain't dead until we find a grave for her. And that we ain't done."

Philemon had an answer. "Maybe she was just throwed in the ground. How could she live long with holes in her brain? And who'd want to go to a lot of trouble on her account?" Gilmer seemed actually to be listening, and Philemon felt bolder. "You take my word for it: she died one night from another fever and them Hobbies they just planted her out back with the others and no fuss about it."

Gilmer cursed under his breath as a passing car threw slop on the windshield of the rented car. "All the bodies were identified," he said musingly; "and all of them were old people. No twenty-seven-year-old woman buried in that yard."

"Well, maybe they missed one."

The detective shook his head. They waited out a traffic light silently. Philemon glanced at Gilmer and discovered something: Gilmer was tired. There was a twitch at the corner of his right eye and his mouth drooped. It was a revelation; Philemon had never seen him look tired.

"We don't know the Polanski woman taken her away, though. There ain't no proof of that."

466

"No proof," Gilmer said, squinting at the sun. "But a lot of little things." He seemed momentarily unsure that the little things, after all the hours they had spent in search of Wanda Polanski, added up to much after all. "The way Polanski treated the other patients, and the way she doted on Mary Kate. Dressed her up real fine, like she was a baby daughter. Bought her special foods, sat up round the clock when Mary Kate was in a fit, singing lullabies to her. No, Mary Kate didn't die, at least when the Hobbies had hold of her. Polanski took Mary Kate along when she disappeared. That's why we ain't found either one of them. If Polanski reads the papers, she must know by now old man Hobbie cleared her of any blame for what went on in that house. She's out of sight, and using a different name, because she's afraid somebody might show up and take Mary Kate away from her."

"Don't see why she'd want to bother all this time," Philemon grumbled. "Taking care of a stranger and for no pay; she must be a little crazy her own self."

"That ain't the right word," Gilmer said, seeming more tired than before, "but warped would do. I don't know whether to feel sorry for Mary Kate or not—provided she's still alive. Maybe she'd be a whole lot worse off in a state institution. Polanski couldn't get along with many people, but she did take good care of Mary Kate, and what difference does it make what her reasons were?" He became silent as they crossed the black iron bridge in the middle of town and turned north to follow the river.

"Could I see the picture again?" Philemon asked timidly, and Gilmer without taking his eyes from the road reached into his shirt pocket.

Philemon accepted the small photograph, reproduced from one in the files of a city hospital in southern Ohio, and gazed at the rugged features of Wanda Polanski. At best it was a totem-carving face, the expression implacably hostile. There was a four-carat cleft in the center of the heavyweight's chin, and her brow was flat and very broad. She had dark hair in the picture, possibly braided. She was wearing a nurse's cap. She had not been a very good nurse at the hospital in Ohio, nor had she done well elsewhere. Gilmer had traced her progress south, through a succession of dowdy private hospitals and nursing homes. Eventually she had reached the medieval establishment run by Charles and Martha Hobbie in Granite City, Tennessee, and there had found total acceptance of her methods for dealing with the aged and the infirm.

It was surprising that a woman whose appearance was as distinctive as Wanda Polanski's could have dropped from sight so effectively following the horror stories that had come out of the Tumblestone Mountain Retreat when the authorities started poking around there. But of course—as Philemon reminded himself—nobody really cared where Wanda Polanski was, except them.

He yawned; the stomach mints had taken effect, and he felt a little less like he'd swallowed a sackful of horseshoes. Gilmer had slowed down and was studying street numbers. He pulled up in front of a remodeled house, painted a cheery and not offensive shade of yellow. There was a small sign in the front yard, identifying the Ridgemont Avenue Home for the Elderly. Philemon scarcely gave the house a glance, and handed the photograph back to Gilmer. He thought of all the time they had spent tracking down former employees of Tumblestone, seeking a clue to Polanski's whereabouts. The single lead had been irritatingly tenuous: a Negro cook, while on a visit to Charleston, West Virginia, had spotted a woman who looked like Polanski, boarding a bus for Teal. The woman had been blond, though, garishly blond, the Negress admittedly suffered from poor eyesight, and the encounter had happened eighteen months previously. Still, they had nothing else to go on.

"This looks like one of the clean ones," Gilmer said, getting out.

"She ain't here," Philemon said, smugly.

The detective leaned against the car for a moment, and Philemon began to fidget as Gilmer's stare pierced his tender hide. But all Gilmer said was, "I'll ask in this place, then the other. And if I don't hear nothing, then"— he made a fist and tapped the car roof several times—"then I reckon that's the end of it. We've been on the road forty-two days. Polanski might be anywhere in the fifty states, working at any kind of job. I doubt forty men could find her. If Mrs. Amos wants to keep it up, that's her business, but I'm heading back to Atlanta." With that he walked briskly to the front door of the house, rang, and was admitted.

For the first time in quite a while Philemon sensed freedom, and as he did so he felt unexpectedly homesick, for the best home he'd ever had, which was the Gospel Train. The Train, he knew, was somewhere in Texas; he'd find out just where, and be on a bus headed west by noon at the latest. He almost wept at the thought of how glad his dog would be to see him. And he'd have a lot to tell Jeremy; probably she wouldn't quit pestering him for days until he'd described his every move for the past weeks. Philemon rolled down the window and sucked clean mountain air into his lungs. Abruptly he was able to think of the future again, of all his plans. He lovingly unwrapped the memory of more than eight hundred dollars safely hidden aboard the Train, and then to that sum mentally added the three hundred dollars which Mrs. Amos would pay him as soon as he returned. Today was the thirteenth of March, and if he rejoined the Train by the fifteenth, then, no later than August first—Philemon clenched his hands anxiously as he counted out the days—he could head for Clearwater with over two thousand dollars in his pocket for Brother Hazelman, and at last make good on his promise to contribute substantially to the building fund for the Archangel Temple of the Healing Grace. The church he had been promised as his own!

On two occasions since he had said good-bye to Brother Hazelman he had struggled to compose letters to the evangelist, and recently Mrs. Amos had forwarded a note from his friend and benefactor, breezily inquiring after Philemon's health and saying that all was well with them. Philemon carried the often-creased note in his wallet and he read it through every night before going to bed. It had provided needed comfort when things had seemed to be going so badly, what with the nightmares and his suspicions of Gilmer.

The detective returned as quickly as Philemon had expected. "No luck," he said, with a shake of his head. "It's a well-run place. But from what I gather the other one ain't. The people in there didn't bad-mouth Wycliff when I mentioned it; they just got a funny look like I'd dropped a cigar butt on their floor." He set the car in motion and rubbed his freckled face and continued north on the state highway. They had some distance to go and Philemon dozed off. When he awakened he was alone in the car, and shivering.

Gilmer had parked in the shadow of the Wycliff Private Nursing Hospital—which was what the place was called, according to a sign tacked to one of the posts of the gracious old-style Southern veranda—and Philemon had no way of knowing how long he'd been gone. He looked dubiously at the hospital and saw no sign of life, without or within. All the windows were barred.

Philemon made a number of rude noises which relieved his swollen abdomen, but he soon found that he couldn't tolerate the atmosphere he'd created for himself, so he got out of the car, taking pains not to fall on the crust of ice along the driveway. He waited in the open air for nearly ten minutes, and then he became uneasy. Why was Gilmer taking so long? Philemon hitched at his belt and wandered up the steps to the front door. He was mulling over the variety of warning signs posted above and below the bell pull when the door opened and Gilmer looked out.

"Come on in," the detective said urgently, "and keep your mouth shut until I tell you otherwise."

"I could use a Alka-Seltzer," Philemon informed him. "Wouldn't they have one in this place if it's a hospital?"

"Shut up," Gilmer replied, and looked like he meant it. Philemon shrugged and entered. It was dark in the hall and Philemon's eyes smarted as he strained to see. They went through a low gate and past a cubicle in which a woman in a white uniform was whacking at a typewriter, and turned left into a second hallway paved with brown and black squares of linoleum. There were a lot of insulated pipes up and down the walls and across the shadowy ceiling, and an exhaust fan high up in one wall rumbled loudly.

Gilmer stopped Philemon short in front of a door marked ADMINISTRATION and gripped his arm tightly. "Polanski was here until six months ago. Then she had a funny sort of accident. She was in the pantry one Sunday afternoon. Nobody knows why; she didn't have authorization. Stealing food for her pet, probably. A five-pound can of lard rolled off a shelf and hit her in the head. She shook that off but two days later she started having drunk symptoms. By the time they got around to drilling her skull she was gone."

"Dead?"

The detective nodded.

"What about—"

"We'll let Mrs. Danjeau take it from here. Just stick to your story when and if she asks."

He knocked on the door and then opened it, ushering Philemon in with a hand against his back.

"Mrs. Danjeau, this is Philemon Love."

She was a joyless, famished-looking woman with a coal-black eye to match her dyed straight hair. She had the smile of a dead horse and a slow, cold, nasal voice. "So nice," she said, rising from behind her desk and extending her hand. Philemon grasped it, looking elsewhere. There were no windows in the little office. The walls were lined with extremely old wooden file cabinets and the grimy wallpaper looked as if it had been breathed on by the paperweight dragon atop one file.

The woman resumed her seat and fiddled with her glasses, which were tied to a frayed ribbon around her neck. She looked expectantly at Philemon, who was avidly studying the legend printed on a yellow pencil lying on her desk. When she finally realized that he wasn't going to speak first she said:

"You must be overjoyed to find your cousin safe and—safe, after so long a search."

Philemon managed a series of winces to indicate his joy.

"It's quite a load off his mind," Gilmer assured her.

"I want you to know it's entirely a surprise to me that she wasn't . . . related to Mrs. Polanski. I was amazed when Mr. Gilmer told me the true story. It's unfortunate that this situation—"

"No harm done," Philemon said, and he looked helplessly at Gilmer.

"Could we see her now?" the detective asked.

"Yes, certainly." Mrs. Danjeau made no move to stand. "We've done our best to look after Mary Kate since her . . . since Mrs. Polanski died. Our directors suggested more than once that I . . . turn her over to the proper state authorities." She peered up at Philemon. "You understand that we're not equipped here at Wycliff to handle cases like Mary Kate. This is primarily a convalescent home. She created no real problems for us, however, even after Mrs. Polanski died. And many of our staff liked her. So I held out against the directors." The woman gestured with one hand as if to suggest a slashing sword.

"Mary Kate must have eaten her share of the groceries, though," Gilmer said, in case Philemon had missed the point.

Mrs. Danjeau smiled her cold clenched smile. "What matters is that Mary Kate has had a *home* all these months, and friends."

"Philemon means to see that the hospital is repaid for its kindness."

"Yes?" the woman murmured, sizing up Philemon again on the strength of this offer.

"Right now, though, he's anxious to see Mary Kate."

This time Mrs. Danjeau didn't hesitate. She popped from her chair and led them, with keys jangling in her hand, to the rear of the house and up a stairway. The second-story porch was glassed in to provide a maximum of winter sun for patients, but at the moment there were no patients around. At one end of the big porch a crop-haired young woman in a faded denim dress was wringing out a mop as she prepared to wash down the linoleum floor.

"Oh, Mary Kate," Mrs. Danjeau called. "Would you come here for a minute, dear?"

The scrubwoman obediently draped her mop over the edge of the pail, looked doubtfully at her hands, wiped them on a greasy apron, and came toward them. She shuffled somewhat clumsily because of her shoes, worn-out loafers splitting at the seams. They were a couple of sizes too large for Mary Kate's dainty feet. Philemon stared. This, then, was the big moment, the meeting with Mary Kate Ransom which he'd assured himself would never happen. He felt baffled and disappointed, finding it difficult to believe they'd actually found her. But Gilmer had described Mary Kate for him, and, despite six difficult years, her basic features were the same. Her black hair, with whorls of gray visible, was cut close to her head and looked clean. Her face also was clean but abnormally pale, except for overgrown brows and blue eyes. Philemon noticed that her legs were pathetically bowed and fleshless, like an underfed child's.

When Mary Kate was within a few feet of them, Mrs. Danjeau said out of the side of her mouth, "You mustn't expect too much. Her memory isn't good. I don't think she remembers anything about Mrs. Polanski, and *that* was only six months ago. I haven't seen Mary Kate myself for three days—she probably won't be able to call me by name."

But Mary Kate said with a tiny smile, "Hello, Mrs. Danjeau."

"Yes; how are you today?"

"The sun is shining," Mary Kate said, obviously pleased that this was so.

"And aren't we glad after the terrible winter we've had? I want you to meet—"

"I have to scrub the floor."

"It can wait for a few minutes. Mary Kate, this is Mr. Gilmer. And this is your cousin Philemon. Did you know you had a cousin?"

Mary Kate blandly pondered each face. "No," she said, when she was through inspecting Philemon. He looked at her hands. They were knobby, scabbed, each nail bitten to the quick. He felt uneasy because of the purity of her blue eyes. He'd expected a madwoman, a slattern, a violent, screeching thing, and he didn't know what to make of Mary Kate, who was almost pretty, despite her gaunt face and bowed legs. He was put off by her simplicity of expression—as others had been put off by Philemon himself.

"Mrs. Danjeau," said the detective, "there are a few things I'd like to talk over with you while Philemon is visiting with his cousin."

"Mary Kate, why don't you take Philemon over to the windows and show him the orchard, and where the goldfish are during the summer?"

Philemon looked pleadingly at Gilmer, but was ignored. The detective went away with Mrs. Danjeau. He was left alone with the eyes of Mary Kate on him. He didn't like the idea of being alone with a crazy woman for even one second. But she was such a little thing after all; he glanced quizzically at her forehead. For the first time he wondered about the story Gilmer had told him. Did she really have holes in her brain? He knew it was no lie about the fever—but holes in the brain! He smiled as if he had just told himself a good joke.

Mary Kate returned his smile. "I'll show you where the orchard is. Then I have to scrub the floor." She turned and walked promptly to the east windows, dragging her feet to keep the outlandish shoes from falling off.

"Is that what you do here?" Philemon asked, joining her. "Scrub floors?"

Mary Kate looked at him as if wondering how he could ask such a foolish question, and nodded. Then she brightened, pointing to a field of wild-looking trees. "That's the orchard." She licked her lips tentatively, as if trying to remember the good taste of apples. "Wanda . . . " she began, tugged at an earlobe, and then sighed, perplexed. She looked at him for help.

"Wanda Polanski?"

Her eyes became opaque. There was a tremor in her throat.

"She brought me . . . apples. Every day."

"Did she treat you real good, then?"

Mary Kate's throat constricted again, and her body tensed. She made no move but she looked ready to run. Her right hand flew toward her mouth; there were no nails to bite.

"I don't like to talk," Mary Kate said, drearily. Her eyes closed and she turned her face like a flower toward the sun. "If you look, maybe you can see the goldfish," she told him. "I thought I saw them yesterday." She stood there for a few moments longer, drinking in the light, then walked slowly away and picked up her mop. As Philemon watched, Mary Kate began to do the floor, her thin arms working as efficiently as pistons, and she paid no further attention to him.

Philemon knew what it was like mopping floors and he wished she didn't have to work so hard. He felt more or less at ease now because Mary Kate didn't seem crazy to him at all, just dim-witted. He wondered what she had been like before the fever nearly took her life in the Sugar Tree Valley. Better off if she'd died there. He knew almost nothing of Mary Kate's life before the fever; Gilmer hadn't wanted him to know. But Philemon hoped she'd had a happy life, to sort of make up for what was happening now.

During the fever Mary Kate's brother-in-law, a man named Boyd Ransom, had come to the Valley to look after her. He was in his late fifties and owned a good farm back in Kentucky. When Mary Kate was able to travel he took her home to the farm. The fever had severely affected Mary Kate's brain; she was little more than an invalid, but perhaps she might have been all right, given time and loving care.

Boyd Ransom's wife didn't like Mary Kate, however; she was unreasonably jealous of the poor little girl, and in a year's time she nearly succeeded in driving Mary Kate to suicide. Boyd Ransom reluctantly agreed that Mary Kate might do better in a hospital where she could receive professional care. But he balked at letting the state take her. Instead he found a private sanatorium he could afford. At the time it seemed like a good idea.

Mary Kate just got a lot worse at Tumblestone, according to all Gilmer had been able to learn about conditions there. When Boyd Ransom died unexpectedly, Mary Kate might still have escaped to the relative peace of a state hospital, but Wanda Polanski had arrived in the meantime and taken a fancy to her.

Polanski had protected Mary Kate from the Hobbies until state investigators discovered Martha and Charles were incredibly lax about filling out certain forms when patients died on the premises, and quite forgetful about notifying relatives, who continued to shell out dutifully for the safekeeping of their loved ones.

Philemon munched on a stomach mint and watched the broad sweep of the mop in Mary Kate's hands. It was quiet in the hospital and the sun had made him drowsy. As he waited for Gilmer he thought how remarkable it was that someone had always come along at the right time to give Mary Kate a helping hand.

Now it was Mrs. Amos' turn.

45

The Key and the Book

About ten minutes after the Gospel Train had stopped, Jeremy heard voices in the Pullman corridor—angry voices, it seemed to her—and she rolled away from the cold window, reaching for a robe. She hadn't been able to see much, although the sky was clear and there was a three-quarter moon above the frost-streaked plains. They were smack in the middle of nowhere, Jeremy repeated to herself as she got up from her bed. And what time was it, anyway? If they didn't quiet down outside, King would wake up—after all she'd gone through getting him to swallow the two tiny tablets Dr. Matthews had provided. She wrenched open the door, sharp words at the tip of her tongue. In the hall outside were two porters and the conductor.

When he saw Jeremy the conductor suddenly lowered his voice and gave her a troubled look. "Mrs. Windom . . . I'm sorry about this. But I need to have words with your husband."

Jeremy shook her head. "He's asleep right now. Can't you—"

"I wish I didn't have to bother him, but here's how it is. Some men have blocked the track up ahead to stop the Train, and they're armed. They won't budge until the preacher comes out and talks to them."

"They've got guns?"

"I don't mean they're looking for trouble. They have a sick relative home, wherever that is. They heard Reverend Windom on the radio, and they're hoping for—" The conductor was new to the Gospel Train, and he had his own ideas about King Windom, based on hearsay. He didn't believe in healing miracles and he tended to look upon his present assignment as a cut above working a carnival train. "If your husband wouldn't mind coming with us," he went on, "then maybe we can talk them into clearing the right of way."

"Why don't you call the sheriff and get him to clear the tracks?"

"Sheriff's a good thirty minutes away. Meantime here we sit, blocking the line between Austin and Sweetwater."

"Jeremy?"

She turned back into the room, reproachfully. "What are you doing up? Get back into bed now."

The preacher came out of the other room, buttoning his shirt. "I heard," he said faintly. "I don't mind going."

"No such thing!"

He looked at her with an obstinate smile, and grudgingly Jeremy removed herself from the doorway.

"Then I'll come too."

King shook his head. "Won't be but just a few minutes. Promise you."

"Take your jacket," she said, half angrily. He touched her cheek with the fingers of one hand and she sighed, relenting. "It's just that they won't *ever* leave you alone so long as you're willing to get up in the middle of the night—"

"Well, Jeremy, the conductor's right; can't let these men tie up the tracks. A little fresh air would do me good, anyway; I'm getting a touch of cabin fever." He zipped up his jacket, opened the door, and squeezed out. By the light in the corridor Jeremy saw how wan he looked, and her throat burned with emotion. Still, how could she have stopped him? Sometimes talking to him was like talking to a post, and the sound of her own voice going on and on, ineffectually, could really terrify her, because all she really wanted when she lit into him was the reassurance that she was needed.

Jeremy had tacitly promised not to follow, but she wanted to see what was going on, so she took her red coat from the wardrobe and left the Windom apartment. No one else seemed to have been awakened by the disturbance; she glanced at the floor-level grills in the doors of the five apartments as she went by, but all the rooms looked dark. The porter was missing from his cubbyhole at the end of the car. Jeremy went out into the cold air of the vestibule. King's motorcycle took up much of the space there and blocked the right-hand door so Jeremy opened the top half of the opposite door. She peered the length of the Gospel Train and saw the smoky fire and the men who were waiting for King.

The blockade consisted of several concrete blocks liberally soaked with gasoline and set afire. Behind the wavering screen of bright-yellow flame three men stood watchfully. They all wore denim of various hues, boots, and deeply creased ranchers' straws. Two of the men were half-pints and one was a youthful sagging giant who looked thoroughly ashamed of himself. They carried rifles, all right, but not with attitudes of great purpose.

On the other side of the fire Cowboy and Dr. Matthews were standing around, just waiting, with members of the Train's crew. It was near freezing, and when the fire died down a little, one of the half-pints carefully fed it again with a squirt of gasoline from a weed-killer tank.

"Evening," King called out, when he was close enough to be heard. "Cold as a pickle, wouldn't you say?"

"It is that," said the half-pint with the gasoline, and his smarting eyes studied the preacher hopefully.

"I guess you men are all prepared to spend your summer in jail for this stunt," the conductor snapped. He hadn't much enjoyed the walk out from the Train, which stood a hundred yards to the south, headlamps blazing upon them.

"Let's keep our tempers," King warned, with an annoyed look at him. He stopped in front of the fire and warmed his hands appreciatively. "Friendly enough to give me your names?" he asked the blockaders.

"Ezra Westerall," said the first half-pint, who seemed to be

477

the spokesman. He nodded to his left. "My brother Wade." Another nod. "His boy Hollis."

"Pleased." The preacher gave them a broad smile. "Why'd you all stop us?"

Ezra Westerall stared into the fire. "Only way I knowed. It's our older brother Jim that's ailing; he has been for two years now. Doctors can't do a blessed thing for him. We been hearing about you on the radio—how you was in Texas, and healing some folks, and it didn't seem to be no lie. Sometimes you can tell by a man's voice, on the radio or not, whether he's a honest man. Seemed like you were honest, and you meant it when you said everybody who needed God's help was welcome to meet with you at the Train. And maybe if the Lord was willing . . ." He fidgeted, and looked down at his half-frozen snakeskin hands. He was worried and scared, scared of being a fool.

"I meant it. Why didn't you come with your brother to Austin this afternoon? Or plan to see me in Sweetwater; that's not too far off, is it?"

Hollis, the big horse, wiped his leaking nose with a handkerchief. "Jim, he can't travel."

"Bones like piecrust," Wade Westerall croaked. "Danger to let him get up and walk in the house. Couple good wallops in a pickup, why, he'd come apart."

King looked around at the doctor.

"Could be a dozen things, depending on his age. Osteoporosis is most common."

"Jim's got aches and pains all over," Wade Westerall volunteered. "But he's not on dope the way he would have to be if a cancer had a hold on him."

King nodded absently; he was already concentrating on the bedridden man he'd never seen. How far do we have to go?" he asked Ezra.

"Bout five miles. Our pickup's there on the road."

"Room for two of my friends?"

"One of 'em will have to ride in the back with Wade and Hollis."

"That's me," Cowboy said promptly.

King turned to the conductor. "Where's the nearest siding you can wait for us?"

"About seven miles north."

"Would you tell my wife where I'm going and when I'll be back?"

"I'll do that." The conductor claimed King's attention for a few moments more by grasping his elbow. "You know, I'll have to report this to the division superintendent, right away. Lucky for these men there's no mail car on this Train."

Ezra Westerall overheard him. "Worth a stretch if Jim gets all right." And he shifted his eyes to the preacher.

"I don't make big promises, Ezra. It all depends on what the Lord wants and thinks best."

"I know that, and thanky. Come on, Hollis, them blocks ain't all that hot; get a move on."

When the fire was out, the six men tramped across the barren ground to a barely discernible dirt road and a stake-sided pickup truck with a couple of bales of hay in the bed. Cowboy climbed in and was followed by Wade Westerall and the boy.

The five-mile ride could have been much worse if he hadn't had the place of honor. But there was a thin cushion of feed sacks under him, and he had the bales on either side to keep him from being thrown helplessly about. The Westeralls braced themselves as best they could, and took the inevitable punishment with hardly an indication that they felt it.

Cowboy had plenty of time to think about the Westeralls—whom he admired for their resourcefulness and fortitude—about where they were headed, and what King would attempt to do. He was anxious for the meeting with the stricken Westerall brother to go well, because the weeks that had passed since the healing of Joe Mabry hadn't been good ones for the preacher. Abnormally bad weather had held the Train up many times and had resulted in canceled meetings. In states like Michigan there were sunny skies and snow-melting temperatures; in Tennessee and Arkansas and east Texas there was ice. Molly had cut their schedule drastically in an effort to get them to a warmer climate, but even along the Texas Gulf Coast they met days of rain and wind. They lingered an extra week in the citrus-growing country of southern Texas, and at last began to draw the crowds they had become accustomed to during the best days of the tour in Florida; at last the afflicted people whom King appealed to every day on the radio began to appear, seeking his help.

But then his Power of healing, which had brightened the long days of darkness and ice like a torch, began, inexplicably, to fail.

A particularly vicious jolt from the road unseated Cowboy

and he wrapped both arms around one of the bales. He coughed as the cold air cut too deeply into his lungs, and studied the brilliant grainy sky. He was at peace with himself, and here on the Texas prairies it seemed to him that a very long time had passed since he had fled in fear and panic from the visible miracle of Joe Mabry. He had run, he knew now, because he had been afraid of the supernatural in King, whose friendship he needed so badly. But in the pages of the New Testament he had found enlightenment, and reassurance. King was just a latter-day disciple after all, he'd decided, and many of the Twelve had had the Power to heal, a Power passed to them by Jesus. The Twelve had been touched by Divinity but they were not inhuman; they had struggled to teach and reveal the Word just as King Windom was now struggling, and they had known failure. King also had been touched by the Divine, inescapably blessed. But he was a man, his future as uncertain as any other man's. Cowboy had recovered from the shock of Joe Mabry rather easily once he reached these conclusions, and he was more devoted than ever to King.

He had stuck close to his friend after the first disturbing failures, which King had accepted humbly, with courage and prayers. But Cowboy knew that if he continued to fail then surely he would begin to agonize, and to doubt himself. Perhaps his great confidence in the ability of the human body to respond to faith was almost as important as the erratic Power itself, and it was questionable how long he could hope to comfort the sick when he felt as empty inside as a cast-off pitcher.

Cowboy gritted his teeth and, despite the numbing effect of the cold on fervent, constructive prayer, he devoted the last minutes of the ride to an appeal for help. When he again became aware of his surroundings, he saw a cluster of low trees, as if by a little river or a branch, and a propeller windmill against the sky.

Presently they pulled up in front of a small flat-roofed house and the Westeralls clambered stiffly out of the truck, rifles in hand, as if they'd returned from a coyote shoot. There were faces at the fogged glass door of the little house and dogs all around. The animal clamor made only a small disturbance in the immense night, a volume of sound like a pin dropped in a mason jar.

Two women came out of a trailer next to the house, and one

of them had a swaddled baby in her arms. Cowboy grimaced slightly, worried that all the people would be a bother to King. And inside there was family everywhere; the house seemed overheated from their bodies. The preacher, however, scarcely saw them. He had his mind on Jim Westerall, and somehow—perhaps old Ezra had told him—he knew just where the ailing man lay. He passed through the hushed living room and entered one of the tiny back bedrooms with everybody on his heels.

Jim Westerall's eyes were feverish by the orange light of a bedside lamp. They flickered uneasily at the sight of the tall preacher, whose face was set, harsh-looking. Then King's sharpened-sickle mouth turned up in a smile; he put his hands inside his belt and rocked on his heels slightly and said, drawling, "I know at first glance I look like the devil to you; but it's God's mercy I've come to talk about."

Jim Westerall raised his head from the big pillow on his bed, which was damp from sweat. He sucked in a breath of dry hot air and gasped for more. "Howdy, King Windom," he said, in a sprightly voice. "I'm an old sinner, and I ain't done my full share of repenting about it, neither. You better face that fact before you sit down."

"That so, Jim?" The preacher cleared a place for himself on the bed and when the man looked as if he was trying to move over, King motioned for him to be still. One of Jim Westerall's arms was encased in a grimy plaster cast.

"Broke that arm four times the past two years," he said when King expressed interest, "and this last time it's stayed broke. Won't heal. Lot of my bones got little cracks in them like the cracks in a porcelain sink. Waste a time to put on a cast everywhere but this arm's the worst." He slowly scratched at a stubbled cheek with his good hand and looked shrewdly at King. "You aim to fix me up?"

"Do you think I can do it, Jim?"

"Hard to say." His tone said it for him: it was all hogwash. But he laid a cheerful eye on his worried silent brothers, who had crowded close to the bed. He was not offended by their efforts on his behalf, and a preacher was as good company as any for a lonely and bedfast man.

Cowboy planted himself by the doorway and wondered what approach King would take with this resigned and not particularly God-fearing old man. It was not long before he found out; the preacher returned to Jim Westerall's great pride, his extraordinary sinfulness. To the apparent dismay and bewilderment of the family, he encouraged Jim to tell it all, and he laughed as heartily as Jim himself did at the escapades which the old man related. A couple of times Cowboy glanced at John Matthews, who leaned sleepily against one wall, arms folded, apparently enjoying the frequently bawdy stories as much as King was. A few of the women left, and soon Cowboy heard them in the living room furiously discussing King's lack of seriousness and his tolerance of the old man's behavior. Cowboy suppressed a smile and went on listening.

After Jim Westerall had laughed until he couldn't catch his breath, King said, "You know, Jim, I could use a bracer. What do you say?"

A shaken Ezra mumbled, "Women got some coffee on the stove."

"Coffee?" King thought it over and shook his head gravely. "I believe Jim here would sooner have hard liquor."

"Hardest you got," Jim cackled, shaking with laughter again, and he winked at the preacher; they were quite at home with each other now.

Cowboy saw that King's left hand had come to rest casually on the plaster cast. Ezra pushed by him, his eyes thunderous and his mouth white, and presently came back with a pint bottle of whiskey that had no label on it. This he handed, unhappily, to King. The women had returned to the doorway, having run out of recriminations; Cowboy could feel the weight of them at his back, and the velocity of their scorn for King Windom.

King held the whiskey at arm's length and stared at it. Jim smirked and waited, then crowed with delight when the preacher casually opened the bottle and sipped the whiskey approvingly. For some reason Cowboy felt a chill of anticipation across the back of his neck; he realized King wasn't doing this just to entertain the old man.

"I got to admit," Jim panted, as King handed him the bottle, "that I expected you to be a stiff-neck. You should get a load of the preacher at the Stronghold Fellowship Church, which is where Ezra and his brood go. Why, you couldn't squeeze a drop of red blood out of his veins if you wrung him with both hands, and good liquor would poison him!" He lifted the neck of the bottle to his lips. "I bet you raised hell in your time too! I bet you could tell some stories . . ."

"I could tell some stories, Jim," the preacher said softly, his eyes half closed, and he watched the old man take a nip of the whiskey. And then he said, in a completely different voice, "Keep drinking, Jim. I want you to drink it all. Don't take the bottle from your lips. Because you aren't drinking whiskey any more, you're drinking God. You're drinking God's mercy. You're drinking His forgiveness. You're drinking His love of sinners. Drink God from God's bottle, Jim. Feel His love spread like a tide through your aching body. Feel Him helping you." He paused for an instant, and Jim Westerall's throat muscles pumped as he pulled steadily at the whiskey that King would have him believe was no longer whiskey; surprise glittered in the old man's red eyes but though he seemed to want to fling the bottle away, he wasn't able to do so.

"He'll choke," someone said, horrified, but King began to speak again, commanding attention.

"You won't ever want whiskey again, Jim, no matter how long you live. You'll be filled absolutely with the goodness and mercy of God, and you won't need a drink. Feel the Power of God flow into your weak bones. Don't stop now—only a little left. Drink, Jim. Drink it up! Drink all of God. Drink it. Drink." The hand that rested on the cast began to tap gently. "Drink," King repeated, insistently. His hand hit the cast harder—the blow caused Cowboy to stir and wince. "Drink"—and King's hand moved quickly, tapping the chest and thigh and ribs of the sick man.

Gasping, Jim let go of the drained bottle and fought his way up from the pillow. With his free hand he touched his lips in a dazed way, then his throat. He tensed and suspicion burned in his eyes.

"What did you do to me?" he demanded. "What happened?"

"God's fixed you up, Jim. You're not a sick man anymore. Your bones are as strong as a boy's. Even that arm that wouldn't heal is healed now. Tomorrow a doctor will tell you the same thing—but tonight you can rejoice." King settled back, satisfied.

"It was give to me to die in this bed, and I know it!"

"That may be the truth, but you're going to live many long years first, praising God every day of your new life."

"I'm sixty-one now," Jim said, bewilderment straining his voice.

"You've got years to go, Jim—who knows, ten years, twenty."

"Oh, blessed Jesus!" one of the kinfolk exulted.

Jim rubbed his face uneasily. "I feel all right," he said, testing himself. And then, "Yes, I don't feel sick anymore. Yes, I know I can get out of this bed right now and not worry about fallin down." He bounced up and down on the mattress. "Yes, I can! I'm well. You made me well!"

"Tell God," the preacher suggested, with a smile.

"I'm sure going to tell God," said Jim Westerall, crying, and he climbed out of bed in his underwear to embrace them all.

The sheriff was waiting at the side track to arrest the Westeralls when they drove King back to the Train, and it took the preacher more than half an hour of negotiation to get them off the hook. Dr. Matthews went promptly to bed. Cowboy stayed around keeping a watch on the stars until they vanished one by one in the paling sky, then the two men walked to the Train.

"It was different tonight, wasn't it?" Cowboy asked.

"That's the wonder of the Lord. I didn't have much hope of helping that old man when I went to see him. I was pretty discouraged, I'll have to admit. But as I sat there talking to him, God revealed a way to save his soul and his body too."

"The whiskey you called for."

"Yes. It was one way of passing the Power into his flesh."

"But the Power wasn't in your hands tonight."

"Not the Power I've come to expect. Something different was there. Eyes."

"Yes?" Cowboy said, startled.

"I don't know if I can explain. I had eyes in my fingertips, tiny eyes, and with them I was able to see beneath his skin. I saw the cracked bones he was telling of. Then, after he drank the whiskey, God's holy whiskey, I looked again. The cracks were healed. The Power in my hands tonight was the power of sight. Maybe you think I've got a crack in my brain when I—"

"I don't doubt you," Cowboy said, but too hastily, and King looked at him for a long moment, distantly, almost with contempt. Then he turned his head somberly away, and shuddered.

"I'm beginning to believe . . ."

"Believe what?"

"That I'm in worse shape than my mother ever was." Cowboy looked sharply at him. They'd had several long talks about the preacher's boyhood, and Cowboy knew how often he thought about his mother and her short, sad life. "Maybe next it'll be bells in the night, and spooks talking to me."

The landscape was becoming clear as dawn approached. King stopped and glanced around, hands in the pockets of his jacket. Steam from the Train drifted white in the air. It was a peaceful scene, but there was a look of loathing on King's face; Cowboy guessed that the Train itself had prompted such a look. But within a few moments the preacher shook the mood that was hurting him and they said their good nights.

Jeremy awoke to find King sitting on the side of her bed, and, with a sigh, she rolled over, putting an arm around his waist. He smiled down at her.

"You're still wearing your jacket. Don't you want to try to sleep for a little while?"

"I'm not tired," he said.

"I wish you'd take it off, though. Wearing it makes me think you're about to run away."

Obediently, King slipped out of the jacket, his smile like a glaze.

"Did you help that man?" she asked, burrowing closer.

He was far away. "What? Oh, I think I helped him."

Jeremy listened to his heartbeat, and to the breath on his lips, and then she said timidly, "Tell me what you're thinking."

"Foolishness, just foolishness."

"But tell me."

"Oh, I was thinking of the summer I joined up with the Reverend Mr. Bonner—my first crack at being an evangelist. We preached two months in the Brasstown Hills, in a parcel of sour gum and hornbeak beside a clear river. When I'd get up in the morning the river would be as green as jade, and by nightfall it boiled with a ruby's fire. There were rosy, speckled trout a foot long in those waters, washed down from the mountains close by, and many times I pulled supper out of stone pools on the other side, with no more effort than to drop a line in. Middle of the river there was an island flooded over with sweet grass and bees, and all summer long the wind parted those grasses with a sound like a mother hunting for her

485

babe. We owned an old trailer, but most of the time Bonner and I slept out in the open. Some nights after the dew had fallen we could hear hounds in the hills, calling down on their fox with the horns behind them, and you just knew those skinny dogs would run all night and have the best time that could be found under the stars."

"Ummmm," said Jeremy. She wasn't really paying attention but she was pleased by the sound of his voice.

"Do you recollect watermelon Saturdays when you were little? Now, that was a feast! Give me one of those long striped melons that hum with juice when you plunk a finger against them. Remember big slippery blocks of ice wrapped in crokersacks and sawdust? I always liked the work of chipping those blocks down and packing ice around two or three melons in a washtub. You talk about a cold treat on a sultry day, I mean! Yehp, and all the little kids with juice on their faces and dripping down their bare legs. Whole rafts of towhees and meadowlarks going crazy over piles of black seeds in the dust. I can just see Bonner standing and licking the juice from between his fingers, then commencing to preach with folks still face down in their melons, with the sun low at the bend of the river and breaking fire through the trees. Bonner did some of his best preaching those Saturdays, everybody listening, played out and peaceful until the sky was dark behind him."

Jeremy waited contentedly to hear more, but instead of speaking King tightened his arms around her convulsively. She looked up; his eyes shone tearfully.

"What's the matter?"

He trembled. "Oh, Jeremy . . . God help me, I want to be free! But I don't know how to—to get out of this!"

"Why, it's easy. All we have to do is get up and walk off the Train. Then we're free."

King didn't reply, but he shook his head in annoyance as if she'd misunderstood his meaning. He continued to hold her in a death grip. Jeremy was calm, and when she felt him weakening at last she shifted her weight, easing the pressure on her sore ribs and breast, and pushed him gently down until his head was on the pillow of the little bed. She sat up with her back against the softly lighted window, watching him protectively. His eyes were open, filled with pain and apprehension.

"Talk to me," she begged. "Talk to me again."

He whispered something.

"Yes?"

"I . . . love you."

"Oh, yes! And we *will* leave this Train together, won't we? Soon."

"I don't know. The key and the Book . . . say we will. But that's just superstition."

"I don't understand."

"Years ago my mother taught me . . . one way to read the future. You take a Bible, and a skeleton key, and place the key in the Book of Ruth, on the page where chapter one, verse sixteen are found. You close the Bible on the key, leaving the loop outside. Then you bind the shut Bible with string, and wrap the string around the key so it stays in place. When that's done you can hold the Bible by the loop of the skeleton key with two forefingers, repeating the sixteenth verse of one Ruth before each question."

She nodded, a shade grimly. "Superstition is right."

He grasped her hand. "Jeremy, it does work! I've tried it over and over. If the answer to the question is No, then nothing happens. But if the answer is Yes, the key . . . heats up. I swear it does. The key gets hot, and tries to twist free of the string tied to it."

"Don't be upset—please. I believe you. If the key and the Book say we'll leave, then it must be so."

King muttered, "I asked the same question, over and over. The answer was the same each time. But I don't know when, and I don't know how."

"You don't need to know. God wants you to have a good life, He wants you to be happy."

"He wants *us* to be happy. Doesn't He? How could He possibly let anything hurt you? But the key dropped from the Book, Jeremy, it fell like a burning brand from my fingers when I asked about our happiness."

"You're imagining things now. I'm here . . . and I'm happy."

The Train had begun to move, quietly, and Jeremy's head grazed the window. She turned a cheek against the glass and its coldness effectively froze the tears in her eyes. She was glad of that, not wanting to destroy all the confidence she had claimed by weeping. And she was grateful for the clockless sky, for this hour, for the unfinished look of the earth. The Train shot on, across a broad coulee. The land rose, almost like a wave of the ocean, and she looked up, fastening her eyes on the crest of the hill, on a single tree taking flight against the mercury-colored sky. Below was a farmhouse, with unequal squares of light beneath the roof, and a mule and a wagon and a hatted man, wonderfully motionless, as if the stiffened light of dawn held them all prisoners. This scene lodged in the tail of her eye long after the Train had passed, and Jeremy felt a sharp hunger for the home place this man enjoyed. There was all her happiness, like a speck at the edge of her eye, and in her heart was a great litter, an inventory of emotions she could not bring to life in the cramped train apartment. In a home she could take out all her treasures, one by one, she could search her heart and fill a house. For him. For King Windom. And be the kind of wife he deserved.

No use thinking about it, though, as long as the Train rolled on. Jeremy bit her tongue. No use hoping for a home place until he realized he was wasting himself. Jeremy knew her husband's weaknesses, but she could not find fault, she could not show him his errors or make him change, although she was certain it was a serious mistake not to try.

King stirred, and she felt his grip on her hand loosen. She looked and saw his eyes were closed. He was breathing easily. Probably he wasn't asleep, but he looked calm, and that, she thought, was something to be thankful for.

46

Blackmail

Molly didn't notice the police car the first time it cruised slowly past her, going in the opposite direction; she had been oblivious to her surroundings for some time. But if she had noticed it she might have made some effort to straighten up and walk a little more briskly, indicating to the curious cops that she had a destination in mind, a place to get in out of the cold. Even then they probably would have stopped her, because her face was almost luminously pale and she was wearing a swank beaver coat, and quite obviously she didn't belong at the tumbledown fringe of a Mexican ghetto.

As it was, the cop at the wheel of the car turned around in the street without saying a word to his partner. For a few moments he silently kept pace with Molly, driving a few feet behind her, then he speeded up, nudged into the curb half a block down, winked at his partner, who shrugged indifferently, and got out. His name was Perez, he was young, and he was good with all kinds of women. He thought he had Molly pegged very well, from his preliminary look at her.

"Evening," he said, with a winning smile, when Molly was close, and she reared back, startled. She looked around the dark street, where only a few pale flecks of saloon neon caught her eye, and fumbled in the pocket of the long coat for her glasses. Rigidly she put them on; sharp vision seemed to cause her agony.

"What do you want?" she said, her teeth clenched.

"Way you were walking back there, I thought you might be . . . sick," Perez replied.

"I'm not sick—and I haven't had a drink for hours. I'm just out for a walk. And I want to be left alone."

Perez shook his head. "This is not a good section to be alone in."

"What's wrong with it?"

"Just take my word, miss."

"Mrs."

Perez had her pegged, all right, because he'd met dozens like her. One of the Juárez divorcees, killing a night in town before the main event in Mexico the next morning. She'd been drinking, but she couldn't get drunk. Maybe she wanted to kill herself—but few of them ever did, at least not right away, not there in El Paso. If Perez was any judge, this one just wanted a man to help her forget her troubles. But she didn't have the knack or the guts to pick one up.

"I wouldn't kid you," he said. "This section's real bad. It's late to be out walking, anyway. Why don't you let us help you get back to your hotel?"

"What time is it?" Molly asked, staring blankly at him, her lips compressed.

"Two-thirty."

She rubbed her jaw and moaned in a quiet despairing way

that made the cop, who was used to the sirens and sighs of human misery, flinch slightly and reconsider his judgment of her: maybe she *was* on the edge, a potential suicide, and she walked the streets because she was afraid to be in a room by herself.

"Do you know what time it would be in Los Angeles?"

"L.A.? An hour earlier."

She took hold of herself then and Perez felt encouraged.

"I didn't know it was so late. I'm expecting a call, an important call from Los Angeles."

All right then, said Perez to himself, let *him* handle you. "What hotel you at, Mrs.—?"

"The—I don't know—something Inn." Molly fumbled in her pocket again and produced a tagged key. She squinted at it. "Colorada Inn."

The cop whistled. "You sure a long way from there."

"I—" Molly shivered as if she had just become aware of the cold, and looked earnestly at him. "I have to get back. It's urgent. Could you give me a lift?"

"You don't want to ride up in front of a place like the Colorada in a cop car; be glad to call you a cab. Meantime have a seat inside."

He held the door for her and Molly sank down on the back seat. Almost instantly tears of relief rolled down her cheeks. She had walked for over two hours and her legs hurt her fearfully. Out there on the sidewalk she hadn't been aware of pain, of time passing. She sobbed, not caring what the two cops might think of her. *Found her alive, what do we do now, Mrs. Amos?* Molly lifted her head, shocked anew. *No, I don't want her alive, I don't want her at all!* But she hadn't told Gilmer that. She hadn't told him to forget Mary Kate and go home. She'd said, Wait. Wait, I'll call you later. Then she'd caught a westbound flight by the skin of her teeth at the Austin airport, leaving the Gospel Train behind.

Molly pressed her fists against her temples. It was two-thirty in the morning in El Paso, Texas. Gilmer was still waiting to hear from her. And Mary Kate lived—mercilessly patient—in the dark cloud of Molly's mind. She had lived all this time to rejoin the husband who had abandoned her.

There Molly stopped; she could not make herself think further of Mary Kate, and of her relationship with King Windom. That only caused her stomach to knot horribly and her wits to vanish like birds at the bellow of a gun. It was better to consider Mary Kate as a particularly complex problem; then she could function halfway intelligently. Then with a little luck she might hit on a way to use Mary Kate for the good of them all, without driving the preacher insane.

The cab arrived, and Molly rode back to the Inn, an imposing resort-style hotel with a magnificent view of mountain and desert and city lights. The telephone was ringing as she unlocked the door and she made a limping dash for it through the spacious darkened bedroom. It was long distance.

"This is Mrs. Amos."

Martin Handwerker came on the line. "Molly, where have you been?" he said, annoyed. "I've tried you twice since midnight."

"I'm sorry, I lost track of time. What—what did they say?"

"I don't know if I have good news or not. The Southland Ministerial Association has conditionally reconsidered its decision to withdraw support of our Los Angeles crusade. I guess that's good news."

Molly groaned with relief.

"But otherwise I didn't get far with them. They want complete assurance that King won't hold healing services. They're upset with the publicity he's getting with his radio broadcasts. They want a Harlan Gray-type revival, something for the family, no suggestion of miraculism."

"I'll talk to Lundgren myself in the morning; he'll have all the assurances he needs."

"Molly, he wants to hear from King himself, and no later than noon on Tuesday."

"I hope you told Lundgren he'd call!"

There was a silence. "No, I couldn't in all honesty tell him that. I think King has committed himself to a course and nothing will change his mind. Molly, is there any chance we can go ahead on our own?"

"Martin, we owe thirty thousand dollars."

"I didn't know it was as bad as that." He sounded stunned.

"I'd say we're about three weeks away from involuntary bankruptcy. The Los Angeles guarantee will save us. Put us in the black, even."

"King must understand that—"

"He says the Lord has always provided money when we needed it, and He'll do so this time. I can't talk to King about

491

money. He's afraid of debt. But he's more afraid of changing his mind, of admitting he's wrong. Something in him is haywire, and I can't fix it by sitting down and holding his hand, by sweet talk, by reason. I'll have to fix it another way." Her voice shook. "Martin, I swear to you he'll have Lundgren on the phone personally within three days. Now, Martin, I want the contracts for the Los Angeles crusade right away. I have to have them to keep our credit good. Work it out somehow with the Association. But get them to me."

The Reverend Mr. Handwerker thought it over. "If I tell them tomorrow King is willing to cooperate, I should get prompt action. A call from him would be a boon. You understand."

"Yes. Good night, Martin. Thanks for waiting up. We'll see you in Los Angeles."

Molly put the pedestal telephone down, then nearly knocked it over with her unsteady hand. Yawning, she rose to her feet and was staggered by her need for sleep. But she didn't dare lie down and close her eyes; the Gospel Train was on its way, and King would be in El Paso by five that afternoon. She searched through her handbag for something to keep her going full tilt for the next twenty-four hours. Molly was afraid of pep pills, they made a shambles of her nervous system, but tonight there was no choice. In the bathroom she drew a glass of water, swallowed the pills, and rinsed her parched throat.

Returning to the bedroom, she pulled a lounging chair close to the partially draped terrace doors and, still wearing her beaver coat, she gazed out at the moon and the mountains. For several minutes she nodded, insensible, her vision blurred, and then she felt the first effects of the pills: her heart labored and was sore, as if teams of tiny horses were hitched to it and pulling for all they were worth. Molly gripped the arms of the chair and sat up straighter. The unpleasant sensation of heart strain faded; she began to feel alert and competent, really competent for the first time in weeks. Wonderful little pills! So kind and helpful now, but later they would rob her, send her to her knees in agony. Molly smiled cynically to herself. She didn't care what happened . . . later. It didn't matter what price she was forced to pay. No, not as long as she had the strength and determination to deal with King in the meantime.

The powerful pills were slowly lifting her to new heights of detachment, of insight, as she stared at the faintly luminous mountains. Looking back over the past month, Molly found it incredible that she had knuckled under so easily, let the preacher have his way at every turn. He had held her in his arms and cried out that he needed her, and she, instead of taking advantage of his weakness and uncertainty, had weakened herself, had given in to passions a rosy-cheeked fourteen-year-old could have handled. And then she had blindly, permissively, helped him to take those first steps to destroy the Southern Cross Crusade, to turn it into a—her detachment was overcome momentarily and she quaked with indignation—chamber of horrors. But no more; she would deal with King now.

Was Age a liar as she had assumed he was; had he known all along that Mary Kate was alive? Well, that didn't matter, because King didn't know; he believed as he had been told that his first wife was dead. Molly felt a deep tremor of anxiety in her stomach despite her new mood. What would happen when he saw Mary Kate? She nearly shot out of her chair at the thought, and her heart pounded. But he didn't have to see her, not if he didn't want to. And that might make all the difference to King; she needed to plan carefully so the shock of learning about Mary Kate wouldn't unhinge him.

The night wore on and Molly plotted. From time to time she smiled buoyantly. She was running terrible risks by bringing Mary Kate to El Paso, but she felt equal to all the risks, thoroughly in control. What she had in mind was blackmail. It seemed to Molly that King would agree to anything to protect Jeremy, and all she really wanted from him was a phone call, and a pledge. For his cooperation she was prepared to help him. He would need an annulment from Mary Kate; that could be worked out. Everything could be worked out, Molly told herself. There was a humming and a ringing in her ears; the sky shimmered as with the light of dawn. She felt as if she could walk barefoot out over the bald mountains and knock heads with the stars. She was beyond caution; she could not see even a glimmer of trouble ahead. She had plans for her doll people, and they would perform as required.

Impatiently Molly waited for the sun to rise.

47

The Flight to El Paso

Ordinarily it took a well-placed charge of dynamite to get
Philemon awake and out of bed if he was fast asleep and
content with his dreams, but Gilmer had no time to waste on
him this morning. He dumped Philemon and the mattress on
the floor and then deftly packed a handful of snow from the
doorstep of the motel into his crotch when he still refused to
stir. He got Philemon's full attention right away.

"It's a quarter to nine," Gilmer told him. "A plane's flying
over from White Sulphur Springs to pick us up. Get your
clothes on; Mrs. Danjeau promised to have Mary Kate ready to
go when we get to the hospital."

Philemon was as prudish as a maiden aunt and he had
reddened from mortification and anger at Gilmer's casual
violation of him. But the detective's words kept him from
kicking up a fuss. At last they were leaving—and by plane! He'd
been thinking about a lengthy bus ride at his own expense, so
he was even more thrilled by the prospect of his first flight.
Without hesitation he dressed in corduroys and a travel-soured
flannel shirt, put on his oversize Army coat, grabbed his duffel
bag, and jumped into the car outside. The sky was flawless, the
sun blinding. He covered his eyes with a pair of dark glasses he
had picked up in the washroom of a filling station—it wasn't
stealing; people never came back for stuff they left at filling
stations—and had breakfast, a Coke and what was left of a box

of day-old Cheez-Its. His favorite gospel quartet was singing on the radio: "Amazing Grace." Philemon babbled happily all the way to the hospital. He was friends with the world today.

The stop at the hospital was a brief one. Mary Kate was waiting, accompanied by the nurse Mrs. Danjeau had recommended. Mary Kate was nicely dressed: she had on a brown coat with velvet trim, warm red stockings, new black shoes. He wondered how Mary Kate, who was a pauper and alone in the world, could have such pretty clothes, but then he remembered the late Wanda Polanski and her generosity.

Despite her clothes Mary Kate didn't look too well. She couldn't stand by herself, and her head drooped. Philemon said hello and smiled but Mary Kate seemed not to hear. As soon as she was helped into the back seat of the car she fell asleep. Her nose would run, and the nurse would wipe it with a Kleenex. The nurse's name was Mrs. Coleman, and Philemon didn't take to her. She was short and blocky and wore a hearing aid like a beetle in her ear, and she closely resembled a teacher who had made life miserable for him in the fourth grade.

The chartered seven-passenger Super Beechcraft was waiting for them at the Teal airport, one engine running. Gilmer drove right out onto the field and parked beside the little airliner. The copilot helped Mary Kate aboard: she walked but she was out on her feet. Philemon stowed the luggage away. He chose a seat in the back of the plane opposite the door, where the wing wouldn't block his view, and the amiable captain showed him how the seat belt worked. He sat there for ten minutes strapped in, working up a sweat of anticipation while Gilmer settled with the rent-a-car people.

By the time the plane had reached its maximum altitude west of Teal, Philemon was so gaspingly airsick that he couldn't get up and make use of the small toilet in the compartment behind him. Mrs. Coleman had to help him in his seat, and her contempt for him as she scrubbed everything down was more difficult to bear than the stabbing pains in his upset stomach.

They stopped in Nashville around noon and Philemon laid in a supply of Marezine, which put a stop to the seizures; a nap calmed his nerves. They were near Hot Springs when the southwesterly sun settled on the port window where he slept and gradually awakened him with its heat. He took an interest in the landscape below, and weathered some tricky bumps over the Ouachita Mountains with hardly a butterfly. Then he became bored, because one mountain looked like another this season of the year. He made an unnecessary trip to the lavatory to stretch his legs and stopped on the way back to his seat to see how Mary Kate was getting along.

Her face was shiny, with a blue cast to it, and there was a puffiness around her closed eyes. She slept with her head well protected by pillows. Philemon wondered how she could sleep so long and so soundly. What would she think when she awakened, so far away from the Wycliff Hospital? Well, she'd been moved around a lot the past few years; maybe she wouldn't care. He felt sad, though, looking down at her; he felt vaguely responsible for her well-being. Gilmer had told him only that Mrs. Amos had found Mary Kate a better place to stay, and that was why they were flying her to El Paso. He hoped it was true, hoped the new place would be less like a jail; maybe they would have a garden there. And hired help to scrub the floors.

The nurse had her eye on him; she looked ready to leap up and bite if he so much as reached down to straighten the blanket across Mary Kate's lap. Philemon stared back at her to show he wasn't intimidated or indebted, then resumed his seat and thought about how hungry he was until the plane touched down in Texarkana.

It was dusk when the Gospel Train reached El Paso, and, as usually happened when they arrived for an extended stay in a good-size city, a crisis was waiting. This one involved local Army brass. The siding Molly had leased from the railroad was needed temporarily by the military. Cowboy eventually worked out a compromise by agreeing to take the Train elsewhere immediately after the night's revival, but he handled the problem himself only after wasting a lot of time on the telephone trying to locate Molly.

She had not been at her hotel since shortly before noon, and she had not left word where she could be reached. This was decidedly strange behavior, for even on her rare trips away from the Gospel Train Molly had always called on the hour to keep herself posted. Cowboy expected to find her at the siding out by Fort Bliss where the tent had been pitched for the Southern Cross Crusade, but she wasn't there either. By eight o'clock Molly was still missing, and Cowboy couldn't spare any more time to find her. The revival was under way, and he was needed in the tent.

Philemon heard Mary Kate groaning, a sound which snatched his attention from the terrors of Isaiah, and he looked up, blinking foggy eyes. Except for the reading light above his seat and the one above Mary Kate, the cabin was dark. Gilmer and Mrs. Coleman had both left their seats and were talking with heads together. The noise of the engines kept Philemon from overhearing, but Mary Kate groaned again, loudly. He closed his Bible and went forward to see if he could help.

"Give her another shot," he heard Gilmer say.

"I wouldn't want to be responsible," the nurse said. "She's reacted so badly to the one she had this morning—" Her mouth clamped shut as Philemon approached, innocently.

"Is she sick?"

Gilmer turned his head a fraction. "Nothing she won't get over."

Philemon saw that Mary Kate was waking up, but she was having a terrible time of it. Her skin looked like soap with a blue glaze on it and her half-opened eyes were weak and rheumy. She was strapped securely in the seat, perhaps too tightly. Her hands lay lifeless and wet in her lap.

The airplane wavered and Philemon, with a glance out the window, watched the left wing dip; far off across the desert void the little star cluster that would become El Paso and Juárez was now in view.

"Can't you do nothing?" Philemon asked, returning to Mary Kate. "She looks bad."

Mary Kate moaned, and her lips parted to reveal tooth gaps and a few flecks of foam at the tip of her tongue.

"She's just hung over, and the pressure up here bothers her. Once we're on the ground and she gets the knack of walking again she'll be fine." The detective chomped down on a toothpick and winced as it stabbed the underside of his tongue. "Thirty more minutes," he mumbled, as if he didn't really believe it, "and she ain't my problem anymore."

Gilmer had spoken to Molly during the short layover in Nashville, and Molly had assured him that she would be waiting at the International Airport with a car when they touched down. As it turned out, the car, a funereal Ford sedan, was there, but Molly was not. Gilmer returned to the airplane, which had been parked a good distance from the terminal in an area reserved for noncommercial aircraft, after several futile attempts to learn where Molly was, and what her intentions were now that Mary Kate had arrived. It was half-past nine, Mountain Time, the massive knockout shot administered to Mary Kate sixteen hours before had almost worn off, and the detective didn't know what to do next. The logical thing would have been to wait aboard the plane for Molly, but they were all sick to death of being cooped up in the small cabin. Philemon was complaining, Mary Kate was a trial now that she was almost awake, and Gilmer had the beginnings of a nervous headache from the constant throb of the engines. After all, the car was there, Molly had arranged for it, and although the rent-a-car agent apparently had not received instructions, it seemed reasonable to believe that Molly expected him to drive to the tent grounds and contact her there.

The longer he considered this course of action the more he cherished it. Gilmer was a good detective and he had built a fair reputation by being methodical and conscientious about his work; ordinarily he would have given this situation the most careful analysis, picked at all the traps with the detachment of a burglar sizing up a job, and then rejected any move until Molly made her wishes perfectly clear. But one thing made him overanxious, made a broth of his judgment. He had taken a liking to Mary Kate, just as Philemon had. From her color and the forced rustling sound of her breathing he suspected that she had been given too big a dose of narcotic at the Wycliff Hospital for her weakened system to handle. In his opinion Mary Kate needed medical attention, despite Mrs. Coleman's indifference to her condition. And if something went really wrong—if, for instance, she died on his hands—investigation undoubtedly would show that there was just cause for a permanent revocation of his license.

Despite Philemon's feelings to the contrary, Gilmer was human. He wanted to wind this thing up, and badly. He felt a little sorry for King Windom, whom he'd never laid eyes on, because King Windom had two wives and was going to have to face that fact. Gilmer wasn't interested in Molly's motive. He was perfectly certain she was going to create more trouble than she could handle, but it wasn't his worry. He'd been paid well and he'd done his work, and that was that. If and when it got hairy he'd be a long way off. He hankered for his home. The hell, he thought. No sense sticking around here any longer. She's not coming. Wires crossed. Let's go.

They were all happy to get off the stuffy plane. Even Mary Kate seemed to benefit from the cold dry air; still, she needed help to walk to the car and she couldn't hold her head up for more than a few seconds at a time.

Just before driving off, Gilmer had misgivings. He quickly got out and went into the office of the flying service that was looking after the airplane. It wouldn't hurt, he figured, to leave word for Molly, on the chance that she would come to the airport after all. The way things were going, they might chase each other around El Paso all night.

Molly hadn't spent a nickel to promote King's visit to El Paso, but the two-hundred-thousand-watt radio station in Mexico that carried his broadcasts was not far away, and so a crowd of over three thousand people had been attracted to the first meeting of the crusade. All seats in the tent were taken, and half a hundred latecomers stood outside the west entrance, as close as possible to fires which blazed in metal drums. The big tent was just east of the spur track and the Gospel Train; in between there was a wide stony road with a triple line of cars parked along it. The road provided access to a highway. It was an ill-lighted location and even the crystal brightness of the moon over a nearby mesa wasn't much help.

The dark and the crowd and the mass of cars and trucks made the detective's headache worse. The revival was in full cry, and he knew it would take a lot of looking to find Molly. He sent a reluctant Philemon to comb the Train for her and got out himself; he closed the door to keep the light off Mary Kate and Mrs. Coleman, but he didn't start for the tent right away. Mary Kate was groaning and crying. She was half sick and half scared. She didn't want any part of Coleman, which he found understandable. She huddled deep in the back seat, and sobbed for her bed, for all that was familiar in her life, and peaceful.

"Listen, can't you keep her quiet?" Gilmer said through gritted teeth.

"Don't get horsy with *me*, I'm doing the best I can. I think she's got a cramp—is that the trouble, honey? Tell Mrs. Coleman."

"I want to get out," Mary Kate begged.

Gilmer cast around, feeling jumpy and vulnerable. He heard the preacher in the tent, although his words weren't clear. A jet whooshed into the sky from the airport. About a hundred yards away a train crew worked between cars on a faulty coupling or broken hose connection. But the road was empty, and no one was observing them.

"Let her have some air," he said. "Stay close to the side of the road."

As soon as she was out of the car Mary Kate calmed down. With her head back she studied the stars while Gilmer rocked on his heels and smoked. Then Mary Kate went for a short walk, Coleman a step behind her, to catch her if she stumbled. Gilmer was pleased with the way Mary Kate handled herself; she walked as if there were only a tightwire under her feet and not the earth, but she was steady. Good girl, he thought, more relaxed than he'd been for hours. He eyed the jiggling lights of the train crew. One of them appeared to be wearing a coat of reflector buttons—some sort of safety gear.

A car turned off the highway and came toward them, very fast, with a sound of small rocks chunking fenders. Caught by surprise, Gilmer drew back from the lights and motioned violently to Coleman, who tried to get Mary Kate into the Ford. Mary Kate had understood that she was to be free, and she screamed in protest. Coleman had a lot of muscle but Mary Kate in her bulky coat was hard to hold. Screaming again, she fell to her knees and wrapped her arms around the front bumper of a light truck that was parked next to the Ford.

Gilmer was there in an instant to plead with Mary Kate. He crouched over her as the headlights from the recklessly speeding car lit up the scene; unthinkingly he pressed a hand over Mary Kate's mouth. He waited, motionless, his back to the road, for the car to pass. But it stopped, twenty feet away, lights blazing, and he sensed, as he had once before that night, that it was all about to go wrong, and there was nothing he could do.

He heard a car door grate open and lifted his head. "For God's sake hold them off," he whispered to Coleman, convinced they had somehow attracted the police. But she was staring rather stupidly into the lights and he knew she'd swallowed her tongue. He looked down despairingly at Mary Kate. He had her pinned against the truck bumper and she wasn't struggling. There was undiluted terror in her eyes.

"Just get in the car with us," he said earnestly. "That's all I ask. For a little while longer. Then we'll let you go."

He heard quick footsteps, stones scattering, and looked over his shoulder.

"You fool," Molly said wrathfully, "why didn't you wait at the airport?"

He'd already asked himself that question, and he wasn't in the mood to take a licking from Molly. "Why weren't *you* there?"

"I had to drive to New Mexico to find the right place for her." She stared at Mary Kate. "What happened? What did you do?"

"Turn those lights out!"

"Oh," Molly said, looking startled and confused. She took a step toward the car she'd left in the middle of the road, then stopped as if someone had built a wall in her way. "Oh, my God, it's the nigger!"

Gilmer understood by her tone that they were in for a lot of trouble, and his first concern was for the back of his head. He could move fast for a middle-aged man. He jumped to one side, away from Mary Kate, then rose in a crouch with his fists ready. A nigger was standing there, all right, come out of nowhere. He had on a crazy-looking yellow raincoat with bicycle reflectors attached to it. A kid's joke, but he was no kid and looked like a hard man to stop. Gilmer was particularly concerned about the steel flashlight he carried in one hand. Then he realized that the nigger was going to be easy. The nigger was in a state of shock. He was seeing a ghost.

"Mary Kate," Age said hoarsely. "Mary Kate!"

"She fell," Gilmer said. "You'd better pick her up." He was on the lookout for other intruders, but if anybody else had heard Mary Kate scream, they weren't making it their business. If there were no cops around, he told himself, they could get out of this. They just needed a piece of luck now. "The lights, Mrs. Amos," he said again, sternly. "Dim the car lights and be ready to go." She jumped to obey him.

"Mary Kate . . . don't you know me?" Age raised his hands pleadingly and edged closer. "I thought you were dead—I saw your grave, Mary Kate, right next to your little daughter's grave!"

"What do you know, you made a mistake," Gilmer said. "Go

501

ahead, touch her—she's real." He glanced at Mary Kate, who was quiet for a moment, but uncomprehending, badly frightened. Gilmer counted his moves in his mind. With a little piece of luck . . . "Pick her up!" he ordered Age. "Can't you see she's hurt?"

At that instant the headlights clicked off. Gilmer leaped at Age and met him in midstride. He slugged Age on the cheekbone with his left hand and a bolt of pain exploded up his arm. A split second later his right hand hooked Age in the throat as he fell.

Gilmer groaned, holding his damaged left hand. He knew at least a couple of knuckles had split, but the nigger was thoroughly stunned, lying helpless on his back. "Coleman!" the detective growled. "Put Mary Kate in the car!" He reached down, seized a handful of the yellow slicker, and dragged Age to the side of the road. Then he picked up the steel flashlight. He heard Mrs. Coleman gasp and turned the light on her face. She was some shucks in an emergency, he thought angrily. She raised a trembling hand and pointed to the tent.

"I couldn't stop her—she ran that way!"

Gilmer cursed and aimed his light. It burned through a couple of windshields and gave him a glimpse of Mary Kate, headed straight for the tent's west entrance, for the knot of people standing there. He shoved the flashlight into his coat pocket and followed her, trying not to run. She wasn't running either, he saw, as he worked his way through the staggered lines of cars, but walking very fast across the dark space of ground to where the barrels flamed.

Several heads turned toward Mary Kate when she came into the firelight. The sudden attention stopped her in her tracks. After a moment's indecision she veered off into the darkness, heading away from the entrance. Gilmer was overjoyed; he felt sure he would catch up to Mary Kate, and then . . . It was too much to hope she'd trust him. If he could just divert her, keep her calm, then Molly could help get her back to the car.

He was sweating and his face felt deathly cold. Mary Kate had a good lead on him but she was tiring, beginning to drag her feet. Gilmer closed in as fast as he could, but he was climbing now because they were on a slope, rocky and deeply scored in places, with sharp little desert plants that pulled at his cuffs. His eyes were now used to the dark: he saw a chain-link fence ahead, slanting to the horizon. Mary Kate saw it too but she drove herself straight to the wire. There she sobbed hopelessly, hands raking the icy metal. Gilmer stopped, watching her drift along the fence. Too bad, he thought. Too bad it had to be there. He switched on the flashlight and went to collect her.

But he'd underestimated Mary Kate again. She shied at the touch of his light and plunged down the slope.

"Don't," he called, "don't run; you'll fall and hurt yourself." He shot the beam ahead of Mary Kate, giving her a path to follow. He wasn't afraid of losing her—how long could she keep up the pace? He was only afraid of an accident, of broken bones.

He was so absorbed with Mary Kate's safety as she ran toward the tent that he didn't see the two men blocking his path until one of them grabbed his shoulder with a hand like a piece of machinery.

"What you want with that girl, mister?"

Gilmer took them in at a glance. "She's my youngest, boys," he said, "and she's feeble. I brought her to see the preacher, but a nigger scared her there on the road. Wasn't his fault, but niggers have always scared her bad. Would you help me with her? I could sure use the help."

The two behemoths exchanged glances. Gilmer tried to keep Mary Kate in sight while they decided whether to believe him or welt him some. He picked her up standing near the tent not far from a refreshment wagon. King Windom's voice sounded faintly to his ears. Was she listening to him, and would she know his voice? Gilmer tried to slide away from the hand clamped to his shoulder. His captor held him fast a few moments longer, then let go.

"If it's family, don't know we ought to mix in."

"I think she's over her scare, boys—she'll come with me. Thanks, anyway." Gilmer broke around them and jogged along to the tent. But he was a little late. After catching her breath, Mary Kate had slipped inside. Panic-stricken, Gilmer ran, hoping to snatch her from the tent. It would be a terrible thing to happen, it would be a blow to kill a man, whether he deserved the blow or not. He wished fervently that he had not come to El Paso. He had done the job he was good at: he'd put together bits and pieces and found a missing woman. He could have left West Virginia the day before, gone home to Atlanta, and been at peace with himself. As he pushed canvas aside and found his way blocked by a wedge of people between two tiers of seats, Gilmer was just aware that after this night it might be a long time before he would be at peace with himself again, and he placed a heavy curse on the soul of Molly Amos.

Molly had got out of her rented car after switching off the lights, looked blankly at the prostrate and semiconscious Age, whom she recognized but could not name, and then gone straight to the tent, ignoring Mrs. Coleman. After two days without sleep Molly was half blind, and even if she'd looked in the right place for Mary Kate and the detective she probably wouldn't have seen them. That afternoon the pep pills had begun to let her down, she'd felt as if she were in a falling elevator, so she'd gobbled more, and the elevator, made of cut glass and filled with pink air, had shot up to hit the moon. In many respects Molly was as alert as ever—she had a clear if distant vision of disaster—but the lofty mind and the earthbound body were not in harmony. They were like an ant and a boulder of sand that had at all costs to be moved.

There was no way she could get through the crowd, not without creating a scene, but as she peered around she discovered in the bracework beneath one tier a figure, moving formally through the maze. It could have been a child or a small woman, but Molly thought it was Mary Kate and so she followed eagerly, bruising her unwieldy head and bumping her shins against the pipes in her haste. If she'd stayed where she was, by the entrance, for another minute or so, Mary Kate would have run right into her.

She was attracted by the voice of the preacher, not because it was a familiar voice but because it spoke of Christ, and the Bible, and the love of the Lord, and she knew what those things meant. He will love you, the preacher said, He will look after you—what harm can befall you in the arms of your Shepherd? Why should you fear Him? But she wasn't afraid of Jesus, she knew that. Only of people—only of being pursued. Jesus is here; Jesus is waiting, said the preacher. What reasons can you have for denying Him even one second longer? Tears of exhaustion rolled down Mary Kate's cheeks, her legs trembled, and she had to hold tight to a stanchion to keep from falling, but there was gladness in her heart. Jesus was near, and the preacher was calling to her. Come. Come. She looked at the backs of men standing in her way, and at the fortress of seats overhead. How could she reach Him, there in the depths of the tent? She was afraid of being seen; sometimes eyes made her melt away, just as ice melted in the sun.

The sound of a cough sent her darting, like a shadow, to her right, into a waiting cage beneath the seats. Here she was alone, and she quickly discovered, before she could react to fears of entrapment, that she was slight enough to force her way between the rigid supports and the drum of dirty canvas. There were plenty of handholds to help her along and she moved quickly, drawn by the voice of the preacher.

Soon she came to another passage between tiers and, cautiously, she crept out into the open. There were people here too, but she was not afraid of them—she was accustomed to invalids. A terribly deformed woman sat in a wheelchair, holding a cross in one hand, gazing vacantly at the pulpit. An emaciated yellow man lay on a stretcher, covered by a sheet. The blind tended the blind; the deaf prayed soundlessly and talked to one another with frantic fingers. Mary Kate moved slowly past these unfortunates, blinking at the harsh lights that were focused on the pulpit and the tall preacher. His back was to her, but Mary Kate was not all that interested in the preacher: she was looking for the Lord Jesus. And when she didn't see Him, fresh tears formed in her eyes. Was she too late, had He come and gone? It seemed to her that she had been to visit the Lord Jesus before, long ago, and she had not seen Him then either, because only certain holy men were allowed to look upon His face, only the beloved and faithful.

The preacher seemed to be such a man. There was great confidence in his voice. Mary Kate, who did not like eyes, relied on voices to tell her about people. She was disturbed by the crowd and by the lights, but she trusted the preacher. He would help her find safety in Jesus.

Someone had entered the tent behind her; Mary Kate's sensitive ears warned her of possible danger. His breathing was harsh, like that of a stricken man. She turned. Age had pushed aside one of the blind in his anxiety and was bearing down on her, a black apparition in a magician's coat. Blood dripped down his face from a formidable cut on his cheekbone, and glistened hotly on the shoulder of the yellow slicker.

"No," he pleaded, "no—don't go near him, Mary Kate!" But the sight of his bloody face and inflamed eyes was too much for her. She turned on her heel and ran, into the small arena, and as she ran she cried out to the tall man on the pulpit for sanctuary and understanding.

King had been thoroughly involved with the mood of religious conversion which he had labored to create, and Mary Kate's cry cut through his whole body like a circular saw. His shoulders quaked, and he had to grab his Bible with both hands to keep from dropping it. Looking back, he saw Mary Kate, but his eyes stayed on her for only a fraction of a second before shifting to Age's cut and battered face. His first thought was that the tiny, frail woman had assaulted Age with a knife and was now after him. But she had stopped just below; her thin white hands were empty, open. King heard a wooden chair hit the platform as Cowboy jumped to his feet. The next instant he recognized Mary Kate.

His second thought was, Yes, Lord, it had to be. I should have known. He gazed down into her mild beseeching eyes and was mostly puzzled that he felt so little shock, that he could accept Mary Kate's return with hardly a flicker of emotion, and he was still puzzled when his knees locked and his eyes glazed and his tongue hardened in his mouth like a petrified lizard and he crashed headfirst down from the pulpit, striking the hard ground with a wallop that could be heard, in the silence, even by those gathered outside the fires that burned in the barrels.

Age could not look away, nor move a step. At the sight of his friend lying crookedly beside Mary Kate, outrage burst in his head like a large artery. How far had he come with this boy and how many unwitting lies had he told to save him? He brushed at the hardening blood on his cheek. Around him the crowd began to seethe and boil, and Age trembled. His lips felt as caked and dry as a dead man's, but that made no difference, he could not have asked forgiveness. Too late for him to go, or stay, to speak or be silent. He turned and walked slowly through the ranks of the invalids, who would not now have the chance to benefit from the healing touch of King Windom, and passed out of the tent into the dark.

He walked on to the road and met no one. With sober eyes he looked at the hated Gospel Train. The noise from the tent assaulted him like a monumental earache. He swung down the stony road, his breath a whisper of sorrow.

Despite his grief, the pain in his hammered throat, Age knew his strength would last long enough. When he reached the highway he shied from the first pair of headlights like a horse refusing a jump. Then a truck was coming, shaking the air, and he steadied himself. So this was to be the violence he had expected, even longed for, during his weeks of uselessness. But the giant truck thundered by and he found he could not do it—or perhaps the time had not come.

With a grimace of self-loathing Age lifted his head. The mountains to the north were strange to his eyes, not wooded but harsh-looking. He was afraid of these mountains, of their barrenness—but they were all he deserved. Tearing at his yellow coat as if it were skin, Age shed it, ripped and glittering, by the side of the highway. And then he resumed where he had left off, before the advent of King Windom, as a wanderer.

48

Not the End of the World

Dr. Matthews earlier had gone into town to have dinner with an old friend of his father's; fortunately the evening had been a dull one and he had excused himself around nine to return to the Train. He was settling down in his apartment with a snifter of cognac and an occult book he had looked forward to reading, *The Boy Who Saw True*, when word reached him that the preacher had collapsed during the meeting.

By the time he got there half the congregation had left the tent. There was a lot of dust in the air from the cars, but under the circumstances confusion was slight. He shouldered past people who seemed to have nothing more to do on a cold night than stand around blocking the entrance, and went inside. King was sitting up on the ground, his back braced by one of the visiting preachers. He had a reddened goose egg on his left temple; otherwise his face was drum tight and pale. Too many people were trying to be helpful. "Let him sit," Matthews ordered. "Don't crowd." He glanced at the edge of the pulpit, which was raised about five and a half feet. He noted the absence of Cowboy—and stranger still—of Age. Then he knelt to look the preacher over. King was barely conscious. He couldn't speak, or understand what was said to him.

Matthews assumed King had fallen from the pulpit, and, as he gently pressed fingers against the back of King's head, his neck and his collarbones, he questioned the bystanders without getting an exact picture of what had happened. Looked to me, said one man, like he was having a heart attack. Yes, but what about the woman? asked another. The woman that run up at him. What woman? This question resulted in a controversy. None of them was too sure what she looked like. Daniel, Mab's husband, had been up in the seats, and he'd noticed her as soon as she had darted out of the passage where the invalids awaited King Windom. He described her as small-boned, girlish but somewhat gray, and said that she was wearing a brown or an off-red coat. She'd called something to the preacher, but he didn't know what. The preacher had turned, seen her, and then, after a second or two, had faltered—slipped?—and plunged off the platform. Daniel and the others who'd had a glimpse of the woman were agreed on one point: she was no longer in the tent. Where had she gone? A latecomer nosing around the group overheard some of this and reported that he had seen another woman, in a fur coat, leading her by the arm out the back way.

The doctor had no time to speculate about the woman who had suddenly skimmed like a bird of ill omen out of the passage and given King such a scare that he'd lost his balance and fallen. A stretcher had been brought into the tent by two crewmen from the Train, and Jeremy was right behind them. She'd just had a bath; her face was shiny and well scrubbed, and her hair was pulled back and tied with a bit of ribbon. Apparently she'd been led to believe King was dead. When she saw him upright and with at least a flicker of life in his face, she staggered and then clenched her hands, separately, prayerfully.

King fainted as they eased him onto the stretcher, and he was still unconscious when they lowered him to the floor of his study aboard the Train. Matthews talked quietly to Jeremy for a minute or two and persuaded her to go with Mab Shaw after promising to let her know as soon as King came around. When the study was cleared he set to work reviving the preacher. This was no more difficult than he had thought it would be, although it took a good five minutes. He was ready to call for an ambulance when Cowboy came in, breathless and red of face, his clothes cloudy with dust.

"I lost them somehow," he said unhappily. "There were too many cars, all of them leaving at once."

"Are you talking about the woman who ran into the tent? Was Molly with her?"

"Molly? No. I saw a man in a trench coat, and a nurse. I'd say she was a nurse, from the stockings she wore. . . ." He dropped into a chair, trembling from the chase he had given, and glanced at the preacher, who was trying to lift his head from the stretcher and doing a poor job of it. There was such a look of terror on King's face that the Cowboy felt uneasy. Was he seriously hurt? Matthews didn't know and couldn't be encouraging. But a little color had returned to King's cheeks; he appeared to have the use of his arms and legs and he was restless. As the two men tried to make him more comfortable with pillows from the sofa, tears formed in his eyes and trickled slowly down his cheeks. He hadn't yet uttered a comprehensible sound although Cowboy talked quietly to him, trying to focus his attention. The doctor cleaned the knot on his forehead. Suddenly King sat up, lurching, flinging up his hands, and nearly unbalanced Cowboy. The preacher strained with effort, face liverish, eyes staring whitely.

"Mary Kate!" he said, and grew rigid with fear. He repeated her name until he was choking for breath, and he beat away the hands that tried to calm him. Filling his lungs, groaning, he threw back his sore head and stared blindly at the ceiling. "*Aaaaagggggeeeee!*" he screamed; it was a crash, a knife thrust, a curse; and an image of the devil was locked in his blind eyes. Then he fell back, swooning, into the doctor's arms.

Almost immediately someone was pounding at the door; they heard several voices, among them Jeremy's. She begged to be let in. "Must have heard him all over the Train," Matthews muttered, shaking his head. "Boy, boy—I hope it isn't true." He dragged himself up and went to the door, smiling remotely. He opened the narrow door a scant inch and tried to reassure those waiting outside. It was nothing, he told them, a mild delirium. In an hour King would be his old self.

Dimly hearing what the doctor had to say, Cowboy stared at

King's perspiring face. Even unconscious he was restless; the shocks he'd suffered were visible as a dozen small tremors of the flesh. At each one Cowboy winced and struggled to bottle up his own shock. Now he knew what he'd been chasing out there in the dark. He arose stiffly, tasting the dust on his lips. But if she'd lived, he thought, groping, why hadn't she tried to get in touch with King before this? Why should Mary Kate suddenly leap at him out of a dark space of canvas, scaring him within an inch of his life? Why would she act so senselessly cruel? Try as he would, he could not remember cruelty in the face of Mary Kate. Anguish, yes—but then he had not seen her clearly. His concern had been King. He had gone looking for Mary Kate as an afterthought, hoping she could explain what she had wanted.

But, Cowboy thought, puzzled, suppose she didn't really know? King had recognized her almost immediately; he wondered now if Mary Kate had recognized the preacher. Somehow he couldn't believe she had, and he was not the type of man you forgot. And what about the people whom she'd run off with—Cowboy corrected himself. There was a dark blaze of excitement, of discovery, in his heart. She'd been taken away. Not by friends, not from the look of things. By jailers.

He needed no further answers. If Mary Kate had been incompetent all these years, shut away in an institution, then, even in rational moments, she might not have wanted to think about the husband who—it seemed—had abandoned her.

Someone, though, had gone to a lot of trouble and expense to find her after six years. Someone had been quite anxious for Mary Kate to see her husband again. For King to see *her*.

Cowboy turned and hunkered down again beside King. Thoughtfully he touched the preacher's cheek with the back of his hand and felt a certain warmth there. Friend, he said to himself, solemnly. My friend, I will take care of you. Cowboy was close to tears, and he had never felt so much hatred for a living soul as he felt for Molly. He was more than a little afraid of his feelings, and he doubted his self-control. But he was also convinced that if he didn't find her now she would vanish as Mary Kate had vanished.

Matthews was still at the door, patiently explaining something. Cowboy wondered what thoughts were in the doctor's mind as he tried to appear amiable and confident that King would soon be on his feet. He wished he had the time to

510

talk to Matthews, but he had felt a slight lurch at his feet that signaled the departure of the Train from the tent grounds, and it occurred to him that the whistle had been blowing for the past two or three minutes. He was startled, then he relaxed, remembering his promise to vacate the siding. There would be another place for them in the city and perhaps it was just as well they were getting away from the tent.

Quietly he opened the other door of the study and slipped out, unobserved, at the end of the corridor.

Molly had no intention of letting the Train stay in El Paso. It can still be fixed, she had told herself as she spirited Mary Kate from the tent. I'll fix it.

She was like a fly with one wing and winter coming on, blowing a paralyzing gale, but she was doing her best to fix it. Gilmer and Nurse Coleman were well on their way out of town, headed for a seldom seen part of New Mexico and the sanatorium Molly had found for Mary Kate. Molly had butted her way through the slow-moving crowd and the traffic on the road to get to her office. She had spent ten minutes on the telephone making arrangements for a full train crew to take them north to Albuquerque, then west to the little city of Tecopa. There King would have a chance to rest and recover while she made amends to the backers of the short-lived El Paso crusade, and schemed to keep the possibility of the Los Angeles crusade alive.

Just let me keep going for another two hours, Molly thought as she tried to rub the pain from her rigid eyeballs. Even the slight swaying of the car as the Train rolled at twenty miles an hour toward the Southern Pacific yards was enough to make her want to screech with agony. She fumbled with the telephone, preparing to make another call, this one to a local newspaper. She had scrawled her version of King's collapse on the back of an envelope while negotiating with the railroad and she was sure the paper would accept it. Most likely the team the city editor had sent out had covered only the first hour or so of the crusade. A real break, as Molly saw it. If only she could hang on, and keep her voice . . .

The door at the end of the car opened.

"Out!" Molly said furiously, not looking up. "I don't want anybody in here, I'm busy, just *stay* out!"

After the usual time lapse the door clicked shut. Molly wept, as she had been weeping off and on, emotionlessly, and quarreled with the telephone operator. "I don't *know* the number, I'm half blind and I can't look it up! You do your job, I'll do mine."

The receiver of the radio-telephone was taken from her hand. Cowboy hung up.

Molly leaned back and peered at his face; he was close enough to be recognized. But to her dim eyes he had no more expression than a concrete block. She did not see, at first, the worn leather belt in his right hand. "Everybody stay out includes *you*, Cowboy!" she said venomously.

He smacked her across the right shoulder with the belt, nipping the lobe of her ear.

"God!" Molly yelped, leaping from the swivel chair, clutching at her shoulder.

"I didn't think you had the hide to feel that one, Molly," he said dispassionately. "I wasn't really trying." *Whop!* This time he struck her hip and she screamed hoarsely and ducked behind the chair. Cowboy snorted at her attempts to evade him; he snatched the chair, threw it against one wall of the car and again laid into Molly with the tough leather belt. He was not quite as careful or accurate as he had promised himself to be, and he knew he was going to leave welts. After half a dozen swift strokes she was defenseless and hysterical. She knelt on the floor with her butt in the air, holding her head with both hands. It was all the target he needed, the prime target, but he held back, doubling the belt between his fists, snapping it briskly so she would hear. He felt both evil and content.

"Don't you want to know about King, Molly?" he said.

She fell trying to get up and lay limply against the couch next to her desk. "Jimbo, it was an accident! Mary Kate ran away from—from us. I didn't plan it! I'm sorry, I didn't want him to be hurt!"

Cowboy sat on the edge of her desk and waited for her to stop sobbing. It didn't take long. Either she was too exhausted for further tears or the beating had calmed her nerves. He stared out the window above the desk until she came around. He couldn't bear to look at her.

"Oh," Molly moaned, tragically, "you blistered me!"

"Where's Mary Kate?"

Molly crept onto the sofa and lay full length, on her stomach, to spare her smarting backside. "Where nobody can find her,"

512

she said, seeming eager to please. "A little place out near Deming, Cowboy. Expensive but good—I'm paying for it myself. King doesn't have to see her. He never has to see her if he doesn't want to."

"Molly, why in God's name—"

"I had to do *something!* The Association threatened to cancel out on us in Los Angeles—they don't want to back some grubby faith healer! I had to make him stop what he was doing." She had begun to whine slightly as she attempted to reason with Cowboy. "He was ruining us; making us look like fools."

"He was doing God's work as he saw fit, that's all. Molly, he has a precious gift, there's nothing grubby. . . . What difference does Los Angeles make?"

"Without Los Angeles we can't keep the Gospel Train going. I figured too close, and the bad weather last month all but broke us. Don't you know what it costs—"

"I know," Cowboy said glumly. "What were you going to do, blackmail him with Mary Kate? Force him to stop healing the sick?" He hit the desk with his belt and she raised her head, fearfully. "Why didn't you just cut off King's hands, Molly? Blind him? Even that would have been kinder than bringing Mary Kate back." He stood up, looking sullen and defeated. "I don't think he'll be able to preach in Los Angeles, or anywhere else, for a long time."

Her breath hissed. "How bad is he?"

"Bad enough to worry Dr. Matthews. King needs a couple of days in the hospital for observation. I know he's got a hard head, but . . ."

Molly nodded. "We'll find a hospital for him just as soon as we reach Tecopa."

"Tecopa?" He gazed at her for a moment or two, incredulously, then reached for the telephone. Molly felt weak; she was vaguely terrified and filled with unexpected shudders, but her head was clearer again.

"Don't! " she said sharply. "Don't be stupid. We can't afford to stay in El Paso. Not after what happened with Mary Kate. Somebody will hear a rumor—somebody will snoop. I sent Philemon to track down Mary Kate, and he probably knows enough to fill every newspaper in the Southwest. I think I can still save us, save the Gospel Train. Jimbo, I *have* to save it! But we're not staying in El Paso. If you can hole up with a

513

fourteen-car train, then that's what we're going to do—as long as it takes to get King on his feet again. Just as long as I can stall, and stall, and rake up a little money to keep us in business."

"He knows about Mary Kate—and knowing will kill him."

"You're wrong. He forgot her once, and he'll forget her again!"

"You don't know what you're talking about."

Her eyes glittered. "I know what King wants," she said slowly, "and he'll do anything he has to do to keep her."

Cowboy was silent, and Molly decided his silence meant agreement.

"Just get him on his feet, Cowboy. You're the one who can do it. *Talk* to him." She hesitated and then said, ruthlessly, "It's not the end of the world, you know. Not for him or for anybody else."

Cowboy could have hit her then, with all his strength; he could willingly have murdered her. But when he made himself look full into Molly's face he was stopped. No life was there for him to take. This unnerved him; he felt horrified and alone. He turned away.

"Save him," she demanded.

"Molly, I saw his eyes when he said Mary Kate's name. Molly! I don't think anything can save him."

49

Host to the Devil

So many people had been kind and helpful. Yet, despite the helpfulness and solicitude of Cowboy and Dr. Matthews, Jeremy couldn't be rid of the feeling that they had plotted to keep her from her husband. She'd tried arguing, she'd tried tears, and finally she had made a scene, and everybody had been understanding, and still she hadn't seen him.

They were traveling very fast; the shaking of the railroad car and the abundance of dry heat had given Jeremy a rare headache. Of course she couldn't sleep. She didn't know what time it was, but it seemed as if they had left El Paso hours ago. From her bed she watched an occasional town light flicker through the window and across the ceiling of her bedroom. She rolled her head on the pillow and saw mountain peaks by moonlight as the Gospel Train took a long curve. She had waited for him, thinking he would come at any minute, and smile at her, and make a joke about the knot on his head. Jeremy wondered how he could have been so careless as to step off the pulpit without looking. Then she began feeling miserable all over again. If he hadn't come, it was because he was hurt worse than she had been let to know. That was the only plausible answer.

Jeremy decided she had been obedient long enough, and done what others wanted her to do. She wanted to be with King, and that was what mattered to *her*.

Quickly she got out of bed and put on a robe and slippers. She let herself into the corridor, furtive as a thief. King's study was in the coach ahead. Jeremy worked both doors as quietly as she could and then stood for a few moments in the coach she had entered, blood throbbing in her temples. Besides the study there were only two apartments in this car, she recalled; one was the Reverend Mr. Handwerker's and the other generally stood empty. Nevertheless she listened intently for nearly two minutes while the Train rocked on, thinking that perhaps Dr. Matthews was sitting up in one of the apartments, close to King in case he was needed. Jeremy was in no mood to argue again with the doctor, and she wasn't about to be sent back to bed. Biting at her lower lip, she proceeded cautiously down the corridor. Both apartments appeared to be dark and unoccupied as she passed. She stopped in front of the first door to the study, which King loved more than their own apartment, and grasped the slide bolt.

The door was stuck, or locked from within. Jeremy had an impulse to shout to King through the door but controlled her nervousness. She glanced down the remaining third of the corridor. From where she was standing the other door seemed to be ajar. Jeremy broke for it and entered the unlighted study. "King?" she said, joyfully. Her eyes searched for him; her smile faded. Despite the absence of lights she could tell the study was empty.

Just to make sure, Jeremy cracked the door to the bathroom. That too was empty. Somewhat morbidly she fished for the light switch. What was she expecting, she thought scornfully—blood? Now she was encouraged by the fact of the deserted study. If he were badly hurt then he would be there. Jeremy backtracked and turned on a lamp. Something on the desk caught her eye. She reached for a white coffee mug, finding it two-thirds full and still warm. There was spilled coffee on the desk top, as if he'd set the mug down hard. Jeremy wiped it up and went to the little kitchen annex that backed up the bath. The little two-burner stove and the kettle were also warm, almost hot.

He'd made himself some coffee, she thought, and then he'd gone out. Suddenly. Where? Jeremy knew King hadn't passed by their apartment. She'd been alert for the slightest movement in the hall. She'd have seen him walking by.

The chapel, she thought.

Jubilantly she left the study, closing the door, and hurried toward the front of the Train. He would be praying there in the domed chapel, in front of the altar, and she would kneel beside him, unobtrusively, and before long as he became aware that Jeremy was with him he would reach for her hand, and they would pray together. If only he'd come in the first place to fetch her! But it was late at night; she understood that he hadn't wanted to disturb her. That was the only reason he hadn't come; for no good reason she'd let her nerves get the best of her.

The choir car was empty and dark—no choir along on this trip. She was respectfully quiet pushing open the chapel door. But this car too was empty. Jeremy couldn't believe it; she'd been so sure of finding him there. She sat down in an aisle seat, staring at the altar and the old brass candlestick.

There was not much up ahead—just the lounge, the office, the baggage car. Clamping down on panic that filled her throat, Jeremy decided he must have gone to the office. Should she wait in the chapel for him? But Jeremy wasn't able to wait any longer to see King. She got up and half ran down the aisle, stumbling once, bruising her ribs against a seat back as the Train shifted on the tracks.

In the office Molly slept asprawl on the couch, face down, with her beaver coat covering her bare legs. It was quite cold here and Jeremy didn't pause. She thought she had heard King's voice, faintly, as if he were preaching above the racket of

516

the speeding Train. Curious, she hurried on, out of the office, and crossed the lapped metal platforms that jerked and jolted beneath her feet.

She saw him then, through the glass in the baggage-car door.

A single work light burned inside, casting his tall slanted shadow—as grotesque as a grave robber's—the length of the car. At first she thought he was talking to someone. He was pacing up and down, sometimes throwing up his hands, occasionally ducking his head in a mime of agitation. Jeremy gripped the door bar with both hands to steady herself against the swaying of the Train and stared at her husband. He was shouting, and the dog of Philemon's, locked inside his kennel, was barking hideously. Jeremy, deafened by the noise of the Train, couldn't hear too well. She thought that he must be taking advantage of the long night to perfect a sermon or two and she started to push the door open. Then she stopped, not really knowing why. Perhaps it was because he looked upset, and talked far too fast and too wildly. Perhaps it was because she was startled by his appearance. His face was yellowish, and the sockets of his eyes were ghastly smears of brown. His eyes were pale as his skin, filled with distress. Occasionally the rhythm of his preaching, or speaking, was disturbed by a violent seizure which he quelled by squeezing his face between his hands. Jeremy, unwilling to break in on him, pressed her ear to the glass, her lips drawn tight.

"I say Jesus who is coming after me is mightier than I. He will baptize you with the Holy Spirit and with fire and how *long* will thou hide thy face from me, O Lord? Amen and if you die *unsaved* you will live with the devil forever Sinner Friend behold the nail-scarred hand *believe* in the Lord Jesus Christ amen and thou shalt be saved if you bend your knee I say unto you surely if you bend your knee and *receive* our Lord Jesus it shall not be said of you he was not found written in the Book of Life O foolish and senseless people who have eyes but see not who have ears but *hear* not amen will you spend Eternity among the fearful, the unbelieving the abominable the murderers and whoremongers sorcerers and idolators and all *liars* who shall have their part in the Lake which burneth with fire and brimstone?" He quaked and fell silent while the dog snapped and snarled in its cage. Apprehensively King raised his eyes. In a more normal tone, which Jeremy could barely hear, he said, "God help you not to live another day without

Jesus. Without . . ." His lips parted and his throat strained, but it seemed as if he could not speak. "Without . . ." Still at last, he swung around and faced the kennel. Jeremy couldn't see his expression. She closed her eyes and clung to the door bar. When she looked again King had advanced to within a few feet of the kennel. There he appeared to steel himself, or to resolve something. He turned and walked quickly toward Jeremy, but if he saw her he gave no indication. On the left-side wall next to the sliding baggage door there was a glass-front case containing emergency equipment—an ax, a crowbar. King opened the case, hesitated, then lifted out the ax. He carried it in both hands back to the kennel.

Powerlessly Jeremy whispered, "Oh, dear God—don't let him do it!"

King raised the ax and brought it down on the kennel with all his strength. Philemon's dog howled madly. As if he were splitting kindling, King continued to pump his ax. The top of the kennel collapsed and the tawny dog tried to leap out, like a bucking horse; his back already was flowing blood. King drew back the ax, changing the angle of his swing, and Jeremy saw the glitter on the blade's edge. She sank down where she was, below the glass, sickened, stopping her ears. The forward rush of the Train and clacking of the wheels obliterated the cries of the dying dog.

When Jeremy felt able to stand she pulled herself up and looked through the smudged glass. The kennel was a tangle of splintered wood and wire. King had the lumpish blood-darkened body of the dog by its hind legs and was dragging it to the open baggage door. His shirt and forearms were splattered with gore.

She felt as if she were going to faint, but Jeremy forced the door open and made herself walk into the car.

Still not seeing her, King dropped the dog and went back to the kennel. Something had attracted his attention there. Stooping, he picked up several dollar bills from the floor. Then he pried at the thin foam-rubber cushion on which the dog had slept. Apparently some of the ax blows had ripped into the cushion. He held up a thick wad of currency, all the money Philemon had stolen and carefully squirreled away—in a place where nobody would ever have the desire to look.

"King," Jeremy said, her voice sounding strange to her ears.

He struggled up and rushed to the baggage door. For a

second or two Jeremy thought he intended to throw himself out of the car. But there was a steel rod across the doorway and he held fast to it as he scattered the money in the slip stream.

She ran and grabbed him around the waist. "Come away!" she said hysterically. "Come away from the door!" King gaped at her but continued holding tight to the bar. Jeremy raised her eyes. "I'm afraid!" she screamed, as if sensing he was far away from her and couldn't hear. "I need you!" She continued to pull at him with all her strength. And then she felt his arm around her waist.

"Let go," he said. "I'm all right, let go." Jeremy backed away and stepped on the dismembered dog. She groaned and fell painfully to her knees beside a collection of trunks. The baggage door rumbled shut, sealing off much of the cold air, but she was already drenched with cold as if she'd fallen into a winter river, and her teeth chattered uncontrollably.

"Why did you kill Philemon's dog!"

Vaguely she felt King's hands on her. She had wanted him to come to her but now she fought him, unthinkingly.

"Why!"

"Jeremy, that dog was host to the devil! It came at me in the tent one night—I should have killed it then!"

"It was just a plain no-account dog. What's wrong with you!" Jeremy turned her head, frightened anew by his antics, by the violence with which he had attacked Philemon's pet. She was prepared to see almost anything in King's eyes—even lunacy. But despite the sinister smudges beneath them, his eyes revealed only the depths of his fatigue. She glanced at the discolored knot on his temple, and sympathy overcame all other emotions.

"Come with me," she said tenderly.

He stiffened. "I can't be with you anymore, Jeremy!"

"Don't say that—I'll take care of you. We have to get out of here." She began kissing his face. He was limp and sad and uncaring; each jolt from the Train went right through him. But as she continued to kiss him she felt his fingers tighten on her upper arm. There was no other response, but Jeremy was gratified. He no longer said *I can't*. He simply waited, exhausted, to be led.

She found the strength, as she had to find it, and took him away.

50

The Long Fast of King Windom

By the end of the month nearly everyone was gone. There was no extra money, no way to maintain a full staff in anticipation of the next revival. Mab Shaw and her husband departed finally on the fourth Sunday in March for Clearwater. The atmosphere aboard the Train had begun to get Mab down and Daniel had become aware of certain dangerous symptoms—restlessness, an expressed desire to return to Los Angeles for a little while, "since it was so close," and so he'd decided he must take her home where she could live simply and without anxiety and sing in the church when the Spirit so moved her. Then only ten people were left, not counting a skeleton crew from the railroad, and in most of the cars there was neither heat nor electricity.

Molly, her secretary, and the comptroller were busy in the office, sometimes until late at night. Molly slept there as well, because the telephone seemed always to be ringing, sometimes at three in the morning. Molly had a lot of lines out, fishing for money, and she always answered. Usually it was some distraught soul wanting to talk to the preacher. Where was he now, and how could they get to him? When was he coming to such and such a city? Molly dealt with these people patiently, almost reverently. They were a reminder that King was still being listened to, that he was needed, that he was alive.

Molly was breaking her back to keep the preacher on the radio throughout the South and Southwest. Fortunately she'd taped dozens of his track-side sermons and counseling sessions, so despite his current silence she had enough new programs to last at least six weeks. It was essential that King continue to preach, for the only source of revenue for the struggling Southern Cross Crusade was the contributions made by his radio audience. Even motionless, the Train was a hideous expense, but they had to keep it.

Involved as she was with money problems, Molly managed to know everything else that went on aboard the isolated Train, though she seldom stirred from the office.

None of them had seen King for eleven days. During this time he had been locked in his study and had fasted—except, perhaps, for coffee and sugar and canned milk, the little kitchen had been well stocked with each. He had not said a word to Jeremy, or to Cowboy, or to Dr. Matthews, all of whom took turns day after day talking to him through the door. They'd heard his voice, because he prayed, often, aloud but unintelligibly. Yet whenever one of them approached to pray with him through the steel door, he had stopped and withdrawn completely from their attempt at communion.

After the fourth day of this Cowboy had wanted to break the lock for King's sake, but Jeremy had stopped him.

Of all those left on the Train she was the most bewildered by King's retreat. Because she'd led him so easily from the baggage car, because he'd made love to her with an intensity he'd never shown before, she was certain that all the demons which had led him to slaughter Philemon's helpless dog had been exorcised, and she had slept peacefully in his arms for a few hours. But by daylight he was gone; he was back in his study and the door was locked against her.

Jeremy, unable to think of anything she'd done to hurt him, sometimes blamed his erratic behavior on the head injury which he'd suffered. Dr. Matthews wouldn't say yes or no, but he pointed out that King had been badly shaken up after weeks of brutally hard work and needed a rest. Although it was difficult for them to bear, possibly his period of isolation might be doing him good instead of harm. And, because the doctor was calm and reassuring, Jeremy halfway believed him.

She moved into the vacant apartment next to the study to be near her husband. Half a dozen times a day she tried talking to

King, and frequently Dr. Matthews had to come and lead her away, sobbing.

"He's going to die in there!" she said, fearfully, after a particularly heartbreaking hour.

"No, he'll come out when he's ready. Here, drink this." And he handed her a thimbleful of cognac from his stock, a drink with which he soothed her nerves and for which she had developed a certain amount of affection.

"But what are we going to do!"

"Jeremy, please don't take what I'm going to tell you the wrong way. I think first of all you should call Frank Henderson down in Florida."

"What good—"

"I'm not saying that he should come here." The doctor sipped his own cognac. Lately he had thought relatively little about King's predicament and quite a lot about Jeremy's, and he was determined to spare her as much as possible in the days ahead. He knew that before long he and Cowboy and perhaps other men would be compelled to break into the study and carry King away to a hospital before he became weak beyond hope of recovery. He could only imagine what a combination of severe physical and emotional strain had done to the preacher, and he was so jittery about the situation that he was afraid of making a serious error of judgment. If it were possible that only one life could be saved, he was determined that life would be Jeremy's.

"I don't believe it would be a good idea to let King's family"—he paused briefly, considering the word he'd chosen, then nodded—"his *family* know about the trouble he's having. Because, Jeremy, I'm morally certain King will snap out of it and be none the worse for his fast." He smiled up at her. "This is a period of religious trial for him. The experience is intensely personal. He can't share it."

"But I know he's suffering!"

"Just as many religious leaders have suffered. He'll survive, and his faith will be stronger than ever."

Jeremy nodded, meekly, because he seemed to know what he was talking about; and Matthews saw that she was questioning herself and her anxiety.

"This is what I want from you, Jeremy. I want you to call Frank Henderson and tell him you're flying down there for a visit. Say a week. Now, don't get upset. I think I can promise

you that after a week King himself will be down to fetch you."
He nodded at the window they were sitting by. It was a gloomy
afternoon. The wind was blowing hard and there was a
pebbled crust of snow on the ground. "You've been doing some
fasting yourself, and losing sleep. The shape you're in now, you
won't be much help to King once he decides to end his retreat.
But if you take advantage of the opportunity to get away from
this bitter weather, soak up some sun, why, you'll be full of pep
when you see him. . . ."

He stopped, because her eyes were filled with tears,
accentuating the haunted hollowness of her eye sockets.

"I couldn't." Jeremy's lips trembled. "I'm afraid to leave this
Train without him. You see."

"Nonsense, Jeremy, we'll be right here to look after King if he
needs—"

"He has to . . . need me. You see. He has to want me. Soon.
Or otherwise I'll—" She looked down at her knotted hands. "But
he *will* ask for me, won't he? Soon? He knows I'm waiting, that
I'm so . . . worried."

"He knows," Matthews said, and though previously he'd felt
able to argue Jeremy into taking the first plane east out of
Tecopa, he found that he didn't have the heart to abuse her
even for her own good. "Will you give some thought to Florida,
Jeremy?" was all he said. "I know King would want you to go.
I'd swear to that. Please think it over."

"I'll think about it," she said, automatically.

Philemon had buried his dog, or what was left of the dog, not
long after the Gospel Train reached Tecopa. Without help he'd
tied the remains into a strip of tarpaulin and lugged this burden
half a mile from the tracks and the town and made a shallow
grave in the icy desert with the same ax which King had used to
do Cosh in.

The ax was still in Philemon's room, still flaked with blood
and skin and tawny hair that hadn't rubbed off during the
grave-digging.

Why? he'd asked Jeremy, and she hadn't been able to give a
decent explanation, though she'd seen King do it. She muttered
something about a demon living inside the dog, an answer
which only infuriated Philemon. Of course he knew why King
had killed his dog! The nigger had told King about the stolen
money, and he'd figured out where it must be hidden. There

523

had been no way to get at Philemon's money without killing his dog first. That was all there was to it; now Cosh was gone and the money was gone and so, brooded Philemon, was his chance for a life.

He'd visited Molly a dozen times a day and at first she simply put him off, and then she admitted they couldn't afford to pay him. Philemon suspected the truth, however. The preacher had instructed Molly not to pay the money Philemon was rightfully owed. So there he was, a thousand miles from Clearwater with less than a dollar to his name; spring was near and his hope of returning home to a church of his own was gone.

His anguish over this predicament was packed deep inside of him; it was like a monstrous sore tooth that could not be reached. It throbbed even in his sleep and sent out shocking rays of pain when he least expected them. Each time he experienced this pain he longed to cry aloud for relief, for help—but who could help him? He had no friends aboard the Train, least of all Jeremy, whom he now despised for her treachery. He thought of telephoning Brother Hazelman and blurting out his troubles. Yes, God bless Brother Hazelman, he would listen! But Philemon trembled, and reconsidered. He would listen, listen sternly—that shining man of God would not be pleased.

Philemon knew why he could not expect Brother Hazelman to sympathize. Even while burying his dog Philemon had told himself that the least he could do, as a man, would be to give the preacher a severe whipping. During the first three days he waited for King to emerge from the study, Philemon had considered such an action and had become sick with anxiety. King had threshed him once before with a minimum of effort and Philemon was sure the same thing would happen this time.

Anxiety gave way to frustration: what would be gained if he got himself beat up? Philemon took to his room, perplexed, still in pain. Inevitably he suffered from nightmares. He dreamed of the long-buried torments of childhood, of strange landscapes and faces; he dreamed of King Windom's religious eye and moaned. He awoke after a particularly murderous nightmare clutching the ax in his bed. He was both sweating and cold but in a surprising new frame of mind: he felt no fear.

It was the preacher who was afraid, Philemon thought gravely. Otherwise why should he have hidden in his study for so many days? He studied this phenomenal thought with detachment. The preacher had murdered Philemon's dog, and he knew what he deserved for such a cowardly act. Horsewhipping, or better. He knew, and he couldn't face the threat of punishment. He was hiding from Philemon.

Philemon tested this conclusion cautiously, waiting for his judgment to collapse, waiting for pain to scissor through him. Instead he continued to feel calm, even dignified. He felt, for the first time in his life, something like a free man. King Windom was the coward. He'd done his best to ruin Philemon, and, failing, he'd hidden himself like a child. Philemon began to soar. He was on the verge of marching to the study and denouncing the preacher in a voice everyone could hear. He visualized his denunciation and rejoiced, but, after a while, after he'd rehearsed it a hundred times, he realized that the satisfaction which he'd gain would not be enough, and he was saddened.

Philemon dozed and for the most part went hungry during this period of sadness. As any Christian man should do in a crisis, he prayed for guidance. At first prayer came easily. He came to realize that the Lord had placed a great deal of trust in him. King Windom was a bad, if not an evil, man. He had stolen from Eli; to say that he had actually killed Eli was not far from the truth. King had married Jeremy, but he cared nothing about her. For, if he did care, how could he let her stand for hours outside his door begging and weeping, and not say a single word to comfort her?

Philemon had reached the point where his emotions easily confused him. He forgot his earlier antagonism toward Jeremy, and shed tears for her. Something had to be done about the preacher. Philemon groped, sensing the depth of his responsibility. Now when he prayed he confused the Lord with the resplendent Brother Hazelman.

How can I deal with King Windom? Philemon asked again and again. He was no hand for horsewhipping, and although he'd won a few rough-and-tumble fights in his time, he realized that his recent stomach troubles had sapped his strength.

Help me, dear Father! cried Philemon in desperation. The blond head and ruddy face of Walter Hazelman lighted his thoughts. What should I do to be worthy of your loving me?

And, to his joy, Brother Hazelman spoke, in comforting tones. At last Philemon rested. For Brother Hazelman had a plan.

51

The Andreson Boy

The train had attracted a lot of attention in Tecopa at first; then after the weather turned bad not too many people came by to gawk at it or to try to arrange a tour. But a little encampment sprang up in a space of hard-packed desert ground between Route 66 and the railroad line. The people who settled down there to wait for King Windom to come out of his study all badly needed help for loved ones. They had brought the poor invalids in camper trucks and small trailers. One penniless family from up above Santa Fe was forced to pitch a tent in the biting weather. Cowboy tried several times to deal with these self-sufficient people, but they politely declined to accept the comforts of the Train. All that they wanted was a few minutes of King Windom's time. He had helped others; they had heard all about his miracles on the radio. Why, then, wouldn't he come out to help them? Cowboy explained that the preacher had suffered a fall and was ill, but the people stayed. He was their last hope, and there was no place else for them to go.

On that same gray afternoon John Matthews made his attempt to get Jeremy away from the Train, Molly hit on a way to force King from his retreat. She sent for Cowboy right away.

"Isn't there a child in one of those camper trucks? A three-year-old boy? What's wrong with him?"

"He has a deformed heart."

"Is he going to die?" Molly asked, staring intently out the window over her desk. It was the first interest she'd shown in any of the supplicants.

"Probably. When he's a little older and a little stronger he'll have an operation, but his parents have been told that his chances are one in five, one in six."

"Does King know about the boy?"

"Molly, I've told King about all the people waiting to see him. Over and over I've told him! It's no good at all. He doesn't hear. He keeps his shades drawn."

"It's time we made him hear."

"What difference would that make, Molly?

"Giving up on him?" she asked, in a nasty tone of voice.

Cowboy shook his head grimly.

"All right; if we can get through to King, remind him who he is, and *what* he is, then I think he'll come out. If he isn't planning to die in there—and I honestly don't believe he wants to die—then he must come out."

"What are you going to say to him? We've tried everything."

"*I'm* not going to say a word." She switched on the tape recorder on her desk; King's voice came from the speaker. "He's going to talk to himself—one voice he won't be able to ignore. And that pathetic little boy is going to talk to him too." She waved a hand toward the encampment. "In fact, we'll have the gang of them make appeals. We'll play the tapes over and over until—"

"The whole idea turns my stomach," Cowboy objected. "No. It's terrible. We can't."

"You've had *your* chance, Cowboy!" Molly stopped the tape. "Break the door down and drag him out, if you can."

"I'm afraid . . . he'll go berserk, Molly."

"Then I'll get him out my way. If you want to help, fine. Otherwise get out of here." She glared at him for a few moments, then softened and said reasonably, "Cowboy, there's no time to waste. The crusade in Los Angeles has to start in three weeks. Trust me, please. This time I know what I'm doing."

He reached past her and switched on the tape recorder again and listened, eyes closed. "I wish I knew what this will do to him; I wish I knew his mind right now. How many speakers, Molly?"

"One outside his door, two more under the windows." His

silence displeased her; she folded her arms and leaned tensely against the desk. "I know what I'm doing," she repeated.

"At least it's something to keep us busy," Cowboy said, without opening his eyes.

Philemon ducked in off the wind-tunnel main street of Tecopa and paused inside the door to wipe his streaming eyes with a cuff of his Army coat. The hardware store was long and narrow and filled with hung brass and a dry-goods austerity. Near the door the display case on the wall picked up light from the windows and the hunting pieces racked inside looked newly polished; there wasn't a finger print to be seen on any of the barrels.

"Help you, sir?"

The clerk was an old cuss in a Pendleton shirt and a string tie, but he looked friendly.

"I'm needing some shells for my twelve-gauge," Philemon said.

"What size shot?"

Philemon hesitated. "Oh, number two."

"Sure thing." The clerk brought out the box. "Do much deer hunting?"

Philemon shrugged.

"Wrong season for it here, you know."

"I just want—" Philemon's mouth dried up. "I ain't hunted in a long time. Thought I'd walk up in the hills a ways with my dog, see what he scares up."

"Weather like this you probably won't find much to shoot at. Coyotes. Won't get close to no coyote, though."

"Well, it ain't no never mind. But I aim to walk some."

"Sure. Stretch your legs. Good idea. That's three forty."

"Don't expect I need a whole box of shells."

"How many?"

"Four," said Philemon. He didn't want to seem cheap.

The clerk counted out the shells and put them in a little paper sack for him. "Now, rabbits. Plenty jackrabbits in the hills. Go blasting them with shot this size, though, you won't have nothing left but four feet and a ear or two."

"We'll see," Philemon said glumly. He collected his change and walked out. There was a drugstore on the corner with a menu posted in the window. Philemon decided that he could afford a milk shake. He dawdled at the fountain until the steam heat made him sleepy—he'd done precious little sleeping for several nights running. It was strange, he thought, that he had talked about his dog as if Cosh were still alive. During his long stay in his room aboard the Train he'd imagined that Cosh was right there. A time or two he'd even spoken aloud to the dog. And just a few minutes ago, while he'd been in the hardware store buying shells, he had really felt that all he had in mind was a tramp across the desert with his friend.

His eyes stung with tears; he missed Cosh terribly. Since running out of prayers, out of words to invoke the protective image of Brother Hazelman, he'd been unbearably lonesome. But there was no need for Brother Hazelman to stay with him at every moment. He was a man; he could be trusted.

Philemon shifted his weight on the stool and clenched his hand around the shells in his coat pocket. He had been doing this quite often while sipping his milk shake and the paper sack was beginning to come apart from his sweaty hand. He pushed what was left of the milk shake aside and left. He still felt intolerably hungry but his stomach had shrunk after days without much food and the oversweet drink had sickened him.

It was growing dark. The wind was colder after his stay in the drugstore. But the sky had begun to clear. Looking up, Philemon saw the early moon like a watermark in the sky, and streaks of orange, featherlike, in the west. He felt more cheerful, more energetic. Out of doors his unasked-for burden of responsibility seemed much lighter. Now that Brother Hazelman had decided what he must do, the idea of hanging around the Train waiting for his opportunity seemed dreadful.

He was no fool and he knew he was going to suffer. The threat of jail alarmed him. How he hated jails! Yet it was all a man could do. He was proud of his acceptance of the right; a man could stand jailing if he knew he was right. The weight of the shells in his pocket gave him a melancholy feeling of manhood. One would be enough, he reminded himself; but he'd had to buy at least four. It might have seemed suspicious, buying just one. He was confident that, so far, no one was suspicious of him. No one gave him much thought these days, or expected him to be a man. Well, all that was due to change.

Philemon was thinking of himself sitting stoically in a cell while Brother Hazelman and Little Rose wept outside the bars, when something half seen disturbed him greatly and claimed all his attention. He was on the western edge of town, walking along a sandy path beside the railroad tracks. A slow-moving freight was strung out on the innermost track. He shielded his watering eyes from the wind and looked through the spaces of the train, at the narrow, uphill streets of the Mexican settlement. He saw a Negro man walking, fast, toward a doorway. Then the train cut off his view. When he was allowed another glimpse the Negro had disappeared. Was it really King Windom's nigger? Philemon couldn't believe his eyes.

He knew that Age had disappeared in El Paso. Nobody had seen him, or heard from him, in nearly two weeks. Philemon clenched his hands against the cold and lingered until the freight had cleared the tracks. Then he peered at the unpaved streets beyond the railroad. He saw only a couple of black-shawled Mexican housewives hurrying along, clutching sacks of groceries.

Philemon almost laughed with relief. They were a long way from El Paso.

He walked on, but his concern over what he had seen slowly returned.

So what? he asked himself brusquely. It isn't him. If Age was back, Philemon reasoned, then he'd be at the Train, where King Windom was, not in this part of town. There was no reason to worry. Yet some of his pleasure in having made a decision, in being free, had vanished. He hated the nigger; the nigger had almost driven him crazy back there in Florida; he was nothing but bad news. If he was back, if he was hanging around now, then maybe it meant—

Philemon winced. It was all due to the fact he hadn't taken care of himself, that he'd been under such a strain, but there were times when his mind was no more than a net of transparent flesh on which the reality of his world was printed in fine and proper detail, and the wrong thought dropping with swift blackness into that net could cause it to sway and twist in a horrifying manner, bringing on panic. But if he was quick enough and on his guard he could keep the harmful penetrating thoughts away from the precious, frail, and tattooed net of the mind. If he concentrated on the Right, on the long hours he had spent in discussion of his course with the Father, he would remain unshaken. And so, because it was darkening, Philemon walked more quickly, and rejoiced that happier times were near; and when he was close enough to the Train he saw that there was considerable activity outside one of the coaches. He forgot everything else but his curiosity.

Scrap lumber for a fire was being stacked along the strip where the camper trucks had stood for several days. A radio-TV-shop panel truck had been backed up to the rails and two men were unloading loudspeakers. Cowboy supervised the work, his hands sunk in the pockets of a shearling coat which Philemon greatly admired.

"What's all this?"

Cowboy gave him a glance. "We're going to try to talk King into coming out—I mean, they are." He pointed at the encampment.

Philemon looked at the windows of the study; the shades were still down. "Do you think he'll—"

"How do I know?" Cowboy said rudely, and drifted off to confer with Molly. Philemon tagged along and, by keeping his ears open, he got a fair idea of what was planned. He was elated. The preacher wouldn't refuse a little child, he thought, not a poor doomed child with a defective heart. Philemon personally had been deeply moved by the plight of the good people who had come for King Windom's blessing. He was also sorry for them because they'd been so easily fooled. King Windom was not a healer. Since rejoining the Train Philemon had furiously disbelieved all he'd heard about the preacher's miracle-working. It was impossible; the Father, who was all-wise, would not have granted the Power of healing to a man He intended to punish severely. Philemon trembled and recalled an expression of Eli's. The preacher was a *scheming fake.* Philemon had tried to be of some service to the people who waited; he had wept for them and offered to lay his own hands prayerfully on the sick bodies, but they'd had eyes and ears only for King Windom, they had paid little attention to him.

He was reflective and sad as he thought about this recent humiliation. Philemon could not conscientiously blame anyone but the preacher, however, and his dearest wish at the moment was that he catch up to King Windom before more helpless people became the victims of lies and deceits.

With a roar the woodpile was set afire. Fascinated, his eyes round, Philemon watched the blaze and thought again of how it must happen. He was certain that the loud cries of the suffering would bring the preacher out at last. Philemon turned, picturing the scene as King Windom left the Train and walked slowly toward the encampment. Perhaps he would have a Bible in his hands. Well, Philemon would not be stopped because King Windom carried the Holy Word, which was just another act of blasphemy. No, he would step quickly into the preacher's path with his shotgun cocked. He would stare into the preacher's eyes and say, firmly, loud enough for everyone to hear, "The Father is tired of your transgressions." And then—before the preacher could turn and run, before anyone could move to stop Philemon—he would aim his long-barreled shotgun and with a single blast turn one of the preacher's knees into a pincushion of splintered bone.

Philemon looked from the fire to the cracked ground at his feet. His mouth was terribly dry, and the wind hurt his tender cheeks. It would be over in seconds. King Windom would never again rise in the tent to bewilder the people with lies. He was not a fit man to speak of the glories of Christ, the wonders of the Kingdom of Heaven. He was not fit, Philemon repeated, relishing his anger. And only Philemon could stop him.

He trudged, half-frozen, to the coach in which he lived, and bit his lip at the pain in his stinging ears. He was more lonesome than ever, and he craved to talk to someone. Jeremy, perhaps. But, although he prayed for her nightly, now that he no longer resented her, unfortunately she did not care about him. Later he would be able to talk to Jeremy. He would need to explain just why the Father had decided to punish King Windom. In the meantime it was better for him to keep silent, say a prayer or two, and make his preparations.

In his room Philemon pulled the shade, then turned on the light and took his shotgun from the closet. The fifty-year-old Winchester was in excellent condition and, while he held it in his hands, admiring the craftsmanship that had gone into its making, time faded from him and his eyes glazed. He loved his shotgun as he had loved his dog, he had turned down offers of two hundred dollars and more for it, and he knew full well they would take the gun away from him and he would never see it again. Yet to be a man he must give it up, and say nothing.

The bellowing of the loudspeakers aroused him. He started toward the window, turned back, switched off the light, and then raised the shade. The huge fire attracted his eye. Men were heaping more wood on it. He could just hear the crackle of flames whenever the amplified voice of King Windom stopped. Philemon was puzzled and upset. Why were they broadcasting one of the preacher's sermons? He sat down at the edge of the window seat, the shotgun across his knees. He thought, They only want to get his attention before playing back the voice of the little boy. Philemon pressed his cheek against the icy glass and stared out, listening. At the moment he felt relatively nerveless, and he hoped he wouldn't have long to wait.

King Windom's study was two cars down. Philemon decided that he could remain in his room and still see the preacher almost as soon as he left the Train. There would be time for him to leave his room and intercept King before he reached the encampment.

Philemon yawned hard enough to crack his jaws, and reached into his coat pocket. He picked at the shotgun shells there. Then, without having to think, he lifted his Winchester and loaded it, just to be ready.

The three of them waited gloomily in the apartment next to the study while the voice of King Windom blared on and on. Jeremy's face was particularly bloodless, her lips thready and blue although the car was well heated. She had twisted a scarf around her hands and pulled at it until the material frayed. Dr. Matthews sat with his head heavily in his hands, wearing the same suit he'd worn for the last six days. Occasionally he looked up to smile, vigorously, at Jeremy, or to gaze out the window at the night and the wind-blown fire.

A number of people from the town had been attracted by the fire and by the voice, but it was well below freezing out and Molly had reported that not many were staying. The cops occasionally drove by, but Molly had cleared the fire and the loudspeakers with city authorities, and they didn't find it necessary to stay, either.

Cowboy lounged in the doorway, watching for King, but after an hour and forty minutes there was no sign of him. Cowboy rubbed his matted head; the roaring speakers had given him a crushing headache. He was disappointed and disturbed by their failure to get through to the preacher. But as he pondered the failure it occurred to him that, although they had the right method, they were using the wrong voice.

Molly tramped in once more, during a lull. She was bundled up to the mouth and her glasses were misted over, but not so much that Cowboy couldn't see she was enjoying the little drama which she had devised.

"Still hasn't budged, hey?" Molly helped herself to coffee.

Jeremy gave her a weary venomous look.

"We're all wrong, Molly," Cowboy said.

"I'm not convinced."

"I mean we've played enough of King's voice. We ought to be playing the tape we made of the Andreson kid. Over and over until morning, if it takes that long."

Molly nipped at her coffee, intent on him. Then she nodded.

"That's what King ought to be hearing. Once just wasn't enough. I was thinking the same—"

Cowboy went outside, buttoning his coat. He climbed into the Volkswagen truck and instructed the operator to put the little boy's appeal on the tape machine. Then Cowboy situated himself a few feet back from the Train, in front of the windows of the study, and there he waited, his head thumping with each cold breath.

The Andreson boy began to speak, prompted in a whispery, sometimes inaudible monotone by his father. *Ask the preacher to come see you. Ask Brother Windom to help you pray. Now, what you 'fraid of? Tell him how you honor the Lord Jesus. Don't you love Lord Jesus? Sure you do. Why don't you sing for Brother Windom? Sing the song they learned you in Sunday school. "Je-sus loves me, this I know . . ."*

The halting but inhumanly loud voice of the child: *Cause the Bible tells me so.*

Giggles.

Cowboy looked up, hating every second of this, and saw Molly behind glass in the vestibule of the coach. For some reason she was grinning broadly, and she waved her clenched hands encouragingly at Cowboy. He wondered if the preacher had given some indication that he was alive, and almost bolted for the Train. But Molly didn't appear to be signaling him. He dropped his head once more, shivering. It was all preposterous and obscene, but there was nothing else to do. If King was still functioning, rational after eleven days of self-torture, then— damn Molly anyway!—he had to respond.

They played the tape again.

The wind blew chillingly, and Cowboy discovered what it was like to be so cold that his knees knocked together.

One of the onlookers hauled a few more broken timbers out of the back of a pickup truck and fed them to the fire.

Cause the Bible

Sing the song they learned you in Sunday School.

Loves me this I know

Oh, my God, put an end to this, Cowboy sighed.

When he looked up, his eyes nearly rimmed with ice, he saw the preacher. King had lifted one of the window shades and was leaning forward in order to see through the opaque glass, bracing himself with both hands against the sill. He was wearing the old blue sweater, his favorite, and by contrast his face was as pale as the stars. Cowboy was quite close and despite the clouded window could see his friend clearly. The eleven-day growth of beard was an unexpected shock. But despite his beard the preacher did not look like a wild man. His eyes were alert, appraising. He had command of himself.

He was coming out.

Cowboy ran for the vestibule, shouting. But it was Jeremy who reached King Windom first. She rushed through the door which King had unlocked at last and then stopped short as he turned from the window.

Jeremy suddenly found that she had nothing to say to him. She had waited like a mother waiting for a child in a well and had prepared herself for anything but a casually unlocked door, which he banged against the wall. Her face was a fiery color; there were blisters of tears on her cheeks.

"Jeremy," said the preacher, a wan hint of happiness in his eyes. "Jeremy, I'm fine. Don't worry—it's over!"

"You . . . love . . . love . . . me . . . then," she said, choking on every word. And she stared at his half-grown beard, generously—and pitifully—trimmed with white and gray. Then her knees weakened and she fell toward him. He took a step, reached out, caught her in his arms.

"I—I gave up," Jeremy moaned. "I lost faith! I'm sorry—I gave you up!"

"Never mind, Jeremy." He soothed her and looked guardedly at the faces in the corridor outside. "I'm not free yet, God knows if I'll ever be, but I won't stop loving you; somehow it'll be all right for us."

Ask Brother Windom to help you pray, shouted the speakers around him, and King frowned, lifting his head.

Cowboy wedged into the study, nearly trampling Molly and

535

John Matthews, who had timidly remained outside. Molly's glasses were askew, but she had a glittering look of triumph in her eyes.

Now what you 'fraid of? Tell him how you honor the Lord Jesus.

Cowboy had an arm around King's shoulders and he shouted to nobody in particular, "Turn that thing off!"

"Hold on, Cowboy," the preacher said somberly, looking at him.

"Those people have been patient," Cowboy replied, feeling less joyful, "but don't force yourself tonight. They'll wait a little longer—if I pass the word that you intend seeing them." The preacher looked famished and there was a perceptible muscle spasm in one eyelid, but he was steady on his feet and the hand that caressed Jeremy had no tremor in it. Cowboy wasn't misled, however, by this appearance of strength: King had been wrenched from his isolation by a blatant emotional appeal; his own emotions must be chaotic, possibly ungovernable. Cowboy didn't miss the preacher's reactions to Jeremy's weeping presence. He was by turn fitfully consoling, bewildered, enamored, appalled.

"I don't want to make them wait," King insisted, "I don't want to put anything off." His eyes were luminous with determination and zeal. "I have to get my life straight, Cowboy."

Was he in a confessional mood, then? Cowboy suspected this was the case and he wanted to say, Spare her a little longer. But it wasn't up to him to decide. He discovered that he no longer cared whether Jeremy was protected. What mattered most was King's sanity and his ability to preach.

"Come on then," the preacher said, aware of Cowboy's indecision. "Let's all go." Jeremy was clinging still; without difficulty he held her at arm's length, where she was as frantic as a trapped squirrel. She tried to protest.

"Not yet—stay with me awhile!"

He smiled sternly at her. "Think of those poor people out there. The Lord God has brought me out of the wilderness for their sake."

She shook her head furiously. "I don't care!"

"But, Jeremy, this is going to be a happy night! I have a feeling we'll all have reason to rejoice before long."

536

"Stay, stay!" the oblivious Jeremy groaned, her eyes pressed tightly shut.

His smile was taut and there was urgency in his voice, a hint of something shattering. "Jeremy . . . let this be a happy night! *Trust* in the Lord our God."

Cowboy turned his face away. Jeremy stared at King, then she ceased struggling. He let her go and she took a step back. All of them were very quiet. King smiled and smiled. It was difficult to say if he was agonized or ecstatic.

"I have my friends with me tonight," he said in a low, husky voice, and tears ran down his cheeks. Jeremy held her breath and looked amazed.

Cause the Bible tells me

"All of you come," said King Windom.

52

The Shooting

Philemon awoke with a jerk of his head against the window, and he clutched the shotgun lying across his knees.

For a few moments he was panicky. He had slept, dreamlessly, but he didn't know for how long. The fire outside had become a pile of incendiary rubble covered with little yellow leaves of flame, and the loudspeakers were silent: perhaps the silence had awakened him.

Philemon half rose from his seat, blinking madly—his eyes felt coated with grease—trying to see. It was difficult for him to tell what was going on at the encampment without the fire. But, as he watched, two figures drifted close to the upwind side of the hill of embers, seeking warmth. Jeremy and Cowboy. Where, then, was King Windom? Had he left the Train already? Philemon was close to strangling on a hard lump of rage and frustration in his throat. Had he missed his best chance?

He pressed as closely as he could to the window, holding his breath so as not to fog the glass, and framed a field of vision with his hands. One of the camper trucks seemed to be the center of attention. He saw a man on his knees behind the truck, hands together in prayer. He realized then that King Windom had indeed been lured out for the sake of the little boy with the crippled heart.

Philemon drew back his fist and beat at the window ferociously. It was no use now—he could not get at the preacher, and take him by surprise. There were too many others around. Philemon knew he would be seen as soon as he approached with his shotgun, and of course they immediately would understand what he had come to do, because he had the nobility of avenging angels in his eyes, and the good wishes of the Father in his heart. Again Philemon hit the glass, bruising his hand. He sobbed. It could not be tonight. He would have to wait.

Yet he sensed that he could not possibly wait. Not another hour. The Father's wishes were clear, His strength was not Philemon's for the asking, and Philemon knew from harsh experience that the Father was changeable—He could become indifferent, and withdraw His favors. If Philemon did not find the means to carry out the punishment of the preacher tonight, then he might as well not return to Clearwater. The Father would not welcome him.

His stomach felt raw, blood-raw. Philemon thought he could taste hot metallic blood at the back of his tongue. Do it another way, he told himself sternly. Be a man. And with this thought he was inspired, precisely when he needed inspiration so badly.

The shotgun was too long for him to conceal, even beneath the overlarge Army coat he was wearing. But was anyone left aboard the Train to observe him? He couldn't tell by counting the figures gathered back of the fire. Philemon trembled with indecision; then he stood, scornfully. Too much caution might cost him his second chance. He opened the door of his room and walked boldly down the lighted corridor, but he was tense and his face itched and throbbed from the heat of his blood.

The chapel was three cars ahead. Philemon pried open each door with care, listened, then went on. His confidence increased; he was sure he was alone on the Train. He stepped over one of the loudspeakers that had been placed outside

538

King's study, paused for a glance through the doorway, then hurried on.

As he was about to leave the last coach before the chapel, he again felt the critical need to be careful. Someone had wedged open the door, so he didn't have to make a sound in his passage. He gripped his shotgun more firmly, right hand on the pump, and walked lightly across the metal platform. It was a good thing he had slowed down. Both halves of the left-hand vestibule door were standing open and, just below, on the tracks, its back to Philemon, was a demon more terrible than any he could have dreamed.

A wonder he didn't cry out in his horror, or jump back too quickly and betray his presence with a clattering footstep. The tight membranous net of his mind expanded like a bubble, like a great exploding eye in which the image of the demon was threateningly multiplied. This pitch-black demon had a manlike head, but otherwise there was little human resemblance. The demon wore a lustrous black cape of wings, intricately ribbed and folded. From under the cape long claws protruded. Philemon had seen this much; he cradled his shotgun and pressed his hands against his face, breath hissing into his cupped palms. Somehow he kept the net of his mind from collapsing. Concealed in the bellows between coaches he also fought the collapse of his hopes for revenge against King Windom.

The Father came to his rescue: the purifying light of the Father filled his head, driving out in an instant the image of the winged evil that was King Windom's guide and his protection on earth. Grateful as he was for this intercession, Philemon still might have turned back, for he sensed that the night was aswarm with these creatures. He could not attend to King Windom and fight off all the demons of hell at the same time. But the light of the Father continued to burn in him, and he was pacified; he felt more at ease than he had for days. Look again, said the Father, and Philemon looked, and was puzzled.

In place of the demon he saw the less fearsome figure of Age, who was not dressed for subfreezing weather: the collar of his suit coat was up around his ears and he was shivering miserably. Philemon pondered this transformation. Was Age flesh and blood, or merely another reflection of the devil's ingenuity? He waited, clenching his teeth to keep them from chattering. Age had a look of suffering on his face as he turned his head, which told Philemon enough. He was possessed, but he was real. Philemon lifted the shotgun. Was Age about to come aboard, or would he move on toward the encampment? He stepped back into the bellows, ready, if he heard Age on the metal steps, to lash out and crush the nigger's head with the butt of the shotgun. But he heard nothing except the wind. Again he looked out. Age was gone.

Feeling encouraged, Philemon entered the chapel. The generator had been kept on day and night during King's retreat, just in case he decided to visit the chapel, and the single small spotlight above the altar was burning. Philemon made his way down the aisle and stopped beneath the dome, looking up. He had poked around the chapel many times by himself and had become familiar with the operation of the dome.

He took the steps two at a time with a burst of nervous energy and found himself under a clear black sky, under brilliant whirlpool of stars. For a few moments he admired the spectacle, and then he pushed the button that activated the dome. The quarter-horsepower motor whirred for a couple of seconds, stopped. Philemon raised his head a little at a time and looked out at the encampment some two hundred feet away. The fire illuminated, redly, a quarter acre of the camp ground.

Philemon could see unexpectedly well and he was pleased. He lifted his shotgun experimentally, to find out if he had room for a shooting stance. The encampment was at an angle and he had to stand a trifle awkwardly to bring the stock to his shoulder, but he was afraid to risk another movement of the dome.

Forty-five or fifty yards to the fire, he estimated, beginning to line up his shot. Nothing at all for a marksman with a rifle, but most shotguns were either erratic or completely ineffective at that range. Philemon stroked the barrel of his tight-shooting Winchester proudly. He had once won a ten-dollar bet by destroying three out of four targets, each the size of a box of shells, from forty-five yards away, with almost no scattering of the number-three shot he'd used. He knew he would be able to hit the preacher almost exactly where he wanted, with a knockdown charge, even if King was standing in a crowd. Chances were nobody else would even be nicked.

Philemon turned his shoulders to see how much of the target zone he could cover effortlessly. Like many other self-taught hunters, Philemon had no use for a gunsight; he shot by the feel of the gun against his shoulder. Shooting was the one thing he did really well, and the prospect of making the most important shot of his life gave him an extra measure of determination.

Now he had carefully planned and checked out his every move and there was nothing to do but wait, as he had waited many a dark and frost-deep morning on line for ducks and geese. Philemon found it pleasant to think back over some of the days he'd hunted with particular success. It was hard to say what kind of shooting gave him the most pleasure—he'd guess foxes, maybe because they were so difficult to track, even with a good dog like Cosh. But, then, a crafty pheasant was hard to beat.

He lowered the shotgun to keep his shoulders from tightening and looked away from the fire, along the shimmering roofs of the coaches. The moon was somewhere behind him. The shadow of the Train along the tracks was well defined. Someone stirred in that ribbon of shadow and Philemon saw Age moving along, slowly, hands in his pockets. From his eminence Philemon looked curiously at King Windom's man, wondering what was the matter with him, and where he'd been. Apparently Age and the preacher had had a falling out. Philemon was vague about that situation; he'd been intensely absorbed by his own problems the past two weeks.

As if aware that he was being intently studied, Age stopped his restless prowling and lifted his head slightly. Philemon continued to stare at him and he felt a jagged malevolence across his heart. An alien sensation followed the malevolence, followed it like a rising sea. Then his head whirled, as if the gentle immense pressure of stars was lifting him upward like a dry leaf. Philemon resisted, tongue bulging in his mouth, but he was badly frightened; he thought he was in danger of being separated from his soul. He took a step back, almost losing his hold on his gun. But within moments he was his old self.

Cries of "Hallelujah!" and "Bless the Lord God!" rang in his ears.

Philemon raised his head and focused on the fire again. He saw that the door to one of the campers had been opened, and a cluster of worshipers was forming around the steps. King Windom appeared, stooped, in the doorway, and in his arms was the blanket-wrapped Andreson boy.

Someone, presumably the father, took the baby. The wind

changed direction and Philemon could hear their voices more clearly. "Miracle!" they shouted. "Praise God! He's healed." Philemon felt detached as he lifted his shotgun. You must not be fooled, he thought. Forsake him! He is not a healer.

His finger curled around the trigger of the Winchester. But the preacher was, for the moment, surrounded. Philemon took his eye off the target and looked again for Age. Then he shifted his attention back to King Windom. They were all walking toward the fire.

Philemon fought a spasm of shudders. He still did not have the clear shot he'd hoped for, and he was very concerned about wounding someone else too. He began to experience doubts. Maybe, he thought, it's too far. Maybe if I wait—

King stopped suddenly and looked toward the Train. Philemon understood that he had seen Age skulking there. He heard the preacher calling to his friend. Age was motionless. After a short hesitation King broke away from the people around him and circled the fire.

Philemon had no time to think, or delay. His hands had stiffened and for a second he couldn't feel the trigger properly. Then he had it, and he had King lined up. He could see the preacher plainly against a sudden outbreak of flame in the pile of charred wood. He was certain he could make out the exact color of the preacher's eyes, but of course at that distance . . .

The gun boomed. King was caught by a charge of buckshot at the knees, in midstride, and whipped around. He fell face down inches from the hot embers of the fire and turned over on his hip.

Philemon saw him grimace with shock and pain, but he felt no emotion himself: he felt only that it was not enough, somehow. A second ago he had seen the motes in the preacher's eyes and he had felt a surprising kinship. Now he knew, with a twinge of regret, that wounding the preacher just wasn't enough.

Not enough, not enough, he thought dully, and brought the stock of the shotgun hard against his shoulder. Perhaps five seconds had passed. King, with at least one knee demolished, had made no attempt to rise. He was looking in astonishment at a bloody uplifted hand. Had he just realized that he was shot? Jeremy knew, or perhaps Jeremy was quicker than the others. She was running to help him. Philemon stood up calmly against the moon and shot King Windom again, this time in the head.

Jeremy was less than four yards away from her husband when it happened; she screamed and threw her crossed arms up in front of her face. Philemon looked hazily down the barrel of his shotgun at her. The front of her coat was redly splattered, as if a bright gout of blood had jumped from the preacher's exploding head. Or had some of the shot gone astray? Philemon didn't know; he only knew, with a forlorn sense of excitement, that he still hadn't had enough. Bagging one bird in the field wasn't a day's work, as long as birds remained, and there were shells in his gun. He shifted his shoulders and brought the muzzle of the Winchester to bear on Jeremy, who stood, frozen and anguished, over the heap of her husband's body. An instant before pulling the trigger Philemon heard Jeremy's second scream, and he flinched, his concentration disturbed.

When he opened his eyes he saw Jeremy lying on her back, and he knew that something was wrong: if he'd hit her breast-high as he'd planned, the charge would have knocked her right into the gray and smoldering fire. Then he saw Cowboy stretched out on the ground behind Jeremy, one hand clutching the collar of her coat. Somehow Cowboy had guessed that Jeremy might be the next victim.

Philemon was indifferent as he pumped another shell into the chamber. He had missed, but he would not miss again. He would shoot all night, until they were all dead. It was good shooting; there were plenty of birds in the field. And who could say when they would let him have his gun back, to shoot again?

Out of the corner of his eye he saw a running man in the ribbon of Train-shadow below. Philemon laughed aloud at the sport he was having and snapped a shot at the runner. He was a little hasty, a little low. Age skidded to a stop, almost falling in the loose ballast, and clawed at his face as if stung by ricocheting gravel. Then he leaped to safety between coaches. Philemon grinned broadly and turned back to the survivors at the fire. Cowboy had dragged Jeremy to her feet and apparently was trying to wrestle her away from the fire, but she could not take her eyes from the fallen preacher, and her sobs were appalling.

"He's in the dome!" someone yelled, and someone else called in a panicky voice, "Damn it, get away from there, get behind the trucks!" And Philemon was so tickled he could scarcely keep his shotgun steady. He caught a glimpse of the Cowboy's strained face, turned toward the dome. Philemon went for the face, confidently.

The dry snapping of the hammer alarmed him. He pumped, and pumped again. Had he fired six shots already? The protective net of his mind began to crawl and shrivel and he closed his smarting eyes. No; for some reason he'd only loaded four shells. He'd thought just one would do.

Philemon put one hand and then the other into the pockets of his Army coat, rummaging for ammunition. At the same time he heard a ringing of iron as Age entered the chapel car.

He dropped to his knees, still anxiously searching himself for shells. He wondered bleakly, as the seconds of his life were sucked away into the whirlpools above, why he had not brought more. The problem was too complex for him to solve. He'd come unprepared for the best shooting of his life. Why hadn't the man in the hardware store made him buy more shells? He felt vaguely betrayed. He felt as if someone had given him very bad advice. Why, Philemon asked himself, had he killed King Windom? He hadn't been thinking, even for a second, about killing the preacher.

It was incredible that he'd murdered a man, but Philemon wasn't remorseful, he had other things to think about: Age was in the chapel below, and he was trapped.

A way out occurred to him. He reached for the operating button of the dome, found it in the dark, and pressed it. The dome slid back all the way. Philemon heard the nigger on the stairs and threw the shotgun butt-first at him. He was rewarded when Age grunted with pain.

Quickly Philemon hoisted himself and wormed out onto the roof of the chapel car.

He balanced awkwardly there and was in immediate danger of hurtling to the ground. He felt exposed to all eyes and wondered with a grating horror if someone else had a gun. Sensibly he restrained himself from looking down, from looking over his shoulder at the encampment. He heard voices, but he'd lost his ear for the meaning of words.

Philemon bent over with his hands ready to grab anything at all and shuffled to the end of the coach. His eyes were filled with tears from the treacherous wind but he saw town lights, and, closer, the narrow streets of the Mexican settlement. Rising beyond the settlement—but, it seemed to him, comfortingly close—was a range of hills.

He figured that Age was hurt and would not be able to follow, yet when he reached the gap between coaches he risked his balance with a look back and saw his pursuer rising slowly but doggedly from the pit where the dome had been.

Heights were intolerable and ladders had been a lifelong terror, but there was something worse in the dark behind him, so Philemon scrambled down the handholds at the end of the coach and fell backward to earth with a jolt that caused him to cry out. Dizzily he picked himself up and ran.

He had thought that Age was an old man who would lose both his breath and his will to give chase, and the hills had looked so close from atop the Train. Now that he was on the ground he could barely see the hills in which he planned to hide, and after a block of hard running he glanced back to discover that King Windom's man was staying with him.

There were boxcars to dodge around, rails to stumble over, then a low wire fence, which he jumped, snagging and ripping his Army coat. The frame and stucco buildings of the Mexican settlement were close, just across an empty blacktop street with a shallow tide of sand on it. On one corner Philemon saw an iron lamppost, giving off a light that barely touched the ground. He slipped, staggered, caught himself, plunged on.

Philemon heard his own footsteps above the sighing wind. Because it was so bitterly cold there was no one else out. He had glimpses of golden lamplight behind thick and barren walls and entered a shadowy street, a dirt street but packed as hard as asphalt. The street angled upward, narrowing as it did so. Philemon felt as if he could not force another blade of breath into his raw lungs, and dragged his feet, looking hopefully around. There were other glimmerings of light along the way, but every door was shut, every window heavily curtained. Dogs barked perfunctorily. The wind pummeled his back, shifted, and ceased; he heard, or thought he heard, the nigger coming on. Holding his stomach, Philemon struggled up the street. He began to whimper in the dark for help and mercy.

Two-thirds of the way along, he saw a dab of yellow-green neon on his left, a step-down doorway. He left the street and skidded down the two worn stone steps and hammered at the windowless door. It opened under his fist, revealing a small bar: half a dozen tables with chairs, all empty. The bartender looked sleepily away from the blue screen of his television.

"Hide me," Philemon said, snarling for breath, casting

around. It was just a tiny room, apparently with no other way in or out.

The bartender shrugged, as if he couldn't understand English, as if his eyes couldn't see that an emergency existed.

"*Hide* me!" Philemon begged, but he knew it was no use.

Half-paralyzed by the agony of his body, he turned back to the street and hauled himself up the two steps. There, against his will, he looked for his pursuer, and thought that he saw Age moving toward him in the dark, but deliberately, as if he too was suffering.

Philemon blundered on toward the saddle-horn hills he had so foolishly chosen for sanctuary. He understood now that they were miles away, that there was a great deal of open desert which he would have to cross between the town and the hills.

The buildings dwindled on either side of him and abruptly the land slanted away at his feet. Just as he was thinking of a change of direction, of a new flight toward the lights of Tecopa, he slipped and slid fifty feet or more on his back into a dry wash. The fall jarred him badly. Slowly he picked himself up out of a clump of mesquite and flexed his scraped, bleeding hands.

Looking back, as he knew he must, Philemon saw a dreadful figure outlined against the moonlighted sky at the top of the wash. It was not moving. It was just standing there, watching him, with its winkless eyes, sulphurous and sharp-edged and hypnotic; the eyes and the acquiring claws were plainly visible to him.

His instinct for sanity was strong and so, in the expanding distances of his mind, he leaped, wiry and doubled, for the mind-net, on which he knew the reality of the world existed indelibly. But he plummeted on through this sanctuary as if it were cheap paper; the realities on which he depended hung in tatters, and the reality of the world which he feared remained, up there on the brink of the dry wash.

Nevertheless, for a few precious seconds he was calm, even still, despite his physical pain. He was able to concentrate on the simple words that would save him from the horror that was about to descend and make off with his immortal soul. He lowered his head; his lips trembled and he bit down viciously with his teeth. What was it he must say, whom was he to call in his hour of need? Tears wriggled down Philemon's cheeks. As he had been about to struggle across empty miles of desert, he

546

now struggled with a blank and depthless mind. Who? This word in his head was like the numbing wind. He had no answer to the question. He knew that his immortal soul was to be protected at all costs, he knew *that* without having to think, and he knew he was in danger of having this valuable soul clawed from his flesh and flung into a roasting pit where it must remain forever. But what could he do; he had forgotten the words that would summon help.

The wind stopped; in the desert stillness Philemon ran. He ran through tough dry mesquite and bled himself on cactus and ocotillo. Then the land became flat and cracked and gray-white under the stars and the budding moon. It was easier for him to push step by momentous step across this flatness toward . . .

If he could just keep on, then, perhaps, he might reach the hills ahead of the demon that was humming along in the dry air behind him. And he might find a crevice, a cave, a patch of darkness to swallow his body. There, Philemon thought, yearningly, he could have time to think of the incantation that would cause the relentless demon to vanish.

Unfortunately, Philemon had about run out his string. He lost track of his progress and his pursuer. For a few seconds he blacked out on his feet, if such a thing is possible, and regained consciousness to discover that he was no longer running, or trying to run. He was simply standing in the desert looking up at the sky, groaning with every tight breath.

The lights of Heaven were like a scalding shower for his frozen consciousness.

"Father Glorious!" Philemon shrieked, as a part of the mystery became clear to him. And he fell down gibbering on the crystallized earth.

When Age arrived, walking with a tall stagger, with his numbed hands knotted in the lapels of his coat, he heard Philemon singing rapturously in the unknown tongue.

"Habba lamai shettum hobeth—sholo wetai zabachthani!" His hands flapped weirdly as if he were trying to beat his way up off the ground.

Enraged, the Negro kicked at the soles of Philemon's shoes, expending a precious part of his remaining strength. "Get up!" he cried, unable to believe that Philemon had escaped him in this unexpected way. The tragedy of King Windom, as fresh as the rock-shrapnel wounds on his own face, would not let him believe.

547

"Get up, you trash! Get *up* from there." Philemon sang on. Age wandered all around his prone body, kicking at random, choking with grief.

Presently Philemon's song ended. For a while he lay powerless but trembling, opening and closing his mouth. Age backed off, drawing the knife which he'd earlier placed, with the blade open, in his belt.

Philemon found strength to lift his head; then, with a ponderous effort, he dragged himself to his knees. He was silent, except for the rasping breath in his throat. His eyes were solemnly fixed on Age. He might have been seeing a loathsome demon, or merely a man as worn out and despairing as he himself. But he had discovered a source of pride, apart from fear, that urged a fight for his immortal soul. He groped with his hands and came up with a good-size chunk of crumbling rock.

Age was immobile, watchful, glad. He held the knife with its five-inch blade close to his chest, almost shoulder high.

Philemon raised up with his potential weapon in both hands and sighed, chest heaving, building the pressure of his bleak courage. The two men were perhaps five steps apart. Suddenly Philemon raised the rock and charged, screaming. Age was surprised by his speed and quickness. He took a buckling step backward and threw up his left hand as he sank to the ground. The outflung hand deflected Philemon's charge, but the rock came down anyway, accurately, on Age's scarred head.

The rock was as porous as a clod of dirt, bursting into a thousand fragments on impact. Age was only slightly stunned. It was the most unpleasant surprise of Philemon's unhappy life, but he had little time to dwell on this failure. Age's right hand flicked out and the upraised point of the knife, invisible as a snake's fang, struck Philemon's throat. Philemon had lost his balance and needed a step to regain it. The step he took impaled him as the blade drove deep into his windpipe between tough rings of cartilage.

Age felt the jarring weight at the end of his arm and looked up swiftly. One of Philemon's hands grasped his raised shoulder in a comradely way; he didn't fall but stood over Age, hunched slightly, his mouth open. Philemon knew something terrible had happened to him but for a couple of seconds he didn't know just what it was. Then he tried to catch his breath.

Blood gushed out of the wound and over Age's knife hand.

Philemon reached tentatively for the unbelievable obstruction in his throat. He fingered the remaining inch of the cold blade, his eyes wide and startled. The fingers of his other hand gripped Age's shoulder convulsively.

"Ahhhhh," Philemon pleaded.

Age rose to his feet, and Philemon followed him with his eyes. He moaned again, frightened.

Age hesitated, feeling shocked by what he had so blindly done. Then he tightened his hold on the hilt of the knife and with a quick hard jerk to the right cut Philemon's throat as he would have cut the throat of a badly wounded animal. The blade was free in the air and Philemon turned, collapsing, hands loose. Age looked away, breathing deliberately and slowly. He had no more use for the knife and so he dropped it, then reached for a handkerchief to clean his soiled sticky hand.

Three or four minutes later he bent over and rolled Philemon on his back. The boy's eyes were open and glum, his face sunken, haggard, and white. Blood was already thickly caked on his torn throat. Crystals of salt glittered on his cheeks like the tears of a lost and out-of-favor child. There was Philemon, the murderer.

Age had no taste for revenge; all he tasted was bitterness. He could not even say for sure he had intended to kill this—lunatic—boy. His thin body vibrated from the cold, but he would not go. He continued to hover over the corpse, feeling perplexed, aching for some sign from within his heart that the assassin of the preacher had met a justifiable end. But Philemon, dead, was no more of a satisfaction than he had been while living.

Now why? Age thought, kneeling, as if by peering more intently into the slick Heaven-petitioning eyes he could divine some sort of explanation. Why had Philemon taken up his gun against the preacher? He continued to kneel but soon began to feel angry with himself. There was nothing to be learned here—perhaps nothing to be learned at all. He straightened and thrust his hands into his coat pockets. Someone would look back and say, This is where the tragedy had its beginnings, and someone else would contradict him, and it would go on like that as long as men were interested in the death of King Windom.

Stock still, Age stared at the town lights as intently as he had tried to fathom the eternal expression in the dead boy's eyes. It was a long way to town, and he felt no pressing desire to go back. He'd failed the preacher in every way, at almost every turn, and the sum of his failures was to be a funeral. Age felt an almost maddening grief, but, unexpectedly, his grief dwindled to nothing, leaving him clear-headed, sharp-sighted. He looked questioningly at Philemon's Heaven, sensing a release. He had failed but he could not—no, he was not permitted to—condemn himself for mistakes honestly made.

Once more Age turned his eyes to Philemon's corpse, this time with a sensation of sorrow, this time with forgiveness. The tragedy of King Windom had begun long before Philemon came on the scene—and long before Age first looked on him in the Sugar Tree Valley, passionate, zealous, headstrong, and basically protectionless. The tragedy had been born into him, he had always been the sort of man to inspire other men to tears, or violence. Age had fought for King without half understanding why. Perhaps Philemon had killed him with the same lack of understanding in his heart.

There were ways he could still be useful if he wanted, Age thought. Probably she would never need him, or care to have him around. But if he stayed within hearing distance, then, someday, Jeremy might have reason to call. He knew that he wouldn't mind waiting, no matter what.

Age walked away, but after several strides he stopped. He lofted a sigh, turned patiently. Still there—and Philemon could not be ignored in his silence.

Returning to the body, Age reached down, grasped the ankles, and began the hours-long task of dragging it back across the desert plain to the town of Tecopa.

JEREMY

53

The Shrine

After the complex affairs of the Southern Cross Crusade were more or less settled, the Appalachian and Atlantic Railroad had the Gospel Train brought back to Clearwater. There the Train was placed on a seldom used and fairly inaccessible siding not too far from the marshaling yard in which Molly had first seen it. The railroad did not advertise the presence of the Train in Clearwater, but from the beginning it attracted quite a lot of attention. After the fatal shooting *Life* magazine published a truncated version of the story which they'd planned to run about King Windom, and other magazines, some of them shoddy and generally unheard of, published articles which capitalized on the preacher's alleged powers of healing and the sensational murder. Because those who had been closest to King made themselves unavailable for interviews, the Train itself became the focal point for a number of the stories.

Long after the press lost interest, the Train remained as a sort of shrine there on the spur track in Clearwater, to the annoyance of the railroad. The people could not be kept away, so special guards had to be hired to protect the property, and all in all it was quite an expense. A big carnival offered to buy the chapel car, from which Philemon had done the shooting: the carnival owners planned to install a waxworks depicting the gruesome murder. But Mrs. Cobb found out about the scheme and quietly applied pressure in the right places to make sure nothing came of it.

Four evangelists tried to buy or lease the Gospel Train for their own purposes. Each was turned down.

A seventeen-year-old boy in Texas attracted quite a following by claiming that at the instant of King Windom's death the preacher's fabulous power to heal had passed into his own immature body.

An unknown number of sick people on pilgrimages to the Gospel Train reported that they had been completely healed merely by touching the Train; this news got around slightly faster than the speed of light. The railroad fathers debated several courses of action. Only get-rich-quick promoters had been interested in buying, and for pittances, so they considered splitting the Train up, sending one car here, another car there; then, they reasoned, there would be no Gospel Train, and nothing to attract the pilgrims. But it was pointed out that by doing this they would compound their problem: sightseers and worshipers would be swarming over a dozen railroad yards and fouling up operations.

The railroad fathers eventually decided to do the one sensible thing: they spruced up their shrine, hired guides, granted concessions, and proceeded to make a pot of money.

And two years passed.

Not long after the second anniversary of King's death Molly returned to Clearwater for a couple of days to visit her mother, who had suffered a heart attack. It turned out to be less of an emergency than Molly had been led to believe, and she discovered that even after a prolonged absence her mother got on her nerves as quickly as she always had in the past. So Molly had time on her hands before she could decently fly back to her new home in Chicago.

She'd heard about the Gospel Train shrine but of course had never seen it, so on a fine March day that was only a change in the wind away from spring she took a taxi to the site.

It was not a hasty decision, for Molly had wondered many times over the two years if she'd have the desire to look at the Train again should circumstances permit. And, although she'd made up her mind, she was quite nervous as the taxi rattled along. She really didn't know what she might be letting herself in for. Two years ago he died, Molly thought, feeling prickly and strange. But his passing had created a knot of difficulties, legal and emotional. This knot had half-strangled her for many long months before she could escape to a new place and piece together a satisfactory new life. She tended to be smug about her new life, at times, and self-congratulatory. A wonder she'd survived at all. Molly gave her spirits a boost with a cigarette and assured herself that there was no reason for nervousness. One look at the Train wouldn't wipe out the gains she'd made, or threaten the new life. He was dead and gone, but it was a mild March day and in only a few hours she'd be back in Chicago, and it would all seem slightly unreal, as the days of the Gospel Train properly should.

When the Train finally came into view from the windows of her taxi, Molly was unprepared for the feeling of elation and pride that rose, strongly but peacefully, in her breast.

In the brilliant, high-noon sun the Train looked just as it had on the day they'd left Clearwater with the blessings of Harlan Gray and the Governor. Today there'd be no speeches, today there were no hillbilly musicians and there wasn't a crowd, not a soul in sight—something of a surprise, yes—but Molly was transported; it seemed all about to happen again. Absently she paid the driver and stood alone outside the chain-link fence which had been erected both to call attention to the unusual shrine and to protect it from vandalism; she quaked with anticipation and wonder.

The sunlight hurt her sensitive eyes, so she slipped on bulky sunglasses and walked slowly along the fence. She had forgotten the power of the Gospel Train, the power to attract the eye and rule the senses. Many times during the Train's brief tour she had looked out at the crowds and marveled at the sameness of expression on so many faces. The common expression was one of total seriousness and respect. They had been staring at King Windom, listening to him preach, but they didn't know him; despite his abilities he really hadn't earned those looks of seriousness, of sublimated awe. Molly paused, still in a vague trance of admiration for the gleaming coaches. Their respect had been for a concept, for a bold idea imaginatively carried out—her idea.

Near the entrance gates to the shrine and just inside the fence was a half-ton of plaque done in aluminum and black marble, very much like a marker commemorating a historic battle. The story of King Windom and the Gospel Train had been condensed to a few paragraphs, in severe raised letters, on the plaque. Molly read, then looked again at the medallion above, at the black marble face of King Windom, without a definite sense of having known him. He had lived brilliantly for such a short time, for a matter of months, and perhaps it was a puzzle to some people why he should be here now, in marble, proprietor of a shrine in his name. Molly too had been puzzled by the endurance of his name and his legend, but now that she was so close to the Train, she understood perfectly. He had been young, and brilliant in the service of his God, and he had died sensationally, and all these circumstances helped make the legend attractive. But the real power of King Windom had been the Train, as Molly had intuitively realized during the first flash of creation two and a half years ago; his power to attract the emotionally needy lived on, lived here, and not in the flesh of some dim-witted publicity-seeking boy in Texas.

With a last look at the plaque Molly passed through the gates and entered the little building through which all visitors to the shrine were funneled. She found no one on hand except a receptionist, a well-groomed girl of nineteen or twenty with a calm experienced smile.

"I'm so sorry," the girl said when Molly expressed interest in going aboard. "You just missed the last tour. But there'll be another in twenty minutes, if you'd care to wait."

Molly smiled, feeling jaunty, feeling wonderful. "I was hoping I could look around on my own."

"No, ma'am. That isn't possible. But the tour is very complete." The girl hesitated, and although her own smile didn't vary by a millimeter, Molly realized she was being thoroughly studied. "Of course, if you've come for personal counseling . . ." She dropped her eyes to one of the telephones on her large desk.

"I can tell you I didn't come for counseling," Molly said, admiring the setup. The reception area was spic and span, furnished with comfortable folding chairs for those waiting for the next tour.

Molly's eyes lighted on a poster, the only ornament in the sunny room. SO FAR THIS YEAR, read the poster, $\boxed{28,657}$ HAVE VISITED THE GOSPEL TRAIN AND PAUSED TO PRAY IN THE CHAPEL OF KING WINDOM. IF WE MAY BE OF SPECIAL SERVICE TO YOU, PLEASE LET US KNOW. Molly pursed her lips. The girl said, tapping a pencil on the desk top, "Last year we welcomed more than one hundred thousand people. The total this year is running ahead of last year. During the summer——"

"Don't you have anything for sale?" Molly asked with a slightly cynical smile. "I mean I've heard about the King Windom long-play records and the——"

There was a fractional look of pique in the girl's soft brown eyes, as if she'd had to deal with too many smart alecks that day.

"Mementos and keepsakes are available aboard the Train for those who want them. Quite a few of our visitors take away the collected sermons. And, yes, we do have long-playing records available." The girl looked at her watch. "I'm sure you'll be pleased with the tour if you have the time to wait."

Molly decided to throw a little weight around. Maybe the tour was very complete, but then she'd had the tour, thanks. "I'm really in a large hurry, and if you could bend the rules for me I'd be grateful. You see, I'm Molly Amos."

The girl didn't make anything out of the name right away, and Molly was annoyed, but after a slight double take she came halfway up from her seat. "Oh . . ."

Molly nodded, modestly.

"Oh, well . . . I'm sure it would be all right then, if you want to go ahead by yourself. Let me write a note in case anyone . . ." Flustered, she scribbled something on a card, and Molly could read every thought she had in her sleek head. There was more to the legend than could be printed on the plaque outside. She was a well-meaning girl, though, and Molly rather liked her.

"Thank you," she said graciously, accepting the card. The girl accompanied her to the path outside and Molly went on alone toward the Train, adjusting her plump mink stole around her shoulders. But her sense of high holiday, her feeling of being just another tourist, had evaporated, confusing her. Several yards from the end of the Train she stopped. All right, there it is, she thought. And she knew every inch of it by heart. Why, then, had she been so keen to climb aboard and prowl around this one last time? The Train was cold metal, nothing more, and inside were cold forgotten lives stored away and dim to the eye, strangely pathetic like featherless baby birds frozen in ice. She didn't have to go inside to be reminded. She didn't want to go.

Aggravated, indecisive, Molly lingered on the crushed-stone path. She knew the girl was still in the doorway of the reception

557

building, watching her. Molly found herself wishing she hadn't worn the knitted green suit she was so fond of, the one that unfortunately made two of each of the excess pounds she had been carrying around the past year. There was no way she could make a decent retreat without giving the girl something to jabber about to her friends. . . . "Couldn't go through with it; she just stopped about thirty feet from the Train and came back. I wonder what she was thinking. Ha-ha."

Molly gritted her teeth and pretended to be looking in her handbag for something of great importance. Despite the pleasantly cold air the sun was bringing sweat to her forehead. Finally Molly grasped a small camera and brought it out with a flourish. There was no film in the camera, but all the same she began snapping away at the Gospel Train. Now maybe the little twat would get tired of staring at her and would go back inside!

She remembered how it had felt to be aboard the Train and to want a drink, desperately. Molly's mouth watered. She reckoned that it would take three stiff ones during the flight back to Chicago to rinse the taste of this visit out of her mouth. She lowered the camera and glanced back over one shoulder, was relieved to find that the girl was gone. For that matter, Molly discovered, she was utterly alone, and it was unnaturally quiet for broad daylight. She decided to walk up and down the path for a couple of minutes, then breeze back and ask the receptionist to call her a cab, as she was in a tearing hurry to make the airport.

But even two minutes was too long. Too long for her to keep her guard up, and to keep the memories away. She felt uneasier with every glance at the impenetrable windows, at the dazzling reflectant surfaces of the convex coaches. Molly began to feel haunted, and she smiled a strained smile. Of course there were ghosts, she thought. It's overrun with ghosts and it always will be, as long as a single person comes to stare, and prowl, and remember.

There he had stood, there he had preached . . . there he had lived with his bride.

Molly fixed her eyes on the dome of the chapel car. None of them had realized, that night, where the shots were coming from. If just one of them had kept his wits, had been quick, then the preacher might have survived the first shot. But it was pointless to think about how his life might have been saved.

Pointless, Molly repeated to herself, feeling the beginning of a headache—too much bright sun. No one could have saved him, and no one was to blame. Not even that poor idiot Philemon. Who would have thought he had the backbone for a murder?

Molly had closed her eyes behind the dark glasses and now she felt a little dizzy. Why, she wondered, angrily, why should I go through this . . . *sickness* . . . again? It was all pointless; there was nothing more to be said. The preacher had fixed his own fate by killing that helpless dog. Perhaps he and Philemon had had some sort of undercover feud going. Only Molly knew how strange some of the preacher's notions were. And so he was dead, he had asked for it— Oh, stop! Molly thought, her throat muscles straining in a silent scream, and she stared up at the open blue sky. No one can be blamed! But her heart trembled like a water-filled balloon and lost a beat. Why, why, does he still come to me in dreams with half a ruined head, a bloody martyred eye?

"Molly?"

She jerked around convulsively, not having heard the footsteps on the gravel path beside the Train.

"Molly?" he said again, smiling his friendly-dog smile.

She was put off by the neat plaid suit, since she'd never seen him in anything but rancher's gabardines. But she recovered from her brief scare and managed a wooden smile.

"Well, good Lord, how are you, Cowboy?"

"Not too bad, Molly." He had paused a dozen steps away, aware that he'd severely startled her, but now he approached. "I was beginning to think you wouldn't show up."

"How's that? I mean, how'd you know I was—" Molly swallowed; her heart was still giving her fits. "Oh, sure, your grandmother and my mother." She shrugged, self-consciously, and tugged at the knitted wool suit as if willing herself to look smaller in it. She had not counted on running into anybody she knew; in fact she hadn't had the vaguest idea where Cowboy was these days. "Good to see you," she said, sounding baldly insincere. "Still preaching, Jimbo?"

His own smile became a kind of grimace as he squinted amiably at her. "Right, I am. I've tried school, off and on, but, just like our preacher, I think I'm cut out for evangelism and not for a church."

"Well." She had her wits about her and was sizing him up.

He'd let his hair go carelessly long and it was a poor style for him, but otherwise he was much better-looking than she remembered. The rambling-bear look was gone. So, regrettably, was some of the brute sensuality in his face. Molly looked into his eyes. Impossible to tell what he was thinking, as always. Apparently, though, he'd gone to some trouble to see her. She wondered if there were still hard feelings—not that it really mattered to her. Molly gestured toward the Train.

"Do you have anything to do with this enterprise?"

"Matter of fact I do—I'm one of the counselors in the chapel. Last summer I organized a full-scale revival here, and it came off well, I think. Probably I'll do the same this summer."

Molly clutched at her heart, discreetly she thought, but Cowboy caught the movement and tilted his head. "Feeling all right?"

"Sure, I'm in the pink, Cowboy," Molly said crossly. "I'm just getting over a bout with the flu, that's all."

"Come on inside, I'll buy you some coffee. Give you a chance to sit down for a few minutes."

"I don't think I want to go inside."

He had turned his head a fraction and his smile seemed to have a trace of mockery. "Nothing to it," he said.

"I mean I—" She was about to say that she had a plane to catch, but the excuse now seemed foolish; Cowboy knew better. Molly nodded abruptly, made a lead-on gesture with one hand, and followed him aboard, flushing a little at the difficulty she had climbing steps in the tight suit. To cover her discomposure she became highly talkative until they had settled down in the recreation car with steaming cups of coffee from a dispenser.

"New city, new job," Cowboy murmured, making random quarter-turns in his swivel chair as he sipped coffee. "Any other big changes in your life, Molly?"

"Well . . . last but not least, new husband."

Cowboy smiled, but his eyes seemed rather bleak as he studied her. The unaccountable bleakness and sobriety made Molly uncomfortable, but she had halfway decided it was no reflection on her; Cowboy looked as he did simply because he had settled down to being a dull boy. There was no further room in his life for high jinks or flights of fancy, and that seemed a shame.

"Tell me all about him."

"He's . . ." Molly found herself unable to speak as glowingly as she usually did of the man she'd married. "He's somewhat older than I am. In his late fifties. A real solid dependable guy. He has two grown-up children—his first wife divorced him. What can I say? Kurt's just what I wanted—just what I needed. I couldn't be happier." Cowboy's bleakness seemed to be contagious. She stared down into her coffee cup. Her surroundings were putting knots in her stomach, but she was holding fast, keeping control of herself nicely, until somewhere in the depths of the Train a door opened, echoed; a featureless voice called out: Molly's head jerked up. Cowboy was watching her closely.

"Sometimes it even gets to me," he said, with a meditative look. "I'll be alone in the office waiting for the telephone to ring, waiting for anyone at all who needs help to call, and then I'll hear a door open, or a footstep between cars . . ." He brushed fingertips across his forehead and looked moodily out the nearest window. "Some things stand out in my mind, scenes too real to be called memories. I feel helpless, in chains, I feel as if I'm back there in Tecopa looking on while he lies on the ground in agony, while Philemon . . . draws a second bead."

I know, I *know*, Molly wanted to shout, but instead she gripped an arm of her chair and said harshly, "How the hell can you stand it, Cowboy, being around this Train? What do you think you're doing, anyway? What keeps you here?"

He frowned as if her question was senseless, and sat up in the swivel chair. "King was my friend, Molly—and my inspiration. I like to think that in a small way I'm carrying out plans he made. Being here isn't as . . . painful as I made it sound just now. Actually I have a wonderful sense of contentment most of the time. I enjoy working late, spending the night. An hour of prayer usually puts me right when I'm blue. I know I can count on his friendship. I really don't need—"

"Whose friendship, Cowboy?"

"King's." He acknowledged the soured look on Molly's face with another, faintly indulgent smile. "It sounds like I'm losing my grip, I suppose, but I really believe that King, or his spirit, is here much of the time, encouraging all of us who are trying to do God's work aboard the Gospel Train. I sense his presence, and so do others—they've told me so. I *know* King is responsible for whatever success I may be having as an evangelist. Strangely enough, when I get away from the Train, when I try preaching somewhere else, I . . . dry up. I'm no good." He leaned forward. "You should visit the chapel before you leave. If you meditate for a few minutes there in a halfway receptive frame of mind I guarantee you'll understand everything I'm talking about."

"No," Molly said, shaking her head, her lips compressed, "I wouldn't understand. Because he's dead and I know that for us—all of us who knew him—it should be as if he never was. We're better off with that attitude. Far better off."

Cowboy politely said nothing.

Molly's face was twisted by a paroxysm. "I know what you think—what a lot of people think. *I'm* responsible. I killed him." She throbbed with anger. "But I won't take that. I won't accept it!" Cowboy looked troubled and started to speak, but Molly cut him off. "I loved him, remember, and it really didn't matter how he treated me. I loved him, and I wanted what was best for him. Maybe I made mistakes, but nobody can say I haven't paid for them—and I'll go on paying, believe me!" She clamped a cigarette in her mouth and lit it, glowering. "I can imagine why you were so interested in seeing me today, Cowboy, and not for old times' sake, hah!" She choked for a few moments on cigarette smoke but kept her eyes hard upon him. "You're worried, aren't you, you're afraid Molly's going to spill the beans after two years. But what satisfaction would I get from ruining what's left of that girl's life? What do you *take* me for, Jimbo?"

"I wanted to see you because you're a friend," Cowboy said patiently. "And I know you wouldn't hurt Jeremy."

"I have no interest in her at all—none at all," Molly reiterated with a jab of her cigarette in his direction. "I don't even know where she is. I—suppose some young buck's come along and carried her off to the altar." Cowboy half-closed his eyes and settled back in the chair. "That's inevitable; she's just a kid still." Molly faltered, as if she were listening to her heartbeat again. Her expression became bitter, disconsolate. "She'll never know he had another wife. Hear that, Cowboy? As long as I'm able to work for a living, as long as I can keep sending money out there, Jeremy will never know. And how long can Mary Kate live?"

"I don't know, Molly; how long?"

"Well, she—she had a terrible case of pneumonia this winter, pulled through somehow, but . . . Dr. Danvers—he's the one keeps me posted—said she's very weak. Very susceptible. Who knows? Mary Kate might outlive us all—and one more illness might kill her." They sat silently together, Molly smoking, Cowboy looking thoughtfully at the ceiling.

At last he said, "I've prayed for her—and for you, Molly. I knew what you were doing. I wrote to the sanatorium a while back and they told me Mary Kate had the best of care, thanks to your generosity. I'm still wanting to help out, though, if you—"

"Oh, no, no, Jimbo," Molly protested. "Thanks, but it's . . . no strain. I've got a good job. I can manage." Thinking of Mary Kate, Molly felt a certain amount of pride. *Maybe I acted badly; maybe I made a lot of mistakes—but it's all right now, everything has worked out for the best.* She felt close to shedding a few compassionate tears, which wouldn't do; she'd certainly overstayed, and they really had nothing more to talk about. Cowboy was happy with his cloister and his mission, no mistaking that. And Molly felt reasonably sure she'd satisfied him that she wasn't holding a grudge against the widow Jeremy.

Cowboy didn't urge her to stay, and they went out again into the sun.

"Seems a shame that the Gospel Train just sits here," Molly remarked, needlessly. "It was a wonderful idea, Cowboy, if I may say so. And it worked for a while, it really worked."

Cowboy shaded his eyes. "We're not the only ones who think the Train should roll again," he said seriously. "The group of ministers who sponsor the King Windom evangelists are talking about a tour. Who knows what'll happen, if the Lord is willing?"

"Who knows?" Molly echoed, finding his attitude and choice of words spookily familiar. *Maybe,* she thought, *he'll be a good evangelist someday, if he can just break the spell, if he can stop living only for the cold breath of approval from a dead man.* Molly sadly smiled good-bye, but after a couple of steps she turned back to him.

"Where is she, Cowboy?" she asked, throbbing with curiosity. *Have you seen Jeremy lately, talked to her? How is she getting along?*

He shrugged. "I don't know, Molly. Your guess is as good as mine."

Molly lingered, disappointed; but Cowboy had no more to

say on the subject of Jeremy. With a hint of his old insinuating smile, he swung aboard. "See you around, Mol."

She popped on her sunglasses and trudged toward the reception building. He was lying, she thought. As God makes green little apples he knows all about her! But with the next breath Molly wasn't so sure. Maybe Jeremy had dropped completely out of sight, after all, behind that screen of Cobb family lawyers.

Molly sighed. It was frustrating in a way; she would have liked to be able to visit Jeremy, spend a leisurely afternoon or two. Molly felt quite friendly toward the girl, despite all that had passed between them; there wasn't a speck of envy or malice left in her bones. Naturally Jeremy would feel less charitable toward her. Molly sighed again, wounded by Cowboy's distrust. All Molly wanted, actually, was the chance to reassure Jeremy that she was safe, that she had a friend she could count on. There certainly wouldn't be any harm in that.

She entered the building, feeling delicately miserable. Jeremy would never know that Molly had practically broken her own back to protect her. But that was as it should be.

At least I can hold my head up, Molly thought philosophically.

And then she cheered herself with another thought.

If I do decide I want to see Jeremy again, I know who can find her for me.

He can find *anybody*.

54

A Sense of Good Times

Actually Jeremy was not that hard to find, but she was certainly well protected, and had been from the day of King Windom's funeral. Those reporters and magazine writers who made efforts to exploit Jeremy's youth and attractiveness as well as her bereavement found that carnival people are a clannish bunch and not inclined to discuss anything with strangers. If any made themselves particularly obnoxious they were likely to come to a few hours later drifting toward the Gulf of Mexico in a rotting old rowboat or hanging head down and naked from a tree in an orange grove miles away from Fort Myers.

When Dr. John Matthews felt that his manuscript had reached the point where it could and ought to be shared with those most concerned, he spent a day and a half composing a long letter to Jeremy; he then devoted himself, for the first time in two years, wholeheartedly to farming, and found the discipline helpful in keeping his nerves under control as the days went smoothly and monotonously by without a word in return from Florida.

Finally, on a morning late in March, as he was about to give in and conclude that Jeremy wanted no part of him or his cherished project, a short polite note arrived.

The same afternoon Matthews had old Babineux drive him to the airport in Lafayette. He flew to New Orleans, made a dash for a Florida-bound jet, and arrived at International Airport in Tampa in time to catch the late flight for Fort Myers.

In his haste to get to Florida he'd neglected to send a wire, so, as eager as he was to see her again, Matthews had no intention of bothering Jeremy—or the Hendersons—until the next day. He got off the plane with the moldering, soft leather briefcase that had belonged to his grandfather secure under one arm, and walked across the wet parking strip to the gate. There, leaning thoughtfully on the fence, eyes fixed on a distant point of the field, was Age.

"Hello, Age," the doctor said, with an exuberance unnatural for him, and extended a sweating hand. Age unwound and straightened up and took the hand with no mutual display of enthusiasm.

"How do you do, Doctor. It's been a good long while."

"I'm flabbergasted—I had no idea I'd be met."

"Jeremy had the notion you'd come right down soon as you got her letter. Tomorrow if not today. So I'm here." He looked, frowning, at the distended briefcase. "What about your luggage?"

"Change of shirt and underwear, shaving gear. All I'll need is in here."

"Then we'd better go. We've got a piece of driving to do—the family's all down at Sanibel for one last weekend before the carnival season starts. Car's this way." Age hesitated, then turned and walked away.

Matthews smiled slightly at Age's stiffness and reticence—but there was no reason why he should have mellowed during the past months. In most respects he was just as he'd always been—aloof, preoccupied. It was too early for the doctor to tell if the death of the preacher had done the Negro man permanent harm—if it had stolen years from his own life. At a glance Age did not seem strong, and there was a whisper of sadness in the words he spoke. He was also quite worried, but the doctor could account for that. When Age turned his head from the windshield of the sand-stripped old pickup truck, it was not to look at Matthews' face but rather at the packed briefcase in his lap.

"I hope she's well," Matthews said for the third time.

"Oh, yes."

"I've been working pretty hard. It's a treat for me to get away from the farm."

"So Jeremy says."

The doctor smiled wryly and tapped his briefcase, having decided to dispel Age's apprehension if he could.

"My book's almost ready, Age. I hope to be able to read it to you all while I'm here. Of course, I'll send Jeremy a typed copy later."

Age inclined his polished seamed head over the wheel of the truck and stared as if there were something in the road he couldn't quite see.

"You'll hear with your own ears, but I just want to assure you now that there's nothing in my book that will harm her."

They drove another mile, and Age seemed not to have been listening. Then he settled back in his seat, his hands loosened on the wheel, and he half-closed his eyes for a few moments.

"As you say, I'll hear for myself. And . . . welcome to Florida, Dr. Matthews."

There were mile-high thunderstorms out over the Gulf, and soundless waves of yellow-gold lightning. The long shell road in front of them was wet; it had rained and would rain again, but now the air was still and cool. The two men rode silently and at ease. After a while Age pulled up beneath a cluster of coconut palms in front of a cypress-board lodge with a roofed porch on two sides. There were other cars, a menagerie, children, and a fire on the beach shooting sparks high into the blackness; there was a sense of good times and good living.

Matthews climbed and stood looking down at the beach trying to find Jeremy but Age came along and turned him by the elbow toward the house. He saw her then, behind the screen of the front door, and he half ran up to the porch, lugging the briefcase.

"Hello," Jeremy said shyly, coming out.

She was taller than she had been, or maybe she only seemed tall because he'd never seen her in a pair of shorts. And she'd cut her hair; it was unfashionably short for that year but the sunstreaked style suited her. She is lovely, he thought, such a lovely child; then he smiled, feeling foolish. No longer a child, Jeremy carried solitude with her, in the depths of her eyes, in the firm sad line of her mouth.

But she was glad he had come, Matthews could tell that, and he kissed a cheek that was still warm from an afternoon's sun.

"I'm so pleased," he said. "I was beginning to think you wouldn't let me come."

Jeremy lightly crossed her arms, and looked calmly into his eyes. "I needed— Well, I'm meaning to say I wasn't sure if I trusted you." And then she shrugged, dismissing her indecision. "I'm over all that now." She looked speculatively at the briefcase. Matthews took her hand.

"I'm not much of a writer; there were times when I ached to throw the whole bundle in the fire. But I kept at it, Jeremy. I finished the book. I couldn't not finish. Maybe when I read it aloud we'll both know why."

She laughed. "Well, I've been trying to get ready. But don't mind if it . . . upsets me from time to time. It won't be hurting as bad as it seems, Dr. Matthews. I promise you that."

There was a disturbance behind Jeremy, a great clacking and gooselike honking that startled him. Jeremy turned leisurely, with a look of forbearance. The little boy who wandered into view hadn't been walking long, but he was getting the greatest possible pleasure from his pull toy: he showed four front teeth in a wide Jeremy smile as he looked up at them. He wore only a diaper and he was as brown as a beach baby should be.

"Hong," he said, grinning up at his mother. She reached down and lifted him. This was not what he wanted at all, and his smile turned to a scowl that Matthews would have recognized anywhere.

"Down," he said, wriggling, but Jeremy paid no mind. Dreamily she laid her cheek against the top of his head. She appeared to forget the doctor was standing there beside her; she was aware of nothing but the weight of her baby in her arms. Then she glanced up, disconcerted, and smiled an apology.

"I forgot," she said. "You didn't know."

The doctor shook his head slowly.

"Downnnn," the baby demanded.

"This is my love." She lowered the baby and he walked sturdily away with his pull toy, crooning to it. Then Jeremy turned her eyes back to Matthews.

"This is why I can't be hurt anymore," she said serenely.

IN THE DARK OF THE MOON — TERROR AWAITS!

Stories of the Occult

CREATURE FEATURES

☐ 52116-1	THE CLAW by Norah Lofts	$3.95
☐ 52178-1	THE DJINN by Graham Masterton	$3.95
☐ 52179-X		Canada $4.95
☐ 52110-2	FLESH by Richard Laymon	$3.95
☐ 52111-0		Canada $4.95
☐ 52093-9	THE HUNT	$3.50
☐ 52094-7		Canada $4.50
☐ 52598-1	MRS. DEMMING AND THE MYTHICAL BEAST	$4.50
☐ 52599-X	by Faith Sullivan	Canada $5.50
☐ 51848-9	THE PET by Charles L. Grant	$3.95
☐ 51849-7		Canada $4.95
☐ 51636-2	QUARREL WITH THE MOON by J.C. Conaway	$3.95
☐ 51637-0		Canada $4.95
☐ 51579-6	SINS OF THE FLESH by Don Davis & Jay Davis	$4.50
☐ 51680-X		Canada $5.50
☐ 51557-9	WEBS by Scott Baker	$3.95
☐ 51558-7		Canada $4.95
☐ 58270-5	WILDWOOD by John Farris	$4.50
☐ 58271-3		Canada $5.50

Buy them at your local bookstore or use this handy coupon:
Clip and mail this page with your order.

Publishers Book and Audio Mailing Service
P.O. Box 120159, Staten Island, NY 10312-0004

Please send me the book(s) I have checked above. I am enclosing $_____
(please add $1.25 for the first book, and $.25 for each additional book to
cover postage and handling. Send check or money order only—no CODs.)

Name _____

Address _____

City _____ State/Zip _____

Please allow six weeks for delivery. Prices subject to change without notice.